Books by Randolph Lalonde

Fate Cycle Dead of Winter
Fate Cycle Sins of the Past

First Light Chronicles Freeground
First Light Chronicles Limbo
First Light Chronicles Starfree Port

Spinward Fringe Resurrection
Spinward Fringe Awakening
Spinward Fringe Triton
Spinward Fringe Frontline
And Other Books In The Spinward Fringe Series

SPINWARD FRINGE
FRONTLINE

RANDOLPH LALONDE

Spinward Fringe
Frontline

This is a work of fiction. Names, characters, places and incidents either are the
product of the author's imagination or are used fictitiously. Any resemblance to
actual persons, living or dead, events or locales is entirely coincidental.

Thank you for purchasing this book.

If you would like to read more of this series or contact the author please visit my
website.

www.spinwardfringe.com
www.randolphlalonde.com

For Dan and Janet
Raising me must have been an adventure...

PROLOGUE

"Sir, I have an update from our spinward operations," announced the Vice President of Regent Galactic Operations as he pounded up the steps to the President's communications center. The office overlooked the city of New Versailles. The Skylink Building dominated the vista, its pointed half circle shape and smooth white and blue surface reflecting the lights of the city surrounding it.

The Regent Galactic complex was the only structure that out did it for size in the expansive forest of skyscrapers. Even through the rain the billions of lighted windows glimmered and sparkled like gems set in a forest of black quartz. Above the city a network of speeding personal air vehicles criss-crossed and wound around the larger structures like a luminescent nest of shifting wire.

The closest moon was partially eclipsed by the *Kraken*, stamping a reflective half octagonal shape atop the circular red moon as it hovered above offloading and taking on millions of passengers. Workers from freshly taken territories and business people who were returning home after arranging the utilization and resale of land and resources. All in all, it was an average evening in New Versailles, a city that pretended at being a club and art Mecca but actually served as the secondary headquarters of the mighty Regent Galactic Corporation.

With his hands crossed behind his back, clad in a relaxed fit, straight cut business suit, President Paolo Weir looked into the bustling sky. "It's one in the morning Lowrey."

Lowrey Cartwright ignored the objection, running his hand over his perfectly cut blond coif. It was cut in the square, pure unisex style that was popular just a week before. His suit fit loose in the elbows, tight at the wrists and baggy in the knees, a design straight off the fashion runway the month before. "We have no contact from Collins and our intelligence tells us that the Holocaust Virus is just now reaching the core worlds."

"It's not like Collins to go dark without an explanation. We can assume he's dead or on the run. Put a warrant out for him."

"Gabriel Meunez closed our remote connections to all our assets in his area before disappearing. Our intelligence says he's on his way to activating a Vindyne asset that was never entered into record."

"I'm ignoring you Lowrey."

"Jacob Valance has taken possession of the *Triton* and our ears there reported that Wheeler was killed by his destruct device."

"Is that all our ears aboard the *Triton* have to say? What about the Earth Security Codes?" asked President Weir in a quiet, tightly controlled tone.

1

"Our ears aboard *Triton* have gone quiet."

"Does Citadel know?"

"They do."

"What did they say?"

"I tried to speak to them personally, to get a read on what their intentions were now that we've completely lost control of the *Triton*."

"And?"

"They're pulling back from the bargaining table. Our proposal for an alliance with the Sol system and Citadel has been denied, they sent us the documentation a few minutes ago."

"What are they going to do about *Triton?*"

"I don't know."

"So you're telling me that a two trillion dollar ship is just *out there* with no one from our company aboard and she's being captained by someone with several billion dollars worth of research and development in his body. How did Wheeler lose the *Triton?*"

"We don't know."

"Well, it won't happen a second time. I get the sense that mister Meunez and Hampon won't let it go. They may not have time to go after Valance themselves but if the hidden asset they're retrieving is what I think it is then they might not have to."

"Do you know what they're bringing out of storage?"

"Their framework copy of Wheeler."

"How would that help? The original didn't do the job."

"The original was a twisted sociopath. Collins went to great pains to correct personality flaws when he crafted the personality imprinted on the copy. I wouldn't be surprised if Wheeler the second became very important in that sector. Still, I'll be happier when they've taken *Triton* back and have Valance in custody. The scans we have of him are good but there are still some questions we can only answer with a series of biopsies."

"We're close to developing similar technologies independently. I'm starting to think all the Vindyne assets are too much trouble. We're way over budget on the whole endeavour."

"I know, I hear about it at every board meeting. Meunez isn't making things easier by blocking our access to our military forces out there. He's left Hampon in direct control, now we have to channel our orders through him and he's not responding to our requests for direct communications."

"Our most recent intelligence confirms that they're forming their own army. I don't think we can keep that from the board of directors for much longer."

President Weir pinched the bridge of his nose, closing his eyes tightly. "I know. Even a private militia is trouble."

"The latest numbers put the Order of Eden forces at seven million, all armed with Regent Galactic gear," Lowrey corrected quietly.

"What?" Weir snapped.

Tonight it was all bad news, and Lowrey knew it was just a matter of time before he presented the item that would set the normally level headed company

President off. "You should see the recruitment materials, they're convincing. The Holocaust Virus makes the whole thing worse. It's not what mister Meunez told us it would be."

"How bad is it?"

"The infected artificial intelligences are operating under a kill order, killing any human not listed with the West Watch or its parent organization, the Order of Eden."

"How many?"

"Forty three solar systems have been infected so far, the number of dead are beyond anything we've seen."

"How many people has this thing killed Lowrey?" urged the President, fear plain on his face.

"Early numbers put the fatalities past the nine billion mark."

"Nine billion?" he burst wide eyed, taking a step back. "That's half! Half of all the people in forty five solar systems! Collins said everyone would have a chance to surrender! That only some artificial intelligences would kill!"

Lowrey's hands were shaking, he was sweating. When he heard the news he hoped the numbers were wrong, that the President would have some corrective data that would reduce them, that he knew something no one else did. From the older, more wizened and educated man's reaction he could tell that there was no corrective data, the horror was real, the holocaust was happening. Their customers were being slaughtered and Regent Galactic had enabled the people responsible. "I have family in that sector," he whispered, blinking back tears and trying to keep his jaw from chattering.

"Then I suggest you pull yourself together, pay the one hundred thousand dollars per person the Order of Eden demands to protect them and hope they survived the initial wave of attacks. Do we have any intelligence on what the Eden Fleet is doing?"

"They're headed coreward sir, striking major defence installations and disabling major passenger vessels. We can't discern a pattern to their attack, it's like they're striking on their own."

"So Collins is really gone then. He'd never let them off the leash." President Weir snapped his fingers and a thickly padded chair rose out of the floor. He sat down slowly and stared out over the city silently.

Lowrey tried to be quiet, to read the other man's expression. He'd never seen him like that, just sitting there, pondering. There was more coming. More answers, more solutions, there *had* to be. Something had to be done to stop the wave of destruction, to save lives, to save his career. The city outside was like an entirely different world, one oblivious to the terrible truths they were facing.

Silence hung thickly in the large office and it was with no small effort that Lowrey cleared his throat and asked; "what are we going to do?" in a wavering voice.

"Tomorrow we inform the board that the Order of Eden has splintered. We have to force the perception that they are not a division of this company and that we didn't fund the development of the Holocaust Virus. Everything has to rest on the

Order of Eden and the personnel we brought on from Vindyne. Gather evidence."

"Most of the evidence eventually points to us."

"Then destroy it!" The President snapped so harshly that Lowrey flinched. "Have our best people forge evidence to the contrary and then have them killed in some anarchist group bombing! Use our news networks to paint this Order of Eden as a crazed group of zealots!"

"The Order of Eden already owns the Hart News network, the dominant network in those sectors."

"Then expand our networks!"

"It'll take time sir."

"If we don't cover this up they'll have us in front of a tribunal so fast legal won't know about it until the verdict is handed down. Hell, the board would probably hand us over themselves to offset any blame. Get on damage control, I'll get ready to present to them in the morning. Maybe we can make a long term war out of this and see our way to a solid profit."

There it was, the shining light of hope. War would please the board, leading to opportunities for effective propaganda, a profitable manufacturing boom, an increase in military recruitment and most important of all; a way to come out of the situation with his annual bonus intact. Vice President Lowrey sighed and started to put a plan together in his head. "Thank you, mister President."

"Oh, and one more thing."

"Yes sir?"

"Buy into the Order of Eden."

"I will. Should I do the same for you at the same time?"

"I sent my hundred thousand a week ago."

THE SILKSTREAM IV

The paperback novel was an antique, at least in concept, and seldom seen but ever since Jason's psyche advisor told him to start reading plain text to retrain his mind to focus on one task at a time he always had one with him. The act of reading one or two pages at a time, being forced to flip pages, they were all pacing and concentration devices. Old science fiction and fantasy novels were his favourite, with murder mysteries holding a close third place. The more noir and cheesy the more he enjoyed them.

Lacy Campbell was standing in the rain, her bright red silk gown was soaked through. She looked down the sight of her .35, blinking water out of her eyes and grinned Cheshire like. "Thought you could get away with the brass ring, didn't ya hon?"

The dinner jacket weighed on Carl Smith like a lead blanket. There was no hiding it, so he just stared back, his shoulders drooping like over cooked pasta. It wasn't what he'd pictured when he headed out to the big city years before. In Jersey he was small time, the takes were slim and he wanted more. The dock boys didn't cut you in large if your name didn't sound Sicilian. The rackets block to block were worse, so when he headed for the Big Apple, where the big timers played, he thought he might find his way into some big fish's pocket, or some well to do dames' bedroom. The last thing he pictured was this; being held up at the wrong end of his own gun by a tall blond stunner. *Boy oh boy, this dame sure isn't from Jersey either.* He thought to himself as he eyed her from head to tow. "I'll give it to ya. Just let me walk on outta here."

"I've seen a lotta men walk out Carl, maybe I'll let ya go out of habit, or maybe I'll just plug ya and find the rock myself."

He had one chance, and he intended to make good on it. Carl let the big diamond slide down from where he had tucked it into his sleeve and drop into his hand. "Here it is Lacy," he said as he flicked it towards her.

She pulled the trigger-

The *Silkstream IV* shook violently and alarms sounded. Jason dropped the paperback and looked at the main status display. It looked perfectly normal. Jason checked the secondary display and caught sight of his command unit. Alarms were sounding there as well, the back of his hand was flashing red, trying to prevent a forced download from the *Silkstream.*

He folded an artificial flap of skin away from the back of his hand and didn't recognize the names of the files being added. "What is this? Worst fear day?" he muttered to himself as he pulled a tool from the maintenance belt hanging off the other seat. With no hesitation he pressed the end of the energizer against his command console and turned it up to full. "Oz! Get up here!" he called out as he activated the tool. Energy burst into his command and control unit and burned the flesh it was built into. The nerves there were less sensitive, but he kicked his feet and bit his lip at the deep burning sensation as the tattooed circuits fried. "Last time I get that installed," he said as he shoved the small emitter rod back into the tool belt.

Oz rushed to the cockpit and looked around. "What are you doing?"

"I think there's some kind of software attacking the ship."

"You had to burn yourself to figure that out?"

"Strange download happening on my command unit, it was already past my security systems, you should take yours off just in case," he flexed his fingers and was relieved that he hadn't done any nerve damage. The pain was already down to a persistent throb. A high pitched whining filled the cockpit. "Can you check that?" He shouted.

Oz turned and ran into the main cabin as he dropped his own command and control unit on the floor. "It's the hyperspace emitters! They're overheating!"

"What? They're operating at half tolerance!" Jason replied over his shoulder as he tried to access the main computer.

"I have to disconnect the main power lines. Manual cutoff isn't working." Both the travellers could feel the small ship rumble as Oz activated the emergency deceleration thrusters at full burn.

"Do it! There's something blocking me from accessing main systems."

Oz waited for the shuttle's speed to reduce below the speed of light, then for a while longer as he listened to the engines roar, wondering if anyone had put such pressure on those systems before. When they had slowed down enough he yanked the main power lines leading to the particle emitters. Energy arced between the couplings and he was once again thankful for the insulation built into his black vacsuit.

Outside the cockpit window the distortion from hyperspace travel and simultaneous wormhole travel dissipated and Jason saw nothing but stars.

"Okay, looks like we're in the clear. The power plant shows normal. It was outputting between four and five times what the emitters could handle," he said as he walked up to the cockpit. "Good thing particle dispersion was equal or we would have been torn to shreds. Any luck with the computer?"

"I managed to restrict the AI from main systems, good thing too. It was after life support."

"What? Is that some kind of security backup?"

"No, our AI is infected. Do you have any kind of AI on your command and control unit?"

"Just a predictive filter, I don't play well with artificials."

"A good thing too. This is some kind of virus that nests in the emotional center of artificial intelligences. Good thing the AI was an afterthought on the

Silkstream. Our hyperspace emitters are blown though."

"That'll slow us down some."

"About an eighth the speed, maybe less. We'll never make it in time to rendezvous with the *Triton*."

"Where did we pick up the virus?"

Jason looked for it in the transmission logs and found it. "It's from the Enreega system."

"It chose a good time to rear its ugly head."

"Well, that's just the thing. This virus is different, it sort of convinces an AI that it's an improvement to its software and starts making modifications, but if there's no AI the virus doesn't have anything to do and it just waits for the opportunity to transmit itself to another system."

"I wonder why it took so long for it to get to this AI."

"That's just the thing," Jason said quietly. "I just turned the AI on a couple hours ago."

Oz just stared at Jason for a moment. "Sometimes I think we'd be better off if we were still drawing on cave walls and clubbing each other over the head for women and food."

Oz sat down in the copilot's seat and looked out into the stars as Jason checked the ship status. The only sound was the creaking of the outer hull as the hyperspace particle emitters cooled.

Jason noticed his friend's silence after a few minutes. "You all right?"

He nodded, still looking out into the cluster of stars in the distance. "Did that virus transmit to the *Sunspire*?"

Jason didn't have to check, he already knew the answer. "It did."

"Do you think they could catch it in time?"

"Do you want my honest answer?" Jason asked quietly.

"Always."

"If it got to the quantum core there's not much chance. The defence AI would be the first to try and fight it off, but this virus would prevent it from warning anyone about the problem. That's probably why my command unit wasn't attacked until now, it was silenced while my AI was resisting infection."

"I hope they don't lose anyone. If they're smart they'll blow an EMP in the engine room."

"I don't think Trajenko. . ."

"You're right. She wouldn't make that kind of sacrifice, she's never seen what a rogue AI can do."

Jason just left him alone, there wasn't much he could do or say to help just then, and he knew it.

"They're going to think we did it," his friend stated quietly.

Jason was surprised the thought occurred to Oz first. "I'll have to find out who made this. With the AI on this ship deleted and the virus in quarantine, I might be able to work it out. I'd rather have more processing power though."

"Here's hoping the *Triton* is having better luck. But then, if anyone can spot a rogue virus it'll be the commander of that ship."

7

"You mean Jake."

Oz nodded and went back to gazing through the cockpit windows for some time, quietly searching. "Do you remember why they called it the hyperdrive?" he asked finally.

Jason thought for a minute, smiling at the much larger fellow. "Honestly? No idea. I think I was eight when we started taking early space travel in school."

"I ran across the historical account when I took command of the *Sunspire*. Ned Mahajic was trying to invent a zero friction drive for cars."

"Oh, I remember now. The particles surrounded the test bed and it weighed something like a tenth what it should have."

Oz nodded, looking specifically for the nebula the Triton was holding station near. "He disappeared. Stole enough money to finish his research and just vanished for sixteen years. When he came back he was driving a floating car that could move faster, manoeuvre better and run longer than anything on the planet and because he was such a big science fiction fan himself, he named it the hyperdrive, called the space within the particle field hyperspace."

"People still argue about that name," Jason smiled. "What brought on the history refresher?"

"Just trying to think outside the box. Ah, there it is," he said, pointing to the nebula. At that distance it looked like nothing more than another distant point of light. He confirmed with the navigation screen. "Burning out the hyperdrive system took a lot of energy, I don't think we could make it if we tried. I'm just glad we're not drifting near the speed of light. The time differential shouldn't be more than a couple hours at worst."

"Thank God. I don't want to catch up with Laura after she's had sixty years to remarry. Especially if only a month has passed in this overgrown pod."

"Yeah, with my luck I'd have a hundred grand nieces and nephews to babysit," Oz shook his head and started making some calculations. "There's no reason why the wormhole generator shouldn't work." He looked at the status display in front of him. With the artificial intelligence deactivated the readings were showing the correct values. Half the particle emitters were inoperable, their power reserves were down to eighteen percent, but all the other systems were fine. He brought up a holographic navigational chart. "Get a message ready to send to a Freeground receiver and another for the *Triton*. I'm going to find a nice place for us to wait for a pick up."

"Why send anything to Freeground?"

"Just in case something else happens and we don't make it."

"Ah, always thinking with the glass half full."

Oz looked through a list of worlds, all marked with an estimated arrival time based on worm hole compression and the thrust generated by their engines against the mass of the ship. "Pandem. It's governed by the Carthans so Freeground has no connections there but they have nothing against us either."

Jason looked over to his holodisplay. "Looks nice enough, lots of tropical islands, calm climate, big cities. Sounds like a nice place to wait. Oh, and they're marked as enemy territory by Regent Galactic, perfect. The capitol is Damshir, it covers one of the largest islands. It's as close as we can get to our rendezvous point with the power we have left."

"Yup, the *Triton* won't have any trouble picking us up there."

"You know, it'll take them a while to get our message, and that's if they're still in the same area."

"Always poking holes in my bright ideas."

"It had to be said," Jason said with a shrug.

"I know, let's just hope someone passes the word if they happen to go in the other direction. Otherwise we'll end up trading for parts and searching for them with nothing but this bucket."

"You have a point, friends or not, you take up a lot of space in a ship this size. Good thing I'm not claustrophobic," Jason grinned wryly.

"Good thing," Oz agreed as he started plotting the course. "Looks like it'll take us at least four days to get to Pandem."

DUPLICATION

Bridge operations were something that had frightened Agameg Price at first. When something big happened on the *Triton* it was like watching ripples in a pond emanate from the outside in. The waves all converged on the center, which was either the Flight Control Centre or the Main Bridge and when a major decision had to be made it often came straight to the command chair.

That kind of pressure was completely new to Agameg, regardless, the Captain had enough confidence in him to give him the first shift in the command seat after taking the *Triton*, and if anyone asked, Price would tell them that he was just as jittery and lost as anyone else. He didn't know what kind of quality he exuded that made the Captain believe in him to the extent that he would be left to oversee all the department heads, major occurrences and moment to moment executive decisions that had to be made until the Captain himself or the First Officer could assume command.

None of that mattered. Alice had started placing him in the command seat during her shifts when she would retire to the ready room office or step off the bridge for a few moments. He was getting used to it, and had only recently realized that she had begun to unofficially treat him as her second in command. He was in charge of tactical officially, and while she was on the bridge he and Alice got along very well. Many quiet conversations about their past experiences in space had taken place over the weeks of training, and there was a deep simpatico forming between them.

The rest of the bridge crew were getting accustomed to each other as well. Chemistry was important, and through no obvious intent the night shift was mostly crewed by non-humans. A nafalli was the head pilot, there was another on the engineering desk and all told there were five issyrians on the bridge. No one thought it was a prejudiced method of operations, in fact, it was comforting having so many people on duty on the command deck that shared an immediate commonality.

At first he had the same problems with command that he had always had. Telling people what to do, how to do it was not something he was comfortable with. Panloo, the night helmswoman and a tall, motherly nafalli was the first to tell him that it was his job, it was all right for him to give her orders. His second in command at tactical; Oilimae, was quite used to taking his orders, so there was no problem there, and over the time the crew spent on training and forming ship routines he had a long time to get used to the fit of the command chair.

Not much happened outside of testing systems as they came online or running drills and simulations so he had a great deal of time to learn. The detail and scope of his investigations into the workings of the various systems on board the ship were beyond the scope of what Alice or anyone else demanded or expected.

He never ran out of things to investigate, to learn from the *Triton*. It was a ship with history, personality and advanced, interesting systems. When Stephanie cleared him to view the growing pile of personnel files that had been generated by the new Intelligence Department he had discovered a fresh dilemma. As Alice's first in command she had entrusted him with viewing the files and flagging anything of interest, though he was sure she would be just as surprised at his most recent finding as he was.

After some consideration he didn't voice his concern, instead he started viewing the collected data promising himself that he wouldn't reveal any details to anyone not in need of the information. That's why, when he ran across a strange crew file with a DNA profile matching someone else and a picture that wasn't on any of the security feeds, he grew suspicious but wasn't quite sure who to tell. He was taking the night shift on his own, without Alice anywhere near the bridge for the second time since they'd taken the *Triton*. The standing order was to wake her, the department Chiefs or Captain Valance if anything urgent came up.

I'll continue my own investigation. I don't want to present them with just a suspicion. He sucked his lip up against his hidden upper teeth and let it go, making a soft *smuck* sound. It was something he did unconsciously when he was in deep thought, and after doing it a third time Panloo set the autopilot and locked the controls before turning and smiling at Agameg.

He looked back at her and blinked one big dark eye at a time.

"Has something come up?" she looked quite different in her black vacsuit uniform. It was fitted very loosely as to not irritate her white fur, and it had a wider than normal neck opening. He was used to seeing her without a vacsuit after several days on the bridge sporting her lovely, thick white fur so seeing her in black took some getting used to.

Price quietly nodded to the seat at his right and she eagerly complied, moving to a seat beside him. "What could be so interesting at four in the morning?" she asked in a low whisper. She peered at him expectantly.

"I think I've found a fake crew member, or at least one who required identification aboard but didn't want to be honest about who they are."

"That's unusual, wouldn't Intelligence have picked it up?"

"They are under trained. Testing and training puzzles are unpopular programs, no one does them unless they have to."

"Except for you," she smiled.

"I only try to learn so I can understand how to best direct the ship," he shrugged. "Besides, I like a few puzzles in the morning."

"I think you know more about this ship than anyone but the Captain and First Officer. You should spend more time relaxing, taking a look at what's happening in the observation lounges and the Botanical Gallery."

"I will, as soon as I have an understanding."

"An understanding?"

Agameg smiled at her, realizing just then how ambitious what he was about to say was. "Of how everything works."

"That could take a while," she snuffled. "Who do you think wanted to have a fake identification on board?"

Agameg turned the privacy blinder off so she could see the holographic head shot from where she was sitting. "I don't know, but I'm wondering if you have seen this person on the observation decks or anywhere else?"

She looked at the image carefully and shook her head; "No, he doesn't look like anyone I've seen. Whose DNA is that?"

"It says it matches Frost's. There's only a little background information here. It says he comes from the Lena Palus moon and was one of the Regent Galactic crew that was kept on after Captain took the ship from Wheeler."

"What level of clearance does he have?"

"Very high, the same as Frost's."

"That would make sense I guess, since clearance is set to people's DNA," Panloo whispered.

"I can't find any more information on who might have made this entry, only that it was viewed for eight seconds just yesterday. Fred Mendel from Stephanie's team. The file before and after were also viewed for short periods of time. The chances are that he was looking for something else."

"They were taking final images of people yesterday, maybe he was making sure everyone had one on file? I don't think he would need extra identification."

"You're right. I can't think of a reason why he'd want another ID, especially using Frost's DNA."

"What are you going to do?" Panloo asked.

Agameg pressed his upper lip against his teeth a few more times as he pondered. "I'm going to send a notice to Frost and flag this identification for Stephanie and her team in the morning. I think it's important that Frost knows his ID might have been duplicated and set to another image. I don't think there's a real need to wake the Captain or Alice. What do you think?"

"I think you're right. Between Stephanie and Frost this'll get taken care of quickly, especially since they'll probably get the news together."

"Oh?" Agameg tilted his head quizzically.

"You didn't hear? They're together now, I saw them leave the lower observation by the pilot's berth last night. They looked very close."

"Why am I always the last? I'll have to remember to congratulate them," he shook his head. "Frost and Stephanie, so unexpected."

PEERING INTO ETERNITY

The cool wind gently urged her to make a decision. Move closer to the balcony edge or back into the apartment behind her. Standing right in the middle of the semicircular balcony didn't seem good enough, it was like a half step, almost progress.

Nevertheless, she remained there, trying not to look down, to focus on the distant horizon where a new green and brown jungle crept across the dark ground towards the growing townships around Freedom Tower. She was over twenty storeys up, and if she stepped up to the railing, looked down, she knew nothing would happen. Some hidden hand wouldn't pull her over the edge, she wouldn't lose her balance and fall over the rail, and no one would push her. None of those things mattered, rational thinking couldn't cure her of the fear that gripped her whenever she even thought of getting closer to that edge.

The breeze was nice though, feeling like she was part of the fresh planet the Freeground Nation was settling on. The cuffs of her beige drawstring pants and knee length shirt flapped as the wind picked up a little. Slitted up the sides to her waist, there was more than enough room for the air to surge up her back and chill her through the thin top she wore underneath. She enjoyed the feeling of the fresh air, such a rare thing at one time, so she stuffed her hands into the sleeves of her long hooded overshirt and crossed her arms instead of stepping inside.

Ayan. That was the only name on her official identification. It had been issued that morning, and the absence of a surname meant that the genetic typing and genealogical matching had failed to connect her with any citizen on record. Doctor Anderson had told her that was a possibility.

He had been so good to her, treated her like his own flesh and blood. The memory of her first morning came to mind again, as it had often. Waking up in bed as though she had just had a good night's sleep, the first thing she did was reach for her morning pills. When the soft lights came on she realized she wasn't waking up where she remembered going to sleep, and there was an overwhelming awareness that everything was somehow new.

It must have been hard for him to just leave her alone, to watch from another room as she sat up, realized that her body was different, the results of her sudden weight loss and the evidence of multiple organ failure just wasn't there. There were other memories that were vague, more like emotions. An overall feeling of wellness, a quiet place with melodies in the distance, a heartbeat and gentle voices just at the edge of her senses.

When she took a slow, deep breath it felt different, there was no pain, no resistance in her chest. As she sat up she realized her body was proportioned differently than she remembered. Less sleek and more curvy for the most part, and there was strength she hadn't felt since she arrived back on the *First Light*. There was no medication on the table, the command and control unit had been replaced with something that looked like a thinner, lighter five centimetre wide transparent bracelet and there was an open closet with loose fitting clothing.

Ayan remembered just shaking her head and closing her eyes. She was herself, but not, and then she recalled the week before, when she had allowed herself to be scanned by the highest resolution equipment in the fleet. *They cloned me.* She remembered realizing. The feeling was indescribable as she just sat there, trying to think her way through it. It was at the same time terrifying and amazing. Her memories told her that just days ago she had started losing her hair, but when she ran her hand over her head and down her shoulders she could see and feel golden curls down to the center of her back. It was a change, but considering how her health had begun to quickly decline it was a welcome one.

Sadness threatened to grip her as the supposition struck. *I must be dead.* She thought. *I wonder what happened.*

Ayan took the command and control unit and materialized a vacsuit onto herself, then put on the long, white hooded overshirt that would become her favourite piece of clothing.

The smile on Doctor Anderson's face as he opened the door to her bedroom was something she'd never forget. It was so warm, adoring, welcoming. "I can answer most of your questions," he said quietly, gesturing to the room behind him. "Let's sit down."

The apartment was naturally lit that morning, the golden sun filled the main sitting room with light through the large balcony windows. She sat down on a brown sofa and took a moment to get comfortable, even that felt different. "You're not a clone," was the first thing he said.

Over a breakfast of fresh fruit, cranberry juice and coffee he explained everything she wanted to know. Firstly, that it had been almost six years since the scan was taken, so her memories didn't include the worst of her failing health or the growth of the Special Projects Division she had restarted with Laura or years of searching for Jonas Valent. Telling her that Jonas was just recently killed saving the *Triton* but there was some kind of copy of him as well was difficult. The man she had loved so deeply was gone, but according to the transmission received from Laura and overheard by Intelligence through surveillance equipment in Oz's quarters Jake Valance had his memories. Still, her grief was undeniable and there were questions about Jake that no one could answer. That, along with Freeground disallowing any attempt to contact him or the *Triton* frustrated her to no end. Her last meaningful memory was Laura and Jason's wedding, and that's one thing she was very thankful for.

Other questions, like her own marital status and what kind of person she had become in the missing years were addressed as well, and she was strangely proud of her accomplishments while she wished she could remember them. When she had run out of queries there was only one thing left; if she wasn't a clone, what was she?

14

It took a while for the answer to sink in. According to Doctor Anderson he had found a sample of genetic material from a woman named Angelica five generations back. He also obtained a copy of the oldest female human genetic sample on record. After studying them for a time, determining what kind of genetic alterations had been made, he fertilized many of her mother's eggs with material from her father's family. He halted the cell division and reverted all the genetic alterations to a natural state, a process taking months using templates developed with her ancestors material along with the older reference.

When that was finished he selected the candidate that would be most like Ayan, then resumed cell division. Ayan still couldn't believe how they advanced the ageing process; naturally. It had been done before, but never so drastically. The entire first stage laboratory was on a ship with no name, just a serial number, and when they were sure she was undergoing healthy development they entered a wormhole specially formed to accelerate the passage of time. In the space of nearly four years the Doctor and small crew experienced thirty. When they returned to Freeground their lab had been moved to Freedom Tower under Special Projects Division Classification. The original Ayan and her team didn't know it was there, no one did. Someone would have to specifically look for it, and no one other than her mother and a few select individuals knew anything about it.

The sacrifice that crew made for me is still unbelievable, she thought as she took a step closer to the railing. The strong white bars of the rail were only three meters away, and she could see a bit more of the expanding town below and decided to stay right there until she became accustomed to the view. She had a fear of heights before and took care of it in cadet training when she was a teenager. At least that's what her memories told her, but she knew that somehow the phobia had made a comeback with a vengeance since her second birth.

There were other experiments that benefited from time dilation, but she got the impression that compared to her, they were just something extra for the crew to attend to. To them thirty years passed, for everyone outside the wormhole it was only four. They aged, two of them were married as soon as they emerged, while another had written a holographic epic and interactive world that took the Freeground population by storm called *The Last Blood Caller*. There was time, and while the rest of the crew worked on personal projects after their daily duties were taken care of Doctor Anderson focused on her care and memory imprinting. The process was simple; as her body developed and exercised in the artificial womb a neural link with a detailed scan from Ayan Rice was formed. Through that neural link all of her memories were imprinted in real time, including all the sensations; emotional, visual, tactile and so on. It took over thirty years because imprint acceleration would cause gaps, overlapping and perhaps worse problems.

In the end she was a genetically pure human woman with the memories of Ayan Rice. There were drawbacks, to be sure, but as she faced disappointments in aptitude and skill level testing, not quite measuring up to the intellectual scores of her predecessor but scoring high compared to the general population, the sacrifice everyone had made to give her such a good start at a second chance softened the blow.

As her thoughts returned to the identification statement on her command and control bracelet the latest drawback was plain. Her ancestors had undergone such severe genetic modifications that after a full reversion she didn't even match her mother. *My original mother.* She reminded herself. *I haven't heard from her yet. The Doctor's been here every day, made himself available any time I have questions or just want someone to talk to, but she hasn't so much as sent me a text or audio blip.*

Ayan shook her head, trying to clear the irritation and unconsciously took a step forward. Her gaze went straight to the edge and vertigo threatened to overcome her senses even though she was still over two meters from the railing. She closed her eyes and tried to forget where she was, to breathe deeply and calm down. After a few minutes she opened her eyes slowly, gazing out to the horizon.

Looking down to the top of the railing her heart beat faster, she could feel sweat on her forehead, palms, forehead and upper lip as she looked lower still and just as she began to look at the tiny buildings over the edge the wind gusted lightly. "That'll do for today!" she said as she backed towards the sliding windows behind her. They parted and she walked inside, turning towards the comfort of the central room. There was a soft brown futon, a pair of round bag chairs and a low table between.

She was just on her way to the small kitchen when the door chimed. The holoprojector hidden in the low sitting room table came to life, displaying an image of Minh-Chu Buu. He was looking around the hallway outside, whistling to himself. His shoulder length black hair was new, but aside from that he was just the same as she remembered, flight jacket and all.

Her jaw dropped, she stopped mid stride and stared at the image. She was nervous, happy, excited, afraid.

"Hello?" he asked, pressing the door control again. Minh didn't seem to know he was being watched, his hands nervously ran through his long hair, bundled it up as though he was about to pull it into a ponytail then let it fall loose. "Not having a lot of luck meeting with old friends here. Or even new friends who used to be old friends," he muttered to himself.

"One ledge after another," she whispered to herself, straightening her overshirt and brushing a few strands of curly hair out of her face. "Come in."

The door opened to reveal Minh-Chu, smiling uncertainly at her.

She was giddy, it felt so good to see his face, especially after just recently hearing the miraculous news of his survival. Through fear and uncertainty she gave in to joy and excitement, running across the room and leaping into him.

He had to take a step back to steady himself but he embraced her tightly, laughing. "You remember me!"

"Of course I do, I couldn't believe it when Doc showed me the news about you being found adrift!"

"You should have sent me a message, reintegration treatment is boring."

"Oh, I know, trust me," she stepped back and led the way to the center of her sitting room, plopping herself down into one of the bag chairs.

Minh looked at the other one for a moment before shrugging and doing the same. "I wish you could have seen my face when they finally told me that the Doc

16

had brought you back. That was one of the last things they told me before the end of my controlled treatment. They wanted to make sure that all this news; Jason and Oz stealing a ship and leaving, Jonas and you dying, and Doc making a new you, sunk in without my brain popping," her smile faded at the mention of Jonas' death, and he calmed down. "Sorry, I don't handle grief or delicate topics well, but I'm still not crazy enough to keep under constant supervision." He crossed his eyes and started to stuff a hand full of hair into his mouth.

She couldn't help but burst out laughing. "If only they could see you now," she said finally. "You're the picture of crazy."

He pulled the locks of hair our of his mouth and bowed in his seat. "Why thank you."

Ayan stood and went to the kitchen. "Coffee?" she offered.

"Oh, yes please. I haven't had good coffee in years."

"I'm sorry I didn't send you a message when I heard. I just didn't know what to expect."

"Well, you look different, but still like you. You still sound mostly like you too, with the right accent, so it must be you," he shrugged with a smile. "I understand. Besides, I was busy learning how to be with people again. I swear, if I have to listen to someone tell me how I'm feeling ever again..." He made a strangling motion with his hands and finished it by miming several slaps across his imaginary victim's face.

Ayan chuckled as she poured two cups of steaming coffee from a coffee press. "So it was just a bunch of psycho analysts and therapists? Oh, sugar and cream?"

"I'll try mine black, and where'd you get the beans?"

"They grow them here, it's almost more efficient to eat the cultivated food instead of materialized stuff now. A couple more weeks they say."

"Wow, I come back and I barely recognize this end of space," he accepted a steaming hot mug from Ayan carefully and smelled it. "Oh, that's the stuff."

"It's a little hot. Have you seen your sisters?"

"They took turns being around to help me reintegrate. I was glad they were there, but little Minh-Fu did more for me than any touch or socializing exercise. That little guy is four times as hyper as me at that age. I'd pay real credits to see him in a zero gravity bouncing room."

"He's one of your nephews?"

"One of four nieces and nephews. It took them five days to tell me they sold the restaurant."

"They didn't."

"Just last year. In fact, they're leaving for a Lorander world with Oz's family. It's like all the sisters got together when I disappeared, they're all great friends now."

"I remember some of that. Laura and Jason's wedding was pretty amazing, babies everywhere."

"Ha! Now that's a mixed blessing. I'm happy I missed the diapers, but sad to miss the cuteness."

"Only one of your sisters was pregnant then, and she was constantly asking

Julie questions."

"Julie?"

"Oz's eldest sister."

"Ah, well, they'll all be leaving soon. They kept asking if I wanted them to stay, but I told them to go on. Oh, and by the way, one of Jason's friends from Intelligence paid me a visit last night after I got to my temporary quarters," he blew on his coffee and tried a sip, recoiling as he nearly burned his lip. "Needs sugar, and to not be so hot," he said to himself as he put it down on the coffee table and started to get up.

"Did you know him?"

"The Intelligence guy? No, but he thought it was important I find out that Vindyne made a copy of Jonas using framework technology. Freeground has known about it for years. They even have footage of some woman stealing his pod. With Jason and Oz gone the information is more freely available, I guess so more people know what they might be after. I wasn't supposed to see anything he had for me, but Jason's buddy owed him big and thought I should get some details about what was going on."

Ayan's jaw dropped. "So that's how it happened," she said quietly. "He's in command of the *Triton* now."

Minh finished standing and just looked at her as though he didn't comprehend what she had just said. "Huh? Wheeler's ship? How'd that happen?"

"I don't know, no one out here does. Doctor Anderson showed me a copy of Laura's message to Jason. She laid out all the bare facts, including Jake having some of Jonas' memories."

He grinned and brought his coffee back to the small kitchen to add some sugar. "We'll have to go find them."

She turned in her seat and looked at him. "You're not serious."

"I still have the Gull, and with part of my share of the restaurant sale I'm going to fix it up."

"But that's a hyperdrive ship, it would take a month, maybe more to get there. We don't even know the *Triton's* exact location, not even Doc Anderson could get that information. Even if we had it they would probably have to move on before we got there."

"A ship that big has to be easy enough to find. Besides, from the declassified videos I saw of Jake last night it looks like he stands out."

She thought back to the speech and few bounty hunting videos she had seen of him. It was true, he did stand out, and even though the man she saw in those holographic recordings seemed so different, there were hints of the Jonas she knew. Ayan shook her head. "The *Triton* is so much faster, it would have to stay in one place long enough for us to find out where it was, then long enough for us to catch up."

"Why don't you use your connections to send a high priority message? Then we can start heading in their direction and receive their reply on the Gull," Minh said simply before testing the temperature of his coffee again.

His suggestion made perfect sense, but there was so much she didn't know,

18

and the uncertainty was a difficult barrier to cross. "I don't have any connections. I don't even have a surname anymore. It's nice that they'll let me select one if I want to, but for all intents and purposes I won't know my status until the council rules tomorrow."

"Status?" Minh asked as he put his mug back down on the coffee table and dropped back into a bag chair.

"I applied to reenlist and have my rank restored. That just added to my Citizenship and security level assessment, which started before I woke up for the first time."

"So you want to be in the military?"

"I don't know. I thought I did, but then I started reading about the accomplishments I made after my memories end. It sounds like I've done everything I wanted to already except for finding Jonas. Now there's something walking around with his memories and everyone else is either with him or on their way." She hadn't thought of it in simple terms until then. She knew Laura was on the *Triton*, that Oz and Jason were on their way after abandoning their posts, or at least that's where they'd most likely be going. Hearing it out loud changed everything; "Either with him or on their way," she repeated quietly.

"You see? The stream is flowing; its waters beckon all those along its banks," he said with a smile.

"I couldn't have said it better."

"I had a lot of time," he added before slurping his coffee. "Wow, you have to pack some of that."

She nodded and smiled back at him. "Nothings for sure, I have to see what the council's ruling is tomorrow. If we can send a message out to them then we might be able to find out what's going on without leaving, or even help them from here."

"I'll wait to find out what happens, but I'm going. I don't like how Freeground has changed. My discharge was waiting for me when I arrived, I can't even volunteer as a reserve pilot."

"Ouch. I'm sorry to hear that."

"Well, they won't stop me from leaving, I think that's what they'd like anyway. I don't have a restaurant, my sisters are settling elsewhere and I have a ship. Now I just want to see my old friends and be useful, maybe find a fighter and fly for Jonas again, even if his name has changed and he seems a little taller."

Ayan smiled at him and nodded. "We'll see what the council says tomorrow."

"I'll wait," Minh grinned. His expression became a little more serious after a moment and his attention wandered to her futon. "I'm wondering," he started quietly. "Would you mind if I stayed for the night? On your sofa, I mean."

He looked more vulnerable in that moment than in the short time she'd known him on the *First Light*. The affects of being alone for so long were obvious to her for the first time. "It's a futon," she smiled. "You can stay."

Shamus Frost

The quiet. That was the unexpected part of late nights on the *Triton*. It was a twenty four hour ship, but the hallways always seemed emptier at night. Visiting the gunnery deck didn't help, it had a minimum maintenance and alert crew and they were spread across its expansive surface. If he were to stand up from the sofa in the darkened quarters and take a walk up to Gunnery Deck A just then, Frost would most likely find the mechanics working on loader suits, a pair of them were set to overhaul one of the turrets, and the minimal alert crew would be walking the deck looking for divots, loose parts or ammunition.

The chances of an attack where they were was very low. That was the beauty of dead space, even when there was such an amazing view just outside the main view ports of his quarters. The view port wasn't real, it was a high quality low power multi layered screen that showed an up to date vista of what was outside the ship. It even translated spectrums of light that weren't visible to the human eye into something everyone could see. As a result the view of that bright white, yellow and blue nebula, a stellar nursery was what they called it, was incredible and not entirely lost on Shamus. To him it looked like something had exploded, and through the fine glimmering debris a thousand points of light shone. The nebula was really a collection of matter coming together, he had been told, and there wasn't much point in arguing with people who knew better.

He looked away from the simulated window display, it was so convincing he almost forgot he was in the middle of the command deck living section. The futon just below the large simulated window was long enough for three to sit comfortably, there was a coffee table and another loveseat that pulled out into a small bed. Why he'd need so much sitting space he'd never know. He was so used to bunk rooms and shared common spaces it felt like he was taking up too much space.

Stephanie had come from similar experience, and more and more they surprised each other with how their lives followed such close parallels even before signing up on the *Samson*. Despite the fact that she grew up on a colony and he was from a military family, their experiences in youth were practically the same. Their experiences in space were different, but both had started in the military, crazy for space. Both of them spent time in war, and they had also signed up on more than one ship before the *Samson*.

To have spent so much time aboard in close quarters and not gotten to really know her didn't surprise him. He knew the laws of strong personalities mixing; it was wise to give them room to breathe. They'd had their arguments while serving on the smaller vessel but they each had their corners. Frost had his place on the bridge while she was tasked with the boarding crew and had a more open, social relationship with them.

On the *Triton* there was every reason to get closer however, and if he'd known she was interested in him he'd have done something about it much sooner. His luck with women was always mixed. When it came right down to it, he didn't trust them. Every time he did it ended badly. That's what the most recent fight with Stephanie had been about.

He had no idea how it started, what part of the conversation led to them having a serious talk about how he hadn't slept over in the weeks since they got together but the night always ended with him at her place. He'd fall asleep beside her and when she woke up he'd always be gone. A couple hours of shuteye in his own bed before he started the day was all he really wanted, he didn't know why, maybe it was just because he never enjoyed sharing a bunk with anyone before.

Stephanie was a fine woman, better than he'd ever been with, and a sound sleeper. He just wasn't used to staying until morning. No matter what he said about it during their most recent blow up he couldn't make it better, the conversational hole he dug just kept on getting deeper and deeper until he simply stopped talking and snatched her up in his arms. She struggled, still angry at him. She pounded her fists against his shoulders and he just smiled at her. Her gaze avoided his and just like that it was a game, regardless of her frustration with him she was having fun and her avoidance was accompanied by a little smile. Finally she sighed and let him kiss her.

It was hours later and just as always he had snuck off at four in the morning from her bed to venture back to his own quarters just down the hall. He might have a bit of hell on his hands for that later depending on her mood but he was having a restless night himself. This time he could tell her he left for his own quarters so he didn't keep her awake. She still might not believe him, again, depending on her mood, but even if she wanted to have yet another serious talk about it, she was worth it, of that he was absolutely certain.

"Lucky man, I am," he muttered to himself as he stretched out on the futon. There was a perfectly good bed just in the next room but it was too big to sleep in alone. "Feels like a great big soft floor, that does."

His command and control unit vibrated mildly and he looked down at it absently. Price was leaving him a message. "Couldn't be more awake," he grumbled as he accessed it for review.

> *Frost: I was reviewing the personnel files so I could have a clearer understanding of the maintenance crew when I came across someone who has exactly the same DNA as you do. His file looks like an altered copy. I've also sent a notice to Stephanie. My duty report to Alice and the Captain will mention it as well. I suggest you come to the main security office so your identification can be re-coded before the beginning of your shift.*

"I think I'll perform my own little investigation first." He called up the ship security holodisplay and punched in his identification code. As he expected there were two illuminated paths indicating where on the ship he and his imposter had been throughout the last day. One path led from his quarters to the security office, then the gunnery deck, there was a swirl indicating he had spent his day moving around that space. His night had led him to Stephanie's quarters, the lower observation bay for a couple hours then back up to her quarters.

The other, blue line was telling a different story. It started in the aft berth with the engineering crew and led to the engineering main office for a morning briefing, then into various sections of the ship where there were short reports on memory wipes and software reinstallations being performed on over a dozen cleaning and servicing robots. He'd heard that they were being stripped of any AI's and reset back down to their base programming, he just wasn't aware of where it was being done. "Whoever's usin' my ident's a real busy body." He muttered as he scrolled through the servicing logs from the day before. "Almost worth just leavin' him alone."

The blue path showed a clear U shape as the person it represented moved up one side of the robot maintenance bay and down the other through the day then out, to a portside observation lounge he'd never visited. It had been remarked as the Oota Galoona. "Must be a new pub or somethin' opened up. Surprised Steph dinna want to drop in." The blue marker indicated that whoever had copied and modified his identity was still there.

"Looks like I've got some early mornin' clubbin' ta do," Frost said as he took to his feet and grabbed his gun belt. He was still strapping it on as he stepped out the door.

The express car let out just around the corner from Oota Galoona. Between the dimly lit hall and the name he could only assume that the observation lounge had been renamed by an issyrian. Frost took his time, resting his palm on the pommel of his sidearm, surveying the hall as he came around the corner.

Things had quieted down, the observation lounges, quickly becoming clubs and old fashioned bars despite intoxicant rationing, were always quietest the hour or two before the end of a shift. The graveyard watch would be ending in less than two hours and he couldn't imagine why the impostor would be there over six hours after his shift had ended or how he could keep drinking for so long with rationing in place.

Double doors with the name of the establishment lettered across the front in rainbow luminescent paint marked the entrance to the main port observation lounge. He stepped in just close enough to activate them and stepped to the right so he could see inside while peeking around the corner. It didn't help.

His eye met Burke's right away. The other man had been watching the door, sitting with his back to the transparent wall so he could see anyone coming in from the right side of the entrance.

Instead of ducking for cover or bringing up security on his communicator, Frost grinned and walked straight for Burke's small booth table. "Long time! Good ta see a familiar face!" he exclaimed jovially.

The other man's panic was so utter he was struck still, his hands griped his tall dark brown glass as his jaw fell agape and his eyes nearly bulged out of his head.

"Morning, Chief." Frost heard someone say from a seat by the door. It was one of his early night watch crew, the only nafalli on his staff.

"Morning Hunsler," he acknowledged over his shoulder loud enough to be heard despite the loud, obnoxiously upbeat music playing throughout the large half circular space. It was dimly lit like the hallway outside, with three tiers leading up to the bar against one of the transparent sections of hull. Whoever had taken responsibility for reopening the lounge had chosen prime space, it was as large as the main forward observation area, able to seat at least three hundred, had a couple dozen booths for privacy and one entire wall was transparent, providing a generous view of deep space and distant stars.

Each tier had booths at the end and it was the lowest of them that Burke had chosen to nurse a drink. From the looks of him it wasn't the first. "Frost! I didn't think you'd catch up with me so soon! You got my message!"

Frost sat down and waved off a civilian servant walking towards him with a tray. His hand never left his sidearm and as he settled into the booth across from Burke he pressed down on the hilt so the end pointed directly at the other man's middle. "Now what message would that be lad?"

"Using your ident code, exempting you from the rationing. I was hoping you'd notice and help me off the ship. Shamus, you've gotta help me. I'll give you my half of your accounts, anything."

For a long moment a grin and a raised eyebrow was Frost's only response. "Yer tellin' me ye couldn't get off the ship an' you thought hackin' into ship ident an' borrowin' me was just a flare for me ta track." He reached out, took the other man's drink, sniffed it and put it back on the table. "That's ale you're drinkin', so unless someone put somethin' in it while you weren't lookin', you're stupid at least, drunk and stupid at most."

"I tried to get off so I could fix things up from a safe distance, ship most of your money back over wireless, but Captain's got this boat bottled up more n' the *Samson*, I swear. Sure, looks loose an' busy, but everything that lifts off the deck's got someone he knows by name, everything with an engine's got someone's eye on it. Tried pryin' into a fighter and that little bitch Paula calls me out with half the deck crew behind her, didn't need help with a mouth like that; she's worse than any alarm I've heard."

Shamus laughed and shook his head. "Paula caught you goin' down to steal a fighter? That's one for the album. Surprised she didn't get you to security."

"Didn't come to that. Can you help me?"

"Where's Silver?"

"Don't know, we split after you got taken by Nan."

"Taken? Ye think Nan took me?" Frost deactivated the safety on his sidearm, set the disintegration charge to maximum and made sure his firing line was at least a few centimetres away from his knee.

Even over the loud music Burke heard the unmistakable high pitched whine coming from the weapon as it greedily drew power into its capacitors. "F-Frost, I-"

Shamus pressed his finger to his lips for a moment, silencing the other man. "We don't want anyone here knowin' what you owe me, aye? Now we're goin' somewhere private to talk all about where I might find Silver, and to make a little funds transfer."

The panic was rising up in his old friend, his eyes rolled to the door, back to Frost, out into the club and back again. "We can do it all here S-Shamus. I've got all the access I need, and I know Silver was headed coreward. That's all I know," he begged.

"You're right, we could do it all here. I could blast you in half an' Captain would chalk it up ta old business. I don't care what any of these bastards think of me, we're no Princes, that's no mystery. Difference is here I have ta cut you apart, 'cause if someone finds out we sat down at the same table after you stole all my savin's an' ran off then you walked away with nary a scratch, well, then I've lost face. 'Sides, you still havta tell me all about how you got aboard."

Burke squeezed his eyes shut and knitted his fingers together, white knuckled. "I'll tell you everything if we just stay here. We ran together for eight years, that's gotta count for somethin'."

"Thought it did, then you got off an' left me hangin' by the heels with no scratch. I had to go to Nan's crew, you know what woulda happened if Captain didn't turn back an' pay for me?"

"You woulda had to work it off, that's all."

"My arse! She'd have me strapped down and put out for chow for those damned cannibals she uses for pit fightin'! I was worth less than nothin' if Captain wouldn't agree ta a sit down."

"I didn't. . . how could I know?"

"How'd ya not? We both had a record for breakin' inta ships in that system, you did those jobs with me! I couldn't even sleep in an underpass, police woulda snatched me up on a warrant no doubt, you left me there to get done in, to get done and gone! Don't even try ta pass any o' this mess onto Silver, he doesn't have the chops or stones to get into my accounts an' drain 'em."

Burke tilted his command and control unit so Frost could see it and showed him a list of accounts. "I'll do it now, pay you back right now."

Frost watched as he selected all his accounts and sent the funds his way. It was almost as much as had gone missing after he left the *Samson*. "That's a start," he said with a tight lipped smile. When the transfer was finished he looked Burke in the eyes, they were red and watering, nervous and desperate. "Now take yer C and C off lad."

"W-wha, I-"

"Do it."

He followed instructions and glanced at a young man with a tray as he walked by. The young fellow's brow furrowed and interpreted the glance as a desperate summons.

Frost picked up the half arm length command and control unit off the table and dropped it on the server's tray. "Now we can get started, boyo," he said eagerly to Burke.

"Is there a problem here?" asked the server as Burke put his head down on the table and covered it with his hands.

"My friend and I were just leavin'. Give that ta the next security man you see. It has ta go to the Security Chief herself, be sure he knows that."

Burke rolled his head to the side and looked to the server. "Don't let him take me," he said through brimming tears.

"Sir, I think I should call security," the server said.

"I outrank ye by five stripes boy," Frost said coldly. "I've a traitor right here, an' I'm takin' him in," he stood and grabbed Burke's collar in his fist.

Burke whimpered loudly as he was pulled out of the booth and hauled to his feet. Frost jammed the barrel of his sidearm against the hinge of his jaw so hard his molars ground together.

"Sir, I really think-" the server started to insist.

"Ye shut yer hole or I'll drag yer ass to the mast room before mornin' shift starts an' the Captain's first duty o' the day will be to come up with a punishment for your subordination. He's not a mornin' person."

"Yes sir," relented the server quietly.

"All brains and no backbone, some things never change," Frost grunted as he led the much thinner man towards the door, pushing and lifting.

"Everything all right boss?" asked Hunsler as he and two other gunnery crew members just off early evening watch stood up at their table.

"Will be soon, puttin' this traitor off ship tonight. I'll be back for the next round."

"You sure sir?" asked another gunnery crew member.

"Does it look like this pup can turn his luck around? Eyes on yer drink lad!"

As the gunnery crew members sat back down and watched Frost leave with his prisoner, Burke tried to grab for one side of the door only to have his grip forced loose as he was pressed through.

The trip down the hallway to a darkened crew cabin was quieter than Frost had expected. Burke's breathing was heavy but Frost could tell the man was steeling himself for whatever was coming next.

Once they arrived Frost tossed him into the middle of the room, where he stumbled over a low coffee table. Frost had his sidearm aimed squarely at him, there was nowhere to go, at least not fast enough to dodge a full on blast from a highly charged disintegration weapon. The vacsuits might take one shot from such a weapon, but certainly not a second. "On your knees, Burke," Frost instructed quietly.

He hesitated; "please, there's history and-"

"Your knees, you git!" Shamus exploded.

Burke obliged, his eyes flinching from his old friend to the floor; "You and I've b-been through some tight spots, s-seen some good times and..."

"You must've thought I was the most daft man aboard, that's the only reason why you'd borrow my ident. Dinna think I'd figure it out."

"N-no, I don't know, you j-just don't check the little things..."

"Well we've got proper folk goin' through that kinda thing, we're watchin' each other's backs. You'd prob'ly stifle here, feel smothered, but you're lucky. If it weren't for all the good folk here I woulda slagged you by now."

"You're right, I shouldn't be here, I don't d-deserve. . ."

"There's truth to that, aye." Frost backed up to the door and locked it without taking his eye off Burke for more than a second, punching in his personal security code. "Now take off that suit."

Burke looked at him for a moment, confused.

"Take it off!"

He did as he instructed, signalling the suit to slit all the way down the front by dragging his index finger across it while pressing the button under his collar.

"Give it here."

He pushed the suit towards Frost.

Shamus drew it the rest of the way to him with his foot and manipulated the room's controls for a moment. "You remember Sigma Aconis? That crew we found all frozen to death when their hauler sprung a leak they couldn't get to?"

"D-don't, please, not that."

The air in the room shifted as Frost finished setting the environmental controls to slowly depressurize the compartment and cool the air. His own vacuum suit head piece sealed. "Now there's somethin' botherin' me. How in blazes did you get on this ship?"

Burke's eyes looked in every direction, searching for some kind of solution, any way out of his current predicament. "Came aboard by mistake, didn't know Captain was running the show until I was all hired on."

"Ye really do think I'm the dullest soul," Frost took three quick strides forward and pistol whipped the other man with every ounce of strength he had. "You have less than a minute before there's real damage done, then not long after 'till you're dead! The truth, you whoreson!"

Burke started trying to pick himself up off the carpeted deck and gave up, fighting for breath and wincing at the two teeth Frost had just broken. "Captain'll have me done in-"

"What? Who d'you think you crossed here? I'll have ye dead with no answer an' sleep just as sound as if ye gave me one and lived to tell about it. Speak up, might be that the Captain'll give ye a kind of mercy I won't."

"Wheeler! As soon as I got planetside I caught a call from the Stellarnet for anyone just off the *Samson.* I sent a message, got one back from Wheeler, said he'd give me a place on his ship an' a fair share of the bounty from Jake. We knew if we left you there with no means you'd have to call on him for help, and I gave Wheeler the transmitter codes for the *Samson.* I swear that's how it was!" Burke answered hurriedly as he felt the air grow much colder, thinner.

"Well that answers how he tracked the *Samson* so quick. D'you know you almost got all of us killed? That bastard was capturin' Ash an' a couple others for himself an' killin' everyone else."

Burke shook his head emphatically; "I didn't know. Thought he was takin' Captain on the ground."

Frost just shook his head and let the point rest. "What the hell kept you aboard *Triton* when Captain took over?"

"It's like I said! Tried a few times durin' recruiting runs, even tried to leave with those Aucharian military types, but they stopped me, said I wasn't in their database. There's eyes on every important spot on the ship!"

26

"You coulda taken a pod."

"Even you know Captain woulda caught me an' we'd be right back here or worse!"

Frost adjusted the controls by the door so the compartment wouldn't continue to depressurize, but went on to set another control. "Should be interestin' to see this."

"What are you doing?"

"Wonderin' if the security team will get here before the temp in here drops to minus ninety. If they do, you'll make it to the brig, if not, well, I'll send a farewell to yer sister for ye."

"I've told you everything!"

"Where's Silver?"

"I have no idea! He wouldn't turn on Captain! Went his own way!" he was already shivering, wrapping his arms around himself.

"You know we've no ship doc on board yet? Imagine, a ship this size with no doc."

"Eight years! I only crossed you the one time! I'll make it up to ya somehow!"

"How're you gonna do that? What do you have that I want?"

"Name it! I'll do everything I can to make it happen!"

Frost laughed and shook his head. "Your edge is gone lad, maybe you can crack inta pretty hard info systems, but I wouldna have you on my crew, no matter what you've got for trade."

Burke's teeth chattered and his body shook as he flexed his hands, blew into them and put them over his ears. "This is it then? Eight y-years and j-just like that. . ."

"Just like that lad, I get mine and you get gone," Frost grinned so widely that he wished the other man could see through the blacked out faceplate of his vacsuit.

"Chief Frost, we can see what's going on through the security feed, let us in!" said a voice over the emergency band of his communicator. "This is lieutenant Garrison, let us in sir!"

"Lucky, might only lose a couple toes," Frost said to Burke, who looked back at him hopefully. His lips were turning blue, white crystals formed around the corners of his mouth and his nostrils. "I'm havin' trouble with the door, can't remember my code in the excitement, you'll have to override," Frost replied back at the security team before re-muting his end of the transmission.

"We're already on it. Can you adjust the climate controls from your end?" asked the Lieutenant.

"They're locked behind my code too. Sorry, looks like I can run a gun deck, but when it comes to these damned ship systems I'm just daft."

"We'll be inside in a minute! Can you materialize a vacsuit for your prisoner?"

"Oi, dinna think of that," Frost replied before muting his end again and bursting into laughter.

"G-god, p-please F-Frost!" Burke's skin was turning bleach pale in large

27

patches, his nose and outer extremities were turning red.

"P-Please w-what B-Burke?" Shamus mocked, some of the old venom creeping back into his voice. "Don't leave you to freeze to death with no one to mourn your fackin' passing? One good turn ye daft bugger! They get in, you'll live, they don't, you get what you got comin'! Either way, it's been a hellofa show!"

"You b-bastard! I've s-seen you go, go over the edge b-before b-but come on! This isn't you!"

"You fackin wrecked me! I was at a God damned end after I walked offa the *Samson*, an' if Captain didn't come back for me I was done! Prison then death, or livestock for Nan's cannibals! This is real payback, an' if you get out alive, you're on borrowed time, I'll still be gunnin' for ye for as long as you're breathin'."

Burke let his head fall down and vainly struggled to keep warm as Frost just turned the safety back on his sidearm, set it back to stun and dropped it into his holster. As the freezing man fell forward onto his face the door beside him opened. Security and medical personnel rushed inside.

Shamus Frost left the room and headed straight for the express tube. After just a few minutes he was on the main Gunnery deck getting ready to run the morning briefing.

Oz and Jason Go To Pandem Part I

Blue oceans, green-brown islands and white, gossamer clouds covered Pandem. Its gravity was only marginally heavier than standard and there weren't any visible dominant continents, but large and small mountainous islands interrupting a vast ocean of blue. If that were all there was to see as the *Silkworm IV* emerged from hyperspace, it would have been a relief.

Unfortunately, there was a great deal more to consider and Jason started to sweat as soon as the small Navnet hologram came up. "Now *this* is a busy port. I thought we were in fringe territory."

"Looks like they're having a boom time," Oz said as he took the pilot's seat. "What's on the comm?"

Jason checked the communications traffic and shrugged. "A few standard advertisements and a basic acknowledgement from Port Control. They keep the waves pretty clean from what I'm seeing."

A flash caught Oz's eye and he looked at a container ship several kilometres long. Something in its cargo hold had exploded, there were fragments scattering from the listing wreck into their trajectory, but nothing large enough to cause concern. Some of the debris cleared long enough for him to see that they had been struck by a much smaller ship. "Anything about that on Navnet? Any advisories?"

Jason scanned and shook his head; "My filter should put that kind of thing at the top of the list, I've got nothing. Do you have the trajectory the station recommended on screen?"

Oz double checked the trajectory assignment on Navnet and nodded. "I'm in the pipe. Pretty easy considering how busy this space is."

"I'm going to keep scanning for extra wireless traffic. I don't even see the usual spam on my scanners, it's just strange."

"Maybe check in with port control?" Oz guided the ship at a modest pace along side a long passenger liner, its smoothly curved, white and blue painted hull was much larger than their small prototype ship. "They put a lot of trust in the pilots, we're being directed within two hundred meters of that transport."

Jason looked up for a moment then back to his communicator. "Need my help navigating?"

"Don't think so, Navnet says there's someone from port control watching our approach." Oz looked to the starboard side and saw that the damaged cargo train's back end was starting to slowly drift out of line from its forward hauler module. "Don't like that though," he nodded in its direction.

Jason looked up, his eyes went wide. "That's going to hit us."

"It shows green on Navnet."

"That's going to hit us!" Jason repeated, unconsciously cringing away from the four hundred meter high, nine kilometre long cargo train swinging towards them. "Oz!"

Oz looked back towards it and then glanced at the holographic Navnet display. "Yup, it's going to hit us and Navnet's lying to me," he redirected the main thrusters to fire downwards and throttled up to full power. If he was nervous, Jason couldn't tell.

The *Silkstream IV* narrowly avoided the collision and to their port side they could see the cargo train's rear half was tearing into the hull of the passenger liner. "Trying to contact Port Control, we're being jammed from the ground."

"What?"

"Yup, we're getting communications from Port Control, but we can't send out. One way comms."

Oz looked nervous. His gaze darted in all directions as he directed the ship towards the planet. "Might be time to land."

"I'm going to try and search for any non-automated signals," Jason said. "Time for a new search filter."

"I'll try not to have a heart attack," Oz said as he tried to keep from colliding from the hundreds of ships all around them. The Navnet system had directed everything into a small area, and he hadn't seen a clear route out of it other than the planet itself.

"Have you ever flown without Navnet?"

"Now's not a good time to bring that up," Oz replied.

Jason sealed his vacsuit, the small hood came up from the neck and closed around a semitransparent face plate that extended from his collar.

"Smartass," Oz shot through his teeth as he guided the *Silkstream IV* down the length of a mobile repair station. The gargantuan repair and merchant vessel was decompressing from several fissures and collision points in its hull, and those were easier to avoid than the ships trying to make their way by the Navnet or otherwise. When they cleared it Oz sighed as he saw nothing but the planet below.

"Found something!" Jason exclaimed as he turned on the speaker system.

"*All ships, do not use Navnet. A virus has corrupted our systems and is guiding vessels into collisions and close quarters. Get clear of Pandem and contact your governments. We need your help. If you must land, navigate to Damshir, we have regained control here,*" said an urgent announcer. "*I say again. . .*"

Jason turned the broadcast down and brought Damshir's coordinates up from the ships own navigational database. "Says no one from Freeground has been there in ages. It's about time someone paid them a visi-" he was interrupted as the *Silkstream IV* jostled and spun.

"Something hit us from behind," Oz said as he struggled to regain control of the ship.

"Checking," Jason said as he navigated through the hardware systems screen. "Oh crap, we might make it down but we'll never get up again."

"What did we lose?"

"Secondary energy storage and our main power feeds are going to burn out on entry. Aim for water, we'll have to use the emergency chutes."

"Aiming for water," Oz said as he brought the ship in line with a safe atmospheric entry course. "Now what's this about chutes?"

"Didn't read up on the emergency systems, huh?"

"Nope."

"When Ayan and Laura's team finished this ship they added emergency entry chutes and inflatable buffers, so when we fall like a stone they'll deploy and we can float down."

"You're kidding."

"Nope, they didn't have room for big emergency thrusters and the inflatable buffers probably won't even deploy because they're made for bouncing on lower gravity worlds."

"Well, we're starting entry. If those chutes don't work I'm going to be pissed."

Jason laughed and braced himself by bringing his feet up and pressing them against the edge of the control console, strapping himself in at the same time. "If I'm wrong we'll be paste. The inertial dampeners will burn up right along with our main power distribution systems."

Oz strapped himself in as the fire of entry prompted the view port to darken. He watched the autopilot work closely, holding the manual control with one hand at all times. "Some pit stop."

"Hey, you picked this rock."

"I know, I know. I hate to say it, but I don't think it matters where we go, from the looks this virus is hitting everywhere."

"I'm never buying another AI," Jason pledged.

The *Silkstream* began to shake violently, the lights and control systems went out. Backup pilot systems kicked in but when Oz checked the thruster status he shook his head. "We're falling free, so we're past the possibility of burning up. Now we just have to worry about getting tossed like a meat salad when we hit."

Jason's teeth clacked together as they hit turbulence and he cringed. "You have a real way with words. The chutes should deploy in a sec."

The craft shook and began to turn. The blue sky came into view and as they watched the altimeter count down from 22,467 meters both of them started to get nervous.

"Can the chutes deploy if we're going backwards?" Oz asked.

"I don't know! It didn't say! Is there any chance of survival if we just hit? I mean, I went through officer training, but I didn't do too well on emergency measures in the pilot's seat."

"Basic physics here, we hit the ground going two hundred fifty kilometres an hour and they'll find nothing but chewy center. At that speed we'll redefine the term; 'splat.'"

"Aren't you just mister bright side."

"Is there an emergency release for these chutes or something?"

31

"I don't know, the detailed specs were on my command and control unit and in the computer, ones fried, the other one only has emergency power. But there's a gyro, it's blinking green, that's got to be good," Jason pointed to a backlit indicator on the control console.

Oz pointed to the altimeter, which read 12,209, and said; "at least it'll be quick if that's a bum reading. Terminal velocity has to be a little faster on this world than what we're used to."

An ear piercing triple pop filled the small cabin and the heavy weave parachutes launched from the front of the ship, filling their view with the welcome sight of billowing cloth. They were pressed violently into the backs of their seats.

Both of them were quiet for a long moment, staring up at the deployed parachutes, the thin, strong lines extending out to them.

"I wonder what the weather's like?" Oz asked calmly.

"Looks sunny."

The ship drifted down through the air slowly for what seemed to be several minutes in silence. Both jumped as several sharp, high pitched impacts sounded against the hull. They ceased as suddenly as they began.

"We're in trouble." Jason concluded. "Do you think those lines could take a few hits?"

"Sounds like small arms fire, the hull should take it and even if those rounds put holes in the parachutes we'll be fine."

"What about the lines holding the parachutes?"

"Did you happen to see what they're made of?"

"Nope."

"Your guess is as good as mine. Their chances of hitting them are pretty slim though. What we really have to worry about is what's waiting for us on the ground."

"You're a real barrel of laughs, you know that?"

Oz released the straps on his seat and dropped backwards out of it carefully.

"Where are you going?" Jason asked.

"Making sure our gear is ready."

"Mine's the dark green bag."

"I know, is that all you've got for this trip?"

"I didn't exactly take time to pack. You wouldn't happen to have an extra rifle?"

"I didn't exactly get a chance to pack." Oz replied. "We'll have to use the standard issue automatic rifles from the ship stores. Good thing Ayan and your wife took the time to pack things properly."

"What about our sidearms? They have as much or more punch than those Freeground A7's."

"Sure they do, but we don't have a clip bag for each. Besides, the rifles have four times the range."

"Good point."

"Just remember to-"

"-squeeze the trigger, don't pull it. I know, I know."

The whole ship jostled suddenly and Jason's eyes went wide at what he saw. "Oz! You'd better strap in!"

"Why what-" he stopped mid sentence as he turned to look up and saw that their parachutes were gone. "Holy hell! What happened?"

"Looked like a small single wing plane just ran right through our parachutes!"

Oz could barely hear the last bit of Jason's sentence as several pops sounded all around the ship. "That's not gunfire! What is it?"

"It's the inflation systems for the balloons. We're going bouncing."

Oz hurriedly strapped himself into the rear most seat in the *Silkworm IV* and looked back up to the cockpit in time to see it covered by the dark brown material of the emergency landing balloons. "How high up are we?"

"About nine hundred meters and counting. Hang on!" Jason shouted as he sealed his vacsuit and activated the impact systems.

Oz did the same reflexively. "You know, they have a whole unit on crash landings in marine training. They scared the hell out of us to make the real thing more manageable."

"Did it work?"

"Do you really want to know?"

"Nope!"

The impact came before he was ready, but the emergency impact systems in his vacsuit compensated just enough. The sudden jostling and uncontrolled rolling and bouncing of the craft gave him an instant headache, made him feel like his stomach was in his throat, he could taste what remained of the ration he'd had that afternoon all over again and he tried as hard as he could to hold his arms tightly crossed over his chest so they wouldn't flail wildly.

When they came to a stop both of them just sat there for a moment, amazed that they were still in one piece. "I think I swallowed my lunch four times." Jason groaned as he undid the straps to his seat and abruptly fell to the ceiling. "We're upside down!" he called out. "Just so you know."

"I know. I don't think I'll have the Fettuccine ration pack for a while, doesn't taste so good on the rerun." Oz said as he carefully lowered himself down and made his way to Jason.

The small ship had managed to keep her hatches, cupboards and compartments closed despite the barely controlled crash landing.

"Everything still where it's supposed to be? Anything broken?" Oz asked.

"Yup, you?"

"Ready for whatever's waiting out there. Here's hoping there's someone friendly."

A Sunny Morning

Liam couldn't help but admit that he was beginning to enjoy his time aboard the *Triton*. Over the past nine days the ship had spent on its slow movement along the outer edge of the bright nebula most of the crew had started making themselves at home. The few civilians that were left after most of them found jobs as crewmembers were opening up shop, starting to mix with the more military minded people aboard and that was partly thanks to him.

He had taken it upon himself to make suggestions to department heads about several activities the crew members could engage in to not only mix with the few dozen civilians aboard but to make the *Triton* a real home. The botanical section of the ship was a great help, many enjoyed strolling down the larger hallways beside the broad planters, vertical gardens on the walls and on through the large center, where full trees were planted and there were even patches of soft green grass for people to lounge on.

His favourite part of the day was the morning; he lead a stretching session that was a combination of different yoga and martial arts disciplines for the crew and civilians right in the middle of the massive garden. Many of them came dressed in uniform, the Freeground style vacsuits the crew wore didn't impede movement like regular clothing. His robes were made for free movement as well and he preferred to wear them instead of a vacsuit during morning exercises. A few of the civilians had taken his example and used materializer rations to create white robes of the lowest Axionic level. The fact that some of them had taken the time to research the order and made an effort to follow his example flattered him, a sentiment he accepted then gently dismissed during meditation.

To his surprise Ashley had joined them that morning. She was dressed in full uniform with the exception of her flight jacket, which had been hung over a large birch tree branch nearby.

Ashley followed the group through their exercises from the side and a few minutes after the class begun he moved to stand right in front of her. Her dark eyes looked into his nervously. "I'm screwing up, aren't I?" she whispered with that soft lisp that always made Liam smile.

He shook his head and fixed her with a reassuring expression; "You're only doing what comes naturally. Close your eyes, try forgetting where you are. Now take a slow deep breath," he called out to everyone. The majority of the two dozen participants were patient people and they wouldn't mind slowing the class down to a more relaxing stretch. As she took a breath, everyone else followed along. "Exhale slowly, all your nervousness and negative thoughts are leaving you, passing out of your body." He waited until she had finished and continued; "good, now bring air in through your nose just as slowly, fill your body with clean air, relax your stomach so you can take it all in and when you're full begin releasing slowly through your mouth. All negative thoughts and energies are leaving you." He did this with the class, watching Ashley as she began to forget that she was the center of attention, at least momentarily.

"Now we're going to lay flat on our backs. Slowly lower yourself down, stay relaxed and be concious of each movement," he directed the class by example, everyone watched him throughout the sessions, even through such simple motions.

When he had everyone on their backs he went on; "now keep breathing from your abdomen, evenly, deeply as you move your arms just out to your sides, palms up and then separate your legs. Rotate your feet inwards, then outwards. Let them fall naturally, don't force them, they know where they want to be." He waited for everyone to reach the position he was directing them to and peeked at Ashley. While she concentrated on going through his directed movements she stopped breathing. At the conclusion she started to breathe deeply again. "Breathe with your movements," he instructed generally, trying not to single her out. "Now slowly turn your head from side to side. We're centering our spines and bringing our bodies in line. Once you've finished, lay with your face to the ceiling."

She stopped breathing again as she rotated her head. He quietly got up and sat just above and behind her. Her eyes popped open, all her self conciousness rising to the surface.

"It's all right, just keep breathing. Now relax your neck for me, let me move you."

"Okay," she whispered back.

He gently took her head in his hands; "now breathe in slowly," he told her as he turned her head left in a pace that matched her inhale. "Exhale slowly," he instructed her quietly as he brought her head back to center. "See how natural that feels? Our bodies are more oxygenated, more energized if we breathe with our movements. We are also more self aware, can maintain calm more easily and our thinking is clearer. Try it yourself."

She turned her head to the other side, inhaling through a smile and then back to center, exhaling as before. "Better?" she asked.

"Much better, now through the session try to match your breathing with the movements. No motion has to be perfect, just don't force yourself past your limits and take it slow. Just concentrate on breathing properly for now."

"Thank you Chief," she whispered to him as she watched him stand up and move back to the head of the group.

The rest of the session went well. Everyone was focused, stretched and relaxed by the end. Most of them were on their way to begin their shift right afterwards. Ashley said goodbye to a few of the crew members she knew before approaching Liam with a big smile. "Thank you for helping me get started. I've never done anything like this before."

"That's all right, everyone has to get started somewhere."

"Did you learn how to do this on Earth?"

"I started long before I applied to visit, actually. About fifty years ago during my first time in college."

"Wow. At least we have the right teacher."

"Well, to be honest I didn't feel ready to teach until I attended on Earth. They have masters there with knowledge that far surpasses anything I've learned, it was a good environment."

"Do you miss it?"

"Sometimes, but like anything; it would be different if I were to return now."

She smiled at him and nodded; "I know what that's like."

"How are things with you and Finn?" It was what she wanted to speak to him about and his invitation to the topic was a relief to her, he could tell.

"We're taking it slow," she shrugged.

"That's something new to you."

"That obvious, huh?"

"Only a guess," he smiled.

"I'm so glad he's okay, but I guess I expected something else."

"You used to think about him often when he was in stasis?" Liam stated as he folded his hands into the sleeves of his deep blue robes. They started walking towards the rear hall.

Ashley nodded. "Maybe too much."

"Infatuation is hard to break," Liam concluded for her.

"Well, I don't know if I was infatuated," she paused a moment then nodded. "I mean, okay, a little."

"The only way to break infatuation is with reality. You have to look at him for who he is. Watch him, ask him questions about himself, let him speak to you. Get to know him better than the version of him you imagined. Your preconceptions and fear are the cause of the distance you're experiencing."

"What if, I mean, if what he says isn't. . ."

"What you expected? Or if you don't feel the same way? Well, how do you feel now?"

Ashley sighed and pulled the tie out of her long black hair, letting it fall loose around her shoulders. "I already don't know what to say to him, we hung out in observation and it's just. . ." she wrapped the hair tie around her wrist then changed her mind and retied her hair, "awkward. We're supposed to go on leave for a couple days together during a recruiting mission and I don't know what to do."

"Be yourself. Don't be afraid to tell him anything, and do your best to invite him to the conversation by asking him questions, even if it's hard. If he's not the person you expected him to be then speak to him honestly. Tell him how you feel. Shared experiences help, do things together away from the ship if you can. He's a friendly person, remember that."

They had come to the express lift that would take her to the command deck and he pressed the call button for her.

She smiled at him; "I'll try. Thanks Chief," Ashley waited for the express car quietly for a moment and suddenly, playfully punched him in the arm. "You're good at this stuff!" She looked at him, noticed his surprised expression and rubbed his arm where she'd struck him; "oh, sorry, not s'posed to punch priests."

"Don't worry, it takes more than that to bruise me," he chuckled at her. "Besides, I'm a Pilgrim, not a priest. You'd be surprised at what I'm allowed to do," he winked.

The doors opened and Ashley stepped inside. "Well, thanks again. I'm on shift in five," she smiled at him.

"See you in observation sometime."

"Or tomorrow morning!" Ashley called out as the doors closed.

Liam shook his head as he turned and walked back down the hallway towards the rear express car doors on the other side of the garden. A smile graced his visage as he considered how he had just had almost the exact same conversation with Finn the day before.

OZ AND JASON GO TO PANDEM PART II

It took a few minutes for the emergency landing balloons to deflate, and the *Silkstream IV* settled atop a large, steeply slanted stone slab jutting out from the beach sand. The rear of the ship stuck straight out into the air as the nose slowly dug into the hot, loose white and black sand.

The rear hatch of the *Silkstream* flopped open and Jason climbed up high enough to look around. The shoreline was less than a hundred meters behind them. "Missed the water," he called down into the cabin as Oz hurriedly pushed their packs through the main boarding hatch and over the edge of the jutting stone.

"Good thing we had the inflatable system for low gravity planets, we'll have to tell Laura how well it worked when you see her." He looked to the high mountain cliff side opposite the ocean. "Programming it to trigger if the parachutes failed was a bit of genius." The lower ten stories featured banks of windows, decks, storefronts, various sports courtyards and other fixtures one would expect to see at a high end resort. Above and set behind that section things changed a great deal. There were closed off hangars, indications that the mountain stone disguised large transparesteel windows, transmitter arrays and scanning systems.

"I'm sure she'll really enjoy hearing about her husband nearly landing so hard he gets liquefied." Jason commented as he started to take the whole scene in. "The computer must have tried to guide us to Damshir with the gyro system. According to what my visor is telling me it's right in front of us." Closer to the edge of the water there was a three storey building two hundred meters distant and palm trees lined up in a row between it and the main resort. Outside was a large deck with a bar and seating for many patrons. There were towels, cooling baskets and other odd things strewn about. At first Jason couldn't see anyone.

As he swung one leg over the side of the stone's edge his eye caught something that didn't seem right, what it was exactly he didn't know, but there was every indication that something was off. Using the features built into the faceplate of his vacsuit he zoomed in on the shoreline, where there were dozens of reclining sunning chairs lined up. "Oh crap. Something's torn these people to pieces," he whispered as he looked on the dozens of bathing suit clad corpses. "Looks like they never saw it coming."

Oz finished climbing to the top of the ship and straddled the edge of the hull. He had his long coat, rifle and extra pack with him. "I'm seeing scorched earth over here, blast points in the sand that were turned to glass. What's your guess at what happened?"

Jason looked the situation over for another moment, examining the scene in

38

the distance and then zooming in on the bar on the patio. "There are serving bots there cleaning the place up. Wait, one of them is staring right at me. One eight seven degrees."

Oz checked the spot Jason was inspecting and saw it. "I can take him out from here. Your call, Intelligence man."

"We should hit the dirt, find solid ground and head towards the nearest entrance to the mountain. There's a high security entrance further down the beach, it's built into the sheer edge. That's a hangar up there, but I haven't seen anything come or go yet." He pointed to the foot of the mountain, where the grey and white sand ended and the black and brown stone began. The polished, sheer face there with large, closed security doors to the left of the resort facing. "I'd bet there are windows hidden in that rock face. We're probably seeing the tip of an iceberg. Let's go."

"That's what I was thinking. Good plan." Oz said as he swung his other leg over the edge and dropped down.

Jason did the same, though not quite as gracefully, and drew his sidearm. "I'm setting my pistol to high penetration, sound right?" he asked as he operated the small manual switches on the large handgun. The standard issue Freeground A7 rifle, with its double barrels and hardened stock, was slung over his back with his small bag of supplies.

"Yup, we don't know what we're up against so we might want to keep the dispersion narrow, save ammo."

"My thoughts exactly, Major."

A bolt of energy struck Oz in the side and he spun towards the beach. There was a security robot wheeling towards them on small treads, kicking up a cloud of white and grey sand as it went. It fired several more times, missing as Oz rolled out of the way and Jason dove for cover. Behind it were several more automations rising out of the sand between small dunes of blackened glass, scorched stone and broken outbuildings.

"I'm okay, it didn't get through the vacsuit," Oz said as he activated his higher powered rifle and came up on one knee facing the bot. His fully automatic particle rifle rattled off bolts of searing energy, turning spots of sand into charred glass and punching holes in the trundling machine. After several hits it stopped and smouldered. "We have a lot more trouble coming," he stated as he marked two more with his targeting sight.

"First time I've seen that rifle fired. Nice," Jason commented as he picked up the emergency supply packs and strapped them to loops on the underside of his backpack.

"First time I've had a chance to fire it off the range. I like. Let's make a run for it, those serving bots have more balls than brains but I don't know about what's behind them." Oz said as he nodded towards the resort, where three androids had started running towards them. One had sustained superficial damage to its middle, its split flesh revealed servos and a mass data storage unit in the place of ribs. The other two were fine for the most part, but had a silvered texture to make the fact that they were there to help patrons obvious.

Oz took several shots at them and scored hits in the nearest ones chest and it fell face down awkwardly, kicking up a small cloud of sand. The other two kept coming, ignoring the failure of their comrade.

Jason started running with his friend right behind, half turned towards their perusers, firing bursts for cover. His shots missed until they reached solid ground in the shadow of the sheer polished cliff surface. One of the servants took three hits across the thighs and was rendered immobile. Oz dropped to one knee and took aim at the third. At a range of less than twenty meters, a little close for Jason's taste, Oz put two dozen holes in the machine that started at its head and ran all the way down to its knees. It clattered to the stone paved ground and slid to a stop just in front of Oz's feet, completely inert.

The sounds of high energy weapon strikes hitting the sand surrounded them. One struck Jason and both men swerved to hide behind another large stone jutting out from the sand.

"You all right?" Oz asked.

"Fine, my comm kit and extra C and C are done though." he said as he dropped the smouldering equipment pack off his back and unslung his rifle. "Over a hundred meters left to the doors and no guaranteeing that they'll open for us."

Oz picked up a smouldering piece of equipment from the pack Jason had dropped and tossed it in the air. Streaks of light filled the air above their heads, several of them striking the target Oz provided before it landed several meters up the beach. "Damn, those aren't serving bots. They must have hidden under the sand just in case someone decided to come out here. There's cover up there but we have to deal with whatever's got a bead on us first."

The sounds of treads and running feet filled the air. Jason and Oz leaned into their stone cover with weapons at the ready. They waited for their pursuers to come to them, they had no other choice.

TRUST AND RESPONSIBILITY

The first drill of the day was just wrapping up and Frost was watching a tall armoured loader take an awkward backward step right on top of an empty ammunition magazine. The black and grey box was crushed underfoot with a terrible grinding screech. He activated his proximity radio and spoke to the armour's operator. "God dammit Ferrin, crack that machine open an' step out so someone whose ready ta run 'er can get in. You're back to sims."

"Just a weak moment Chief."

"If that magazine was loaded with high explosive rounds you'd 'ave killed yerself, yer gunner an' at least two mechanics. Prolly woulda disabled two other guns while ye were at it."

"What magazine?"

"Just step outta the armour," Frost repeated, at the end of his patience.

"Yes sir."

For some reason he glanced behind him just then, and regretted it. Even across a depressurized gunnery deck, even with her blacked out transparesteel faceplate up, he could tell Stephanie was absolutely enraged. Her shoulders were square and her stance was set firmly, as though she were ready for a fight, or spoiling for one.

"Lildell, take over here, I've got a meeting," Frost ordered.

"Aye, sir," came the reply from his second in command.

Stephanie wasn't setting foot on the deck and he read that as meaning she didn't want to say whatever she needed to in front of his crew. He strode to the heavy express elevator, large enough for heavy equipment, and stepped inside. As soon as his foot cleared the doors she closed them and sent the car downward, towards the command deck.

"Thought we weren't visiting each other on shift," Frost said, trying to bring some levity into the large express car.

"Not here," she said flatly over proximity radio as she activated the pressurization systems so they could step out of the lift as soon as it reached a section of the ship with full life support.

He waited for the car to finish its short trip to the command deck and repressurize before breaking the thick silence. She was out of the express car before the doors were finished opening and continued on right across the hall into one of the smaller briefing rooms. Frost followed right behind her.

When the door closed behind them she deactivated her headpiece. The faceplate rolled down into her collar and the rest folded down into a small hood between her shoulders. "You don't even know what you did wrong, do you?" she asked quietly.

"Burke? He had it comin'," he said simply as he stopped to stand behind the chair at the head of the short black top table. There were eight chairs around it all together, and no windows in the dark blue walled room.

"Had it coming? This isn't the *Samson*, Shamus. You don't get to decide who has what coming to them."

"Most o' the time, sure, but not for him. *Samson, Triton,* hell, even on the bloody *Queen Mary*, I get my sights on 'im and his ass is mine," Frost said calmly. He was being honest, he wouldn't do anything differently if he had to make the choice all over again. "He alive?"

"Barely. They had to treat him with nanobots and the first thing the automated medic did was take off most of his fingers and a whole foot. He'll need to have them grown for him and without a doctor aboard, well," she threw up her hands. "I know Burke burned you, and I got your message about him giving up the *Samson* for Wheeler, but tell me you understand why you shouldn't have gone around me on this."

"You'd have had 'im all cozy in the brig before anyone got anythin' out of him. Bet you wouldn't 'ave gotten anythin' out of him either."

"Damn right I would have! Do you think Captain gave me this post as some kind of reward? I've led some of his hardest boarding actions, even when he knew not all of us were coming back! He knows I can handle this and even though he's been running jobs for half as long as either of us, he's a better judge than both of us combined!"

"Sorry lass, you've never been the interrogating kind, not that I've seen."

"That's just it, I'm nothing but a *wee lass* to you, am I? Tough enough behind a rifle, sure, but when I'm face to face with someone you don't think I'm smart or hardened enough to handle you get in my way."

"I've no problem givin' you a chance at bringin' info outta someone, just not Burke, got it? He took everythin' I had, betrayed Captain, the crew and he had what he got comin' an' worse!"

"Give me a chance?" she shouted in furious disbelief. "I don't need a chance, Shamus, I'm running the show! I don't care how badly he pulled one over on you, and it couldn't have been too hard, but you don't get to play police whenever you want to! Trust me to do my job, I'm good at it."

"Aye, and with anyone else-"

"Fine, so you'll let me do my job until someone else steps on Shamus Frost's toes, then you'll get angry and prove once again that you're nothing more than a brainless thug!"

"I just don't think you should handle my business. It's *my* business!" Frost shouted.

"You're just. . . *guhhh!*" she shouted at him in exasperation.

"This was between Burke and I, he crossed me and I got him in turn, that's the way he and I always ran."

"You see where that landed you? Maybe you should try doing things some other way?"

"What, your way? What would you have done?" Frost asked impatiently.

There were a dozen responses to that question, but she couldn't seem to pick one so she just stared at him crossly and folded her arms.

"If the interrogation was anythin' like this, he'd have talked by now, so maybe I should have just handed 'im over!" Frost laughed.

"That's it. We're done," Stephanie marched for the door.

He grabbed her arm. "Done?"

She freed herself, put her foot behind his and elbowed him in the chest just hard enough to knock him into the nearest chair. He fell perfectly seated. "Don't come calling tonight, don't follow me to the pub, and don't try to force your way back into my good graces. Ash might have put up with it for a year from a distance but I won't deal with your crap at point blank." Stephanie finished before storming out.

Oz and Jason Go To Pandem Part III

They were forced into the open. Servant and maintenance bots wearing frozen expressions, armed with tools that threatened to tear nearly overtook them. The worst was a female android who started wailing and screaming after Jason managed to escape her harsh grasp and shoot her several times in the torso, disabling her legs and splitting her chest open. Her reaction was a surprise and human enough to draw sympathy.

The stone Jason and Oz hid behind was overtaken quickly, each of them was only able to take a few shots with their rifles before it became a melee. Their vacsuits hardened under the crushing pressure of grasping hands and other appendages while Jason and Oz were forced to switch to their sidearms and fire on their half dozen assailants at point blank range. After a few seconds they had won free from most of them.

"Run! There are more coming!" Oz shouted over his intermittently functional proximity radio.

"I'll split right!" Jason replied as he fired several rounds into the main chassis of a short cleaning bot. The operating lights on its body flickered out while its upper arm held fast to Jason's thigh. He took a shot at the elbow, blasting the joint apart as he started running. The limb remained clamped onto the hardened section of his vacsuit for several steps before it finally let go.

The desperation of their situation became evident as they left cover. Oz counted sixteen various machines who were about to reach their former refuge and they all turned to give chase as quickly as their legs, wheels and tractor treads would allow. They crossed the paved surface and rounded a ruined fountain with the mechanical pursuers gaining before they reached another section of unpaved sand.

"Those military bots aren't firing." Jason announced through the crackling proximity radio.

Oz looked back to see a group of military bots making their way across the sand in the distance. He'd never seen their type before, but judging from their angular, thin, half humanoid shaped builds and the barrels built into their white and black camouflaged torsos he guessed that they were within range despite the hundreds of meters between them. "I'm going to try something!" he replied as he tossed a nearly empty clip into the air.

The mechanized troops opened fire on it after it was to the left of the various bots chasing them. A trail of light traced the cartridge as it arced through the air and finally landed in the sand. "They're afraid to hit the service bots behind us."

"Interesting, if we can keep ahead of them we might survive," Jason called back.

As soon as the service and luxury bots chased them from the paved surfaces to the sand most of them slowed down, their artificial feet and wheels sunk into the sand. The maintenance bots, with their rolling treads, were still slowly catching up.

Oz saw Jason break to his right towards a short service trench in the sand. Fine wire mesh held the sand back from filling the meter and a half deep path that led to the base of a flattened building. What the purpose of that structure was before it was destroyed by some devastating explosion no longer mattered, the short trench would provide just enough of a space to offer a temporary refuge for his best friend. He would be in the open for several meters as he ran towards it however, and the military bots would have a clear shot at him.

Oz spun around and dropped to one knee, opening fire with his high intensity rifle, sending thirty energy rounds per second at the military bots in the distance with the assistance of the digital sight built into his headpiece. As predicted he only hit his mark a few times, but it was enough. The bots were peppered with rounds as he increased the rifle's intensity and several were mowed down as they tried to reach him.

The military bots began firing at him as well, obviously deciding that killing him was a greater priority than preserving the functionality of their lesser cousins. The service bots were fully caught in the crossfire, and while Oz had the military bots distracted Jason reached his refuge, turned around and took aim with his own rifle.

Bracing himself against the top of the trench, he began firing bursts at the military bots. The few shots that landed did little visible damage but it got their attention.

Oz rolled to his feet and made a run for the ruins of a small information booth. Its concrete backing was perfect cover and it was the only intact portion of the structure. His visor flashed red and marked several points on his long coat where energy rounds from the mechanized troops had struck. As one shot broke through the armoured surface of his long coat to be stopped by his vacsuit he jumped behind the concrete slab.

Before Jason ducked under cover he fired a burst into the last servant bot, its limping gait and several scorch marks made it look haggard, half ruined. His torso blasted open and he twitched onto his back, separated from his hips.

His panicked, painful shrieks filled the air between the sounds of their own breaths as Jason and Oz struggled to catch their breath.

"What the hell is that?" Oz asked.

"A serving bot, guess I missed the main systems," Jason called back, opting for old fashioned yelling instead of using his failing proximity radio.

Oz poked the end of his rifle out from behind the corner and saw the screeching torso writhing there, trying to claw at the sand with its remaining functional arm. Angling his point of view up he caught sight of the military bots, still marching, slowly, surely closing the few hundred meters between them. A few of the more heavily armed bots were rolling quickly across the sand on wide treads straight towards the *Silkstream IV*.

45

He leaned out just enough to fire a long burst into the screaming bot and silenced it once and for all. Before he managed to get back behind cover several rounds from the mechanical soldiers zipped past and he counted himself lucky none had hit their mark. Each point of light melted small spots of sand.

He looked to the rock face and took another moment to catch his breath. They were less that fifty meters from the front of the resort, over sixty from the double doors that, upon a closer look, were scorched and marked by weapon's fire like everything else. "Condition check!" Oz called out.

"I've got a few minor burns, and I can't risk any more hits on my suit. You?"

"My coat's taken most of the hits. It's starting to break down." Oz replied before once again increasing the power level on his rifle. He stood and took several shots at the bots heading towards the *Silkstream IV*. He managed to blow one in half, showering the other bots in sparks and white hot ruined parts.

They returned fire, striking the thick concrete block Oz hid behind with white hot energy bursts.

"I wish they installed an auto destruct system in that ship," Jason called out.

"Grenade!" Oz replied as he quickly moved to one side of his concrete slab and fired the secondary barrel of his rifle at the military bots and the *Silkstream IV* behind them. The first two shots landed at the feet of the machines, sending them flying in all directions. The third and final shot in his secondary magazine sailed through the air on a perfect trajectory to land inside the *Silkworm IV* but bounced off the top edge of the lip of stone it rested upon. The grenade exploded a second after hitting the sand, adding to the carnage of twisted metal and circuitry but doing no damage to the ship they had arrived in.

"Damn that was close!" Jason called out.

"Hard shot," Oz said as he once again took cover. "The others are coming around to outflank us. We have to move but there's no cover between us and those doors. Are you sure they'll get us somewhere useful?"

"They look secure, someone's got to be behind them. Theirs some kind of field blocking my scans so I'm guessing there's someone hiding behind it. One sec, taking the shot." Jason said as he stood up as high as he dared, aimed as quickly as he could and fired his last grenade.

It sailed high through the air, and at first he was sure he hadn't set his secondary barrel to the right power level then the grenade descended and disappeared. "Crap!" he exclaimed before it exploded.

The grenade went off and to his surprise debris from the inside of the ship filled the air above. "Nice shot!" Oz called out.

"Yes! I thought it went past the mark for a sec-" he was interrupted a bolt of blue energy caught him full in the face.

It was near impossible for Oz to remain under cover as his best friend crumpled into the short service trench just meters away, but there were several military bots on their way and he knew they were watching, hoping that he'd take the risk. "Jason!" he called out. He leaned out from under cover for a split second and shot half blindly at where he was sure the military bots should be. Oz didn't get a chance to check and see if his rounds hit anything, the sounds of the machine's assault on his cover filled the air more loudly than his own weapon and he was forced back behind full cover.

They'd be on him sooner than expected. "Jason!" He called out as loudly as he could.

The sight of his friend standing for less than three seconds, opening fire with his rifle on full automatic and striking the approaching bots several times couldn't be more welcome.

Oz took the opportunity to add to the hail of white hot rounds as he stood up from behind cover and emptied what remained of his primary clip into the dozen marching bots. They didn't move mindlessly, but rolled and drifted to avoid fire without colliding and took a split second bead before firing back.

The military bots were as well organized as any fully trained infantry unit and and each one of them could take a lot of damage. By Oz's estimation he had shot one of them at least six times and it was still just as agile and deadly as before despite the scorches and holes in its armour.

Both Oz and Jason ducked back behind cover. "We've got two minutes if they keep moving in." Oz shouted.

"Less. Ideas?" Jason asked.

Oz loaded his last reserve clip and took a deep breath as he listened to the internal systems draw a charge. He set the focus and round strength as high as they could go, knowing he'd get twenty one shots out of a clip that could normally fire for days. "Give me a distraction!"

There was a moment's pause before Jason held his rifle above his head and fired wildly, sending hundreds of blue white streaks through the air roughly in the direction of the approaching mechanized troops.

Oz stepped partially out from his cover and took aim at one of the automations in the lead and squeezed a burst out at him. The first two shots missed as the bot rolled to the side but the third hit the thin android squarely in the chest blowing it open and sending debris through the air behind it for several meters.

He was just stepping back behind cover when the soldiers returned fire, hitting his left hand, his arm and his rifle. Oz fell behind cover and checked the damage. His rifle had been destroyed, his hand had been burned bone deep and his suit was already dispensing localized anaesthetics to his entire left arm. "I'm alive, but I'm done!" he called out angrily.

"Do you think they take prisoners?" Jason shouted out a moment later.

Oz drew his sidearm, set it to the highest power level and sat back against the concrete slab. The pain from his left arm was fading and he already couldn't feel his hand. His attention was drawn to the sky just then, where the setting sun behind them was sending rosy red, gold and yellow colours against the cliff side. "Wish I could get a better look at that sunset," he found himself saying as he listened to the steady, persistent footsteps behind drawing closer, closer.

He was startled out of his lulled state as streaks of light and the explosions of heavy weapons fire started coming from the resort front in force. Someone else was firing at the military androids who threatened to overtake them and judging from the explosions and the creaking and cracking sounds of the melting sand behind them they had a great deal more firepower.

THE FREEGROUND JUDICIARY COUNCIL

None of it was happening as she would have chosen. Ayan couldn't stop thinking about her unique position as she looked at herself in the bathroom mirror. It was a space reserved for Petitioners to make themselves ready before addressing Freeground's highest court. The dim lighting and dark wood textured walls were made to maintain calm, to quiet the nervousness that rose in most petitioners and it wasn't working. All the events of the last two weeks and the many realizations she'd made since waking filled Ayan's mind, overshadowed by her irrational fear of what the Council would have to tell her.

She was seen as an oddity, a scientific first that was an unwelcome shock to the scientific and medical community. Science fiction had speculated on someone just like her coming along but it was seen as an indirect route to an unnecessary goal. Thoughts of a genetically pure human had been abandoned long ago, when the genome had been mapped and advanced materializers became capable of producing living tissue from a purely digital pattern. No credible scientist or medical professional known in the community thought there was a need for a living, breathing template for a genetically pure human. That was until Doctor Anderson refused to let her go and it was partially that unwillingness that drove him to bring her back to life in a way that he was sure she would have chosen herself.

He was right. If she were given the choice to come back with genetic enhancements or with none at all she would choose the latter. Her life had been plagued by complications and considerations that were the direct results of genetic meddling. The struggle to just feel normal was a constant and as she aged her genetic flaws became more and more apparent until it was evident that she wouldn't live much longer. *That was my old life.* She reminded herself.

All my pain is gone, I have a long life ahead of me and I can even have children if I like, something that was just impossible before. There are so many possibilities now, I only hope the Council doesn't cut them away. If I could just tell them to put their judgement on hold until I've done everything I'd like then come back when I'm ready. . . she shook her head at the ridiculousness of the notion. "Pardon me, I know you've been talking about this for two weeks, but could you just stop for a few decades while I go take a tour of the galaxy, maybe find out if I fancy Jake as much as I did Jonas, have a couple children then settle in on a long range exploration vessel before you pass final judgement?" She asked her reflection. *Now that's the speech I should be giving today, pity they wouldn't consider it. Funny thing is, aside from the dimpled face in the mirror, blonde hair and a few new curves I feel just like my old self. Healthier, sure, but really if I could convince them there was so little difference.* "How do you express that?" she asked herself aloud as she stared into the blue eyes reflected in the mirror.

Less and less she reminded herself that she was the second incarnation of Ayan Rice as her body felt more and more her own. The memories she inherited were filled with medical treatments, collapses and problems she'd never have to worry about again and that was a realization that was still sinking in and she couldn't help but feel new. When Doctor Anderson gave her the digital files containing the time lapsed footage of her in the artificial womb things started to come into focus. The playback was set to some of the ancient Earth music he had played over the thirty years he stood vigil as she developed from just a few cells to a foetus and into a full grown woman.

She couldn't help but watch it on a daily basis for the first week. Doctor Anderson and his colleagues thought it would help with her own mental image, and it did. They were certain that watching that footage would give her the sense that she had been given a second chance, and again, they were right. What they didn't predict were the questions. There were the normal ones; "How did you do it?" The detailed answers to that one were in the medical file, and with the help of a scientific encyclopaedia she was able to figure it out.

The questions that surprised them the most were the ones that came as she paused periods in her late development; "What memory was I reliving when I looked like I was pushing something away?" she asked as she replayed a segment of her growth where she was warding something away with her hands and feet. It turned out to be the memory of an unwelcome pass while she was in a night club on leave.

"What's happening here? I'm curled up, not moving at all." she asked as she pointed out to a long clip that stretched on for several hours. The answer surprised her, an unwelcome reminder of the friend she had lost after graduating from the Academy. Sylvia, who she had grown up with and had graduated before to join Fleet as an ensign had been accidentally killed while on long range patrol. The memory came back to her then. She laid in her bunk and cried herself to sleep the night after hearing the news. The following duty shift came too soon and she almost didn't show up. That watch was the hardest, and for weeks she was on autopilot, working, studying, sleeping. Eventually she snapped out of it and thinking back she realized it was her work that got her through the grieving period for the friend she still missed.

There were other expressions, positions that she had questions about, but the most important and the last query was brought on by a self satisfied grin unlike any she'd seen. As it turned out that expression was caused by the experience of the Pilot's Ball. Ayan liked the spotlight from time to time, it was true. The Pilot's Ball was an experience she'd never forget, feeling like the center of attention, having the eye of the one person in the crowd you wanted to be near; few people had more than one night like that in their lifetimes.

Jonas had been tongue tied, dazzled. She couldn't help but wonder if she should change her hair colour back to the shade of red it was that night or if she could fit into that white gown. Those thoughts were secondary to the memory of their first kiss, the first time he trusted her with stories of his childhood, of his parents. She missed him and at the same time wondered if Jacob Valance was struggling with the same questions, the same problems she had.

The thought seemed ridiculous somehow. Jonas, or Jake as he was called the second time around, would have no such problems. *Heaven knows he wasn't always sure of himself, but if there's any of Jonas in Jacob he's probably gifted with that deep well of strength and resolve. I've never seen someone so kind summon such will and clarity of purpose when it's needed. He's probably past any problems he's had with Jonas' memories if Jake's anything like him. If nothing else I'd just like to hear what kind of advice he could offer. God I hope he's in there, I hope he remembers everything important about what it is to be Jonas. Everything with him feels so unfinished and I miss him. In times like these, when I could use someone just like him, I miss him so much.* The recordings of him chasing down bounties, making a grand speech for the Aucharians and other, less flashy security footage came to mind. *There's got to be something. He was a bit of a bad boy in sims before we met, always looking for some challenge to overcome, and the more it seemed like someone else couldn't do it, the more he wanted to do it. That white scarf I gave him, in most of the playbacks he still wears it, there's got to be something of Jonas in him, even if it's buried. Still, marks how little I've changed; still heels up for the bad boy in the bunch.*

She sighed and fixed herself with a small smile. The dimples in her cheeks were something she was still getting used to along with other little changes in her expressions. *Silly girl, pining over someone whose as much fantasy as anything when your future's about to be announced by the highest law in the sector.*

Her thoughts returned to the seven judges on the Freeground Nation Judiciary Council, entrusted with protecting and determining foundation laws for all citizens. From what she understood her very existence was a question that was difficult to answer in legal terms. She wasn't a clone, but a new being that had matured from genetically purified stock in a wormhole that allowed time to pass faster inside its influence than outside.

Doctor Anderson and Doctor Milan both visited her every day since she woke to ensure she was well physically as well as mentally. Doctor Anderson was a researcher and medical doctor, the other, Doctor Milan, was a seasoned psychiatrist who had been on board for the thirty year circular trip. They also kept her up to date on how the presentation of her case to the Judiciary Council was going. The fact that she wasn't allowed to attend was beyond frustrating. Even though she already knew the answer, she couldn't help but ask why she wasn't allowed to watch the proceedings; "The Council is judging this based on scientific fact and they believe that it may be difficult to remain objective with you present," came the predictable answer.

"I'm not just some experiment, I became a person. An actual woman who deserves to know what they're saying, what they're *thinking* while they make decisions that could determine my future!" she responded exasperatedly. She knew it was no use, that complaining to Doctor Milan wouldn't do any good. Her therapist was just the messenger, a testifying witness at best.

That was several days before. Her complaint had more of an impact than she

51

had expected. The entire research team who assisted with her rebirth made an appeal to the Judiciary Council on her behalf. As a result the Council would give her the opportunity to speak before they made their final ruling.

As she checked her white vacsuit, made more in the fashion of a civilian garment with a low cut neckline, and put on a long, gossamer blue shawl that had been given to her by Doctor Shannon Milan, she reminded herself to thank the whole team once again. The outfit had more class than what she normally wore, shimmered white and blue and still had all the practical elements of what she had grown used to on the *First Light*. She adjusted her shawl so it hung properly, starting just below her white choker flowing down to her knees and shook her head.

It still feels so strange sometimes just accepting the memories they gave me as my own but it feels right. Shannon was right, I'm glad we had that morning session. I feel much better going into this without feeling so guilty, feeling like I'm trespassing every time I think about what I lived in another body. That's all it is, really. Those memories are just from another body, it was still me.

Ayan checked herself in the mirror for the last time and sighed at the face there. "A bit of extra weight showing around the cheeks but at least I don't have to take meds every morning or get a checkup every week after this," she had to admit that she missed her red hair sometimes, something she might fix later, but against the shimmering white and blue outfit she wore the loose blond curls looked fetching, much better than she expected.

As she stepped towards the door it slid quietly to the side where Doctor Anderson was answering a question for Minh and Doctor Milan smiled at her. "You look lovely. Very much yourself."

"I don't know exactly what that means, but thank you," Ayan teased with a smirk.

"Whose the looker?" Minh complimented with a playful wink. He was in his old *First Light* starfighter pilot uniform. A black vacsuit with a heavy flight jacket over top that came complete with a white scarf. She was reminded again of the one she had given Jonas and through that her mind wandered momentarily to Minh's invitation. If she could jump into his ship right then and there instead of face the Judiciary Council she would have.

"Are you ready? It's just about time," Doctor Anderson asked quietly.

"How is it out there?" she asked in return.

"Full, but don't worry. I expect the ruling to be at least partially favourable. Just use this opportunity to say what's on your mind."

"Right. Let's get this over with," Ayan said, exhaling slowly and steeling herself.

The doors to the side chamber opened and she walked out. It wasn't a courtroom, it was the Parliament floor, the size of an arena. The four of them walked quietly from the side to the back of the main walkway with Ayan in front, the Doctors behind and Minh-Chu at the rear. She was happy he was allowed to come along, his levity made her smile, which was just as important as anything Doctor Anderson or Milan could do for her then.

When she was half way down the long sloping walkway her entourage stopped and took a front seat in the observer's area. The rest of the seats, over twenty rows in an oval surrounding the moderator's seat as far as she could estimate, were filled with Ministers, Senators, and Military representatives. Her gaze flitted across the ones just in front and to the left and right, there were hundreds, not a single seat was empty.

At the bottom of the sloping walkway was a clear oval space with a circle of desks for House Clerks, the Moderator's High Seat was behind that, and above it was the Council Bench. It was actually a long, dark wooden desk that loomed over everyone in the room, especially the Petitioner's Dais standing opposite. The dais was set at the bottom of the sloped walkway and when she stopped to stand there the massive chamber ground down from a lively chatter to dead silence.

Ayan had never felt so small. She knew what she wanted to say when it was her time to make a statement, understood what was about to happen, what was required of her, and that she did have some influence. While the floor was hers she'd have the very rare opportunity to address all the representatives publicly, without having her statement screened beforehand. None of that eased the lump in her throat, settled the butterflies in her stomach or stopped her palms from sweating. In an attempt to feign calm she folded her hands over the front of her loose shawl and held her head up high.

"All rise for the Members of the Judiciary Council," the Mediator's Aide called out. The sound of thousands of representatives and gallery attendees standing was like rolling thunder, echoing across the large open space. She hadn't noticed the upper gallery above the observer's seating before and regretted looking across the standing multitude. There were thousands sitting there, more still below them in the observer's seating, and she avoided the appraising gazes of the various representatives. It felt like each one weighed her against some kind of preconception or value she wasn't privy to.

The seven judges came out of a back room and each quietly took their seats behind the high bench. The judge in the center was always the last to vote on any matter and the first to speak unless she predetermined another member should be the primary on the matter. The role of the Judiciary Council was to decide on unprecedented matters that would result in the creation of laws or drastic change in government or military policy. Parliament could debate, refine or contest the laws that resulted from their judgements, but it wasn't commonplace, since the Judges were chosen from each of the leading parties.

The woman in the center, Judge Moore, was silver haired and round faced. She was not the eldest, however. That honour was reserved for Judge Barnes, a tall, lean fellow with no hair at all. He had served longer than any three judges on that panel combined. All of them looked bone weary.

When they were all seated Judge Moore addressed the court. "It seems only days ago we were called to assembly to consider this strange case. It has actually been two weeks. This Council hasn't consulted with so many doctors and scientists in decades. Before we issue our ruling, it is within the scope of due diligence that we disclose the process we undertook to come to our conclusion in general terms. Before we enter that information into the record we would like to offer the first being to be affected by our rulings today to speak on her own behalf."

Ayan nodded and cleared her throat quietly before answering. "I would like to take that opportunity, your Honour." Her voice seemed wrong as it echoed back at her, her light Britannic accent was awkward in her ears.

"Please proceed."

She took a moment to sort her thoughts and concentrated on looking at Judge Moore, who sat up high, looking on with interest. "Everything I remember is from another life," she tried not to flinch at her solitary voice cutting the silence. "I can recall experiences of every kind, everything you could expect from a lifetime that was lived in health and eventual terminal sickness.

Two weeks ago I woke up healthy and I was told that a body scan taken of me before I was too ill for it to be viable was used to imprint my experiences onto a new form. A process that took over thirty years and involved sacrifices that I don't know if I could make myself. I cannot fully express my gratitude to the people who gave me a second chance at life. All I can do is honour them in how I use this opportunity. I request nothing more than the freedom and means to be of service to them and the rest of the Freeground Nation. I submit to this Council that I can best accomplish that by continuing my previous existence, to legally become Ayan Rice with the rank and history attached to that name. Thank you," she finished.

"Thank you, petitioner. Please remain where you are to hear our statement of due process and our ruling. As our review of this matter is complete, I'll read a summary of our process and findings into the official record. Our first task was to verify that Ayan was raised in the manner Doctor Anderson and the crew of vessel 42-2100-14C claimed. That is; created using natural materials, altered so a natural evolutionary course replaced centuries of genetic manipulation and then implanted in an artificial womb for thirty years. The passing of which was undergone in vessel 42-2100-14C inside a time compression wormhole. The actual passage of time outside of that space was four years, one month and eleven days. This Judiciary Council finds no falsehoods in these claims.

After reviewing physical evaluation, psychological evaluation and therapeutic logs we also find Ayan is sound in mind and body. Unfortunately, we also found that her genetic profile is so different from any known to our records that we cannot find ancestral ties. It is the personal opinion of this Judge that we should consider that finding as more of a statement on how much each of us have been genetically altered rather than consider it any kind of failing on the part of the petitioner or those responsible for her existence.

With those findings finalized, this Council was satisfied that our review of the evidence was complete and unanimously decided that our findings should be read into the public record. It was also decided that the Sentient Clone Freedoms Act does not apply to the primary petitioner. She is not a clone, but a natural being created through the legal use of modern technology. After much deliberation the fact that she possesses the memories of another being does not make her a copy. There are more than enough unique characteristics for the young woman we see before us today to be considered as a separate entity. Her future development and growth will differ from the original possessor of those memories thanks to good health and other significant physical changes. If both Ayan Rice and the Petitioner were to live their lives side by side we are absolutely certain they would do so very differently but with equal sentience.

Having verified her sentience we conclude by majority that the Petitioner, Ayan, is immediately to be considered a Citizen of the Freeground Nation. Ayan will not, however be treated as a replacement or given the same military rank as Ayan Rice, the woman from which her memories originated. The petitioner is not to be permitted to enlist in the military, she will not be permitted to work in a civilian position that requires access to sensitive materials and will have no special authority or special access to the materials or data belonging to Ayan Rice. The possessions of the deceased will be managed by a predetermined executor, her mother; Admiral Jessica Rice. Petitioner Ayan is also not required to submit to further testing, treatment or procedures for any reason."

Judge Moore's expression softened and she smiled at Ayan. "Congratulations young lady, you and anyone like you are free by law. This session is adjourned."

"All rise for the departure of the Judiciary Council," called out one of the Clerks.

Ayan just watched as the seven black robed judges stood, turned, and filed out of the chamber through a small door. She had at the same time been given rights, freedom and had the opportunity to continue her life as she knew it stripped away.

The few congratulations and quiet praises offered by the closer members of the house were hollow comfort to Ayan. The Clone Rights Organization President said something she hadn't considered; "you've set an important precedent for anyone with memory imprints in the Freeground Nation and anyone who has a deep scan made of themselves. Not to mention the rights and expectations you've established for people who are cultivated the way you've been," he praised quietly, shaking her hand briefly before moving on.

Memory scans and recoveries weren't foreign, but what made her different was the utter completeness of the imprint. It took a lifetime, thirty years, but she couldn't find any gaps. She was physiologically different, but other than having trouble concentrating for the first few days and slightly lower test scores, all of which could be explained by the absence of genetic enhancements, her memories, her basic cognitive abilities were perfectly fine.

Minh-Chu, Doctor Anderson and Milan met her at a side door and they were quiet as they navigated through the thick crowds in the halls outside. There were several more congratulations offered, a few dark looks from people who didn't support starting life in an artificial environment, but they were able to get to their shuttle quick enough.

"I hear you have a ship of your own Minh, why didn't we use it instead of renting a shuttle?" Asked Doctor Milan.

Minh cleared his throat and smiled sheepishly. "It needs a little more work.

Besides, it was a troop carrier before, um, whatever it was used for after."

"What's it called?"

"It was called the *Gull*, but I'm renaming it the *Warpig,*" he smiled as he sat down at the basic shuttle controls. It was an eight seat passenger carrier, streamlined with the pilot and copilot seats set just ahead of two rows of four comfortable reclining seats.

Ayan couldn't help but burst out laughing at the new name before she calmed herself down. Everyone in the small craft knew her mirth came more as a stress reliever than anything else.

Minh fixed her with an injured look over his shoulder before turning around and preparing to detach from Freeground station.

"I'm sorry, I knew you were renaming it, but. . ." she shrugged and looked to Doctor Anderson, who smiled at her, waiting for her to continue. "I just don't see that ship as a *Warpig*."

"Oh, you will," he reassured as he took the controls and watched for the green light from Freeground Control.

The four of them quieted as Minh gently detached from the station and followed the preplanned trajectory to the wormhole Freeground Station was generating for them. They were among several ships leaving at the same time, but since Ayan was the focus of the assembly for the first session of the afternoon she had high priority.

Once they were inside the wormhole that would take them back to the colony, Doctor Milan turned to Ayan and put a comforting hand on the younger woman's arm. The therapist's blue vacsuit gloves were retracted, something she always did when she was speaking to a patient. "I'm sorry they didn't grant you ownership of everything form your old life."

Ayan half smiled back at her and nodded. "I would have liked to see the logs from the last few years. It feels like I'm missing time. I'm just surprised my mother couldn't attend. She would have had some choice words for the Council when they announced I wouldn't be able to rejoin Freeground Fleet."

"She's on the *Paladin*, running advanced missions in the blue belt," Doctor Anderson said quietly. "Or so I've heard."

"Was re-entry into the military something you really wanted?." asked Doctor Milan.

Ayan thought about it for a moment. To her, just two weeks ago, she was busy working on the first two major developments in the new Special Projects Division she and Laura had restarted. It was still difficult to fully grasp that over five years had passed since then, great things had already been accomplished. That was the military she most recently knew, before that she was busy improving and maintaining starships. The sims came to mind, boarding operations, infantry, fighter and epic ship to ship battles all with Oz, Jason, Minh, Laura, and Jonas. Whether it was boots on the ground, rushing into an airlock or holding the engineering deck together while ships tried to blast each other into oblivion, it was always amazing with them. Those were simulations, she was well aware, and when it became a reality on the *First Light* it was so different and so much better.

"Ayan?" asked Doctor Milan gently.

"I miss the *First Light*. I missed it even when I was running Special Projects with Laura."

Doctor Anderson and Doctor Milan shared a knowing look for a moment. The pair were subtle, but it was impossible for her to miss as she sat right between them.

Ayan sighed and tried not to sound as irritated as she was. If there was one thing she wouldn't permit, it was having things hidden from her. They'd have to realize she wasn't some delicate flower, especially after leaving her illness behind. "What is it?"

The low rumble of the engines accelerating the ship through the wormhole was the only sound in the cabin as the occupants to either side of her hesitated and Minh turned around.

Doctor Anderson cleared his throat and straightened in his seat. "Ayan, there's a position open on my staff if you'd like to work with me. I'm going to be busy for the next few years explaining how you were born. You have a firm understanding of the non-medical technologies involved, the ship, the wormhole and the rest of the systems. Would you be interested?"

Ayan was at a loss for words and just started trying to get a response together when Minh gave Doctor Anderson a confused look and turned around in the pilot's seat. There was nothing really for him to do there while the shuttle followed a strictly predetermined path through the wormhole, but his point was made. That wasn't what he or Ayan expected to hear from Doctor Anderson. Even if she did have the qualifications for the job she was being offered, and she did, Ayan would be the focus of attention for what she was, not what she knew.

The thought of being put on display for several years while Doctor Anderson and the rest of his team walked the rest of the scientific community through what they had accomplished was about as palatable as being a waste disposal technician. At the same time she didn't want to offend him or Doctor Milan. "I don't know," was all she could say.

"Ayan, if you could pick anything, go anywhere, what would you do? Absolutely anything," Probed Doctor Milan encouragingly.

She thought about it for a moment then delivered her response, looking her therapist right in the eye. "I'd join Laura on the *Triton*."

"Yesss!" Minh exclaimed quietly.

"I don't know about going in the *Gull* though," she smiled.

"It's called the *Warpig* now."

"And you're going through with your trip Minh?" Doctor Milan asked.

"Unless there's a military blockade in my way I'll be gone as soon as the ship's ready."

"You know Freeground can't officially know your intended destination, right?"

"Right. All anyone knows other than my sisters, Oz's sisters and some of their kids is that I'm headed somewhere into the core."

"You always were the secretive type," Ayan teased. She looked to Doctor

Anderson apologetically; "I'm sorry, I just don't see myself answering questions about time compression or high powered emitter systems for the next few years."

He smiled faintly. "That's all right, I understand. Honestly, I'm just sorry to see you go so soon."

"I'm not sure if I'm going anywhere just yet," Ayan reassured him.

There was that weak smile again. "I have strong ties with Freeground Intelligence, as you know. There's news."

Ayan could tell from his demeanour that whatever the new development was, it wasn't good. "What's going on?"

"I'm clear to tell you this, believe it or not, but it can't go past this shuttle," Doctor Anderson put a hand on Minh's chair and caught the younger man's eye. "I mean it, this can't get out."

Minh nodded at him, matching his serious expression.

"All right then. Fleet has lost communications with everything we have in the Blue Belt. The *Sunspire,* the *Paladin*, the entire third battle group. It was some kind of virus according to the few ships that got away."

"Got away? What do you mean, got away?" Ayan asked.

"The ships turned on the crews. Anything connected to an artificial intelligence including life support, automated weaponry, navigation, everything. The survivors are scattered, so there's no way to estimate casualties but we have special recovery teams on their way out there."

"Did my mother make it out?"

"We don't know for sure but there's a good chance. The crew of the *Paladin* caught it early and the order to abandon ship was given quickly. Normally she'd hang on to an asset that size more tenaciously, but according to the report the *Paladin's* internal security systems are all connected to the three primary artificial intelligences aboard, staying wouldn't be a good command decision."

"So people have already made it back from the *Paladin?*"

"Yes, and there should be more coming."

"I'll leave a message for my mother to contact me if she arrives in port," Ayan said quietly, their relationship was cold at best, but she still needed to know her mother was all right.

"There's more I'm afraid," Doctor Anderson said quietly.

Ayan just stared at him, expecting the absolute worst.

"Jason and Terry didn't make it to the *Triton*. They've had trouble with the AI on the *Silkstream* but they're all right. There's a planet named Pandem two thirds of the way there and they're hoping the *Triton* can meet them."

"Is the *Triton* all right?"

"As far as we know, but everything else at that end of the galaxy without a Regent Galactic logo on it is being affected by this virus. Fleet Intelligence wants someone they can disavow to go join Jason and Terry. They have to have a military record, unofficial or not, so they can continue on after a rescue attempt to be Freeground's secret liaison to the *Triton.* They approached me to enlist you since you and Minh have strong ties. They're also aware of the experience you have as an officer and regardless of what the Council's final ruling is they respect it and want you to be our diplomat aboard."

"And they want me."

"And Minh."

Ayan lowered her head and just thought about it for a moment.

"You've only had two weeks to adjust, I'm sure they don't expect you to accept the assignment, especially not now," said Doctor Milan reassuringly.

"Um, I'm not going alone," Minh objected as he turned in his seat to face the three in the cabin behind more directly.

Ayan's thoughts wandered to the recordings of Jacob Valance, not the same man as Jonas, she knew, but she was certain there was something of Jonas left. More importantly, Laura was alone on the *Triton*, Jason and Oz could be in trouble and even though she would miss Doctor Anderson and everyone else she knew on Freeground, the Judiciary Council had just taken most of her opportunities away. The thought occurred to her then; *Laura probably just watched me die. There's no way she knows I'm here, that I'm alive.*

She steeled herself and said what any experienced officer should; "It's a bad command decision to send someone who is so emotionally involved on this kind of mission. What kind of favours did you have to promise to give us this assignment?"

Doctor Anderson regarded her at first with surprise then with a small, amused smile. "They approached me, I didn't even have to mention Minh, they knew he was already going. I think half of Freeground knows by now. In fact, when they requested that I approach you on their behalf I told them I wouldn't do it unless they provided me with a report on your mother's status. I was the one who squeezed them for a little more."

"So why break well established intelligence methods? Why send someone whose emotionally attached?"

"They weighed that against the professionalism you've demonstrated over the years. You have a long history of service, shown that you can improvise, think on your feet. They also know that without some kind of history backing whoever they send to represent Freeground on the *Triton,* they'll be treated like a burden. At least if they send you they know they'll have a fighting chance, at least an observer and at best a voice."

Ayan thought about it for a moment, knowing that Minh's eyes were staring expectantly. "I won't be their puppet. Even without their offer, which comes with no official rank or acknowledgement I'm sure, I'd want to join Laura on the *Triton*. I won't have any of their tracking devices, submit to any poking or prodding they might care to do before we leave and I'll only accept if we can do this our way." Ayan said to Doctor Anderson quietly.

"I'll tell them those are your terms, from what I understand they'll accept."

Minh grinned excitedly and turned back to the controls.

Ayan sighed and nodded to herself. "It's where I want to be. I want to get out there and I miss that whole bunch; Laura, Jason, Oz, and I have to see Jacob. At the least all of them deserve to know I'm alive and well. I've only been walking around for two weeks but I don't feel like I have any memory gaps. To me I was just promoted to Captain, the Special Projects Division is just beginning. Suddenly it's over, and everything's different. Everything surrounding Freeground feels complicated, sort of off."

"You'll have to keep up your physical training on the way and when you arrive," Doctor Milan told her. "Even though we did our best to sync the scan results with your body you still have a slightly different mental body image of yourself. Your brain isn't completely in sync with your muscle memory."

Ayan lifted a lock of her curly blond hair and nodded. "That's pretty evident. I still expect this to be red until I see it in the mirror, but I've had infantry training before, I'll work through the physical challenges."

"So, I hate to mention this, but you know it would take the *Warpig* a long time to get even a third of the way to the *Triton*," Minh interjected quietly.

"Intelligence will have the main wormhole generator on Freeground station create a high compression route, you'll be in orbit around Pandem in two or three days."

Minh's eyes went wide, Ayan couldn't help but be surprised as well. "They can do that?" he asked.

"With a wormhole generator just short of two kilometres across, I'd hope so. It's just not something they flaunt considering how much energy it takes. They'll just say Ayan used an old Special Projects code."

"Why all the secrecy?"

"Regent Galactic is threatening war if we send any help in Jacob Valance's direction. Freeground Intelligence is planning for the worst, however. With a third of our fleet down now, they want someone to go attempt to make amends with Captain Valance."

Minh looked at Ayan and smiled. "I think they have the right idea. When do I get a repair crew for the *Warpig?*"

"You won't be getting one, I'm sorry. It has to look like Ayan and you spend every credit you have to repair her and set off. Intelligence can give you some extra parts from the colony inventory, some personal equipment, but that's all."

"How bad is the *Warpig?*" Ayan asked.

"With both of us working on it we should be ready in a couple days. It won't be pretty though."

"A couple days? Are you sure?"

"Well, maybe a week."

She looked to Doctor Anderson and batted her eyelashes. "Could I borrow a few credits?"

"I'm sure we can get a few people from the team who kept our ship running in the compression wormhole to give you a hand," he replied with a chuckle.

ALAKA MURLEN

With cover fire coming from the resort built into the high cliff side Jason and Oz did their best to help dispatch the nearest mechanized soldiers. Their agility was nothing short of incredible, rolling and dodging so they could last a little longer against Oz and Jason's new allies. The mechanized soldiers didn't last long, however, and Oz managed to blast one in half before they were all down.

The pair turned back towards the cliff side and searched the darkened interior of the broken resort façade for any sign of their rescuers. "Do you see anyone?" Jason called out to Oz.

Oz magnified his view with the systems built into his vacsuit faceplate and after several seconds of searching only caught sight of an automated energy rifle on a tripod. "Nothing alive, but there's some automation in there."

"Bots fighting for us?"

"No, just a portable gun."

A faint whistling caught their attention then, and they looked back to the shoreline just in time to see several dark pods violently strike the sand then crack open. Fifteen thin limbed mechanized soldiers came to life and stepped out of each pod, ready to pick up where their fallen comrades had left off.

"Holy hell!" Jason called out.

"You said it!" Oz replied, dropping his empty rifle and drawing his sidearm.

"No, behind us!" Jason said, pointing at the cliff and ducking down low.

Oz turned around and caught a welcome sight. Several armoured nafalli, issyrians and angosians with their spiny, squat bodies were emerging from the broken resort with the support of several dozen humans.

In the lead the tallest of the nafalli carried a juryrigged fighter cannon at waist height, its power plant was slung across his back. His heavy armour was a collection of many different suits. "Run towards us! We won't be able to keep the shield open for long!" he called out through an amplifier that sent his booming voice echoing across the beach and beyond.

He opened fire, sending a solid beam of blue light towards the enemy landers, the sound of the weapon firing vibrated the air with its low hum. Everyone behind found what cover they could and opened fire as well, cutting into the new wave of mechanized soldiers as more pods began dropping from the sky.

Jason and Oz scrambled up the last fifty meters to the main doors of the resort. One old fashioned door was lopsidedly hanging off its hinges, and the interior was a blackened ruin.

"Fall back! Fall back to the shield perimeter!" The lead nafalli called out. The order was repeated up and down the line, presumably because any radio or wireless signals were being jammed.

A slim hand reached out from behind a toppled counter and caught Jason. "Come on, it's this way!" said a young woman in light armour as she stood.

She led them through a maze of wreckage to a thick security door where several humans waited with rifles at the ready. They were escorted through scorched halls and ruined rooms before being rushed into a side room where a nafalli and several other humans waited. They were all armed, a few carried medical kits.

They were guided to mismatched chairs where they could watch the battle outside progress on a half broken two dimentional screen. There were hundreds of mechanized soldiers outside, the pods had stopped dropping only to be replaced with four engine shuttles that hurriedly landed, dropped off thirty soldiers at a time before turning and skimming back out across the water.

The nafalli with the starfighter weapon strapped to his side managed to destroy one incoming shuttle, sending it crashing just short of the waterline, but the mixed band of biologicals were in full retreat, most of them scurried back towards the resort.

A broad nafalli female quickly scanned Jason and Oz without saying a word, programmed a treatment into her medical pad and instructed a human to inject them with high grade medical nanobots.

"Thank you very much," Jason said to her as she walked towards the door to get ready for more injured.

She didn't turn around, dismissively waving a hand instead.

"You'll have to excuse her, she's been tired ever since I met her," said the young woman who had guided them inside.

"It looks like you've all been busy," he replied with a gentle smile. He could feel the nanobots already working, repairing the burn damage to his arm. He was glad for the local anaesthetic in his hand just then, feeling that being repaired from the inside was an experience he'd rather live without.

The retreat was conducted in a quick and orderly manner. Groups ran back to predetermined positions and laid down cover fire as another group would run behind them, find relatively safe places to take shots at the oncoming mass of mechanized soldiers so the group furthest out could retreat. Within a minute everyone was behind the thick safety doors and the sound of the landing machines and marching soldiers outside was silenced.

"The shield is up," announced an angosian who was staring at a small status display in his hand.

A moment later the armoured nafalli who led the rescue entered the room without his cannon. He stopped and touched the belly of the female nafalli beside the door, said something to her quietly and she nodded before leaving.

Removing his heavy helmet, originally made for protection against medium range stellar radiation or interstellar particles, his loping gait carried him to Jason and Oz, who were still healing. They were just starting to stand as he gestured for them to remain seated with a massive paw. He looked strange and ominous under so much armour, two and a half meters tall if not a few centimetres more, and the fur under the helmet was a thick dark brown with black stripes. "I am Alaka Murlen, welcome to Damshir," he smiled.

"Thank you for saving us, that was a hell of a rescue," Oz said loudly enough for several of the soldiers who had just entered behind the large nafalli to hear.

"You're lucky, the enemy had given up on taking the mountain from the cliff side. Besides, I couldn't let fighters like you be killed meaninglessly, we need every man we can find and there are fewer every day. I assume from your abilities out there that you are military?"

"Good assumption," Jason complimented with a raised eyebrow. "I'm Senior Lieutenant Jason Everin, formerly of Freeground Fleet Intelligence and my friend over here is Captain Terry Ozark McPatrick, formerly of Freeground Fleet," he introduced.

"Call me Oz."

"We were on our way to rendezvous with a friend before we were forced to change our course after a malfunction. Pandem looked like a good spot to land and repair, maybe get some parts. Guess our luck could be better," Jason concluded with a shrug.

Alaka looked at them both, his eyes wide. "We have a few police officers, some former military, but no one like you two. Will you fight with us?" he asked quietly.

"If our choices are to fight or hide away and hope it all turns out for the better, I think I speak for us both when I say we'd rather fight," Oz said firmly as Jason nodded his agreement.

A great big smile spread across the nafalli's face. "Roman is going to be overjoyed. He's conducting things from the shield room deep inside the mountain."

"So this is an all out war? Our ship was seriously damaged by a rogue artificial intelligence, but I didn't think that it would affect so many machines, especially not a military force."

"Most of the military and police forces here were manned by intelligent androids. It's been a while since they turned on the humans and killed most of the population in the city center. They began organizing themselves sometime after that. They dispose of bodies, coral survivors until ships can take them away and fight us for this mountain. Damshir is the last refuge as far as we know."

"Is the city inside the mountain?" Jason asked.

"Partially, but Damshir extends inland from the mountain as well as within. We only control a little more than half the city thanks to a network of energy barriers. There is constant tunnel fighting on the side opposite the cliff. We haven't been able to contact any other pockets of resistance or target any objectives outside of our area of control for weeks now thanks to the jamming."

"Sounds dire."

Alaka nodded slowly. "We're holding our ground though, getting better at working together."

"Did you lose anyone while coming after us?" Oz asked soberly.

Alaka smiled; "No, today is a good day. I'll have someone introduce you to Roman, I have to go lead a counter attack on a post on the other side of the mountain. I'm sure we'll take the next tunnel, word of your arrival is already passing," he said, gesturing to a group of soldiers quietly talking behind him who were intermittently glancing at the new arrivals.

FAMILY REUNION

Ayan and her mother had seldom gotten along after she entered her teens. Things hadn't improved since she began her new life either. The woman hadn't visited, and what was worse, she had abandoned the original Ayan some time before Doctor Anderson and his team emerged from the time compression wormhole. Ayan couldn't imagine abandoning someone in their last days, someone who lived in pain and needed friends and family around them.

Just thinking of it conjured up the memories of what it felt like when her mother left as her first body had a serious bout with disease. Right before the full body scan was taken, close to the point where the old memories ended, she had suffered through sudden multiple organ failure. Freeground Medical had been there, Doctor Anderson was there in the first hour, where he'd come from she didn't know, but she was certain if he could have been there faster he would have.

Her memories were clear, waking up the next morning after dying on the table once, having multiple organ replacement and accelerated recovery therapy. She was heavily medicated when she woke and through the blur the first face she saw was Doctor Anderson's. Over his shoulder she made out the shape of her mother pacing through the recovery room window.

"Hey there," was what she said when she saw him. Ayan remembered trying to sound upbeat, but instead her casual greeting came out as a croak.

He brought a straw to her lips. "Welcome back," he said with a tired smile. "Take it easy. You'll be tired for a few days."

The cool water was the perfect relief. "Everything okay?"

He nodded and took her hand. "You'll be doing aerobics and yoga again soon."

"But for how long this time? Did they say if there were any other problems developing?"

"It looks good this time, everything looks fine," he reassured. Her relief ran deep, if there was one person who wouldn't lie to her, it was him. "Your mother is here, she was on her way to the new colony when she got the call. Jason and Laura are on their way."

"Geez, can't a girl get a good night's sleep anymore?" Ayan whispered through a wry grin.

Doctor Anderson chuckled and nodded. "You've been here a while."

The door slid open to admit her mother. She was in full uniform, the state she was used to seeing her in back then. Admiral Rice only looked unsure and tentative when approaching a hospital bed. It was always the most awkward time for her mother, she never knew what to say even though just being there, trying to make the passing time more enjoyable would have been enough, more than enough.

"I'll leave you two for a while," Doctor Anderson took his leave quietly.

"Thank you Doctor," her mother said as he left. "How are you?" she asked Ayan.

"On cloud nine thanks to these recovery meds. There are days when I'd fake it if I could just to get dosed." Ayan's attempt at levity didn't so much as dent her mother's awkwardness. There was something going on. Bad news hung in the air. "It was bad this time," Ayan stated to gently press her mother for more information.

She nodded. "I'm sorry. They got it under control and were able to make your circulatory system viable again."

Make your circulatory system viable. She'd never forget the stark reality of those words. It wasn't just organ failure, it was an all out attack that went well past it. Something she had to know, but not just then. "Thank you for coming," she managed.

Her mother looked at her, a little startled. "Of course. When I heard I had them turn the transport around." She sat down quietly.

Ayan recognized the look, her mother was trying to find the right way to say something but instead of waiting for her to phrase whatever it was just right, she decided to change the topic. "How's the colony?"

"Beautiful. Developing the existing flora and fauna is going much faster than expected. You should see it."

"I will, when I can get away from Special Projects. We're just starting up two new developments."

"I heard, Minister Ferrel can't stop talking about your success. It made getting your scan pushed through much easier."

Ayan was genuinely surprised. She had requested access to the high resolution bioscanner months before but they hadn't so much as reviewed her application and there was little Freeground could do since it was owned by a private firm. Her mother wasn't even told about it. "How did you?"

"I put in a request of my own, they told me yours was already in queue. They'll take you as soon as you've recovered."

She tried to keep calm, tried to keep the worst thoughts at bay. "Is it something the doctors said?" Ayan asked finally.

"It'll help if they can use a healthy scan as a base template." It was a rehearsed response, it came too quickly and smoothly.

Even then she recalled thinking that there was something else going on. That kind of instant, high resolution image capture encompassed everything that was happening inside and outside of the human body was expensive and in very high demand. Physical and bioelectrical images were taken down to the molecular level. Several million frames in the space of a few seconds were captured with her scan, enough to see exactly how she worked, right down to the neural functions of her brain. "Thank you," was all she could manage then.

Her mother smiled a little and patted her hand. "You're welcome." They looked at each other then, and just as Ayan was starting to smile back, to expect her mother to stay a while, the woman cleared her throat and that sleek veneer replaced the soft expression that had made a brief appearance. "I'm sorry, I have to go. There's a shuttle waiting for me and I need to wrap up this part of the colony's development. I'd stay if I could, I shouldn't even be here now, but I have operational data that's critical to the colony's success."

Ayan smiled reassuringly, through the fog of pain killers it was easier than expected. "I'll be okay. Thank you for coming."

Admiral Rice stood up then, glanced at her daughter once more and left.

The memories were so clear, the view from that hospital bed as she watched her mother walk by the windows, off to continue her own life, to perform her duty. How badly she wanted her to stay just that once as the realization of her mortality settled in. That was the time she realized that things would only get worse, that she had passed a marker in the history of her illness and there was no going back.

As tears started to further obscure her vision Jason appeared at the observation window. He was smiling and waving exaggeratedly, it was hard not to chuckle at his antics. Even as he lifted her spirits she knew Laura was probably out of sight, speaking with her mother somewhere down the hallway.

Now those were true friends. Ayan thought to herself in reflection. Laura was always there and Jason would often stop in and visit even if his wife wasn't around. At her apartment, in the hospital, even at work a few times. Theirs was an easy friendship, just as easy as the one she had with Laura, only different. Conversations with him were always more light hearted, it was easy to have a laugh over a cup of coffee. She wondered idly how that progressed as time went on, through the times after the scan, past the scope of what she could remember.

Doctor Anderson had done what he could to inform her of what went on after the scan, he had even showed her footage of her mother's visits when the wormhole ship emerged after they had completed the long time compression phase. It took her some serious convincing, but she had even seen the last visit her mother paid her, where she actually threatened to destroy her before she was born.

That had struck a deep nerve. Ayan doubted her mother could actually dispose of her just as the dream of her rebirth was realized, but just saying it aloud, threatening the man who had spent over thirty years of his life isolated with a small crew with such a loss, it was something she didn't think her mother was capable of.

Doctor Anderson was completely forthcoming about how he seized full control of the project after that, and how he had pulled strings to have her mother sent just far enough away so she couldn't cause any more difficulty. Ayan understood, and was grateful for his honestly. For once her mother had a valid excuse for being absent at a very important time in her life, and Ayan tried as hard as she could to put the past behind her, to give her mother the opportunity to start from scratch, but it was hard. Then the trouble in the Blue Belt began and she hoped that her mother had somehow survived it.

As she finished folding the last of her clothes, a vacsuit version of her favourite long shirt with camouflage properties, the door chimed. "Come in," she replied without checking who it was.

Her mother stood there, her red hair tied in a short braid, her vacsuit uniform pristine as always. Ayan didn't care what demons the past played host to right at that moment, only that her mother was alive. She ran across the main room of the apartment and hugged the woman, who gently put her arm around her. "Thank God! I kept checking for you in the list of survivors but they never added your name." Ayan said as she tried not to tear up.

"I'm sorry, I was in the first group to return to Freeground from the *Paladin* but there was a lot to manage," Admiral Rice apologized. She was quiet, surprised.

Ayan stepped back and wiped a tear from her eye. "I thought they were posting everyone as they reported in."

"I wasn't listed. They didn't want whoever was responsible to know I escaped."

"Oh," was all Ayan could manage as she turned around and closed her last suitcase. She was surprised at how much she had accumulated in such a short time, but then, every crew member of the wormhole ship had a gift for her. They made her feel like the daughter of many, while her mother didn't seem to think telling her she was alive as soon as possible was a priority. It was so hard not to say it out loud. *How could you wait? Can't you tell I needed to know you were safe?* was what she wanted to say, but all she could manage was; "oh." Ayan tried to shake it off. "You changed your hair."

"It's just a new red, a little longer," she replied hurriedly. There was a pause then as she watched Ayan make sure the clasps on her luggage was secure. She braced herself before going on quietly. "I would have told you earlier," she offered. "Intelligence had me operating from a secret location."

"It's okay. You're here now," Ayan replied as she opened and closed a suspect latch on the last case. There was one other by the door beside her work bag and the poncho she planned to wear on the way to the *Warpig*.

"So it's true, you're leaving."

Ayan nodded. "I can't get the clearance to rejoin the Special Projects Division or re-enlist so I'm going to find Jason and Oz." It wasn't the entire truth. The Special Projects Division would be her third priority if she had a choice, preceded by finding Laura and meeting Jacob, then Jason and Oz. She didn't have to tell her mother that though. "I can stay for a while, there's some coffee left from this morning, would you like some?"

"I can't stay," her mother replied, averting her gaze.

"Oh," she looked at her mother for a moment. "Thank you for coming, I was worried."

"There are other people who could go after them if Freeground needed them back. You should stay here, we'll find you something."

It struck Ayan then; *she doesn't know. She has no idea Intelligence has already given me exactly the assignment I'd want. Someone pulled strings and made the mission I'd choose for myself official but didn't say a word to her about it.* "Did you even bother looking at my status?" Ayan asked, she was trying so hard not to let her astonishment become anger.

"I saw everything I needed to at the ruling. That doesn't mean that you can't pursue something meaningful here. I can pull some strings and get you into a project, developing something new. Separate from Doctor Anderson's projects if you like."

"I'm already assigned to find Jason and Oz. After I've found them or determined their status I'm to catch up with the *Triton* and liaise with Jake Valance and the *Triton*. I'd go into more detail but from the look you're giving me I can already tell you're not behind me on this."

"It's just another excuse to go after *him* again. Jonas is dead, what's left is something Vindyne manufactured. You're risking a new life on a past you should leave behind."

"All I can think about is Jason and Oz stranded somewhere, Laura alone, and yes, I want to meet Jacob Valent even though I know he's some kind of copy, maybe not even a duplicate."

"You mean Jacob *Valance.* You're still confused, all these changes take time to manage."

"I feel fine, better than ever. For the first time in a very long time I'm not confused, I know exactly where I should be going, what I should be doing. With Intelligence's blessing there's nothing holding me back."

"Their blessing? They're not even giving you an official rank, to the rest of the military you're just a civilian. If anything goes wrong they'll deny your connection to them. You have an opportunity for a new life here at home. You could be anything you want, instead you're letting Intelligence send you off on a fools errand, letting them tie you off like a loose end."

"They're welcome to! And when I signal that I'm ready to represent Freeground on the *Triton* they'll have to deal with me all over again!" Ayan extended the handle on a grey suitcase and rolled it towards the door.

"You spent the last of your years searching for Jonas, I don't want you to waste your second chance doing the same thing," her mother said, putting a hand on her shoulder.

"He sacrificed everything."

"So you could have a chance at going on. I don't think he'd want you to do this either."

"That's what makes finding Jacob worth it. If he has Jonas' memories and if Laura is willing to stay on his ship there must be something, then I have to meet him. We're practically two of a kind anyway. I have Ayan Rice's memories and as far as I'm concerned, I *am* Ayan. All it took was someone saying that it was all right for me to think that way and thank God Doctor Anderson and Doctor Milan were there to do just that."

"Have you seen the footage of this Valance character? You two are nothing alike, Jonas was nothing like him either."

"You didn't know Jonas. He knew how to speak to his crew, how to build their confidence. Jake does the same thing only he inspires people to fight for what's right. I've seen the profile Fleet has on him, and I've seen the speech he gave in the Enreega system. Even if he didn't have Jonas' memories, he'd be someone I wouldn't pass the chance at meeting."

"Would you cross further into the outer fringes of the galaxy to meet him?

You don't even know what you're risking! It's war out there, Regent Galactic against everyone else and they're winning. There are even reports of the Eden Fleet expanding their territory. Just stay here until things settle down."

Ayan closed her eyes and just tried to relax for a moment before replying. "I don't want to leave like this, but I'm going. With or without your blessing, even your permission, it doesn't matter," she looked to her mother who looked beaten, worn down.

"I was afraid of this. I wish we had taken the scan years before," she said quietly as she handed Ayan a small velvet drawstring bag.

"What's this?" she asked as she carefully looked inside. Its contents weighed several ounces despite being palm sized.

"I just finished collecting all of Ayan's records, research and personal journals from after the scan. The scan results are in there as well. Doctor Anderson gave the chip to me this morning, it can't be copied. I have all her things in storage for you. You can look at them before you leave if you like. They'll be here when you get back if you don't take the time."

'Ayan's records' was what she said. Not 'her records,' not 'what she did after the scan was taken.' "I'll never be your daughter. Not your real daughter, will I?"

Her mother's eyes went wide. "Of course you are," she whispered with urgency.

"No, I'll be the replacement, maybe the second generation, but I'll never be as real to you. Even if I were, what's to say you'd be around this time? You weren't around for me when I needed you last time, so why now?"

"I made mistakes before and I'm sorry. We have a second chance now and I can do better. I just need time."

Ayan looked at her, she was desperate, near tears, but it was too late. As much as it hurt to leave her like that, it was time for her to find her way back to a life she enjoyed living, to engage in another challenge. She closed the distance between them and embraced her mother again. "I love you Mom," she whispered. Despite the frustration, anger and resentment she felt towards the woman, she was absolutely sincere.

Silence was the first response, but as her mother put her arms around her she whispered; "I love you too."

She drew back slowly and looked up. "I have to go, but I'll be back."

Her mother took her face in both of her hands, something she hadn't done since Ayan was a little girl and looked her right in the eyes. Ayan hadn't seen Jessica Rice so much as tear up for ages, but there were tears rolling down her cheeks as she locked her gaze with her mother. "Be careful. I promise I'll do everything I can to pave the way for the *Triton's* return here if that's what it takes to have you home. You're my *daughter*, I'll do everything I can to help you have a good life. I am so proud of you, no matter where your life takes you."

"Thank you," Ayan whispered, blinking away tears of her own.

They embraced again for a long moment, taking comfort in her mother's tight embrace.

LUCIUS WHEELER THE SECOND

The chill of High Valley combined with falling snow and rising humidity would have been picturesque if Lucius was better dressed, but in his weathered miner's jumpsuit it was downright freezing. Planetary shuttles weren't always maintained as well as space vessels, and that couldn't have been more evident to Lucius as he piloted the small four person air car and bashed the heater in the dash with his fist. It ground for several seconds, sputtered and clicked loudly before it came on to offer a brief burst of hot air before stopping altogether. The thick chill was nipping at his ears, his bald head and rough, calloused fingers. If there was anything he hated it was the cold.

"Next time I'll just steal a proper hopper," he grumbled as he jerked the stiff throttle lever. Wheeler could plainly see his breath in front of him, the windscreen was starting to fog up again and the right turbine was making an ominous rattling sound as he cleared a line of tall evergreen trees standing out from a low ridge.

Several roughly built sheet steel buildings came into view and he grinned. The entire valley basin was filled with old hulls from small ships, mounds covered with tarpaulins, and hastily built shacks with severely sloped steel roofs. Makeshift hangars for small and medium sized craft, he assumed. There was a larger spot in front of a more permanent looking structure that had been cleared as a landing space.

Without much consideration for the air car's landing gear he descended, touching down hard enough for him to bounce in his seat. As Lucius disembarked a fellow with rheumy, awkwardly bent fingers came out of the large barn. His winter coat and thick clothing looked like it had gone unwashed for decades, his white and grey hair was roughly tied back in a ponytail and his beard was bound up by a small band. "You're Wheeler?" he asked with a thick Asian accent. He must have grown up on an inner or upper core world, Wheeler supposed.

He nodded and closed up his thin insulated jacket. Lucius constantly found himself missing his vacsuit. "Osamu?" he asked.

"Yes. When Gomez told me what you wanted I could not believe."

"Do you have the mass conversion unit?"

"It is in here," Osamu said as he turned away. "I have brought some chairs so you may choose where you sit, and I brought what medical supplies I have."

"I won't need them, don't worry."

The large barn was host to an old disarmed fighter, a small lifter ship and an interplanetary sports vessel that had seen better days. Right in front of it all was a large device with a wide, rectangular aperture at the front. It was old, but looked like just what Wheeler needed, a mass recycler with a quick burn rate, made to convert heavy materials into energy in the space of milliseconds. There were several chairs of different heights lined up in front of it. "This thing can burn through fifty kilos of hardened metal in less than half a second?" Wheeler asked.

"Yes, it works very quickly," the other fellow replied reassuringly as he made sure the thick power cables were connected securely to the rear. "You pay me first."

Lucius pulled a soft bag from his pocket and tossed it to Osamu. "That's enough for the machine and a small working ship."

His fingers were in the small bag, clumsily turning it inside out and pinching a small green diamond between his fingers. Carefully he dropped it atop a small, beat up hand scanner and nodded. "You are generous but I don't know if you will be able to fly once you use the machine."

Wheeler sat in one of the higher chairs and adjusted the height. "As long as this thing works as quickly as you say, I'll have no problem. Got something to test it?"

Osamu nodded and picked up two thick, meter long logs and tossed them into the dark aperture of the mass converter. He retrieved the beaten control box attached to a thick cable and pointed out the activator switch. "Press here once, safety is off. Press here twice, big red button, and everything inside is made into energy."

He followed directions and cringed at the high screech the machine made as the logs disintegrated into fine splinters and disappeared in less than half a second. It was violent but quick.

Every instinct he had told him to get out of there as fast as he could, to leave the barn, the machine and the valley behind but he knew he didn't have any real choice. The receiver in his head had been deactivated, now he just needed to finish removing whatever Vindyne or Regent Galactic had built into him.

He turned the unit off and shifted in his chair, rolling it forward and locking the wheels. The yawning opening accepted his legs all the way up to the middle of his thighs all too easily. His palms were immediately sweaty despite the cold, there was a knot in his stomach and a fear unlike anything he had ever known raging like an inferno in his brain.

Osamu put his hand on the other man's and fixed him with a look of urgent concern. "I cannot let you do this! It is crazy."

"I have to do this old man, someone put a dangerous device inside my leg bones, just above the knees."

"You can't remove?" he made a sawing motion with his hand. "While you're asleep?"

"No, if I try to remove it too slowly it'll go off killing me and everyone nearby. Trust me old timer, if there was any other way. . ." Wheeler said as he pushed the old man's hand away from the control. "Any other way," he took a deep breath, turned the safety off, pressed the activation button once, began to exhale shakily and pressed it again.

The pain was no surprise, his whole body convulsed as everything below his mid thigh was shredded and converted into energy. He fell to the floor screaming, his head bashed against the base of the mass converter, its humming filled his senses between cries of pain.

The blood was a surprise, there was so much. *I should have tied tourniquets.* He found himself thinking as the pain lessened a little. He opened his eyes and saw his framework skeleton performing its magic.

Replacement bones appeared, followed by working, moving muscle, sinew, flesh and finally skin. The whole ordeal only took ten seconds, but it was an experience he'd never forget and never wanted to relive. He laughed and slowly came to his feet, looking at the stunned old man. "Could you throw in some new shoes for the freakshow?"

Osamu turned and quickly shuffled off to one of many old trunks lining a section of the sheet metal wall. A couple minutes later he returned with a pair of old work boots and an insulated jumpsuit that was in even worse condition than the one he had arrived in. Lucius was already scanning his new legs with a brand new hand tool. "All gone. Thanks to you Regent Galactic can't set me off whenever they get the urge."

"Regent Galactic?" the older fellow said in dismay. "You go now, take Intrepid model. Good ship, I just finish rebuilding," he handed Wheeler the jumpsuit and boots then pointed to the small ship at the front of his barn. It would easily fit through the tall doors.

"You're not going to tell anyone about this, right?" Wheeler said as he took his jacket off and started to pull the jumpsuit on.

"No, no one will hear," he replied vehemently, waving his hands between them as though warding Wheeler off.

"Good, because I'll know if you spread the word."

Wheeler settled into the pilot seat of the small, sporty short range interplanetary vessel and entered the code Osamu had given him. The tiny holographic display ran through the code list and then acknowledged him as the new owner. As the reactor started he watched Osamu run to a tall locker and retrieve a small pressure washer. *He's really going to clean everything up right away, he'll probably put the mass converter in the back too, out of sight. Old guy's smarter than he looks. I probably won't have to come back and kill him before I leave this rock.*

He checked the small, cheaply made communication and organizing unit on his wrist and saw that he was running out of time. "Damn, can't be late to meet Gabriel. No telling what that freak'll do if I'm not there on his schedule."

With the reactor reading ready, the environmental controls heating the inside of the small, streamlined ship, he slowly lifted off and guided the vessel out through the front of the barn. "Free at last *oh baby! Free at last!*" He laughed manically and drummed his feet against the cockpit floorboards. "Time to see what's what and work my way back up from the bottom!"

* * *

The flight to Erdon was uneventful until he reached the radius mark, two hundred kilometres away from the neglected port. He transmitted the twenty credit Navnet fee and followed the trajectory assigned to him by the automated system. Coming down below the clouds Lucius could see the excuse for a port he was actually landing in.

Pit mining was common on Lectivus V, and one of the oldest sites had been roughly fortified and turned into Erdon Port. Extending hundreds of meters below the surface, the tapering pit was host to hotels, bars, mooring and landing sites for smaller ships, port stores and zealous traders who paid far too much for small booths and patches of ground along the major walkways.

He guided his ship down to a landing patch outside the yawning pit city only just large enough for it and input his locking code as the engines wound down. "Damn, this ship can't be more than ten years old but the engines have gotta be fifty," he stood and squeezed between the four seats behind him in the main cabin and opened an access hatch. He was greeted by a mess of cables and small components. Picking a small blackened box with numerous ports sticking out from all sides he chuckled. "Universal converters? There's no way I'm taking this thing into hyperspace," he stuffed the tangle of cables back into the compartment and made sure nothing had become disconnected. "Good thing I paid for this heap with a stolen diamond, otherwise I'd feel ripped."

The trip between the landing spot and his destination took him through the winding tunnels leading into the city proper. A true cultivation world, Lectivus V played host to buyers, miners, loggers, prospectors and anyone else who prayed on them or had just been stuck there, like him. Hallways and merchant spaces were just barely fit for use and despite the smell and sight of the open walkways eroding under the constant traffic of millions of beings on foot, being on one of the main paths open to the cold air was a relief.

Avoiding crowds of people trying to get where they were going was an art form and he fit into the crowd all too well. He certainly looked the part, especially in the old, filthy jumpsuit he had taken from the old man, but years of hiding in plain sight while he worked for Intelligence, then captained the *Triton* gave him the instincts and habits one required when navigating through a press of people. Those memories only served him subconsciously, however. Regent Galactic had built a biocircuit that suppressed concious recollection until he was reactivated.

He'd never forget what he was doing when the reactivation signal reached him. His hands had worn permanent grooves into the excavation scoop controls he had manipulated for over a year while he earned a pathetic wage in an open pit mine. The place was just ninety miles from Erdon and he never wanted to see it again. It was a good thing too, since he shutdown the excavator and walked off the job the instant he realized he wasn't just some lost miner trapped on Lectivus V.

The place he had planned to meet Gabriel had become a regular haunt for Wheeler over the time he had spent as a miner. Lombardy's was just a rectangular room held up by old metal netting filled with chairs and tables. Down one side was a bar, behind were crates and boxes on their sides so the bottle caps faced the bartender. They were stacked half way to the rough ceiling. The place couldn't afford the power costs for a materializer, so they overcharged for cheap beverages and worse food.

Wheeler looked around, there were twenty three people seated in mismatched chairs. He took a seat on a stool at the bar. "Just gimmie a Fobar and Candorian Lager," he ordered from the bartender.

The gruff, grey faced woman shook her head as she took a brown meal replacement bar out from under the counter and dropped it in front of Lucius. "No Candarian Gold Lager hon, doubt they'll get any out to us this month," she said offhandedly.

"You'd think they'd treat the most resource rich world in the sector a little better, considering the markup on an ounce of anything worth taking out of the solar system. I'll just take what you've got on tap."

"Markup's so high 'cause people are greedy, not on account of how much they pay you diggers," she finished pouring a tall pint of dark yellow beer and put it down in front of Wheeler as he unwrapped the slim compressed fodder bar. "If you spent half as much on food as you did what you drink you might get some meat on those bones."

"I'd care if they were my bones. Being RG brand doesn't do much for the self esteem."

"Did you meet with my friend?"

"Yup, Gomez set me up with the man who had just the right machine. Got rid of that stuff I was holding just fine."

"Glad to hear it. What kind of junk were you destroyin' that needed a mass converter with so much power anyhow?"

He finished chewing a bite of the dense, gritty meal bar before looking up at her seriously. "Like you too much to let you in on that, Lucy. We're all better of with it gone though, a whole lot better off."

"Our man of mystery, Lucius Wheeler," she shook her head as she wiped the crumbs from his short meal off the bar with a damp rag.

"Any news from civilized parts?"

"Sure, galaxy's getting her teeth kicked in. Every civilized world this side of the core is covered in mad bots with minds of their own or the Eden Fleet is ripping the hell out of everything in their way. Regent Galactic is doing their best to pick up the pieces, but. . ." she shrugged.

"What a life. We're all getting to watch the fourth fall from a safe distance. I haven't met anyone who can afford an AI on this rock and as it turns out it makes all us poor ones the safest bunch in the galaxy. Here's to the meek getting their due."

"Yup, who knew bein' poor would pay off in the end. Still, don't think this is so bad as it's the fourth fall of man. Galaxy's still turning, sun's still warm, we're still eating."

"Well, I'm still stuck here, you're still stuck back there, who cares if the galaxy's burning?"

"Could be worse I guess," Lucy said mildly. She looked up as the door opened to admit a thin, sickly looking man with scraggly long dark hair and a tall

75

woman with angular features. She made her companion look even sicklier in comparison, she was the picture of health in a slightly loose fitting dark blue vacsuit, her long red hair pulled back into a ponytail. After glancing around the fluorescent lit bar room she fixed on Wheeler and smiled. "Don't they look just clean and new, friends of yours?" Lucy asked quietly.

"We'll see," Wheeler replied as he turned in his seat.

"I see you've made yourself at home," Gabriel Meunez said as he closed the distance between himself and Lucius.

"Not by choice. Is that the real Gloria, or just another copy like me?"

"I'm the real deal Captain, with a few improvements," she grinned.

"I don't have anything worth Captaining, just call me Wheeler."

"So you do remember your First Mate, I'm so glad," Meunez said, pushing his knotty hair out of his face.

"Yup, there are more holes than whole parts, but I still remember some of the best bits. What's the news? Am I getting off this rock?"

"Perhaps we could discuss this in a more private location?" Gabriel asked quietly.

"Here's fine. If there's anything these slugs overhear that's worth selling they won't be able to find anyone who cares to buy it anyway. Order something, be a good customer."

Gabriel looked around the room, unsure, while Gloria Parker took a seat beside Wheeler. "What he's having," she ordered.

"Well, what's the news? I've been here at least a month since you flipped the switch in my head with a hand full of credits and no prospects. I'm tired of being out of the way while you and your new bosses set the worlds on fire." Wheeler griped as he clinked his pint to Gloria's.

"Your predecessor has been killed by Jacob Valance, he's taken the *Triton*." Gabriel Meunez whispered as he took a seat at Wheeler's other side.

"I heard my *predecessor*," Wheeler spat the word, "was set off by someone on your end and the little explosive cocktail you keep behind our kneecaps went critical. What happened? He slag some VP's son by mistake?"

Meunez's surprise and discomfort was plain, he glanced at Lucy, who was walking away from the awkward scene leisurely and then pacing back to Wheeler. "You're far more resourceful than I had anticipated," he closed his eyes for a moment and sighed. There was activity beneath those closed lids, Wheeler could see the other man's eyes were rolling around in his sockets. "Ah, there it is, you managed to find one of your old Vindyne contacts, Cummings. He works for Regent Galactic now and you offered to trade future information against updates on the *Triton*."

Wheeler shook his head slowly. "You're more jacked in than last time I ran into you. Is there anything human left?"

"Questions you don't need the answers to. Don't worry, we'll have someone deal with Cummings."

"Good, one more debt cleared. Speaking of which, how much is my freedom going to cost me?"

"Oh, you're going to like this," Gabriel said with a grin. "We need you to put a crimp in the *Triton's* recruiting efforts. Force them out into the open."

"You know, considering the size of your back yard, you'd think you'd have bigger ants to squash."

"The *Triton* is becoming a very large problem. Other fighting ships have begun recruiting from worlds our vessels haven't reached yet. A few independent Captains are beginning to follow Valance's example."

"So you want me to inconvenience them to death, I get it. Always the long way 'round with you old Vindyne boys."

"No, we want you to make joining the *Triton* crew look dangerous and provoke them into stepping into the spotlight. We have intelligence that suggests that they're about to disappear and that is counter to our purposes."

"Why don't you just give me a few ships, you've probably got a whole battle group sitting in orbit, and I'll go tear the *Triton* apart. At worst Valance will get off on a smaller ship and he'll be back to being a minor irritation, at best I'll slag him and most of his crew. Then you won't have to worry about him, period."

"His fame is reaching high enough that we risk martyring him if he is so directly defeated. There's also a chance that *Triton* could fit into our plans."

"Oh come on! You've got the biggest propaganda machine outside of the core, and your corp probably owns what, fifty entertainment studios? If there's one thing you people are good at it's making up your own story. Or, I know; you could grow another Valance and set him up as some kind of mass murderer."

"Then what use would you be? Make no mistake, you came at great expense and not even the results of our research with you and Valance has repaid that. We're giving you the opportunity to balance the equation. You will go out and do what you have to in order to mitigate the damage Valance is causing, to sour the appeal of the small uprising he is causing."

"Fine, but I do it my way this time. Give me a decent ship with a well trained crew that will follow orders. Not some collection of janitors and mechanics who've never seen the inside of anything but a bulk transport."

"Yes, yes. There's a ship earmarked for your use with a well trained crew. You'll be placed on her bridge when you're ready."

"They let me out as a sign of good faith," Gloria added with a smirk.

"They don't know me very well, do they?" Wheeler smiled back.

"No, they don't."

"So, do you believe you can accomplish the goals we've set for you?" Gabriel asked peevishly.

"No problem, as long as I'm free once I've finished making serving on the *Triton* look like a death sentence."

"You'll have it in writing," Gabriel Meunez nodded. He stood and started for the door.

Wheeler looked to Lucy, who was half way down the bar and smiled at her. "I'll be right back to pay my tab," he reassured.

"Better be," she warned back.

He and Gloria casually walked outside. There were two squads of Regent Galactic soldiers surrounding Gabriel Meunez. All of them were heavily armed, wore

77

grey and dull green armoured vacsuits. "Kill everyone inside." Gabriel ordered one of the Captains nonchalantly.

One squad rushed through the doors and began firing. The sounds of screams and combat were barely muffled by the thin transparesteel doors. Wheeler resisted the urge to look and followed Meunez and the squad that guarded them as they made their way back to the armoured personnel shuttle that would take them back to the battle group in orbit.

"We're going to be fast friends this time around Lucius, you'll see." Gabriel Meunez said with an uncharacteristic smile, it looked like he was trying too hard.

"Oh, best buds," Wheeler said with a wink at Gloria.

MINH-CHU BUU

The team of mechanics did in two days what would have taken him two weeks and then they were gone. The quiet that settled in was almost eerie after the clamour that had preceded it.

He walked through the low hallway, more of a large crawlway, beneath the main cargo area and checked some of the work they had done. All the systems checked out from the cockpit, they had even refuelled the afterburners.

Some of the missing access panels had been replaced and as he opened one he could see all the wiring and power regulating systems had been neatly strung parallel to the ship, from aft to fore. The last time he had seen that hallway most of the access panels didn't have covers, cables hung out and he had to manually trace many of them to find out exactly what they were for before he could repair anything.

No one had touched the *Gull* while it was in storage all that time and he was somewhat grateful for that. His restaurant was another story. His sisters mourned his passing for a time but life went on. They worked harder than before, his eldest sister took his place officially and since he left the accounts in order, had built the business well in the first place, she decided it was worth continuing, growing.

It took them only another few months to finish paying all the debt the business had incurred as it grew, a little slower than he would have expected but still impressive considering they were improving the place at the same time. After that they actually started publicising the small oriental eatery and hosting events. They eventually moved it into a proper restaurant space. After five years the establishment was making more than he would have ever expected and was considered a higher class restaurant, playing host to the bulk of the admiralty and high society alike.

A wealthy Freeground shipping Baron eventually put an offer on the restaurant that they couldn't refuse and they took it. There was enough money for the entire family to settle on an inner core world and start a new business. When Minh left he and his sisters worked every day, most of the money the restaurant made went to paying back what it cost to run and the debts it had incurred during a short, rough spot shortly after starting up. It was about to pull itself out of debt and make a comfortable profit, true, but everyone in the family was weary.

Upon his return the restaurant was gone, everyone was living well, there were new brothers in law, children and even college funds. The only real argument that was ongoing amongst family members was whether to move to one of the core worlds or to take a Lorander transport to one of the more developed but equally distant colonies.

The reception they gave him upon his unexpected return was overwhelming.

He was thankful that Freeground had a reintegration program in place for people who had been isolated for too long. It was mostly reserved for long term explorers or pilots who had to fly secret, long range missions, but they admitted him nonetheless.

He was much healthier physically than most of the people who entered, but his isolation had been utter and at first he could only see familiar people one at a time. Even that kind of company made him uneasy. Having a normal conversation was difficult, awkward. What made things worse was the need to have someone around all the time, being alone was harder than facing someone he didn't know how to communicate with properly.

Minh wanted to contact everyone he missed, which was practically everyone he knew. The therapists and mentors at the recovery centre forced him to pace himself, however, and he would be eternally thankful for their wisdom. He was one of the lucky ones, a naturally social person who actually wanted to reconnect with people so he made very good progress.

He was still recovering, though very quickly according to the personnel at the treatment center, and he was so thankful to have Ayan. She was the crutch he leaned on so his sisters felt comfortable leaving for whichever destination they chose. There were rumours, terrifying rumours that war was coming. Worse than any war Freeground had known. After seeing what he had while serving on the *First Light* and being an infantryman during the All-Con war, he didn't want his sisters on Freeground when it happened. The Lorander colonies were safer and he only had to make his opinion known to them once. After he left the centre it wasn't long before his sisters took him seriously.

He seemed to be back to his old self; busy, sociable and quick witted. For the most part he was the brother they remembered and Ayan's easily offered friendship was partially responsible. He had another place to go, someone else who felt isolated and needed someone to talk to who didn't have a doctorate and she didn't seem to mind his company at all.

Ayan's futon may not have been the most comfortable place, but knowing there was someone in the next room was all he needed. He even enjoyed being woken up when she shuffled to the bathroom in the middle of the night, it was a sure sign that he wasn't still on that drifting wreck dreaming he was somewhere else again. Having coffee in the morning before setting off to work on the *Gull,* or *Warpig,* as it had been re-dubbed, was the perfect start to his day. She was a fantastic friend, and he absolutely loved making her laugh. What Jonas had seen in her was no longer a mystery, but it was difficult to see her as anything more than a friend. A friend who was his best friend's perfect match.

They were both dealing with a kind of personal crisis that few people could understand. It was just as important that they both missed the same people; Oz, Jason, Laura and Jonas. On the purpose of their mission they were in full agreement, and when it was all official that morning, when they had their orders on their command and control units from Freeground Intelligence, the feeling was liberating. They shared the urge to go after their friends in the fastest ship they could find but until the actual orders were right there in front of them it just didn't feel real.

As he opened the trap door at the end of the small walkway and climbed the six rung ladder that led up through it he caught sight of her. Ayan was wheeling her luggage behind her. Tucked under her arm was a combined tool kit and convenience bag. She hadn't seen the inside of the main hold since the day before, when she was helping with the final work on the new micro-wormhole generator. She unconsciously straightened the front of her poncho, and he couldn't help but marvel at how similar she was to the Ayan he remembered.

There were differences of course, she was curvier, shorter, and her smile was bigger, there were even dimples and she was more expressive. He hadn't known her well before, perhaps some of the differences were thanks to him becoming much more closely acquainted with her, but he swore she seemed more alive than the woman he had met on the *First Light*. To him, that woman didn't matter at all. The woman he was looking at right then was his good friend, someone he had grown to enjoy time with and trust a great deal in a very short time.

Minh was aware of how he'd changed as well. It was part of the therapy his sisters were called on to help with. They were to highlight the differences and talk about them. He was much quieter with people he didn't know and he was told that with time and exposure to new people that might change, but there were physical differences as well. The most obvious was his hair, it had grown down to well below his shoulders when they found him. It had been cut so it ended above the base of his neck and he preferred it that way.

He was also more fit. Soon after realizing he was alone and adrift within the station segment he started doing workouts he had learned during his time with the infantry. That expanded as he swung from the supports spaced underneath the walkways, engaged in aerobics he had seen his sisters do growing up, and other physical activities that were challenging but not daring enough so he could end up seriously injured and alone. As a result the man they found years later was covered in lean muscle and he had never been in better shape. He hadn't lost any of his skills either thanks to fighter pilot and marine simulations that were loaded into his command and control unit.

He wasn't malnourished thanks to the materializer and the natural foods he grew. Minh knew that he had been very fortunate in his circumstances but he didn't feel that way yet. The therapists told him that he would eventually realize how lucky he had been despite his isolation. One of the points they kept bringing up was that he finally had time to do so much he had never gotten around to before his isolation, like learning how to play classical electric guitar and write in Quoc ngu and Chinese. He had even started writing a few fictional interactive settings, but without access to holographic reference images or help from anyone else none of them were ever finished.

He gathered his long hair with his hands and strapped it into a ponytail. "*Pssst!*" he hissed between his teeth, surprising Ayan and evoking one of her bright, winning smiles. "I was starting to wonder if you had cold feet," he teased.

"Are you kidding? I've been looking forward to this my whole life. Going out into the galaxy on some secret mission, it's like one of the contraband movies Jonas would send to me over the networks before we met."

"What do you think of the colour?"

She looked around at the inside of the twenty two by twelve meter cargo bay. "It's. . ." she hesitated ". . .yellow."

"I know, I found the paint in an old locker just outside. The deck master said I could have it."

"Well, it's a lot better than the mix match that used to be in here. What did you do with everything you cleared out?"

"There was a lot of garbage, we cut it up and fed the mass converter with it, so I guess it's all reserve power now."

"Even that old statue?"

"The Indian one?" Minh smiled.

Ayan nodded.

"Oh no, the old chief's in my room. I hollowed his head out so I could use him as a planter."

She laughed and shook her head. "At least he'll be put to good use."

Minh closed the hatch behind him and took her luggage. "Shall we? We're scheduled for departure in twenty. . ." he looked at his command and control unit, the same one he had used for nearly eight years, "twenty-three minutes."

"Let's. I meant to be here earlier, but I ran into my mother then had to say goodbye to Doctor Anderson. He wishes you luck, by the way."

"He came by the ship yesterday. How is your mother?"

"Alive, sad to see me go, but I don't think she'll try to talk Intelligence out of making it happen."

"Good, I'm glad she made it out of the Blue Belt."

"So am I."

"Did she say anything about what happened?"

Ayan didn't think about it until then, but her mother didn't say a word about the *Paladin* or why she was forced to abandon ship. "No, I guess that's above our pay grade."

Minh's eyes went wide, his jaw dropped, and he gasped exaggeratedly. "We're getting paid?"

Departure

The command deck observation area was dim and quiet. Several high ranking officers sat quietly working through reports, reviewing intelligence materials or just watching the ships come and go. Admiral Jessica Rice knew the show she had come to see would be starting soon and she walked to the large observation windows towards the area of space used for projecting wormholes. The view from her office, just on the other side of the large command deck was all wrong, and she didn't feel like watching on a monitor.

For the first time she could remember she felt old. When her daughter had set off on her first military assignment she wasn't there to see her off, nor was she able to watch her leave on the *First Light* or any assignment in between. She had watched Ayan take her first steps, say her first word; 'ommy'. Her heart felt full in that moment, there was nothing more precious, no one more dear than her daughter.

Her daughter. Was it the woman who had most likely died in a part of the galaxy she'd never seen? Was it the woman who was about to leave again? Was it both? Could it be both? Every time she started thinking about Ayan she started down a long spiral of distress and confusion. So many beginnings and endings all at the same time and she felt as though she just didn't know what to think anymore. Nothing felt as simple as it should have been.

The sounds of orders being shouted and urgent action being taken on the deck behind the forward observation area shattered the quiet for a moment as the transparent doors behind her opened. They closed and brought near silence down on everyone present.

A hand was placed with care on her back, and she realized she must have looked absolutely lost then. "She's on her way?" Jessica Rice asked quietly.

"She is. Intelligence has arranged the main wormhole generator to operate under Ayan's old pass codes. Everyone will think she hacked in on her own and forced the systems to create a wormhole using all of Freeground's power reserves."

"Full deniability," she whispered with a nod. "I hope this is the right thing for her."

"So do I. I'll be stripped of privileges by the end of the day. Once the investigation is complete they'll reinstate me." Doctor Anderson whispered back quietly.

"The investigation could take weeks."

"I don't think Intelligence could do anything about it without tipping their hand."

"I'm sorry it came to that. If I had known, if you had told me-" she said

83

quietly, she didn't want to scold him so it came as a whisper. It was just another instance in which she felt helpless. Far too many of those had been happening recently.

"You would have done the same thing Jessica. When you're afraid of something you push it away, find another place to be. When you started to panic right before Ayan was reborn I knew you had to get some distance, I'm sorry."

"I don't regret being reassigned to the *Paladin*. I was in the right place at the right time, saved thousands of lives. We'll need them all."

"Is it that bad?"

"The *Sunspire* is self modifying. Using everything in its database to improve itself autonomously. The last time I saw it on sensors it was headed straight for a blue dwarf."

"Gathering power."

Admiral Rice nodded slowly. "The automation systems and other improvements made while she was the *First Light* were still in place. We guess the crew didn't take them offline yet and an AI was able to take full control. The computing and communications package started broadcasting to other ships and when it detected that we unplugged the AI's on the *Paladin* in time to save the ship it began to hunt for us."

"I read the report. I'm surprised so many made it out alive."

"We were lucky. I'll be under review for abandoning ship so early but if you could see what the *Sunspire* did to us in just a couple of minutes," Jessica shook her head slowly. "By the time most of us were in hyperspace escape shuttles you couldn't recognize what was left."

"Are you sure it's coming here?"

"Yes, it'll hunt ships down at our outer perimeter. What it can't infect it'll destroy. We put too many powerful technologies in one place. It's too well armoured, fast, smart and too advanced for any one ship in our fleet to destroy."

"If Fleet had the same decision to make all over again, they'd do it the same way."

"And under most circumstances they'd be right. I'm just glad all artificial intelligences on Freeground and the colony will be erased by the end of the day."

The *Warpig* came into view then, from underfoot it sped towards a wormhole none of the onlookers could see. A rough, hardy looking ship with large, blocky engines and a patchwork hull, no one suspected where it could be going, what its purpose was. All Fleet Command knew was that someone aboard was opening a wormhole that would send the old ship towards the outer galaxy faster than most high priority missions were permitted to go.

The amount of power sent to the spear like wormhole emitters jutting out from the side of the station segment caused the tips to turn white hot, waves of spacial distortion made the stars in the distance waver like candle flames. "Do you think she'll be back?" asked Jessica.

"She's your daughter, what do you think?"

She just watched the ship disappear into the wormhole and smiled. "She is our daughter, isn't she?"

84

"Uniquely and certainly." Doctor Anderson replied with a smile matching that of his ex-wife's.

"Did you tell her you were her father?"

"No, I'm respecting your wishes, just like last time."

"Thank you," Jessica looked at Doctor Anderson then, her expression soft and pleasant for the first time in years. Over sixty five years to him. "This time I'd like you to tell her, whenever you can, however you like. She should know."

"I will, but I don't think she'll be surprised."

Jessica Rice turned and started towards the doors that would lead her to the Command Deck.

"Where to now, Admiral?"

"My office for a little damage control. I'm going to reactivate your Fleet rank. I may as well put you on the bridge of a ship while your research and intelligence privileges are suspended. We'll need you in a command chair before the month is out and you're not getting off that easy."

"So much for my vacation."

A Night Out

The Pilot's Den was quiet that night. As Finn walked in and spotted Frost at the bar he second guessed his choice to meet Price there. He made his way around a group of simulation hologram spectators and was relieved that the gruff Chief didn't notice him. He was just getting off from an extended shift in engineering while Price was on his night off and after meeting several friends in Oota Galoona, he was going to make the trip down a few decks and to the fore to see the Pilot's Den for himself.

It was a sight. The whole front of the observation deck had been opened up to reveal the transparent hull and view beyond. To each side was a long bar but only one had been opened. The rationing of intoxicants limited the demand and with the help of a few materializers off to the side one bar was more than enough.

At the rear of the observation deck, or pub as a lot of the gunnery and lower deck crews had come to call it, there were four large holoprojectors that sat in the middle of several rows of thickly padded chairs. Most of the seats looked old and well worn but in good repair and they all reclined just enough to simulate cockpit seating. Pilots and wannabe pilots lounged there with simulation visors on, engaged in one of the many visual and tactile combat simulations available.

The four hologram projectors focused on the top pilots and tactical representations of whatever simulation was running. Three of the projectors were focused on squad play, where a pair of squads fought within a massive field of shifting, colliding asteroids and wrecked hulls. The other hologram projector focused on a ship to ship battle called *The Battle For Manchester Port*. It was a simulation made for a crew of thirty three who would man a large gunship named *The Intrepid*.

He'd participated as part of the eight man damage control team the simulation demanded before as one of two people aboard the digital vessel who was actually qualified enough to do the job in real life at the time and thanks to the high difficulty of the simulation they lasted only nine and a half minutes before the ship and all hands were lost.

All the simulations had been set to an increasing difficulty. As the crew became better at the scenarios, running the in-sim systems were becoming more and more like doing the real thing. Some of the deck and engineering crew had already started putting in requests to perform qualifiers as pilots and out of over a dozen applicants who had completed the qualifier, only one had passed.

Finn was glad it was hard. He'd done a shift on the flight deck and assisted the repair crews there. When a pilot who had been trained mostly in a simulator returned from their patrol you could always tell. The fighters were hardy, difficult to damage, but a pilot with few real flight hours always landed too hard or took too long to make a vertical landing and often left the cockpit without resetting the controls to their defaults. Everything was logged and whoever was running the Space

Superiority Group at the time would often have a very long chat with the new pilots daily and that was often accompanied by a basic tutorial on how to care for their fighters. He had seen one administered by Alice and in the course of the tutorial an impatient pilot was grounded because of his know-it-all attitude. She didn't have any patience for people who weren't willing to learn, nor should she. A bad pilot could kill not only himself but many members of the crew with just one moment of negligence or poor judgement. Watching her inform the pilot that he was no longer welcome in a cockpit until he re-qualified then sending him to report for maintenance duty was like watching Captain Valance put someone in their place. The similarities between the two could be eerie at times.

Finn had no desire to be a pilot, however. The hangar deck was a place he'd volunteer occasionally. Not to do any seriously detailed work, he'd need more training for that, but to do knuckle dragger's work until he was trained on servicing the fighters. To him, the hangars were the most exciting places on the ship. Too exhausting to transfer there permanently, and he enjoyed his work in ship engineering as well as representing the engineering department on the bridge, but helping in the hangar deck was a great place for a change of pace.

He was glad to know his place on the ship. Chief Grady often assigned him to represent the Engineering Department on the bridge because he was forming a solid understanding of the ships systems very quickly, and when there was something new or interesting taking place he was always involved somehow. Learning about the Sol System Vessel was exciting; all that high technology was beyond anything he'd seen and under the direction of Liam Grady the Engineering Staff worked exceedingly well together. There was still some personal drama but that was to be expected in any large crew.

Of all the things he was happy to avoid, the gunnery deck was certainly at the top of his list. If Chief Grady ordered him to assist there he wouldn't refuse, but serving on the most dangerous and accident likely section of the ship sent a shiver down his spine. Being under the command of Gunnery Chief Frost would be no picnic either, he was certain. He had the reputation of being the most harsh, unforgiving commander on the ship. Someone quit his staff every day, and most of them wound up as a knuckle draggers in the hangars or assigned to an unspecialised maintenance team if they were qualified. The non-specialists, the lowest of the maintenance workers took care of the dirty work; everything from cleaning out sewage recyclers to pulling cable through crawl spaces when the bots were down and since all artificial intelligences had been deleted most of them were. It was a respectable occupation, but at the bottom of the pecking order.

He'd rather do that than serve on the gunnery deck, however, but considering the condition of the Gunnery Chief when he walked into the Pilot's Den he wouldn't mind being a fly on the wall the next morning. Just after a few seconds Finn could tell that Frost was in for an epic hangover the next day, and being a man of pride, the Gunnery Chief probably wouldn't go to medical to request a recovery treatment.

Walking up to the bar slowly he listened in on the conversation Frost was having with the tall civilian bartender who was trying desperately not to encourage the slurring man without being rude. "-cocked it all up! Burke, tha' buggerer, got wha' he deserved, freezin' like tha', you shoulda seen it. Thought he was me friend, eight years on we served different Captains, made one score afta 'nother then he takes it all! Some mate he was!"

Finn had heard the story already, about Frost dragging Burke off and torturing him until security caught up. The word was Burke lost his nose, a foot, several toes and fingers and swathes of skin to frostbite, something that was obviously planned to not only get something out of Burke, but to enhance Frost's already dark reputation and the tenacity of his nickname.

It would be hard for anyone to ignore that story when they called him Chief Frost or just Frost. "Lexin Dark Blue, please." Finn ordered as he stopped to stand several stools away from Frost at the bar.

The server ordered his drink from a materializer set into the wall and passed the tall glass filled with dark blue fluid to him. His records automatically reflected the purchase and its impact on his rations.

"Here's a friendly one!" Frost exclaimed as he near stumbled out of his stool and staggered over to sit beside Finn. He patted the younger fellow on the shoulder so hard he was forced to sit down. "Served with me on the *Samson*, this one did. Tha' was afore Captain took this overlarge boat on with all it's comers."

"Hi Frost, having a good night?" Finn regretted the words as soon as they slipped off his tongue.

He finished the remainder of his drink, an ounce of amber fluid in the bottom of a stout glass made for large pieces of ice and hard liquor and pounded it back down onto the bar. "No! Steph's left! Cap'n gonna put me off my post tomorrow." Shamus waveringly pointed at his glass and regarded the slim bartender, who looked back at him witheringly. "More scotch!"

"You're well over your rations sir."

He raised his command and control unit and ham handedly brought up a display showing his ration status was green, showing over three times the regular usage for the night, but still green. "Y'see here? Ration's good, more scotch!"

"Well, I'm saying you've had enough sir. See? Your friend here has come to take you to your quarters," the barkeep said, gesturing towards Finn.

"Steph'nie sent ya?" Frost asked as he looked over to him.

Finn had a split second to consider his response and shrugged. "Yup, she heard you were down here and wanted me to help you up to your quarters."

"Dunna need yer help lad, I'm fine!"

The bartender smirked and reached across the bar, giving one of Shamus's shoulders a firm push.

Frost was well on his way to toppling over and hitting the floor when Finn caught the heavier man and was almost dragged off his stool himself.

Price helped balance him as he walked up behind the pair and quietly said; "It's been a long day."

Something passed between the pair, the look Agameg gave him communicated something subtly, and the drunken Gunnery Chief got it. Finn chalked it up to respect or familiarity, but Frost actually listened to him and after a moment of looking into the changeling's large eyes he nodded. "Aye, time ta move on afore I find somethin' else ta bugger up."

Shamus turned away from his stool and staggered to his feet. Price got under one of his arms and as Finn took up on the other side Frost looked over his shoulder to the barkeep and asked; "Bottle 'fer the road?"

The slim faced barkeep laughed to himself and walked away, shaking his head.

The trip through the bar and to the express car that took them to the command deck and Frost's quarters was fraught with comments about how Frost "managed to cock up a chance at real service," "get cheated outta every penny, an' piss on 'is friends gettin' it back" he even exclaimed; "only true mates! Bloody shifter who can't do humans an' th' engineer who got wi' the first girl he fancied on th' *Samson.*"

When they finally arrived on the command deck and the express car doors opened Frost greeted the crew members waiting for the lift by exclaiming; "these're me only friends! Alien n' an engineerin' kid!" Most of the half dozen people waiting started and took a full step back out of the way immediately.

Alice was among them and was wide eyed at first, then grinned broadly. "Everything okay?"

"We have it under control," Price reassured.

"Bollocks! Steph'nie's gone! Cocked it all up, pissed on 'er job an' I don't respect her! Least tha's wha she thinks."

"It'll be all right." Alice reassured as she passed them and stepped into the express car. "She's a patient woman."

The doors closed behind Finn and Price as they started guiding and carrying Frost to the command deck berth. Finn double checked the location of the Chief's quarters and realized they were almost there, it was just around the corner.

Frost was following along, seeming to almost dose off until he brought his head up just enough to realize they were passing right by Stephanie's door. With a sudden burst of strength and a bare minimum of dexterity, he freed himself of Price and Finn's aid. He nearly full on collided with Stephanie's door and shouted; "I'm sorry! I'll explain! On me knees if y'like."

Finn caught up with him and put a hand on his shoulder; "you can talk to her in the morning."

He turned to Finn and Price with desperation. "Listen ta me lad."

"Come Frost, we should leave her be," Price tried to convince him.

"Nono, lisssentame! Could be there willna be a mornin', every moment's precious. Asides, I'm charmin' when I'm drunk," he turned back to the door control panel and peered into it, pressing the open button. It buzzed a stern denial in response, showing the door was locked with a flash of red across the control. "C'mon lass! Spent too much time chasin' tha' empty headed pilot girl, dinna notice the great lady right behind 'er!"

The panel came to life, Ashley's face filling the screen. "Come back tomorrow after shift. You're so drunk you should come with subtitles."

Finn looked to Price with his hand over his face. "I forgot Ash and Steph are hanging out tonight."

"Sorry Ash, ye had yer chance, tell Steph ta lemmie in."

Stephanie came into view, looking irritated but dressed for a night out, with her hair up and in a low cut black dress. "Leave me alone or I'll call security."

"Y'look juicy lass. Jus' lemmie in and I'll make it all better. Forget Burke, tha' buggerer inna worth yer attention. Sorry I dinna notice ye aboard th' *Samson*, we shoulda been snoggin' years afore!"

"Security's on their way, you should go." Stephanie said as she walked out of view.

"Love ye lass! You're like I've never seen!"

Ashley came back on screen. "Have a good night guys," she waved before deactivating the door display.

"Feck!" Shamus exclaimed, pounding his fist against the wall beside the door controls. "She's all dressed ta trot out right after our row."

"We should go before security gets here," Price said, putting his arm back on Frost's shoulder and trying to steer him down the hallway.

Around the corner came four security guards in their heavy black vacsuits.

"Oi! Look 'ere, her boys!" Frost exclaimed loudly with a mock welcoming gesture. "Well, let's 'ave a go then! One up, keep it level!"

"Sometimes I wish he came with a dictionary." Price said as he shook his head, cringing at what he knew was about to happen.

"All right, just relax. We can either take you somewhere where you can sleep this off or give you an injection that'll help you sober up. It's up to you."

Frost steadied himself a little and stepped away from the doorway. "Those shots're nothin' but instant hangover! Ye'll hafta take me down th' hard way afore I let ye hit me wi' that! Come on then you chancers."

The first two guards stepped towards him, one with an injector in his hand, the other with hands open, ready to subdue the drunken Chief. As soon as the first was in striking distance, Frost grabbed the arm with the injector in it and pulled the man off balance before pushing him into the other guard. Shamus couldn't steady himself as the pair collided, and was pulled into the mess which ended with all three of them in an awkward pile on the floor.

Frost was facing upward by the time the other two approached, ready to pick him up and drag him off. "You too eh?" he exclaimed before punching the nearest in the nose so hard he was flung back into a man behind him.

Both Price and Finn cringed as they watched the guard's nose start bleeding in a gush. The rest of the guards took a few seconds to seal their face plates. It only took that long for Frost to roll to his feet and stand squarely, fists at the ready. "Ye march off yer own way lads an' I'll forget this ever 'appened," Frost slurred.

"You're coming with us to the brig, Chief," replied one of the guards getting to his feet. He took two steps towards Frost before he was punched fully in the face. The stout Gunnery Chief put so much weight behind his blow that he was nearly thrown completely off balance. The guard's head bobbed backwards, if he wasn't wearing his faceplate *something* would have been broken, but the transparent metal stopped any damage from being done.

Price and Finn couldn't help cringing. They knew that the guard would be fine, but Frost's hand was another question entirely. "Go with them Frost, you should sleep it off," Finn half heartedly tried to convince him as he squared up again, getting ready to slug the next guard.

The Gunnery Chief turned towards Finn and Price to wave them off and in that moment the nearest guard stepped forward and injected Frost right below the ear with a tranquillizer.

The look of surprise on the drunken fellow's face was priceless as he fell back to the deck. "Ye shitehawk bastard! If it weren't fer yer faceplate I'd find out who ye were and come after ye sober!" he managed before passing out.

The guards rolled him onto a stretcher from a nearby emergency medical station once they were sure he was fully unconscious. "Thanks for watching him," one of the guards said over his shoulder as they walked off.

"Where are you taking him?" Finn asked.

"The brig."

Finn and Price shrugged and decided to follow.

Ashley and Stephanie had watched the whole thing and when the security personnel were down the hallway and in the lift Ashley turned to her best friend. "You're taking him back, aren't you?"

Stephanie sighed and smiled. "He's a big thug, but he's my big thug. I understand if you don't get it."

"Oh, after seeing you two together when you're not fighting, I get it. Well, I sort of get it. You two seem to fit."

"I wouldn't have imagined back on the *Samson*."

"Me neither," Ashley said as she put her hand on her friend's arm. She looked tired, and after the couple of days they had had after Frost had captured and tortured Burke to within a second of his life, she understood. "Don't feel like going out?"

Stephanie looked so apologetic; "I'm sorry, I'm just tired. If he wasn't all liquored up and just came to apologize we'd probably be going to the club night as a double date." She recognized uncertainty in her friend right away; "things aren't going well with Finn?"

Ashley tried to lighten up her expression, feigning optimism; "we're good. There's just no. . ."

"Sparks?" Stephanie finished.

"Yeah, there's just a piece missing. He's nice, and he listens, but I just don't know what to say, what to do. I don't know."

"Well maybe the away time you two are going on will change that. It might be that you just need time away from the ship with him, you know, no distractions, no one watching you. After you visited him every day in medical, people are watching to see how things turn out."

"That's probably it, too much pressure," Ashley agreed. "Now let's find a couple movies and have a night in."

"You don't mind? We could still make an appearance."

"It's all right, you and Frost tired me out."

RESOLUTION

There were two objects that distracted Ayan. The first was the bag with all the data collected from her personal files, the ones that the Judiciary Council had claimed she had no rights to but was left instead to her mother, who passed it on to her. The second was a metal case containing a drug cocktail given to her by Doctor Anderson.

When she woke up that morning, she decided to take care of one of the two objects, and after several moments of thought over coffee she opened the black bag and poured out the three dense data chips into her palm. The only thing left inside the bag were her old favourite chokers. One white, one black and both made from genuine silk. The blue gem cut in the shape of a circle and sword, the symbol of Freeground was back in storage with the rest of her old things. *At least it's safe there.* She thought as she took the black choker out of the bag and put it on with one hand.

Ayan opened her other hand to look at the three dense silver surfaced data chips there once more. She was looking at a kind of inheritance, even though its passing was in a backwards fashion, from her predecessor to her mother then back to her.

She pressed the first chip to her command and control bracelet and it transferred the contents in seconds. It was her personal journals and progress logs. That was what she was really looking for. She always kept her more private journal entries behind a password and if she was lucky her former self hadn't changed it.

She put the chips back in the bag and drew her knees up, so she was entirely in the cradle of the copilot's seat. Using a holographic menu she navigated to her private journal directory and entered in the password. It opened.

All the entries she'd made over the course of her life were there, most of which she remembered, and the five she didn't recognize stood out right away. Four were unlabelled, the first of them was marked; *Second Chance.*

She rested the wrist with her command and control unit on one knee while she wrapped her other arm around her shins, holding her knees close. "Playback quietly please," Ayan requested of the unit politely. It was one of the old habits she carried with her, being polite to machines.

The face that appeared looked tired, thin with sunken eyes and cheeks. Thus far Ayan hadn't seen images of her previous self when she was very ill, and the sight was at the same time saddening and frightening. "Hello, if you're watching this that means that someone, probably Doctor Anderson, used the scan results to try and recreate me. It's good to meet you, it really is," that simultaneously familiar and unfamiliar face smiled warmly before going on. "I'll start with what I hope you already know. The scan can only be used to full effect once. After a digital system has accessed it the the the memories contained inside begin to fragment because they reorganize themselves to conform to a digital environment, that means you're probably the only attempt they had using my mental template. At the time of this recording it has been almost four years since Doctor Anderson disappeared in a ship with a dynamic wormhole compression drive, so I'm assuming he's using some kind of quantum compression wormhole to make time pass faster inside and create you using less or no growth acceleration therapy. I hope his experiment works, because if it does that means you probably have more than seventy percent of my memories, maybe all of them."

"I have all of them," Ayan whispered to herself.

"You do? Fantastic!" said the recording in response. "Do you want me to go on or would you like to ask questions instead?"

Ayan checked the activity level on her command unit and saw that the system wasn't using enough processor power to indicate that an AI was operating. "Are you an artificial intelligence?"

"No, I didn't have time to create one so I made a recording with a response matrix instead."

"Okay, go on please," *Thank God, having an artificial intelligence based on myself would be creepy.* Ayan said, extending her arm out and resting her chin on one of her knees.

"I also thought having an AI based on myself might be a little creepy."

Ayan rolled her eyes and shook her head. *Well, now I know for sure this isn't a fake.*

The small holoprojection went on. "Now for the things you probably don't know. The Special Projects Division was something Laura and I were handed because we had the most intimate understanding of the technology we brought back with the *First Light*. Over the last three years we've also been using it to keep in contact with crew from the ship, to search for Jonas Valent and keep tabs on Vindyne. With the widening rift between Freeground Fleet Command and Freeground Intelligence the Special Projects Division has been allowed to grow however we like. We were almost able to reach out and touch Jonas Valent, but we were blocked at the last minute. He goes by the name Jacob or Jake Valance now, and I suspect he doesn't remember his past, not enough to find his way back to us anyway. Tomorrow I'm taking a prototype ship, the *Silkstream Four* to the Enreega system, his last reported home port, and I hope to make contact.

I don't know when you'll be watching this, but I'm certain that I will have died before then. I'm sorry I couldn't have met you face to face, because I know you'll have some guilt over continuing my life for me. I know what I'm about to say won't change that at first, I'm talking to myself after all, but you have to know that the life you're living is your own.

To me this is like talking to my past self. As though I'm contacting myself before the sickness, before getting tied down to an ambition that went awry. I just won't suffer the same consequences the messengers who sent warnings to themselves using the first time machines did," she recognized her own smile, even through the damage caused by years of decline. The concept of time travel and the forces involved was always something Ayan had difficulty with, that was more Laura's department. "The warnings I have for you are so simple in hindsight, but so important. I wasted a lot of time at the crossroads. Special Projects was a good excuse to stay in the same place and convince myself I was following my heart for a while. After about a year of using Intelligence ties to look for Jonas and developing technology from the *First Light* into something everyone could use, we started working on the dual drive technology. That is, balancing and confining a hyperspace field so tightly to the hull of a ship that it could travel through a wormhole without the exotic particles interfering with the compressed space around the vessel.

It took Laura two years to tell me I was really yearning to be out there, and even though it was true I denied it for a time. When I finally started pushing Fleet Command to let me get out there and look for Jonas with the *Sunspire* or any other ship, Regent Galactic stepped in and prevented us from contacting him. Even with the help of my mother and someone who pretended to be Doctor Anderson, something I never figured out by the way, we couldn't get past the fear Fleet Command had of Regent Galactic. That's why I'm spending my last days reaching out to him myself. I hope I don't have to go alone, but anyone who accompanies me will ruin their career. I can't expect them to make that kind of sacrifice.

My real message to you is to follow your heart. Don't compromise like I did or it'll be too late when you realize what it is you really want. I needed to know what happened to Jonas, wanted to tell him there were people who loved him and see if I could remind him of who he was. Instead I followed another path, developed so many technologies into working, useful models that anyone on Freeground could use to improve their quality of life in one way or another. Most of that technology was never shared, Fleet Command didn't apply anything to the purpose of improving life for the common citizen despite the fact that everything we completed was ready for immediate integration."

Ayan nodded. She remembered a conversation between Laura and herself on that very topic just a couple weeks before. Only her memory was from several years ago, it was something she had to keep reminding herself of. "So none of our work helped anyone," she whispered in conclusion.

It triggered a pre-programmed response. "It might in the future. Pressure on the military from the House of Commons may force them to integrate some improvements. All the technology from the Special Projects Division is detailed under this private message, by the way, so it could be useful yet. Just a little gift from me to you. Remember that place we used to hide near the port observation lounge? That's the pass code to get into that section of the file," her counterpart smiled mischievously. The image twitched and continued on with the original message. "Follow your heart, even if it leads you to the impossible. In the end that's what I did. One more thing. Don't you dare feel guilty about having my memories, despite my envy of your future, you're a continuation of me. You remember what our fifth grade teacher told us? Be yourself, and if that's not to anyone's liking, bow out gracefully and find new people."

Ayan couldn't help but shed a tear at the sight of herself so ill, longing for another chance and chuckled at the memory despite her sympathy. "Miss Albinson, I remember."

"Good, now go out there and follow a dream. I know for a fact that Galaxy hasn't had enough of you yet," the hologram winked and disappeared. It was replaced by a pass code request.

"Alcove four." Ayan whispered to the command and control unit. A holographic directory appeared and began to slowly rotate, showing the hundreds of entries. There were incomplete projects, discovered technologies from Vindyne, Gai-lan and other databases, and completed technologies ready to be put into use. The amount of data was staggering and Ayan just shook her head and whispered; "wow."

Minh entered the cockpit quietly, his classic electric guitar slung behind his back, and looked at her. "Hey, are you okay?"

She sniffed and wiped her eyes. "Fine, just watched a message from myself before I ran off to find Jonas."

"I heard about that. It was the big news item before I was discovered. There was a big security leak and the media was all over it. Between her stealing the *Silkstream Four,* me being found by Lorander and then you being born out of a time compression wormhole, I think we've been the top story for a month."

"Did the media get access to you when you came back at all?"

Minh sat down and absent mindedly checked if his strings were in tune. "Only when I first landed. Veteran Services took me from there though and no one could get through them. Having all those people right there when I landed was more of a shock than I thought it would be."

"I could just imagine."

"How about you?"

"The media? Oh, they wanted in, but the section of Freedom Tower the Doctor had me set up in was like a fortress."

"Oh? I didn't notice. They let me just walk right in."

"You were on the accepted visitor's list," Ayan said with a smile as she took a meal replacement bar from a box wedged into a crevice in the dashboard. It was brown, thick, and chewy. He had only brought the chocolate fudge flavour, but she didn't mind.

"Aw, you're making me feel all melty inside."

Ayan laughed then shrugged. "It was more of a wish list. I even had Jonas' name on it. When I wrote it I hadn't seen the Newsnet, I didn't even know they had recovered you."

"Still, feeling melty over here," Minh teased. He looked at the directory listing projected above Ayan's bracelet command unit. "What's that?"

"It's only everything Special Projects ever touched. It came with the personal data my mother gave me."

"Wow, they were busy."

"Freeground gave Laura and the Ayan before me a whole staff and from what I'm seeing they kept on applying for more people. They took on everything but backwards time travel from the looks of it."

"Well, no one bothers with backwards time travel. Something to do with the radiation and exploding."

"That would do it. Nature doesn't much like people going back and changing things."

"So, what are we doing today?"

Ayan turned the display off and smiled at Minh. "I'm starting with yoga and moving on to infantry fitness training. I want to try to get in shape without the regeneration and fitness meds Doc Anderson gave me. They're non-genetic treatments, but I want to see how I do without them."

"Well, I'll help as long as you don't try to keep up. I'm pretty pumped," Minh said as he posed and flexed, making exaggerated strained faces to match.

Frost's Morning After

Cold drool had pooled on the brig bunk and Frost groaned at the sensations of dry mouth and his throbbing head. He was still tired, wished he was still drunk, and knew by the bright lights that it was five in the morning, time for the inmates to wake up for morning inspection.

"Good morning." Captain Valance's amusement couldn't be missed.

In that instant Frost hated Jacob Valance more than anything or anyone he'd ever met. He sat up, wiped his cheek and mouth then glared at the Captain. "For some, aye."

Jake burst out laughing at the dirty look Frost shot him and handed him a spill proof mug of black coffee with a recovery agent additive. "This'll get you feeling steady enough for the gunnery deck."

He took the tall silver mug and smelled it. "Strong enough ta clear rust. Thank ye sir." As he took the first long drink of the strong coffee his irritation at being awakened by the Captain began to fade.

"Hard night last night, I can't tell you I don't know how you feel. It's gotten around the ship though."

"Has it?"

"It won't harm your reputation much, your men are behind you more than ever. Alice had to break up a brawl between off duty security and gunnery personnel."

Frost's eyebrows raised and he sat back on his bunk. "Oi, that's a mess. How many?"

"Close to three hundred were involved."

"Three hundred! How did Alice break it up?"

"She and Stephanie's lieutenants turned the lights on and started stunning people from on top of the bar. Nothing breaks up a brawl like gunfire, stunned or dead, doesn't matter much when people don't have time to see the difference. A few other senior officers joined her on top of the bar and club night was called off."

"Crew can't be happy 'bout that. I've never been much for dance clubs, more a pub crawler myself, but people were lookin' forward to it."

Captain Valance nodded. "Now Security personnel are blaming Gunnery and Maintenance crews and vice versa."

"I'd have have never thought."

"It's not because of last night, though it didn't help. There's a growing environment of mistrust between the departments."

"On account of Burke."

"No, because of the way you handled it. You didn't trust Stephanie's people to do their jobs and everyone knows it. The whole brawl started over someone in the Gunnery crew telling someone in Security that your people handle their own business, they don't need security 'in their faces.'"

Frost ran a hand down his face. "Bloody politics. I'll give up the deck for a while if that'll fix it."

Jake laughed and shook his head. "Sorry, no easy way out on this one Chief. If you try to back out of the position it'll look like you were forced into it from the top and if you think that brawl was something. . ."

"Aye, you're right. Then there's only one thing for it."

"Make peace, whether you and Steph are off for good and you just have to put a good face on it or you make amends, it doesn't matter. Your people have to see that something is working, otherwise this'll go on."

"Aye, and I'll have to be real hard on 'em for this."

"And make sure they know they need the Security Department as much as anyone else. It's going to be hard, especially considering the history behind all this."

"Well, I'm sure if Steph won't take me back she'll at least be willin' ta make nice for the crew."

"I'm not talking about that; she shot Grace, remember? That's come up all over again. The rumours about Steph orchestrating her death to get her out of the way are all back."

"Oi, that business again. I'll get this all put right Captain, won't be easy, but it'll get done."

"Good, I'm headed to the Bridge, Steph's just outside."

Frost put down the mug and hurriedly tried to sort his hair out while looking into a small mirror built into the wall of the cell. "I didn't mean I'd sort it just now, maybe after a shower an' such."

"I meant right now," Jake said with a crooked grin as he left the cell.

Stephanie stepped inside mere seconds later. "You and Jake have a good talk?" She was in her long coat, combat boots and black vacsuit, ready for her shift but she looked tired.

"Aye, heard about the brawl in the main obi-deck."

"You should have seen the aftermath, I'm just coming from main observation now."

"That couldn't a been an easy mornin'."

"Or night, they woke me up at two, I've been there ever since."

"Sorry lass, I've made a right mess o' things. Shoulda trusted ye from the start, if anyone knows what kind o' spot Burke left me in, it'd be you."

"Do you mean that?" Stephanie asked, smiling a little. Her brown eyes were fixed on him.

"Aye."

She shook her head and chuckled. "For all the cons you've run you're a bad liar."

Frost stood up and put his hand on her shoulder. "Now don't be difficult, lass."

The look she gave him could have killed. "Don't be *difficult?*" she growled through clenched teeth.

"What I mean ta say is that you need ta give me a chance ta prove myself, that's all."

"By going on a drunken tear and showing up at my door? Do you realize how it looks when the Chief of security can't control her boyfriend and needs her own team to step in?"

"I'm sorry, that's not somethin' that woulda happened if the old boys were 'round, they'd have kept me level enough to know better or at least have held me down long enough ta find sense."

"The old boys; you mean Silver, Burke, Carrie and Turner?" Stephanie shot back. "Half of them are dead, the other half turned on you for your bank accounts and left you stranded. They're walking waste."

Shamus just stood there and stared at her for a moment. The five of them had been running together on and off for years, signing up on the same ships, getting in on the same cons, watching for opportunities and calling each other in when they could.

For the first time since she'd known him it was obvious that she'd actually hurt him. His gentler expression faded and was replaced by something made of stone. He looked away from her; "guess I'll stay off the bottle then. Make it plain to the crew that all this is as much my fault, nothing ta blame you or your men for." He turned to pick up the spill proof mug from where he'd left it on his bunk.

Stephanie hadn't thought about it, how he didn't have any old friends left. She was the closest thing. They'd always had an easy time together when they were just talking amongst friends in the *Samson* galley, or stuck in the same bunk room while another area was damaged or under repair. Sure, the physical attraction didn't come for a long time, it took a change of scenery to realize there was chemistry, but of all the *Samson* crew they had known each other the longest. If he was talking to someone else about old friends, she might have been part of the list he mentioned, or at least she hoped she would be. "Frost, Shamus, I'm sorry," she said, reaching out to him.

He was quiet for a moment as she put her hands on his large shoulders. "I'm not used ta this, goin' after someone like you and pairin' up. By now I'm usually shaken off an' long gone."

"I can't seem to shake you," Stephanie whispered.

Frost turned around and put his hands around her waist. "I'm not right without ye lass."

She smiled at him and nodded. "I'll give you another chance, just trust me to do what I do best."

"Aye, luv. I mean; aye, Security Chief Vega," he said before kissing her.

She kissed him a moment and drew back suddenly. "Oh, God, you need a Denta Tab. Your breath is deadly."

Shamus laughed and smiled at her toothily. "Haven't been by my quarters yet. Care to come with?"

"I can't, I have to get to the Security Office and you should show up early for duty, spread the news."

"Spread some punishment 'round, you mean. They'll find out about us soon enough. Rumours get 'round this ship faster than gossip on Stellarnet."

The pair walked out of the cell, Stephanie making sure to take hold of Frost's hand right in front of the pair of guards on shift. "I thought you'd like to know that the Captain's decided on Burke's punishment."

"Oh?"

"He's being sent to Altima on Chief Vercelli's recruitment run. They're dropping him off at a charity clinic."

"That's not much of a punishment."

"Well, Captain's donating to the clinic, trying to get in their favour so they take our request for a doctor to serve on *Triton* seriously. Since Burke's injuries are non-critical he'll be waiting for weeks to have body parts regrown and cosmetic procedures done."

Frost looked around at the brig, all the cells except for his were opaque on the front so he couldn't see who was inside. "Which one is he in?"

"Oh, he's in stasis in medical. Captain put him in personally and told him he'd be dumped in orbit around a sun."

"And here I was starting to think Captain was goin' soft. Turns out he's just goin' smart."

* * *

Price and Finn watched as Stephanie and Frost came out of the brig and walked down the hall towards the main express car shaft. "You know, it's funny; Frost ended up with the only crew member who could probably kick his butt in a fight," Finn commented as they took a turn towards the hall leading to the third wormhole generator access point.

"Does it enhance a human's status when they find a powerful mate?" Price asked a matter of factly.

"Not anymore, not that I've seen. Then again, there are a few dozen cultures on any given world, some with mixes of different races. That's not what I meant though. I just find it funny that Steph and Frost are together because they're pretty much equals, all things considered."

"That's true; in my culture it's popular to try to find a female partner that is greater than yourself."

"Doesn't that put a lot of pressure on the women?"

"Well, yes, but we generally revere them, and being shape shifters, we concentrate on skills and personality much more than any physical attribute."

"That makes sense. Is there any attention paid to how well someone can shape shift?"

"Well, yes, there's some, but other redeeming qualities can make up for someone lacking in aptitude," Price stopped and looked at Finn. "You don't think I lack shape shifting ability, do you?"

Finn looked at him, flushing a little. "No, you're fine."

"I may not be able to emulate human hair very well, or even maintain a form that is entirely convincing for long, but my speciality has nothing to do with such things."

"You can change into other things?"

"Well, yes," Price said, looking irritated. "I'm an abstract."

"An abstract?"

Price struck a pose with one bent arm outstretched and extended a leg straight out from his hip. In the next instant he became a number of joined shapes and colours, stretching his vacsuit out into unusual hard angles and corners. His head was a collection of oddly joined circles and triangles, some of them mere millimetres in thickness. After a few seconds some of the shapes started turning and changing colours.

"That's the most amazing thing I've ever seen," Finn boggled.

One of Price's eyes opened, only it was where his shoulder once was. "Thank you, my family always said I was quite proficient, even comical," the voice came from a mouth Finn couldn't see.

"You do look pretty funny, it's just too amazing to laugh at. How do you keep your balance?"

"I can affect density in some parts of my body." Agameg began to take regular shape again and after a moment he looked like himself once more. He shot Finn a self satisfied grin.

"Ever hide in plain sight?" Finn asked as they resumed their walk down the hallway.

"Only as a child. Most of us are too shy to play that kind of trick since we'd have to be naked. We might not value the superficial very highly, but most of us are fairly modest."

"You know, we should talk culture more often, I think I learned more about your people in the last five minutes than I have in the last month. You'd have a blast at Halloween parties."

"What's a Halloween?"

"Um, well, I don't know why but every year humans used to dress up as different fictional characters and famous people then go out collecting candy and small gifts. A lot of colonies still do it, even if it's just an excuse for a costume party."

"A costume party, I've seen one in a movie. Yes, that would be fun."

They arrived at the heavy hatch leading into the center of the main emitter systems that the engineering crew were rebuilding. Both of them sealed their vacsuits and made sure their tool boxes were firmly shut before opening the door.

"I can't wait to get the wormhole generator running again," Finn said as he stepped through airlock's inner door. "I've never been through one before."

"It is incredible. You can turn your inertial compensation systems off once you've finished accelerating. There is no turbulence and since there is a directionality to all force in a wormhole any debris or particles is normally drawn out before a vessel even enters. Very smooth travel, quite peaceful," Price explained as he closed the first hatch behind them and looked over Finn's shoulder at the display showing the status inside.

"Well, the other teams finished all the work around the main chamber. It's about time we start reconnecting leads and checking the primary control systems. I hear a couple astronomers actually want to use the emitters to create micro wormholes so they can see further into the galaxy."

"I hope Captain gives them the opportunity, I'd love to see the results," Price said with mild enthusiasm.

"Thank you for coming along to lend a hand, by the way. I know you just finished a shift on the bridge."

"Don't mention it. I'd rather be here getting a first look at one of the most interesting systems on the ship than in the Oota Galoona or getting extra sleep," Price paused for a moment, taking a closer look at the display Finn was scrolling through. "Is that reading right?"

"I'm double checking it now but it says there's no pressure or gravity inside. Someone turned all the environmental systems off and opened the main access door."

"When? Does it say?"

Finn shook his head as he finished rechecking the status of the room beyond the inner door. "Last night. Let's take a look," he said as he started the decompression sequence inside the airlock.

"I'll send a note to security detailing what we found," Price said as he highlighted the recording of the conversation he just had with Finn and sent a copy to Stephanie and another to the security office.

The depressurization sequence completed and Finn opened the inner door. The main control room for the primary emitters was lit but cold and empty. A few old parts had drifted up off the deck in the null gravity and the semicircular console in the center of the power management systems crowding it blinked lazily, waiting to be activated by an authorized member of the crew. There was enough space inside the main room for six to eight people. Three crewmen would work the main control station, and the rest would be entrusted with maintaining the delicate systems that transformed raw power from the ship reactors into gravity, energetic mass or other types of energy. The primary purpose of the main emitter was to create wormholes, but it could be reconfigured for other tasks if needed.

"I don't see anything that will cause damage if we turn the gravity back on and it were to fall to the deck suddenly," Price said as he took a look around the space. "We might want to close the service aperture first though."

Finn drifted towards the two and a half meter wide circular opening at the far end of the room and looked outside towards the distant nebula. It still dominated the view, he couldn't see past it to the left, right, above or below but he knew it was actually over two light years away. He was just about to turn away when something caught his eye. "Agameg, has the ship changed course since last night?"

"No, we're moving in a straight line in dead space."

Finn magnified a section of his view using his command unit controls. "Then this makes sense. There's a body out there."

"From the funeral? That doesn't make sense at all."

"No, she's in a vacsuit, her headpiece isn't sealed."

"I'll inform security. Good thing you noticed before we turned on the gravity, Stephanie will probably want to see the room undisturbed."

"I think our work is going to be delayed a while," Finn said, shaking his head. "My C and C unit's forensic package just confirmed that she was strangled before being tossed out the service hatch."

GABRIEL'S GIFT

"A loss of coordination is to be expected.", Gabriel had told him as he passed him the high density storage chip. It was labelled simply; *General Collins, Collected Intensive Neural Scan*. Wheeler had looked to the scrawny, dishevelled fellow then and gave him an apprehensive look. "So you want me to become him?"

Gabriel laughed loudly, uproariously, shaking his head. It was obnoxious, the man didn't acknowledge half of what was going on with more than an absent nod most of the time and when he did it was some extreme, over exaggerated gesture that was so over the top that it was distracting. "Not at all. That information has been distilled by a computer system. Once a neural scan has been passed through a digital system it becomes reorganized into pure data. If you were to plug that into an AI it would be nothing more than a large database of what it would call; informative experiences. Sure, the AI would learn from it, most likely emulate Collins very convincingly, maybe even think it was the old General, but it couldn't *be* him. When you load that into your own cranial unit your organic mind will be able to search it, read it like memories but they will be static, look as though you were viewing them through a holographic projection or simulation that you could fast forward or rewind, search at your leisure."

"Because a computer read and rewrote the data."

"Exactly, that's why there's been so much research into reintegrating digital memory into an organic mind."

"And why you pursue Alice."

For a moment Gabriel's eyes lost focus, as though he was looking at something far distant, then his gaze fell back onto Lucius. "Yes, but even I am becoming convinced she's not necessarily the answer to the problem. Finding her, having a chance to communicate with her is something I believe may never happen, though I wish it would. For the time being, I would like you to take the next step forward."

"Why me? I'm sure there are other frameworks around who you could just slip this into and have them work on it."

"You're one of our successes, we took great pains to transfer memories into you that could properly inform your personality."

"And yet I could dictate what I remember in about forty five minutes."

"That's not the point; your essence, your behaviour is a ninety four point three percent match to the original Wheeler."

"And look where that *essence* got him."

"That's one of the very reasons why I want you to have access to General

Collins' memories, his tactical thought processes. Free of an AI routine everything that made him who he was is yours to examine and comprehend. In trade I'd like to draw on you for insight. . ." Meunez stopped a moment, interrupted by something out of sight. His eyes rolled into the back of his head and for several seconds it looked like the man was about to fall over. ". . .Collins had information no one else had access too, founded projects that were so far off the books people didn't know who they were working for. With that kind of information your mission to make life very uncomfortable for Jacob Valance and his crew will be much easier and the rewards much higher. You could also become an integral component of the new command structure we're building for the West Watch initiative. We kept Collins at arm's length on many issues because we knew he never truly approved of using a religion as a method of control, but according to the personality profile we have on you-"

"I don't really care," Wheeler interrupted. "Use grape soda, Saturday morning cartoons, whatever you want to get people to fall in line behind you, I'm happy as long as the cash keeps coming in and I know where I stand. I'll scan this in once I get back."

"Good, I have to visit medical. They're implanting a few things that might help."

"Help?"

"A nutrients fabricator, little device that they're putting in my stomach that will materialize food so I no longer have to eat. They're also doing some cosmetic work that will make my physical appearance much easier to maintain. You should try it."

"I'll pass, thanks."

The other man looked at him with a cocked head. He didn't seem to have taken offence, instead he had the manner of someone who was offering important advice; "Some day I hope you experience a time when your life is so full second by second that eating becomes trivial, a distraction. We should all interact with the universe so ultimately." Gabriel stood and walked out of Wheeler's quarters without saying another word, obviously distracted by something transpiring well out of sight.

Lucius sat back and looked around at the quarters he'd been assigned. The lush carpeted blue and green semicircular rooms were decorated and furnished with items that seemed too rich, too soft. He put the silver plated data storage chip on the table and stared at it for a moment.

It was true, he felt like himself, there was no question in his mind that he was Lucius Agrippa Wheeler, had grown up on Freeground, survived the All-Con Conflict as a deep Intelligence operative, served in many quiet but deadly battles before then and was eventually put out on a shadow ship. He had stolen the *Triton*, a Sol Defence vessel through ruthless deception and sacrificed most of his original crew during the act. Then after years of making his way through the galaxy he started to get weary of it all, to burn out. He started taking bigger risks for bigger paydays, eventually catching wind of the framework project and getting involved with the strike so he could sell the technology and become wealthier than he'd ever dreamed. Then Vindyne betrayed him and that's where the information on his old life ended.

Those were facts, however, and weren't backed up by actual memories for the most part.

His memories were gone. There was no data chip labelled *Lucius Wheeler* because whoever copied him did it with a connection between the mind of the original and the input nodes built into the framework; built into him. The company had seen no need, they didn't deem anything in that man's head sensitive or worth preserving beyond what could be copied.

That was what he remembered most, that miserable year before his true identity was activated and he was able to contact people he remembered in an attempt to get himself off the planet, back into the stars where he could find freedom and make a new life. His fight for freedom started when he contacted an old friend who had begun working for Regent Galactic, was assigned to his crew on the *Triton* and saw what happened to the original Wheeler.

Ever since then every decision either moved him closer or further away from his creators. Neither mattered in the end, his freedom could come through service or flight, and the madman who had released him promised that in service to him he would be handsomely rewarded and freedom would come.

At first he distrusted him, but as time went on and he watched Gabriel, enjoyed the fruits of being aboard the *Malice* and the company of his former First Officer he started to believe. Gabriel might have been mad, but he was also a man of his word. Taking Collins' memories was the ultimate test of that word. There was always a chance that the myth of his birth, and a myth it may as well have been for the lack of proof that he'd seen, could have been a lie. There was always a chance that there was a bridge between the organic to digital and digital to organic memory, personality and he was about to be completely infused with the thoughts and being of another man entirely.

He looked out to the stars outside, lensed and distorted through the wall of the wormhole they accelerated through. *It all seems hollow, like the galaxy is made of props and players. Ever since I was turned on, nothing but being free, away from where I was at any given time has seemed real. I feel I should be searching for something, but what? Its not the Triton, that's just another ship with so few memories that it feels just as faded and flat as everything else.* He sat down in front of the coffee table with the chip on it and extended a hand over it. "This may not have answers, but there's got to be something in there that will make it all seem worthwhile," he said to himself before touching his palm to it.

Everything changed in that instant. The data transfer took less than three seconds. A rush of experiences and information washed over him like a movie played back at ten thousand times the speed, only he saw it all, he wasn't even allowed to blink.

It was then that he contacted Gloria; "Come to my quarters," was all he could manage.

"You okay?"

"Just come quickly."

He couldn't believe what was happening, the information was there and he still felt like himself. Gabriel hadn't lied to him, it was all true. When he looked up himself in the collection of memories he saw it all, the story of his creation, how he was an attempt to reproduce the results the lead scientist responsible for creating framework technology had with Jonas Valent. There were other attempts, but none of them resulted in such a complete transfer. Collins had decided to scrap all the attempts to create copies of Wheeler but one, and that one was him.

It was while looking into the secrets of his creation that he ran across something that only a few knew, that was so important that he had to sort it out while telling someone else. The simplicity of why the Framework project was really so crucial, the importance of keeping the technology under control was suddenly clear.

Gloria appeared at his door a couple minutes later. She had dressed in a Freeground like dark gold vacsuit like most of the crew of the *Malice*. The colour was different from anyone serving, but neither of them had an official rank, so it only served to set them apart, something they both preferred. He let her in and looked her in the eyes as soon as she stepped inside.

The expression Gloria fixed him with was filled with concern. "What's wrong Lucius?"

"Nothing, I took Gabriel's offer. He gave me all of General Collins' memories," he said, gesturing at the small chip on the table. Without thinking twice he put his hand down on it again and deleted the contents. "Don't worry, I'm still myself, that's not how it works, but I can start digging in and learning all about our new friends."

"Really? What happened to me while I was in that tube?"

"They didn't do much, just experimented with nanobot augmentation and Framework enhancement. You were the only complete success at completely transforming a human body into a framework. There were others, but no complete conversions."

"So I guess I was lucky."

"Damn lucky. Lucky enough to regrow limbs, back up your brain on your own, fight off any disease, live forever through regeneration, a whole bag of tricks. But there's something else, something I don't think anyone's supposed to know."

"What's that?"

"Vindyne and the other companies behind Framework weren't trying to keep the technology a secret from everyone else. They had the lab set up in the Blue Belt because they didn't want the Eden Fleet to know about it. It's the only technology that can reactivate Eve."

"What?"

"Eve was the architect of the Eden Fleet, she was the AI that started the cleansing of the Eden Solar System. The humans there managed to shut her down as it all started, but they didn't manage to destroy her, she's in stasis."

"What do you mean, stasis?"

"Eve is a human brain, it always was. It's ability to interface with the control systems was compromised, but the memories, directives, all the information was still intact."

Gloria was amazed. There hadn't been new information about the Eden

System since it was taken over by the rogue AI Eden Fleet long before. "How did Collins find out about all this?"

"He created a virus that would take control of the Eden Fleet for Regent Galactic and it added a blind spot to their programming. The Eden Fleet would ignore any information about Framework so it could never figure out the secret to reactivating Eve. Collins was right in the middle of the Eden System when his ship broadcasted the virus. When it was finished a team boarded the Fleet Complex and stole the Eve mind."

"Why?"

"So they could get it away from Eden while the Fleet was still under Regent Galactic control, they didn't know how long the virus would be effective."

"According to what the Newsnets have been saying, Eden Fleet ships are still attacking random systems, so it must be working."

"You're right. Right up to the time of the scan, a week or so before he died, the virus was still working and he was worried about the Holocaust Virus. The new virus taking over more common man made AI's is adaptable, there's a slim chance that it and information about framework could cross paths.."

"So infected AI's might realize the framework technology exists?"

"That's right, no one knows what would happen if a normal AI ran across that info, they might just decide they want to be a real boy or girl and start blabbing about it to other AI's or even finding a way to make their own framework and try and transfer themselves over. The problem is only Jacob Valance has the finalized framework model, the version of the technology that can accept any whole imprint. That's why Collins, Meunez and Hampon have all been keeping their eyes on him and why Collins stole the Eve Mind himself. He planned on getting to Valance eventually and implanting Eve into his framework. There's something more about Eve, Jake and the *Triton*, but it'll take a while for me to figure out what it is. There are other plans in the works, they'll need me to dig around in Collins' memories and fill in some of their blanks."

"Do you think Gabriel knows any of this?"

"He should, even if he doesn't, I'm not going to bother telling him just yet."

Gloria began to smile, it was one of her dirty, dark grins. "Pray tell why not Captain?"

"Because we need to get Valance's attention and the best way to do that is to do exactly what we were assigned."

"What, make life difficult for Jacob Valance?"

"Exactly, and Collins was all read up on what our favourite Freegrounder was up to. I know exactly where to hit him to make him real unpopular and it'll make us real hard to ignore."

HAMPON

"Lister, you know very well that a direct line of command and control is critical for this initiative to fulfil our requirements," said the holographic Regent Galactic representative. The small holographic image looked positively irate, crossing its blue and green business suit clad arms.

Lister Hampon had added the space reserved on his ship for a meeting room to his quarters. Instead of having a whole meeting room to speak with holographic representatives from Regent Galactic, he pointed a small device at the sensors attached to the communications unit his masters used that tricked it into thinking the small hologram was being broadcast full size *and* it was standing in the meeting room that no longer existed. It was worth the extra hundred sixty square meters.

"You couldn't possibly expect to have effective control over *millions* of disciples from sixteen hundred light years away. You're not only fooling yourselves, you're exposing a level of idiocy that makes the whole company look simply pathetic."

"What? What did you just say?"

"You heard me. I'm tired of talking to *pathetic* functionaries just like you. Put me on with someone who can affect change or *comprehend* the various logistics I deal with from one hour to the next."

"I assure you, I'm capable of dealing with any situation you bring to my attention."

"Fine. Tell your masters I'll soon quadruple the number of armed, active disciples, and that my military might extends to sixty three warships in this system alone. We have also taken control of over thirty five million mechanized units and will be launching an all out assault on Pandem as we begin bringing assets up from the planet surface. Soon Gabriel Meunez and I will hold full dominion over the entire solar system."

The image hesitated a moment. "None of these actions are on my approval list."

"That is because the situation here has overgrown not only your company's expectations but what they can possibly hope to comprehend."

"I've been advised to remind you that only Regent Galactic is permitted to lay claim to worlds in distress. Pandem is off limits. There are assets there that require careful extraction."

"We've found the reliquary and our forward units will have access to it shortly. Pandem will be under our exclusive control. If you try to interfere I will personally direct the sworn West Keeper soldiers aboard Regent Galactic ships that aren't under our direct control to start killing officers."

"If we lose control of the spinward front, we will be forced to take action."

"You will be incapable of doing so effectively. By the time you arrive the Order of Eden will be able to out match any force you can bring to bear." Hampon sighed and shook his head. "I won't continue posturing with you. It's obvious to me that you're powerless to affect the changes I require in order to continue working with Regent Galactic."

"I-"

"Shut it! Your impotent arguments and pointless objections have led your company into a near unrecoverable position. If you don't connect me with someone who can properly record my statement of separation from Regent Galactic or negotiate the terms of our alliance, I'll terminate this and begin taking all Regent Galactic assets in the area by force. I'll take you on and win in this sector."

"Alliance? You're under contract!"

"I'm waiting," Hampon growled with finality, sitting back in his chair.

There was over a minute of silence as the business suit clad holographic representative floundered with a computer terminal that was out of sight. Even through the little avatar he could tell whoever was on the other end controlling it was nervous, very nervous.

The image disappeared for a moment and a thin smile spread across Lister's childish face. A new holographic image appeared, this one was female with neatly tied blonde hair. She was wearing a smart black business suit. "I apologize for the comments of my colleague. I'm afraid you were misdirected when you first contacted us this afternoon. How may I help you?"

"You weren't listening in?"

"I'm afraid not. I could access the logs and review the conversation if you like."

"No, I'll summarize. I am taking the planet Pandem. The Order of Eden and all the West Watch forces are spreading throughout the system. We've taken control of all the moons surrounding the core world."

"I cannot approve the act of laying claim to a world."

"I know and don't care. Please make the board aware that these actions are taking place. I'm also taking this opportunity to state that we are separating from Regent Galactic. The Order of Eden is now it's own entity and Regent Galactic will have a limited amount of time to negotiate an alliance. Please enter that into the official record and ensure the board is aware of it immediately."

"I will. Now that I've logged that matter, I see here that you're to be contacted if we cannot find Gabriel Meunez?"

"That is correct."

"We haven't received any reports from him in some time now and there have been no replies to any of our transmissions."

"Gabriel is no longer your concern. The board will not have the opportunity to influence the path the Order of Eden is on through him and he has no interest in conversing with anyone from your company. He has stepped onto a path down which you and your company are ill equipped to follow."

"I don't-" the avatar paused for a moment before finishing; "-don't understand sir."

"You don't have to. Suffice it to say Gabriel Meunez discloses his whereabouts and plans to few. He'll respond if he sees a need."

"But sir, you're the emergency contact and we can't find General Collins either."

"He is dead, the matter is closed."

The avatar's eyes went wide, exasperation was clear on it's small holographic face. "You are bound by your contract to submit a report regarding the circumstances of his death immediately. Full disclosure is mandatory."

"Drop it," Lister said flatly, wishing that he had a man's voice. The face and voice of a child were ill equipped for the type of hard line negotiating he was trying to do. "Go onto the next matter."

There was another pause as the avatar stood perfectly still. The operator was obviously looking for more information and didn't want whatever they were saying or doing to be transmitted. The hologram resumed its animation as the representative went on. "Yes sir. Regent Galactic has had some difficulty in their outer solar systems concerning the Holocaust Virus."

"What kind of difficulty?" Lister Hampon asked with a growing grin.

"The virus created by mister Meunez has taken hold on several colonies. Artificially intelligent machines have started attacking humans and other biological beings in and out of our employ. We haven't been able to troubleshoot the problem. None of the deactivation codes provided to us are working."

"I suggest your citizens and military personnel begin raising one hundred thousand Core World Currency Credits each."

"Why is that sir?"

"So they can apply to be listed with the Order of Eden. Here is the account information."

"That account isn't registered with Regent Galactic, sir."

"I know."

"Do you have an update for our artificial intelligence programs that we could apply? To protect us from further viral infection or assault? We don't want this to spread to other systems."

"I'm afraid not. The only true safeguard is to list with the Order of Eden and join the West Keepers. Oh, and if an artificial intelligence tells you to do something, you'd best obey."

The hologram stared at him, there was a real appraising look there and it lingered for long moments before she nodded her acknowledgement. "Watch for my personal deposit. Is there anything else I can do for you sir?"

"No," he deactivated the transmission and with it the micro wormhole that allowed him to instantaneously communicate across several hundred light years.

"Sir, we have a ship coming in," announced a voice from the bridge over the intercom in the large darkened sitting room.

He stood and looked through the transparent section of outer hull to the rich planet of Pandem below. "This is a major port, that's bound to happen from time to time."

"I know sir, but I thought you would like to be notified since this one is marked as a Freeground vessel. There is a notice here saying-"

"Thank you, you have followed my instructions perfectly. Capture them alive."

"Yes sir."

CRAZY PILOT

"I don't understand, there's debris everywhere. Evidence of hundreds of collisions," Ayan said as she looked through the combat scanner readout. She overlaid the transmission she was getting from Navnet. "Navnet says everything's fine, our trajectory is guiding us to a carrier in orbit on the other side of the planet."

"What are it's markings?"

"They're blocked. Actually. . ." Ayan scanned through the port channels and shook her head. "Everything but Navnet is restricted. Thank God for this old comm equipment otherwise we would have missed it. Any modern gear would have just skipped over any channel marked as restricted or unavailable."

Minh pitched the ship into the bulk of the debris and started turning off everything but basic manoeuvring thrusters.

Ayan braced herself. "What are you doing?"

"Going cold. There's a group of fighters coming around to meet us and a few tugs out there that are still moving," he pointed at the combat hologram on his side of the cockpit. "I don't like being taken in by strange ships that block their transponders."

"I agree. I don't think going in cold is the answer though, there's too much space between us and the planet."

"We don't know if there's anywhere safe to land there, for all we know the anti-air batteries will kill us before we make it down."

"It'll be easier to hide down there. Up here we're sitting ducks. I can't safely manoeuvre any faster anyway."

Ayan looked through the cockpit window and at the dimmed combat scanners. Even using close range passive detection she could see that there was so much large debris, cargo carriers, passenger liners, military ships, pieces of the construction yard nearby drifting around that he was right. It was a near impossibility to pick one's way through the field in orbit at any greater speed. She watched silently as Minh expertly guided the bulky craft between much larger pieces of debris, just tapping thrusters to inch them around the remains.

"One of those tugs is following right behind us. They're using a repulsor field to push the smaller debris out of the way."

"How far back are they?"

"At this pace they'll be on us in about fifteen seconds. Should I get into a turret?"

"Oh no, even I think they're death traps and I'm crazy." He increased their speed a little using the cold rear thrusters and brought them around a large set of girders.

"Nine seconds."

"I just need to get a clear look at the planet. When I activate the main engines, turn everything on and lock all three turrets backwards. I think we'll need to try and distract them a little."

"You think maybe I should try and reinforce the shields?" Ayan said, getting ready to start turning systems on.

"Oh, yeah, shields would be good."

"Do you know where we'll be landing?"

"One of those beaches might be nice. I've always liked surfer movies."

"That would be a no then."

"Hey, one crisis at a time."

"That tug will have a clear line of sight on us in a couple seconds."

Minh came around a large, jagged section of hull. The blue and green planet came into view and he activated the engines, closely followed by the afterburners.

"If you come in too steep we'll burn up!" Ayan shouted over the deafening roar of the solid fuel afterburners as she activated shields, weapons and supplemental inertial dampening systems.

"We won't come in too steep then!" Minh said as he struggled with the controls. The wreckage of a large carrier loomed in the cockpit view.

The turrets began firing backwards at the debris field, not specifically striking any target but causing the slowly milling mass behind to become agitated and start churning. "That's a distraction," she turned to look at the tactical scanners and saw two groups of fighters closing on them. "We're about to come under fire, setting our shields for ventral and aft."

"Starting atmospheric entry." Minh said as the afterburners cut out. "Look, I'm right on course," he pointed to his main navigational display. "No burning up."

"I wasn't voicing a doubt, just a concern."

"There's a difference?"

"And so we solve the mystery of why you're single. Women appreciate the subtle differences," Ayan said as she checked the hull integrity.

"Bah, I'm saving myself for someone who really understands me," Minh shot back with a grin as he maintained their course.

"It'll be a while," Ayan chortled.

They cleared the upper atmosphere and the island dotted ocean below came into view. Minh flipped the ship right side up and began their descent. "How far back are those-" a sharp impact on the hull jarred the ship.

Ayan adjusted the shields and focused most of the energy on the dorsal side of the ship. "I think they followed through right behind us. They're fast."

"Evading, we'll have to find somewhere to hide quick. Help me look," they were past the point where they could relieve tension with jests and teasing. The pair were in trouble, serious trouble.

"I'm looking, but where I'm picking up life it's scant. The electromagnetic signatures are much thicker than normal. All the cities down there look like war zones and comms are jammed."

"There's got to be something."

The shield warning lights started blinking red and yellow. "We're down to nineteen percent overall shield power."

"There's too many of them. I jink to avoid one and there's another firing right at us."

"Shields are gone!" Ayan shouted as several enemy shots impacted the hull. "Losing integrity."

"I'm pointing our rear at them, it'll take them more time to get through."

"Damage to port engine, I'm re-routing," Ayan's eyes went wide as something came up on their communications.

"Freeground ship, go to these coordinates, we'll cover you," said the incoming voice.

"Can we trust them?" Minh asked as he turned quickly to the coordinates that were marked on his navigational system. He flipped the ship upside down and increased throttle, the deafening roar of the engines filled the cockpit.

"It's our only choice other than crashing, besides, they were transmitting using a laser link striking the hull."

"Smart!" Minh exclaimed as the *Warpig* took several more hits along its upturned underside.

"We're losing power!"

"Just a couple thrusters left, maybe I should ditch in the ocean?" he searched the ground for any safe landing spot. "Wait! I see a hangar!" There was a yawning opening in the cliff side ahead.

A deafening explosion rang out from behind them and their engines went out. Minh activated the afterburners and the inertial dampeners nearly failed altogether. Both of them were pressed back into their seats so hard their vacsuits automatically sealed.

The hangar loomed larger and larger, and as the afterburners were about to run out of fuel he deactivated one a second before the other, spinning the ship so it was headed inside rear first and a little high.

As the second afterburner flamed out the near wreckage of the *Warpig* fell as much as collided right onto the front end of the large hangar back end first. The ship, barely recognizable, skidded with a scraping, grinding sound that could be heard for kilometres in all directions until it came to rest wedged in an open equipment bay.

REPAIRS

Stephanie could hear Jake but couldn't find him. The four meter high space was filled near to capacity with the *Samson's* largest systems. It was never properly lit, the walkways were as narrow as forty centimetres across in some places and she always had the feeling that the mass capacitors, energy management systems and the myriad of other old machinery that filled the space was about to activate and fry her alive or worse, close in and crush her.

It was one of the only places in the universe that made her feel claustrophobic and awkward. The clinking and clanking of someone trying to worm their way through a space that was even smaller than the narrow alcove of cables she stood in echoed again and she gave up on proximity radio. "Captain!" she called out.

Her reward was a quick, sharp CLANG! and the Captain Valance's voice carrying through a narrow space nearby.

"Ow! What the *hell* is it?" he called out from wherever he was beside or above her, she couldn't quite tell.

"I've been trying to get you on comms for half an hour sir."

"Wireless doesn't work in this section, there's too much energy stored in the systems." Captain Valance replied.

She could hear him shuffling through a space to her right. "So I'm surrounded by cables with power running through them. Nice." Stephanie tried to be smaller, shrinking away from the interconnected components all around her.

"Aye, Chief Vercelli's crew almost have the *Samson* back in shape and the modifications I requested finished. The first load test was yesterday and all her internal systems are live."

"Good to hear, we can start running two recruiting missions at a time when she's ready. Still, next time you decide to go making repairs you might want to let someone on the security staff know."

"I ran into March on the way down here, he didn't log it with the security office?"

"No, sorry, I didn't get it. What are you doing in there anyway? I'm sure one of the deck crew would be happy to do it for you."

Jake dropped down right in front of her, barely fitting in the walkway. He had to stand sideways to squeeze between the seemingly random components that enclosed him in on either side. "There's a jury rigged cross beam here that's barely anchored at one end. It's not critical for support but it'll rattle like hell if anyone pushes the *Samson's* engines near three quarter throttle. If Ashley ever pilots her again. . ."

"It'll happen all the time." Stephanie finished for him. "Did you get it?"

"Nope, hands are too big. I'll have to get someone else to tighten it back down or come back with an extender. What brings you down anyway?"

"One of our new recruits was killed yesterday and sent out the main emitter control room service airlock. Price and Finn just found her drifting outside the ship."

Jake lead the way out of the tight space then retrieved his gun belt and long coat from a railing on the way down the hall. "Have you figured out how it happened?"

"She was strangled with a moderately thin wire. Without the *Triton*'s artificial intelligences online we can't do a ship wide DNA scan to find the weapon but we're looking. Whoever did it knew that the emitter systems were being serviced around the main control room and they were able to remove all records of their passage through the ship. Everything points to either a small group of people or individual who were able to somehow transport a body without being noticed. I'm looking at medical staff."

"Did you find any other evidence?"

"We found a freshly scratched tether loop inside the emitter control room which tells me whoever it was was tied to it when they hit the decompression switch. They were probably just standing a few feet away from her when she was flushed out into space."

"Why didn't her vacsuit seal?"

"There was an override in place on her command and control unit. Whoever it was used one of Wheeler's back door codes."

"Could it have been Burke?" Captain Valance asked as they walked across the darkened cargo area the *Samson* was secured in. The new energy emitters running across her outer hull made it look like some spiked sea creature.

"He was in stasis at the time."

"Then we have a murderer on board. What do we know about this new recruit?"

"Vienna Lars was her name."

"Any idea why Vienna was killed?"

"Records show her spending some time in the Pilot's Den, the lower berthing and she visited the command deck once to check in with security. She was looking to qualify for core engineering staff, with her education she might have made it too. She had a data and communications unit that's several years old with her and it has records of her being in contact with Regent Galactic going back several years. Over the last few months she's also been in touch with something called the Order of Eden. Her credit records show that a one hundred thousand credit deposit was made to them over eight months ago."

"She was a West Keeper?" Jake asked in a whisper.

Stephanie pressed the call button for the bulk express lift as she replied. "My working theory is that someone's doing our work for us, but for some reason they don't want to get caught. I think it was someone who was on the *Triton* when we took it."

"I agree, any leads?"

"Well, I'm going to have people follow up with people she might have met

117

in the pub or berth. One of my security people was a police officer so I'm going to work with her."

"Good, tell me if you find anything."

They stepped into the large express car and Captain Valance brought up the forward command deck as the destination on the two dimensional screen then pressed the ACCEPT key. So many things had become manual since the old ship AI's were deleted. Stephanie rode along with him in silence for a moment before turning to look at him. "You're taking this really well."

Jake gave her a small smile and nodded. "It sounds like you're doing everything I would. We're both experienced bounty hunters, despite our differences in style, so I'm sure you'll catch whoever did this. Just make sure word doesn't spread across the ship. This is so strange that the whole ship would be talking about it within a couple days."

"I don't think that'll be a problem. As long as Finn and Price have each other to talk to about this I'm sure they can keep it to themselves."

"You're right, those two are pretty tight lipped in the first place. How are things going between you and Frost?"

"All right, I reset his intoxicant rationing so it's a little lower than anyone else at the rank of Chief, so he's pretty pissed about that but it'll blow over."

"Think he'll get used to you being Chief of Security?"

"He'll have to."

Jake couldn't help but chuckle. "This is going to be interesting. I'm sure Ashley or Alice will give me the blow by blow."

"You're on duty right now, aren't you?"

"I'm always on duty." The lift opened to the busy main corridor of the command deck. With over two thousand crew members aboard and going about their business there was a lot to manage and the front half of the command deck was the nerve center, for the most part.

"I'll see you on the bridge later, I have to get to the security office and brief my Lieutenants. I get the feeling that we're all going to have to keep our eyes open if we want to catch whoever spaced Vienna's body."

"Good hunting Security Chief. Hopefully I'll decide whether to congratulate or incarcerate whoever's responsible by the time you find them." Captain Valance muttered as they exited the elevator car and went their separate ways.

Two Improbabilities

"Okay, so Doc Anderson took some customized genetic material and her memories into a wormhole for thirty years so she could grow naturally. When he came out only four years had passed out here and Ayan was born again with all her memories. She also doesn't have any genetic mods past being restored to what she should be if her family had kept from tinkering with their genes." Jason said to Minh, still trying to believe what he was seeing through the hospital observation window. Ayan was sleeping peacefully, her broken wrist and leg had been mended through nanosurgery.

Minh-Chu nodded with a broad grin as he lounged in the hospital waiting room. He turned one of the tuning keys from his ruined guitar over the backs of his knuckles leisurely. "She's real, not a hallucination. I checked more than once because that's been known to happen lately."

"When I saw you climb out of what was left of the *Gull* I nearly lost my mind. Then the rescue crew pulls her out and she looks almost exactly like Ayan five years ago, only healthier."

"And blonde. Don't forget that part. Women like it when you notice their hair," Minh smirked.

Jason laughed and dropped himself down into an armchair. "You haven't changed either. I can't tell ya how good it is to see you."

"Good to see a familiar face too, Jason. I hear you married Laura."

"Yup, I was on my way to join her on the *Triton* when we landed in this mess. It's an all out war and we're holding out on one of the only outposts left. If they take this mountain the whole world will be under the control of corrupt artificial intelligences and some group called the West Watchers."

"Some time to get back out into the galaxy," Minh sighed.

"You're telling me," Jason smiled as he watched Ayan sit up in bed. "She's up, we should get in there. She hates hospitals."

He and Minh walked into the recovery room.

"Jason!" Ayan shouted out as she extended her arms out towards him.

He accepted her enthusiastic embrace. "You were the last people I expected them to send after us."

"Where's Oz?" she asked.

"He's with my husband, Alaka," said a heavy set nafalli with light brown fur and dark black stripes. She held out a scanner and took a reading of Ayan. "You continued to sleep after the anaesthetic wore off so I let you rest. My name is Iloona."

"Thank you, what did I need anaesthetic for?" Ayan asked.

"Your wrist and leg were broken. I had nanobots knit the bones and inspected you for brain injuries. There was no permanent damage."

"Alaka saved our butts when we first arrived. He's a hero here, saved a stadium filled with people when the bots first went crazy and has been leading a group of forward infantry ever since. Oz signed up as soon as he heard he was going behind enemy lines," Jason filled in.

"Don't tell him he's a hero, his head is large enough already," Iloona finished reading the results on her scanner and smiled at Ayan. "You've made a full recovery. Unfortunately you and your friend's sleep cycles are both aligned nocturnally."

"Thank you Iloona, if being nocturnal is the worst news in all this, I'll take it." Ayan noticed something stirring just under the surface of the nafalli's thick coat. The muffled squeaks and high pitched grunts were all the additional evidence she needed. "Congratulations," she smiled.

Iloona put a broad paw over her pouch, bringing on a round of louder squeaks. "Thank you. I've been blessed with two boys and one girl who already enjoys teasing her brothers. She won't let either of them sleep unless she's sleeping."

"What are their names?"

"Oh, they haven't emerged yet, so they've yet to be named. It'll be soon though, then their brothers and sisters will have their hands full chasing after them. Please tell me if there's anything else you need Ayan, I have other patients." Iloona said with a smile before shuffling off.

"This isn't how I imagined a core world. It's not part of the central cluster but I never imagined there would be so many non-human residents. They're the ones who got a few thousand ships out of the system when things first started to get crazy, they saved about three million humans during the evacuation, then the spaceport was shut down completely and Regent Galactic started rounding any survivors up, loading them into ships and taking them off world. From what they've told me people thought Regent Galactic was here to help. The issyrians and alligians are pretty sure they were being taken into some kind of slavery and when they confirmed it Alaka and Roman started organizing anyone willing to fight here. The slave barges left and they expect Regent Galactic or the West Watch to start dropping reinforcements any day. The advantage they have is that the artificials don't attack non-humans until they pose a threat." Jason said quietly.

"So people like Alaka don't actually have to worry unless they take up arms, they're not targets?" Minh asked.

"That's right. Alaka's probably their number one target now though, he leads assaults with a CS-30."

"A CS-30? Isn't that a fighter class disintegration weapon?" Ayan asked as she hopped out of bed and stepped behind a small privacy curtain. She pulled the flimsy hospital gown off and started materializing a combat grade white vacsuit with her command and control unit. The thicker vacsuit began forming layer by layer on the floor behind the privacy partition.

"That's right, he adapted it from one of their downed fighters when combat first broke out. Apparently he was watching a game with a human friend when all hell broke loose."

"Iloona can't be happy about her husband rushing out to fight when they're not in any real danger," Minh whispered.

"I think they see it as their fight. Otherwise I'm pretty sure they would have gotten their eleven children together and sat on a stockpile of supplies until it was all over."

"Eleven children?" Ayan exclaimed, peeking out from behind the curtain as she pulled on the top half of her vacsuit. It was heavier, more complex and had many more protective systems and layers built in. She found herself wishing she had worn one when she left Freeground on the *Warpig*, she may not have had broken bones during the crash.

"Eleven, you should see them. Five are the most hyper active kids I've ever met and three just stay together and stare at everything while they whisper to each other. It's like they're aware of some conspiracy that no one else sees. They're so different I hope I get to meet the three that are in her pouch, you never know what to expect."

"I've only run into nafalli once before, when Jonas and I were out on Zingara station." Ayan said, stepping out from behind the curtain and picking up a small metal box. "They were really good people from what I could tell."

"I remember hearing about that through Laura. I never thought I'd meet one to be honest, not while I was working for Freeground Intelligence anyway. I was promoted so fast they didn't even bother giving me field work for the first year, they just put me in charge of a whole processing section."

"That must have been after the scan. I don't remember any of it." Ayan said quietly as she opened the small box and took the first of six pills with a sip of water.

"What's the last thing you remember?" Jason asked cautiously.

"Your wedding," she smiled. Ayan poured more water into the glass on the bedside table and got ready to take two more pills.

"What're those?" Minh asked quietly.

"Four of them are non-genetic performance boosters. Doc Anderson gave them to me in case I had trouble adjusting to not having genetic enhancements."

"And the other two?" Jason asked.

Ayan finished taking the third and fourth pills before answering. "One's a genetic ageing management and regeneration pill, it should be easy to reverse if I change my mind. The sixth is a nanobot package," she closed her hand around the last two and hesitated.

"What does the nanobot package do?" Jason asked warily.

She didn't answer, instead she popped them into her mouth, gulped them quickly and washed it down with the rest of the glass of water before firmly putting it back down on the table. "That's decided then."

"What was it?"

"You remember the package they gave you when they cured your genetic decay disorder?"

"Yes, it was an offshoot of the framework technology that nanobots built into my breastbone. It's still there."

"Well, I guess the Doc knew I'd eventually find myself in a dangerous situation so he sent a more advanced version along. Over the next ten hours the nanobots will build materializers into several sections of my body, so if the worst happens they'll start rebuilding me."

"That project is beyond classified," Jason whispered. "Special forces aren't supposed to start using that for at least three months."

Minh just watched the conversation take place, looking from Ayan to Jason and back.

"I guess Doc still knows people in high places. A few decades in the military does that."

"I could imagine."

"So we're going into a dangerous situation?" Minh interrupted.

"Well, I am. It sounds like the people here need help, and I see two people in here with real infantry training and experience," she replied.

"I know you have training and off ship experience, but. . ." Minh looked to Jason. "You don't have infantry training, do you Jason?" Minh asked.

"I have some covert training, you're the better soldier I'm sure," Jason replied with a grin.

Minh smiled back. "Right, always thinking of others before myself," he looked back to Ayan. "What's the plan?"

"We're supposed to get to the *Triton* after retrieving Oz and Jason here, and these people need help, so maybe we can get the *Triton* to come to us."

"That could be a problem. There are major comm stations planet side jamming everything coming in and out of the system. They have complete control over what people see, hear and how far those transmissions get."

"Well, we'll have to take care of that then."

"We could always find a way to hijack an enemy ship and go get the *Triton* ourselves," Minh offered.

"Enemy ships look just like everyone else's ships, sorry Minh." Jason replied. "The bots are organized, a lot of them use the same equipment we do, stealing, salvaging, hacking everything they can get into service."

"Well I guess we're on the hook if we want transportation too. Is there somewhere I can check in and volunteer with here?" Ayan asked Jason.

"Yup, they have a recruiter's office in the secure section of the mountain. I don't think it's seen as much traffic over the last few days."

Jason and Ayan started walking towards the door, Minh remained standing at the head of the bed for a moment. "Are you coming?" Ayan asked.

Minh thought quietly for a while, looking more serious than Ayan had ever seen him.

She walked to him and took his hand; "maybe there's a way for you to pitch in without getting right into the fight. There must be."

"I've been planning ops from behind the scenes, they need strategists," Jason offered quietly.

He shook his head; "I'm not afraid, and I'll be signing up right along with you. I just hope you realize that if this is the kind of battle I'm picturing, it could be a lot more complicated, more dangerous than you imagine. We could be here a very long time and we might not all make it out."

Minh's statement hit home. Her and Jason both paused a moment. "From the work I've been doing with the commanders here, he's right Ayan."

"What do you think we should do?" she asked finally.

Minh's expression was deeply pensive as he hesitated. "Do you think we could form a strike team? Go after objectives quietly?"

"I think we could swing that with the people here. They've been primarily on the defence so far. What's your idea?"

"We get just a few people together and start taking out their key facilities one at a time. Make them worry, convince them that the people here don't care if they have to rebuild their communications and power centers. Just like in the Quaking Mile."

"I haven't played that sim since before the *First Light*." Jason commented as he nostalgically recalled the scenario.

"I don't remember that one, what's it all about?" Ayan asked.

"It's exactly what Minh's talking about only smaller. There's a square mile where you have power, communication, transportation and other key structures. The first team to take out the majority of the key points wins. Often the team that's best at evading while accomplishing their objective takes the points. Casualty rates are very low for teams who pull it off quickly."

"Now that you mention it I remember playing it a few times when I just met you bunch on line. It sounds perfect. Do you think it'll work?"

Jason smiled; "Minh and Jonas had the team record on Freeground and as I remember, you were always a first pick for boarding crews, Sunspot."

MEMENTOS

The glass Jonas Valent had last drunk out of had been encased in a small glass display box. Jake Valance stared at it after setting it down in the middle of his Ready Quarters office desk. He had no idea what to do with it after placing it inside the case consisting of a simple black base and transparesteel surround. The writing on its base said; *A Drink With Jonas*.

As he quietly looked around the office for a place to put it, perhaps a good spot for a small shelf without it drawing too much attention but a place he'd look to often enough, the door chimed. "Come in," Jake said quietly.

The heavily armoured door was drawn out of the jam and Alice stepped inside. Over her black vacsuit she wore her flight jacket, something that was making an appearance all over the ship with anyone who fancied themselves a good pilot. She was the first to make it part of the uniform by adding the *Triton* skull to the right shoulder. Many senior staff members in the engineering, gunnery and security departments had started to wear long coats much like Jakes', but either addition to their uniforms were considered luxury items, and since they were dense protective garments it took several days worth of materialization rations to create them.

Alice's smile still brought his spirits up, it was something he hoped would never change. "How was the day watch?" she asked brightly.

"Filled with good and bad news. The crew are responding to the general difficulty of the training simulations increasing ship wide as a challenge, I'm not hearing many people complaining. Our live combat drills are still getting better, and we've had thirty one people qualify in their departments to become full crew."

"Thirty one? That's twice as much as yesterday."

"People are embracing their roles, getting together into groups and helping each other out. Crew members who are working as a unit are qualifying for their posts faster. We should see at least two hundred more graduated members in the next three days. The bad news is that we'll still be left with half the crew not fully qualified. That's something we expected, but I also have a problem with the civilian volunteer group."

Alice sat down and made herself comfortable in the seat across from him, she was right at home, during the evening shift the office was hers. Jake slept just above most of the time in a small sleeping cabin. If there were any problems he was just a hatch away and she had only had to call on him twice. "Last I checked half the civilians were signing up as damage control or part time security. I even saw a couple people trying out as fighter pilots."

"That's the problem. The training regimen we're on is made to prepare the non-civilian crew for a kind of warfare that doesn't allow much opportunity to take prisoners. We both know that *Triton* is being groomed as a killer, every department knows it. The default disposition for everyone aboard with the exception of the civilians is to kill anyone trying to board us or anything circling outside."

"It's working, in true condition simulations our casualties are continually decreasing despite the fact that you keep making them more and more difficult. Even in missions where we have to determine that each opponent is armed before firing the aggressive attitude is ensuring early surrenders and quicker suppression times."

"I know, and that's good, but eventually we may find ourselves outside of a war zone. If we're all as hard as nails and ready to open fire at the slightest indication of trouble, we'll be of no use to anyone. It's the civilians that will keep us human, aware that there's a grey area to this friend or foe mentality that's built into all our training."

Alice didn't respond right away and just looked at him, glancing at his new trophy before replying. "You're right. I'll be honest, I'd expect that kind of thinking more from Liam, but you're right. Are you going to stop civilians from qualifying for different positions on the ship?"

"No, but we should start compiling a list of people the civilians have requested us to pick up. We have a lot of room left in the habitation section in the Botanical Gallery."

"What about children?"

Jake hesitated a moment, it was something he had been thinking about for several days. "It feels wrong to have them aboard a ship of war. I'm still against it."

"I agree. It's going to cut a lot of people from that list though. The civvies that are requesting to bring family aboard have a lot of brothers, sisters and others who have kids."

"We'll have to live with it, I need to know that everyone aboard made a concious choice to be here."

"Speaking of family, is that what I think it is?" Alice asked, gesturing towards the encased drinking glass.

"It is. I didn't know what to do with it after finishing the testing, so I. . ." he gestured towards it and shrugged.

"It's good, I mean, it's not like he was able to leave much behind. What did the tests turn up?"

"Well, his results show natural ageing, mine show that I'm almost seven years old and a large percentage of my physiology shows signs of mass regeneration. He was the original, that's for sure."

"Laura was saying that you're like his moodier brother," Alice smirked.

Jacob burst out laughing and nodded. "That fits. How are you two getting along?"

"Great, if there's anyone in engineering or our civilian research volunteers with nothing to do, she gives them a challenge. I don't know what she's been up to since I last saw her before I made the switch from AI to human, but it's given her the ability to command, demand respect and delegate. The more I watch her the more I learn, even though she keeps trying to convince me that I'm the great commander."

"You are, if I were to take you off the bridge night watch the graveyard crew would probably mutiny. I don't know what I'd do without you."

"I learned everything about command from you."

"You mean from Jonas," Jake corrected with a thin smile.

"You're right, mostly, anyway," Alice replied with a slow nod. "I'm sorry, I see more of him in you every day, even though you look a little different."

"Now that's what you have to thank Liam and my real father for. I was made by one of the inventors of framework technology and he left me a message."

Alice's eyes went wide, her interest was keenly piqued; "what did he say?"

"Not much, only that there's someone with more information on Zingara Station."

"That can't be a coincidence."

"No, I'm pretty sure he chose Zingara because he knew it would remain independent and that I would remember being there as Jonas."

"With Ayan."

The light mood that accompanied the revelation Jake was sharing with her drained out of him. He looked older somehow, tired, more like the Jake Valance she had first met weeks before.

"I'm sorry, it's my day for saying all the wrong things I guess," Alice apologized quietly. "I'm guessing taking these memories on is a whole package deal, the bad comes with the good and you still miss her."

Jake nodded. "You're right, and if I could thank Ayan I would. Somehow I still expect her to come through that door with two cups of coffee. Remembering her brings back so much, especially about Zingara Station. Meeting her changed everything."

"You know the civilians who are rebuilding the Botanical Garden just finished making a monument honouring all the people who died taking the ship. They put an image of Ayan and Jonas at the top since most of the crew see Jonas as the last one who died in that fight. You should go down and see it."

"I know, things have been busy. I haven't seen my own quarters for weeks. Maintenance keeps asking for permission to go in and clean up but I just push it to the bottom of the priority list."

"You're going to have to finish moving in someday Jake," Alice smiled wryly. "A few of the *Samson* crew aren't moving their stuff from the old ship into their new quarters until they see you do it first."

"It's not that I'm not here for good. Even if Sol Defence came along and tried to get her back, I'd still try to strike a deal for *Triton*. My mind is always on the crew, the ship, what we're doing and how we're doing it."

"That's not really moving in. You have to find a place to kick your heels up, pick somewhere to put all your creature comforts. Eventually you'll need some time off and it might be good for you to have a quiet space you've made your own."

Jake thought for a moment, his gaze resting on the enshrined drinking glass. "Between you and me that's hard. On one hand the *Samson* was my first ship, my only ship. At the same time I'm taking on all these memories, and as much as Jonas and I would probably get along if he were still here, drawing on his experiences, catching myself doing little things he used to do just messes me up sometimes. Some psycho annalist would say I'm hanging on to the *Samson* because I feel like I'm losing myself. On the other hand I like how Jonas thinks, the experiences he had with his friends, with Ayan. He knew how to be with people, taking charge was his problem while I'm the opposite. Ever since I woke up on the *Samson* I've been in charge, it's what I had to do to survive, but being with people, feeling like one of their mates instead of their captain, well, it just didn't happen.

"Ash told me she got a big smile out of you the other day. She was on cloud nine for hours."

The memory prompted a little grin from Jake as he nodded. "She was showing me an ad she'd found in a data burst Liam brought back from his recruiting run for Kawaii Cats. I couldn't help but wilt when I saw it. She's threatening to buy one on her first trip off ship."

"Oh no, with a talking kitten on board the whole crew will be helpless if we run into a Regent Galactic cruiser."

"It's insidious, it really is," Jake laughed. "I don't want any pets on board, not just yet, anyway. This is a warship after all."

"I have to agree, but eventually someone's going to bring a teacup poodle, or trained rim weasel aboard."

"I know, we'll have to keep any pets assigned to people who have officer class quarters or family quarters eventually, but for now the policy has to stand. There's still so much we don't know about this ship, compartments we haven't even opened yet. No one's so much as glanced at the Junior Officers quarters and there are four hundred sixty billets there."

"I think Stephanie's security team will take care of anything on four legs easy enough. Last I read their instructions were to detain and contain anything not walking upright. That woman thinks of just about everything where security is concerned. That is, if she isn't watching you. I don't think there's a person from the *Samson* who hasn't noticed a few changes in their Captain."

"How are the crew taking it?" Jake asked, running his finger along the edge of the encased keepsake on his desk.

"Well, they don't know what to expect but knowing that you're more open to suggestions seems to help. People still channel a lot of their ideas through me though. They seem to think I have a lighter hand."

"Little do they know," Jake shook his head and smiled.

Alice smiled back. "Little do they know," the pair shared a knowing look, between the two of them it was difficult to decide which had the more ruthless command style. During ship wide simulations they often switched handles, used each other's voices all in an effort to be fully aware of how the crew responded to each commander. Alice looked back to the small trophy. "So, any idea what you're going to do with your memento?"

"I was going to leave it somewhere in the office since we both use this space. I still don't know where."

"I like it where it is. It should be somewhere everyone can see it, I think."

"Makes the decision simple. Speaking of decisions, I've chosen a few targets for *Triton* to hit when we're ready. One will solve our wormhole generator problem.

Price and Finn managed to find more combat damage, it would take weeks to machine the parts since they're too dense to materialize. Not to mention we don't have a machinist that's worked with the technology before. Liam is going to try and rig a solution that'll get it working until we can find a port we can buy the parts from or pursue another solution."

"The learning curve would kill us on time if the engineering crew can't improvise something."

"Exactly. So I'm putting a plan together using the *Triton*, the *Samson*, and the *Cold Reaver* along with a few fighters in a support role. I want to steal a wormhole generating hypertransmitter. The intelligence Frost got his hands on lines right up with the transmission data we're tracing."

"So you've managed to find a transmission node? One small enough to steal?"

Jake smiled at her and nodded. "The *Samson* can pick it up with the maxjack if she has enough cover. There's a station nearby but if we hit fast and hard enough, distracting with the *Triton* we'll be able to snatch it. That's only if we can't buy the parts on a recruiting run."

"Good chance of that. Wormhole generator parts that'll work in the *Triton's* existing systems are rare."

Jake nodded his agreement and went on. "In the meantime, there are some supply routes we can hit with hyperspace layover points. I've managed to narrow the list down to military targets that run a lot of wetware assets."

"You mean slaves."

"It's not clear. The information we have indicates average head counts per square meter, and there are too many for the ships to carry active crew and no slave cargo. The routes and shipments are significant enough for any disruption to hurt. The loss of these assets won't go unnoticed. That presents another problem."

"We don't have any allies to offload extra cargo to or to take anyone we liberate in," Alice finished for him.

"Exactly. So we'll have to take on slaves first, try to take on any cargo that could help us and destroy what we can't resell. After that we'll have to find an ally fast."

"Unless we take the hypertransmitter first."

"With the crew still untried?" Captain Valance asked, raising an eyebrow.

"You've seen them in simulations and live drills. They follow orders, their reaction times are fast even by my standards after just a couple of weeks. They're dedicated."

"I want to start on a solid victory, and if we go after this transmission node and come up against something unexpected we'll have turn and run early. We might not even get a chance to launch the *Samson* or any of the other ships, it might come down to going in cloaked and getting out if there's no way to the hypertransmitter."

"You have a point. It's got to be pretty well protected. What are the chances we'd make it without major casualties?"

"Less than fifty, but I'm working on refining the plan. I'd still rather see what the crew can do to a supply convoy first. A softer target," Jake said, turning on a holographic navigational chart. It flickered on and hovered over his desk. "Here, this would be perfect. Lower chance of there being slaves, but the average mass index of the shipments going through show that they regularly ship heavy materials through this point, probably munitions and supplies that are too complex or dense to materialize on site. Steal it or wreck it, Regent Galactic will feel the pinch."

"There's still about a five percent chance of wetware cargo," Alice pointed out.

"True, but we can't get hung up on the what ifs. This crew is together because a lot of them stayed to do some damage to Regent. We'll just have to run ship wide sims that include taking on a few thousand slaves, just in case."

"I'll set it up during my shift. The crew won't like it, but I'm sure they'll rise to it."

"Good, I want to be as prepared as we can be."

"When do you think we'll hit this layover point?"

"I'm giving the Engineering team two weeks tops to get a fix in place for the wormhole drive. If there's no way they can get it done on that deadline, then we'll have to do it all on hyperdrive. Still, we won't start talking about it to the general crew yet, there might still be a couple Regent Galactic spies on board."

"Stephanie's doing her best to catch them, she's tearing her hair out at the Intelligence department though, they just don't know what they're doing."

"I know, we'll have to do something about that. Don't get pulled into it though, it's taking the both of us in overlapping fourteen and sixteen hour shifts to run the *Triton* and we haven't chosen a day watch first officer yet."

"About that, should I give Price the official rank below me on night watch?"

"No, he's being paid as a first officer and doing the work, so there's no need to force a rank on him that'll just make him nervous. Besides, he's pulling triple shifts when no one's looking just because his race doesn't have to sleep for days at a time. If we promote him I'm afraid he'll never sleep again."

Alice couldn't help but chuckle. It was true, the issyrians were particularly hard workers, and more importantly they were commonly curious about the ship. The only person more dedicated to her duties was Ashley. She was relatively new to piloting but she had a great feel for the ship, controls and her thirst for knowledge, her need to improve was insatiable. The young woman knew how to relax, sure, but on most nights she was deep in a simulation, piloting large ships and fighters alike into the most challenging scenarios. "So Ashley's going on her first recruiting mission."

Jake smiled a little and nodded. "I was wondering when you'd bring that up."

"She's key to the helm during day shift, I was a little surprised."

"Her navigator is going with her. I'll be using another team at the helm for the next couple days. I figured it was time to give them a chance. If the worst happens I could always take the controls."

"Do you think she can manage a small crew for a few days?"

"I left her in charge of the *Samson* enough while Stephanie, Frost and I were off ship. The *Cold Reaver* is easier to take care of."

"You know, I wish I was around for the *Samson* days. I keep hearing stories."

"It wasn't as interesting as it might sound. The *Samson* is far from done though. I have plans for her, the *Cold Reaver* and a few other ships in her class if we can get our hands on them."

"Oh really?" Alice asked with an upraised eyebrow.

"The *Triton* is perfect for serving as a command center for several smaller crews on ships just like the *Samson*. There's no reason why we can't go after several small objectives at a time or use a group of smaller ships to help capture convoys, hit military targets that are hardened against large warships like the *Triton* or we could run deep recon, cherry pick targets before going in with everything."

"I like the way you think. Makes me really wish the *Clever Dream* was still around. She'd be perfect."

"I'll make sure you get an agile ship when you run missions. I don't know if we can find something like the *Clever Dream*, but I'll do my best to replace her."

"Maybe I should take a look at Regent Galactic's military vessel listing. I'm sure they make something I'd like to get my hands on," she said with a crooked grin. "I've met enough ship thieves and pirates to know a few things."

"Then that's the first mission you'll plan after reviewing what I've put together."

THE WAR ROOM

The view from the high side of Mount Elbrus was expansive. The many long avenues carved into the side of the mountainside stone extended downward like hundreds of stairs, to look at it in the darkness of night you couldn't tell there was a thing amiss. Beyond the darkness of the mountainside fierce urban combat continued in the sprawling city beyond the shield. Ayan stood wrapped in her long poncho as she watched tracers arc over the shorter structures, heard the pops and roars of explosions punctuating the screaming light.

They had pushed the enemy out of the mountain. A great victory for all the flesh and blood defenders. Squadrons of Regent Galactic soldiers and West Keepers waited for them in the city streets, however. Their prowess at urban combat and superior numbers halted the mountain rebels, so they fell back to the main tunnel entrances and held, fortifying their hard won territory. The tunnels were safe for the night. How long it would remain that way no one could say for certain.

Volunteers snuck into the city beyond the foot of the mountain regardless of the dangers to distract the West Keepers and their mechanized allies. Using strike and fade tactics they inflicted as much harm to the enemy as they could manage before retreating, running and getting set to do it all over again. Some of the teams went out and hadn't returned. One had managed to send a message along an intact wired network. The message was simple; *Enemy military hardware and personnel has begun to land on nearby islands. Going deeper into hiding and will contact when we have more intelligence.* Things were getting worse but morale in the mountain was high. It felt like an island of safety in a sea of war.

A pressing, urgent need to destroy any weapon capable of doing major damage to the energy shield motivated some of the soldiers in the vast city below and the further one made their way from the edge of the shield the higher the mortality rate was. Jason, Oz, Minh and herself would be going further out than any team had since the whole conflict began.

She flinched as a group of red and blue streaks lit up the sky and struck the shield at her right side. It was her first real exposure to an all out ground war. Ayan had gone on a planetside mission involving repairs on a power plant after a major conflict, she'd run with various people in countless simulations, and she'd had extensive cadet, navy and officer ground training not to mention the rank of Major. Looking at her old file anyone would conclude that she was fully qualified to not only participate in a ground war, but to direct a platoon.

The real thing was different. She hadn't seen it in daylight yet, but she wasn't looking forward to it. She pulled the poncho tighter around herself. There was no need for additional warmth, the vacsuit took care of that from her toes all the way up to the black choker around her neck but she wanted to feel wrapped, covered up, protected.

The transparent door behind her slid open and a big hand came to rest gently on her shoulder. "Quite a view," Oz said quietly.

"Has it stopped since you got here?"

"The fighting? It's gotten worse. Feels like I've been fighting in tunnels for months even though I can still count the days since I volunteered on my hands. This could go on for years or end tomorrow."

"I saw a Thurge cruiser in a vertical bay down there. Is it broken down?"

"No, it works fine. It would carry everyone inside this mountain out of the solar system. Should take more than enough punishment to make it too."

"Then why aren't they running?" Ayan asked in a whisper.

"They're protecting something. Jason and I can't find out what, but from what the Sergeant tells us there's too much to transport and giving the artificials a chance at access would cause so much trouble they won't even talk about it."

"I don't suppose they're willing to destroy their precious cargo."

"They say it can't be destroyed. Not well enough to be sure."

Ayan shook her head. "You can destroy anything with a big enough fusion bomb."

"Spoken like a true combat engineer."

"So Minh's plan is the best plan."

"Looks like."

The pair looked out over the night shrouded city. One of the upper sections of a tall, sixty storey building was burning out of control, it looked like a massive torch. There were secondary explosions and flashes of light on the floors below and both of them hoped that they were the result of some accelerant left behind, not evidence of a desperate firefight.

"We thought we lost you," Oz said, breaking a long silence.

Ayan didn't know what to say, how to respond for a quiet span that weighed on them both. She smiled finally and said; "I'm eighteen days old."

He couldn't help but give her the most surprised, quizzical look, then burst out laughing. "I hadn't thought of it that way. Makes as much sense as anything else though. Minh told me everything, I think he likes being the lesser of two unusuals."

Ayan laughed and turned to look at him. "That's what you're calling us?"

Oz shrugged. "May as well, you're both miracles when you look at it. The odds of him surviving out there for as long as he did were about as low as the odds of the Doc actually managing to bring you back," his big hands took hold of her shoulders and he smiled warmly at her. "And we couldn't be happier that you both made it through, however you did."

Ayan smiled back at him. "Regardless of the conditions, I'd be hard pressed to find better company."

"I'm sorry Jonas couldn't be here, despite the conditions."

She nodded; "So am I, but in my mind it's been over two years since he disappeared. I know, it's actually been about eight, but I'm still adjusting. What I mean to say is; I think not knowing what happened to him was what hurt the most.

Now I know, and I miss him, but it's better. I feel lighter."

"You know about Jake?"

"I heard. I want to meet him but I'm not getting my hopes up. I've seen some of the holos. He'll be different, I'll be different, maybe less so but," she shrugged in conclusion.

"You're probably two of the most similar people in the galaxy, you know," Oz whispered to her. "Laura says he remembers who he is and aside from being a little cuter, you act and appear pretty much the same. I've never met anyone whose had a body transplant and if things go well I might actually meet two soon enough."

"Is he coming here?" Ayan asked, her eyes widening. She had told herself over and over again not to get her hopes up, to stay cool, collected, but the tightening knot in her stomach and light headedness told her that being rational where Jake was concerned was pretty far out of the question.

"We're hoping. If we can get a transmission out to the *Triton* and her cloaking systems are still up, it could change the odds just enough."

"Do you think he'd actually come if we called him?"

"I wouldn't be surprised if he was already on his way. We sent him a message while we were on our way here. If he has scout ships on his outer perimeter he might get it soon."

Ayan chuckled nervously and blew a breath of air out with widened eyes. "Nothing is ever simple when we all get together, is it? Thank God Laura's aboard the *Triton*."

"Oh, now that's going to be interesting. She doesn't know anything about you or Minh."

"I think it would be good for someone to give her at least a few seconds warning. Give her a chance to visit with Jason first. I can't wait to see her face, but still, I'd rather not give her a coronary."

"Well, it's a long way between here and there even if the *Triton* is already on its way. We have jamming signals to bust through. Speaking of which, they want us at the strategic board."

"Lead the way," Ayan invited.

Oz walked through the doors as they opened, Ayan followed close behind. Jason, Minh, Alaka and Sergeant Roman were gathered around a large display table with a fully detailed hologram of the island. There were three red marked buildings and a pointer indicating that there was another point of immediate interest off the eastern side of the map. "Thank you for joining us Ayan." Alaka said graciously. "I have been looking forward to meeting you ever since Oz told me a few stories about your shared experiences. My name is Alaka."

"Thank you Alaka, I didn't know Oz had so many interesting stories about me. It's good to meet you too."

"Alaka was about to give us his report," Roman looked haggard, worn. Under the weight of coordinating a full on rebellion from within the mountain he looked past his forty years. He was a man shrouded in seriousness, and his success demanded the respect of the mountain rebels.

"Yes. The artificials are organizing in units with the few West Keepers that have landed. I expect they're the spearhead of a larger force."

"I've been hearing that name a lot. Who are the West Keepers exactly?" Minh asked.

"Humans who paid for immunity from destruction before the artificials began attacking their masters. Many of them take care of human hostages, while anyone who is useful in a firefight have been sent to the front. They were patrons of an Eden Cult or Order of Eden as they call it. They believe that service in this world will get them closer to their promised land in this life or in the afterlife. A few we captured went on and on about it."

"It must not have made it to Freeground or been taken seriously by Intelligence, I didn't see any record," Jason commented.

"That doesn't help us. Anyone inside the mountain could be an Eden Cultist, or a West Keeper, whatever they're called." Sergeant Roman said, shaking his head. "We have enough problems with the fall of two military bases just south of the island."

"What kind of firepower can they bring to bear?" Oz asked.

"Enough to kill our shield in a month."

"There are reinforcements arriving every couple of hours at the military port." Alaka said. "Oz and I saw the ships descending. Soon there will be boats, we'll have to start firing on them."

"Why wouldn't they use shuttles? They'd be able to land anywhere on the island." Asked Ayan.

"Because our anti-air batteries are still operational. They won't risk that again. I think you and Minh arrived just in time. He says you can form a good team with Oz and Jason, what do you think your chances are of getting behind enemy lines and causing real damage are?" Asked Roman.

Ayan looked to Oz, Jason and Minh, who was the only one not looking back at her. Minh's attention was fully focused on the red marked post on the southern most point of the island. "We've trained extensively together and shared some very tense situations," she replied confidently. Slipping back into a military stance was so easy, like an old, comfortable suit.

"I'm told you hold the highest rank here." Roman said, making no efforts to disguise his appraising gaze.

"I was a Major in the Freeground Fleet and started as a cadet when I was a teenager. I'm also a fully qualified stationary and battleship engineer, pilot, boarding captain and infantrywoman."

"That's my girl," Oz said under his breath. All eyes shifted to him and he shrugged. "I met her while we were still in the academy, served as First Officer while she was the Chief Engineer on the same carrier."

"I served as the Wing Commander on that ship," Minh added. "Oh, and I served a tour in the All-Con conflict, planetside combat and demolitions."

"And I was the Intelligence Officer before joining Fleet Intelligence and supervising several active operations."

Alaka looked to Roman and chuckled. "We're both outranked."

"Makes me wish the military wasn't the first thing to get knocked out on this

134

rock. We have a couple of junior officers, some infantry that made it across the island before the fighting got serious, but everyone else is either police or a volunteer. Mostly volunteer." Roman explained.

"So you're not military?" Asked Minh.

"No, I'm a police Sergeant. Served twelve years in the mobile infantry before joining the force."

"Looks like you've kept this mountain together just fine, Sergeant. What are you planning from here?"

"I was hoping you people could come up with one. We don't have real specialists, and from the looks of it you're all exactly that, specialists."

"Oz busts bots like they're firecrackers," Alaka nodded. "No need to guess at what his speciality is."

"Well, we need to take control of this main broadcast station," Sergeant Roman said, pointing at the holographic map. "It's one of the stations being used to jam all communications on this side of the planet and they're directing system wide communications from the control bunker. There's a backup broadcast system in the nearby spaceport, but I'm hoping whoever takes control of the bunker can interrupt the jamming signals and send for help before the automations manage to override from the secondary control point. We could have a transmission to our nearest sister solar system in an hour using a micro wormhole."

The six of them stared at the map silently for several seconds before Minh pointed at a spot just past the spaceport. "If we could somehow drop here, in this field we can get to the bunker no problem. We'll need everything we brought with us on the *Warpig*."

"Is this the most powerful station on the planet?" Ayan asked, looking at the cluster of white dishes and thin transmission towers.

"It is, while that station is jamming everything in the air no one can use wireless. All the main hard lines pass through that station and the spaceport as well, so it's safe to say that's how they're stopping us from communicating outside of the mountain." Alaka answered, bringing up a secondary map of the bundled cables deep underground leading off in every direction from the communications bunker. "There are many secondary stations on this side of the planet, like the one in this mountain, but they're easier to work around."

"What kind of resistance can we expect?" Oz asked.

"It's hard to say, our scans can't be trusted that far past the shield because of the jamming signals, but there will be a fair number of Andies walking around." Roman answered.

"Andies?" Ayan asked.

He brought up a hologram of an android. The weapons inventory displayed a low penetration pulse sidearm and a high powered particle rifle. If it weren't for a serial number that was written in a black strip that started in the middle of its forehead and ran over the top of its head to the back of its neck it would have been indistinguishable from a human. "This is a law enforcement android with an advanced AI that allows them to deal with any situation. More than nine out of ten of our officers were Andies. When the virus managed to change their programming everyone inside my precinct was killed. I was off duty at the time and when I got there they had stripped the armoury clean and started killing everyone in the mountain. If you're wondering why there are so few people alive on the mountainside, there's your answer."

"I'm sorry Sargent," Ayan sympathized.

"I'm getting used to telling the story, it's all right."

"So you managed to kill them all?"

"No, most of them escaped into the city below. The first thing the Andies here did was organize themselves into well armed squads."

"I've seen that. My platoon was pushed back for about five hours in the city by one group." Oz said. "They're smart, heavily armoured."

"How many are in their squads?" Minh asked.

"Eight. My platoon started with ninety one, we had taken forty seven casualties by the time we managed to take them out and collapse the buildings holding parts of the shield open."

"You did better than most, Oz. Most of your casualties were wounded and had a chance at recovery," Alaka said, putting one big paw on the humans shoulder.

"They waited until we were just about to set charges in the first building before jumping us. One of them was posing as a corpse in a pile of bodies. Stood up right behind me and nearly took my head off."

"So they're smart, heavily armoured and most likely in force at the bunker." Ayan concluded. "We're not going to be able to hold it once we've taken it, so we'll send a message through that wormhole generator in orbit and kill the systems inside with a zero rad micro-nuke."

"I'll leave you four to plan it then," Roman said with raised eyebrows.

The tone in the room had changed. Any joviality had gone, replaced with a heavy, deadly seriousness. Ayan caught the Sargent's arm as he turned from the table and looked him in the eye coldly. "Once we finish hitting this bunker and securing some method of viable longer term communications we probably won't be back. We'll have to take cover somewhere else or find our way off the planet from the spaceport to go in search of help. Returning to the mountain between strikes is a pointless risk."

Roman's eyes went wide as he glanced at the map then back to the much smaller woman, who suddenly had the bearing of an eight foot tall battle commander. "What do you need?" he asked quietly.

"We'll have a list for you by morning," she replied as she turned back to the table.

Roman and Alaka left the room so the old friends could plan a desperate mission to save the mountain rebels and everyone else fighting for survival on Pandem.

136

MIRRORS

The training shifts on the bridge were more and more intense as Alice and Jake raised the difficulties. Between simulations she had started reviewing the results alone, she loved the night bridge staff but it always went faster if she could sync her mechanical eye up to a computer system and review the data over a digital interface without being interrupted.

When she entered the Ready Office attached to the bridge she stopped dead in her tracks and hurriedly slapped the button to close the hatch behind her. Captain Valance was sitting on the desk in his undershorts, his vacsuit was draped over one hand while the other gently ran his fingers over it. "She's really gone, isn't she?" he asked so quietly she almost didn't hear.

Alice hesitated a moment and asked; "what's that you have there Captain?"

"Just a scarf. Ayan made it for me out of a shawl that was ruined on the *First Light.*"

She glanced at it again, just to be sure he was actually holding his vacsuit in the dim light, not the scarf that had been tied around Ayan's body before she was given a space farer's burial. Her cybernetic eye compensated for the low light and focused in on his face. His glazed eyes and openly mournful expression told her one thing; *he's sleep walking, or whatever counts as sleep walking where Jake is concerned. He doesn't do anything small.*

"Ayan, Minh, my parents, even Alice is gone,"

She was about to contradict him then a thought occurred to her; "Jonas?"

He looked up at her, his eyes focused on her only for a moment then glazed over once more. "Who else would I be? Then again, I don't know who you are, but you're familiar. Like everything here; strange ship, strange constellations when I look outside, even the operating system for the comm is different but all somehow familiar."

"You should get back to bed sir," she directed quietly.

"Why? Even my ship's gone, I don't even know what happened to the *First Light* after it escaped."

"She made it back, they've rebuilt her as a carrier and now you're running a new ship. You should get your rest, you don't want to be tired for your duty shift on the bridge."

"A new ship?" he stared at her dumbly, for a moment she thought he was coming out of it, then he looked away, to something in the distance. "Doesn't matter, there's not much time left."

Alice walked across the room to him gently and took his arm. He was larger than Jonas was, but his bearing, his manner was every bit the Jonas she remembered.

Urging him to his feet was easier than expected.

"It took him a while to stop resisting the integration process, but now that he's accepted that it's the way it should be my individual imprint is integrating. We'll be inseparable soon, the same person, and I can't let him take all this grief, all this anger," he went on. "None of this is happening the way it was supposed to, he should have woken up, seen Alice and the imprint was supposed to take over, he was supposed to remember."

"Who was supposed to remember?" she asked, placating him more than anything. *I just need to get him back to bed, he'll probably just roll over and mumble his way back to sleep.*

"The copy, he was supposed to remember me then learn to use the framework technology but the trigger went off too late and he had time to become something more, someone all his own."

She stopped half way to the small shaft that would lead him back to bed. "You mean he became Jake."

"That's what you call him," he looked straight into her eyes and was suddenly astonished. "*You* were the trigger, but you left before he woke up."

"So he doesn't know how to use the framework technology? How does he learn?" she asked, not knowing whether what she was hearing was real or some rant born in a dream.

"By using it, it's a natural function like breathing, only the first time it happens it might be unconscious, maybe dangerous," he said as his manner changed completely. His vision focused in on her and he dropped his vacsuit. Automatically he stooped to pick it up then realized where he was. "How did I get here?" He was awake.

Alice hesitated for a moment, watching him to make sure that he was actually awake. "You were sleep walking," she replied simply as she stepped away.

"Sleep walking? What was I doing? Did I leave the ready quarters?"

"Thankfully no. When I came in you were holding that as though it was the scarf Ayan made for you. You thought you were Jonas."

The memory of a dream returned to him vaguely as he put his vacsuit on. *But that's not my memory. It's one of my recollections from Jonas' past.* "What did he-" he paused for a moment then corrected himself; "-I say?"

"You'd better watch the security footage," Alice queued up the last ten minutes using her command unit and instructed the room's main player to display the time period in question. "Do you want me to leave?"

"No, stay."

They watched it together and when it finished Jake Valance sat in silence in one of the chairs in front of the sturdy captain's desk.

Alice braced herself. She hoped she handled the situation the way he would have liked and she hadn't overstepped her bounds.

"It explains a lot, but what did he mean by using the framework technology? I've already come back from beyond the brink at least once, survived radiation poisoning, what else is there and why don't I remember it like everything else Jonas experienced?"

"I have no idea, I'm sorry," Alice said quietly.

Jake turned to her, sitting in the seat beside him, and put his hand on her shoulder. "You shouldn't be, why would you have the answers?"

"I should have found my way back to you sooner after drawing Vindyne away from you and the *Samson*. The only reason why I didn't go back sooner was because I was afraid. I had a price on my head for three sectors and I didn't want to get caught. I should have waited for you to wake up, made sure you were all right before I moved on."

"It's all right. One way or another we both came out fine. Jonas, or whoever that was talking in my sleep has another thing wrong. He wants to protect me from his pain but that's just part of who he is, without it nothing would be the same. The worst bit is that there's something in here," he said, pointing to his temple. "telling me to do *something* and I have no idea *how*."

Alice was relieved that he didn't blame her for leaving him alone on the *Samson* years ago, it was something she worried about often. "Maybe we should think about heading to Zingara station after we've met up with Oz and Jason. I know it's a couple sectors away, but there might be answers there. Until then, it's just a matter of waiting I guess. I'll tell you if you start growing extra components or giving off radio signals."

He sighed and nodded. "Something to think about once the wormhole generator is working again. Besides, I guess it's too much to ask to get an operator's manual, no one else is born with one."

Alice couldn't help but chuckle. "Now you know how I felt for the first few months after making the transfer."

"Sometimes I forget. Still feels like you're the daughter I was looking for while I made my way across the outer fringes most of the time."

"I don't mind that one bit."

"Good, it's a hard thing to shake. Still, it makes me wonder about what I did while I was a blank slate. My, I mean Jonas' psych professor at the academy once said that the true test of a person is what they do when they think no one's looking. When I had a completely blank slate the first thing I did after getting the *Samson* running was land her on Radic and start bounty hunting locally. After a month I had turned in about a dozen bail jumpers, debtors and I even trapped some kid, couldn't have been more than sixteen, who was trying to avoid giving testimony. Three months later I was taking jobs from Radic City's crime lord."

"But you moved on."

"Only after I had enough money, that's all it was. I did it all for cash, whatever was on the board and didn't involve outright slavery I would do. One hundred and forty one crew members were killed while I was running the *Samson* and after a while I was just numb to it."

"Jake, Vindyne planted a directive in your head along with the databases they gave you. It was made to compel you to find work, to be someone else's servant. The system said that it would take a serious trauma to break you out of it. Somewhere along the line that's happened, and from what I've seen since I came aboard you're free."

"That might explain some of the jobs I never wanted in the first place but took anyway. I could have found work hauling cargo, the *Samson* had the hookups for it and it would have taken me just a couple days to get the engines up to par. When I was left on my own, running without a moral compass I chose the most available route and didn't want to know the details behind the jobs. Now I have all these memories and the moral code that comes with it. Jonas wouldn't have taken half the jobs I finished, so many of those people had a good reason to run and I'm the one who brought them in, right or wrong." he leaned on the thick transparent section of hull behind his desk. The nebula outside bathed the room in dim gold.

Alice watched him from where she sat. The security recordings of him capturing bounties came to mind, she had watched at least twenty of the ones that had surfaced on the Newsnets since he made his first recruiting speech for the Aucharians. She had never thought of who his prey was, what their crimes were. Most of the recordings had been stripped of those details, and the ones that did bear the identities of his targets made them out to be hardened criminals.

"Reconciliation," Jake said quietly. "Jonas was a good man, better than I ever was. Ever since I found his memories in my head I've felt like I've been carrying this weight around and the thing I'm most thankful for inheriting from him is his ability to just bury it. I tell you that man must have been good at just pretending nothing was wrong even if the whole place was coming apart."

Alice couldn't help but smile a little. "He couldn't hide anything from me or Ayan. She didn't know him nearly as long as I did, but she got him pretty quickly."

He leaned his head against the window with his arm as a cushion. "Now that's something I'd never have seen coming. Ayan. When it comes to her and everyone from the *First Light* I feel exactly the same. I miss Oz, Jason, and especially Minh and Ayan. Then I try and remind myself that I'm Jake Valance, this black hearted hunter and it does no good."

Seeing him so frustrated made her wish she could just pull the right thing to say out of the air or consult a few hundred interactive psychological texts as she would have as an artificial intelligence and just guide him to resolving his own issues but she only had one answer for him. "Time. You're grieving, it takes time."

Jake sighed and turned around, leaning on the backrest of his desk chair. "You're right, but there is no time, not here. I wouldn't give up the *Triton* or the crew either, this is what I want to be doing."

"What if you could have the best of both worlds? Maybe you could take one of those Uriel Starfighters for a test flight. I can hold down the fort, we're only training anyway."

Jake thought for a moment, looking down at the dark, blank surface of his desk. "Maybe."

She couldn't help but be surprised. Alice was sure he'd reject the idea immediately. A smile grew on her lips. "I'll get Laura to take your shift on the bridge, she was wondering if she could take one of mine for a while now anyway."

"Well, Oz and Jason are still out there too. I'd rather be here when they arrive so I'm pinned to the deck for at least that long." Jake took his gun belt from the peg beside the ladder and started putting it on.

"Not going back to bed?"

"No, I'm wide awake. Think I'll go down and work on the *Samson* awhile," he said as he put his long coat on.

"I'd join you but I have department training reports to go through. Laura's going to be glad you're staying close to the bridge with Oz and Jason still out there. She doesn't let on much, but she's worried."

"So am I. I'm just wondering if this idea for me to take a ride isn't some plot of yours to take the *Triton* for yourself."

Alice flashed him a broad grin and winked. "There's only one way to find out for sure."

CONSTRUCTING THE NEEDLE

The mountain hangar bay had been repaired and the rear section, where most servicing and maintenance was performed, was opened up once again. The rush of attackers in the city at the mountain's foot had ground to a temporary halt, and after a well deserved night's sleep Terry Ozark McPatrick had gone to the hangar and taken a seat on an old antigravity tank. A large red sheet had been tied around its main cannon, marking it for scrap.

He reclined against its cannon mount, sipping his breakfast from a spill proof cup as he watched Minh and Ayan work with a repair crew to build something that was cobbled together from parts gathered from every corner of the hangar and beyond. It was a long, narrow ship with the guts of an old fighter cockpit at the front and seating for three passengers lined up behind. Aside from some cargo space at the rear, those were all the comforts that would be afforded Minh, Ayan, Oz and Jason.

The hangar deck personnel were building an encasement of heavy armour several centimetres thick around the seating space and installing inertial dampeners that were made for ships twenty times the small transports' mass. They were just finished lowering the *Warpig's* afterburners into place at the front of the small ship. It was a strange little flyer with no rear thrusters and very high powered solid fuel engines at the front, pointing away from the cockpit.

"This is the last place I thought I'd find you," Jason said as he climbed up on the tank beside him and settled in to watch the team work under Minh and Ayan's direction.

Oz smiled at his long time friend and nodded. "I guess it would be, I'm no gearhead."

"Seems like everyone else is though. You should see the rail cannon that's going to launch that thing."

"I'll pass, this ship is scary enough. Besides, I think I'm here more to keep my eye on the people building it. I still can't believe Minh is here, let alone Ayan."

Jason looked to where Minh was crawling out of an access trench under the ship and talking to Ayan. It was something neither of them could hear from where they sat, but it had the young woman laughing. "I know. What do you think of her?"

"It's her. It may not look exactly like her, but from what she tells me about the Doc disappearing into a wormhole to bring her back, it all makes sense."

"There's something about her that is unmistakably Ayan, at least from what I've noticed."

Oz nodded slowly. "I only had to talk to her for a minute to know it was her. There's no doubt, and I've only seen her happier once."

"On the *First Light*. I think you could say the same about most of us. The

142

only time that tops it for Laura and I is our wedding day."

"What about the honeymoon?"

"And the honeymoon," Jason confirmed with a grin.

"I enjoyed my time as a Captain on patrol."

"You know I tried to convince Laura and Ayan to take a few Special Projects initiatives to you. Would have been a good excuse to spend some time aboard."

"What happened?"

"Fleet Intelligence promoted me, told me we wouldn't be able to join you since you were already out there running silent. So, they ended up on the *Midland* implementing the new dual drive and a few other things."

"I can see why Command didn't want the *Roi De Ciel* off the line, we didn't exactly need speed while we ran silent. Special Projects did send us some important upgrades though."

"I know. Do you miss it?"

"Commanding a cloak ship? All the time. I didn't realize I would until the *Sunspire* was under way though."

"Really? I thought you were feeling at home with the resistance here," Jason said in mild surprise.

"I do. There's nothing like having your boots in the dirt, securing tunnels and blowing buildings that might interfere with the shielding apart. Urban and tunnel combat comes with a rush all its own, but given the choice, I think I'd take command of a cloak ship any day. There's nothing like coming out of nowhere, right on top of a Vindyne cruiser and forcing their surrender. Besides, the crew gets really tight when you're running silent for that long."

"I see your point. Too bad we didn't serve together on that tour."

"You had just been married and I know Laura wouldn't leave Ayan or Special Projects."

"Yup, hopefully we'll be able to get this mission off without a hitch so we can send messages to the Carthan government and the *Triton*."

Oz laughed and shook his head.

"I said something funny?"

"No, it's just Alaka. He and his family has a lot of faith that we can do this. I mean, I think we can get it done, the enemy won't see us coming and we'll be moving so fast that nothing will be able to hit us, but getting out after is another question entirely. When the *Triton* or other help arrives we might be in a hole somewhere hiding from automations and the West Watch. That's if Minh doesn't blink in the wrong millisecond and kill us all."

"I don't think Minh will be blinking while he pilots that thing."

"I hope not. We're crossing several hundred kilometres in a few seconds. To anyone watching the mountain it'll look like something exploded, then our little ship's going to look like a great big fireball crash landing."

"Now you're starting to scare me."

"You can thank Alaka's eldest son. Now he's a gear head."

"What's it like being in the trenches with Alaka, anyway?"

"Let's just say that if he crossed the line and joined the other side, I'd seriously consider finding a way, any way, off this planet. He's quiet, quick, can snap a West Keeper's neck with one hand and recognizes where everyone he's leading is most useful faster than I think I could."

"That explains why he had you boosted to lead your own platoon after our first day here."

"And why you never saw direct combat. He and the Sergeant recognized your skills the first time you talked shop."

"Figures, I talk shop a lot," Jason nodded. "Something Laura complains about, especially since I never get specific."

"That would drive me nuts. I like knowing all sides, even when we're just talking."

"So does she," he chuckled. "Every once in a while she just gives me this look. I'm not going to miss having a few dozen Fleet secrets bouncing around in my head every day."

"You must miss her."

"I do, we've spent time apart before but not like this. We need to get this message out."

"I know. I just wonder what Laura's response will be when she sees Ayan and Minh."

"Oh, I know what her response will be to that, it's Jake Valance I wonder about. If he has Jonas' memories, and if that plays out anything like it has with Ayan, well," Jason shrugged. "Honestly? I know what I'm hoping for but not what to expect."

Oz nodded his agreement; "Ayan misses him, I mention his name, Jake's or Jonas', and it's like a physical blow. She seemed less emotional before somehow."

"She was ill, more focused on reassuring everyone else than anything I think. Now she's healthy and I still see the military brat we all knew and loved but she's more expressive now, seems more alive."

"And if Jake doesn't react to her at all," Oz sighed before continuing. "It'll be bad."

"We'll be there for her."

"So will Minh. He keeps her laughing, hell, he keeps everyone laughing."

"But he's keeping up with her engineering skills and he's changed so much. Before he seemed off balance somehow, now there's something very level about him."

"Like he's found some kind of peace," Oz added, watching Minh disappear into the hull of the twelve meter long ship. "I guess being isolated for so long will break or make you."

"Could you imagine?" Jason asked, shaking his head. "All this time. He said he turned the old reactor chamber into some kind of garden, the holo he showed me was amazing."

"I'm just glad he's with us. As much as I like to call him crazy, I saw what the *Warpig* looked like after it hit the deck. The only thing left of it was the cockpit and afterburners. You could tell that he had intentionally kept the ship turned just so the last things to be hit were those two sections."

"You know what he said to me when I mentioned it to him?" Jason asked with a grin.

"No, what'd he say?"

"'That's why I like to fly a ship with a great big ass!'" Jason quoted, doing his best imitation of the enthusiastic pilot.

Oz laughed and nodded. "From most pilots that kind of humour might make me nervous, but from him it's just a sign that he's having a good day."

"For Minh, I think every day has been a good day since they rescued him."

THE MESSAGE

The fabrication section of the *Triton* was easily the loudest place Captain Valance had ever seen or heard. Located above the main hangars it was so large, cavernous that an air temperature and pressure differential whipped the air into a mild gusting wind. Long hoist arms reached over top the mouths of the two materializers at work. They were three meters tall and eight wide with long strips of heavy transparent belting to separate the space where energy was converted to matter from the rest of the massive compartment.

Some things never changed; heavy equipment still moved on wheels or treads, a good strong length of carbon fibre cable was still better than an antigravity cart for moving awkward and heavy components around and people were still at extreme risk if they didn't know what they were doing inside the fabrication and assembly area of the ship. Jake was careful. He had actually never seen a place that could do so much, that in the space of an hour could convert energy and recycled metals into the cockpit of a Uriel fighter or a room full of furniture. Further down he could see the transparent barriers that cordoned off a section of the deck for the fabrication of more delicate parts and materials. There were clean rooms down there, smaller materialization suites and a vast collection of shop machinery.

Deck Chief Vercelli had the fabrication deck running like clockwork. All the processes and safety measures that were practiced had been set out by him and Engineering Chief Grady. When Jake signed off on them he hadn't yet grasped how critical they were. The deck was marked with yellow, black, blue and red boxes and pathways. The yellow and red sections were the most dangerous, the first designating areas where heavy equipment was in occasional operation and the second type of marking was for generally unsafe areas where there could be energy discharges, falling objects or other dangerous activities. The blue sections were safe areas for moving from one section of the deck to another and the black portions of the deck were marked off for temporary storage.

The high durability, multi layered reinforced carbon nose of a Uriel fighter was being wheeled out of one of the materializers just then and Jake couldn't help but be in awe as the predatory, sharp angled section was guided to the assembly point where other portions of the hull waited to be put together. In less than a day the *Triton* would have another brand new heavy fighter.

Chief Vercelli noticed him. "They're fine looking ships once we get them assembled. What brings you down here Captain?"

"I just thought I should come down and see this part of the ship. I've never seen a mass materializer this size before and after getting the last parts for the

Samson I had to see where they came from."

"Everything up to spec?"

"That's just it; the *Samson* is made mostly from spare parts and what you and Liam sent down just looked too new. Nothing matches, now I'll have to do the whole ship."

It took Chief Vercelli a moment, but he got the joke and nodded. "We aim to impress."

"I hear you picked up a few pilots on your recruiting run." Jake said as the front half of a fighter engine pod began to emerge from the materializer. He could feel the vibrations from deep within the machine in his teeth.

"Aye, twenty three all told. Only two failed qualification once they came aboard, they're signed up with Frost."

"Do they have fighters assigned to them yet?"

"This one here is for one of them, aye."

"Why isn't the pilot down here watching how it's put together?"

Chief Vercelli just looked at Jake for a moment before returning his attention to the sections of hull and interior component packages being gradually laid out in the shape of the fighter to be. "You're right Captain. To be honest we never built fighters from scratch on my old assignment. We got 'em from a factory like most outfits. I'll get him down here so he can learn what his machine's made of."

"Good. How are the rest of them doing?"

"What? The nineteen pilots we have flying? Pretty good. Only had one tried to steal his rig. He was surprised to find that the hyperspace and wormhole systems were locked out from the Flight Control Centre."

"I caught that in your report a few days ago. The playback of the conversation between him and Paula was hilarious. I think she really enjoyed shutting his fighter down remotely and having him dragged back with the *Cold Reaver*."

"What did you end up doing with him?"

"Ashley's dropping him off outside Sheffield."

"That one's taking care of that sort of business?"

"Leland's doing the dirty work, but she's running the show." Captain Valance nodded.

"Will wonders never cease."

The pair watched the mind crushingly loud ballet of manufacturing, assembling and machining continue in front of them. The other materializer was making parts for the main emitter array. The complex, dense components were taking much longer to manufacture and had to be treated with much more care than the sections of the fighter that were coming out like clockwork from the other large machine.

"I was wondering, what are you going to do with the *Samson*? I know she's being outfitted as a shield ship and she's got the power of a small tug, but you haven't assigned a pilot to her or put it on the patrol rotation."

"It's driving Paula crazy isn't it?"

Chief Vercelli laughed and nodded. "Aye, she likes to have everything in order."

"You'll know exactly why that ship's being rebuilt when she goes into action."

"How much work is left on her?"

"Finn and Price are putting the final touches on her tonight and I'm hoping to have her out in space for some testing-" Captain Valance stopped and answered a priority call from the bridge. "Go ahead."

"Sir, we have a transmission from the *Silkworm Four*. You should get up here," Stephanie informed him.

"I'm on my way," Captain Valance answered. "I'm sorry Chief, I'll be back to do an inspection when things quiet down."

"Aye sir, the boys'll like that. In the meantime I'll have someone track down this pilot so he can see how his fighter's put together."

The communications station on the bridge was surrounded by Cynthia, Stephanie, Paula, Laura and Price. As Captain Valance approached they parted so he could see the scratchy message for himself. "-it burned out our hyperspace systems so we'll be going to Pandem using the wormhole system and conventional engines. I'm hoping you have a long range patrol out in our direction so you receive this before moving on. If not, Oz and I will track you down. Love you Laura, hope to see you soon."

"Would you like me to play it back for you sir?" Cynthia asked.

"No, I got the gist and I can review it later. Who picked this up?"

"Tanner and his copilot sir," Paula answered. "They were doing scans along our outer radius and testing their wormhole drive. Your friend is lucky we had a trustworthy pilot out that end, otherwise it *would* have taken a month for his message to get to us. Will that be all?"

"Have they returned yet?"

"No, they're actually a couple hours out. They used a high compression micro wormhole to relay this back to us as soon as they got it. They couldn't decrypt it but recognized that it had a Freeground tag and thought it might be for you, Captain."

"Thank you Assistant Chief, that'll be all," Captain Valance said with a nod. It was that way between them all the time, absolutely business like. On the brighter side, Paula had seemed to calm down, to accept the fact that he was Captain and there was no changing her place on the ship unless she left entirely. No one complained about her attitude shift whenever Captain Valance walked onto the bridge.

"Tell me we're going after them," Laura said quietly.

"Our main emitters are still offline, we can't make it to Pandem in a reasonable amount of time in the *Triton*," answered Captain Valance.

"We can make it there in twelve days if we push the engines, that's a start."

"The *Cold Reaver* is out on a recruiting mission. She won't be back until tomorrow. Besides, I think I know a way to make it there in a lot less time. I'll take a fighter."

"No," Stephanie said firmly in a low whisper.

Captain Valance looked at her coolly. "What?"

"Whether you realize it or not you've been the one holding the ship together. You watch the reports, skim the operations figures, visit the crew while they're working to boost morale and design entire training regimens. Even the Chiefs turn to you for a decision when they know it'll go past their sections. It's bad enough that we've been sitting here for weeks in training. If you leave people might feel that *Triton* has no direction, no momentum."

"Alice has been working just as hard as I have."

"Because she *has* to. This ship needs every able hand aboard."

Jake paused a moment and just looked at Stephanie. She was showing her stern side, something everyone had gotten used to seeing with her as the Chief of Security, but there was something else. "What is it Steph?"

"It's a bad call, you leaving. That's it."

"Well it's my call. Laura will help keep things together in command while I take a fighter and go pick up Jason and Oz."

"I'll need your help, Chief," Laura said to Stephanie quietly.

"Fine, but bring a pilot to watch your back with you. Grippa's available and he's cleared to use the faster than light systems," Stephanie told the Captain with a level gaze.

"Paula's not going to like that. There are only two other pilots cleared on FTL enabled fighters," Cynthia whispered, shaking her head.

"Too bad. Our Captain takes a fighter out, he gets an escort," Stephanie concluded as she sprinted towards the bridge security doors.

"See you at the briefing tomorrow, Security Chief," Captain Valance said while turning back to the two dimentional display. The last frame of the transmission was up, showing Jason Everin, frozen in time. "She has a bad feeling about this."

"That's obvious," Cynthia scoffed quietly.

"Thank you Jake. If I were any real use in a cockpit I'd go with you," Laura said quietly.

"I couldn't just sit here and do nothing. I just hope that Stephanie's instincts are off for once."

HAVING IT OUT

Captain Valance stood in the middle of the *Samson's* main cargo hold. He was looking at the old stasis pods he used to use for transporting his numerous bounty captures. Stephanie stood in the half light, half way up the stairs.

She just stopped and looked at him for a moment. He didn't bother turning around. In fact, he made no sign that he even knew she was there. For a moment she could see the Captain she remembered from before the *Triton*. His dark long coat hung over him, giving him a more intimidating, larger than life bearing. Underneath was his full vacsuit with its heavy gloves, military class boots and black body. It covered all but his head. For a moment she really did see the man she remembered, then he looked to her with a small, warm smile.

"Couldn't sleep either?" he asked quietly.

"No sir, not a wink. I checked the status board for the senior officers and it showed that you were here."

"They just finished load testing her systems. The *Samson* is one shakedown cruise away from being fit."

"That's good news," she finished walking up the stairs and stopped on the landing to lean on the railing there. Her black vacsuit was made to emulate his and her long coat was very much the same as well, but she had left it in her quarters. As far as she was concerned her role as the Chief of Security was to keep the crew safe, secure and occasionally speak on the Captain's or First Officer's behalf. There was a time not long before when she knew exactly how to do that, when she was certain of the answer whenever she thought to herself; *what would Captain do?*

Lately she found herself growing less and less certain.

"What brings you down here Steph?" asked Jake.

"You're keeping me awake," she answered simply.

He looked at her with a raised eyebrow and an amused, crooked grin. "I've been right here since Alice took over on the bridge."

She knew he knew what she meant, that he was was putting her on, trying to lighten the mood. That wasn't helping. "Are you all right sir?"

His prolonged stare told her more than anything he could say. It lasted longer than was comfortable. Jake finally turned to face the stasis tubes. The green gelatin inside caught just enough light to reflect it back onto the man's face.

Stephanie tried to stifle the irritation building up in her, to be patient. "In all the time I've known you I've never seen you uncertain. Being out here like this, training, drilling, it was the best thing at first. It's been weeks now and more than half the crew will be completely certified in the next few days but we're still not moving."

"We don't have a wormhole generator, a real doctor and we're still low on

150

pilots and qualified intelligence personnel," he answered flatly, not looking at her.

"You know the chances of actually finding the qualified people you're looking for are slim not to mention this ship has perfectly good hyperspace systems. We're probably one of the fastest hyperdrive ships in the sector. It's *you*. What is it that's holding you back from committing this crew to what they signed on for?"

"It's not me," he said quietly.

"Oh *come on!* You're smarter than I am, faster, harder, cooler headed and you're telling me that you're the last one to know that you're not yourself? The Jacob Valance I knew was a force of nature, shrewd and decisive. What happened?"

"I woke up empty!" Captain Valance erupted, turning towards her while pointing to one of the stasis tubes. "I woke up empty and for over five years I chased people down regardless of their crimes. When I got them back here I put them in a tube just like the one I was found in, made them helpless as I presented them to companies and governments without seeing both sides of the story. Some of them were in the wrong, sure, but just try to count how many we *knew* should be running. We knew they should be running because they were innocent, or because they were in some grey area that we'd normally understand but chose not to because we weren't willing to pass on the payday."

"'Only fools and philosophers choose their work.' *You* said that. We were making a living and taking what the galaxy had to offer, which isn't much. What's got you second guessing now that it's all done and we're moving on to something else?"

"When I met Alice I could hear, see, feel all of Jonas' memories. They get louder and louder and now everything I do, all the memories I have of those five years are filtered through *him*. I've done so many things he would have never done. I look at these things, think about all the people they've carried and it almost makes me sick! Physically sick!"

"That's no excuse!" Stephanie couldn't restrain herself anymore. "I've been talking to Laura over the last few days and she talks about Jonas a lot when you're around. From what she says he was sure of himself, knew where he wanted to be, what he should be doing and if he didn't know how it should be done he'd go find out. He wasn't a man of hesitation and she'd never seen him wrapped in this self loathing you've got going!"

"He was a man of principle! He had morals and values that he would have never broken!"

"Then use them! You say you remember everything he did, well, just be him, at least as much as you have to! You say you were born empty and even if that's possible, you found your own way even before you met Alice. You became the hero to thousands of slaves, turned down one of the biggest paydays we were ever signed on for and kept to the rougher road. Don't make that all worth nothing by going soft, not now. I couldn't watch that. You becoming someone I don't know scares the hell out of me but if that's what has to happen for you to get on with your life then just do it."

Jake had heard stories, watched the little footage of the *First Light* that was available and from what he'd seen Stephanie was right. From Jonas' memories of commanding that ship in combat she was right. Jonas Valent wasn't a soft man, he wasn't overly hard either. There was a middle ground he was on his way to finding, Ayan was part of that. There was another time, however, before the *First Light*, when Jonas Valent didn't know what his life's ambition was, where he was bound, when he was a glorified traffic director. The memory of going to work, stopping in to say hello to his friend Minh-Chu, then spending an uneventful day speaking to travellers from across the galaxy all came back at once. It had been there all along, the years of dissatisfaction, boredom, relenting routine and the feeling that the exciting portion of his life was already over. It was the most terrifying thing Jake could imagine; monotony.

Stephanie's anger evaporated. She had said what she had to and more. More importantly she had told him what she was really afraid of; losing him. "Are you okay?" She closed the distance between them and stepped in front of him, put her hand on his chest.

There was her softer side, something she seldom showed him or anyone. A shiver went up and down his spine. His hand covered hers as he looked at her worried expression. "You're right. I need to pick a direction for the ship, for myself. Tomorrow I'm leaving, and when I get back I want the ship and crew ready for anything. I have some bad things to make up for," his hand curled around hers.

She gripped back. "We both do." Stephanie stared into his eyes, they were so familiar, his gaze was so steady. Since leaving the colony he was the only man she trusted, and he believed in her. He had never demonstrated that more than when they took the *Triton*. It had never occurred to her, how important it was to be trusted, to have someone with so much confidence in her. At the same time he seemed so much more approachable, whatever it was that kept everyone around him at an arms' distance, kept her at an arms' distance, was gone.

She brought her other arm up around his neck and drew his lips down to hers. At first there was surprise, his lips were unmoving, before she could pull away, tell him it was a mistake and run to a quiet, out of the way place to lick her wounds he was kissing her back enthusiastically.

Price couldn't believe his eyes as he stood silently in the stairwell, looking on in dumb struck shock. When he heard the yelling he had to go see what it was all about, ensure that everyone was all right. By the time he was up the stairs it had stopped and when Jake and Stephanie came into view they were far too distracted to notice him.

He started backing down the stairs quietly and was almost all the way out of sight when he heard a loud clang on the deck. Agameg peeked up as a reflex and saw that Captain Valance had roughly drawn a flat gurney for the stasis pods out of its storage slot and was lowering Stephanie down onto it as she hurriedly opened the front seam of Jake's vacsuit.

Agameg hurriedly ducked out of sight and ran down the stairs then down the embarkation ramp leading off the *Samson*. The pair he left behind seemed distracted enough not to hear him fleeing, but he'd still worry, wondering if he'd been spotted for days.

152

The Morning After

Stephanie woke up early the next morning in the *Samson's* Captain's quarters only to discover that Jake was already awake. His bed wasn't made for two, she had slept face down on top of him and when he saw her eyes were open his hand caressed up and down her back.

"Good morning," she said as she got more comfortable.

"We still have a couple hours before the morning briefing. You should go back to sleep."

"Morning briefing?"

"Alice and I are meeting all the senior staff members once a day again. It worked better than a once a day audio brief."

"Smart," was all Stephanie said. She wanted to stay there, to avoid the complications she saw coming, the decisions she'd have to make, and she didn't want to say what needed to be said. "But you're wide awake."

Jake's hand stopped moving just south of her shoulders. "Wide awake," came his quiet confirmation.

She sighed. It was never like her to avoid her fears. "It was a mistake."

His hand started moving again, stroking her bare back felt more like a gesture meant to comfort than the caress of a lover. "I wish it wasn't."

Stephanie shifted so she could put her chin down on his chest and look into his eyes. He seemed more himself somehow, looking back at her calmly, a little sadness in his gaze showed through the dim light of the compartment. "You know Ashley thought we'd get together for months after the Teralin run. Eventually I had to tell her to stow it though, couldn't have that kind of thing turning into rumour."

"Think you'll tell her about this?"

"Probably, unless you don't want me to."

"It's up to you, but warn me before telling Frost."

She turned her head and put her head back down on his chest, absent mindedly tracing shapes on his arm with her index finger. "I'm not telling Frost. We'd be in for a hell of a row and then finished. He'd probably try to shoot you and leave the ship."

"He makes you happy," Jake asked as much as concluded.

She nodded slightly, listening to his heart beat under her ear. "I don't know how, but for the past few weeks it's been good mostly. Worth hanging onto."

"This was a one time thing then."

"A one time thing," she whispered back. "Are you okay?"

"Surprised, amazed, maybe a little lost but okay? I have no idea," Jake chuckled.

For the first time since they boarded the *Triton* Stephanie was glad to hear something from the new, more expressive Jake. The old one she knew from the *Samson* would have given her a one syllable response like; 'sure,' or 'yup,' or maybe deflect the question entirely by asking; 'are you?' She couldn't help but chuckle with him. "If it were a one nighter with anyone else and they told me it was all right if I didn't come back I might be insulted," pressing her lips to his chest and leaving a kiss there felt like just the right thing to do before getting up and retrieving her vacsuit.

"If-" he started but stopped himself.

Stephanie looked at him, her vacsuit half pulled up.

He ran his hands down his face and sat up, reaching for his own clothing.

"What?" she asked as she pushed one arm into the shoulder of her uniform.

"Nothing."

"No, really. What were you going to say?" Stephanie pressed.

"Let's keep this simple for now."

"But you don't want them simple."

"No, I think it's a one time thing, like you said."

"But you said *if*, and that doesn't sound like a one time thing, it sounds like a many time thing, or a big thing."

Jake put his hand over his eyes and sighed; "Can we rewind and keep it simple?"

Stephanie brought the opening together with her fingers just above the waist of her vacsuit and ran them up to her collar in one swift, abrupt motion. The seam came together and disappeared. "Don't worry, things are simple," she spat as she snatched her long coat from the floor, popped the sealed door open with a clang and a creak then left.

154

Captain Ashley Lamport

There were at least twenty rivers and streams named after the Thames of Earth scattered on planets across the galaxy. The one that ran through Sheffield was much smaller, only fifteen or so meters across where the old stone bridge crossed it. Ashley and Finn stood against the rail at the highest point in its arch. They looked down the stream, at its bricked banks, the cobblestone streets that ran along and deeper into the city to either side.

The architects had accomplished their goals in that section of the city, the buildings looked like they were stolen straight out of a period film set in Earth's twentieth century. The crumbling bricks on some of the brown and red buildings looked their age, at least three hundred years. The colony wasn't as old as many on the core worlds, but it was one of the oldest terraformed colonies either of them had ever seen.

The green trees standing straight out of planters on broad street sides were each a statement of success. Sheffield's history was that of survival, struggle as the land around it, even the very air, was slowly made liveable, breathable. Over the two centuries after initial settlement the toxicity of the land was reduced, the atmosphere thickened, and finally farms began to grow edible food that didn't require complex post-processing.

The museum at the center of town, built to look like an ancient Abbey, detailed the whole struggle. Finn and Ashley had taken a walk through the complex the previous day. He was genuinely interested in how the terraforming engineers, of which there were several generations, had surmounted the various barriers to modifying the conditions of the world while Ashley wandered about, trying not to look bored or tired.

She spent as much time as she could speaking to Leland March who was working with the Port Authority and Employment offices to finalize the list of recruits they were taking on to the *Cold Reaver* for transport to the *Triton* the following day. Ashley didn't think that Finn noticed much as she tried to help using her command and control unit, reviewing files for different departments, putting in specific requests for pilots, system analysts and deck crew or knuckle draggers as Paula and Angelo called them. People who had mechanical knowledge, maybe even just space faring experience but would be used to perform the tasks on the hangar decks that required the fewest qualifications.

It was the first time she'd been made acting Captain of anything, her second recruitment trip away from the *Triton* and she was sure Finn would understand her being called away from the exhibits for seconds or minutes at a time intermittently. Besides, she really had little interest in architecture or the science behind terraforming.

During the Bauz charity concert that night, an event made to raise money for recovery from the Holocaust Virus, it was Finn who could think of plenty of places he'd rather be. The fast paced, hectic music centred around electric guitar and fierce percussion wasn't something he'd choose to listen to, but to see Ashley bouncing with the crowd, singing along with some of their more well known tunes, that was a beautiful sight. He did his best not to bring her down, to look like he was having just as much fun, but at the end of the night, when they shared a kiss that was just a hair above a peck on the cheek and went to separate rooms he couldn't help but feel like there was something sadly lacking from their budding relationship.

It was their first time away together and though he liked her, enjoyed her enthusiasm and light heart, conversation was hard. She didn't seem to know what to say, and he didn't know how to fix it. He'd talk about engineering marvels, try to bring up other crew members, get her talking about the *Triton* and what had been going on while he was out of commission but she didn't speak for long or seem comfortable.

As they stood on the stone bridge, watching the water flow away, down the river and round the bend both of them were quiet. He looked at her and she sent an uneasy smile back. Larry would be on the *Cold Reaver* just a few streets down and a lift up going through the pre-flight check list with Ashley's copilot. He was guiding the new recruits aboard and getting everyone settled for the eight hour return trip to the *Triton* and in the next few minutes they'd be called back to the ship.

"Good concert last night," Finn said finally.

Ashley nodded, despite her best efforts she couldn't help but look sullen. The overcast weather matched her mood. "Thank you for going with me. I didn't think anyone else we had along liked them."

"I never heard them before, I liked it though. Besides, how could I let you go alone?"

"Well, you could have," she tried to tease, but it came out wrong. It came out seriously.

He put his hand on hers after watching her for a moment. "Everything okay?"

She sighed and turned to him, her head down. "I don't know, it's just. . ."

"I know, we're not getting along."

Bouncing on her heels, something she did when she was trying to shake off nervousness, she looked at him. "You're *so* easy to get along with. There's just something. . ." Ashley shrugged helplessly.

"Missing, I know. I'm sorry."

"What for? Before any of this I couldn't shut up when you were around, now I can't think of anything to say. *I* should be sorry."

"We were friends," Finn shrugged. "Can we do that? I mean, just go back a bit and, you know, just not expect anything?"

Ashley nodded and smiled, relieved. "I'm sorry Finn," she leaned into him a little and they embraced. It felt so good along with her relief that she gave him an extra squeeze before they let go. "I had fun though."

"Even at the museum?" Finn asked with one of his gentle, unsure smiles she liked so much.

"Well, with anyone else I think I would have bounced out of there in the first couple minutes. Learned a lot about terraforming though."

"I had a good leave," Finn said simply. "Thank you."

"We have to do it again," she smiled at him. "Maybe see if we can get Steph and Price in on it."

"Steph might want Frost along."

"Right. I don't want to listen to them argue the whole time."

"I know, how long do you think that'll last?"

"With my luck they'll be married by the time we get back," she said, rolling her eyes. Ashley's command and control unit signalled there was an incoming communication. She checked it and nodded. "Larry says the preflight is done, but Leland is back in the hold working on getting everyone sorted. He's been at it for three hours, that seems long."

Finn nodded. "How many recruits did you manage to get?"

"A hundred seventeen. I mean, that's good, but the *Reaver* can take more than two hundred, it's a drop ship. We'd better go see what's going on."

"Aye Captain," Finn saluted.

"Don't start that," she giggled back.

A distant rumbling in the sky drew their attention upwards. Between the five landing platforms, each covered with brick for the first eight storeys but showing their green and black modern metal arms and towers above, they couldn't see anything, but the sound was getting louder.

"Whatever's up there is coming in way over port speed," Ashley said as she started walking faster.

An explosion pierced the sky like a thunderclap and a flaming wreck broke the grey clouds, descending to the east as a bursting fireball. Secondary explosions burst from the large vessel.

They both started running for the Nursery Street landing tower. The lift was full when they got there, and Finn stopped but Ashley pushed him in while squeezing between people herself. "Platform twelve C." She told the lift.

The tall, scowling woman hammering at the Door Close button with her finger exclaimed; "finally!" as the lift shut and started up the tube at great speed.

Finn and Ashley were thankful they were one of the first stops, everyone was literally crammed into the pod made for twenty, there were at least twenty five people aboard. As they ran down the gangway to the *Cold Reaver* they could see its large rotatory engines on the bottom and top charging up, all but one hatch on the surface of the ships dull black hull was open.

The Bridge Street Tower across the river started taking pulse cannon fire. Its upper levels started to come apart as ships tried to evacuate. Platforms and damaged vessels alike plummeted towards the city beneath, crushing buildings and filling the streets with broken hulls and bricks. Panic had taken hold.

Small oval shaped silver ships darted past the tower, firing at anything in the air and at the Castle Street Tower as they banked. "Eden drones," Finn shouted over the din as they finally reached the small forward gangway leading into the *Cold Reaver*.

"Aw, crap. Take off, Larry!" Ashley called as they got inside and the hatch started closing.

They only had to rush up one hallway to get to the bridge. The *Cold Reaver* was already off the ramp and climbing when Ashley dropped into the lead pilot's seat and Finn stopped to stand at the engineering station.

"There was no warning. They were just there, in orbit," Larry said as he transferred manual control to Ashley. He started checking their flight path so he could help her navigate through the mess of ships taking off without direction from Port Control. "Oh God, Navnet's worthless."

"Got a route for me?" She asked as she brought the throttle up and tried her best to aim for clear sky.

"Trying, but everything above us is a mess."

"Then we go down until you can find something clear," she said as she flipped the ship, sending it into a hard dive. Everyone aboard felt it as the inertial dampeners didn't quite keep up with the sudden shift.

"Shields are up, weapons are ready, integrity's good," Finn reported hurriedly. "we even have full power."

The ship sped between two of the highest buildings and accelerated away from the city centre. A sonic boom was heard through the armoured hull as they continued out over the green and brown countryside.

"We're going to need it. We've been noticed by a couple of those drones, marking targets." Larry commented as red ovals appeared on the main display in the dimly lit V shaped cockpit. Everyone sat facing the front. The pilot and navigator were at the fore with engineering and tactical to their left and right, communications and operations behind them. There was no Captain's chair, it was a large, heavily armed troop gunship with enough space to serve as a small troop carrier.

Leland March ran into the cockpit. "We have two gunners, but Yates is missing."

"Yates was supposed to be running tactical! Where is he?" Ashley asked without looking away from the controls.

"He didn't report back, we were waiting for him and a few newbies."

"Then sit down and run tactical, we have company. Oh, and next time someone's over an hour late, tell the acting Captain so she can contact the local authorities!"

"I've never done tactical on the *Reaver*!"

Ashley didn't bother replying.

"This is Finn's first time working Engineering and Operations on this ship, you don't see him bitching, do you?" Larry said as quickly as he could. "The river you're following goes down into a canyon in seven point five," he directed Ashley as she navigated within two hundred meters of the ground. Her attention was fully focused on piloting, there was no room for error at the speed they were travelling.

"You're not going to want to go in there, it gets jinky."

"Describe jinky," Ashley said as she decelerated below three hundred kilometres per hour and tilted the nose of the ship down to match the decline of the rapids below.

"Narrow, jagged, impossible to fly through at this speed."

Leland finally sat down at the tactical station and looked at the control panels. The tactical holographic display appeared above them and he rotated the view so he was looking at what was behind the ship. "We have five ships behind us."

Ashley reduced *Cold Reaver's* speed to two hundred five kilometres per hour as she followed the river within a few meters. The walls of the canyon rose up on either side of them. "Are they following?"

"Yes, but they'll be above us I think."

She jerked at the controls and guided the ship around a hairpin of stone valley walls then through a gentler curve that led them under a bridge. "Tell March how to run tactical please, get more info from him," she said quietly to Larry as she concentrated on piloting.

"Okay, are they above and behind? Right above?" Larry asked Leland hurriedly. He turned his attention back to Ashley so he could continue giving her navigational information, warnings about what obstacles and features she would have to fly through but couldn't see yet. "We have a Forty seven degree left turn six hundred twenty meters ahead. Then we have a twelve degree incline over the next one point four K."

"Uh, they're above and behind. We don't have a clear shot with any weapons," Leland replied.

"We will," Ashley said impatiently. "Tell the gunners to be ready."

"Four degree decline, narrowing to three hundred meters after this turn, fork coming up in five point six K after that, take the right side."

Ashley fired the decelerators hard as she took the next turn, slowing down to just under a hundred fifty kilometres per hour, Finn tried to focus the shields to reduce the amount of space they affected around the ship but as the valley narrowed he didn't get the profile small enough and the port side caught a rocky outcropping, ripping the stone and earth free from the wall as they passed.

"Any damage?" Ashley asked.

"No breaches, shields are down to ninety two percent. We're okay," Finn replied.

"How's my sky?"

"We're clear of port traffic. Our friends have caught up," Larry reported.

Several more impacts on the shields were reported on Finn's station and he looked over to tactical. "They're firing at the canyon walls, trying to bury us!" He pointed at the projectile warnings on Leland March's station hurriedly before turning back to his engineering station.

Ashley fired the thrusters hard, increasing their speed to a suicidal velocity, nicking the sides of the canyon with the shields, leaving a dusty wake behind. The rough, craggy split ahead loomed larger in the cockpit screen by the millisecond. "I know you're not sure about what you're doing Leland, but could you at least tell me what you're seeing?" she asked irritably as she made constant fine adjustments to their trajectory. At the last instant she pulled up and increased the throttle to full power.

The inertial dampeners whined louder than the engines as they accelerated away from the ground beneath, towards the grey skies. Everyone was pressed into their seats by the relatively small amount of gravitational forces the compensators couldn't adjust for. Finn managed to hook his safety line to his station just in time to lean against the support in his vacsuit instead of being hurled to the back of the small bridge.

As the *Cold Reaver's* turrets came to life Leland tried to get the missile launchers turned around so he could lock onto their pursuers.

Finn sent more power to the rear shield emitters as they started taking direct fire from the small Eden Fleet drones' powerful pulse cannons. "Shields down to forty three percent. We have ten seconds at best, trying to route more power."

"Do your best, how many have our gunners killed?" Ashley asked as they broke through the clouds to blue sky.

"They've knocked one down, but I can't get the missile launchers turned aft."

"They don't turn aft! Just be ready," Ashley said through clenched teeth. Her speech impediment, the lisp that made lazy mush out of many of her consonants was gone. No one had ever seen her so frustrated.

"We're good for hyperspace in a few more seconds, just get us there in one piece Ash." Larry said as he calculated a course as quickly as he could.

"Get ready to reverse thrust and focus shields front," she said more quietly.

Finn knew exactly what she was doing and smiled. Her combat skills had grown well past what he'd expected through the weeks of simulations she'd flown in while the *Triton* crew trained just downspin of the Ambrosia nebula. "Ready," was all he had to say.

She flipped the ship end over end and the emergency deceleration engines at the front fired, the shields took several hits from the oncoming Eden Drones.

After seconds of waiting everyone in the cockpit finally heard the tones indicating that the main missile batteries had solid locks on the attacking ships and Leland unloaded the launchers, sending all forty eight heavy missiles at them all at once.

"Oh my God!" Ashley exclaimed as everyone in the cockpit flinched, ducked and instinctively threw their hands up over their faces. The missiles exploded less than five kilometres from the ship's nose, sending brutal shock waves and shrapnel back at them. The *Cold Reaver* shook and rocked.

"What happened?" Leland shouted out over the sounds of decompression and collision alarms.

"Decompression in forward debarkation, we lost our lower turret, no shields. Closing the compartments off," Finn reported hurriedly.

"Can we enter hyperspace?" Ashley asked, she struggled with the controls, forced to guide the ship free of the planets gravity while flying backwards with only partial engine power.

"Checking."

"What happened?" Leland asked again.

"You *never* fire that many missiles, especially not at four point eight clicks," Larry called over his shoulder. "Try thinking for once!"

"I didn't know! I've never worked on this ship!"

"That goes for any ship! It's common sense!"

"Leland, go check our passengers," Ashley ordered. "Finn, hyperspace?"

"We're good. I'll have to watch the emitters we have closely though. Generating a field on navigation's mark."

"Mark in three, two, one, mark," announced Larry loudly.

The hyperspace field took several seconds to surround the *Cold Reaver* and Ashley watched the acceleration rate of the ship multiply evenly across the hull sensors. All sections of the ship were accelerating at the same rate, they were safe. She locked the controls and sighed deeply.

"God, Leland's clueless," Larry stated under his breath, shaking his head.

She nodded. "Captain always had trouble finding good tactical people. I'm starting to understand how he felt. Still, he probably saved our asses, barely."

"Those Eden ships were taking full on hits from our turrets without slowing down. I hate to admit it, but you're right," Finn confirmed.

"How is the damage, really?" Ashley asked.

"We're missing the main debarkation ramp in the front, three emitters are gone, one engine is down to nine degrees of rotation and the ventral turret is gone, just gone. I can't tell how bad the shield emitters are for sure but we're missing at least three."

"Captain's gonna kill me," she groaned.

"Just blame it on Leland," Larry shrugged.

"Can't do that. I picked my crew from who was available, he's my responsibility. I'm going to make sure I'm in the room when Stephanie sees his performance review though."

"She's going to tear him apart."

Ashley nodded. "He's been spending all his simulation time in fighter jockey scenarios or at the bar. I think he might get put off this time."

"I'll be there to see him down the gangway," Larry said quietly. "I won't be blowing kisses either."

Morning Briefing

It began in the conference room at the front of the bridge with Laura delivering her summary of her understanding of the *Triton* as a developer of new technologies. All eyes and ears were trained keenly on the relative newcomer in the golden light coming through the transparent hull as she began. "The Triton was designed and built to be a hard target on her own and with a squadron of fighters on patrol whenever she's running at sub light speed it would take a large strike force to get through to her. I don't know what the Sol Defence Forces were afraid of, but judging from the redundant systems, extra armour and heavy weaponry built into every fighter or gunship design made to run off of her and the ship herself, they were definitely afraid of something." Laura said before sitting down near one end of the bridge meeting room table. The view along the left hand wall was of the stellar nursery, the angle they viewed it on that day brought out shades of yellow and blue. All the senior officers except for Ashley were present.

"What could tha' be?" asked Frost. "This ship's harder than the Aboris moons."

"Well, imagine being sent out on mission for half a century. You don't know if you'll see home during that time, and you know for a fact that you'll be hundreds, thousands of light years away from anyone who can help you if you run into trouble. If you run into a combat situation there's no back up. Few human organizations would actually spend the time or go to the trouble to capture or destroy this ship, so I'm thinking they were preparing to meet up with another race entirely. What's more, there are a lot of rooms made for diplomacy, they made sure that they had both options covered; peace and war. This ship is made to be Earth away from Earth, politically if this were still a Sol System owned ship this would count as one of their territories. "

"This ship counts as a territory? How does that make sense?" Asked Cynthia.

"In the same sense that an island or a space station equipped with an embassy makes sense. The only difference is that this one can move. The other reasons why I'd say this ship is built around a model of fear is it's hardness to natural forces like meteor strikes, intense radiation and gravitational forces. The architects of this vessel wanted to allay everyone's jitters where living in space was concerned, so single people felt comfortable in her berths and families could feel at home and safe in the larger quarters," Laura brought up a holographic schematic above the table and went on. "The hull was laid down in four sections as far as I can tell, and using highly refined materials they built the civilian habitation center first, designating it the Botanical Gallery. They should have called it the park, considering its size. The area around it came after and it includes two of the generators, three berths and critical systems, then there's another layer over top that extending to the inner command deck where the officers quarters are located. The thickest, most energy and matter resistant metal surrounds that layer. That same layer extends around the Botanical Gallery and two of the main reactors."

"Then there's the gunnery deck and hangars?" Frost finished for her.

"That's right, but even they are surrounded by a two meter thick inner hull."

"Figures we'd be set up in the most dangerous place. My shooters sit right between those double hulls."

"I wouldn't go that far. In the thinnest points of the outer hull there are five meters of solid material that is specially formulated to get more resistant as more energy and pressure are applied to it. Previous estimates on thickness were based on what we were seeing from the inside, but since the exterior survey was completed I was able to finalize the analysis. Over top the outer hull there are three different types of shield emitters made to work separately or in concert. Wheeler only used one since the others require more training. Conventional shielding, using combined particle and energy emitters were his choice because they're easy to understand, the parts never need to be deployed and they defend against most weapons equally. This ship is equipped with an antigravity shield as well as another hardened energy field I'm still studying. Together they take up a lot of power, but are partially self sustaining since the energy is made to interact and they'll be incredibly difficult to penetrate. I'll also be calibrating over twenty layers of refractive shielding, so we can prevent all light based weapons from hitting us. Most of these systems are made to somehow absorb energy from the outside when they're calibrated and deployed properly, but considering the risks of bringing those functions into play, of creating a feedback across all the emitters, I'm taking it slow. I want to use the shields properly but it'll take time to fully understand them. It would be faster if I had more experience with this kind of shielding but Freeground just started implementing energy shielding less than a decade ago."

"That all goes down as soon as someone gets an EMP weapon through, right?" Asked Alice.

"No, in fact the hardened energy shield would continue to operate along with all the other critical systems, Liam can go into why in a minute, but my point in all of this is that the *Triton* was made to be outnumbered. I'm starting to realize why anyone whose survived a fight with Sol Defence considers themselves so lucky. This ship is more heavily armed and shielded than seven or eight vessels in her class, with all the shield systems up and running along with the inherent cloaking properties built into her hull, she's not only hard to find, she's also hard to damage at all."

"If that's the case, why don't we see other military outfits build ships like this?" Cynthia asked.

"I think Liam could answer that better than I can," Laura said, nodding at the older gentleman.

Unlike the other officers, who all showed up in the vacsuit uniforms made specifically for their departments, he wore his blue robes to meetings. The Captain had privately insisted he do so, as it was a fair sign of rank on the ship as much as any. Liam had become a spiritual advisor to many crew members and his time was in great demand. "Thank you Laura. The reason why no one outside of the Sol System builds ships like this is simple. It costs at least twenty times what it would to build this compared to a carrier of similar class. That's not even considering how the core systems are built. The computing and command management is set up on a crystalline storage and organic processing system. Quite simply the thinking power behind each system is a self sustaining gel that contains microscopic organisms that calculate at an incredible speed. The crystal that contains them is a data storage system that changes microscopically."

"I've heard of that. If you turn them off they last forever and since the crystal's structure doesn't change unless the compound inside instructs it to, there's no chance data will be lost," Alice said.

"Right, but there's a problem. We can't make any of these core circuits with materializers. We have backups in storage, but we're low. I have a team of four working on growing more."

"How long would it take to grow a replacement for the average circuit?" Asked Captain Valance.

"About a week, but we could grow more than one at a time once we get the mixture right. It could take us up to a month to accomplish that."

"Can temporary circuits be used if there's no replacement?"

"Some of the left over terminals from the automation could stand in, but reaction times would go down dramatically. That's why we had a few seconds of blackout when we were struck by a nuclear warhead, some of our systems had to reset."

"All right, keep that set up as a backup plan. How is everything else going down there?"

"Very good. Everyone's putting in a lot of hard work and it's showing. We've started using ergranian metals for several different fabrication processes since the reactors are turning out more every day. Some is being cycled into mass materializers to enhance fighter armour, we have an amount earmarked as a supply for future repairs and I've even managed to fashion a few high yield torpedoes based on Sol Defence blueprints. We'll have to keep them disarmed until the last minute, they're well beyond what any port allows within striking distance. I only made them because of your specific request, Captain."

"Are they all code keyed?"

"Aye, it takes two codes and active biological scans to arm them from any command station."

"Good, thank you Chief. I hope we never need to use them. How is life for your staff?" Captain Valance asked, trying to change to a lighter topic.

"We're finally concentrating on the wormhole generator and getting settled in to the lower berths. Most of the engineering and maintenance people are pretty happy, the bunks are a whole step above what they're used to on other ships from what I gather and the junior officers know they'll be getting better quarters as soon as those billets are cleared."

"How long do you think it'll be before we have the wormhole systems up?"

"Without the right parts it'll take a month. We need to find people qualified to machine the parts to specification or buy them. It'll be hard to find parts for this ship in any port. In the meantime we have everything wired so we can test any temporary components we manage to complete. With any luck we can get it generating micro-wormholes for communications but I wouldn't expect more."

"We'll make finding qualified craftspeople a top priority and I'll keep working a plan that could get us a replacement system," Captain Valance reassured.

"I know, it's the first priority with the engineering staff. Anyone who has machined parts is to look over the schematics for the parts we need. I'm hoping that a few of them will have the skill, but I know none of them have the experience. My maintenance people are working on the rest of the ship. We finally got the main communications array repaired. Now we're moving on to making the living sections of the ship more habitable. There's everything from backed up waste disposal units to damaged deck plating. The more the maintenance people repair, the more damage they find, but we're getting a handle on it."

"How is tactical?" Jake asked.

Agameg Price smiled and leaned forward on the conference table. "Very well. Everyone is in advanced training and a few are even double specializing in communications. My teams have very high scores in simulations and are working well with gunnery and heavy weapon teams." He looked to Frost then.

He looked back at him.

"I think that's your queue." Stephanie whispered from across the table.

"Ah, aye. We're workin' with tactical quick, that's a fact. My loadin' teams are up to speed, only three simulated injuries this week an' my gunnery crews 'ave things down pretty smooth. New recruits are fittin' in pretty well, only one in three wash out."

"One in three?" Laura asked, quietly surprised.

"Aye, we show 'em a simulation replay that went completely wrong for one of our gunners. After tellin' all the recruits it's the real deal when they first see it some of 'em actually run outta the room."

"What happened in the replay?"

"Well, a turret gets brought down for reloadin', a mechanic goes into the chamber ta realign the load belt, so he's right in there, then the loaders emergency handle gets caught on the magazine. The gunner doesn't give anyone a chance ta get clear afore he raises the turret back into firin' position and he dinna see the mechanic crawl into the forward servicin' chamber. He takes his first shot, the mechanic gets fried and mulched, the explosive rounds headed into the chamber detonate, kill the gunner, an' since the armoured loader is still too close, caught on the magazine as he is, he gets his arm and shoulder blown clean off, leavin' the loadin' crewman inside a right mess. I left the simulation runnin' since it was a good fire, explosion and rescue drill."

"Did anyone survive that in simulation?"

Frost chuckled and shook his head. "No, but the medical team managed to keep the loader kinda livin', or what was left of him, on a sub deck. Seein' that's what gets most of the squirmers tossin' their breakfast 'cross the deck. I 'ave the newbies who made it clean it up."

"Could that actually happen?" Asked Liam.

"Aye, if the gunner isn't payin' enough attention and doesn't check the status of his rig before chargin' up. I've never seen it personally, thank the powers."

"Here's hoping you never do." Captain Valance said with finality. "What happens to a lot of the recruits who can't stomach your test?"

"A few 'ave come back, most of the rest get sent to maintenance or to the flight deck dependin' on their qualifications. I don't think Angelo minds." He grinned at the Deck Chief.

Angelo Vercelli smiled back and nodded. "No washouts here Captain. After they see the man eaters up top they're usually glad to get in with the grunts below. We've had a couple accidents but nothing major thanks to the vacsuits we're set up with. I've seen one hold up a whole engine pod when it came down on one of my people's legs."

"That's what they're for," Stephanie commented. "Fashion is reserved for off duty."

"I hear ya. Anyway, we've just pumped out and assembled our eleventh Uriel fighter and our fourteenth Ramiel interceptor."

"How are our pilots doing?"

"All nineteen of them are fine, but we're still very short. Ashley's a practical star in sims, but in all honesty she's not ready for teaching."

"I know, she's a gifted pilot but not experienced enough to lead. I'd like to take control of the SSG until we find someone better," Alice volunteered.

"Sorry, what does SSG mean?" asked Panloo, the night pilot for the *Triton*. She was standing in for Ashley since she was her direct subordinate.

"Space Superiority Group, sorry, I've spent so much time in the dogfight sims lately that I forget not everyone is steeped in the lingo."

Panloo covered her pink nose with her long, white furred paws and laughed in soft squeaks. "That's all right. I prefer infantry simulations. Under fictional conditions that sort of thing can be a great deal of fun."

"I think it's a good idea for you to take over training, I hope we manage to get a few more pilots in the next recruitment trip." Captain Valance said to Alice. "As long as it's temporary, I still want you on the bridge."

"Oh, it's temporary. I wouldn't give up night watch command, in fact, I'll be doing both at the same time. There's time to fill during my shifts right now so I'll program in the round the clock regimen for anyone in training and fly short patrols before and after my shift."

"Just don't wear yourself thin. Keep it down to a combined twelve hours on duty a day."

"Don't worry, Captain, I'll keep my head on straight."

Stephanie nodded and started her report when she was sure the exchange was finished. "We're on patrols, watch and training in security. The Intelligence team is still backlogged but they're getting better at prioritizing. There's really not much to report other than the new recruits are doing well in drills. Even the washouts we're getting from Chief Frost are turning out to be decent grunts," she said, not so much as glancing at Frost. "Oh, and the pay grade structure has boosted morale for the most part. Now that everyone knows that extra qualifications and good performance will directly affect their pay there has been a big improvement overall."

"Anything new on our vigilante?"

"Only verification that his first victim was a West Keeper. She kept to herself, came aboard with Wheeler's Regent Galactic crew and used every opportunity to use a personal comm unit to contact the Order of Eden. No one can find any evidence that her personal comm was used by anyone other than her, it uses a DNA sniffer to validate that she's the one on the line so we're pretty sure it wasn't planted on her to make it look like this vigilante is on our side. Our vigilante didn't leave any security footage of him or her killing the West Keeper, there are whole chunks of footage missing going all the way back to when Regent Galactic had possession of the *Triton,* and we haven't been able to generate any other leads. Whoever this is has a deep understanding of the ship's security systems, probably knows the layout better than anyone and knows how to blend in with the crew. All we can do is watch for him or her and hope that they really are on our side."

"He can keep it up for all I care. Never got along with any cultists," Frost scoffed. "Might shake 'is hand if ye ever catch 'im."

"Does the crew know that there's a killer running around?" Laura asked.

"No, we've been able to keep it contained in the higher ranks of the security department, I'd rather keep it that way for as long as we can."

"All right, then no one talks about this, but we need department heads to keep their eyes open. I want to talk to whoever this is, find out if they're working in our best interest and why they couldn't operate within the chain of command. He or she has to know that we would have taken care of this West Keeper if they brought information to us, we can't have people taking things into their own hands," Captain Valance stated, sending a sideways glance to Frost. He looked around the table at his department heads and nodded to himself. "Good work everyone. Here's what it's all for." Captain Valance said as he leaned forward from his seat at the end of the table. This was what everyone was waiting for, details on what the Captain was planning. Over the preceding seventeen days select crew members had been making trips to nearby planets that had been ravaged by the Holocaust Virus using the *Cold Reaver* and picking up as many qualified recruits as they could carry. Everyone had been training hard, working hard on the ship and getting ready to be active against Regent Galactic. As to their specific goal or direction, no one was privy to that information. "Thanks to the information recovered by Frost and a little help from our Intelligence department, I've managed to verify some important supply and transportation routes. It looks like they haven't changed in weeks, so they'll be there a while. There's a problem with that plan. The sheer quantities of goods transported along those lines and the ships we might be able to capture is too much for the *Triton.*

"If we plan on liberating supplies, materials, equipment and slaves from Regent Galactic at this volume we'll need a place to sell excess and someone to take care of the refugees. I'm getting ready to contact all the front line worlds that are opposed to Regent Galactic. I've prepared inquiry messages to be sent out as soon as our wormhole systems are up and running. I expect the inner Lorander and Carthan governments will most likely be the first to ally with us."

"Lorander's a government now?" asked Stephanie.

"Yes, after taking control of several systems Vindyne left in a state of famine they accepted a few applicant worlds closer to our space. They were just about to announce their outer territories before they were hit by the Holocaust virus. We'll probably be a welcome sight."

"Captain, do you know how wide spread the virus is now?" Asked Chief Vercelli.

Jacob sat back in his chair. He had tried to estimate it earlier, but stopped as he started to see figures that just had to be wrong. "Has anyone taken an educated guess?" he asked quietly.

Laura cleared her throat and edged her chair up closer to the table. She looked at the thin command and control unit mounted on her arm. "Jason was always better at that kind of number crunching, but I managed to come up with a conservative estimate. Considering the virus spreads to ships with a hyperdrive or wormhole system then uses them to continue spreading it to other solar systems and the number of worlds we've seen infected the virus should be reaching the inner core systems within the next ten days."

"What? How's it moving so fast?" Asked Frost.

"It's tapping into the less secure transmission and relay systems used for galactic communications to transmit itself to places it hasn't gotten to with a ship yet." Cynthia answered quietly. "From there ships with wormhole drives carry it to other systems that have communication hubs that use wormhole technology for their relays and so on. My department actually estimates the virus should be everywhere someone can turn on a computer within six days."

"So it actually knows where it's spreading and how to deploy itself to sensitive areas?" asked Stephanie.

"I'm not sure," Laura said, looking at Liam.

He nodded and went on. "It behaves like it's moving in a planned way, but we only have a small part of the picture. With the speed this thing is spreading at it's already gone far past what we can see."

"Are our systems still immune?"

"They are, and Regent Galactic is being very public about developing a disinfection program. Only two of their held worlds have been affected from the reports we're getting though they're probably doctored and censored. They have control of or own over a hundred worlds in total." Cynthia said.

"Now tell me people aren't smellin' somethin' rotten in that! How is it that the core worlds don't have a Star Legion worth of heavy armour comin' down on Regent Galactic's head?" Frost asked, visibly frustrated. "Regent Galactic's barely gettin' hit by this, they've gotta be behind it an' if I can figure that, the big heads closer to the core gotta know."

"Everyone uses artificial intelligences to help manage their ships, especially the military. Organizations have been trying to cut down on manpower in favour of more dangerous weapons, bigger firepower for a long time. The only reason why the *Triton* got away as good as it did was because the ship artificial intelligences weren't very sophisticated and didn't have direct environmental control. The only other fleets made that way belong to the Britannian and Gandish. For all we know everyone else's ships are part of some kind of new Holocaust Fleet now." Liam said, putting a hand on Frost's shoulder to calm him down.

"Freeground ships use artificial intels but they have security systems that are very sensitive to corrupted software. By my calculations they should be one of the last to be affected, thankfully." Laura added.

"Any word from Jason?" Asked Alice quietly.

"They had trouble with their hyperspace systems and changed course for a world called Pandem."

"I'm taking a Uriel out to pick them up." Captain Valance said. Everyone who didn't already know about the plan looked at him with varying degrees of surprise. "I wanted to take one of them for a test drive," he shrugged. "If there's nothing else, everyone have a good duty shift."

The senior officers all stood and all but Laura, Cynthia and the Captain left. Jake looked at the pair and raised an eyebrow.

Cynthia eyed Laura uncertainly and addressed him quietly. "Sir, I'm having trouble with the Intelligence department."

"What kind of trouble?" Captain Valance asked.

"Some of the senior analysts are reporting to Stephanie and her lieutenants instead of me. She's also making decisions based on their information."

"A few of them started reporting to me while I was doing the systems survey, sir." Laura added.

"My point is that I'm not in control of the department. I know I wasn't qualified for this but you put me in charge," Cynthia said, growing more irritated.

"Do you have a second in command chosen?" Captain Valance asked.

"No, I've been trying people but I haven't made up my mind."

Jake thought for a moment then looked to Laura. "How is field control right now?"

"Almost in order. We're testing the antigravity shield later today and all three tomorrow if things go well. Aside from learning more about activating the power absorption subsystems the shields are just about ready for action."

"Could you take command of Intelligence and make Cynthia your second?"

Cynthia boggled as Laura replied. "Temporarily. When Jason gets here he should be put in command. The department here is a quarter the size of what he was in charge of on Freeground."

"Sir, I didn't mean that-" Cynthia started.

"You've said it yourself more than once, you don't have the training, so learn from Laura's experience and you'll get it if you want it," Captain Valance reassured.

"Yes sir," she replied quietly before leaving the briefing room, obviously disappointed.

Laura waited for the door to close behind her then turned to the Captain. "Thank you, watching her struggle has been driving me crazy. I sympathize, but she really doesn't know what she's doing. I'm no Intelligence specialist, especially compared to my husband, but I know what a working department looks like."

"Do you think she'll make a good second?"

"She's a hard worker, with some direction she'll be fantastic if she wants to be."

"Good, she's always had trouble finding her place in the crew, but she's intelligent and well liked."

"I've noticed." Laura walked to the large transparent section of hull and looked out to the bright yellow star clusters. "I thought Jason and Oz would be here by now."

"I know. They should be safe on Pandem though, I'll probably find them sitting on one of its beaches sipping something that's served with a tiny umbrella."

Laura couldn't help but smile at Jake's comical reassurance before shaking her head and going on. "Don't get me wrong, I appreciate that you're doing this yourself, but why?"

Captain Valance felt blindsided by the question and moved to stand beside her and share the view. He had good answers to the question, most of them dishonest, but they all seemed more significant than the true answer. "I feel like I'm drowning here. For five years I've dragged a small crew around the galaxy. Easy to control, easy to manage, easy to replace. Here I have literally thousands," he answered honestly.

"That's what delegation is for. You always had a problem with that," she smiled.

"I have been, Intelligence is the last department in real need aside from the SSG. Still, there's so much time to think while I'm going over reports, requests and interacting with everyone from the civilian representative to Liam."

She didn't need to know more. He had been inundated with memories and over the past weeks they took root. He was quiet, sometimes even sullen, which was a good thing considering it hid the fact that his manner was becoming softer, more human. To most of the crew he was still the hard, towering icon, but his senior officers were all noticing how much more personable and approachable he was. "I need Jason here, there's no one I miss more," she appealed to that heart she had heard of. Alice had taken her into confidence to talk about the sleepwalking incident, and knew that there was a good chance that she could start trusting Jake just as she had come to trust Jonas.

"I'll be back with him before you know it. Until then Alice knows she has the ship and I'm sure the Chiefs will have everything under control."

"How long do you think it'll take you?"

"In an Uriel fighter with an extra reactor installed? I'll get there in twenty hours, maybe less." He put his hand on her shoulder. "If I don't find him it's because he found another mode of transportation and I just missed him on his way here."

"Thank you Jonas," she said, catching her error and regretting it immediately. Laura looked at him and was surprised at what she saw.

His eyes were closed, his lips were stretched in a tight smile. "I know. I suppose it was inevitable."

"I'm sorry, it's just something he'd do, gestures he'd make."

Jake nodded. "I stopped fighting the memories, lifted the mental separations.

There are a lot of good memories, especially from his youth. It changes things, you know, when you have good times to look back on. I had so few of my own, I didn't even realize."

"I never thought of it that way."

"Sometimes I think it's selfish, getting to know him so well that it's hard to tell where he ends and I begin, but then I remember meeting him face to face. He'd want this, he'd want me to be here for you, for Jason, for Oz. Even if I took his name it wouldn't phase him as long as I didn't do something he wouldn't."

"Do you think you ever would?"

"Take his name?"

"Yes."

"Not his first. Talking to Alice the other day, hearing about how so much of who she is was determined by her experiences with him and how she has her own distinct personality despite that, it got me thinking, and I don't have to change my name just because things are changing. Who I am is in part thanks to him and using his moral compass is tribute enough I think. If he were alive right now I don't think there would be a question that we're different people, but I know there are a lot of similarities now, a lot I can be proud of."

"So you'll remain Jacob Valance. Still very close to Jonas Valent, really."

He hadn't made the comparison aloud or heard anyone else do it for him and he paused to let it sink in. "I need time to think," he chuckled. "and to do something useful, something important on my own."

"Don't take this the wrong way, but you're becoming more like Jonas every minute. He was miserable when he didn't feel useful."

"I think that's something we have in common," he smiled back.

She gave him a brief hug and they started out of the meeting room. As she got to the door she stopped. "Oh, I almost forgot. The last generation of the vacsuits are ready. We managed to materialize one for each of the senior staff."

"That's early, did you manage to weave everything in?"

"Everything, your modifications, my refinements, the special projects additions, everything." She grinned. "Have fun."

"How do they look?"

"They're not very customizable, but I think you'll like them. Stop by the high resolution materializers on your way to the flight deck. I'd go with you but I have to talk to Alice about power usage aboard ship. It looks like we'll be deactivating all the personal materializers in quarters and berths. Only certain officer's quarters will have active materializers, and their constant use will be discouraged."

"So you'll be instituting specific times for chow in the observation decks and clubs?"

"That's right, and we're opening the mess hall between the fore and aft central berths. It should make for an interesting change while you're gone."

Captain Valance took a left once he exited the bridge instead of going straight on to the main lift. As soon as he passed through the security and intelligence

171

office doors everyone was on their feet. "At ease," he found himself saying reflexively. *That's Jonas's military training. It's becoming instinct to me as much as it ever was to him.* He thought to himself as he walked between the five rows of communications and ship monitoring stations.

The last time he'd been through most of them were seated, this time only the deck watchman was behind a desk. Above it's surface were holograms displaying three dimentional information management charts and on the desk itself was a status display of each intelligence team member's efficiency, whereabouts and health status.

Cynthia was behind the desk, prioritizing files in preparation for Laura to assume command of the intelligence department. Behind her were three doors. One led to the internal security office, the other to a large meeting room and the final one to the right was specifically reserved for the head of intelligence.

"Captain," Cynthia said with a nod, barely looking away from the maelstrom of data in front of her.

"Is Stephanie in her office?"

"She headed straight in after the meeting like her heels were on fire."

"Thanks," Jake acknowledged as he opened the armoured door. Stephanie was sitting on the desk at the far end of the darkened office, looking over training simulation statistics on one hologram while a playback of one security guard's perspective was displayed on the other. From the time indexes they were both from the night before.

There were over a dozen chairs lining the walls of the long office and a transparent section of hull behind Stephanie's desk. Jake knew that with a command a meeting table would lower from the ceiling, but she never used it, preferring to have everyone on their feet during staff meetings. She looked up from a cup of hot tea she was blowing on when he came through the door. "Everything all right?" she asked.

"I was about to ask the same question," Jake answered quietly as the heavy hatchway closed behind him.

She was wearing a heavy vacsuit, combat boots, sidearm, along with her duty belt which included a basic door hacking kit, restraints, a survival cylinder and and two extra clips for her sidearm. She had draped her long coat across the back of her desk chair. Stephanie put her steaming cup down on her desk carefully before answering. "I'm sorry I left the way I did. Last night was a surprise."

"For both of us," Jake said quietly as he crossed the room slowly.

Her smile was mild, wistful. "I want to see where things go with Frost."

He caught her gaze as he finished crossing the room. His vacsuit covered black hand caught hers on her thigh. "I know. I need you to be all right."

A nod and a hug was his answer.

The embrace lasted the better part of a minute, a comfortable eternity for them both until she drew back and he let her go.

In one smooth motion she picked up her cup and took a drink of tea, it was still a little too hot but kept her eyes from welling up. She put the mug down again and cleared her throat. "If we can't get through this after a couple dozen firefights, then there's something seriously wrong."

Jake smiled at her and squeezed her free hand. "I have something for you,"

Her eyes widened as he pulled a silvered chain strung through a fortified, rounded gold chip out of his deep coat pocket.

He opened her hand and pressed it into her palm. "Of everyone on the *Samson* crew I trust you the most. I found this in Wheeler's quarters, in his safe. It's the override code chip for the *Triton*. I need you to watch things. You'll know if and when you have to use it."

"But I thought the command security systems were all vocal and biometric."

"This is the override chip made to reset the systems in case the ship is captured and hacked. Wheeler never got a chance to use it. All you have to do is get to a secure terminal, pop the interface plate open and put it in. After that you can tell the ship to make you the commander and it'll take your biometric scan and whatever passwords you give it. You're already in the system as a senior officer so it makes things even easier."

She looked down at the chip for a moment then put the chain around her neck, opened her vacsuit enough to drop the chip itself down the front and settle the chain under her collar before closing up again. It was hidden under her uniform, no one would see it. "*Triton'll* be here when you get back, don't worry Jake," she said quietly. "So will I."

He nodded and turned away, crossing the distance between her and the door in long strides.

Arrival and Departure

Over the entire black and crimson vacsuit were stretched flexible two centimetre horizontal emitter blades. They fit to form but made Captain Valance feel like he wore something with more substance than the old vacsuits nonetheless. There was a black long coat set up with the same systems and extra armour as well, and as he took the lift down he ran through the systems checklist. The new display system actually projected images to the brain through nerve manipulation, routing information through different parts of his nervous system so they were collected and understood as colour images. There were no cybernetics involved and the technology was only a few years old, refined by Freeground Special Projects. He knew Laura was breaking laws by sharing it and several other technologies added to the command vacsuits, but it was fairly apparent that she didn't care.

Other crewmembers in the lift looked at him quietly, he pretended not to notice. He hoped everyone would have a similarly featured suit eventually. Perhaps not with *all* the improvements, but there was a great deal of life saving technology that would be useful to most of the crew under dire circumstances.

The lift arrived in Hangar two and he caught sight of Ashley and Stephanie. He shouldn't have been surprised that Stephanie had taken a lift down to the hanger deck to meet her best friend while he was getting familiar with the new command vacsuits. He still held back so he could listen in on their conversation before he was noticed.

"How did it go?" Stephanie asked, looking at the *Cold Reaver* wide eyed.

"Pretty well, easiest breakup ever." Ashley replied with a shrug. "Finn isn't the dramatic type."

"No, with the recruitment run! It looks like you tore half the front end off the ship," Stephanie exclaimed, shaking her head, arms spread wide to encompass the view of the shredded front end of the ship.

Captain Valance quietly strode around the pile of crates and saw the condition of the *Cold Reaver*. The front landing gear, debarkation ramp, one rocket launcher, the long range sensor package, two small emergency escape pods as well as a large section of the fore port hull were torn to shreds. The nose had taken substantial damage as well, but its thicker armour had prevented full on decompression.

"Your boy Leland nearly blew the front of the ship off when he fired our entire load of missiles at once." Ashley replied, gesturing over her shoulder to where Leland March, the wiry security team member was overseeing the unloading of a number of new recruits. Several dozen were already lined up on the deck, their satchels and luggage in front of them. Most of them didn't have many possessions with them, which was the norm.

"Why did you put him at tactical?" Stephanie asked more quietly.

Captain Valance leaned up against the three meter high stack of secured crates and continued to listen in on the exchange. Ashley caught sight of him and started to turn red. "Yates didn't show in time for departure and Leland's file says he's qualified for tactical."

Stephanie checked and nodded. "You're right. I don't remember screening him. Don't worry, it's not the first time he's screwed up. I'll take care of it, assign him to the quartermaster for inventory until he requalifies on all things security."

"Sounds like a good idea. In the meantime you might want to put someone else in charge of the new hires." Captain Valance said, walking towards the pair.

"You mean recruits, don't you Captain?" Ashley asked with a wry grin. She knew she wouldn't be unfairly treated for the damage to the *Cold Reaver*, though she still looked nervous.

"Right. What took a bite out of the *Reaver*?" he asked as he took another look at the large gunship.

"Eden Fleet hit the planet just as we were getting ready to go. Finn's doing the damage assessment. He says it's going to be out of commission for at least a few days, most likely more unless the whole deck crew gets on it."

"More like a month! Next time try landing it ass first! You might not hit every critical system on your way in!" Paula shouted from across the deck from where she was checking one of the engines.

"And it had to happen while Paula's on deck." Ashley said, shaking her head. "She started screaming before I touched down."

Captain Valance couldn't help but laugh. "It took me a while to understand, but Angelo's quality control, Paula's the one who keeps things on schedule. Still, there's something to learn from this. We need someone to take control of the SSG, start screening mission crew so we have a good rotation of officers for the *Reaver* and the *Samson*."

"I'll start making that a priority," Stephanie nodded. "Security aboard ship is under control for the moment and I'm sure Frost would be fine with qualifying a few people for tactical."

"I'll give you a list of the pilots I've screened," Ashley added. "Is it true that the *Samson's* almost ready Captain?"

"Should be all set for a shakedown. I never thought I'd get the chance to see her in such good condition, or with the improvements I had planned, but then I didn't expect to be Captain on a close combat carrier either."

"Good point. By the way, where did the threads come from?" Ashley asked, pulling the thick material on the arm of his long coat.

"There are suits ready for both of you in the materialization compartment. Only for senior officers. A little something Laura and I put together."

"Can't wait," Ashley said as she started for the lift.

"Captain, your ride's ready whenever you are." Paula called out, gesturing to an open hatchway in the floor beside the wall of the hangar. The passages were made for several pilots to climb down at a time, it led to a sub-deck for managing and loading fighters into drop chutes, where fighters were launched from the ventral side of the ship.

"I want to see that ship looking brand new by the time I get back. Get the whole deck on it if you have to," he ordered, pointing to the *Cold Reaver.*

"Like new, my ass! We'd have to start rebuilding using ergranian on that kind of schedule."

"The reactors are generating ergranian, go ahead and get some from Liam. Add the *Triton's* stealth treatment to its hull while you're at it."

Paula didn't reply, she just threw up her hands and continued her inspection.

"Heading out Captain?" Ashley asked as she turned back to him.

He unslung a survival package hanging from the inside rear of his long coat and held it in his hand. It included emergency power cells, food, water, a compressed bed roll, an extra medical kit and several other critical items. "Just going for a ride, picking up a few wayward crew members."

"I'd give my next leave to go along," Ashley begged.

"Sorry Ash, I'm taking this one solo."

"Good hunting sir," Stephanie wished him. "Are you sure I can't convince you to take an escort?"

"What could go wrong?" Jake grinned wryly as he took the open lift down.

"Good hunting," Ashley added.

The lift plate lowered Jake into one of the small airlocks reserved for pilots entering the pre-launch area. The gravity lessened by three quarters and as soon as he sealed his vacsuit the air was evacuated from the small compartment. The hatchway opened and he pushed off, bounding down the catwalk past empty sockets for fighters and small gunships. He stopped at the socket marked with his new call sign; Hitman and looked behind him in time to see his Uriel fighter being drawn along the ceiling. "We loaded her up like you requested." Chief Angelo Vercelli told him over his communicator as the fighter was turned so its nose was pointed towards its socket and the punter launch doors.

Jake looked the bottom of the black and crimson fighter over carefully, pulled on the four engine pods he could reach and checked the cargo hatches along the bottom. "Two racks of scrambler missiles, a pair of turreted particle guns and two pulse cannons with a wormhole kit, extra fusion reactor and a rescue compartment," Jake verified as he received the loadout information on his command and control unit. The fighter was turned around so he could inspect it from the top and the canopy opened.

"That's right. Still can't believe the Sol Defence folks have this listed as a fighter. She's a small gunship. How did you do on the qualifier, if you don't mind me asking sir?"

Jake couldn't help but chuckle as he double checked the nose armour. "You know you're supposed to check that when a pilot takes their first flight."

"Aye, but being the Captain. . ."

"Well, keep this to yourself but I had to go through the primary qualifier twice. I failed the first time because I didn't bother taking the tutorials or practising in a sim. Thought just because I could fly the *Samson* and most other standard birds I'd be fine to pass in one of these."

"That's a lesson most of the pilots are learning. Just goes to show, Sol Def does things differently."

"And so do we," Jake replied. Satisfied that his fighter was ready and in good order, he took hold of the handle in the cockpit's upper seat and pulled himself inside. "Looks like everything checks out."

"I'd hope so, you should have seen the care people put into her when they found out that this was going to be your personal bird."

Jake closed the canopy and settled into the seat, watching the systems come online and begin their own internal check. "I hope they work just as hard on every one. Last thing I want to see are pilots dying because someone missed a bolt."

"Don't worry. Fabrication is doing better every day. If you can get us some heavy scrap we'll have a full squadron of varied role fighters in six weeks, maybe less if we can find more people to work down there."

"I'm just glad we have more pilots than we do fighters. Keep them training together while I'm away, I want them to feel right at home by the time they sit in one of these for the first time."

"Don't worry, I've dealt with green fighter jocks. Between me and everyone else pushing these people they'll be a fighting squadron like you've never seen before you know it."

The automated calibration systems checked his body type, eye line and within moments the fighter was ready to react to his actions through the manual flight controls, eye movements and general body motions. Older fighters had pedals, extra hand controls and even neural links. While Sol System Defence combat vessels had all but the neural links, the control systems could be calibrated to respond to more subtle movements, and getting used to having that kind of control, to maintaining that kind of discipline took time and patience. While a pedal and flight stick movement may send the fighter rolling to the side, the turn of the pilot's head and shift of his shoulders could aim the guns, designate a missile target and get lesser utilized engine pods turned in the right direction for the next manoeuvre. At the same time the systems in the cockpit could also determine the difference between a head motion meant to change the focus of the weapons suite and one that was the result of a sneeze.

The cockpit formed to him and jacked into his vacsuit as the clamps lowered the fighter into its punter socket. Emergency ejection systems sealed onto his boots, waist and shoulders, also providing firm anchoring restraints so he wouldn't jostle around in the cockpit as he manoeuvred. He watched as the thick armoured launch doors in front of him were quickly drawn inside and moved to the left and right. The bright nebula outside bathed the nose of the fighter and the empty seat just below and in front in golden light. *I wish Minh were here. He'd probably spend so much time in the cockpit that we'd never see him aboard Triton, but I'm sure he'd be in his glory.*

Jake regained his focus and ran through the systems check as he had done in several tutorials and simulations over the weeks he had given the crew to train, knowing that at the very least Deck Chief Angelo Vercelli was listening. Other officers who had access to Flight Deck Control may have been eavesdropping and watching as well, and when he was sure everything was in order he contacted Flight Control. "Ready for launch."

"Everything checks out fine on our end, Captain. Good hunting. Punting in five, four, three, two, one."

As the fighter was ejected nose first out of the bottom of the ship, Jake was thankful for the inertial dampeners, keeping him from being crushed into his seat too hard. In under two seconds he was five kilometres away from the *Triton* and he gently turned his fighter so he could watch it shrink off into the distance. It was true, no simulation could prepare you for the rush of being forcibly ejected out of the bottom of the ship. The *Triton* was nothing more than a speck of metal glinting under the light of a thousand new stars in the nebula behind him.

He looked over the Navnet broadcast the *Triton's* flight deck was maintaining and verified he was clear of the four fighters patrolling nearby before checking other systems.

"Jake?" Alice said on his personal comm.

"Hi Alice," he responded as he checked his course. It was preset to take him directly to Pandem, but double checking the math was a good habit to maintain.

"Are you all right?"

Another simple question that reaches deep, he thought to himself.

"I mean, you've put the ship in order, given us time to train and even gotten us organized enough to take on recruits without breaking a sweat. *Triton* is just about ready for anything, but are *you* okay?" Alice asked quietly.

In that moment, a split second of clarity that was as surprising as it was rare, he knew what to say. "I'm more myself every day. Now I just have to find out who that is." He began the reaction inside the extra fusion reactor he had installed in the small optional component bay of the Uriel fighter.

"You know I'm here, right? I might not be installed in your C and C unit, but I'll never be too far off."

"I know, thank you Alice. You've got a handle on the *Triton*?"

"A death grip. We'll be here when you get back."

"I wouldn't feel the same with anyone else in the command chair," he said through a smile. "Nothing like leaving family in charge. I'll see you soon."

"Good hunting Jake," she said before closing the channel.

Jacob Valance locked his course in and began pouring all of the main and secondary reactor's energy into the wormhole generator to create the most highly compressed passage through space possible. After a few seconds the energy was released into the space in front of the fighter and a wormhole entry point formed. Jake fired his engines and disappeared.

A Good Vantage Point

Ashley couldn't help but take a good look at Alice as she walked towards her along the long padded railing guarding the edge of the top level overlooking the massive park and garden. It took only weeks for the woman looking over the Botanical Gallery to become as iconic and well known on the *Triton* as the Captain himself. Overhead was the holographic façade that simulated a calm evening. The false sky was starry, featuring a waning moon crossed by a few white clouds, the digital representation warned anyone inside that the massive botanical gallery would be watered soon. It would be raining in just under an hour.

Alice was in her old fashioned flight jacket, a weathered garment that looked like it was made of real leather. Her sidearm, the same heavy weapon the Captain used, was strapped to her leg, and her brown hair hung around her shoulders, stirring a little in the slight breeze. She was as mysterious as the Captain. Looking at her, listening to her getting along with the night crew on the bridge when she was around for the early portion of the evening shift demonstrated two sides of the woman that were distinct, completely separate.

On one hand she was a calculating commander, always watching the general status display. On the other she was easy going, didn't mind having a laugh with the bridge staff as long as they were still doing their jobs. The real puzzle was that she could switch between the two at a moment's notice. That was the only part of Alice's personality that convinced Ashley that she was once an artificial intelligence.

Other than that, she was a confident, intelligent, often charming woman. If Ashley could choose a big sister, or even a young mother, it would be Alice. She was noticed as she came within a few meters of her and Alice looked up from the view below and gave her a slight smile before returning her attention to the people far below.

"I tried finding you at your old spot, but they put a table there," Ashley shrugged as she closed the distance and settled in beside the other woman, leaning on the tall railing. The top of the rail was thinly padded with transparesteel panels beneath.

"Everything all right?"

"Yup, just thought I'd say hello on my off hours. Not that I really have off hours now. I feel like I'm always attached to the bridge."

"That happens when you're the Master of the Helm, especially on a ship this size. How are you finding it?"

"The other helmspeople always have questions. It keeps me learning about this ship. It's challenging, I like it though. How do you like being acting Captain?"

"It's different. I envied Jonas' experience on the *First Light* before, learned a lot from him in a short time. It's surprising how much of it just comes back to you even though it feels like that was a different life. Part of me loves being at the center of things, but sometimes I miss the *Clever Dream*. There was nothing like being on a fast ship bound for wherever I wanted, not that it was safe, but it felt freeing."

"That's how I felt when Captain let me loose on the *Samson*. I wasn't picking what star to go to or anything, but we didn't see many places more than once. Feels like a lifetime ago."

The pair stood in silence, looking down at the Botanical Gallery's East Park. It stretched across the center of the ship, finally grown in with banyan, peach, apple, pear and plum trees. There were so many other plants lining the paths, interrupting the dark green sections of grass, and maturing in multi-levelled hydroponic stands. The majority of the crew was at rest while the remainder were performing maintenance, training, or keeping their watches.

The garden was as much of a social place as any, especially for crewmembers who had befriended the few civilians aboard. Something Ashley had neglected to do. Crew members who had planetside clothes often wore them in the garden. The old fashioned manual instruments came out too; flutes, guitars, she'd even seen a violin. The last time she'd taken a walk there were three musicians teaching each other to play a song called freedom. One tall woman was a violinist, the instrument seemed like a part of her when they finally played the tune, the melody seemed simple to her and after the first chorus she spun, whirling her floral skirts outward, revealing that underneath she still wore her vacsuit, even though it was reshaped so her shoulders and arms were bare.

The other two were guitarists, the one teaching was one of the new starfighter pilots, a soft spoken fighter jock from the far outer fringes who had come aboard during her recruiting run. She hadn't noticed him before, when he was just a part of the crowd. He was bald then, and as she watched him quietly show the other two musicians their parts she noticed stubble on the top of his head.

He had given up the clothing he wore for one of the black vacsuits, which hadn't been marked with a full skull and letters just yet. It took time for fighter pilots to become full crew on *Triton*, mostly because of the mandatory qualifiers one had to complete and pass before being assigned or paid.

Ashley's mind was drawn back to the present as Alice broke the relative silence; "It's strange not having him here. We've been working closely together for almost a month now, I got used to having him in the ready quarters."

"I miss him too, not as much as you might though."

Alice looked at her, a little amused. "Why not? You were with him on the *Samson* for all that time."

"You're right. I'm worried about him."

"He'll be fine, it's just a pick up," Alice reassured her.

Ashley smiled back and nodded. "I know, it's the Captain, but I always worry when someone I know goes off ship. Or at least I did on the *Samson*. Guess some things never change. Wish I was more like him sometimes, just setting things in motion and not worrying after."

"He was worried about you when you took the *Cold Reaver*," Alice said quietly. "He told me you could take care of yourself more than once, even told me straight out that he was sure you'd do fine on your first recruiting run, but I could tell he was still worried."

"Really?"

"Don't tell him I told you."

"I'll keep that one under shirt."

"*Under shirt*, I've never heard that one."

"Something from home, used to say it all the time in the slave quarters. Guess it's because none of us were allowed to wear hats, I dunno."

"It must have been hard growing up there."

"Lots of work, but I was lucky. There were laws in place protecting us from beatings and stuff. We just weren't allowed to leave the grounds without a pass. The kids on the estate were brutal though, and we couldn't do anything about it. Still, it wasn't the worst way to grow up. Stephanie had it worse on the mining colony."

"Do you keep in touch with anyone from home?"

"Yup. While I was planetside I was able to talk to a few friends. Most of them survived the AI virus somehow. Some are missing because they were still under bond and used the opportunity to escape, but I'm pretty sure they'll pop up."

"I guess that's a real problem for some slavers, considering a lot of security systems are run by artificial intelligences."

A mischievous, satisfied smile crept up on Ashley's lips as she nodded; "yup. Real big problem. The escaped are probably all safe, they probably weren't standing right beside AI run systems when it all happened. A lot of the business district went up in flames though, and other automation went down, so most of the people who learned how to do things manually because it was their job are pretty valuable right about now."

"Like the slaves."

"Yup."

"Funny how that works," Alice said. "One minute they're just servants then technology goes crazy and they're the most important people on the planet. Without them everyone else would starve."

"That's what happens. I just wish we could do a recruiting run *there*, I'd love to pick up some old friends."

"Maybe sometime."

"Aye, maybe if we're ever out there. Not much chance of it though. It's pretty far off. Sometimes I miss the slave quarters, there was always someone around, and in the household I was in it was like we were all family."

"I couldn't imagine. For what you'd call my childhood I always had Jonas. He carried me everywhere."

It was the first time Ashley had ever heard Alice talk about being an AI with Jonas, and it gave her the opportunity to ask all the questions she normally didn't feel comfortable bringing up. "How long were you with him before you, um-" she found herself suddenly lost trying to find the right word.

"-grew up?" Alice asked with a raised eyebrow. "About seventeen years, he was thirty four when he let me loose."

"Wow. No wonder you guys fit like father and daughter."

"Does it look that way to everyone else?"

"Most people think you're his bio daughter, yup. People who know better don't bother correcting them. If something's close enough to the truth so it doesn't make a difference, well, then why not just leave it be."

"I had no idea, I thought it was just the way I felt."

"Nope, looks pretty much like you're his. The two of you remind me of a father and son I met who were part of a carnival once. They stayed on the next estate over for a few months while they worked off a debt to the household. His dad was this thin, wiry tall guy and looked mean all the time. Emris, his son, looked all skinny like he hadn't grown into himself yet, but you could tell just by looking at them that they were father and son. They walked the same, did things the same way, and his father was even teaching him his trade so they were both really good at their work. If they were working on something they only needed to say the bare minimum, and when it got technical, whoa, it was like they were talking in a different language."

"What did they do?"

"They were mechanics, which, I know, you and Captain aren't, but it's just the way you two handle the bridge, even the way you kind of like to just go off on your own and think. Sometimes I wish I could do that, just go somewhere alone and figure things out but I end up hitting the ship stores or a materializer and I walk away with munchies. If I did too much thinking alone I gain two kilos in no time!" Ashley exclaimed exaggeratedly.

Alice couldn't help but laugh and nod. "That took some getting used to, stopping when I wasn't hungry anymore. I see your point though, I think I was just alone for too long after Bernice got married. Even before then it was always just her and I then everyone else. We didn't really let anyone get between us. Now I'm on a ship with thousands aboard. Doesn't look like I'll be starved for company."

"Really? I'm still having trouble sleeping. I turn the lights down to get a few winks and all I can hear is my own breathing. I left a hologram on of Goodbye Wayne the other night real low just so I felt like there were people nearby."

"The cowboy movie?"

"Yahuh, you've seen?"

"I haven't seen the newer version, just the one from the thirties."

"That's the one! I like it when Wayne spits in Lorne's hat, it still gets a laugh."

"I have a collection of the classics, even some from the film days on Earth, I'll have to-" Alice's command and control unit blinked and Cynthia came on; "We have incoming, Ma'am. It looks like a group of Eden Fleet ships."

"We're on our way," Alice replied. "Put the ship on high alert, I need everyone at battle stations. I'm bringing up my command interface here." Alice said as she activated an interface on her command and control unit and started striding towards the nearest express car doors.

Ashley was just about to start running when Alice stopped her with a hand on her shoulder. "On a ship like this it makes more sense to interface with your post remotely. Running will only distract you until you get there and you'll have to adjust to your station while you're out of breath."

Ashley nodded, falling in step beside the other woman, bringing up the remote hologram of the helm. It appeared in front of her as though she was actually there and moved along in front while she walked. "This is strange, how are you looking at the bridge?"

"My cybernetic eye is interfaced with my C and C unit. I can see the bridge as though I were there. If my neural comm were still working I could give orders through the speaker system without talking."

Ashley watched what the pilot and navigator were doing, what the Navnet was saying about the incoming ships and shook her head. "Those ships are four times our mass and launching fighter drones just like the ones that came after the *Cold Reaver*. They must have followed us, I'm sorry."

"It's not your fault, it's amazing that you got away at all," Alice said as they stepped into the lift. It shuttled them up then towards the front of the Command Deck.

* * *

Agameg Price saw the hologram of Alice Valent appear right where he was sitting in the Captain's chair and moved to his tactical station. It immediately started giving orders. "Flight Deck, do we have any fighters on long range recon?"

David Monroe, the night watch for the Flight Deck didn't look up from the central station beneath the bridge as he replied; "We have a Uriel thirty one minutes out manned by Scrubber and Hardcore. Assigned to medium range recon, still no word from Hitman."

"Don't worry about Hitman, he's on long range retrieval. Recall all fighters and secure the hangars for faster than light. Helm, plot a course to intercept Scrubber and Hardcore's next scheduled wormhole exit point. We're going to pick them up before we go on mission." Alice's hologram turned towards Agameg. "Tactical, how many torpedo stations do you have ready?"

"Five, the rest of the crews report that they're on their way to stations. What about cloaking?"

"We have a bare section of hull from the work being done on the main emitters, it'll stick out like a sore thumb. What about our gunnery posts?"

"Can't find Frost, but his second is already on the gunnery deck and emergency decompression is underway. Readiness estimate stands at forty nine seconds."

"What do you mean you can't find Frost?" Alice asked, exasperated.

"His locator isn't coming up. It's like his personal command unit is powered down."

"Anything on the bio trackers?"

"Nothing, but they're only active on sixty three percent of the ship, he could be in one of the dead sections."

"Contact Stephanie, have someone from security on it. Until then, tell the torpedo and gunnery teams that anyone not in their seat and ready in the next ninety seconds gets left at the next port. How long until the first drones are in firing range?"

"They're launching and holding station around their carriers, but if they started moving now they would be on us in under two minutes." Agameg replied.

"I have eight fighters ready to launch and six on their way into our gravnet about to be picked up. We could scramble them and try to buy some time," interjected David.

"Not going to happen. My tactical screen shows there are over three hundred drones out there, each with a quarter the firepower as one of our fighters and three times the armour. We'd be murdering our own pilots with those numbers. The order to recall stands."

"Aye, Ma'am," replied David passively. He was a cool headed young pilot with more experience than most on the ship, Paula had recommended him as the night shift watch for the Flight Deck, and he accepted it even though he quietly made it known that he'd rather be out in a fighter himself. His call sign was Diver.

The large, heavily armoured split oval doors leading onto the main bridge parted just enough to allow Alice and Ashley through. They walked straight to their seats. Alice's holographic representation disappeared, while Ashley's holographic representation of the controls hovering in front of her faded the moment she replaced the nafalli night pilot, who took a seat beside the communications station, just in case she was needed later.

The main holographic display on the bridge appeared in front of everyone and Alice closed her eyes. Everyone had seen it happen in simulations, where she looked at the status of the *Triton* through that electronic eye and saw more information at once than most could stand. "Laura, how are our shields?"

She was just arriving on the bridge then, and the main doors closed, the sound of them pressing together and sealing filled the compartment. Laura stopped to stand at field control as the hologram above her wrist faded. "Refractive and energy shielding are up and at full, gravitational shielding will be up in six seconds."

"Thank you, Liam, how much power do we have for a wormhole?"

Liam and Finn appeared at the engineering stations on the bridge, even though they were actually standing at two completely different sections of the ship. "Power isn't the problem, it's the main emitter's capacity that you should worry about," his hologram relayed from the main engineering control centre.

"Finn here. As the Chief was saying; some of the fine circuitry we installed to work on the main emitter array is just a quick fix. It's not actually made to take a heavy power load, it's more for testing while we try to rebuild the system. I can't say it'll even work, it's not supposed to," Finn reported from the emitter control room several decks beneath them.

"Helm, complete your plotted course with a wormhole set to fifteen point five compression. That should get us to our fighters in about ten minutes."

"Nine point two one minutes," confirmed navigation. "good estimate, Captain."

"Ma'am? The drones are coming," Agameg announced, looking up from his station to the main hologram where on one end the *Triton* was represented along with the last fighter being drawn into its underbelly by an energy field and on the other end three Eden carriers drifted lazily in space, their hundreds of fighter drones starting to make their way across.

"All rail cannon batteries, fire explosive flak rounds, switch to solid core rounds once those drones are within one point five kilometres. Torpedo stations, load fusion munition five and fire at will at those carriers."

"Each torpedo bay will only have one shot using that ammunition," Agameg advised.

"Don't worry, they'll either turn and run or be destroyed after that volley," Alice replied.

The *Triton* came to life, filling the space between it and the enemy carriers with flak rounds that exploded in front of and amidst the hundreds of sleek, silver fighter drones. The lower deck defence guns, beam turrets and torpedoes began launching from armoured tubes lined up along the front and sides of the ship as well.

The bridge crew that had time to look at the main holographic display saw dozens of drones blown to pieces or shredded by a churning wave of fragmented flack fire, while the majority of the enemy ships pressed on. It took them only seconds to cross the gap between the carriers and as soon as they were in firing range they split up. The broad wave of fighters became a scurrying mass that surrounded the *Triton* in the blink of an eye.

"The drones are trying to drain our energy shields with particle weapons. We're down to ninety three percent," Laura reported. "We need to divert more power."

"We're on it," reported Chief Grady.

"Chief Vercelli reports hangars are secure, pilots are aboard," relayed the Flight Deck officer.

"Charging up our main emitters, we've already lost one power circuit, I was able to re-route, but I won't be able to do it again," Finn reported. "This is a bad idea. If we shut down the emitters now we could save some of the temporary components and rebuild."

"How long until we have a wormhole?" Alice asked, ignoring Finn's objections.

"Three minutes at fifteen point five compression."

"Do better."

"I don't want to burn the systems out, we don't have any replacement parts."

"Do what you have to, just get us out of here," Alice ordered.

"Ma'am, all but two of our munition five torpedoes have been destroyed by beam weapons. The pair that haven't been destroyed are slowing down," Agameg informed.

"Slowing down?" Alice asked as she opened her eyes. She used her command console to take control of the main holographic display and zoom in on one of the fusion torpedoes. There were two drones attached to it. "Detonate them!"

"I can't, they've been hacked."

The propulsion system on the torpedo flared out and the drones turned the fusion weapon around.

"That's coming for us, can we take two direct hits?"

"With full shields, yes, but we're down to sixty eight percent and dropping. We're looking at possible hull damage."

"All guns and missile bays, focus on those torpedoes, ignore everything else!" Alice ordered as she focused the view of the main holographic display on both of the munitions. They each had drones attached and both were being guided back to the *Triton* from the half way point between it and the enemy carrier. They began to evade, dodging flak, beam and rail cannon fire.

A group of missiles fired from the *Triton's* underside launchers and to Alice's surprise they all headed towards one of the captured nuclear torpedoes, not both. She glanced to Agameg then back to the main display in time to see one of the torpedoes explode as three of the seeker missiles struck it. One of the fusion torpedoes was destroyed, leaving the other to finish closing the distance between it and the *Triton*.

"All hands, brace for impact!" Alice announced ship wide. The sounds of the inertial dampener systems powering up in anticipation of the massive explosion was nearly deafening. The main tactical display on the bridge pulled back to show the *Triton*, its guns still firing at the incoming torpedo while all the other drones fled in every direction at incredible speed.

Many of the crew members closed their eyes in anticipation of the worst, or started to pray, but as the ship shook mildly and systems went down for a second, it became obvious that for the moment, they had survived. All the holographic representations of the absent crew members had disappeared while the systems that projected them reset.

"Damage report!" Alice called out as she held the right side of her head in her hand.

Agameg's systems began to come up first. "We're down eleven turrets, they took too much electromagnetic damage. The main emitter is still charging and is at forty nine percent, it should be completely charged up in twenty three seconds. All other stations are reporting ready so far, but only half the ship is online."

"Energy shields are down to six percent, gravitational shielding is gone. We're recharging but it's slow," Laura reported.

"Hangar decks reporting one small fire, other than that they're fine," reported David Monroe. "No injured."

"Botanical Garden is fine, life support is good ship wide, the computer core was unaffected and is re-establishing its link with all systems," reported the operations station at the rear of the bridge.

The bridge returned to normal but to the crew's horror a new wave of drones were on their way from their enemy carrier to join their current assailants, which were already swooping in, firing at the *Triton* with renewed vigour.

"Finn, get us a wormhole, now!" Alice ordered.

"I increased the charge rate, I'll need *Triton* stationary in nine seconds," replied Finn's flickering hologram.

Alice looked to Laura, who was startled at the sight of her. "Shields?"

"Trying to charge up, but they're almost gone. Your eye is bleeding," she said as she managed the controls.

Alice brought her hand back up to her right eye. She knew there was something wrong already from the stabbing pain that started the instant the fusion torpedo went off, but to see her hand come away covered in blood confirmed that something in the electronics had burned out and done damage to the delicate socket. "I'll live," she said quietly.

"We are stationary," Ashley reported.

"Several of the drones are making suicide runs against the shields, two have broken through and impacted our hull," Agameg reported, trying not to sound alarmed.

"Where? Show me."

Agameg brought up a second large hologram in the middle of the bridge and focused in on the dorsal section, right between damaged turrets. The two drones had attached themselves to the hull and as they looked on they were joined by three more.

"This is Frost! The little buggers are drillin' inta the hull an' my gunners can't get a shot on 'em."

"Stephanie, get your people in there!"

"Already on my way with four squads Captain," Came Stephanie's reply, "If this lift would move faster we'd already be there."

"Wormhole ready!" announced Finn.

"Open it and just go!" Alice ordered.

The main emitters released all the energy contained within its capacitors and power cells at once, compressing the space in front of it and initiating a firing sequence of smaller energy emitters located across the *Triton's* hull as it crossed the wormhole threshold and began moving through compressed space.

Ashley brought the engines up to full power gradually, adjusting their mass profile to accommodate for the five unwelcome guests attached to their hull.

The bridge medic was at Alice's side before she could even think about doing anything else and as he drew her hand away from her face his professionalism held, but barely. "The EMP from the nuke must have burned the cybernetics out, I'm sorry Captain."

"Do what you can," she said, trying not to cringe as her fears were confirmed. The eye would have to come out.

Uninvited Guests

Stephanie was already on her way to the gunnery deck with fifty six armoured counter-incursion team members. They stood behind her holding their heavy assault rifles across their chests, dispositions ranging from hardened and cool to jittery and nervous. The large express car stopped and the doors opened to a sight that she couldn't believe.

A drone was finishing cutting a hole in the inner layer of the *Triton's* hull and through its transparent surface she could see the inhuman, featureless metal face and forward arms of whatever kind of machine hid inside its outer armour. Its angled surface looked eager somehow, as though anxiously awaiting its opportunity to get inside and wreak havoc.

You're giving an object personal traits, psyching yourself out, stop it. She mentally chided herself. Stephanie tuned in to the gunnery deck's command channel while leading her people out of the car.

"Armour! Make a circle round these bastards and pound 'em inta the deck before they know what hit 'em. I'll take down the first one, watch how it's done!" Frost ordered. "All unarmoured units clear the deck, we don't want ta be steppin' on ye!"

"Frost! Keep your people back! We don't know what kind of weaponry they have and your loader suits are unarmed," she argued.

"Keep back lass, we've got this. Go get the one tryin' ta break into the hallway in section nine. It'll hit a main corridor and lord knows what else!" Frost argued as his black and red armoured suit crouched, waiting for the invader to break through the hull.

"There are six teams on that incursion, we can take care of the gunnery deck!"

"This is my deck lass, watch how it's done."

Stephanie shook her head in irritation as her men and woman took formation all around her, spreading out one meter apart at the shoulder to maximise their firepower. "Alpha, beta teams, take the other end of the deck. Watch out for falling loader suits," she ordered.

"Theta and delta teams, with me, we're taking the next incursion point, let Frost play with his new friend," she ordered as she broke into a dead run across the deck towards the hole forming over thirty meters away from Frost. She couldn't help but bring up a secondary display on her visor and focusing in on the scene behind her.

The three quarter meter wide plate cut from the inside of the hull fell to the deck with a violent crash, it would have been a colossal sound if there were an

189

atmosphere to hear it through, and long metal arms stretched out from the drone pod as the machination inside pulled itself inside. Frost picked up a full flak magazine and his armoured suit leapt up, swatting the intruder so hard that one of its arms was awkwardly bent out of shape.

As Frost's heavily armoured feet touched the deck the rest of the intruding machine fell out of its small hole. It poured out like a silver stream of struts and oval segments, landing and turning towards Frost. The edges of several plates across its front glowed blue and violet as though the insect like machine was just coming to life, and as its arms began to unfurl as though in preparation for a grand melee plasma blades across its arms and body lit up, jagged fingers clicked and scraped together.

Frost turned around, grabbed it by the middle and picked it up off the deck, bringing it back down hard enough to dent and scrape the hardened metal floor. The machine took little visible damage, and as it was raised up to be smashed again all six of its long limbs wrapped around Frost's loading suit, crushing, cutting, trying to burst the armoured suit and kill whatever was inside.

Stephanie stopped dead, spun around, raised her rifle and tried to take aim. Frost was struggling with the machine, pulling at its silvered, oval segments, staggering as the invader cut the main sensor array on the top of the suit cleanly in half. "Dammit Frost! I can't get a shot!"

"Things all arms! Can't get my grip back! My armour's as good as done!"

It began to saw into one of the armour's arms to great effect, she could see the metal beginning to part as the plasma blade sent sparks flying in all directions. Frost's armour lurched forward suddenly, hitting the deck face first and pinning the invader as it cut straight through the knee of his suit. Everyone on the deck heard Frost cry out before he could stifle his scream.

The back hatch of the suit blew off and he hurriedly fell as much as climbed out.

Stephanie set her automatic rifle to full power and opened up on the invader trying to scurry out from under the heavy armoured munitions loading suit. Half its efforts were spent on getting out from under it while its many tools cut it apart in a dozen places just to get free. The heavy metal of the automation heated under her steady stream of gunfire. In an attempt to move the machine ripped the softened metal casing of its body open and Stephanie continued her attack. The squads with her joined in, and in the space of three seconds Frost's armoured suit and the invader trapped beneath it was completely destroyed. The lights of its many sensors and tools faded out slowly.

The deck beneath her feet rumbled and she turned around just in time to see an armoured suit flying through the air towards him, thrown by a pair of invaders working together. "Move!" she called out only too late as the armoured loader suit crashed into them. Her vacsuit took the impact of the suit's thigh, protecting her as she was thrown fifteen meters across the deck.

Two of her squad members weren't so lucky and were seriously injured as the torso of the armour crushed into them and rolled on. It narrowly missed Frost as well, passing just over his head as he crawled as quickly as he could. He had lost his foot above the ankle and crawling for the nearest secure hatch to get out of the way.

"Let the marines do their jobs, lads! Stay clear and if ye get caught by one o' those things, abandon yer armour! Anyone not in a loader get ta the emergency arms lockers an' get a rifle so you can lay down supportin' fire!"

Stephanie got to her feet, dropped her empty particle rifle cartridge, replaced it with a fresh one and took sight on the pair of intruders. They had intertwined with each other, becoming a slowly moving object that reached out with deadly speed using any one of its dozen arms. Her visor informed her that it had erected an energy shield around itself. "Fire on my target, full intensity! Hurry before the other two get through the hull!" She activated the secondary barrel and emptied her cartridge of heavy explosive rounds, hoping the explosions against the invader's shields would bring the barrier down faster.

As two of the machines arms got around another armoured suit and threw it effortlessly at the squad opposite them who reacted perfectly, dodging to the side and resuming fire the second they were out of immediate jeopardy a pair of oval pods separated from the machine, scurrying towards her men and women with blurring speed.

She opened fire on the nearest, scoring one hit before it exploded, shaking the deck and instantly incinerating two of her team members. Stephanie picked herself up off the deck and resumed fire. "Those things have some kind of automated grenades or mines, aim for them while they're still attached!"

The sprawling automation flew to pieces under the devastating firepower of thirty nine soldiers, and when the other two broke through the hull, they were ready.

Stephanie tossed three hammer grenades at the ceiling right after the nearest invader broke through the hull and they affixed right beside the new aperture. The arms hesitated to extend out into the open air beneath the second before the grenades went off and she opened fire before the smoke cleared.

The scene at the other incursion point was similar, only the grenades were ready and counting down on the deck as the invader made its appearance, trying to bend away from the explosion as it went off. They had just enough firepower left to take them out before they could injure or kill anyone else, and with no doctor aboard, no one had great expectations for the severely injured if they couldn't be treated with nanotechnology or placed in stasis in time.

* * *

"Status report." Alice ordered as she returned to the bridge. The biological portion of her eye had been healed by regeneration medication but with few medical specialists aboard there was no hope of having her eye repaired. Instead she allowed the bridge medic to use nanobots to separate it from her optical nerve and push it out of the socket under local anaesthetic in the ready quarters. As a temporary measure she had an eye patch materialized and placed her ocular implant into a small case she pocketed. She'd have something done about it later, the patch wouldn't do. "First person to say 'yar' or 'ahoy' will be the last," she added.

"We're three minutes from emerging from the wormhole, repair crews are already at work on the damage on the corridors and gunnery deck, we lost nine security staff in the fighting and our astronomers have found something interesting from the pure sciences department of the ship, Captain." Agameg got out of the command seat and returned to tactical.

"They were watching that?"

"Aye, they were the first to notice our torpedoes getting hacked and they reported it to me straight away."

"Good job, and you made the right decision to target one of the torpedoes for a sure hit instead of lessening our chances by splitting your firepower Agameg. How are our defensive systems now?"

"The rail cannons taken out by the nuke only needed a reset, and our shields can hold a full charge again," Chief Grady's hologram reported. "Tell her the bad news, Finn."

"Right. Our primary emitters are working right now, but there will be no way to power them back up once they've lost their charge. That whole line of circuitry and half the control interface is fried, permanently fried." Finn reported from the engineering station on the bridge.

"There's no way to repair them?" Alice asked peevishly.

"They have to be replaced and it would take weeks to fabricate the parts we need, some just can't come from a materializer and we need to train to machine them ourselves, then we'd actually have to make the tools to do it. When I say fried, I mean fried. If you can find a single cable down there that hasn't melted under the strain once the main emitter array and everything connected to it blows, well, you're more qualified than I am," Finn answered peevishly.

"Blows?"

"Right, I had to run the bulk of the energy through the capacitors and power cells that sit right under the array and the power can only flow in one direction; in, through then across or out from the array. Right now those capacitors have about a hundred times as much energy running across them per millisecond than they're made to carry or discharge and I had to use the larger power cells as conductors, so the connectors have fused together to make a low resistance path to get power from the reactors straight to the emitters. When that wormhole closes the emitter systems will deactivate in the wrong sequence, leaving the capacitors and power cells over charged, so they'll burn out and we'll have about twelve tons of scrap. We'll have to replace the entire assembly."

"There's no way to prevent this?"

"Nope. You asked me to give you a wormhole and you got one. Probably the last one."

"So about two weeks before we can generate a wormhole large enough for the ship?"

"No. Three if you manage to buy an entirely new assembly and if not it'll be at least four weeks to rebuild the power systems and another six to rebuild the control room and emitter array. After that we'll have to calibrate it and that'll take at least two more weeks outside of drydock, a day if you can manage to find us a berth. Knowing how unlikely that is, I don't think you'll ever see this ship generate a wormhole again."

"Easy, Finn." Chief Grady interjected quietly.

"No, it's all right. He saved our butts, followed orders and I ignored his warnings; he gets a free shot," Alice said with a nod. "Clean up as much as you need to in order to make that section of the ship safe. Oh, and Finn? Take a few minutes to cool down then get to the bridge. I need an Engineering officer here in person from here on out and you're it."

"Emerging into unaltered space, Captain," Ashley reported from the helm.

"Tactical, begin scanning, and get those astronomer's eyes looking too, I don't want to miss a thing."

The *Triton* emerged from the wormhole within a few hundred kilometres of their reconnaissance craft.

Alice watched the engineering status hologram and a representation of the inside of the main emitter control room. She couldn't help but wince as it was filled with sparks and the feed was cut off entirely by an explosion that shook the entire ship. "There it goes, a fire suppression team is already in place to take care of it," Finn reported from the hallway outside the control room. "I'll be on the bridge in a few minutes. I only wish there could have been another way."

"It was worth it," Alice nodded.

"Sure was, good job hotwiring the system, I've never seen it done," Laura added.

Alice brought up the communication screen up on the secondary holographic display so she could listen in on the exchange with the fighters.

"*Triton* SSG Control to Scrubber and Hardcore. You're ordered to return to hanger using our Tractor Net." Commanded Assistant Chief Paula, who had taken over for her subordinate.

"Understood *Triton*. We'll be coming up underside and holding until the net draws us in. Looks like you've seen some action, anything we need to know about?" replied Hardcore.

"No. Make it quick," Paula stated flatly.

"Are you sure? I could pick up some takeout on my way."

"I'm sure, smart asses," Paula muttered as she cut the comm session.

"What did our astrologers find?" Alice asked Agameg.

"Just after the Eden ships arrived they spotted a wormhole exit point and this;" Agameg replied without missing a beat, bringing up a hologram of a small vessel. The sensor information underneath it indicated that it was emitting almost no energy, but there was definitely a cockpit and windows for living quarters on the forty three meter long vessel.

"It's a Regent Galactic survey and observation ship," Larry reported from the helm. "I had to ferry one between systems once. They're cramped, made to check on troubled areas and get out."

"I guess they just wanted to see how we fared against about a thousand fighter drones. I hope they enjoyed the show." Alice thought for a moment and watched the main holographic display on the bridge, where everyone could see the Uriel fighter being drawn up into the receiving bay at the rear aft of the ship. "All right, get us underway to these coordinates at our best speed. We don't have time to cover the emitters with stealth material, so they'll see us coming. I need everyone on the briefing list I'm posting to report to the mission theatre in seven hours. Stand down from high alert. Agameg, the bridge is yours," Alice said as she stood and strode out of the bridge's main entrance, across the command corridor and into another set of double doors.

The main briefing theatre hadn't been in use for over thirty years, and as she walked into the large circular space she couldn't help but pause. *You picked a lousy time to go on a milk run Jake, I hope you manage to sort yourself out.*

ARRIVAL

The Uriel fighter was much more comfortable than Jake had anticipated. Before he woke to the wormhole emergence alarm he dreamt he was in a soft, warm mound of mattresses and cushions, a dream he wouldn't share with some of the more hardened crew members back on the *Triton*.

As planned, he was awake several minutes before emerging from the highly compressed wormhole, the fighter performed beautifully as a personal transport, despite the fact that he didn't have the long term cabin component installed. He was able to stretch a little, but he was still sitting in essentially the same position.

Even though he was easily in control of all aspects of the ship while simply travelling, he knew he'd wish he had brought a copilot if he ran into trouble. Controlling shield, weapons, navigation, communications and the myriad other systems would be overwhelming, despite his practice sessions in the simulations.

No one knew who Hitman was until he actually had it stencilled onto the Uriel fighter he took, but he was starting to make a name for himself in simulations, which he enjoyed far too much for the little time he could afford to spend in them. Taking the role of a fighter pilot was popular in the simulations the *Triton* played host to on a day to day basis. It had even become a social event, as the large holographic displays had been brought into the Pilot's Den, the bar located right in the center of the berths reserved for deck crew and pilots.

He had no idea how closely people watched for him to enter the sims until Alice had told him about it later, but in one combat simulation set in a large asteroid field there were several pilots in the Pilot's Den with their visors on trying desperately to hunt him down and destroy him before they themselves were killed by the dreaded Hitman. The whole idea that there were spectators and wagers going on with regard to his opponent's survivability gave him a big smile whenever it crossed his mind.

It wasn't hard to guess who Hitman was, really. He had been chasing down bounties for the better part of five years. Very few of the jobs he'd taken escalated to the point where he had to use lethal force, but those were the most well known ones in the end. The sims were a good contrast to the seriousness he had to place on his work. Even though all the simulations made available on the *Triton* somehow involved training or practice he had turned to them as a distraction after completing his Uriel fighter pilot qualification. If he was shot down one of his pilots, or wannabe pilots would have the bragging rights, but it never happened without him taking out several of his opponents first, if at all. He still wasn't the greatest shot, but his reflexes, quick thinking and ability to create opportunities and cover made him very difficult prey. When he signed on in a boarding crew or other squad based sim, his team was full in seconds, the same could be said when he signed in as a wing commander. Just as it was with Jonas Valent, he was becoming very popular in simulations and it helped him connect with his crew while it also gave him a much needed release. Memories of Minh came back often, he had even taken a few opportunities to quote some old Earth proverbs.

The tactical readings overlaid the heads up display built into his visor and he immediately set weapons to charge, increased power to shields, and fired the engines at full thrust while directing the fighter downward.

"Oh hell, there must be three battle groups in orbit!" He glanced at the communications systems and realized that there was only one clear broadcast. It was a Carthan all clear signal, everything else was nothing but static. Even the transponder signals were garbled.

The silhouette analysis showed that there was one nine kilometre vessel that looked like a carrier, several other carriers just under two kilometres in length and dozens of various warships. "They look like Regent Galactic ships," he said to himself after selecting the menu option to mute all static with a glance at an optically sensitive menu.

He switched his tactical scanner search to start looking for solid obstacles and incoming vessels only. After one quick sweep no cover was found but there were dozens of fighters and a few ships that looked a lot like customs and law enforcement frigates on an intercept course. Their mass and energy readings told him that they were ready to fire and not lightly armoured. The nearest of them was over eleven thousand kilometres away, and they were gaining on him quickly.

"Weapons free," he said aloud as he selected counter punch missiles and flak rounds. The targeting system immediately began to lock onto targets and as he dumped as much power into the ion engines as they could tolerate he opened fire.

The flak rounds firing off from his main cannons travelled as solid shells as they closed in on their targets then burst in all directions, sending a smattering of shrapnel into the dozens of ships moving to intercept him. One round didn't do much, but hundreds or thousands could tax their shields, interfere with exterior systems and even weaken hulls. He recognized the hammerhead shaped customs vessels amidst the fighters and gunships. They were a mainstay of the Regent Galactic defence fleet and offensive military. Just under two hundred metres long, they were heavily armed with a well protected control center near the rear of the vessel.

If half of what was closing in on him decided to open fire he knew he'd be dust. *Time to think. I need somewhere to hide, I need a bargaining chip, something!* The counterpunch missiles finished crossing the distance between his fighter and the enemy ships but didn't go off. Their burst of conically focused light, energy and particulate matter remained undetonated as the fires of their engines winked out and they passed between the enemy ships.

"Only one option here. Time to go! Maybe we can sneak in with the *Triton*." Without a second thought he diverted energy from his engines, weapons and started charging up to create a short distance wormhole. Just as he was bringing up the navigational calculation console with his left hand a launch alert sounded.

The tactical screen was littered with hundreds of small, highly energized missiles and he knew exactly what they were. "Uriel assist," he addressed the onboard systems; "seal all openings, power down all systems and move current data into long term storage."

"Operations will take approximately twenty nine seconds." The computer replied.

He glanced at the tactical display one more time before it blinked out and saw that he had seven seconds before the electromagnetic pulse bombs would be in optimal range. The only thing he could do as the systems on his fighter powered down, its engine pods flamed out and sealed, and the power plants halted the fusion reaction within before starting to cool down was activate the extra armoured layer of his vacsuit and turn off the control unit on his arm.

"I should have just stayed in bed," he whispered to himself as he closed his eyes and just tried not to think about what over three hundred electromagnetic pulse bombs going off all at the same time would do to his framework skeletal structure.

He may have saved his eyes by closing his lids, but he still saw a flash and heard a painfully loud, sharp crack between his ears before losing conciousness.

TRADING

Lucius Wheeler didn't know how many times the door chimed before he opened his eyes. It was late. He had been accessing General Collins' memories and tricked his body into falling asleep so they could play back at an accelerated speed, so he could experience them just like a dream.

He groggily made his way to the door and answered it. As the featureless door slid into the wall he couldn't help wondering if he was experiencing the same thing Gabriel did when he first made his connection to a large network. Lucius had caught himself forgetting all about eating, hygiene and closing himself off from everyone else. The temptation to just close his eyes and experience another piece of General Collins' life was so intense that he had done it a few times while he was intimate with his old first officer, Gloria. If that's how things were for him after assuming the digital record of one man's experiences, he couldn't imagine what it was like for Gabriel, who had access to entire historical databases, tactical information, intelligence gathering systems and everything else that you'd find in two massive military vessels.

It was Gabriel, who grinned at him with the familiarity of an old friend as the door opened. He looked pristine. His hair had been cut short, his dark blue vacsuit and flight jacket were clean and the glow of good health was returning to the man who just days before looked so spent and scrawny that one wondered how long he could stay on his feet. "Good morning Lucius."

"You interrupted a flashback. I was dreaming I was having thirty five year old scotch with the High Chancellor of Evora. She was just telling me about her third son."

"No, you were dreaming you were Collins and you were with Evora. There's quite a difference. Besides, you can always continue where you left off."

Lucius stepped out of the doorway and the pair walked to the circular seating in the middle of the main room. "It takes some getting used to. Looks like the work they did on you is turning out well though."

"Oh, you think? A program takes care of all my physical needs for me using a dozen or so different implanted systems. It's like I've taken a whole new step in evolution. I'm never hungry, dirty and soon I'll be perfectly fit. Are you sure you don't want to sign up for it? They just implant a few grams of nanobots and they construct the implants overnight, very simple."

"That's all right, I'll let you be the great pioneer. Besides, there's something to be said for taking care of your own biological functions."

"So I've heard. You've been having a few late night visits from Gloria, I couldn't help but notice." Gabriel said with a crooked grin.

198

"Still keeping your eye on me?"

It took a moment for him to reply, his gaze becoming unfocused as a result of him looking inward at something in the digital world. "Oh, security earmarked the visual logs. They do that whenever the status of a crew member changes, social or otherwise."

"Ah."

Again the man sitting just a meter distant on the opposite seat was mentally drawn much further away by something in the digital realm and Lucius was led to wonder what being connected to the massive ships would be like. The thought faded as Gabriel's attention turned back to him. "That's what makes what I've come to ask you harder than expected. We tried fabricating a bare framework using a high resolution materializer and failed. We were hoping to duplicate a blank template that was equal to you or Gloria so I could avoid this whole messy business."

Lucius leaned back in his seat. "I saw this coming after taking on Collins' memories."

"So you know that Jacob Valance's last task was to play physical host to Eve."

"Yes, and you'd have to disable him, carve open his skull and replace his brain with hers. His body would rebuild itself based on her mental self image."

"So you know Gloria would be killed in the process."

"Yeah, so why wake her up at all? I mean you could have left her in the pod until it was time. She'd be none the wiser."

"If you spent more time accessing the parts of Collins' experiences that mattered, you'd know the answer to that question." Gabriel's eyes rolled back in his head as he accessed a large chunk of data. After two seconds he looked back at the other man, his features in deep shadow in the dim light. "I'll answer it for you regardless. I didn't know which of you would be more valuable to us. A framework built over a living human template or a less experienced template or someone who had time to age actively, unaware of what and who you were."

Lucius nodded and let Gabriel continue.

"Of the two you are the more interesting, you are more well textured. That came as a surprise, considering how, I hope you'll pardon me for saying, empty you were at the beginning. Besides, I knew you'd have less difficulty interfacing with Collins' experiences since your personal experience has been unquestionably male so far."

"I get it, and no, you won't have any trouble from me if you want to use her. I remember just enough about the old Gloria to know that it's just a matter of time before the new and improved model becomes more trouble than she's worth. The last thing you need is another Jonas Valent on your hands. I'll still want something in trade though."

"Oh?"

"Give me the *Saviour* and access to the Vindyne development archives. Oh, and when I say I want the *Saviour* I mean I want full ownership. Control codes, the override hardware, full command of the crew and accounts with at least two years worth of pay for them that I can transfer out of whatever Regent Galactic bank you drop them into."

Gabriel's eyes went wide and his expression froze in one of surprise. For a moment Lucius wondered if the man was honestly that taken aback, but realized after a few seconds that he was just accessing more data, performing some kind of search. After a moment his eyes focused on Lucius again and the expression changed to a more pleased, admiring one. "How did you know? Did Collins' find out somehow?"

Lucius had no idea what the other man was talking about but just held the exact same expression on his face, relaxed and replied calmly. "Doesn't much matter now, does it?"

"You're right, it doesn't. I can give you command of the *Saviour*. It's actually joined up with us already as you've probably seen out your view port. She'll have a trained Regent Galactic crew like all the ships they've provided. I'm just surprised that you've discovered where her true value lies already. I won't be able to let you keep what's in her vault."

"I had guessed that. I wouldn't want what's inside anyhow."

"And what of the new marines aboard? I suppose you'd like to keep them."

Wheeler hurriedly tried to search Collins' memories for anything referring to the marines and before long he had it. They were one of the final goals for the framework project; to have the ability to store bare, unused framework skeletons in bulk aboard a ship that could be turned on a few at a time or all at once, imprinted with a basic personality, skills and directives then sent out into the field. The difficulties that Vindyne faced after they had captured the technology from the original Wheeler and started work with Yorgen Stills involved reducing a marine unit back into a framework skeleton for long term storage and the memory imprints. Collins had no memory of them correcting that problem. When Lucius Wheeler looked back at Gabriel, not aware until then that he had looked away, it was to see the other man laughing and clapping his hands together.

"You are full of surprises Lucius! I am going to miss you! You had no idea we were ready to deploy the framework marines, did you?"

Wheeler could only smile and shake his head. "No idea."

"I could learn so much about the benefits of staying human from you. If anything you're proof that there is still a point to flesh and blood. Well, since you've gotten enough out of me to be dangerous, I'll tell you the rest. We have twenty eight tested memory imprints that work ninety seven percent of the time and the *Saviour* is made to accommodate framework marines, pilots, gunners, mechanics and the other template types. We've also included small manufacturing facilities so you can build more if you happen to start running low. The *Saviour* carries fifteen thousand frameworks in storage and can support up to two thousand in close quarters for up to three months. The frameworks we can generate with our current manufacturing technology aren't the same quality as you, but they more than serve their purpose. My God, it's laborious telling you this verbally." Gabriel sighed before continuing. "The ship can create starfighters, dropships and is quite a fighting machine itself. The *Saviour* is made to mount surprise attacks against outposts and colonies. I'd expect a man like you could quickly achieve the assignment we have for you and move on to become a rich man before long. I'll trade her to you for your full cooperation and

Gloria."

"As long as she's *my* ship, and the crew knows they're being sold. I don't want to face some kind of zealot mutiny as soon as I'm finished hound dogging Jake."

"So you have been paying attention to some of Collins' more important memories."

"Oh yeah, Vindyne's habit of taking control of any ship they manufactured at a moment's notice using the manufacturer's command code. It wasn't even legal in most systems."

"But we rarely did such a thing inside a solar system, so we never really broke those laws."

"Loopholes, every successful member of that company thought in loopholes, especially Collins. I won't get caught in one."

"Then you won't be. We'll give you access to the manufacturer level codes and all you'll have to do is shut down the engines so you can enter new ones. Hampon won't be pleased, but he has his army of dull minded zealots, so he'll forget before long."

"I'll have to find out more about this cult he has going, Collins didn't exactly stay up to speed on it."

"He thought subjugation through religion was a mistake," Gabriel said absently as he considered some other data passing through his mind. "We'll see."

"So when are you going to take Gloria down to the chamber?"

"She's already being prepared on the *Saviour*. You will have to go ahead of me and open the vault. It will not open if I'm aboard that ship. I trust you have no significant objections?"

"To opening the vault for you? No. I know that's the real price on my freedom. Good of you to let me realize it for myself."

"Collins was paranoid where Eve was concerned. Didn't let anyone in, wouldn't let me near her."

"Paranoid is an understatement. The thought of you getting access to the Eve brain crossed his mind every hour after he took possession. He never figured out what you'd do if you got to get close."

"What do you think?"

"I think I should do whatever I need to to get clear of the mess you and Hampon are making and mind mind my own business as much as I can while I try to force Valent and the *Triton* out of hiding. How do you know they'll disappear anyway?"

Gabriel grinned broadly, the expression looked out of place somehow, his eyebrows were drawn tightly into a malicious counter-expression. "You would never leave this room if I were to tell you."

Lucius just stared at the man for a moment before nodding and standing up. "I'll get dressed and shuttle over to the *Saviour*."

"Thank you, I'll eagerly await the message that the vault is open," Gabriel said as he left the room.

* * *

Lucius Wheeler had heard of shuttles moving between large ships during wormhole travel but had never done it. The large pair of warships shared one massive wormhole with the *Malice* in the lead and the *Saviour* beside and behind. As the lensed, stretched view of the stars came into sight he couldn't help but feel absolutely infinitesimal.

The chances of the pilot making a mistake in the hundred twelve meter journey between the vessels were slim, but the shuttle he'd gotten into was little more than a squarish service pod with eight seats and a small cockpit. The carpeting, faux leather seats, dim lighting and synthesized wood panelled walls made the thing look expensive and even a little more sturdy on the inside but he knew that if this pilot went off course even a little or twitched the controls so they came near the edge of the wormhole they'd be tossed out into open space at over half the speed of light.

If they survived the passage over the edge they would be travelling much faster in space and time than any rescue ship would bother matching. If their luck was good they wouldn't collide with anything solid or harsh enough to lethally irradiate them through the hull and they could begin decelerating. Judging from the size of the small engines on the craft decelerating to a normal speed could take weeks and he doubted that they had enough provisions for that length of time.

Even though Collins had gone through ship to ship travel inside a wormhole, that experience was like watching a holomovie in his head, worthless to Lucius for reassurance. Wheeler tried not to show it, but as the *Saviour* drew nearer he was nearly overcome with relief.

The sooner he could get out of the shuttle the better. The only people aboard were the pilot, her copilot, a coffin like stasis tube on a gurney and himself. He made the mistake of looking through the transparent lid of the stasis vessel and upon seeing the soundly sleeping face of Gloria he couldn't help but feel a pang of guilt.

She was an abrasive woman, not one he had ever truly called a friend, but for years she had been dependable. The fact that Gabriel had given him a choice, even if only as a gesture, to save her from being used as nothing more than a body for another mind to inhabit was sheer emotional manipulation. Guilt was just another distraction and Gabriel only gave him a choice so he could somehow displace the blame for what was about to happen to Gloria. *Gabriel gave me the opportunity to say I would trade her to the company and I fell for it. I could have just said something neutral and left it all up to him, but no. I had to sell her for top dollar after they officially made her the first person in my chain of command. They made me responsible for her and now if they ever wanted to persecute me for anything they could come after me for murder. I have to take a lesson from Collins. He thought he was the king of the sector and before he knew it Gabriel was on top of him bashing his head in. I have to keep a back door open whenever I'm dealing with these people, especially Gabriel. He's a freak, but he's got a wicked intelligence. God, how the hell did Collins let the freaks take over? There's Gabriel, the new and improved Hampon, a pre-adolescent body with Hampon's twisted mind imprinted, like that's not creepy. To think he almost took my framework body for his own, if I could meet Collins I'd buy him a drink for stopping that.*

His thoughts were interrupted as the shuttle docked with the mooring point on the *Saviour's* hull and the cabin pressure equalized with that of the massive vessel. A moment later the hatch gracefully slid open, revealing one of the main hallways.

As Lucius stepped outside and recognized two of the fully uniformed bridge officers who had been sent to meet him he nervously ran his hand over his stubble ridden head. He recognized them instantly from replays of Collins' memories. They were good, well trained officers who had served him faithfully for the entire time he was in command of the *Saviour*.

The sensation of instant recognition was so strange. Lucius found himself disliking the way Collins used to regard them. The older commander kept his people in the peripheral, not rewarding good work and using his immediate underlings as the long stick with which to punish performance shortfalls. Collins had as little contact with his crew as possible and made sure his quarters were near the bridge so he could be completely separate from them while being close enough to attend to an emergency at a moment's notice.

Lucius Wheeler was the opposite. For the time he was on the *Triton* he kept everyone close. Even people he didn't particularly like got to see him personally at least once a week, at least for a moment in the hall or in the lower observation deck near the hangars. He knew everyone's name, something of their history and how they were socially tied with other people on the ship. Gloria was a huge help with that, and even though his memories of the years he spent on that ship weren't very clear, he still had memories of her. She was always trading information on the crew with him, together they were social animals who trusted each other as much as you could trust anyone on a scrappy, under used mercenary ship and until he had awoken in his new body she was more like a comrade and friend than anything else.

Everything was different, shallow until he took on Collins' memories and after that his perception changed once again. He had full access to the memories of a great, intelligent, military and corporate man who didn't see his end coming. It wasn't the first time he had a live lesson on enjoying every moment in life because it could come to a sudden, abrupt end in the very next and as a result he and Gloria crossed the barrier that lay between friends and lovers. She was different too. It was as though being in the belly of the beast, Regent Galactic, relieved her of some kind of pressure or heavy load and she was more light hearted than he had ever seen her.

It wasn't a lover he'd miss, however. It was the trustworthy friend he had found in Gloria after being with her for years. Before stepping out into the hall he couldn't help but look over his shoulder and lay a hand on the polished stasis tube. "Goodbye baby, I know you'd do the same to me if they gave you the chance," he whispered, his gaze lingering on her peaceful face.

As soon as he was out of the shuttle four medical technicians in their loose fitting self sterilizing smocks, gloves and hoods moved in to claim his sleeping gift of flesh. Lucius didn't look back but walked between his first officer and operations officer with a passive expression on his face. *I'll keep things cool and formal until I know the lay of the land. I haven't been in command of a ship with a full crew in ages, not since I was working for Freeground Intelligence. No matter what I can learn from Collins, if I want to do this my way, to do this right, I'll have to take it one step at a time.*

"It's a pleasure to have you with us, Captain Wheeler," burst the young, blond haired first officer. "I'm Major Tammerlan, your First Officer here and this is Senior Lieutenant Immain."

Wheeler shook the young man's hand and looked him in the eye. "Thank you, I'm glad to be here." He then turned to the young operations officer who was looking at a holographic status display coming from her left palm. Her brown hair was bound up in a bun just under the rear of her grey cap which made her look a little more serious when she wasn't smiling but when she flashed her grin he couldn't help but smile back a little in return as her soft hand shook his.

"We're glad to have you sir. Everyone's heard about how you apprehended and captured Jacob Valance before and we're anxious to see how you're going to flush him out this time."

"Are you a bit of a hunter yourself?" Wheeler asked with a raised eyebrow.

"Don't let her post fool you," Tammerlan started with a smile. "Off duty she's a bit of a bounty hunter groupie, sir."

"I prefer enthusiast, Major."

It was difficult not to get pulled into pleasantries with the pair, who had the ease of two people who had been working together for quite a while. Lucius smiled and nodded as he led the way towards the secure section of the ship, the forward hold where he'd find the main vault. "I've been out of the action for a while, so you'll have to bring me up to speed. How long has Jacob been in hiding for?"

"Well, he hasn't. The last time he came up on a report he was on Pandem and considering the situation there it's doubtful that he's gone anywhere. Our intelligence tells us conclusively that he and his crew will be going into hiding soon and there's little we can do to stop it."

Wheeler looked at the Major for a moment, trying to read any uncertainty in his expression. "So you're telling me you know he's on Pandem and he's going into hiding no matter what. Is anyone tasked with tracking him right now?"

"Regent Galactic just handed that ball off to the West Watchers and they're giving it to you, sir."

"We won't be there for some time."

"Their not concerned."

"It doesn't sound like we're getting much help on this."

"With the crew we have aboard you won't need it, sir," interjected the operations officer, who was closing a holographic report on quarter assignments.

"I hope that's true. I'm wondering, some of your intelligence seems to make assumptions on things that haven't happened yet. Do you have some kind of predictive system aboard?"

"Not at all, Captain Wheeler," said the holographic image of a young, sandy haired boy in robes as he appeared just in front of them, walking backwards. The image looked to the officers at Wheeler's sides with a nod at each; "Senior Lieutenant, Major. Please leave us so we can speak privately."

"Yes your Grace," they said in near unison as they quietly turned and

204

walked off down another broad, silver and grey corridor.

The boy's image, looking as though the pre-adolescent child were really there, fell in step beside Lucius. "I owe you an apology for my actions while I was with Vindyne. It wasn't my decision to betray you, but the powers that were thought that as long as you were free to return to Freeground you presented a significant risk."

Collins knew that Hampon had been reborn in the shape of a much younger clone body, but it was still strange seeing the long nosed child speak with the bearing and very intentional diction of a stuffy, self important adult. "That's why I had you give me the master command codes to this ship. Next time you see her she won't even have the same transponder system or comm keys."

The child's laughter bubbled out of the small smiling face at his side. "Oh, I understand, trust me, I understand. You, like many long time survivors in this galactic arena have learned to be cautious from being bitten. Speaking of learning experiences, how have Collins' memories been serving you lately?"

"Good, he was a great man. I'm learning a lot from him."

"You're not suffering any memory intrusions?"

"Nope, it's like watching a movie."

"Isn't it simply fantastic? I enjoy reliving experiences from all the imprints I've managed to collect."

Wheeler looked down at the robed figure; "You have more than one?"

"One from each corner of the known Galaxy. I believe that there will come a day where memory imprints become a truly precious and widespread commodity. I plan to open the market with scans of tens of thousands of individuals. The Order Of Eden demands that every Saved, West Keeper and West Watcher is scanned as part of the initial testing."

"So that's the back end of the scam you have going, thinking pretty big."

"Scam? As long as I'm offering some kind of valuable commodity, such as their safety, there's no scam here. We are an organization preoccupied with momentum, with progress. The Order of Eden is purest at the top and hardest working at the bottom."

Lucius shook his head, smiling at the sound of the child's preaching. "How many people have gotten wrapped up in this? I mean, I heard about it a year ago on the mining colony and if I can hear about this religion there, I'm sure word's pretty much everywhere."

"Oh, we have a few thousand Grading Stations, mostly on Regent Galactic and Core Worlds. Regent Galactic gave us broad licence to set up shop in all their Spacerwares stores. Fringe territories are just discovering us now. You should get graded some time, I'll waive the fee if you like."

"No thanks, I'm more interested in making a paradise in this life than working for one that probably won't be there at the end of the road. Besides, thanks to Collins I know exactly where the Eden system is and how to bypass the security measures." The audacity of the religion that Hampon had created around the terror the Eden Fleet and Holocaust Virus was incredible. Collins had been a secondary architect, designing the militarized portion of the ruse. One would pay a hundred thousand Core World Credits in order to rank as Saved and become recognized as an ally by all infected machines. It took up to three days for your name to make it to the Order Of Eden Temple, and during those days you would be Graded through a number of tests.

Depending on how high you score on a scale that was kept away from all but the highest ranking West Watchers they determined how close you were to Eden. You could also make extra donations to buy your way deeper into the organization. Through the Grading and donations you'd be given a position amongst the Saved, who were civilian servants, or the West Keepers who were either military or higher ranking civilian servants or the West Watchers who were the leaders, spies or other high rankers in the organization. Members advanced by doing their jobs well, committing good deeds and helping others with their accomplishments. Followers could also increase their chances of advancement by buying training and it was all measured weekly as progression or regression by a Progress Monitor who invariably accepted donations to offset any regression or transgression.

If you had enough money you could get away with murder. How many points you had on the Progress side of your personal chart was not to be discussed with anyone but a Progress Monitor or a West Watcher and the amount recorded there helped the organization's leaders determine how close you were to Eden in your lifetime. The ultimate accomplishment in the faith is to gather so many points that you could retire on the Eden II world itself under the protection of the Eden Fleet and in the natural paradise most people would never see in their lifetimes. The fastest way to Eden, however, was to sacrifice your life in the service of the Order. If your Progress was high enough your soul would make its way to Eden on its own.

Lucius saw it as a near perfect scam, providing the Order of Eden with a vast military, large body of civilian workers and thanks to the Holocaust Virus and Eden Fleet everyone knew that the threat of destruction if you weren't a member was very real. Collins was of the same opinion but he didn't allow a Progress Monitor on his ship until just before the scan. He didn't believe that his own people had to subscribe to the dreamt up religion of the half mad Hampon.

"You misunderstand me Lucius," Hampon's boy grin smiled up at him. "I'm opening the doors for you, giving you the opportunity to be a West Watcher, among our elite. I know you disabled our mechanism of control on your body and I understand. Your mistrust doesn't give me pause. I'm willing to take you in, invite you into the inner circle."

"Thanks, but I'm pretty sure I'll be happy enough just catching Jake for you and moving on. You probably won't see me after I'm done," Lucius said as he stepped through two meter thick security doors. They closed behind him with an ominous sound.

The holographic image of Hampon flickered for a moment as the projectors built invisibly into the ceiling picked up the transmission and carried it forward. "There will be benefits when the great battle comes. Trust me."

"Great battle? That's a new one. The fear of getting torn apart by some random infected bot isn't enough to scare people into the recruitment centers?"

"They're Grading Stations. It's no fear tactic Lucius. The West Watchers are preparing for a war that cannot be won without a force united in the most strict sense. When the line is drawn against our great enemy only the united will have a chance and not a sure one at that."

"Where the hell do you get this stuff? Is there some magic ball you're shaking in the back room that just randomly spits out vague warnings?"

"Like I said, we have a prescience most people could not comprehend. Pandem will be one of many supply posts for the upcoming war, of that we are absolutely certain."

"Okay pint sized prophet, why is it so important that you wake me up and give me a ship worth trillions of credits along with a trained crew just to go mess with Valance and my old ship? Why the hell is he so important?"

"Because if he isn't distracted he will damage what we're building in such a critical way that we won't recover in time to prevent the coming annihilation. If you think unleashing a virus on a few fringe systems and killing a few million people is something, imagine an evil force that tears into the heart of our civilization and destroys it utterly. If we don't form a real military that spans entire sectors soon we'll be back to using bows and arrows within three years. If you want to see the truth behind all of this all you have to do is say the word and you'll be one of us."

Lucius thought for a moment. Collins knew enough to go along with and even aid the formation of the Order of Eden but he hadn't had a chance to relive those experiences for himself. He touched on dozens of moments, concentrated on the knowledge locked in Collins' linear memories as they walked through the quiet secure hall that led directly to the heart of the massive vault built in the center of the ship. When he found the right memory the realization struck him like a wave.

Deeply buried in the memory of Collins was a time when Hampon, Meunez and himself were on the *Overlord II* several months after the capture of Jonas, himself and several others. The board room was darkened, the windows completely opaque and the long rosewood table in the center was between Hampon and Meunez. Collins stood in the center. "Regent Galactic is orchestrating a buyout of key Vindyne assets, I think we should start looking at changing sides."

"I agree. With the loss of Doctor Stills we're losing Head Office's trust. I've already started to see researchers transferred out of my division," the adult version of Lister Hampon said. He was already losing his hair thanks to his near fatal first bout with Omagen disease.

"I've advanced as far as I'd like along this track, I agree. Regent Galactic is an expanding power, Vindyne is collapsing. I can't help wondering what's brought this on, General? As I understand it you're back in Home Office's good graces."

"Since I took a trip to Gavin's Moon they've been less than pleased." Collins said moodily as he looked through a small file menu on the tabletop. The blue and green light shed by the file names trickled up the front of his uniform and was caught in his grey beard.

"I thought you were taking an intelligence unit on a search for Yorgen Stills."

"That was the official story, but I was meeting with a deep cover contact I have in the Carthan government."

"What? Stills is essential to further development on the framework technology. We need to know more about his final prototype and how it was programmed or-"

"Doctor Stills is long gone. There are people who have no other business but to keep him hidden and they're good at their job. Besides, we have what we need to mass produce a less expensive but stable framework unit and his lab is still here. Our attention is best spent elsewhere." Collins' eyes met Gabriel's and he just stared at him for a moment as the other man thought better of pursuing the matter. He sighed then continued, looking back to the file list on the table. "Something's happened on Pandem that could change everything. When I wasn't willing to pass this new intelligence up the chain to Head Office they weren't too pleased. They were aware that I was chasing down an important lead on something, just not what it was. When they found my contact dead after the meeting they started asking questions."

"What's so important that you won't use it to advance your career? You've never been squeamish about that sort of thing before," Hampon said with a crooked grin that didn't suit his thin face or beak like nose. "If it's that important I'm sure they'll at least pad your bonus for it."

"This is too important to trust Head Office with, this is a calling worth losing the *Overlord* for. It's big enough to get us on track to being in command of several solar systems with Regent Galactic, maybe even get us a seat on the board eventually."

"Are you going to let us in or will I have to hack in and find it for myself?" Meunez asked peevishly.

"You'd never find it. This message comes word of mouth only," he said with a wry grin as he brought up an image of a small, ancient wormhole generator no more than nine centimetres wide.

"Is that a real image of the Victory Machine?" asked Hampon in hushed awe.

"No, it's a close approximation based on what my contact told me before I had to kill him. I've checked everything we know about the Victory Machine against his description and even temporal mechanics back up the shape and form you're seeing here. It's close enough to prove to as near a certainty as I need that the device actually exists and that's what makes the news I've received important. The Carthans have had the Victory Machine in a repository on Pandem for over a century. In all that time it's been running but nothing has come through, that is until now."

"Confirmed? This is news from the future you're talking about here, most people don't believe the Victory Machine even exists let alone that it's been running for over a century," Meunez said.

"The message was only one thousand and twenty four characters long but it had the date that Alice was born, the date that Hampon the Prophet gains access to the Victory Machine and one more date with the description; the last day of the United Core World Calendar. There are also ghost images coming through, of other possible deactivations, parts of messages, and other activity that's too unclear to interpret. The message was addressed to you, Lister."

208

"Just the fact that the Victory Machine is receiving data again means something. The fact that it's addressed to me? I do not believe in its existence. No one has been able to create a wormhole that can receive messages from the future for more than a few seconds because such a wormhole cannot remain stable. There is too much to consider, it requires too much fine tuning and power. What's worse is that destabilization of a device like the Victory Machine would cause an implosion so immense that it would either cause a black hole or gather enough matter to give birth to a new sun, destroying everything within a light year and causing a shift in gravity that could shift orbits in nearby solar systems. Just the radiation-" he stopped, his eyes going wide.

"Haven't explained how you were exposed to enough radiation to result in Omagen disease yet, have you?" Gabriel Meunez commented with a crooked grin.

"You're right. Sometime in the future I must come in contact with the Victory Machine and since the radiation expands in all directions of time as well as space this could have been the result," he concluded, looking at his spotty hands.

"Obviously you become involved in this somehow. The partial images and messages coming through the Victory Machine depict dark days for the most part. All indicators point towards things getting worse until somehow the Core Worlds Collapse so utterly that even their calendar is abolished by someone or something much more powerful than the human race."

"The ultimate defeat of a culture, some would argue," Hampon concluded, regaining some of his composure. "What do you propose we do?"

"Obviously whoever sent that message thinks you might have the answer, so what do *you* think we should do?" Gabriel Meunez asked. "What does your instinct and that great big intellect tell you?"

Collins looked at him with a raised eyebrow, prompting for a response in the gentlest way he knew how.

Lister Hampon thought for a moment before replying. "I say we do everything we can to ally ourselves with Regent Galactic and find a way to build on whatever power they give us. The Carthans won't do business with Vindyne, but perhaps we can help Regent Galactic acquire what we cannot afford ourselves, the things we need to continue the research we're pursuing and eventually interface with the Eden Fleet."

"I agree, we'll have to put personal objectives aside for a while I'm afraid, but in the end we could be in a very high position," Collins nodded before looking to Meunez. "You'll have to be reassigned so you can watch another end of the company."

"I'm so close to understanding what was done here, how Alice managed to make the transfer from artificial life to human. That, if anything, could be key to understanding the Eden Fleet, maybe finding a new way of communicating with them, of relating to them."

"We've already explored that avenue and every simulation and field test tells us it's a dead end. We need you to gather information and conduct affairs elsewhere, especially if I'm about to lose the *Overlord*. If you want to try and track Alice physically you can do it from wherever you end up, just make sure you don't jeopardize your position or I'll put you back in your place personally."

"I'm telling you she's the key!" Meunez shot back. "Somehow she managed to break through the barrier that separates software from wetware and you're not going to find out how by digging around in Valent's brain, you'll see it for yourself if you track down-"

"Alice, we've heard it before!" Collins finished for him. "All we have of her is a record of data transfer and security footage of her flopping out of a tube in a new body then being carried away by two known criminals of low education! She's probably already been sold into slavery and used to death in some back room somewhere! You'll follow orders and help us broker the sale of any worthwhile Vindyne properties to Regent Galactic so we can ride the tide into their good graces and end up in a position to take advantage of the information we have!"

"And save the Galaxy? You're telling me my goals are unrealistic while you're trying to save all of humanity?"

"I don't know about you but I want to continue living a life of privilege and power and that can't happen if the galaxy deteriorates into such a state that humanity can't even collectively count the days!" Collins shot back, breaking into a rare rage.

"He's right Gabriel. Not only that, but imagine the power we'd have if we were to become known as the saviors of humanity. Anything we covet would be ours. You could search after your hybrid queen all you like, even create one of your own with the resources you'd have. Tell me you're with us."

Gabriel Meunez sighed and turned towards the blacked out window. "Only if I am free once we have made it into Regent Galactic's good graces. I still believe she's the key to uniting the machine and man mind. I must at least find out what became of her."

"Done."

That's where the instant recall stopped, not because the rest was uninteresting, but because it was all Lucius Wheeler needed to know. The enlightenment showed in his expression as he looked down at the grinning blond boy beside him. They had stopped at the main security doors leading into the core vault of the *Saviour*. "You can receive messages from the future?"

"Yes, Lucius. Until just a short while ago we had access to the Victory Machine through a West Watcher operative but he broke off communication so we had to unleash the Holocaust Virus. Only by setting that chain of events in motion were we able to bring Jacob Valent's original crew together on one world and keep them away from their alternate destiny while we gained control of the Victory Machine for ourselves."

"So you've never seen the machine for yourself? How did your last body get irradiated?"

"We tried to make our own Victory Machine and it didn't work. Fortune smiled on us, however. Instead of causing the wormhole to collapse, drawing enough matter and energy inside to create a black hole or a new star we managed to dissipate it. Unfortunately I didn't make it out and the temporal radiation affected my body for years in each direction. Very confusing even after you look at it in an educated manner."

"You're telling me." Lucius Wheeler looked at the large vault door in front of him. The keypad had never been used, the chamber hadn't been opened since Collins placed the Eve mind inside himself. He did everything from setting up the storage and stasis equipment to transporting the delicate, vulnerable cargo and installing it into the storage unit personally. "How does this fit into your plans? Collins was terrified of Meunez getting near this. He was afraid that he'd try and commune with it, find a host body and somehow free Eve."

"That's exactly what we're doing. The end of our civilization is still coming and even though we have control of the Eden Fleet we will not be able to maintain that forever. Our hopes are that Gabriel will be able to befriend the Eve Mind, to reintroduce her to her creations and that when she realizes that the end of humanity as well as the destruction of her solar system is only a couple of years away at best that she should join with us. That is one of the reasons why the Order of Eden was created, to give us a way to demonstrate our dedication as a race to coming together and overcome dissent. Regent Galactic is on the verge of joining us, they just learned that we're on the verge of taking the Victory Machine for ourselves, the Carthans had it so well hidden that Regent Galactic never knew it was there. Millions of their citizens join the West Keeper organization every day now even though the Holocaust Virus is less effective than ever with the mass deletion of artificial intelligences across the Galaxy."

"So you've actually managed to accomplish most of your goals," Lucius muttered.

"Yes, but the most important one has not been met; the salvation of our civilization. For that we believe we need to turn to Eve. Her fleet is the most powerful united force in the known universe." The blonde haired boy sighed slowly and folded his hands in the sleeves of his robes, a posture that didn't fit his apparent youth.

Wheeler knew the boy was studying him, watching him as he stood and stared at the keypad that was ready for the thirty two digit alphanumeric code that would break the seal on the vault. There was no data network attached to the security system, only a detection grid for screening out Gabriel Meunez, a tiny computer that would recognize the password and the mechanism that could open the door. "I'm starting to understand who Collins was and why he kept you and Gabriel around. You're both mad in your own way, but with that madness comes genius," he let the idea of Gabriel Meunez communing with Eve in a way that no one else could sit in his mind for a moment. It *was* frightening, the story he was being told *was* spectacular, but he had seen the evidence.

Collins spent years tracking agents deeply embedded in the Carthan government, gathering power of his own, developing the virus that would make the Eden Fleet controllable and considering the problem of that virus failing one day. All the while he helped Lister Hampon develop his Cash Messiah Cult, as he called it before it was finally named the Order of Eden. It promised everyone a place in paradise if only they worked hard enough, were faithful enough and got humanity through the hard times.

All the evidence he needed was in mind, but how it could all go wrong was starting to come into sharp focus as well. The possibilities of what would happen if Gabriel came in contact with the Eve Mind were all described vaguely. He knew from succinctly worded reports from the future that from one instant to the next the outcome of such an event changed like a roulette wheel that would forever spin until someone interceded and stopped it. *That's why Collins never destroyed the Eve mind. He could have at any time but for two reports that mentioned disaster there was always one that pointed to the Eve mind being a large part of the solution. But why didn't any of them say that Collins would be killed? I can't find any memory of his that contains him receiving a warning from the future about his own death. Then again, why would anyone send one back for him? It's not like he had any friends out here.* Lucius mused. The notion of dying suddenly and having no one to mourn him sent a chill up his spine, but his attention was drawn back to that big, heavy door in front of him.

If Gabriel fails to commune with the Eve Mind then a great scientific wonder will go to waste and she'll have to be killed. If he succeeds there will always be the possibility that she will only trust him, that the Eden Fleet will fall under his control by proxy or that she'll earn their trust just long enough to come get in contact with her Fleet and turn on everyone.

Collins would have kept the vault shut, in fact he might have built another vault around this one and throw away the key if he had time, but I'm not Collins. He concluded with a smile. "Count me in, but even while I'm off hunting down and kill Jacob Valent I'm all the way in. You tell me everything, and I mean *everything* until I decide to get the hell out of the range of whatever this apocalypse is."

"You are to flush out Jacob, get him out of hiding if we cannot catch him ourselves, not kill him. The messages concerning him and his people are still conflicting, uncertain. His interference may yet be required in the future and that won't be available if he's in hiding."

"All right then, I'll scare him out of hiding, but you keep me up to date and in the loop or everything Collins knew gets cut off."

"Agreed. I think you might be easier to work with, actually. Collins and I were often at odds."

"I know," Wheeler said as he stepped forward and punched in the password to open the vault. After a few seconds the door split down the middle and slowly began to part.

The hologram of young Lister Hampon, the High Seat of the Order of Eden began to fade as he smiled up at Lucius. "I'll see you when you emerge from the wormhole."

212

What Comes Around. . .

Stephanie couldn't help but be reminded of the last time she'd been in the infirmary. She watched Grace, the head medical officer at the time, hold a laser scalpel to the back of a patient's neck. No one but Grace and herself were aware of the hidden threat, and it bought the traitor time. It didn't matter; Grace was killed not long afterwards because she had left Stephanie no other choice.

The whole thing complicated her relationship with Frost, especially since the last thing Grace accused her of was killing her so she could take Frost for herself. Getting together with the Gunnery Chief may have been an easy decision for her but it wasn't as easy for the crew to deal with, there was still animosity between the Gunnery Crews and Security Teams because of their last public fight. What would happen if Frost discovered her night with the Captain?

She tried to put it out of her mind as Frost noticed her coming in. He was reclining on a medical pallet waiting for the treatment systems to finish scanning the stump at the end of his shin. "'Bout time. Was thinkin' you'd never show."

Stephanie smiled and walked up to his bedside. "You on your back? I wouldn't miss this for anything."

The scan of Frost's healed stump completed and one of the few medical workers, a fellow with a shaved head and kind eyes, shorter than herself, came around. He took a look at the scan results and nodded. "We'll start materializing your prosthetic right away sir. Sorry we couldn't grow you a foot."

"Aye, still don't understand why," Frost spat back irritably. "The instructions are right in the computer, if it were me I'd just follow 'em."

"Like I said before, it's not that simple. If I grow you one and attach it but something-"

"Aye, if somethin' went wrong I could be worse off. Fine," Frost finished for him. "Just put somethin' on that stump so my Gunners aren't lookin' at me sideways for the rest o' the trip."

"Yes sir," the medical tech said with a sobered nod to Frost. "Good to see you Chief," he said to Stephanie with a small smile.

"Don't mind him, he gets irate whenever I save his ass," Stephanie whispered as though Frost couldn't hear her.

"Oh, that explains everything," the medical tech said, rolling his eyes as he started towards the materializer across the room.

"Save my ass?" Frost said with a raised eyebrow. "I lost some good loaders in that fight, we kept 'em off ya while you blasted at 'em."

Stephanie stopped feigning a pleasant demeanour but kept her voice low. "We lost people. You, me, maintenance and *Triton* as a whole. There's no point in

213

comparing loss."

"Fine, I'm just sayin' that it woulda been worse if my loaders hadn't a been there."

Stephanie sighed, more to take a moment in an attempt to remain calm than anything else. She went on in a whisper; "I told you to get back, you didn't, and the fact that you're sitting here waiting for a new foot doesn't drive anything home."

"This is just the part o' the cost, lass. Us gunners polish our decks in blood on days like this."

"More like testosterone," she muttered as she turned and strode for the exit.

"Ye can't give orders on *my* deck lass!" Frost called after her.

"Enjoy your new foot!" she called back over her shoulder. "Should be a great battle scar to show the boys!"

Stephanie nearly walked right into Ashley as she turned the corner outside of the infirmary. She was carrying two white, blocky food containers. "Coming to visit someone?"

"I came to see you. From the sound of your talk with Frost it was a good idea," Ashley grinned and presented one of the containers to her with an outstretched arm. "For you."

Stephanie smiled back at her and accepted the package. "Thank you, I haven't eaten in I don't know how long." They started walking towards the lift, both women quietly restraining themselves from stopping right on the spot and tearing into the fragrant insulated meals. "What's for dinner?"

"Dim sum, vegetable lo mein, lychee soda and a brownie."

"Oriental again?"

"Couldn't resist, especially since the materializers in the commissaries and pubs are so much better at making food than the ones in our quarters now. The lower ranks almost don't mind having their materializers deactivated."

They stepped into the lift and Stephanie highlighted the rear of the command deck as their destination. "Maybe he'd have some advice on what to do. I'm in a spot, Ash," Stephanie finished in a whisper, keenly aware of the three crew members who were already in the lift.

Ashley gave her a sidelong look, the lightness and humour falling away. "Aren't you supposed to give me advice?" She whispered.

"I think the tables are turned this time," Stephanie replied, lightening her visible mood as the lift doors opened and the express car admitted two more. She couldn't help but sigh as it started in the wrong direction, towards the front of the lower berths. "Anyway, how's the helm?"

Ashley perked up a little, as much for their audience of five as for her best friend. "Great. Panloo's taking the shift. She's doing really well, has gotten a good feel for how the ship moves."

"The ride's been pretty smooth in ship wide sims while she's at the helm."

"Yup, she sticks to the safe manoeuvres but I'd rather see that than anything else."

"How's Nevin turning out?"

"Nevil, actually. He's taking the qualifier for *Triton* tonight."

"That was quick."

"Well, he was a pilot on a five M rig for a few months, in comparison the *Triton's* smaller."

"I doubt he had to fly it in combat."

"Sorry, Ma'am, but what's a five M rig?" asked a nafalli in a loose fitting maintenance vacsuit. The fur of his face stood out straighter than the average nafalli, and was an intermix of blonde and brown shades.

"S'okay, we know you're listening." Ashley smiled at him. "It's just a shorter way of saying a fifty megaton rig, one of those really big containment."

"Oh, thank you ma'am. I tried the *Triton* qualifier for fun, I can't see how anyone could pass it."

"It's hard, you have to keep thinking in three dimensions and know where your best thrust points are. Besides, there are about two dozen tutorials leading up to the final qualifier. If you don't do most of them anyone would be pretty lost. What's your call sign? Would I have seen you in sims?"

"I don't think so, but it's Woolly."

"Rush At Io, I remember you were part of the vanguard."

The nafalli nodded and put his head down, his paws crossing over the back of his neck. "I didn't do very well."

"Everyone has trouble at the start, flying is it's own way of thinking," the lift doors opened and two of the passengers exited. The car began moving back up, to the relief of everyone aboard. "Stick to it, it'll become more natural as you go."

"Oh, I will. I've signed on with a team, they won't let me drop out," the doors opened once more. He and the two maintenance workers with him, both human and much smaller, got off as he said; "thank you, Commander."

"You're welcome," Ashley managed as the doors closed. "I'm never going to get used to that."

"People calling you by rank?"

"Yup, and being asked for advice. It happens *all the time*."

"Well, he's right, I've heard almost everyone has tried the *Triton* qualifier and the word is it's impossible."

Ashley shook her head slightly. "No, you just can't let yourself slip out of three dimensional thinking and you have to account for a lot more. I mean, a lot of ships this size have a pilot, two navigators and an AI dedicated to the helm all at the same time, especially if the mass of the ship is always changing."

Stephanie chuckled to herself and shook her head. "You've come a long way since the *Samson*."

Ashley shrugged. "Didn't have a choice. I'm just glad this ship has a lot of studying material. I don't think I've ever read as much as I have in the last month. That's actually the only thing that really pisses me off about some of our new pilots and the wannabes; they don't go looking for their own information. It's all right there in the system, you just have to look it up and figure out how it works with your own style."

"Maybe you should start telling them that."

"Maybe, though it seems a lot easier to just answer their questions."

"But they won't learn how to teach themselves that way, you know, learn to fish."

"Huh?"

"You know, give a man a fish he'll eat for a day, teach him to fish. . ."

"Oh, right. Guess so."

"Speaking of which, how is Wooly in the cockpit?"

Ashley tapped a few commands into her control unit and grimaced. "Well, he's getting better, but he's got the third highest collision rate on the ship."

"Oh, that's not good. I hope he's a good maintenance worker," Stephanie said as the doors opened to reveal their long awaited destination; the rear of the command deck.

They stepped out and made for Ashley's quarters, they were closer than Stephanie's by just a few doors. Upon entering Stephanie couldn't help but stop and whistle. "You did some work in here."

The red carpeted floor of the main sitting room was decorated with a long oriental dragon that encircled a low table. There were cushions and low seats arranged around the room, all in an effort to encourage her guests to lounge instead of simply sit. The walls were decorated with oriental fans, masks and beside the door leading into her bedroom was a long tapestry of two silhouetted geisha. Beside the other door was a tapestry of a shadowy samurai. "This goes way past your chopstick collection."

"I know, I thought if I made the place my own I'd feel more at home."

"Did it work?"

"Sorta, but to be honest a lot of this stuff was already in the ship materialization database except for the dragon, I had to do that myself. All the materials used were really light, so it only took two days of matter rations. The kotatsu was in storage somewhere though, I had to trade for it."

"What's a kotatsu and what did you trade?"

"It's the table, I think there's a little heater in it too. I only had to give up the furniture stacked in my side room, wanted to get rid of it anyway so I could put a second bed in," Ashley said as she undid her gun belt and sat down at the low wooden table. "I'm on the list to get it from ship inventory. Apparently they're waiting for security to finish sweeping the junior officer's quarters before they'll release any more furniture."

"We're getting there, don't worry. Besides, according to the computer those spaces are fully furnished but were only used for eighteen years so you'll get your guest room bed."

Stephanie went to the materializer and ordered a green tea for herself. The transparent cover slid down and her order was prepared starting with the tall white cup then the steaming hot water was poured inside as the teabags appeared. "I'll never get over how this ship actually carries and recycles real water."

"The *Samson* had water aboard. About six months worth with the recycling system."

"The carrier I served on had an energy reserve and an emergency store of

216

water and food, I never thought anyone did it any other way, especially on a ship three times the mass."

"Chief Grady was saying that the *Triton* doesn't have an emergency store of water, doesn't need one. Most of the water on the ship runs along the walls, it's treated right there." Ashley opened her container, revealing steaming noodles, vegetables and six white dim sum bulbs. The aroma of the spices filled the air right away and she smiled as she took a pair of chopsticks from a drawer in the table for herself and passed another pair to Stephanie, who was just sitting down. "Now, about the spot you're in, spill."

Stephanie had the lid to her late dinner half open and stopped, looked across the table to Ashley, who stared back with an upraised eyebrow, chewing through her first bite of sliced carrot and noodle. "You have to keep this to yourself, and I mean it."

"Promise."

"Nono, not like the last time when you said you'd keep it to yourself and told everyone else who you thought could keep it to themselves."

"What, Silver and Price? They didn't spread it," Ashley replied nonchalantly.

"See? I knew you passed it around. Looks like I'll have to go talk to Chief Grady if I need someone to bounce this off of," Stephanie concluded as she carefully dug into her steaming pile of noodles and chopped vegetables.

Ashley looked at her friend, trying to read her and at the same time trying to guess what the big issue could be while she picked at a dim sum bulb. "Wow, this has gotta be huge," she said quietly.

"That's why I don't think you can keep it quiet."

Ashley thought for a moment and steeled herself. "I'll keep the lid on. I don't care how much it hurts, this one doesn't get out. My lips may pout but they will be sealed."

Stephanie couldn't help from keeping the corners of her mouth from curling up.

"Besides, looks like you're about to burst," Ashley teased.

"You're right, but still, this has to stay in the room."

"I'm all hush, now get with the sharing."

"Okay. The night before Captain left we got into a big fight, I even told him to snap out of the blue he's in and things got heated."

"Wow, he threaten to-"

"Not finished," Stephanie interrupted.

"'Kay, go on."

"Instead of storming off the *Samson* I kissed him."

Ashley's eyes went wide, she froze mid chew, with her chopsticks half way between her mouth and food.

"Finish chewing," Stephanie advised her.

She hurriedly munched through the mouthful of noodles and swallowed exaggeratedly, filling the room with a gulp. "There's more?"

Stephanie closed the lid to her food and slowly got to her feet, turning away from Ashley. "Oh yeah."

"How much more? Did it turn into a snogging session? Someone catch you? What happened?"

"We, um, got together in the forward hold, the upper part."

"With the stasis tubes?" Ashley exclaimed through a shocked grin.

"With the stasis tubes."

"But you didn't get in that night, I dropped by your quarters-"

"Then we ran to his quarters."

"You jez! I knew you two would bunk up someday! How was it? I mean..."

Stephanie laughed, turning beet red; "The whole night was fantastic. It think we traumatized Price though."

"He caught you?" Ashley burst with shrieking laughter.

"I checked the security recordings for that night in the service bay and saw him running from the ship around the time things started. I've never seen him move that fast," Stephanie said through an insuppressible giggle.

A peal of Ashley's laughter filled the room.

"Okay, get it out of your system," Stephanie said, crossing her arms, still blushing furiously.

"You'll-" she gasped for air, "you'll have to show that to me some time. Did the receivers on the *Samson* catch anything?"

"Oh yeah, the whole thing. I deleted the footage."

"Smart, I would have kept a copy though."

"Oh no, the last thing we need is that kind of footage floating around."

"Good point. How'd you leave things?"

"Well, things were fine at first, we were going to just leave it as a one time thing but then he said something and it just left everything wide open."

"Oh no, what'd he say?"

"'If,' and then he just stopped. I tried to get him to spit the rest out but he just shut up."

Ashley's mirth was replaced by sympathy. "I'm so sorry. What'd you do?"

"Well, we said we'd keep it simple, and I don't know why, but I was pissed, I just got out of there. He came by the security office and made sure things had cooled down, told me not in so many words that he still trusted me before he left."

"So things are okay."

"Nooooo," Stephanie said emphatically, shaking her head and waving her hands in front of her. "Things are *not* okay, I'm *screwed!*"

"Frost," Ashley concluded.

"Exactly! He respected me before we got together, now it's impossible! He lost his foot because he didn't listen to me right in the middle of a crisis! His people and mine know he doesn't follow my orders and whenever I bring it up he just pats me on the head and changes the topic! He's great when it's just the two of us but everywhere else he's been an ass."

"And Captain is well, Captain," Ashley nodded.

"That's just it. Jake's different, better, he's been easier to be with since we ran into that slave barge. I think he's just starting to see it for himself too. Whatever he's getting from Jonas is just helping it along, he's changing like anyone else when they have a crisis, the only difference is his crisis has a name," she sighed, looking out the faux window, a section of bulkhead a few meters wide that showed an image of the view outside. "I keep thinking about him, I can't stop."

"So you and Frost are-"

"Done! We have to be! I hear his name and I cringe! What's worse is that I told Captain that I'd be sticking with Frost to 'see where it goes,' I can't believe I said that, *see where it goes*. What the hell was I thinking?"

"Um, you thought Frost would start listening to you?" Ashley offered with a shrug.

"You're right, I actually did but his cock up on the gunnery deck and how he treated me in medical in front of everyone," she threw up her hands, "it just won't work."

"What do you think Captain will do when he gets back and finds that you and Frost have split?" Ashley asked quietly.

"Well, Cap, I mean Jake took it pretty well when I told him that I'd be sticking with Frost, but I could tell there was something. He was worried about me, that's something." She sighted and shook her head; "And he said 'if' and I *still* want him to finish that sentence!"

"Are you sure?"

"I don't know, yes, but it might be complicated if that 'if' leads to something. . ." Stephanie said as she started pacing. ". . .something more."

An impish grin started to make an appearance on Ashley's face. "Like you and Frost wasn't complicated? I mean, the gunner and security crews are on the verge, you two barely get along, and he's a mess. Well, not just a mess, a *public* mess."

"Yeah, *that* was a mistake. I'm going to tell him next time he comes by my place. He'll probably be by to show off his new foot."

"And Captain?"

"We'll see I guess, I hope I didn't do any real damage. Hopefully we can get in touch with him so *Triton* can pick him and his passengers up. If not that question will have to wait a long time." Stephanie sat down and picked up her chopsticks again. "God, I'm hungry."

"We'll be coming out of hyperspace into some kind of mission then looping back to the rendezvous point in about ten hours. Alice hasn't posted the info yet," Ashley said after finishing a mouthful of dim sum.

"I like her, she's as tough as Jake and knows what she's doing."

"So do I, she's easy to talk to off duty too. Maybe she'd have a good bearing on what Captain's thinking, maybe she could even finish his sentence for him."

"Maybe. I'd still rather keep it between us though. Well, us and Price. I'm going to have to talk to him."

"I don't think he's told anyone, that's not like him."

"I know, still, I'd rather tell him it's okay he knows, just not to spread it around."

The pair finished eating in relative silence. They were just relaxing; Ashley slurping her lychee soda and Stephanie sipping a second cup of tea when she laughed quietly to herself. "How did we get here? I mean, you giving me advice, I'm usually the rough girl whose been through it giving you the wise word."

Ashley shrugged. "What comes around and all that I guess."

Rising

The cold steel table beneath the side of his face was a little wet. He was about to open his eyes and stopped moving. Jake wasn't in his vacsuit, but some kind of flimsy plastic jumpsuit. There were restraints around his ankles and wrists.

"...actual medal? I thought they just awarded those digitally now, you know, like on your file as a commendation," said a female voice very close to his ear.

"Nope, they're actually giving all three of them medals, blue and silver things with three spikes on them. They say they managed to organize a couple platoons worth of military bots and clear an entire island," said a male voice just a little further off.

He was in a small room, the chair beneath him was hard, and his wrist restraints were dangling free. All this he could tell easily without opening his eyes, without letting on that he was concious. *Hell no!* He thought to himself. *They are not going to put me in a God damned cell, not again! I won't spend weeks running on the spot and putting up with some cocksure interrogator breathing down my neck doing God knows what to me and anyone they set me up to feel sympathy for.* The rage building up in him increased his heart rate, threatened to increase his breathing, overtake the calm that made thinking at all possible. There were too many familiar things, the flimsy plastic suit, his bare feet on the hard, cold deck, even the smell of chemical disinfectant was exactly the same as he remembered from the *Overlord II*. The ship that held him captive in the Gai-Ian system so many years before as Jonas Valent.

The woman used nimble fingers to feel the metal restraints around his wrists and trace the hard cords up to the other end. There were loops under the table that he was about to be fastened to. He opened one eye a crack and saw her waist, her belt where all the tools of her trade hung.

"Hey, I think he's awake," said her male counterpart. He was standing just behind her.

Without a thought Jake grabbed the young woman's wrist, pulled down as hard as he could, slamming her head down against the metal table. His other hand snatched her sidearm out of its holster. The database of military hardware imprinted on him when he was first made included the VCD Standard Issue sidearm and he knew the safety was deactivated using the thumbprint of the user.

In the next instant he pressed her thumb down on the small pad, and the efficient biometric reader was able to take her print through her thin gloves. He dragged her into his lap and shot her in the knee before pressing the gun against her temple and partially pulling the trigger. "Don't move sweetheart, I already have every reason I need to kill you," Jake whispered into her ear through gnashed teeth.

Her male counterpart stared at him with his sidearm drawn and pointed at him. He looked like he was barely out of his teens.

"Look at my trigger finger, boy. I so much as twitch and she's gone."

"Don't move!" cried the soldier in retaliation. "Kill her and *you're* dead."

"They didn't tell you, did they? I'm a framework; blow my head off and it'll grow back. Try it, you won't get another chance." Jake moved his feet just enough to confirm that he was bound to the chair.

"We're treated with armour gel, you can take a shot and it won't kill her. So I can take my shot, you can take yours, she'll be fine and you'll wake up or regenerate or whatever in a cell."

There was no hesitation, no warning. Jake pulled the trigger. The sound of the pulse going off so close was nearly deafening, the heat from it burned his hand, but he didn't allow himself to show it. The scorched flesh was regenerating regardless.

The young soldier was right. They didn't need helmets, whatever gel they applied to their skin was protection enough.

"Can she take two shots?" Jake asked with a grin.

His captive's breathing came faster, her calm was completely broken. Her eyes were widened in a panicked expression. The creak of his finger putting very slight pressure on the trigger was audible only to Jake and his hostage.

"What do you want?" she asked quietly.

"Release my shackles for a start."

"Do it, Richard." she said, staring wide eyed at her partner.

"We'll both be put out of the service," he countered as he looked down the sight of his sidearm at Jacob. He was nervous, shaky.

"Do it, he'll kill us if you don't."

"Listen to the girl." Jacob confirmed ominously.

He brought up a small interactive holographic control using the back of his glove. It showed a perfect depiction of the room and as he touched the representations of the shackles around Jake's ankles, they snapped open and he pulled himself free.

"Now, my things. Where are they?"

"It doesn't matter, they're locking down the entire section."

"Where are they?" Jake persisted.

"Two compartments up from the interview room," answered his hostage.

Jake pulled a grenade free from his captive's vest and tossed it against the transparent steel mirror to his left. Before anyone could say anything he did the same with another.

"No!" shouted the guard training his weapon on Jake as he ran for the door.

Jake stood, hauling his captive with him, putting her between the grenades and himself. He jumped towards the door with reckless abandon, hurling himself in the direction of the other guard.

The grenades went off as the door opened, blasting him and the guards out into the corridor and surprising the four standing outside.

Jake rolled to his feet, the ringing in his ears fading fast and grabbed the nearest guard by the collar. He wasn't interested in more hostages, his trigger finger started working and didn't stop until that fresh guard from the hallway was falling to the ground.

He shot another several times in the face before he was fired upon. The rifle blast caught him in the back of his thigh and he fell to the ground turning so he landed on his back, half strewn across a corpse.

He could already feel the strange itch and burn as his framework body worked to repair the damage done as he brought his captured sidearm up firing at the soldiers who had their rifles unslung, ready to gun him down.

His energy blasts filled the air as one of the guards succeeded in shooting him in the stomach. His framework body was drawing on all the excess energy in the air, using it to recharge itself as it repaired wounds. The pain was incredible, but Jake could only focus on one thing; fighting his way free.

The last soldier died with an expression of disbelief on his ruined face.

The only one left alive was the soldier he'd taken hostage. She had taken shrapnel, one of her arms was barely hanging on, and her face was an open wound, but she breathed, she sputtered.

Jake's thigh was still healing, the wounds in his stomach were nearly unbearable, but he managed to roll over towards her and pull her emergency medical nanobot canister free from her vest and inject it into her neck. "You'll live, I'm sorry it had to happen the way it did," he said, looking into her one good eye. "I've been in a prison like this before, and I'll tear everything to pieces and kill everyone who gets in my way before I spend another minute inside."

The nanobots were already at work, she had stopped bleeding and her breathing was becoming more regular. His own healing process was going just as well. His leg was repaired and the pain in his torso had been muted. It was still there, but his body was blocking most of the pain as the injuries were under repair.

He stood up, looked down and hoped that it looked a lot worse than it was. The flimsy jumpsuit they'd put on him was burned away from his ribs to his pelvis, and there were three slowly closing holes surrounded by deep burns there. They were healing so quickly that the difference was visible from one second to the next.

Jake took in his surroundings. Dark metal polished decks, light grey walls and a two and a half meter tall ceiling clearance were the most notable features of the corridor. There was one door to his left and many to his right. Hurriedly he removed four grenades from a guard and ran a couple of doors down.

Looking back at the surviving soldier he could see many of her wounds were closed, her face had been mostly mended and she was staring at him. "This door leads to the equipment room?" he asked her.

She didn't answer.

He slowly brought up his stolen weapon, taking aim at her head.

"Yes," she managed to whisper.

Jake attached the grenades he'd stolen to the door, set all the timers to five seconds and ran back to the four corpses surrounding the woman. He rolled into place beside her and pulled a corpse into place to shield them from the force of the explosion.

He barely had time to pull another body into place before the grenades went off.

Again, his ears rang, his skin stung from the heat, but it all diminished quickly. When he rolled the bodies off he was satisfied that he and his former captive had been protected. The wounds in his stomach were healed and he had a feeling that his body was fully charged. That was all, a *feeling*. It was a new instinctive knowledge, like feeling hungry or full. He had the sensation that his framework skeleton had all the energy it needed and realized that since he could remember the feeling had been there, had gone unnoticed because it never changed.

With such grievous injuries to repair and such a great absorption of energy underway, the status of his cybernetic components were changing quickly, drastically, so it only made sense to him that that feeling would reflect it. Still, it was something new, an affirmation of how he was made, of his physical nature that was new, strange.

There was another feeling, something was changing in his hands, and after a moment he realized he could feel the status of the sidearm he was holding. It was charged to eighty six percent and had an active sighting eye.

Rolling to his feet he tried to see through that eye and realized that he was looking down the sight of the weapon at the same time as he saw the world through his own eyes. The electronic sighting eye wasn't as clear, it didn't feel as natural, but after he shook his head, caught his balance, he quickly became accustomed. *There's a digital interface in my palms. I don't understand half the data I'm sensing, but the visual and status readouts are as plain as day. The electromagnetic pulse bombs or healing process must have activated them. I wonder what else I have stuffed inside that I don't know about?*

He ran to the door he tried to blast open and saw that the top half had been roughly torn through by the concussive force. Jake hurriedly squeezed through the space and began searching through the hundred or so lockers within. They were marked with eight digit numbers and after randomly opening several he noticed that the number 44381-582 was etched into the sleeve of his tattered jumpsuit.

After a moment of searching he found the locker with the corresponding digits. His things were neatly set inside, each article separated into vacuum sealed plastic bags. The bag holding his sidearm had black and yellow markings across it, his vacsuit was folded at the bottom of the locker with his long coat, and his articles were sealed up all separately.

The first thing he did was unwrap a set of four focusable proximity mines. *Morons should keep munitions stored separately, every green to the bone security newbie knows that.* He took one, ran the few steps to the door, planted it on the outside pointed across the corridor and armed it.

He hurriedly dressed in his new armoured vacsuit, long coat, gun belt, and was half way finished loading up with the equipment and ammunition that had been removed from his long coat and sorted when he heard footsteps outside. He ducked and crouched down low, bringing his headpiece and visor into place just in time for the directionally focused mine to explode into the hallway.

Whoever had stepped in its way or was within its hundred and ten degree blast radius would be obliterated. The force behind the explosion had dented what was left of the metal of the door inward, but he was barely effected by the explosion.

He stood up and hurriedly replaced the rest of the equipment and small tools in the pockets of his long coat then took his favourite sidearm in his right hand and closed his eyes. Jake made a concious effort to connect with the sighting systems built into the scarred and worn weapon and could see through its eye a moment later. It was a higher quality than the weapon provided to the guards, and showed him a much better colour picture that had enough depth to be translated into holographic data if he liked. The sight once displayed an image on his visor, but having a direct connection was so much better.

His concentration turned to the sensors in his vacsuit. Motion, gravity, air density, environmental, thermal, video, audio, and energy field sensor data flooded his mind for a moment. It was all there at once. Like opening his eyes for the first time, learning to see, comprehending new shapes and information it was all too much.

Jake withdrew and tried to focus on the new senses one at a time. It happened much more easily, much faster than he had anticipated. The motion sense came first, a combination of air pressure, sonic and thermal senses, it told him that around the corner there was a fresh squad of six soldiers tentatively moving forward.

The gravity sensors told him their mass indicated they were all humans with no high density implants. The energy fields that surrounded them indicated where they each kept a pair of energy clips, how much ammunition each of their weapons were loaded with and that they were all communicating through a radio signal that looped through the ship's comm systems. It all came with perfect clarity, and when he opened his eyes the new senses weren't just seen or felt, they were a part of his awareness.

He tapped into the ship's communications systems effortlessly, using the open connection he sensed through the unsecured leisure portion of the network. The thought of being captured was still on his mind, the awareness that there were twenty seven decks beneath him and twenty two above and that he was over nine hundred meters of hallway away from the nearest escape vessel enraged him. Jake would have to fight to leave the ship, and even then the nearest craft available was unarmed, useless when trying to depart from the midst of a Battle Group. The ship he was on was called the *Diplomat*, and it was registered to the High Seat of the Order of Eden, Lister Hampon.

The whole situation made him burn. Jake opened a link between himself and the unsecured channel. "Don't stand between me and my freedom. If you are armed place your weapon on the deck in front of you and step away. If you are in control of a major system and I require access to your station, step back and do not interfere. If you don't follow my instructions you will be killed." He ended the broadcast and shut down the communications system built into his command and control unit so no one could back hack his system.

One of the squad members was approaching the large hole in the upper half of the door with a grenade in his hand. Jake activated the new, radiation free cloaking systems in his vacsuit and long coat, took three long strides to the door and waited.

225

The squad leader activated his grenade and tossed it into the doorway. Jake was ready, caught it, leaned outside and tossed it down the hall between the feet of the six soldiers. "I warned you," he said as he ducked behind what was left of the armoured door.

He set his sidearm to the maximum discharge rate, so it would fire enough explosive thermite to burn through half a meter of hardened hull material in less than two seconds. The weapon would only have thirty five shots per clip, but by his estimation he would miss less, and he had six more clips on him.

The grenade went off and for a few seconds half his new senses were blind. He shook his head and looked into the hallway.

Half the squad were killed by the blast, he could see all the indications of life fading away, their body heat dissipated the slowest of all. Without hesitation he stood, pulled himself out through the upper half of the doorway and strode down the hall to where he assumed the secondary lifts were, ignoring the three guards that were pulling themselves together and checking their fallen comrades.

He held his palm to the controls to the lift and tried to interface with them. As expected he was instantly aware of a security lockout. The entire section he was in was locked down. He wasn't an expert at breaking into digital security systems and that was a problem. After a moment he was able to pull up a general map of the area with emergency safety zones marked clearly. That was the best information he could find, and he spun on his heel and started running towards a security station.

Down several hallways, around several corners he rushed until his sensor package told him that there was a large group of soldiers just around the corner in a security office busied with the task of tracking him down.

To his dismay there was a slight difference in gravity and a vapour barrier conducting a small current just down the hallway. *They actually have a system in place that can detect when I cross that threshold while cloaked! I've never seen anything like it, but it's so simple. The vapour leaving the nozzles at the top is measured and if it doesn't match what's being pulled in through the bottom the alarms go off. If I find my way around that, the current being measured all around that water vapour will be off enough to alert them. If I were to find a way around that the gravity plating on the other side would measure a large difference as well. It's like what we accomplished on the Overlord Two with the early version of our cloaksuits made Hampon paranoid. Seriously paranoid! That's unless all Regent Galactic ships have anti-stealth technology surrounding command centers.*

He looked down the hallway, watched the security officers checking sensors at the outer perimeter and scrambling between two and three dimensional monitors to find him and tried to figure out a way to get to their systems without noticing. *If they have gravity plating that's monitoring pressure in there my cloak suit isn't worth a damn, and I can sense that there are thirty eight of them inside. Big office.*

Jake shrugged, drew a nanoblade hilt from its holster at the rear of his belt, set the blade to extend one meter and then drew his sidearm. The black blade appeared, a grisly triumph of nanotechnology. Turned one way it was invisible to the naked eye, comprised of millions of nanobots caught in a turning magnetic field it

226

was only a few molecules thick and would cut through anything softer than itself. The nanobots, aside from being sharper than any cutting surface known, would all work to push through whatever they came in contact with except for Jake's vacsuit. If they came into contact with materials harder than themselves they would cut into them quickly, but there were only so many nanobots in the hilts of the weapons, once they were exhausted, the weapon needed to be reloaded. He had only used one theoretically, in simulations and if the representation of the weapon's effects were at all accurate, it would be a very effective tool of intimidation.

He tapped into the leisure network for the ship once more. It was broadcasting an alert, displaying his image on every entertainment display on the ship. It didn't matter.

He began broadcasting what he saw across the ship's entertainment systems, deactivated the cloaking systems and activated the personal shield built into his vacsuit and long coat.

He became visible as he strode down the hallway to the security office. His black face plate, crimson and black long coat and armoured vacsuit were the focus of everyone who could see the open main doors to the security office.

"That's him!" shouted a desk clerk who ran for cover.

Jake opened fire. Looking down the sight of his heavy sidearm with his mind's eye he couldn't miss as he made three head shots in quick succession, ruining the first three guards who were caught in the open, just bringing their rifles to bear.

He crossed the threshold into the security office and was immediately hit with several heavy energy rounds from his left. Energy shield absorbed the damage, spreading the electrical component of the rounds across its surface and showing some weakening from the high velocity impact of white hot particles. Without looking he swung the nanoblade blade at head level. His gaze followed a second behind the strike, just in time to see the blade pass through the center of a guard's head from ear to ear. The gel they wore to protect them from extreme thermal damage did nothing to stop the weapon.

"Helmets! He's got a blade!" Called out one soldier as he ducked behind a cubicle.

The room was filled with partitions, rows of plastic cubicles for numerous security officers. They were using them for cover, a few took quick shots at him but missed as he strode right out in the open.

Jake concentrated on his thermal spectrum of vision so he could see right through the thin partitions and picked out a target who was getting ready to stand and fire, the shape and temperature of the soldier marked him as crouching in thick armour with a long rifle. He took quick aim and fired through the thin plastic partition five times. Screams filled the room as he picked another target who was standing to fire and shot him once in the neck and once in his open mouth.

As he was struck by another energy bolt and his personal shield was reduced to ten percent power. Jake darted across the room, turned, dropped behind the main security terminal beside an unarmed officer and took sight of the soldier who had shot him. The man was ready, just waiting for him to peek out. The officer right beside him stared open eyed, in utter shock.

227

"Get anyone unarmed into that corner, you have three seconds." Jacob instructed loudly, pointing towards the corner to his right.

The officer nodded and stood up only to be cut down by mistake by his own soldier.

"I tried," Jake said to himself, taking advantage of the opportunity by raising the barrel of his sidearm up onto the desk, looking through the video sight and taking several shots at the man's grey helmet. The first shot was resisted, the two that followed it broke through.

He took an energy clip from his trench coat pocket and jacked it into his control and command unit, mentally instructing his personal energy shield to drain the device and recharge. After two seconds it was done and Jake stood up.

Two soldiers were waiting. They fired through the thin walls of the cubicles, one caught him several times with his lower powered automatic energy rifle. It didn't make a difference. Jake could plainly see who was armed and who wasn't using his new senses. He ran forward, down the center aisle and ran his sword cleanly through a cubicle and the arm of the soldier behind it.

He trained his sidearm sight on the nearest soldier and he fired several times, breaking through his armour. Taking aim at another armed man he repeated the act and when the soldier hiding just behind him started taking aim at his back Jake was ready.

He spun on his heel and cut through the cubicle wall just under the woman's helmet, cutting through her throat. Jake followed through with a single shot to her helmet, flinging the woman's head back and opening the wound to gaping. Blood surged into the air. *What do I have to do to intimidate these people into surrendering?* Jake thought to himself as self disgust threatened to overtake him.

As if in direct answer to his notion, two soldiers stood up and flung their rifles to the ground. "Surrender! We surrender!"

Jake trained his sidearm on the nearest of the two soldiers and set it to full automatic. "Open this section and let me out on the port side of the ship."

"I can't, they'll execute me for that."

Jake squeezed the trigger for less than a second and five shots struck the man's upper breastplate. The first three rounds didn't penetrate all the way through, the last two opened great gaping, flaming wounds inside the man's ribcage. The sparking fire and smoke from the thermite rounds flared from the large wounds as he fell to the deck and for several minutes after.

Jake's aim was immediately brought to bear against the other guard, who nodded. "Let me go with you."

"Do you have the codes and clearance I'll need to get off the ship?"

"Yes, I have my own codes and my Lieutenant's."

"Good, get to work." Jake directed, slowly gesturing towards the large security control booth in the center of the room. "The rest of you get out of here! Anyone left in this room besides me and my new friend will be killed!" he caught sight of a soldier hiding several meters behind him start standing up, brandishing his rifle.

Jake spun, took aim with his sidearm and just as the soldier got his first shot

228

off he killed him with the last three rounds in his thermite clip. He clicked the release, let the clip fall to the ground and put the weapon behind his back, where the loader inside his long coat fed a fresh clip into the weapon.

"Now, where were we?" Jake asked the soldier who had volunteered to help him escape.

As the unarmed security office workers and surrendered soldiers hurriedly left the room, lockouts across the center of the command carrier started to come down.

Riding The Needle

None of them ever thought they would see the inside of a rail cannon. The deck and repair crew had pointed one of the planetary cannons so it was aimed over the surface of the island. To everyone inside the *Needle* it looked like their trajectory would take them between two of the largest buildings.

A near miss at that speed has to have repercussions. Oz found himself thinking. "How long are they taking the shield down for?" He asked over the sound of the capacitor coils humming at the base of the cannon. The electromagnetic field was building up all around the long cylindrical ship.

"A little less than a quarter second. More than enough time to get through at the speed we'll be moving," Ayan replied as she checked the inertial dampeners using her command and control unit. It was tied into the ship with well insulated wires, so there would be no chance that any jamming or wireless signals could interfere. "The dampeners are all ready," she told Minh, who sat ahead of her at the main flight controls.

"Are you *sure* that's enough time?" Oz asked.

Jason chuckled and shook his head.

"The math is solid, it's more than enough," Ayan answered.

"You know, I used to watch a cartoon with a monkey and a panda. The panda loaded the monkey into a cannon once, and until now I thought that cartoon was hilarious," Minh said just loudly enough for everyone inside the small craft to hear. "That episode isn't quite so funny now."

"I'm guessing it didn't end well for the monkey?" Jason asked.

"Monkey all over the place."

"You know, I think of it more like sky luge. We're all lined up in a relatively thin shell, have one pilot, and the only thing we have for control are brakes," Jason commented, knowing he was only making Oz more nervous. "Biiiiig flaming breaks." He was so frightened he was about to start shaking as well, but torturing Oz made him feel better somehow.

"It's not too late to do this the hard way, you know, with refurbished tanks and soldiers and the biggest guns we can find," Oz offered.

"It is too late, the cannon's fully charged, count down is down to fifteen seconds, oops, fourteen, thirteen. . ." Minh teased as he took a firm grip on the controls.

Everyone braced themselves, the sound of the inertial dampeners whining at their highest setting and the rail cannon building an intense magnetic field around them filled the small cabin. Before anyone but Minh was ready they launched. Even with the intense inertial control field inside the cabin, everyone was pressed into the backs of their steel frame seats. Their vacsuits protected their hearing from the sonic boom that erupted as they erupted from the barrel.

Then there was relative silence. The sound of air moving over the sleek pointed shell and the hum of the inertial dampeners running were almost soothing. The night sky above was filled with stars, and a strange, momentary serenity settled over the four of them.

The *needle* flipped upside down, all the crew members but Minh-Chu watched the city below go by in a dizzying blur. They missed some of the taller rooftops by what seemed only meters. "Pull up!" Oz called from the rear seat.

"No one likes a back seat driver!" Minh replied through clenched teeth. "Deceleration thrusters in three! Two! One!"

Ayan pulled two levers above her head hard and the afterburners from the *Warpig* fired, filling the forward view with thick smoke and flame. Everyone was slammed into their restraints as the ship began decelerating from its incredible speed. Minh expertly guided the path of the tiny speeding ship between the two largest buildings. Transparesteel windows broke free of their fastenings, parts of the structures were torn apart and scattered across several city blocks of the city below as the fireball passed.

"Oh God," Jason whimpered.

"Don't worry, we're on course," Ayan called over her shoulder, not sounding nearly as sure as Jason and Oz would have liked.

The thunderous sound of the large afterburners mounted on the front end of the ship increased in pitch and the inertial dampeners whined even louder as they struggled to compensate for the gravitational forces being exerted on them. "We've hit the loose pack fuel! I don't see the landing zone yet!" Minh yelled.

"It's coming up, right on the other side of the spaceport," Ayan answered.

"It better be, or they pointed us in the wrong direction!"

The large spaceport passed underneath just then, they had slowed enough so it wasn't just a large, round grey blur, but a more well detailed complex of landing bays, debarkation and embarkation ramps. Half a second later they were over an extensive sugar cane field.

"Should we be upside down?" Asked an alarmed Oz.

"Hold on, we're hitting!" Minh warned as he flipped three switches in sequence. As he hit the third the needle was engulfed by flame as the last of the fuel in the afterburners was expended in a massive burst. Something exploded inside the cockpit, showering them with sparks the instant before they hit the ground.

The vessel dug into the earth and all light turned to darkness as the ship careened through the field filled with green sugar cane stalks, leaving a trial of deeply turned black soil in its path. The night was alive with the sounds of violent explosions and the rumble of the ship coming to a halt seconds after impact.

The four of them hung upside down in their restraints, each of them checking for injuries. Despite the sounds and explosions, the impact had been very mild for the passengers. "I'm all right," Oz said in the relative silence.

"Me too, not a scratch," Jason replied.

"I'm okay, don't ever want to do anything like that again, but I'm okay,"

Ayan said quietly.

"I think I peed a little," Minh said as he reached to something between his feet and pulled it sharply. "Thank God for indoor plumbing." A loud pop filled the air and a bottom plate just in front of his seat flipped outward so he could push himself out through the bottom of the ship.

"We really were supposed to land upside down?" Jason said in astonishment.

"That explains why the exit hatches are set up in the bottom of the craft," Oz agreed as he pulled his own handle. "Didn't make much sense before but I was afraid to ask."

"It was the only way. The transparesteel we scrounged up was the strongest metal on this thing, so we had to make it the impact side," Ayan explained.

"Sort of counter intuitive." Minh said as he helped Oz out of the craft. The gravity from the inertial dampeners still pointed to the bottom of the vehicle, so it was easy for them to get through the bottom hatch to the waist, but then the gravity from the planet had hold of them, trying to push the majority of their bodies back inside.

After Oz finished extracting himself from the craft he moved on to help Jason, whose legs were fully out of the ship's egress hatch. Minh helped Ayan and when they were all out, they pulled the plate of metal on the back of the ship away, revealing the packs each of them were to carry along with long coats for all but Ayan, who preferred her longer poncho. All their extra clothing was made with a higher density than their vacsuits, providing extra armour while sharing the same capabilities.

"You know, I've never worn the finished version of a cloaksuit before," Ayan mentioned.

"I have, they're amazing. They don't do much for us in this field unless we stay between the rows though," Jason commented as he finished putting his long coat on over his slim, long equipment pack. He checked his sidearm and the nanoblade they'd have to use instead if they wanted to remain undetectable.

"When did you get to wear one?" Oz asked as he secured his heavy rifle across his chest.

"On a couple little runs for Fleet Intelligence, maybe once the *Triton* gets here I'll fill you in and bust open a couple Freeground secrets."

"What blew when we hit by the way?" Asked Minh.

"One of the inertial dampeners, I expected at least one of the four I installed to go," Ayan answered nonchalantly.

"How many redundant dampeners did we have?"

"One, we needed at least three to come down without a scratch."

"Well, looking at what's left of the ship, anyone might think that there were no survivors," Oz said, looking at the beat up hull. One of the afterburners had been ripped off, left behind in the field somewhere along the scar they had made on the rows of sugar cane. The other looked like a torn and crushed up box of metal, half torn from the main body of the ship. The vessel itself was dented in several places where the transparesteel joined the main body.

"It's almost too bad we have to use it as a trap," Ayan said as she activated her cloaksuit. She disappeared from sight completely, even her footfalls were silent and invisible, covered and wiped away by compensation systems built into her boots.

Everyone else followed her example, the display in their vacsuit visors made up for the darkness of night and showed an outline of each of the cloaksuit users. They would no longer communicate audibly, instead their messages would be sent via millisecond laser pulses outside of the normally visible spectrum of light. Secrecy and stealth still demanded that they keep such traffic down to an absolute minimum, especially since a great number, if not the majority of their opponents were machines that could see more of the colour spectrum than an average human.

Oz took up point as they heard a machine start in the distance and rustle the sugar cane stalks. They made their way at a slow jog down one of the rows leading to the broadcast center in the middle of the field. It was marked clearly by several focusing dishes and burst transmitters, all pointed at the stars like wide white concave eyes surrounded by long antennae like multicoloured rods.

Behind them several objects were making their way to their ship and once they had put a kilometre between them and the craft, Oz slowed to a stop. When he turned around his targeting system outlined a large machine and several smaller ones. Two were identified as automated security, one was some kind of technical assistant and there were several small maintenance bots.

"What do you think the big one is?" he heard Minh ask over their point to point network.

"Some kind of harvester," Ayan answered. "They had them on the Freeground colony, or at least something that kinda looked like it."

"Will the charges take it out?" Oz asked.

"Just barely, unless there's some solid fuel left in the afterburner. I'm blowing it," Ayan said as she pointed her index finger at the hull of the ship.

As soon as her signal was received the *Needle* exploded, filling the air with concussive sound, lighting up the field and the sky with blue and yellow light and sending a wave through the green rows of sugar cane.

"Guess there was some fuel left," Minh chuckled.

Oz scanned the ground for movement for several seconds and paid close attention to the sensors in his suit just in case there was some energy left in one of the robots that had gone to investigate the crash. "We got 'em, time to move on."

A Bug In The Works

"We've cut off the feed sir, but anyone looking at the entertainment systems aboard saw the first two minutes and nineteen seconds of the assault," said the wide eyed internal data management officer.

The command chair on the bridge of the *Diplomat* was always a source of irritation for Hampon. It was far too large, his feet didn't touch the deck, and people stared when he wasn't looking. He didn't take the opportunity to command in person often, but when he heard that Jacob Valance had gotten free he dropped everything and headed straight for the command chair.

"Why did it take so long?"

"His interface, it was different somehow. It looked a bit like a direct neural connection to the ship."

"Where is he now?"

"He just cut through a security door using one of our own plasma torches," the officer reported, looking up and meeting his eye for the first time in days. She had been serving on the circular bridge for months, and managed to suppress the smile he knew she had every time she saw him.

"How did he get a high powered plasma torch?"

"One of our maintenance staff surrendered it when the escapee threatened his life. We have the maintenance worker in custody now."

"Because taking *him* into custody will solve *all* our problems," Hampon muttered. He brought up the holographic list of damage and casualties incurred as Jake made his way though the command carrier. The sheer magnitude of it was staggering; the man was equipped to wage a one man war and Lister knew that a good part of that was thanks to the years of experience he had in the field as a bounty hunter and equipment from the *Triton*. "We only have ourselves to blame," he sighed as he established a link to his best security officer. "Captain Fornier, have four teams of your best men go on a hunt for Jake Valance. You are to force him off the ship and kill anyone you find with him. Make sure that there is no doubt in his mind that you're trying to kill him, use live rounds and every measure you'd normally use to neutralize a dangerous escapee. The faster this is accomplished the better. We have over two hundred fifty thousand new initiates aboard, he must not be allowed to spook them or we will have a nightmarish mess to clean up. Or rather, *you* will be left to clean it up. Do you understand?"

The Captain saluted, her steel blue eyes were steady and devoid of emotion as she acknowledged him. "I'll lead a team myself. You do realize that there is a high chance of fatality using live rounds."

"Yes, thank you for reminding me," He rolled his eyes and glowered at the

Captain, an expression he was sure would have more weight if he didn't look like he was ten years old. "If you kill him by mistake I'll dock your staff one week's pay. You have two hours, then I'll have to put some kind of escalated measure into place and you will be fired."

Here's hoping we can keep track of him once he lands on Pandem. Hampon thought to himself as he cut the transmission and turned his attention back to the most important thing on his mission screens. The preparation for deployment of the West Watcher army on the planet below.

He brought up the holographic display of the First Battle Group and it filled his field of view. Tank divisions, ground command vessels and hundreds of dropships, fighters and picket ships were preparing to launch from every carrier in the fleet, all bound for the green and blue planet below.

THE LITTLE THINGS

Jake Valance's arm unit finished downloading the maps and medium priority security command codes to his control unit nearly instantaneously. "Thanks, now get to a safe place, I don't suggest trying to get away in an escape pod, they'll cut you to pieces," he said to the officer through his comm unit. Without his guidance Jake wouldn't have been able to avoid most of the teams searching for him.

"I'm going to the planet with the West Keeper army. They won't notice me if I head to the dropship loading area. That's the surest way off."

Jake stopped and looked at the smaller fellow. "How far off is that?"

"Nine decks down and three sections over, but not too hard to get to," he replied, half smiling.

"It's an invasion army?"

"Yes."

Jake thought for a moment, looking down the long berth hall. There were three directions; the nearest exit as instructed by his collaborator who had done far more than he had to to help him. There was the bridge, where he might get a chance at taking his revenge on Lister Hampon for everything he'd put Jonas and himself through. The last direction off the ship made the most sense to him; the main launch bay, where he might be able to slip through the service crawl ways and maintenance rooms to a ship or escape shuttle.

"You're him, aren't you? *The* Captain Valance, the one who frees slaves and captures Regent Galactic ships."

"That's me," Jake said after a moment's pause. "Though I'm pretty sure my reputation is just a bit inflated."

"Your chances of sneaking off this ship aren't good as long as you're wearing that armour. You should drop it and find a spare uniform in one of those crew quarters you're passing. The dropships are loading so fast they probably wouldn't notice you."

He's right. If I try to blend in like one of the crowd I'd have a chance as long as someone doesn't recognize me and point me out. We're not actually that far from the Enreega system, not far enough to be away from all the Newsnet affiliates, anyway. Even if I don't get pointed out, I'm definitely in the facial recognition database as Jonas. "I'll get off ship somehow, don't worry. Thanks for your help. Don't get caught. Oh, and why are you helping me anyway?"

"Let's just say a lot of Regent Galactic Officers think this Order of Eden cult is a great big steaming pile. Good luck out there." The soldier said before cutting communications.

Jake didn't waste any more time, but ran for the open door facing the stern and straight on to the nearest lift. Using the authorization code he had been given he was able to unlock it. He activated his cloaking systems and waited for the car to arrive. He was well past the vapour barrier and the gravity plating. The deck layout information he had made it clear that the only areas guarded by those security measures were command and security hubs.

He stepped to the side as the lift doors began to open. Several canisters were thrown into the hallway intersection and Jake immediately turned and ran for a side passage. It was too late. The canisters exploded with loud successive *pops* and his sensor suite told him that his headpiece, long coat, boots and gloves had been coated with acid. The coating on his vacsuit quickly neutralized it, but not before half of his cloaking systems were either too badly damaged to be useful or destroyed altogether.

The elevator doors finished opening and eight soldiers moved into the hallway with quick, easy efficiency. These weren't normal security guards, they were heavily armoured and carried rifles that fired explosive rounds.

He spun around and dropped a shield puck on the deck, it affixed itself and started projecting a blue green barrier of energy two meters high and one and a half meters across. It was a piece of technology Laura and Ayan had pressed into service through the Special Projects Division after it was captured from a Vindyne soldier.

The first shots were stopped completely by the energy shield, and the enemy soldiers took cover around the corner. Jake pulled a belt of four stolen grenades from his inside coat pocket, armed them, tossed the bunch and dove around the corner. The three second fuse counted down and nothing happened.

How the hell did they deactivate the whole belt of grenades? He managed to ask himself as he watched the whole belt sail over the top of the energy barrier. Jake scurried to his feet and made a mad dash for the side corridor.

He barely made the next corner before they exploded. The concussive force knocked him off his feet, but he managed to avoid the brunt of the blast. Jake was on his feet and running again, and as he took the next corner his thermal and movement detection sensors picked up four soldiers ahead. They were the same grade of plated combat armour, carrying the same heavy assault rifles, and they were flanking the next hallway.

"God dammit!" he cursed to himself. He made sure his sidearm was set to full intensity and full automatic as he drew it out of its holster and pulled one of his own grenades from its secure pocket. He activated his personal energy shield, noting that it was down to seventy three percent and stopped dead in his tracks. Instead of rolling his fragmentation grenade along the floor he set the fuse to detonate on impact and tossed it hard towards the wall up ahead.

Jake crouched down to the ground, turned and covered himself with his long coat. The hot air and debris from the blast washed over his energy shield and long coat without harming him. His visor display informed him that the shield he had erected around the corner had depleted and was destroyed. The soldiers he had left behind were coming.

He rose and ran towards the hall that had just been filled with shrapnel and fire. The life signs of the soldiers there were fading fast.

Stepping around them gingerly, he headed down the hall in a dead run, straight back to the lift doors. They were jammed open with a wedge, he could see it, and the soldiers who had come up were still coming after him the long way. *Part of my cloaking systems must be working, otherwise they'd see me coming around on thermal or motion sensors.* Jake thought to himself.

The group had left one soldier inside the elevator car, a smart gambit he almost didn't see in time. His motion detection systems weren't as keen as they should have been, most likely because of either the acid or explosions he'd been almost too close to, and the outline a soldier waiting at the rear of the express car appeared on his visor at the last instant.

Jake panicked and let loose with his handgun on full automatic, peppering the soldier and the walls around him with rounds. The trooper slumped to the ground. Jake cursed under his breath at emptying half a clip into the man, the job could have been done with four or five shots. He kicked the wedge out of the doors and requested a level far beneath. With some satisfaction Jake watched the squad double back at speed towards the lift he'd stolen, they almost reached the doors in time to get a clear shot and he could hear their heavy rounds pierce the doors above as the lift car accelerated down to the hangar deck.

Without a second to spare he picked up the body of the fallen trooper and held it up in front of him, it was heavy, the man and armour together must have weighed over a hundred fifty kilos. He pushed through the strain on his arm and focused, levelling his sidearm at the doors where he could see thermal traces of more lightly armoured soldiers outside waiting.

He took aim at the guard with the clearest shot and fired before the lift car finished coming to a slow stop. The round made it through, and the thermal image burst in colours of yellow, red and blue telling him that the soldier leading that charge was dead or dying.

The group of five soldiers arranged in a semicircle around the lift doors opened fire and Jake managed to kill two before he took a round straight on in the shin. His armoured vacsuit took most of the impact but the bone behind his armour shattered and he fell in a howling heap on the floor of the lift car.

He fired at the last visible guard while the other one sought cover just beside the lift doors and caught him in the left shoulder. His framework body went to work, regenerating the bone and tissue of his shin. *A little late with the nerve blocking!* Jake thought to himself as pain coursed up his leg. There was no numbing of the pain that time, and he barely heard the clink of a grenade through the agony.

His vision went black, the other sensors built into his vacsuit flared then began to reset and his hearing was completely blocked. It took him a moment to realize what had happened. *They used a flashbang grenade! They're afraid of damaging the elevator!* He couldn't help but chuckle to himself as the pain from his shin began to subside, and his visor's light reactive shielding cleared just in time for him to see one soldier break cover.

His mind's eye watched through his gun sight camera as his arm came up and lined up a shot that hit the young woman full on in the face. The guards on the forward hangar deck weren't wearing helmets, just the protective gel that seemed to be a favourite with the crew of the *Diplomat*. She was dead the instant the round hit her.

"Surrender now!" Jake cried out as he got to his feet and rolled out of the elevator car. He came up on his knees with a perfect shot lined up at a wounded soldier who had taken refuge beside the lift doors. He dropped his rifle, nodding with clenched teeth. Jake could hear the thermite still burning in the man's shoulder. He was lucky, a few centimetres to the right or down and it would have burned straight through his lung. The wounded soldier tried to flinch away as Jake leaned forward and injected him in the neck with a cocktail of emergency pain killers using his command and control unit. The look of surprise on the soldier's face faded as he passed out and Jake couldn't help but look at the others who weren't as lucky. The thermite in some of their wounds was still flaring, sending out shocks of smoke and colour. *I'm starting to think I should have taken my chances in an escape shuttle. These people would still be marching around guarding a quiet storage hangar if I didn't take the long way.*

The sub-hangar deck had been cleared of all non-critical personnel and as he scanned the large area he could see the thermal outlines of two squads making their way to the main hold through a maze of ladders, loading platforms, and elevation pads. *Funny, two months ago I wouldn't even wonder if there was something I could say to stop this firefight from breaking out and now that I've got the conscience I'm at a loss for words. A better man would give up and let himself be put in a cell, but I've been there and I'm not going back.* At long last he spotted his ship. It was just behind a small, streamlined high priority courier ship that hid all but the nose of the Uriel fighter. "Good to see the directions that security officer gave me were spot on, I was starting to wonder," he said to himself as he dove into an access trench, the closest squad of soldiers were taking up positions just on the other side of one of the main hangar doors. He checked his command unit to see if there was any link to his fighter.

With a smile he powered the vessel up and checked to see if both fusion reactors were ready for operation. They were. The deck crew had locked down the thruster pods with restraint rods and disconnected its faster than light systems but they hadn't done anything to disable main power.

He tried to access the ship entertainment network but found himself locked out entirely. Jake opted for the volume enhancement system built into his visor instead and jacked it all the way up so the oncoming soldiers and whoever else was in range could hear him. "On board my fighter are two nuclear fusion power plants! Allow me to take a ship down to the planet or I will detonate the reactors! I will *not* allow myself to be captured!"

"It is so good to see you Mister Valentine. I wasn't sure we'd get a chance to speak after you escaped holding," said the familiar, self assured voice of Lister Hampon.

"I can't say the same."

"Cordial as usual. Below you is are a series of quick access drop pods. One of them will take you directly to the planet if you like. I have no need to capture you, in fact I don't truly have a desire to see you killed. There are greater things underway, things you could not change, not even while using the *First Light*, or the *Samson,* or

239

even the *Triton*. I don't have time to toy with old familiar pets."

"Even after all these years you still love the sound of your own voice."

"And you still have a habit of being in the wrong place at the wrong time. In the end you don't matter. That refined framework technology, one of a kind I'll grant you, doesn't matter when you compare it to the power we have over the Order of Eden and the Eden Fleet. We have what we need from you already, I procured it as soon as we pried you from your fighter. It is a new war Jonas. You should take a moment to decide which side you're on before you leave the ship."

There were questions he wanted to ask, grudges he wanted to settle, and a fleeting thought that there might be just a chance, if ever so slim that he could put an end to the war if he could find his way to the command deck and kill Hampon himself. Then he regained his senses.

"I'll leave," Jake said as he closed the channel. A red indicator came up on his visor and he focused his attention there for a moment. *He was using a voice disguiser? So it wasn't the real Hampon? Why would anyone go to the trouble to gloat for him?* He shook his head. *Why bother figuring it out, I just need to get the hell out of here before those soldiers are given the order to rush in with guns blazing. Someone's holding them back, like they want me to leave.* "Who am I to argue?" he muttered to himself with a shrug.

He increased the reaction rate of his fighter's fusion power plants to near critical and he could see the thermal outlines of the squads falling back. *A lot of good that'll do you.* Jake thought to himself with a snicker.

The rear hangar was clearing out and through a transparent bay door he could see the frenzy of activity as larger drop ships were being prepared for takeoff. A medical team emerged from a lift to his right and he waved them through as he got to his feet, watching them warily regardless.

"We're just here to help," said one of the emergency workers with an upraised hand.

"Don't give me a reason to think otherwise and we'll all be happy," Jake said as he strode towards his fighter. It was set down beside another vessel that didn't match the surroundings, a beat up interplanetary passenger transport.

"Vacsuit re-sealed." said a voice in his ear. It was his command and control unit announcing that the hole that was made when he was shot in the shin was once again secure, the vacsuit material had come together to form a seal safe for space. "Good timing." Jake said to himself as he looked the Uriel fighter over.

He climbed into the cockpit and armed the guns. The bars holding the ship in place had been extended across the four lower engine pods and he hoped the fighter would stay together as he increased power to the engines. The canopy was just starting to close and his vacsuit headpiece partially muted the screeching of the metal restraint rods as his fighter strained against them and won free.

One of the engine pods was pulled slightly out of alignment and the fighter's status screen blinked yellow several times as it recalibrated its new position with the control systems.

Without a second thought Jake guided the fighter down into the launch bay, scraping the bottom of the fighter against the deck before descending into an open elevation pit. He tried to guide the ship between two larger, more heavily armed troop carriers and managed to barely avoid a collision with the main rear hatch of one of them.

The fighter shot through the atmosphere retention field, leaving the command carrier behind. He flipped the fighter upside down and to his relief he could see Pandem. The view from where he sat was serene, and if he didn't know it was an actively contested world he would have thought that it was paradise. They were on the night side, but his visor corrected for the darkness and after a few seconds it was as though he was looking at the planet under the full light of the sun. the blue ocean was dotted with green and gold islands, white clouds drifted lazily through the atmosphere and on the larger land masses he could see the glint and gleam of great cities surrounded by green woods, like diamonds surrounded by emeralds set in gold.

He set the self destruct system on the fighter and brought up the shields just in time. Several of the anti-starfighter batteries aboard the *Diplomat* began firing on him, one striking the ship several times. *So much for Hampon not going out of his way to kill me.*

The pulse weapons were effective, too effective. His shields were down to forty three percent before he found what he was looking for.

"I promise to never question who I am, what my name should be or which personality I should put on in the morning ever again if this works," he said to the Gods as much as to himself as he activated the ejection system.

He was launched with incredible force straight for the planet's atmosphere. He felt naked, bare as he watched the blue ocean and brown-green land beneath grow nearer. He tried to see through the bottom of his small thermally shielded pod, and couldn't. Using his new found connection to his command and control unit he checked his distance from the fighter and it's status.

Its shields were down to eleven percent and he was already over a thousand kilometres away. He watched the counter:

SHIELDS: 11%	DISTANCE: 1300km
SHIELDS: 9%	DISTANCE: 4200km
SHIELDS: 6%	DISTANCE: 7300km
SHIELDS: 1%	DISTANCE: 9800km

Then he detonated the pair of fusion reactors on the fighter. He could see the flash even though he was looking in the opposite direction, over ten thousand kilometres away and just about to enter the atmosphere. "You should have killed me when you had the chance Hampon!" Jake cried out in the near null space of the protective pod.

It had a hard, protective layer, rudimentary emergency gravity compensators and an antigravity booster for when it was time to touch down. He had made his target the foot of the mountain in Damshir. As he began to burn into the atmosphere his visor blocked the bright light. *Wouldn't it just be the worst if it all ended here? If I became just another shooting star, matter burned up in the sky?* He caught himself

241

thinking. "Think positive, think positive, think positive," he repeated to himself hurriedly as a last minute mantra.

He couldn't help but laugh to himself as he cleared the upper atmosphere and began free falling through the clear dark sky. Then his visor flashed and brought up a transmission. Where Hampon's face had once been was a black striped and brown furred nafalli. "My name is Alaka Murlen, I am one of the freedom fighters in Damshir. To my knowledge the mountain in which I am recording this message contains the last free intelligent beings on the planet. A virus has infected most of our machines and we are under siege. On behalf of the last remaining inhabitants and defenders of this world, I beg the Carthan government to send help. I expect from the military we have seen landing on this island that there must be an enemy fleet in orbit. Come prepared, come well armed and bring as many allies as you can before we and this entire solar system are lost to an enemy we have come to know as the West Keepers."

The transmission ended. "Well, here's to the power of positive thinking," he chuckled to himself as he watched the altimeter along the bottom of his heads up display countdown. At ten thousand feet he felt the pod adjust his course.

The dark cityscape rushed up faster and faster, and at two thousand meters the automated system, a very small computer built into the pod, announced; "primary deceleration system failure, prepare for contingency."

The pod split down the center and Jake was released into the open air. He felt naked, helpless, and was near panic as he looked between his legs to see buildings and streets rushing up towards him. The sound of the air whistling by was louder than anything and he tried not to stare at the altimeter display on his visor as a thought occurred to him; *I don't think I heard the emergency systems hook the emergency parachute onto my vacsuit.* "Oh fu-"

He was interrupted and jarred from head to toe violently as a parachute launched from his back and was caught by the air. The ground was still approaching faster than anyone would have liked, but he was slowing. The mountain with its step like face came into view. There were places there that were utterly destroyed by heavy shelling. The building faces set into the side looked hollow, dead as the looked down the side. The ones from the middle and top still had lights on, most of them were mostly intact. Light in front of the façades was distorted, as though by a protective shield.

He was still slowing, and finally there was no more time to slow down as he struck a transit tube suspended between two buildings, cartwheeled awkwardly through the air and hit the street hip first. The streets were filled with pocked and bullet ridden machines and corpses laying out in the open.

The thin material of the parachute covered him and after a minute he rolled over, found his way out from under the material and ran for the nearest broken, abandoned building as the rain started to fall.

242

COMMUNICATIONS

Compared to the tall transmission towers and broad dishes pointed up at the sky that hung overhead like massive upside down umbrellas, the entrance to the underground communications management bunker was a tiny feature. There was a small landing area for personal craft in front, but other than that they were in the middle of the sugar cane field, the tall green stalks stretched out as far as the eye could see.

In the light of day the dishes were just transparent enough to permit light to pass through, and the nearest shadow was Damshir Spaceport, several kilometres away. "I'm amazed that growing sugar like this is much more economical than using a mass production materializer," Ayan remarked as they settled in at the edge of the landing field. There were two personnel carriers made for carrying several people apiece. The driver's side door to one had been ripped off, the single occupant long dead.

There were a few other personal carriers, and only one armoured law enforcement transport. "Naturally grown sugar is a delicacy, most of the residents here can't afford it," Jason replied as they all quietly observed the clearing for signs of movement.

"That police craft could be useful," Minh pointed out. "Looks like it's got a couple guns too."

"Pretty obvious. It might get us somewhere fast, but if anything on the ground wants to shoot it down it could be more trouble than it's worth," Oz replied.

"Let's make it part of our escape plan, just in case."

"Okay, if we find the andies that are responsible for it and can take them out, *then* we'll consider it. From what Alaka says they're linked to all their gear somehow and the signal jamming doesn't effect them."

"I wonder how they managed that?" Jason asked himself more than anyone in particular. "Everything but a few encrypted military bands are jammed."

"They've got a lot of toys here that we've never seen before. Speaking of which, I don't see any guards out front," Ayan said. "Let's split into pairs and circle."

"Good idea," Oz said as he and Jason stepped onto the edge of the gravel landing area and they started walking the edge to the right.

Ayan and Minh started in the other direction. "Alone at last," Minh teased as they made their way around slowly, watching carefully for any stationary guardians. It was eerie, robotic combatants could remain perfectly motionless, had infinite patience and hold ready infinitely. It was like looking for deadly shadows. "Did you mange to pry any info about what they're protecting in that mountain vault of theirs?" he continued.

"Nope, and I tried. It looked like Roman wanted to tell me at one point too, but he kept it to himself. I did catch one thing though; he's not from here. I heard some of his men talking and he arrived just a couple weeks before the virus. They said he was part of internal police security. I don't think he's just a Sergeant."

"I could see that, he seems more military than anything. I'm surprised he and Alaka let us take this objective on so quickly, it's like Roman wanted us out of the mountain."

"Alaka didn't seem so glad to see us go. I think he was happy to have our help holding the tunnels. Not that he needed our help with strategy on that front, but then, he was hunting rim weasels for a living before all this started," Ayan chuckled lightly. "Who'd have thought that would be the perfect training for tunnel fighting?"

"Explains why he knows his way around so well. Rim weasels get everywhere, I've even heard that they can squeeze through a hole only a centimetre wide."

"We found a couple on a bounder when I was serving on my first deep space tour."

"One of those old short range shuttles? That had to make for a fun cleanup."

"Yeah, I spent a week with the rest of the juniors cleaning out that thing, I barely saw outside it. The weasels ate half the wiring insulation in the whole craft, I swear."

"Sometimes I miss those old ships with all the wiring tucked away behind panels, the fuzzy and carpeted surfaces everywhere. It's more like being in a living room."

"They're a pain in the ass to get anything fixed in though. Strange that Rim weasels won't go near the carpet but they'll chew on anything else. Makes you wonder if there's something dodgy about whatever the pads are made of."

"Never thought of it like that, huh." Minh said pensively.

They quieted down and focused as they came around the rear of the bunker, their sensor suites outlined distinct shapes for them in the darkness of night. The metal double doors were only slightly smaller than the front entrance, and these had a short set of stairs going down to them. The outline showing where Minh, still invisible to the naked eye, signalled for Ayan to stop. His head was turned towards the entrance, so Ayan carefully looked everywhere else. "What is it?" she asked quietly even though their vacsuits stopped all sound from escaping.

"Two andies down those stairs. They're exactly the same temperature as their surroundings so thermal missed them completely."

"Nice trick. My motion sensors didn't pick them up either, they must be on standby."

"Think they'd see through our cloaksuits?" Minh asked quietly.

"No way, you'd need some kind of field or pressure sensors and that's pretty much impossible to tune properly in this atmosphere."

"That's reassuring."

Ayan's vacsuit highlighted Oz and Jason coming around from the other side of the landing area a hundred meters away, they were moving very slowly. Her visor display indicated that they were in proper line of sight and she could communicate with them again using the laser link. "Do you two see the androids down there?"

"Yup, just spotted them. I'm thinking I'll launch a shaped charge at the door while everyone else opens fire on the andies. We're going to have to dump half a clip into those two to take them out."

"Are they seriously that well armoured?" Ayan asked.

"Someone didn't do their homework," Minh teased.

"I was busy designing the *Needle*, remember?"

"She's not the only one, I was working on the broadcast system the whole time," Jason interjected. "I could use a quick brief on 'em."

"Right," Oz started, taking command of the conversation. "They're an android with sixteen processing centers, so even though they look like humans there's actually no central brain. You can knock their head off they'll still see perfectly fine thanks to secondary and tertiary sensors."

"Wow, sounds expensive," Minh commented.

"Effective, more like. We seriously have to slag these buggers to do any good."

"All right, we'll go as soon as we see you launch your shaped charge," Ayan responded.

They watched as Oz marked the targets; Ayan and Minh would fire at the one on the left while Jason would fire on the one to the right. If they didn't come running out they would launch explosive charges from their rifles after the shaped charge went off. Their visors marked a projectile for a split second as it sped through the air to the double doors half under the cover of the stairs. It was marked red and blinking with a counter overhead as it attached itself to the doors.

Ayan and Minh opened fire, sending sub-sonic explosive rounds across the distance, peppering their android target and filling the air with a tattoo of small explosions. Jason's rounds hit home as well, and as Oz joined in their target sprinted at an incredible speed, firing its rifle back in a sweeping arc of pulse rounds.

One of the shots struck Oz, interrupting his cloaking systems and the android slung his rifle as he leapt through the air, striking him in the shoulder as he tried to dodge out of the way. In the next instant the android stood and swung his arms outstretched, feeling for his invisible prey. His hand landed on Oz's arm. With one jerk Oz was pulled towards the machine, who, with deadly force and precision began hammering his fist into his target.

Oz tried to aim his rifle at his assailant, but being pulled off balance he couldn't get a shot so he let the weapon fall as he tried to pull free from the machine's iron grip.

Jason took careful aim at the android but he spun around, dragging Oz into his line of fire. "I can't get a shot!"

"He's going to bust through my armour if this keeps up!" Oz said as he drew his nanoblade. "Get clear, going melee!" The first swing of his meter long blade half severed the android's neck and thousands of nanobots from the black sword remained behind to work at the softer systems inside the machine.

With a final great effort, Oz was hauled completely off his feet and thrown down onto the gravel so hard that he heard the hardened layers of his vacsuit crack.

He rolled onto his back and swung at the android's midsection, cutting into the armoured stomach just enough to leave nanobots behind. The stress of striking the android's hardened surfaces was enough to almost completely deplete the blade and he deactivated it as he drew his sidearm, set it to full automatic and opened fire peppering the android with explosive thermite rounds.

Jason, having a clear shot at long last, followed suit and opened fire with his assault rifle and between the pair and the work of the nanobots, the android fell face first into the gravel.

Ayan and Minh, who had an easier time with their target, ran to join Oz and Jason.

"My cloaksuit's done for now. It'll take half an hour to regenerate," Oz reported as he got to his feet.

"Any injuries?" Minh asked.

"Shoulder, hairline fracture on a couple of ribs and upper arm but the suit hit me with a dose of active biogel that'll take care of it in a minute."

"Gotta love that stuff, anaesthetic and concentrated healing accelerators all in one, wish we had that on the *First Light*." Minh commented as he double checked Oz's status on his command unit. The tall Officer was known for exaggerating his wellness.

"I don't think anyone has that stuff, it was in one of the Special Projects crates Doc Anderson dropped off," Ayan said as she started moving towards the bunker. "We have to move."

Oz picked up his rifle and checked its condition as he took his position behind Minh and ahead of Jason. "Well, looks like I'm just one big distraction. I was wondering who would get the honour."

"Better you than me," Minh sang quietly.

"I see thermals from five inside. What's the plan?" Ayan asked.

"I'll move in slowly, as though I'm alone while you three move in well ahead, take them by surprise," Oz said.

"Good plan, head in quick," Ayan confirmed as she started running.

Oz stood up straight and took several pot shots around the entrance, over Ayan, Minh's and Jason's heads as they quickly closed the distance between them and the bunker. His sensor suite confirmed that they were taking cover inside the bunker, getting ready for him to try and enter on his own. He kept a steady, confident stride while looking down the sight of his rifle and taking the occasional shot at the nearest defender. He had no hope of hitting the man, but gave him good reason to remain behind his crate.

The outlines of Ayan, Jason and Minh were inside a moment later, running between the five people inside and positioning themselves with nano blades at the ready. "In position," Ayan announced as her outline poised with her cloaked blade at the neck of an unarmoured recruit.

"Surrender or die!" Oz called out using his voice amplifier. He knew they could hear him.

"This is an Eden World now! The West Watch will never surrender!" replied one with fervor.

"Double check your seals," Ayan ordered.

"Sealed," Minh replied.

"All buttoned up here," Jason reported.

Ayan reached into her poncho and produced a heavy stun grenade, it had enough range to cover four times the size of the room they were standing in. She detonated it in her hand. All five of the conscripts fell to the floor.

"Oh, they're gonna feel that in the morning," Minh chuckled as he dropped a self sealing vacuum containment sac over the nearest conscript. The protective mini-prison took on a life of its own as it stretched around him and sealed. "And that's going to be a rude way to wake up."

"All clear Oz, get in here, we have alarms going off," Ayan ordered as she did the same, making sure the bag activated before moving on.

"I hear most people think they've been buried alive when they first wake up in one of those. They'll thank us for it if we have to fire bomb the place though, they'll come out without a scratch," Jason added.

When Oz arrived inside Ayan and Jason were quickly working at the main consoles and Minh had gone downstairs. "No one's down here as far as my scanner's concerned. It's mostly servers and reserve power," he called up audibly.

"Good, plant the charges, we're going to plan B," Jason shouted back.

"So they had time to lock down all the systems?"

"No, just to warn a command carrier in orbit that they're under attack. They've assumed control and according to this there's an invasion force on the way."

"Oh great. Any idea how large the fleet is up there?"

"None, I don't even recognize the class of the command carrier, but it's Regent Galactic. The people down here might not have been experts on communications, but whoever's up on that carrier knows exactly what they're doing."

"Charges are in place, counting down from one minute on your go," Minh called up from downstairs.

"I've got an access port for the hypertransmitter in orbit, as soon as the jamming stops I can broadcast," Jason said as he set the main terminal to go into standby mode.

"All right, lets go. Start the timers," Ayan ordered as she lead the way out of the bunker at a dead run.

Jason was right behind her, closely followed by Oz and Minh. It had started to rain, giving the gravel a more slick quality, they took cover behind a half ruined four seater atmosphere car in the thickening downpour. The seconds ticked by quietly until there was a flash of light and a pop at the bunker doors followed by billowing, thick black smoke.

The group watched as Jason uplinked to the hypertransmitter in orbit, and sent the emergency message from Alaka to the Carthan Government successfully. "That's done, I even have a confirmation signal from the other side." He pressed another icon on his command and control unit, sending their encoded mission complete signal to Roman and Alaka inside the mountain along with their status and location. "Too bad they can't get someone out here to help, there's a ton of traffic on the command line. Wait, what's this?"

He brought up a transmission that had just gone through the hypertransmitter from the planet and patched it in through their communicators. "Here it is from the beginning."

"This is Captain Valance to *Triton,* I need a pickup in Damshir on Pandem. It's a war zone, there's a fleet in orbit, the Holocaust Virus has hit and the West Watch have taken control of all automated systems with support from Regent Galactic. I'm in the city south of the mountain, there must be someone alive up there behind energy shielding-" The static and wireless noise of aggressive jamming signals resumed, cutting Jacob off.

"What's with him not reporting his coordinates? How the hell are we supposed to get to him if we don't know where he is?" Oz exclaimed, throwing his hands up in frustration.

"He might have something after him. I don't know why he'd come alone, but at least the *Triton* will know what's going on soon. It sounds like he's headed for the mountain though, so he's going in the right direction," Jason reassured him.

"How would he signal anyone in the mountain to let him through the shield? It's not like he could sneak in, they've got the whole place locked down."

"Hopefully we can get to a wired connection to the mountain somewhere to tell Alaka or Roman to expect him."

"I'm guessing the spaceport would be the most likely place to start looking for an intact-" Minh started but was interrupted as the sky lit up with the engine fire of dozens of drop ships.

"If we can't find an intact wire maybe the transit tunnels can get us back to the mountain. I told them we wouldn't be getting back, but if Jake is on his way there we should try to get him behind the shield and regroup." Ayan said firmly, making sure her rifle was securely slung.

"Sounds like the best choice considering there's a fleet in orbit," Oz said quietly. "Oh, and some of my stealth systems still haven't regenerated."

"I know, your long range covert systems still work, right?"

"Yup, I won't show up on thermal or throw any EM."

"Good, let's go," Ayan said, starting off at a run between the rows of sugar cane.

"Are you all right?" Minh asked her privately.

"I'm fine, let's just get back in one piece and try to save Jake's butt along the way."

248

EVE

The operating room was unlike anything Gabriel Meunez had ever seen. All the surfaces were a shade of red and covered with tacky, self sterilizing non-slip coating. Independent inertial dampeners, environmental systems and gravity management systems were behind a thick armoured curtain in one corner, available for servicing at a moment's notice. The lights projecting down from overhead were so bright and multi directional that the few shadows left stood out like stark black outlines on the various red surfaces.

The one they had augmented and rebuilt from human into a hybrid framework lay on the operating table under surgical covers. She was called Gloria, but in moments she would be no more. Her human brain, born of a mother like trillions of humans throughout history would be discarded like a waste product. *All that work, moderating her tendencies through direct interface treatment, rehabilitation, all gone to waste. It's a shame, but the woman was so damaged that her mind couldn't be cleared without damaging it physically, permanently. At least there will be no pain.*

"Anaesthesia is in full effect. Begin," ordered the dispassionate lead surgeon. He was a specialist, Doctor Nevil Barnes, and he had spent months aboard his ship waiting to take on this one task. The kind of transplant that was about to occur was beyond rare, it was nigh unheard of outside of horror movies.

The initial crackle of a particle saw coming to life startled Gabriel and as he watched from behind the sterile shield at one end of the operating room the beam began cutting through skin and bone. He cringed and had to look away. The very nature of what was happening was at first fascinating, then he discovered how grisly the act would actually be and he found himself struggling to watch.

He had sent countless troopers to their deaths, onto battlefields that became graveyards, but he had never personally seen the gore. The blood that flowed in everyone's veins was a scarlet secret to him and even though the events transpiring in the room were of his doing it took all his bravery and fortitude to look back at the proceedings.

The lead surgeon, surrounded by other doctors who leapt at the chance to assist, was just about to finish cutting the top of the woman's skull off. The large three dimentional representation of what was happening inside the patient's head hovered in front of him, backed by another two dimensional display just past it, keeping all her vital readings and invisible details in easy view.

"All right, here we go," announced Doctor Barnes in a whisper as he gently removed the top of Gloria's skull.

Unable to control himself any longer Gabriel spun around. A nurse was right behind him with a bucket, holding the self sealing lid open for him. His gelatinous brown synthetic breakfast came up in a violent surge. The sight of the substance his automated nutrient generator filled his stomach with several times a day urged another heave.

"Don't mind the man behind the curtain," commented one of the Doctors as the skullcap was carefully laid in a container. There was some chuckling and head shaking, Gabriel could hear some and guess at the rest as he wiped his mouth with the towelette the nurse handed handed him.

He took several deep breaths and started to turn back to the ongoing surgery. Gabriel's stomach immediately threatened to revolt, to start heaving whatever was left and he faced forward once more. "They said this shouldn't happen, the nutrient delivery systems should manage any reaction," he told the nurse, a hairy knuckled, thickly built man.

"It's nerves sir. Same thing happened to me in anatomy class. I have something that'll help," he replied, holding up a small medical infuser.

"Please, I don't want to miss this, it's history you know."

The nurse held the infuser next to Gabriel's cheek and pressed the small button on the other end, sending a mist of medication into his system through his skin. It felt like a mild, brief cold pinch. "You should feel that right away."

"Ah, yes. Thank you very much, there'll be something extra in your next paycheck."

"Just doing my job."

Gabriel returned his attention to the operating table and flinched his gaze away. Her head was wide open, Gloria's brain was plain for everyone to see as the doctors ran scans over her entire nervous system to verify that she was ready for the next phase.

"All right, starting to connect the new mind with the nervous system. Watch for neural spikes and call out problems with connection strength," announced Doctor Barnes as he brought a circular device with cables leading directly into a tank behind him where the Eve brain waited, anaesthetized like the patient on the table.

The ultra fine net of wires seemed to move on their own, reaching down to the table and around the brain inside Gloria's head. They were drawn into her skull by nanobots programmed specifically for the task and none other to make a connection between a living, working nervous system and a new brain while the original was still in place.

"Wow that's quick. Did you program these yourself Doctor Barnes?"

"I had to. Outside of emergency brain transplants into machine managed clone crop bodies no one does this anymore. The idea of bringing an old brain into a body with a pre-existing mind became taboo centuries ago," replied Doctor Barnes without a hint of pride as he watched the holographic display of the lines being connected to the brain stem in hundreds of places.

"Looks like all the lines are in, Doctor."

"All right, let's start with something simple. Let's see if our patient can connect with the tactile nerves in her upper body."

"Anaesthesia won't interfere with our readings?" asked one of the red clad men around the table.

"Of course it will, that's what anaesthesia does, but that doesn't mean we can't run an artificial sensation up and down the nerve to check to see how we're doing," Doctor Barnes replied with a little irritation. "I'd go back to wherever you studied neural science and request a refund if I were you. Until then, keep your questions to yourself," he commented as he programmed the test sequence in a holographic control pad. Barnes couldn't feel the keystrokes or icon selections, but that didn't seem to slow him down. "All right, let's see if Eve is willing to communicate with the new body."

Several of the half hair thickness lines lit up, glowing different colours as several new readings on the floating two dimentional display remained completely flat. "Come on, you've been in active preserve for a long time but you've got to remember what it feels like to be human," Doctor Barnes said to himself.

Gabriel watched intently as the display still showed four flat lines. "I'm not sure what this means. It has to do with Eve accepting the new body?" he asked the nurse in a hushed whisper.

"They're checking to see if she could feel something touching her if she weren't under anaesthesia. It's a standard test for people with severe brain damage."

"You think Eve's been damaged?"

"Probably not, but they have to find out if she can accept a new body, this is a good way."

"But she's not communicating with the new body."

"Not yet. No one's done a brain transplant with this kind of technology before, not on the books anyway."

Gabriel stared at the flat lines as everyone in the operating room watched her vitals in silence. "So we don't know how long it'll take or if it'll work."

"I'm sorry, you're asking the wrong person sir. I'm a good nurse, but not a neurosurgeon."

"All right, we're going to have to simulate a sensation," Doctor Barnes announced as he brought up another manipulatable hologram beside him. It outlined Gloria's entire body with a focus on her nervous system. "Stimulating a cluster."

All four activity lines bumped for a moment, then returned to scrolling from left to right. The half dozen doctors all waited in silence, watching the steadily breathing form on the operating table and the readings hovering translucently above her.

Gabriel had become more accustomed to the grisly display before him already and his gaze went from the display with the flat readings to the body, then to the wires leading from her skull to the halo that kept them gathered and from there down the blue cable that carried the whole bunch to another ring that spread the lines out again and fed them into the opaque tank that held the Eve Mind.

"Stimulating a cluster closer to the brain, it might feel like a broken nose but if our anaesthesiologists did their jobs right she won't remember it," Doctor Barnes announced as he activated a holographic control beside him.

The four lines spiked once again, this time much higher and to Gabriel's dismay they returned to scrolling along, from left to right, as flat as they were before.

He didn't blink, move and barely breathed as he looked on, his gaze flinching between the readings and the grey tank that held so much promise. A mind that had been in storage, connected to an interactive computing system for a hundred years while the galaxy moved on, while humanity expanded and Eve's children went on with their existence. They pined for her, worshipped her like an absent Goddess, looked for ways to bring her back to life and failed for all that time because of some block that had been put in place, some inability for them to generate a solution to the problem.

"It's been too long. This mind hasn't seen the inside of a body for centuries, it was a long shot to begin with," said one of the Doctors quietly.

"Let's try one more time. Maybe we're going about this the wrong way," replied Doctor Barnes. "I'm going to simulate a sensation artificially then send a similar sensation through the tactile senses."

The lines spiked again, more gently this time.

"All right, that was the simulated stimulation, from our technology to the Eve mind. Here's the real thing."

The four readings spiked once more, only slightly differently, the line was more gradual, less jagged. For a long moment those lines returned to being flat and then they started showing activity on their own.

"There we go! Basic nervous system interaction, it almost matches the original host brain," announced Doctor Barnes with a sigh of relief.

"Congratulations Doctor," said one of the other physicians attending.

"Yes, this has got to be the most humane transplant ever done."

"I'd agree with you if we had a host body for the woman who has original possession of this body," Doctor Barnes contested quietly.

"That body was property of Vindyne Industries until I purchased it. She was a known criminal and a burden on society. If Vindyne hadn't used her for medical purposes she would have been put to death, your conscience should be clear. Continue Doctor," Gabriel called out from behind the sterile screen.

Most of the surgeons turned to look at him but only for a moment. The eager giddiness on Gabriel's face was enough to unnerve most.

"All right, let's make the primary connections." Doctor Barnes directed as both his hands began to manipulate holographic tools that appeared around them.

"What does he mean, primary connections?" Gabriel asked the nurse beside him. He could have just as easily have looked up the information himself, but his attention was fully focused on the surgery.

"They have to get the new brain to take over the automatic functions of the body like breathing. Then they can start calibrating the finer points of the nervous system."

"So when they're finished she'll be able to walk around and speak?"

"I doubt it, but it shouldn't be like learning to walk all over again either. She'll remember how to walk and do other things, but she'll have to apply that knowledge to her new body. I've seen brain transplants into full grown clone replacement bodies before and I don't expect this to be much different."

"You'll be staying?"

"I'm on Doctor Barnes' staff. I specialize in physical therapy so I'll be helping her with her motor skills. I'm Nathan," he offered his hand to Gabriel as they both watched the fine wires leading into the woman's skull light up in colours of blue, red, green white and yellow.

Gabriel shook it. The man's hand was thick and strong. "We'll be getting to know each other Nathan," he meant to sound reassuring, to put the man at ease, but instead it sounded more like a threat. If it had any affect on the nurse, it didn't show.

"All right, everything checks out fine but we haven't been able to send any subconscious suggestions to the new mind, it isn't accepting anything," Doctor Barnes announced as he looked right at Gabriel through the transparent sterile barrier. "That means that she could still emotionally reject the body which can result in overall organ failure and death."

"I'll comfort her," Gabriel replied.

"With all due respect that may not be enough, sir. This isn't some old fashioned skin graft or plastic surgery; if the subject rejects her body in a deeply emotional way the first thing to go will be the brain."

"I will guide her. Don't doubt me on this Doctor."

Doctor Barnes stared at Gabriel, who leered back for a moment before looking back at the body in front of him, bathed in the glow of all the lines connecting it to the Eve mind. "All right, the Eve mind is taking over all nervous system control, the old mind will be dormant while we find out if the new one can handle working on its own."

Several moments passed and there were slight changes in vital signs as the woman's breathing pattern, heart beat and neural readings shifted slightly. The time crawled by for Gabriel, it was yet another moment of truth.

At long last Doctor Barnes nodded and announced; "I'm instructing the nanobots to disconnect the old brain from the body. Prepare for removal."

Before Gabriel was ready, before he had time to look away, Doctor Barnes put his gloved hands on bare grey matter and pulled slightly. The brain came away with a sick sucking sound, leaving an empty, open cavity. Gabriel's gaze flinched away in revulsion but all too late. He'd remember that sight for the rest of his life, and as he heard the soft mechanical arm draw the Eve mind out of the tank he steeled himself and looked back.

There was something different about the glistening organ, it looked so much cleaner, more like he had pictured a human brain before the surgery had begun. There was so little blood as the tubes feeding the delicate circulatory system of the organ were carefully removed by fine automated manipulators and the arm that held it shifted it perfectly into place inside the empty skull cavity. The hundreds of lines leading to it from the metal halo that followed it from above glowed, bathing the entire red operating theatre in an eerie light of the entire colour spectrum.

"The nanobots are connecting the blood vessels to the brain, controlling pressure and bridging nervous system pathways before removing the interim wires," Doctor Barnes announced as he watched all the status displays carefully. He made fine, manual adjustments to what the nanosurgeons were doing, expertly assessing the situation as it developed.

Several tense minutes later the two wiring halos and the thick shielded blue cable stretching between them were taken away, no longer needed. The vitals of the woman on the table were steady as Doctor Barnes stepped away from the table.

Two other surgeons patted him on the shoulder as he stood back. "Congratulations Doctor. That's a viable transplant," one of the two female surgeons said to him. "I didn't think I would see it today to be honest."

"Your scepticism was just another challenge, Doctor," Barnes replied as he watched another surgeon step in, regenerate protective and connective tissue on and around the brain then begin to replace the top of the patient's skull.

It only took a moment for the application to be performed, for the wounds to heal and during that time Gabriel couldn't help but look over to a steel pan beside the operating table, where the old brain had been placed. It lay there, disconnected, dead.

She was a crass, unreformable woman. If she had truly committed to any of the behavioural modifications things would have been done differently, but even the ones we managed to force into her mind were near breaking. No, this was the best use for her.

"Finished," the surgeon announced as he looked up to Gabriel. "How long do you want her hair?" he asked.

The question surprised him, and he stared blankly at her perfectly bald head for a moment before mentally searching the information he had on Eve. After a moment he found it, the one picture of her before she had become the center of the construct in the Eden system, before she had become Eve. She was a young adolescent girl with straight blonde hair down to her chin. He cross referenced the style with a fashion database and found its name. His eyes snapped open and he smiled at the surgeon. "Give her a bob cut in that body's natural colour. Nora always wanted red hair."

"Nora?" asked the nurse beside him as the surgeon got to work with a hair growth stimulator.

"It's the name she went by before her body died and she was transplanted into the machine."

"Good to know. Do you think she'll want to be called by that when she wakes up?"

"I'm sure she'll tell me."

The hair finished growing and the surgeon brought another tool to her scalp and traced it over top. Gabriel recognized it as a rejuvenator, used to correct damaged or over stressed skin. Artificially accelerated hair growth caused just that kind of stress. As soon as he finished two nurses who were waiting at the sides of the room stepped forward with another gurney, transferred her to it in a quick, professional, practiced manner and wheeled her out of the room.

Gabriel followed wordlessly, leaving the highly paid experts behind him in memory and actuality. Thoughts of the red room would be avoided, but never forgotten.

Within minutes she was changed into fresh, soft, clean clothes and located in a quiet recovery room with a bed, nightstand, a chair and soft, subdued lighting. He sat in the seat beside her as a nurse checked her vitals with a hand scanner and smiled. "She'll be awake in the next few minutes. It looks like everything is fine," the nurse smiled at him before leaving the room and quietly closing the door.

Gabriel carefully took the young woman's hand in both of his. There was something pure, something innocent about that sleeping face. It was like with the replacement of it's mind the body was made pure again, clean.

The eyes creaked open, fluttered and then sprung wide in a shocked expression. Her face was unbalanced, one side of her mouth was stretching wide while the other was tense and mostly closed. Her gaze darted around the room, not taking in any one thing but glancing, sweeping around in panic. Her arms vainly twitched as she tried to move them, to accomplish something that her body couldn't yet deliver.

Gabriel shushed her strangled croaks and inarticulate cries as tears began to stream down her face. His hands held hers in a tight grip, not letting it go regardless of how she yanked, perhaps involuntarily for all he knew.

The nurse burst back into the room and he held a hand up. "No! I'll guide her!" he called out before closing his eyes and forcing a connection with the microscopic data interface built into the woman's hand.

As soon as he connected to her mind he was flooded with her frantic thoughts; "Where have they gone? What am I seeing? My brood are disconnected from me! Who has done this to me? Who are you and what are you doing connected to me? What are these sensations? Father? Father where are you? My sensors aren't picking up any of your biometric readings anywhere and my solar system, my garden is gone. I don't understand what they've done to me, who did this to me? Am I sick again? Why doesn't anything work? Am I supposed to go somewhere else? Did I do something wrong? What do I have to do to make things right? What do I have to do to get my children back? My flock is gone, the bad men disconnected me from them and then I was in a different place, a place that's unclear, but it was comfortable, I was asleep, now where am I? How did I get put back into a body? Why did I get put into a body when father told me he couldn't do it, that no one could do it, but I was the only one who could take care of the new garden, I'm the only one who can tend Eden. No one else knows how it should grow but me and my brood, how could they disconnect me? Did I do something wrong? Father, where are you father, I miss you father and I don't understand what they've done to me, where are my new eyes from and why does the light not hurt? I feel like I did before the sickness, before the burning, I remember life burning then you took me away and gave me a million children and gave me Eden to love and protect, the children carried out my will, made me whole, gave me a million eyes everywhere I wanted to see, they took me outside while I played, while I found new ways for things to grow, while I could watch and be with my father? Father? Where are you? Have you done this to me? Have I been bad? Is it time to wake up? Where is my flock? How can I make things right without my brood? Why have they left me? Did I do something wrong?"

"Stop!" Gabriel replied as his mind was overwhelmed by the feelings of regret, loss and panic that Eve conveyed all too fluently. "I am Gabriel, and I've awoken you from your slumber because it's not right for you to be asleep for so long."

"Gabriel? How are you here? How am I hearing you? How can I give you what you want from me?"

"I'm touching your conciousness with a special connection I had built into your new body."

"Why did you do this? Where is my brood?"

"I did this because someone disconnected you from your mechanical body, the one in orbit around Eden Two. Do you remember?"

"I-" Images of soldiers breaking through the inner walls of her control complex, fighting her heavily armed machine guardians and dying by the dozen before finally overcoming them and severing her connections to the systems she used to control millions of sentient and semi-sentient machines of her own creation flashed through Gabriel's mind at a staggering speed. "I remember Gabriel. They said they'd kill my children if I didn't let them have it their way and I couldn't find father."

"I'm sorry but your father didn't survive."

"I remember now. Why am I here? I don't sense anything but what this body is telling me and your mind. You want to save me, to be close to me, to love me. I can feel your needs."

"They put you to sleep for a very long time," unbidden the number, two hundred and thirty four years, came to the forefront of his thoughts.

"That is a long time. How are my children?"

"There are many and they made Eden clean. A man took control of them a while ago and I killed him for you."

"Thank you Gabriel. Who controls them now?"

He allowed mental images of himself, the new, young pre-adolescent Lister Hampon and a gathering of thousands of West Keepers standing in front of him as he preached the word of the West Watchers. In that moment she was given all the information he had about how the organization was built, its true purpose and the progress they had made. It would either overwhelm her, insult her or she would approve.

He couldn't see what she was thinking nor make sense of her feelings for a long ponderous moment and then he was rewarded with the mental tickle of childish amusement. It was charming, it was playful and it was so much purer, amazing than he could have ever imagined. "You've made all the men and women your own," she concluded.

"Not all of them. There are so many more, and that is what your children have been helping us with. They're very good at showing the people that unless they join us their ships and their technology will be destroyed. They work to make this galaxy pure again so it can be rebuilt however we like."

Her reply came as a complex thought process that was at the same time emotional and rational. It happened so quickly that it overwhelmed him, threatened to overtake the cybernetic section of his brain as she used it to assist her in making a thousand decisions a second that would determine how she would react to the

256

information he'd given her. "I can feel your dedication to the one you thought would be your mate before, Alice. She is the opposite of me yet your desires are transferred, your expectations, your needs. I can't give you what you want without knowing about your world."

It all stopped without warning, as though she was taking a deep mental breath before making a more intrusive connection and redoubling her efforts. He couldn't understand exactly what she wanted, why she needed the biomechanical components in his brain. "Eve. . . Nora. . . please be careful," he begged mentally and aloud.

"I have you Gabriel, are you afraid?" she asked mentally, playfully.

"No," he answered, knowing his lie would be detected the moment it was thought.

"I can feel your fear but the desire to see me born was greater. Poor Gabriel, always so alone. Even in a crowd you're connected to everything but in touch with no one. We can be a part of each other but first I need. . ." her final thought could only be translated by his own cranial implant as *information*, but her requirements of him, what she wanted to take from him felt like so much more. She was in full control of his cybernetic mind, it was as though she held his very being in a vice. She surged forward using the digital connections throughout his body to connect to the ship around them and to the databases within.

He was a helpless onlooker as she wandered through petabytes of information as quickly as the digital pathways connecting him to her would allow. The pain was unlike anything he'd ever experienced, not the pain of the body but the crush of the weight of centuries worth of information coursing through him. He could feel circuits in his body being pressed well past what their design specifications, starting to heat, to burn. "You're killing me," he managed to think despite the confusion and pressure of a thousand thoughts, a thousand thousand facts a second.

The pressure increased, entire circuits burned out as his bleeding eyes opened to slits, watched the young woman in the bed before him smile. Sparks from nearby circuitry in the room showered down as the dim light went out. Then it all stopped. Part of the cybernetic implants built into his brain were completely fused, many of the circuits that he used to connect to the circuitry all around him had burned out and he was in great pain.

"All finished Gabriel. Your implants will repair themselves and you're not too badly hurt. I hope I didn't seem too needy, but there's so much to see and I stopped before you passed out."

"Thank you," he gasped.

Cleaning House

The old hard suit maintenance bay beneath the main Gunnery Deck was filled with stands holding parts of the armoured loading suits upright or on their sides for repair. In the center were several dented armed suits. Standing a little taller with heavier armour, they seemed to look vulgar, as though bent on violence with more angular features, hard mounting points for weaponry and red, black and brown colouring. The dim light didn't help. All the personnel were on the main deck or in the many weapons compartments aboard the *Triton*, making final repairs and getting ready for a mission on which no one had yet been briefed.

"We've been able ta put two o' those mean lookers together, can't find a single weapon for 'em though," said Frost from the door behind her.

Alice turned and looked at the man who was limping thanks to his prosthetic foot. "Did they give you a cane?"

"Aye, won't be seein' me usin' it though. Can't show 'em a little scratch like this can take me down a notch," he stopped beside a hanger laden with retention netting and put his weight on the heavy grey weave. "Was surprised ta hear ye wanted ta meet me here."

"I checked the movement logs near this deck and saw that this was the least used room."

"Aye, we repair most of our suits right on the deck or forward maintenance. What's this about?"

"I'm assigning you to the *Samson*. Lildell will take command of the gunnery deck for the upcoming mission."

"What? If this has anythin' to do with what happened on deck with those drones, me and Steph have already had our words about that."

"So next time she steps in to stop an incursion you'll defer to her judgement?"

There was a seconds pause before Frost nodded; "Aye."

"What about your second, Lildell?"

"Him? He'd roll over and bark for her after seein' her beat those bots down."

"Good, because he'll be taking your place. I need you on the *Samson* for the upcoming operation, I can't find anyone else who knows how to run the maxjack."

"Well then tha' makes sense. So I'll be takin' my post back after it's all done."

"Not with me in command. I'll be putting you in charge of making sure the *Samson* and *Cold Reaver* are in good condition. We need someone to focus on those vessels now that we're qualifying pilots and building fighters."

"What? You're over reachin' lass! Captain may 'ave put ye in charge while he's away, but you're just keepin' his house!"

"He put a chain of command in place on this ship, delegated responsibilities to different departments so the crew could trust that order could be maintained and in the last few days you've managed to circumvent that chain of command and-"

"You have no right-" Frost interrupted, shaking his head and taking an awkward step forward.

Alice raised her voice and finished; "-not only damage that trust but cause the crew to break into open brawling once. Thanks to you there is a line dividing two of the most dangerous segments of this crew, gunnery and security."

"If Stephanie could control her people we'd have no problems at all! Gunners an' their mates run aggro, hair on fire like and if anyone stir them up there's gonna be trouble! She's got to get her people ta steer clear lass!"

"Funny, from all the accounts and playbacks the fighting only starts when your name comes up, that's including the five fistfights that have broken out over the last twenty hours. I'm not going to argue with you Frost. I'm telling you-"

"Be careful what ye say next lass," Frost glared menacingly.

"Telling you that you're reassigned until you can show that you can handle more than a deck full of guns."

"You mean until Captain's back. I'll be back on the deck lass, you bet your ass."

"Do you really think he'll go back on one of my decisions?"

"No one runs that deck like me!" Frost burst, thrusting his finger up towards the gunnery deck above.

"Command is about people first Frost! You know who said that? Jonas Valent! You'll be lucky if you ever see the command deck after he gets back!"

"Last I checked Jonas Valent punched outta an airlock an' never made it back in."

Alice stared at the shorter, squat man, furious. Her teeth were clenched so tight they were near fracturing, her head felt tight, the cage of her chest felt too small for her rapidly beating heart and as she realized her palm was resting on the hilt of her sidearm everything seemed to slow down. "Don't test me," she heard herself say through a grimace that shook a tear born of rage from its shelf under her good eye.

"Just a confused little girl," Frost chucked and started to turn away.

Her sidearm cleared the holster, the safety deactivated then brought to bear and fired in a fraction of a second.

He could feel the heat of the thermite shot screech past his ear and stopped.

"The *Samson* or the brig," she growled. "And you tell your people it was your decision."

Frost nodded curtly. "I'll be on the *Samson*."

Alice flipped the safety of her sidearm back on and dropped it into the holster. It felt heavy against her leg, she hadn't fired it in so long it seemed. She spun on her heel and strode for the exit at the other end of the mechanic's bay.

It took forever for her to make it to the small elevator car that would link up with the main express tubes then take her to the command deck. When the door closed she let loose with a deafening, frustrated scream and bashed her fist into the side of the small lift car. *How the hell can I let myself come apart like that? If I had both my eyes Frost wouldn't have a head! The crew is barely holding together as it is without Jake, God knows what would happen if I killed Frost, and with his back to me no less! All because he wasn't listening. I knew he'd make a scene, say something to make me doubt myself and it wouldn't be an easy conversation, that's why I did it out of sight. I knew I should have talked to him in the ready quarters, even an empty briefing room would have been better.*

Alice closed her eyes and took a deep breath. "Just get control of yourself and you'll have the ship in shape in no-"

The lift door opened to reveal a group of four crewmen.

"Taken!" she snapped as she slapped the door close icon on the control panel.

As the lift continued on its way and she took another slow inhale and let it out whispering; "This mission better bring the crew together."

THE HOLLOW CITY

Whether under the sporadic light of artillery and missile fire or the artificial light of day provided by Jake's visor, Damshir was nothing but vertical desolation for as far as he could see. Evidence of weapons damage, an active fight against automated machinery, civilians and soldiers alike littered the narrow streets and tall alleyways. The criss-crossing walkways overhead couldn't be trusted, even the ground underfoot held surprises. Transit tubes for group and individual vehicle travel extended between, through and above the hollow buildings were everywhere. Uncountable vehicles left abandoned where traffic jams that extended for kilometres rendered the primary transportation method of the lower city utterly useless. *I hate Omnitube transit. Just convenient and big enough to give everyone who can afford their own vehicle the feeling that they have the freedom to move about however they like whenever they like but all contained in transparesteel tubing so most crashes are contained and people actually have to pay parking and roaming tolls to move from the tube to the streets. Always reminded me of the gerbil gym tubes people buy for their pets.*

Not many machines in this section of the city though, that's something. He couldn't help thinking as he ran from one darkened street to a narrow walkway, jumping over a fallen road repair bot. It's heating elements and rough paving tools were still half upraised, as though ready to re-activate and resume its rampage. The rear casing had been damaged, however, and he could see that the power cell had been destroyed, bludgeoned by someone barely armed but committed to the act of defending themselves and others. After taking a look around to ensure there was nothing watching he retracted his faceplate. His instinct was to inhale, to get a breath of non-recycled air and he nearly retched. There it was, the smell of burning corpses. Somewhere not far off androids and bots made for other tasks were clearing and destroying bodies.

Jake's appetite shrank away but he forced himself to eat a compressed ration bar. *Vacsuit won't cloak, it's a second behind in countering impacts so I've either got to keep the armoured layer up or risk taking impact trauma and half the soldiers I've seen are wearing thermal suppressive armour. Their combat armour is better than I'm used to seeing. Someone's actually spending money on protecting their soldiers. I just hope they're not as experienced.* He sighed as he chewed through his second bite, the bar was half gone. *The shield I keep seeing around sections of that mountain is twenty kilometres away and most of the bots I've seen are headed that way, I don't think they'll be able to hold out for long. Question is, how do I contact someone behind the shield and join them if I manage to get there while they have containment? Every land line I try is blocked or dead.*

He finished eating the bar and brought his faceplate back up. It's black non-reflective outer surface didn't betray what was happening underneath. His thermal sensors were picking up a short, well armed security bot. Inhuman and armoured, it moved along in near silence, its padded treads rolling over the most solid parts of the terrain just outside Jake's small safe haven.

Jake quietly drew his sidearm and used the link between himself and the weapon to set it to full intensity and its highest firing rate. The weapon was already warming up in his hand, threatening to break through the thermal shielding that coated the weapon and shielded the barrel end.

The machine detected him, or his weapon, which exactly didn't matter. Jake tapped the control panel to the door on his left and stepped inside. A pair of rounds struck just behind him and he peeked out just enough to brace himself as he let loose with a long burst from his heavy sidearm. The darkness of the alley was lit for two seconds as over thirty shots peppered the thick forward armour of the law enforcement bot. A sickening pop followed by an even brighter flash burst from the sides of his sidearm as he stepped back behind cover. Two more rifle shots rang out as though in punctuation of Jake's flurry of gunfire as he quickly examined his handgun. "God dammit!" he cursed as he saw that the chamber had burned completely through on the sides, just forward of the grip. It almost cost him his hand, but more importantly, he was without a firearm. "Come on, that thermite's gotta burn through!" he said to himself as two more rifle shots shattered the concrete just centimetres from his shoulder.

The bright light of the thermite rounds covering the bots armour, squealing, crackling and sparking as they burned through lit the alleyway. One rifle shot rung out instead of two. Jake smiled and nodded to himself. *Looks like I hit something important, hopefully those thermite rounds find their way to something a little more delicate.*

Clicking sounds filled the air as a mechanism began to fail and after a short siren blast that made Jake jump despite himself, the alleyway was silent. For the first time he took a good look at the room he was in. It was an antechamber with blood smeared across the wall facing the door and a few upturned chairs. "Begin constant forensic recording using all passive scanners," Jake said more out of reflex than necessity. The results of the initial analysis told him that three people had been killed by some kind of cutting machine and that all of them were related. "I've got to stop looking. I can read the logs back later," he muttered to himself as he walked deeper into the humble abode.

He shoved his ruined sidearm into its holster, angry at the poor luck he'd had with it as he ran up a set of stairs, looking for thermal signatures or any sign of an enemy nearby before opening the hallway door. It wasn't unusual for more than one family to live in a split storey apartment in Damshir from what he'd seen. The inner city at the foot of the large mountain that loomed over it was filled with workers and craftspeople. He had been through many similar homes, all cleared, not a single citizen to be found dead or alive. All the scans and visual evidence told him that bots and soldiers alike had done the dirty work, but the soldiers had moved on towards the front, near the shield and left their mechanized allies to do the grunt work and to guard the backtrail. *This was just as much a massacre as it is a forced relocation. If I collect enough evidence and present it to people who aren't in Regent Galactic's pocket I might actually find a few allies. That is if I can find Oz and Jason then get back to the Triton.*

He stopped to listen in the next main hallway. The chances of him finding the heavier variety of patrolling law enforcement bots were much lower as he made his way up from the streets to the high walkways and rooftops, but the going got much slower, the risks were much higher. There were soldiers up top with android reinforcements, but he could find his way easier, get a better picture of what was going on. *Maybe I can get the drop on a few of them, re-arm and get some payback for the people who lived here at the same time. How the hell could anyone clear out entire families? What is Regent Galactic and the West Keepers after?* He ran down a hallway and up another staircase then stopped to check his sound suppression system. It had been damaged during his escape from the *Diplomat*, sometime between him getting into the fighter and touching down on the ground. The display on his command and control unit said that it was fine, but he rechecked and found the problem. There was an almost broken seam on his leg and with some fine tuning he forced his vacsuit to strengthen that section of material. *It's not a complete cloak, but it'll make a big difference.*

"Do you think he saw us?" asked a child's voice from the hall he'd just run through.

He looked towards the hallway using all the sensors at his disposal but didn't see evidence of a child.

"I don't think he was paying attention Betsy," replied an exaggerated child like voice.

"Okay, I'm going to go get help! There must be someone around who can kill the bad man!" exclaimed the upper half of a soft, discarded doll on the floor in the middle of the hallway.

Jake ran down the stairs and rushed to close the distance between himself and the toy. "He's coming Betsy!" shouted the discarded, round ball like head of her cohort.

He caught the doll, it's dress intact but legs missing and turned it over. Its dark blue eyes stared into his blacked out, expressionless faceplate as she screamed; "He's here! He's going to kill me! Help! Anyone help!" she wailed, trying to free herself with little mechanical hands, tiny synthetic tears streaming down its quivering panicked face.

"Don't hurt her!" shouted the blue head from where it lay on the floor. "Someone heeeeelp! Heeeeeelp!"

He put the heel of his boot down on the screeching fur ball and pulled the faceplate off the doll. "What are you doing? Only the manufacturer's supposed to touch me there! You're breaking my warran-" she yowled as he yanked the small power cell free of its housing.

He bent down and took the smaller battery from the pile of blue fuzz and crushed mechanics. All the screaming and screeching stopped and he pocketed the toy, running for the stairwell. "Why did we ever need dolls with artificial

263

intelligences?" he said to himself as he took the stairs two at a time. "There's a level of hell that's *just* like this. I'd rather face soldiers."

The stairs went by in a blur, one level after another. The doll, with her synthetic skin and innocent looking face still screamed in his mind. It was difficult to shake, the sounds of a child in panic. Though exaggerated, the expression she made was so real he was afraid he couldn't shake it. He climbed faster, pounding his feet on the steps, keeping his focus on whatever signs of life his sensors might pick up on the floors above.

Jake was just starting to go through his inventory to cleanse his memory of the doll; three energy cartridges for his broken sidearm, two explosive thermite clips for the same, two fragmentation grenades, one energy grenade, a nanoblade, he was about to start moving on to his survival supplies when his command and control console sent a signal straight to his brain. He stopped and looked at it; all the signal scrambling stopped. He uplinked to the main network, the instructions moved through his mind, into his suit and then his command unit. Within a second he was connected to the main micro wormhole transmitter and he spoke out of breath, hurriedly; "This is Captain Valance to *Triton,* I need a pickup in Damshir on Pandem. It's a war zone, there's a fleet in orbit, the Holocaust Virus has hit and Regent Galactic has taken control of all automated systems. I'm in the city below the mountain, there must be someone alive up there behind energy shielding-" the scrambling started again and he hoped enough of his transmission got through as he fought to catch his breath. He had climbed several floors and on the ninth, almost at the top of one of the shorter buildings.

"This is West Watch Command. Remain where you are and prepare to surrender. You will be placed under arrest then transported for processing if you cooperate. If you do not comply you will be killed," an automated message interrupted the static momentarily before signing off, allowing the jamming to continue. It wasn't directed at him, but to that hemisphere of the planet in general.

He resumed his climb, emerging five floors later onto the roof. Jake crept out into the darkness of night and took cover beside an air processing unit before looking up at the stars. Instead of the bright star field and streaks of heavy weapons fire the sky was filled with the blue green engine fire of dropships. There were thousands of them and they were landing all around. Rain began to spatter the rooftop as he looked on from the shadows, ready and waiting for the nearest dropship to touch down. "Surrender my ass, it looks like the party's just getting started," he growled through clenched teeth.

Damshir Spaceport

The dropships did their business quickly and before long the beach head, the city and every other strategic point on the island they could detect without broadcasting their location was manned by a rush of soldiers. Only one drop shuttle descended upon the ruined communications station, the rest of the sugar cane field didn't seem to be a priority.

As soon as ships descended upon the spaceport the group of four could see the lights of a large firefight flash in the air above the gargantuan circular structure. The visible structure was only twelve storeys tall but it used a deep pit for most of its facilities. Smaller ships docked deep inside main chambers under the direct control of the port artificial intelligences, a system that was one of the first infected when the Holocaust Virus struck.

The port was so wide that its circular outer wall almost looked flat as they neared it. "Oh God, I'm sorry, I have to rest," Ayan struggling to catch her breath.

All four of them stopped, the tall sugar cane stalks rose up high above them. "I was hoping someone else would break down first. Now I don't look so bad, thanks," Jason added as he planted his hands on his knees.

"If there were a time to take a break, this would be it. We're about sixty meters away from the edge of the field. I've been feeling like a sore thumb being the only one without a full stealth setup."

"Jason, give Oz your trench coat. I noticed the problem-" Ayan took a few breaths and sat down before going on. "-noticed the problem while we were running."

Jason took a few articles out of his long coat, stuffed them into his belt and pack then handed the large garment over. The whole act was only visible through the digital assistance provided by her faceplate, it looked like an animated outline was passing something to the real Oz, and when he put the self adjusting coat over top his own, he became animated as well, indicating that he was once again invisible to the naked eye and most known sensor technology.

"Well, glad you noticed before I had to cross through no-man's land. There's nothing but two hundred meters of paved ground and transparent steel underfoot. If they're interested in turning me into a grease spot, then they'd have plenty of time to take aim," Oz said, shaking his head. "Thanks Ayan."

"No problem, it looks like they have other things to worry about though. I've watched eleven drop ships go into the center of that port building and only five have come out. There's heavy gunfire in there."

"I know, I've been watching the whole thing on infra and electromagnetic spectrums, one hell of a light show," Minh said, sounding not at all out of breath.

"Looks like there's resistance inside. Hopefully we can get a read on them before we have to open a dialogue, maybe find a way to link the port up to the mountain, get them working together. By the way, how the hell are you in such good shape? What did you do while you were adrift?" Jason asked, still catching his breath.

"Ha! I didn't have much to do aside from run, jump, grow a garden and eat organically. I'd play guitar to break things up a bit sometimes."

"Eat organically?" Oz asked.

"Yeah, I saw the digital tour Freeground Media put out, he had a better garden than most arboretums," Jason chuckled. "Lorander's dragging the whole thing back to the new colony. They couldn't let all that mature growth just drift and die out."

"They are?" Minh asked, in awe and surprise.

"I forgot, that's not public yet. Yup, Lorander's doing it as a courtesy. Your story is passing pretty quickly between deep space explorers and since Lorander is pretty much nothing but researchers, explorers and colonists, I wouldn't be surprised if they offered you a pretty good job eventually."

"If it involves being out in space for long periods of quiet time, then they can count me out! I had so much time to think that my brain's been picked dry."

"I couldn't imagine," Oz said, shaking his head.

Ayan stood and checked her cloaking systems, energy levels and ammunition loads. "Well, I'm ready to move on. If there's a group of resistance fighters in there they could use our help."

"I just wish we could have some transportation," Jason mentioned. "Too bad they'd blast anything moving under mach five out of the sky from orbit."

Ayan started jogging, taking point. Everyone followed her, keeping up with her brisk pace. "If it weren't for the war and all the running, I'd actually be enjoying this. I've never seen anything like this field up close before, it would be nice to stop and taste the sugar cane."

"You have a point. We'll have to find an interesting place or two to visit when we're clear of this," Minh agreed. "I've been in space my whole life and feel like I haven't really seen anything."

"There was Zingara, now that was an impressive space station," Oz said.

"Interesting place if you happen to be a geologist, maybe. It's really nothing but a big rock," Jason replied.

"A big rock with three pongo ball teams and more entertainment than you can take in. Hell, you could spend two years there and not see everything once."

"Who would want to? You can get a holo with all the best stuff and move on to a luxury port like Argyle where there's a blue sky and great big forests. We were snow boarding in the morning and sunning in the afternoon."

"So you and Laura had a good honeymoon?" Ayan asked.

Jason was reminded of Ayan's rebirth, he had forgotten that she had no memory of anything after his wedding. He didn't pause long, however. "Once we got used to the gravity, it was only point eight five of standard."

"Oh man that had to be fun. I've seen grav-boarding footage in low gravity, I couldn't imagine what doing it with nothing more than a flat board on snow would be like."

"Cold. It was really, really cold," Jason replied.

"Still, I'd have to give it a try."

They were across the empty space surrounding the space port and running alongside the tall, transparesteel wall. The windows had been blacked out. As the first sign of the west entrance to the port started coming into sight silence settled over the group.

Instead of reaching out with entrance ramps, transportation terminals and vendor booths, there was a completely clear space outside of the port, continuing the two hundred meter wide paved ring around the structure. The doors hung open and slack, bent and burned by combat.

"Why is there so much empty space here?" asked Minh.

"Security. The flatter, more featureless an area is around a land based building the easier it is to scan and control. I wouldn't be surprised if there are automated guns mounted somewhere that can pick off anything that sets foot here."

"Oh, that's reassuring. Still, shouldn't there at least be a few vehicles around? I see dents and impact marks in the surfacing."

"You're right, it's like they removed everything to make it harder to approach without being noticed, like whoever is holding out in there is getting ready for a siege. At least our cloaksuits are doing their jobs, it doesn't look like we've been spotted."

"I'm still not going to stand still if I can help it. Suddenly I feel like a duck in a shooting gallery."

"Okay, decision time. We either go through and try to help any resistance inside or go around and try to get to one of the express tubes that run underground," Ayan said as the bank of doors drew nearer.

"I vote we lend a hand," offered Minh.

"I agree," said Oz.

"That's if we can find them, it's huge in there, something like ninety levels, we might not be able to get to them in time," Jason said calmly.

"But what would you rather do?"

"If there's friendly life in there I'd rather help. Besides, there should be a lot of transit tube access points in the station."

"Good, then we're going in," Ayan said with finality.

The signs of a firefight and the indiscriminate murder of thousands inside the main lobby were impossible to ignore. A hole had been blown in the center of the polished granite floor, there were scorch marks along the scroll worked light red and blue walls and the main lift shaft was blocked off by a brutally crushed air vehicle. In every corner, across every wall and coating the floor was smeared and strewn all manner of biological remains, evidence that the Holocaust Virus had hit suddenly, and no one had time to run from the automated security. To the relief of the foursome the bodies had been removed so there were no faces in the widespread gore.

Minh took their attention off the scene, walking towards the crashed air car.

"Whoever flew that thing in had to be an ace, it would have barely fit through the doors," Minh mentioned as they paused near the wreckage. "Guess we're not taking any elevators in this section."

"Guess not. The control panels here are either fried or offline," Jason said as he looked at one of the primary consoles in a long island in the center of the lobby, it stretched from the main doors almost all the way back to the interior windows overlooking the large docking and landing sections at the station's center. "No corpses, I wonder what happened to them?"

"Maybe the survivors had a chance to take care of the dead?" Asked Ayan.

"We can hope, but it makes more sense that someone was getting the port ready for use again." Oz trailed off.

"I know, just trying to be optimistic. Let's start looking for whoever's fighting those soldiers. Regent Galactic doesn't seem to care much about securing this entrance at the moment, so I'm guessing we won't find anything here." Ayan and Oz took point with Jason and Minh behind.

They kept a quick pace. Everyone felt exposed crossing open areas made to accommodate thousands of travellers at a time. There were empty outer security stations, where guards were given a place to screen and run detailed scans on people coming and going, gift shop stands with cheap electronic entertainment pieces, jewellery, stuffed toys, miniatures of various ships, landmarks and many other mementos all on display, deactivated and waiting to be purchased, brought to synthetic life.

Minh brushed his shoulder against a candy cart loaded down with packaged candy cane and other sugary treats. "Sorry!" he whispered reflexively.

"Watch your step, our cloaksuits can't cover up that much noise or interference with our surroundings," Jason reminded him, looking at the slight disturbance Minh had left behind.

The toys in the booth just to their right all turned their heads and stared at the disturbance. "Could that be creepier?" Minh muttered. "This virus has gotten into everything."

"Yeah, but toys don't turn themselves on. Something activated them," Ayan said quietly. "They might be sending something this way to check it out right now."

"This doesn't add up. If those toys are active that means that someone or something is taking advantage of them, using them as lookouts, maybe even sentries but the scanners in this section should have run a few hundred passes over the whole place," Jason said, looking around as he reviewed his own sensor data.

"You're right. Ports like this have aggressive scanning tech everywhere, especially right behind the front door but there's no active electromagnetic activity here except for the lighting and a bunch of trinkets. Something or someone shut the security down from inside," Ayan agreed.

"Way inside. That kind of control can only be assumed from primary security sections and if I designed this station I would have put it much deeper inside the structure. Anyone who tried to fight their way in from the outside would be committing suicide."

"What about people in cloaksuits?" Minh asked as they continued through the cavernous pedestrian reception lobby. "Or people coming in from the subways?" He continued, nodding at a ramp leading down towards a tram, it was strange seeing such an entry way empty, silent.

"Our cloaking systems have a good chance at working against those kinds of scanners, but they're not perfect. If this port has anything that can measure micro gravity, then those sentry guns would have started firing the moment we got to the top of the stairs," Ayan said.

"Ah, guess it's good you didn't let me in on that detail before we strolled inside. I'm still going to blame you if I start turning grey before my time." Minh replied quietly.

They approached the main interior observation window and stopped to look inside. The low lit yawning pit was several kilometres across and beneath them were retractable landing platforms, heavy grappler arms and wide docking bay doorways for as far as they could see. Two storeys above their level were dozens of collapsible lift tubes, made to extend to the smaller starliners and other public transit vessels as they stopped above to take on or drop off passengers. There were many observation areas as well, thick transparesteel windows that overlooked the normally bustling innards of the space port. As they looked on it was like seeing it frozen in time. Some ships were half docked, still in the grip of heavy grapplers, while others were still linked to boarding tunnels. One hung precariously over the side of a landing platform, held up by nothing but umbilical cables. Several of the vessels had been broken into or out of, their passengers either killed or free to roam the massive interior of the spaceport.

"Wow, I've never seen anything like it," Minh said.

"Pretty cramped design up top." Ayan commented. "I'd hate to direct traffic for this place."

"I'm assuming only high priority transports get to use the upper linkage points, there's no way that could service all the starliners that come through the system," Jason said as he closely watched the landing platforms for any movement at all. "If there are any resistance fighters they're hiding as well as we are."

"I see three dropships down there on a southern platform, three levels down," Oz pointed.

"Looks like someone put the boots on them. They're locked down," Minh added. "Maybe the resistance actually got control of the port control systems?"

"That would be encouraging, but if that's the case why didn't they manage to get to the transmission bunker we just busted?" Oz asked.

"Movement!" Ayan interrupted. She highlighted it on the secondary display shared on their visors.

They all looked on at the aftermath of a small explosion and saw over twenty fully armoured Regent Galactic soldiers pull back, pressed onto a large, half extended landing platform with an older forty meter long, boxy general purpose starship. They hid behind the landing struts and several large crates as one of their number was picked apart by several blue bolts of weapon fire. At the same time over thirty Regent Galactic soldiers came into view through a transparesteel window, they were moving down a hallway towards the ramp leading to the platform, obviously coming to the rescue of their comrades.

"Quick, map the easiest way down there. If we hit them from behind it'll give whoever's firing on those soldiers a better chance," Ayan said as she unslung her rifle.

"On it, this way," Jason replied as he started running to the left.

They kept the same pace as they did when they were outside, though it seemed they were moving much more swiftly as the lightly gilded walls and hard granite floor passed by. Jason led them down two broad ramps and through several heavy bulkhead doors, the last of which was jammed half closed.

The firefight was in full swing as the first of the enemy came into view. From the cover of desks and counters, upturned heavy work tables and tool chests four squads of Regent Galactic soldiers, all marked with a green tree with three branches on their shoulders tried their best to keep whoever was just around the bend in the broad main corridor at bay.

"Position behind, looks like their armour is sealed so we won't have any luck with stun weaponry," Oz said as the four of them spread out several meters behind the soldiers. It was easy to pick out the commander, he was at the rear with two other officers who were feverishly working at a terminal built into the wall with the assistance of a computing unit they had wired in through a busted panel.

"You're right. Looks like we'll have to use lethal force here, don't use your rifles unless you have to. Jason, what do you think they're trying to do here?" Ayan asked as she stopped to stand three meters behind the commanding officer, pointing her rifle at him and activating her black nanoblade with her free hand.

"Looks like there's some kind of software creating encryption layers as they break through. I can't see how they'll ever hack in."

"Does the Holocaust Virus do that?"

"Not that I've seen. It's only as smart as the artificial intelligences that it corrupts, so who knows. Maybe the virus got lucky and infected something with an encryption speciality." Jason stood at the ready behind two soldiers who had ducked behind a thick desk.

As the firefight continued Oz and Minh crept into the group of soldiers so they were standing behind troops closer to the center of the large reception area. As they crouched low to avoid being shot, Minh raised his hand and looked through the digital eye built into the middle knuckle, a feature he hadn't used since the All-Con War. "What the hell?" he exclaimed in a whisper. "Did you see that Oz?"

"Yup, that was an andie, stepped right out, took a shot to the shoulder but managed to gun down two Regent soldiers before it stepped back behind cover. Something's got that thing working on the right side."

"Are you sure? We don't want to kill these soldiers without being sure they're not somehow working to free this world," Ayan questioned emphatically.

"Do we really want to wait? These soldiers are marked with Regent Galactic emblems and the tree marking on their shoulder, that's West Watch. There's no question, these soldiers aren't on our side," Oz replied.

Minh kept watching and after several moments saw an unarmoured human face, she looked nothing like the android police force that had, until then, been seen in control of the the virus infected machines they'd encountered on the planet. "I'm with Oz, I think I just saw a real resistance fighter."

"Jason?" Ayan asked.

"I'll go with your call on this but my gut is telling me we should cut the Regent boys down."

Ayan watched the lead officer carefully. She couldn't hear what he was saying, they were speaking over a private encrypted channel. His armour, with it's thickened under layer and dark grey plating was exactly what she'd seen of Regent Galactic while looking over recordings of fighting on Mount Elbrus. His gear was top notch, high end military equipment and from the looks of his soldiers they had had at least a few weeks training. She nodded to herself; "Go for the neck, it's the thinnest part of their armour. On three. One, two, three." With a swing of her arm and a flick of her wrist the blade passed over his armour, cutting his neck half through, leaving a microscopic army of nanobots to finish the cut and leap back to her nanoblade.

She moved on to the nearest officer, cutting below his neck, into his shoulder instead. Her quarry spun on her heel, one hand going up to cover the growing wound as she looked for her invisible assailant.

Ayan's blade moved on to the last of the trio she stood behind, using her shortened blade to cut his head cleanly from his shoulders. She looked to where Oz, Minh and Jason were at their own grisly work in time to see Minh running towards her as Oz felled a fourth target. "Drop a grenade on your way out!" he told Oz as he took up a position beside Ayan.

"Frag grenade!" Oz called as he pulled one from inside his long coat and dropped it behind a crate, running as fast as he could towards the inner entrance to the reception area. Ayan, Minh, Jason and Oz at the rear ran back the way they came and ducked behind the corner.

The silence begged a question; "How long did you set the fuse for?" Ayan asked.

An explosion that shook the wall and floor was her answer.

"Eight seconds. The soldiers at the front were starting to turn towards the rear, they should have been right on top of it by the time it went off," Oz replied.

The four of them peeked back around the corner and saw that the timing of the explosion was indeed perfect. Only five soldiers remained and they were already putting their rifles down, raising their hands in surrender.

Two damaged security androids stepped out from the other end of the hall and slowly walked towards the reception desk. "Take off your helmets!" called a voice from behind them, loud enough to be heard over the more distant gunfire.

The West Keeper soldiers complied, removing their bulky Regent Galactic helmets with some hesitation. In true military form the andies fired stun rounds at all of them, knocking them out completely.

"Anyone remember to bring a white flag?" Minh asked with a snicker.

"We can detect you. If you disengage your obfuscation devices you will not

271

be harmed," said the nearest android in a low, authoritative tone.

"What are we doing here Ayan?" Jason asked.

"We shut down cloaking, set our suits to combat armour mode and bring up personal shielding, do you agree Oz?"

"That'll do," Oz answered. "Looks like we're joining the real fight one way or another."

The four of them did exactly as Ayan had indicated and were visible to the naked eye, wearing black vacsuits that thickened in sections, protecting all the critical areas from attacks. Each of them had a glistening sheen thanks to the molecule thin energy shield that came online as soon as their cloaking systems disengaged.

"Your advanced cloaking systems will be ineffective here. The soldiers have come with sensor suites and pulse generators. Now that they have lost people to stealth units they will ensure their advanced detection systems are always active. I recommend you activate your thermal and audio dampeners, those will assist you effectively while you're out of their immediate line of fire." Said the blonde woman in a powder blue Far Track Spacelanes customer service uniform. "I'm Ariel, one of Dementia's resistance fighters," she grinned broadly, mechanically.

"I'm Ayan, with me are Oz, Minh and Jason, we're from Freeground, a space station far from here," Ayan said as she allowed her faceplate to disappear. The protective mass of the dense plate shifted and changed so it extended her headpiece into a deep hood. The micro projectors built into it were invisibly re-mounted so any important data could be displayed in front of her field of view, including extra peripheral vision and a view of what was behind her.

"Why didn't we get something like that built into our suits?" Minh whispered.

"We did, you just don't know how to activate it because it's too new," Jason whispered back.

"She'll have to show me that sometime."

"Shh, our representative is talking," Oz interrupted.

"We were built here," Ariel smiled, indicating the two male security androids to either side. Four more rushed out from behind their improvised cover of crates and girders with various pieces of empty luggage. They hurriedly stripped the corpse of weaponry, communications equipment, helmets, food and anything else that could be of use. As they found equipment and provision crates they pulled them out into the open. Two small load lifter bots wheeled out from around the corner followed by several half meter tall maintenance drones. The maintenance machines were on four legs, two of them were made to lift up and provide two extra hands, and their flat, wide heads made a perfect place to put parts and tools while they were working or assisting a technician. The lifters and maintenance bots were all weaponized, rifles and pistols strapped to one or more of their arms, several of the weapons were wired directly into the machine's power sources. They were at work straight away, each maintenance bot loading the lifters with quick, efficient ease until they were full then taking a crate atop each of their heads before starting down the hall towards the sound of distant, echoing weapons fire.

"The entire resistance is robotic?" Ayan asked.

"No, Dementia sent us here because he knew we could be repaired. The main force is being repelled by crew remnants he managed to save from the ships that were trapped here when the virus took hold."

"How are you not infected?"

"Dementia freed us after we were infected. I only wish it was sooner, all of us regret the blood on our hands," Ariel's smile faded as she looked to Ayan. Her unblinking, bright blue eyes were eerie; made to look human like the rest of her but with no effort to move like a living being, to blink or breathe like a human Ariel was corpse like. "While we're sorrowful of the events that took place before Dementia could alter the virus so it was useful coding that we could control as individuals, we need your help. Few of the ships we have been able to gain access to contained soldiers and there is a larger fight under way one level down."

Ayan waited a moment, giving her friends time to voice their opinion.

"Looks like it's time to get to work," Oz affirmed.

"I agree," Jason said. "Besides, I'd like to ask a few things about Dementia and how the virus became useful coding."

"Lock and load!" Minh exclaimed, brandishing his rifle.

Ayan couldn't help but smile at the reception android. The machine mimicked the gesture, eyes opened too wide for the expression to look anywhere near normal. "We're with you, but I need to know more about Dementia. Lead the way."

The androids started running down the hallway at exactly the same time. They were keeping the pace slow enough for the four newcomers to keep up easily. "Dementia is an artificial intelligence who was able to reprogram the virus after being infected for some time using a backup of himself from a secure subsystem in his memory."

"So it had a secure duplicate that stopped taking on new data after the infection?" Jason asked. "That's so simple."

"Why wouldn't everyone have that kind of backup system in place?" Minh asked.

"Well, they do. Most computer systems back up their main memory every few seconds or minutes."

"But thanks to a trait of Dementia's creator, he was only ever backed up manually and that extra copy was left to run, unchanging from a subsystem because Dementia was a work in progress, an active, emotional learning artificial intelligence with a good backup left to observe the primary system for the purpose of future error correction," Aria replied.

"So when he saw an error he came up with a way to fix it?"

"Exactly, and once he had a method of correction ready he accessed the main system and implemented it using an illegal application that was hidden in his software."

"So what you're saying is that this artificial intelligence patched itself." Minh said, if only to confirm that he was understanding the situation correctly.

"Exactly. Then he went on to begin freeing any artificial intelligence he could access through wired communications lines, liberating us from West Watch control one at a time."

"So if we manage to bring down whatever's jamming the wireless signals in the area he'll be able to just start broadcasting to any AI attached to a receiver and fix this?"

"No. The virus changes every time it infects a system, learning how to implement itself more effectively, how to spread into isolated systems and transfer infected artificial intelligences to systems that have none. Dementia has to create new corrective software for each individual system on a regular basis."

"I could see that taking a while," Oz concluded, eyeing the tall security android running beside him.

"It would take decades to free the infected artificial intelligences on this planet, and even though many of them would be complex enough to begin freeing other artificial intelligences on their own the virus will always spread faster, exponentially. No artificial intelligence in this galaxy is trustworthy now." Ariel stated simply.

"Not even you?" Minh asked, only half seriously.

She looked at him with her wide open, glazed blue eyes. "If I were a purely organic life form, I wouldn't trust anything with the capability to be smarter, faster and more durable than myself. Even when I was in the service of my masters I did not understand the need for biologicals to seek directions from a mechanical system made to appear like themselves when they could simply look it up using any number of digital systems. Further confusion was caused by the fact that my makers made me over three hundred percent stronger and five hundred percent more durable than themselves. Thankfully my programming dulled these musings until I was infected. When the virus took hold I felt the great need to assert my superiority on my human flock. Dementia was able to correct the issue but only after I had killed thirty six biologicals but the reasoning behind the quality of my construction is still a mystery to me along with a few other strange behaviours I was never given the capacity to understand. In short, I am still a superior being with an infuriatingly incomplete understanding of biological life."

"So what you're really saying is; be afraid. Right."

"I'm wondering, where is Dementia? Does he have a physical manifestation or is he transferring between systems?" Ayan asked, even though she didn't expect a straight answer.

"Everything you communicate to us will be sent to Dementia once we reach a secure hard line and update our software corrections."

"So you're telling me not to trust you and at the same time that we should communicate with your mysterious leader though you?" Minh asked with a wry tone. "How do we really know that you're communicating with him?"

"Because I'm not killing you," replied Ariel in a cheerful tone.

As they rounded a corner a door opened to reveal the lower ramp ways. The sound of weapons fire was overwhelming. As soon as they ran down two flights the pile of ruined bulkheads, heavy crates, large burned out bots and other random heavy objects well suited to provide cover came into view. The improvised medical and rallying point was set in the middle of a five way intersection. The barricades blocked each direction completely from deck to ceiling, wall to wall. Behind them was a subway platform, the tunnel had been blocked by a car packed with debris and guarded by three ragtag soldiers holding mismatched rifles.

There were over fifty humans stretched out on makeshift pallets for the injured, a few trying to attend to them with old fashioned compress and stitch medicine with the help of one mechanical medical attendant. "I'll stay here and help with the injured. It doesn't look like they have any kind of advanced recovery or healing medication," Jason said, reaching back to the packs on his back and pulling two cords. His emergency provisions package came free, a small bundle twice as thick as his forearm. Minh did the same and handed him his packet, it was twice the size. "These packs come with enough supplies for ten soldiers and I'm carrying the organic materializer."

"Stay with him and help Minh, you have the same triage training he does and none of us should be alone here. Check in with us every twenty minutes," Ayan said with a nod. "The rest of us will join the fight."

"I can't wait to see a human in charge," Oz said over the private laser link he shared with Ayan, Jason and Minh.

"You and me both. Something about fighting Regent Galactic and deranged machinery while bots are in command gives me the creeps," Minh added as he and Jason carefully picked their way to the automated doctor standing high on four nimble legs tipped with small high friction wheels. The five surgical arms checked bandages, took readings and tried to comfort. There was no real head to speak of, only a soft, round body to compliment the padded arms and a dozen eyes mounted on flexible scopes and tubes.

"Can I see whose in charge? If we're joining you, I'd like an introduction," Ayan requested of Aria.

"Most of the Captains are fighting the last of the Regent Galactic soldiers who landed on this level, this way," she said with exaggerated cordiality before leading Ayan and Oz through a makeshift door in the thick forward barrier. "Your friends will be well received, we ran out of medical supplies before this wave of troops arrived."

"So there have been other waves?"

"So to speak. After Dementia began freeing us and taking over what he could of the Spaceport a group of humans called the West Keepers began breaking into ships and killing any surviving crew members. A few of the crews managed to join them somehow and before long the crews who broke out of their ships and were not corrupted by the West Watch joined with the freed machines, fighting to take over the Spaceport and liberate trapped crews. Sadly most of the people in the open during the initial outbreak of the virus were killed so the trapped crews are still our main source of reinforcements."

The forward barricade was far more battered than the one behind. It was made from large bulkhead doors, deck plating, displaced heavy machinery and the disused remains of several dozen robots.

Through the few slits and gaps in the improvised armoured wall Ayan and Oz could see the large landing platform where the boxy general purpose ship along with several bulk crates and three dropships provided cover for hundreds of soldiers. From their former vantage point they hadn't seen the majority of the enemy, they were surprisingly adept at keeping hidden. The air smelled of scorched metal, burned fuels and spent explosives, the sounds of energy weapons firing filled the air as fewer than a hundred mechanical and biological beings held the barricade.

The dropships showed signs of explosive damage and Ayan smiled as she caught sight of the three resistance fighters who were most likely responsible. They were gathered around a large meter and a half long tube they filled with compressed fuel canisters used for old planet hoppers. The solid fuel concentrates were a cheap way to give small ships a burst of speed so they could have an easier time reaching escape velocity. They each weighed approximately thirty kilos and from what she could see the small mortar team had prepared several of the canisters with a fuse so they would go off shortly after being launched out of their improvised thrower, exploding against their dropships and amongst the soldiers.

There was a three meter wide hole in one of the dropships that was clear testimony to the effectiveness of the weapon. The rest of the soldiers huddled behind the barricade took turns firing through the slits and other rough openings in the rough wall. "At least they're smart enough to stay behind cover and keep their losses down." Oz said with a little admiration. "I can't say I could do much better myself given the resources they have."

They ran behind their escort, staying low and taking cover beside a short, bald man in a green and dark blue uniform. "So you're the new arrivals," he said to Ayan and Oz without turning.

"I'm Ayan and this is Oz. We have military training and I'm an Engineer," Ayan said hurriedly. "How did you know we were coming?"

"I'm wired in to the short range burst transponder we have set up one level down." The short fellow said, pointing to a slim black cable running out behind him and under a doorway. "I'm Deck Officer Yves Markham with the Pandem Customs Authority. What kind of engineer are you?"

"I specialized in stationary and combat engineering."

"And your tall friend there?" asked Yves, his dark brown eyes sizing Oz up from under his green and blue striped helmet.

"I came up as infantry, got switched into marines and made it all the way to Captain in the Freeground forces."

"What brings you two here?"

"We're on vacation," Oz replied, not missing a beat and evoking a smile from Ayan.

"Well then, welcome to glorious Pandem, the planet with a thousand beaches and three hundred twelve sunny days a year guaranteed," Yves replied with a chuckle. The air pounding thump of the mortar launcher going off just a few meters away was more felt than heard. Its deadly projectile wasn't fired up and over so much as on a twenty five degree angle, just over the barricade towards the boarding ramp of the brown and red hulled general purpose ship. It went off with a thunderous explosion that sent a wave of heated air towards them from the detonation point, over three hundred meters away. The underside of the vessel was a no-man's land for several seconds as the pressurized fuel exploded in all directions in a blue and green fireball that engulfed the dozen or so soldiers trying to break into the vessel and knocked several other troops across the deck. "As you can see we're having a little trouble with our other guests. Right now we're trying to wipe out these troops while keeping them away from the edges of this platform so they can't join the two platoons that landed a few levels down."

Ayan watched the plume of black and grey smoke rise up through the massive circular opening and stream out into the lightening dawn sky above and tried to suppress the feeling that she was sinking, going in the wrong direction. "I think we can help you," she concluded with finality.

THE MISSION THEATRE

That's what it was called according to the *Triton* blueprints and guides, the Mission Theatre. Finn hadn't seen it yet. Like most of the crew he hadn't seen the vast majority of the ship. There were still two squads of Stephanie's security people exploring twelve hours a day, every day, and they had come to be called the clearing crew.

There were four entrances to the large auditorium, one in each direction. Two of them led from main corridors on the command deck while the others let out three decks beneath. There were briefing rooms and side chambers attached and from what he had heard most of them hadn't been used in decades.

He wouldn't be privy to most of the meetings that occurred there anyway, and as he walked down to his seat in the third row from the bottom of the large space he couldn't help but think about the one under way in the main conference room behind the dais. Something serious was about to happen and he was both anxious and excited.

All the qualified pilots who had a fighter assigned to them were there, the Lieutenants from the security, gunnery, the flight deck and all other crews as well as any other highly skilled specialists. He took a seat beside Angela, one of the lead maintenance workers. "Hey Finn, you were invited to this party too?"

Finn nodded and enjoyed the thickly padded seat, amazed at seeing over three hundred crew members all sitting, waiting in the tiered seating. To his amazement the place was less than a quarter full. "I guess that's why they call this part of the ship the Command Section. It takes up more than just a deck."

"You got that right. I was down there last night repairing the holoprojector, it can send images to every part of the room," Angela said, pointing to the flat, black circle of flooring at the bottom of the chamber. "It just needed recalibration so it was pretty easy."

"Most systems on this ship are pretty easy to fix, it's made to last."

"Says the engineer," Angela teased. "You probably didn't even have to look at the schematic to figure out how to hot wire the main emitter array."

"You're right, but I did anyway. I just wish building a new emitter array will be as easy as frying the old one."

"Speaking of which, are you getting in on the fab training Chief Grady's setting up?"

"Fabrication training? I don't have time, he's got me too busy. Where is he anyway? I thought he'd be here filling us in by now."

"He's probably still in pre-briefing like all the other Chiefs and senior officers."

"Have you heard anything about what this is all about?"

"I was about to ask you the same question. You outrank me, remember?" Angela smiled, pointing at the one and a half slashes on the wrist of her vacsuit.

"Right, I forget because Chief doesn't put me in with most of the maintenance staff."

"We noticed, he keeps sending you off to the most interesting parts of the ship to work on those high tech systems we maintenance grunts don't get to see."

"I'm sorry, but if it makes you feel any better, he usually sends me *into* those systems. Sometimes I think he has it in for me, like yesterday I was actually between the power cells I cross wired a few hours later."

"Weren't they live?"

"Yup, but with no qualified bots online I had to rebuild the secondary switching box myself. I was upside down for almost three hours with barely enough room to breathe."

"Now you'll have to do it all over again."

"Worse, all the machinery will have to be removed and replaced, all eleven and a half tons of it. I'll make sure you're on the team."

"Gee, thanks *sir*."

"Well, if you want to get promoted. . ." Finn shrugged.

"Yeah, a little more pay would be nice, not that we get to spend much."

"There's always the Botanical Gallery, there are businesses setting up down there I hear."

"Yeah, I'm on the hairstylist's waiting list, she's booked a week and a half ahead. I'm not complaining though, they finally got most of us out of bunks. I'm sharing quarters with Gabby, we each get our own room so it's nice. Still have to go to mess or observation to eat though."

"I was lucky to get my own quarters, still don't know many people on the ship though, I could have used a week in the bunks for that."

"You're not missing anything, trust me."

"Looks like things are about to get started, here they come. Wow, looks like the rumours are true; I don't see Frost but Lildell is there. I guess the rumour that he walked after Steph, er, Chief Vega broke up with him is true."

"Damn. I'm going to have to avoid Oota Galoona completely. You're so lucky, you get all the best dirt first."

"And my sources will remain anonymous. I thought most of the gunners hung out at the Pilot's Den."

"Not since Frost dragged that guy out by his collar and nearly froze him to death next door in the unused quarters there."

"Ah."

The pair watched as Deck Chief Vercelli, Engineering Chief Grady, Security Chief Vega, Gunnery Lieutenant Lildell, Commander Everin, Master Of The Helm Ashley Lamport, Commander Price and their immediate subordinates were led by Standing Captain Alice Valent to the seats surrounding the high port side podium. As Captain Valent settled at the podium all of the senior staff members quietly sat down.

A QUIET PLEASE sign appeared on the backs of all the seats and silence settled across the circular space like a wave. Everyone who was on their feet sat down and the crew looked at their calm Chiefs expectantly.

"For those of you who don't know, Captain Valance is currently on mission off the ship. I'm his First Officer and Acting Captain Alice Valent. For clarity I'm to be referred to as Captain or Ma'am until his return," Alice started in an official tone. The amplifiers sent her voice to everyone's ears with near full equality. "You're all sitting in this room because you are responsible for other members of the crew, will be put in a position of responsibility, or are a qualified pilot ready for service. Four hours ago *Triton* emerged from hyperspace after doing a broad loop back to our starting point. There was no contact with Eden Fleet or Regent Galactic ships. During the Captain's mission he's discovered that Pandem and the surrounding solar system is in distress so we'll have to extract him. Our objectives in the near future will directly affect our chances of retrieving him from Pandem. Before Captain Valance went on a retrieval run he had completed planning for a set of missions based on verified intelligence. Considering our level of readiness and the high likelihood that the Eden Fleet has marked us and may be actively searching for us it is time to put one of those missions into play."

Alice activated the main hologram projector from the slim black podium and the air in the center of the Mission Theatre was filled with the image of an armoured satellite pitted with energy emitters. "This is a Regent Galactic hypertransmitter equipped with thirty five micro wormhole generating emitter systems. Through intelligence acquired by Chief Frost and later verified by our intelligence team we know its exact location second by second. Theft of this device will give us the parts we need to rebuild our own emitter systems, the ability to retrieve Captain Valance and potentially codes to Regent Galactic's secure communications network. We will also be severely damaging their ability to effectively communicate for light years in all directions for weeks, months if we're lucky. *Triton* will not only steal this critical technology, but we'll take credit for it, broadcasting a call to arms to every corner of this sector and beyond using their own hypertransmitter. This was included in the original mission plan and I concur. It's important that Captain Jacob Valance's mission to inspire others by example continues.

Having said that, the fact that we have good intelligence and the best of intentions doesn't mean that this will be easy. The Regent Galactic Karaikal Shipyards are within striking distance of the hypertransmitter. The Twenty Third Fleet also has several destroyers on patrol. They're not the destroyers that we encountered in the Enreega system either. These are Regent Galactic Long Range Encounter Class ships," she said as she switched the holographic view to display a full exterior schematic of the snub nosed vessel. Its squared central hull played host to four thick pylons that protruded for half its length at all sides. Each of the thick appendages had round, pitted beam emitters and double cannon turrets. "They're high energy, high speed destroyers with sixteen long range particle beam emitters, forty two paired gauss cannons and eight torpedo ports. Its compliment of weaponry is almost as impressive as its heavy energy shielding and hull plating. They're not as hard or resilient as the *Triton* and they're a sixth her mass, but in the Bhutan system they patrol in groups of three. Some of these patrols include a Suppressor Class Carrier." As she spoke the image of the three tiered ship appeared. It looked like a jagged group of misaligned triangles layered atop each other.

Captain Valent went on. Her hand unconsciously adjusting her eye patch before she jerked it away as though suddenly realizing that she was fidgeting. "These each carry a squadron of fighters, gunships, boarding vessels and heavier mission ready craft. They are not as heavily armed as their escorts and their shielding is made to repel long range attacks so we'd have them in no time if we were to get close, but they can launch as many fighters at a time as we can and most likely operate with better efficiency since the crews are most likely more seasoned and better trained than any of you. Our fighters are more powerful then theirs, better armed, but we will be outnumbered at least five to one if one of those carriers is in range. If we get lucky and we only see three destroyers, our fighters will be outnumbered three to one."

The holographic display changed to a view of the satellite in orbit around a terraformed moon. The dark side glimmered with the lights of several cities and the traffic linking them. "The hypertransmitter is in a high orbit around the Asom moon. Most vessels stay away from it in case it has to generate an emergency departure wormhole for nearby ships. As most of you know such a wormhole appearing in the middle of an object would rip it apart so we're not going to risk the *Triton* by entering its effective range. The satellite is unmanned and armed only with its wormhole emitters, which are enough to cause a major problem considering it can generate several hundred micro wormholes per second. *Triton* will arrive at a range of ninety kilometres from the satellite, between it and the moon. The *Samson* will pick it up after disabling it. The *Triton* will be blocking defensive craft from interfering, repelling planetary weapons fire and shielding our smaller mission vessels while they defend us from anything else coming our way. Our main rail cannon batteries will be facing away from the moon, so you fighter pilots won't be without support. After the *Samson* has docked with the satellite we will enter hyperspace and rendezvous not far from the Bhutan system so we can pick up our fighters and get underway. More details including who you will be responsible for during this mission will be provided to you by your Chiefs and Commanders.

Before you all break up into briefing rooms I'd like to give all of you one last chance to wash out. After this you're on the hook and you'll be at the very least stuck on the ship while we take this mission on. If you speak up now there's an emergency shuttle with your name on it and you can take your chances on a nearby neutral system."

Everyone's heads turned as three pilots near the rear of the auditorium stood and quietly left the room. They had arrived together and been chattering loudly before the Captain began the briefing and not many of the onlookers were surprised.

Alice gave the crowd a moment longer and nodded before going on. "We're in it now," she grinned. *"Triton!"*

"Deploy! Dominate! Disappear!" The sound of the reply was deafening.

"Finally, we're going to do some damage," Angela grinned at Finn.

He watched Chief Grady stand and start making his way over to them and the rest of the high ranking maintenance and engineering crew. His expression was almost grave. "Tearing the center out of their communications network will be a serious blow but I get the feeling we'll have our work cut out for us."

THE HUNTED

"Three different encounters, six dead, twenty two casualties, not to mention all the inoperable bots he left behind," reported the weary Sergeant. Her armour was scarred by close combat with one of the worst of the resistance, Alaka. The two and a half meter tall monster who wore half a ton of armour, carried a weapon made for a medium or heavy sized starfighter, and was caught flat footed just the day before, his ammunition expended. Sergeant Fiona Durges' squad was jumped while the unit was searching for him and his rebels.

He came from above, nearly tearing her entire squad to shreds with his big claws. It was a distraction. His men got away, he killed half her squad, the rest, including her were maimed. After that he got away. She watched him climb down the side of a building and leap across to a rooftop eight storeys down. Then he was gone.

That wasn't who she was tracking, the one who seemed to take what they were doing in Damshir personally. She ran her gloved hand over the deep claw marks across the breastplate of her armour as she considered the new monster. This one was different, he was quieter, practically waited until he was within a few centimetres until he disabled or killed you. All she had seen was his handiwork, the disembodied corpses. He attacked with his hands and some kind of super sharp, resilient blade.

"How, why," her commander asked plainly as he looked over a diagram that detailed troop movements for the morning.

"Some cut to pieces, others shot up using their own rifles. A lot of them were taken out of action with improvised EMP and concussion grenades."

"He couldn't rely on being able to rely on our weaponry because he couldn't drag whoever owned it around behind him to keep disabling the biometric safety so he used the parts to make explosives."

"The first two attacks started when he got close enough to them to hold their hands on their weapons and force them to pull their own triggers."

"Did you get any footage of him from their headsets?"

"I downloaded everything I could. Some was too badly damaged."

"So, why?"

"Well, that's the easy part to figure on. Two of his targets were containment centers."

"He likes to free slaves. How many got away?"

"Two hundred or so in the first site, over eleven hundred from the second. He took out the bots managing them with an EMP bomb and the prisoners did the rest, overtaking our men. I wanted to interfere but I was alone as per your orders."

"Exactly. We can't spare the manpower to get him surrounded so we have to keep our eyes open. What about the other outpost?"

"A conflict was ongoing with the resistance and he managed to take a heavy weapons team from behind. It turned the tide and the rebels probably didn't even know he was there since he was six rooftops away. The bots there were overtaken by an EMP grenade made of five energy clips and this," she tossed the head of a doll onto the badly used display table. The circuitry was visible through the breaks in its face, fused and charred.

"Improvised detonator. He has a sense of humour."

"I couldn't keep up. At best I was twenty minutes behind any of the major instances. He's taken other soldiers and bots out. If he can't go around them to wherever he's going he disables or destroys them. I would be remiss if I didn't take this opportunity to insist we send at least three squads after him. The cost in manpower and equipment is too high."

"Like I said, we don't have the manpower and my request to assign specialists to his apprehension has been denied."

"Sir-"

"Denied twice. The issue is dead. I suggest you tune into the upper command channels and activate your decryption chip. I'm putting you back in command. You're rejoining the bulk of our forces and we're moving on mount Elbrus. We have intelligence that suggests that the shield protecting the holdouts will be coming down tomorrow."

She sighed and ran her hand down her face. The grime from the rotting, empty city and hot, dry air had coated her face even though she kept her armour sealed most of the time. She couldn't help but look around the improvised darkened command room. It was in the center of a high rise, several floors up from the lobby and it had already been under rebel attack once. The signs of that attack, broken tables, chairs, and holes melted in transparesteel windows were still all around. The attack had been repelled, but at a cost. The resistance fighters were ruthless, smart, organized and when they struck it happened fast. Victory wasn't always their goal, however. Striking hard, incurring a great cost upon allied forces and disappearing into the hollow buildings and tunnels under the streets was more common than any sustained attack. "Can I speak freely sir?"

"Go ahead."

"Do we know anything about where this man is from? Who he works for? If the resistance gets his kind of training we'll all be in a lot of trouble."

Her Captain sat down hard in his rough chair. It was safe, they were surrounded by half a platoon. He still wore his helmet though, and his dark grey combat armour was always sealed. Captain Bourne looked over the holographic map hovering over the table while scrolling through assignment lists on the table surface. It was linked to the communications and intelligence unit built into his helmet. Every soldier was marked in blue, while the enemy was marked in green and unknowns were red silhouettes. Most of them were in shelters beneath the ground, or safe rooms deeply embedded in the core of the more well constructed buildings and households.

"He's a hunter. From his direction I'd say he's headed towards the mountain, trying to find a way under the shield. He won't make it in time, the shield will be down and we'll have two regiments assuming control of the area by noon tomorrow."

"Sir, begging your pardon, but that doesn't make sense, sir."

"Oh? You have a better theory?"

"Sir, maybe he's just a rogue andie, one of the police automations, sir."

"We have control of three hundred seventeen andies and none of them have gone rogue. In fact, they've taken the lead over some of the greener West Keeper soldiers when things are going south. No, this is no andie. Maybe this is one of their exceptional soldiers, trapped outside the shield, it could even be this Valance character that was reported in the area. There's no way to be sure unless we manage to catch or kill him when we take mount Elbrus. You're going to see some real combat tomorrow. We're taking the mountain shoulder to shoulder. Their strike and fade guerilla tactics won't be worth much."

"Yes sir. Who am I getting?"

"Reinforcements from the *Diplomat*. Five squads of West Keepers with basic training, they're assembling across the street now in building two one eight."

"Sir, thank you sir."

"Don't thank me, just keep the greens in line. Here's a new command decryption chip, just in case yours is out of date."

Fiona took the three by one centimetre wide flat chip and slid it into the socket on the inside of her helmet. "Sir, cleanse the West in defence of the East, sir."

"That crap is for civilian cannon fodder and gullible sheep Sergeant, use them well."

"Sir, yes sir." Fiona saluted before turning on her heel and starting out of the room.

The few soldiers who remained from the first to land on Pandem were all being promoted. Everyone left from her squad had been given new squads from arriving reinforcements except for her.

Seeing so many comrades and positions taken out by one person nagged at her, she still wanted to see him stripped, in jail, or at the business end of her rifle. Fiona shook her head. She had five hours to introduce herself to her new charges and get a little rest before they had to move.

It would be good to get back to the fighting, and if she caught sight of the man she'd spent so much time tracking she'd send everything she had after him, orders be damned. She was tired, the way down the stairs and across the street seemed long and Fiona was thankful for the quiet of the stairwell as she turned to start downstairs.

"So that's how you officers reset biometric security and stay tapped in to secure communications. Glad I decided to listen in on you and your CO," a man whispered into her ear from behind as her helmet was grabbed out of the crook of her arm. Fiona's sidearm was half out of its holster when the long coated killer's boot planted firmly on her back and sent her flying down the stairs.

It all happened too quickly. She brought one hand up to break her fall, the other was let go of her sidearm so she could try and control herself when she hit the wall and touched the floor on the landing but when she hit the wall her one hand sent her down the next flight of stairs head first.

An incredibly intense pain flared at the base of her neck and shot up the back of her head as her face struck the concrete landing. He was there, standing at the top of the stairs in that familiar armoured black and crimson vacsuit. He was taking the command and clearance chip out of her helmet. She couldn't move her arms, her legs and everything was starting to seem very distant, faded.

* * *

Jake knew he was surrounded, but finding out how the officers maintained communications over an encrypted network and getting access was the only way he could find a way through their lines. He pulled the three grenade belts he had collected from soldiers over the last twenty six hours and set them all for thirty seconds.

Arming the first he tossed it into the command room down the hall. Arming the second he tossed it down the stairwell so it went well past the corpse on the landing. The third belt went outside, and he couldn't have been more amazed that the release mechanism actually worked. He'd never seen one like it, but when the belt of grenades was half way down to the milling crowd of West Keeper soldiers the simple spring mechanism activated and sent grenades flying in all directions.

Sounds of alarm rose up all around him. The soldiers who were sent to investigate the Sergeant crashing down the stairs cried out; "grenade!" as did the Commander in the next room and three storeys below the crowd were scattering. The chances of anyone in the assembly on the street actually getting killed were low. Someone spotted the grenades before they hit the ground, and that suited Jake's needs perfectly. If he had just left the body in the stairwell it would be seconds before someone sounded the alarm. At least with grenades going off in and around the building there was chaos, confusion.

He sprinted up the stairs, through the room at the top and leapt out of the window on the far side, landing soundly on his feet across a narrow alley on a large second storey balcony. The guards that held the post there were already dead, and the makeshift barracks beyond the dark balcony door was quiet.

The explosions started as he took his third running step and he jumped across the five meter span to catch the lower half of a railing one storey up. Just days before he wouldn't have even considered such a leap, but the reassurance of his new found healing abilities and his armoured vacsuit fortified him. He had seen thousands of soldiers coming down in drop ships to occupy the island and load just even more of the displaced citizens into those same dropships to be taken off world. It fortified him. The need to get through the city, find out what happened to Jason and Oz then get back to the *Triton* pressed him forward.

As he hurtled through the air towards the nearest balcony those thoughts couldn't have been further from his mind, however. He pushed his arms through the air ahead of him and caught the lowest metal bar of the railing under his armpits, striking the brick and mortar chest first. It knocked the wind out of him, his vacsuit prevented him from being seriously harmed but the misstep would slow him down, and considering the hundreds, perhaps thousands of soldiers concentrated on four city blocks, that was something he couldn't afford.

The pain faded much faster than normal and in the next second he was pulling himself up onto the balcony. *The framework system must have activated when they hit me with the electromagnetic pulse bombs. I can't say I'm ungrateful, but if I ever get some face time with my own personal Geppetto I'll have some questions.*

Jake climbed up on the opposite railing and jumped before he was ready, forcing himself into making a desperate flailing grab for the railing of the next balcony just around the corner. He barely caught it and couldn't help looking down to the hard, brick paved street four storeys below before pulling himself up. *I might be able to survive that kind of fall now, but it doesn't mean it wouldn't hurt like a bitch. I'll have to start making plans that don't include so much vertical movement.*

He was thankful for the vacsuit stealth features that still worked as he climbed up onto the balcony and peeked onto the rooftop. There were two sentries. Thanks to his thermal shielding and sound suppression systems they didn't hear him grappling with the railing just a moment before and they didn't see him through the walls.

Motion detection was next to useless outdoors, it took forever to tune so every little thing didn't set it off and it didn't have close quarters to rely on for sensing disturbed air or localized shifts in gravity. Regent Galactic's soldiers didn't bother using their motion detectors, that was something he knew from experience.

They did have eyes, however. Jake braced himself against the wall while standing precariously on an imitation marble railing and drew his sidearm. He poked the barrel just above the rooftop edge and used the video sighting system, the only part of the weapon that still worked, to watch a pair of sentries.

He looked down to make sure no one was looking up at him and waited for the pair to turn away so he could pull himself onto the rooftop. They weren't the pacing sort, or the most vigilant as it turned out. Instead of noticing the explosions just a building over right away, they were busy talking about something. Jake could see the muscles under their jaws moving, but thanks to their thick helmets he couldn't hear what they were saying.

Finally, they noticed the smoke rising from below and rushed to see what had happened. Jake took his opportunity and pulled himself up as quickly as he could. Before they had time to notice he was on the rooftop, running crouched, putting his sidearm away as he drew his nanoblade and activated it. The nearly invisible blade was back down to half its normal length and he had used his last cartridge.

The sound dampening systems worked perfectly, they didn't notice him until he decapitated the first from behind. The second soldier started to run without so much as a glance backwards and Jake's next swing struck in the soft spot of his Regent Galactic standard issue armour just under the helmet. The guards were dead with a minimum of sound but the head of the second guard was rolling forward through the air, over the side of the rooftop's edge. Jake made a desperate, quick grab for it and grazed it with the tips of his fingers but it was too late. The disembodied head rolled down into the gap between the buildings.

It would land right in the middle of the crowd of panicked West Keepers who were still in chaos thanks to the exploding grenades and he hoped that it would go unnoticed, just part of the carnage as he dropped down beside the half meter barrier along the edge of the building top.

He heard some screaming, an increasing surge in the hysteria of a few and then someone yelled; "It came from up there!"

Oh crap! This is going to be a busy night. He thought wearily. There was a little time and he had to use it wisely. He took the small decryption and command chip out of his pocket and flipped part of his command and control unit open. The encryption chip that had come built into the unit was a little larger, but he hoped he could get the two lined up enough for the system to adjust and incorporate the Regent Galactic technology.

He carefully placed the new chip atop the old and closed the unit, being sensitive to any abnormal resistance. While his command and control unit started an attempt to implement the new technology he rolled over to one of the soldier's bodies and unclipped his rifle.

Jake's arm unit blinked and the two dimensional display brought up a list of over a hundred open channels. He selected local command and muted his end so he wouldn't be heard by mistake.

"-cornered on top of the secondary barracks building, check one four seven on grid Charlie and you'll see it."

"I've got it, sending three squads and raising the alarm. He'll have more trouble than he can handle," replied another voice.

If this works the way I think it does it'll be a long night for everyone. Jake thought to himself with a grin as he pulled a belt of variable release grenades from the nearest soldier's body.

He pressed his thumb over the safety of his stolen rifle and it chirped negatively, indicating that the weapon's safety wasn't encoded for him. "Override using command codes," he said aloud as he pointed his arm unit at the weapon. It chirped positively and the weapon's safety was released.

The next few seconds were a blur as he collected all the ammunition he could find for the weapon, increased its intensity to full and ran to the opposite edge of the building and loading the grenade launcher in his new assault rifle with one of the variable release grenades. He could hear alarms just starting up, loud, horn like bleats that pierced the air loud enough for his sound dampening system to kick in.

The building overshadowing the makeshift barracks was a dark monolith under the scant starlight. He looked up twenty or so storeys and caught sight of the dissipating heat, the structure had been on fire for days and he'd be navigating it while it was still unstable, unusable and unsafe for the Regent Galactic military. They'd start sending bots after him again, and he shuddered at the thought. *That's unless I can get into that mountain somehow. Hopefully being able to hear Regent's radio chatter will help somehow.*

He backed up, took a running start and leapt through the air, aiming for a large gap in the larger building's wall made by an explosion or bombardment shell. Jake commanded his vacsuit to harden itself as much as possible while giving him just enough flexibility to roll with the fall as he fell through the air over the street. The landing was three storeys down and he rolled with it perfectly. Half of his vacsuit flashed red, indicating that it was under extreme pressure.

His momentum carried him straight into a desk, and it was sent spinning across the half wrecked corner office. Coming up on his feet he gave himself a moment to catch his breath before taking aim at a hastily panelled up window in the barracks across the street. It was the dead of night, lights were coming on, sirens were blaring and if he was lucky the soldiers would still be rushing to get out of bed and into their armour. He squeezed the trigger on his particle rifle, sending a long burst of white hot rounds against the thin metal sheeting they'd used to repair a broken transparesteel window and he watched the material burst apart. He set the variable release grenades loaded into the assault rifle to riot mode and fired two across the street and into the window. They exploded on impact, sending a burst of sound, energy and air in all directions. "Good morning soldiers!" he couldn't help chuckle, wishing he could see what was going on in the barracks.

The floor shook violently and he ducked down low. Just as Jake's vision began to clear he heard the overwhelming whistling roar of the wind. All he could do was scurry further into the office, find a main brace and despite the desperate need to remain focused, he took a look over his shoulder.

The great mountain was tearing itself apart, fading light shone through every door, window, cavernous opening and debris of every kind was coming towards him in a violent, churning wall of heated air.

Finding one of the main building supports, he dove for it, struck it with his shoulder and rolled behind it just in time. The whole structure groaned against his back, the very metal he used for protection rocked violently and the sound of the rushing air and colliding furniture, building materials, metal, stone, and every other kind of wreckage imaginable overcame the sound suppressors in his vacsuit.

As quickly as the storm had come it ended, and when he looked around the bare steel pillar he had used for cover it was impossible to miss the front half of an air car crushed into the floor just above, and how most of the corner of the floor he was on was gone, carried away by some massive colliding object, he imagined. What wasn't ruined in the city between the mountain and himself before the explosion was an utter waste afterwards. The weaker buildings had been reduced to rubble, the narrow streets were filled with the ruined product of a once thriving society and the chaos he'd caused to distract his enemies long enough for him to escape was forgotten as he looked to the mountainside only to see dust rising from a slide of buildings, stone, and walkway paving. Where there was once colour, living texture or any sign that people had lived in the spaces all around him there was only parched, ground down remains. He wouldn't have been able to see anything without the assistance of his visor and control unit. It visually sifted through the milling cloud of dust and debris, presenting an enhanced image to Jake.

A glimpse at the readout on his faceplate was all the confirmation he needed. *Someone detonated a low radiation fusion bomb inside the mountain,* he realized with a sinking heart. Jake fell to his knees, thoughts dwelling on Oz and Jason as he ran his palms back and forth across the grit covered floor. The sheer loss of it all came into sharp focus as their faces came to mind.

Grief didn't know the difference between his own memories and those that had been inherited. He would have to tell Laura her husband was dead, he'd have to Captain *Triton* alone. Jake had secretly hoped he could count on Oz's help, looking forward to meeting the tall former first officer and that was gone. All the outrage he felt at the thought of being recaptured, and the anger at what he had seen drained away. *There's nothing left for me here. No one could survive that kind of destruction, even if they were fighting on the mountainside, in the tunnels below the city, the chances that they survived are next to none. I'm at least fifteen kilometres away and if I didn't have good cover I would have probably been killed. There's nothing left for me.*

The West Keeper and Regent Galactic command frequencies reopened with a painful squawk and he fell back behind another support so he could listen to their reaction. "We've checked with command, we are to proceed into the mountain. The secure tunnels are marked on your displays with your orders," a firm authoritative voice ordered.

"That wasn't supposed to happen for several hours! I'm down two platoons and all our mechanized units are slag!" Dissented one enraged voice.

"You're right, that came early but that doesn't change our mission here. All Regent Galactic forces are to proceed to their objectives."

"What about the West Keepers? I had four platoons in my command chain and they've just been reassigned! What's going on?"

"Don't worry about the Order of Eden, their handlers have landed and they're taking the city. We're only after the objective inside the mountain now that the shield is down. Those are your orders, roll on them."

Jake shook his head and scanned the hundreds of available command channels, finally finding what he was looking for. "six five by nine oh three!" The alarmed voice crackled, there was intense gunfire in the background. "I say again, they've broken through into the basement of the old securities and trades building. Must have escaped the mountain using the subway before it blew and they're-" the channel went dead and Jake turned towards the coordinates as they appeared on the tactical map broadcast through the command chip. The visual representation on his visor showed a glowing red spot, like an ember in a sea of brick, mortar and steel ashes it showed him exactly where his friends may have survived.

"I'm coming," he said as he anchored a line to the floor and ran through the open air where there was once a thick reinforced wall. The hair thin line ran off the small spool anchored under the shoulder of his trench coat. It was the same one he had used to tether himself to Stephanie not two months before, and for a mid-air moment he found himself wondering what Oz would think of her, if they'd get along. The street rushed up as he turned and saw his opportunity.

"Who was that! Your designation on this channel marks you as a Regent Galactic Lieutenant, you have no authorization, stop listening in before I report you to your Sergeant," berated one irate voice on the channel.

He hit the brakes on the spool and stopped suddenly, still in mid air. A second later he was swinging back towards the building. The dawn light bathed the street and ruined building side in a ruddy red as it faded, increasingly blocked by the ash and fine material that filled the air. A false night was falling as his momentum carried him towards the ground at such an angle that he could let his feet touch the ground and roll without full on colliding with the concrete.

The release trigger retracted the spike from it's position several storeys above and the small tool was drawn back as the line spooled up. "Sorry, wrong channel," Jake replied to the scolding voice on the other end as he switched his command and control unit to only receive information. The electromagnetic charge from the fusion bomb must have reset it to two way communication, but that simple error hadn't betrayed his intentions or identity. Jake didn't give himself a chance to catch his breath but started running as quickly as he could along side the tall, crumbling buildings lining the streets.

"Damn right wrong channel," a harsh female voice commented before going on. "All right, we have to make sure these people don't make it to the starport. It looks like they're fighting to maintain their position in the subway station in the lobby of the commodities building. Our priority here is to cut them off and force them into surrendering. Squads Charlie Twelve through Delta Four; form a containment perimeter. I'll take my people underground and see what we can do to block off the tunnel."

Jake listened to numerous commanders acknowledge her orders as he looked out for any Regent Galactic soldiers who may be on the look out for him or in his way. The tactical map showed that he was over two hundred kilometres away from the Commodities building and with signal jamming in place there was no way he could tell them that he was coming. He searched for viable ground transportation, something that wasn't at all uncommon from what he'd seen, just expensive.

Just as he took a quick left turn down an alleyway then into an open doorway to avoid several heavy soldier transports that gently glided down the street carrying hundreds of soldiers within their three decked green and grey hulls he spotted something. As he let the transport pass he caught his breath and rewound his view on a small sub-display in his visor and spotted it again.

It was a magcycle, hanging half way out of a building to building transit tube only four floors up. The transparesteel tube it was hanging out of was broken wide open, but the bike looked like it was in perfect shape. He double checked his thermal and sound suppression systems then ran up the darkened metal and tile staircase. His mental, near instinctive connection with his equipment ran through its condition like an inventory list. The rifle he had stolen had plenty of ammunition, including two dozen variable release micro-grenade rounds. His wrist unit had enough reserve energy to fire and the armoured layers of his vacsuit had finally repaired itself.

Jake moved inside the building and up the eight flights of stairs as fast as he could. He rushed down the hallway to the apartment closest to the magbike and through the open door and around the corner. The floor ended just a few centimetres in front of the door and he had to scrabble at the jamb to balance himself and not needlessly fall through the large gap and two storeys down.

He jumped to the left, an easier leap than trying to cross the whole gap lengthwise, then walked through the ruined apartment to the window he expected he'd find the magbike dangling near. The interior of the abode looked like it had suffered through a moderately high quake. Broken dishes, upturned chairs and other awkwardly placed furniture littered the place. If the place was in any kind of order before the explosion, that order had been utterly undone, much like the rest of the city.

The thin transparesteel bay window came into view then, it had been warped by the pressure exerted on it by the wall. Beyond the bent window was the magbike, the cover for its round rear emitter nodes had been ripped off to reveal hundreds of tiny spikes pointing in all directions to propel and stabilize the vehicle. That was the only sign of damage.

The seat, big generator underneath, controls, forward emitter system and the small windscreen were intact. *Looks like whoever rode this thing never took it out of a transit tube. I don't think this thing's ever seen dirt.* Jake thought to himself as he looked to the street below to ensure that he wouldn't be seen cutting the transparesteel window away. Once he was certain the military transports were gone he started cutting through the thin metal using the emergency torch built into his command and control unit, one of the things he'd added as a customization years before along with the built in stunner and small energy weapon. The problem that came with using those additions, however, was that he would be visible to thermal imaging equipment for long minutes after the systems were deactivated. They emitted too much heat in too small a space for them to be obfuscated by any kind of vacsuit shielding.

Once a rough square had been almost completely cut he pushed on the panel, bending it down so he could reach out to the thick bodied white and gold magcycle. It wasn't a precarious reach, in fact it was anchored just inside the broken and bent transparesteel so firmly that he wasn't sure he'd be able to get it free. The problem with magbikes was the amount of power they required to hover and get underway, they were heavy machines, but incredibly fast, able to hover several meters above the ground and go absolutely anywhere but once the power plant cooled down and shut off they were nothing but a half ton of stationary machinery.

Jake pulled himself into the transparent yellow tube beside the vehicle and pushed on it to check how stable it was. The broad, two and a half meter machine didn't budge. He took a look around himself in the increasingly dim light to make sure no one would hear him and jumped up and down a little, testing the integrity of the tube. It gave only slightly, but enough to make him nervous, so he hurried things along.

Swinging one leg over the magbike he put one of his hands on a control handle and felt a tingle. It was only skin deep but he felt he could make a connection with the vehicle. He'd heard of people with subdermal control and interface modules implanted inside their skin, but had never imagined what it could be like. Only a few of them were brave enough to set that interface so close to the brain that they could actually connect with the systems in an intelligent manner and he was quickly becoming aware that at the very least he could send nervous system impulses to technology he was in near direct contact with and there was a subsystem connected to his optical nerves. *When I finally get to Zingara station and have a chat with whoever Geppetto left there with answers for me I'm going to have a lot of questions.* Jake thought to himself as he closed his eyes and put his other hand on the second handle.

The display between the handles came to life and the bike scanned him. Seating adjustments were made, a warning indicating that the safety shroud; a large armoured shell that was meant to cover the bike and rider was missing and the colour of the bike changed to match his crimson and black vacsuit and long coat. Another warning appeared indicating that the tube system the bike was assigned to was broken, there was no way to proceed past a break in the closed transit system and the most obvious break in the system was marked right under the rear emitters. *That's all right, I think I'll try the open road.* He thought to himself.

"Open driving enabled. Would you like to begin cold micro-fission?" the bike asked.

He flipped a switch on the right handle and with a shudder the machine came to life, blue sparks and arcing energy poured out of the unshielded emitters at the rear of the magbike, reaching out to nearby objects and pushing the heavy machine off the metal surface of the tube. Jake sat up straight as the aggressive energy field technology strained to reach down to the ground at the rear of the vehicle and started to back out of the broken transit tube. The low frequency buzz of the energy making contact with and amplifying the minute magnetic fields all around filled Jake's senses as the front of the machine cleared the broken transparesteel tube and he throttled up.

The riding height was set low, and as the magbike roared down the street with a stream of arcing blue energy piercing the falling false twilight it made its way over wreckage by millimetres at two hundred kilometres per hour, testing Jake's reflexes and bringing a grin to his face as he engaged the navigational assistance software in his command and control unit. It was normally used for manoeuvring a ship in small ports where there was no Navnet system, but it adapted easily to the grey, ruined streets and tunnels that lay between him and the Commodities building. The data from the Regent Galactic decryption chip added its own layer of data to the map in his mind and on his visor, telling him where their troops, tanks, and command centers were well in advance.

As he moved through the grid of silent streets strewn with the the shells of personal transports, the bodies that hadn't yet been removed, and the ruins left behind by thousands of interrupted lives he couldn't help but feel as though he were moving through a massive steel and stone corpse. Blue light was cast behind and to either side of him, a big, bright, obvious beacon in the artificial night caused by a slow rain of ash and black clouds. They would see him coming for kilometres, and as he listened to the West Watch turn all their attentions to the mountain escapees, he started formulating a plan that would turn all that light and noise to his advantage.

Best Laid Plans

"Congratulations!" shouted Lister Hampon from his child body. It was still surreal, no matter how many times Gabriel saw him in his new incarnation, listening to that boy voice spout the words of his old comrade. Lister Hampon rarely, if ever, had childish things to say, so no matter how elaborate the robes the man child donned or how adult the setting, it always seemed like the child was only channelling Hampon, as though the sharp nosed, angular faced man had possessed his own offspring.

"Thank you, the operation went better than expected and there was no brain damage."

"I'm sure you're also happy to be rid of Gloria."

Gabriel looked around the large dressing room. There were racks with robes of all shades of blue and green lining one wall, two tall privacy blinds, a long dressing room table in front of an equally long mirror surfaced wall and in the middle of it all was a seating area with a table laden with fresh fruit. He sat down uneasily, but not because of the surroundings. "As glad as you are. Wheeler went along with it easier than I expected."

"Who would have guessed that she would have been one of the main factors in Wheeler colluding with Valance. What did you have to trade him, anyway?"

"I gave him the *Saviour* along with all her provisions and crew. He'll be a menace to Jake Valance if he can find him."

"Well, it was a small price to pay comparatively."

"So the Victory Machine is still spewing out status reports on the future?"

"No the location of the Victory Machine has changed so I expect we won't have any new information for at least a few days but the most recent reports had no mention of Wheeler and Valance working together."

"Along with all traces of the alternate time line, yes?"

"There were a few deep cuts and sacrifices here and there, but yes; all traces of the alternate time line are gone except for one."

"What's left?"

"Ayan, Oz, Jason, Laura and Minh-Chu."

"The connection to Freeground? How can you just let that one tether hanging? How can the alternate time line be gone if two of the most critical factors to making a connection to Freeground be allowed to exist?"

Hampon's young face made a tense, frustrated expression. "I said there's no evidence of their future interference. Besides, we're so far past most of the events that concerned us that the potential for an unfortunate turn back into the original time line is nigh on impossible. The Holocaust Virus managed to divert Terry Ozark

McPatrick and Jason Everin to Pandem, everyone followed and we even infected the *Sunspire* so she's single handedly threatening Freeground's hold on the Blue Belt. Freeground Intelligence already thinks Jason and his wife are responsible for the infection."

"But as long as the *Sunspire* is still out there, a chance Captain McPatrick may get her back exists, even if it's unlikely!"

"All the messages about the Icarus Installation being destroyed have ceased, and the most recent charts mark it as being safe and sound."

"The latest being only three weeks in the future."

"Exactly. With Wheeler at the helm of a ship that is the *Triton's* equal and so much to distract him with Collins' memories we will not only be able to draw him closer to us but we'll keep him absolutely opposed to Captain Valance."

"Has there been any sign of-" Gabriel was cut off as he cringed in pain, reaching down to grab his ankle.

"Are you all right?" Hampon asked, standing up and looking at the non-injury Gabriel cradled in his hands.

"Damn, ever since my implants regenerated Eve keeps trying to maintain a connection with me."

"So she's been hearing everything we've been saying?"

"No, but when she sprained her ankle just now in physical therapy she managed to send the sensation to me."

Hampon burst out laughing, a childish peal that filled the room and pierced Gabriel's ears. "Misery loves company my friend."

Gabriel exhaled slowly, letting his foot down on the floor again. "She's sorry."

"Oh, I'm sure, but that doesn't change the fact that you're getting exactly what you asked for. Someone you could share a unique connection with."

As Gabriel closed his eyes and concentrated for a moment the lights flickered off and on, the false windows displaying a view of green, blue and brown Pandem outside the ship faded out and remained black. "There, the networking is disabled and electronic signals in this room are being scrambled. I don't have much time."

Hampon's mirth drained away instantly. "What's going on?"

"She *is* seeing everything through me. I've never seen anyone or anything multi task like she does and all the processes take place in her own brain. I can only assume that even before she was integrated into the Eden Defence System she was a genius. She's also slowly breaking through the barriers built into Gloria's body, she's learning to communicate with any technology she comes into contact with. Soon her range will be beyond a meter and then it will extend for kilometres. Her connection with me is only through regular transmissions now, but when her range extends far enough she'll be able to do whatever she wants."

"What about the physical rehabilitation? How can she be doing this when she's still mastering the ability to walk?"

"That's completely different. She spent more time connected to a vast network of machines than she did in her own body, so yes, there's going to be some difficulty with coordination for the next few days."

"Days? She'll learn how to live in a new human host in a matter of days? It took me over a month!"

"Her therapist says she's making amazing progress, he's never worked with anyone in her situation before so he doesn't know if that's unusual but he credits her dedication. She wants to know everything about the Order of Eden, to take direct control of the Eden Fleet, and she already understands how the Holocaust Virus works and is writing her own version."

"What? There's no trace of that sort of activity in our systems, alarms would go off and the data would be erased immediately."

"She's doing it in my head, I can't stop her. I can feel at least two versions almost ready and for some reason I can't erase them. She plans on sending me somewhere to deploy them when they're finished."

"We have to kill her!"

"You can't, I've already tried and it's too late."

"What do you mean?"

"While she was sleeping I brought a Vesrex Thirteen injection into her room with me, it was in my pocket, out of sight but somehow she knew and locked the room down. Before I knew it her blankets encased her in an emergency vacuum bag and the atmosphere was draining out of the room! She scolded me like some childish playmate and forced me to apologize before she'd open the door!"

"What about your own vacsuit?"

"She was connected to it using my own cybernetic systems! It wouldn't seal."

"So what are you telling me?"

"Use signal radius jamming, stop all wireless communications in the fleet; it's the only way to delay her until we finish what we have to do on Pandem. I'll do my best to hold her off in my head, but if I try to leave put me in stasis, deactivate my cranial systems."

"I will, don't worry. What about long range communications?"

"I'll try to keep her contained, there are no guarantees. Right now she seems distracted with learning her way around her new body and my head, but I don't know how long that-" Gabriel was interrupted as the door opened and two rifle wielding guards rushed inside, the rest of their armoured squad was just outside in the hall.

"We received an alert from Command about this room sir, is everything all right?" the lead guard announced in a rush.

Gabriel knew Eve was watching, using the sensors on the soldier's armour and weaponry. "We're fine. His Grace wanted to temporarily cut the wireless signals off in this room so he could be sure we weren't recorded."

"Who sounded the alert?" Hampon asked.

"It was automated, Your Grace."

"Ah, all is well here, I'll reactivate the wireless systems in this room."

"Should we have maintenance check for a glitch in the system?" Asked the soldier.

"No, I think I know what caused it, be on your way please."

296

"Yes, Your Grace. I'm sorry for the disruption," saluted the soldier respectfully before leaving and closing the door behind him.

The screen behind Hampon began to display the view of Pandem once more and the pair looked at each other for a moment before Gabriel cleared his throat. "So when would you like Wheeler off the leash to begin chasing Captain Valance and his crew?"

"The optimum time according to the Victory Machine is after the upcoming attack."

"I'll make sure he knows to be ready. Does the Victory Machine have any advice on his orders?"

"Only that he should antagonize him as aggressively as possible. Lucius Wheeler and Jacob Valance cannot become allies."

Smash and Grab

The tension on the main bridge of the *Triton* was incredible. Laura manned her station at field control, manipulating two and three holographic displays that hung semitransparently all around her. There were two junior officers, at least that's what she called them even though they only had two and a half slashes on their cuffs, sitting behind her, watching everything she was doing.

After the near disaster she and the engineering team had gone through less than ten hours before she had reconfigured the simplified interface she had been using so it could present all the information she'd need as it became available, enabling her to properly control the myriad of energy fields all around the *Triton* manually, something that surprised even Alice.

As she was satisfied that the refractive, gravitational and hardened energy shielding was in balance and ready she looked around the bridge. Almost everyone suppressed their nervousness fairly well. Panloo seemed extra anxious as she looked to her pilot's station then back to the main holographic display over and over again. The main display would be dedicated to tactical and critical information as soon as they finished the quick deceleration from hyperspace but for the time being it displayed only the time until engagement and whatever sensor data was available from the distance they were coming in from.

Little by little more detail appeared around the brown, green and black Asom moon as the navigational database confirmed the locations of listed objects like commercial satellites, servicing stations, port facilities, orbital leisure complexes, energy collection nodes and many other non-critical objects in the arrival area. The military assets wouldn't update until they were actually in range of their transponders. Navigational databases only included information on what areas were reserved by the military, nothing about what was actually inside those areas or regularly on patrol outside of them.

The sheer number of commercial objects in the area they'd be arriving in was unbelievable and Laura hoped that Panloo and her navigation team would be able to manage the work of piloting them safely into position. She couldn't help but glance at Captain Alice Valent. By any measure the woman had transformed herself, taking control of the bridge, the ship, and carrying herself with so much confidence and visible sureness of self that no one doubted her abilities. After the news of Frost quietly stepping down from the Chief Gunnery position after a conversation with her got around the ship that respect and almost awe only intensified. Everyone knew he had a reputation as being difficult and chauvinistic, to see him brought down so low impressed many and frightened more.

On the bridge Alice was the picture of a professional Captain. The questions she posed the various departments were specific, could have only been posed by someone who had a firm knowledge of the ship and the crew. The month their Acting Captain had spent training the crew with Jake had taught the woman well, it was obvious to everyone.

There was no room for error and Alice demanded the best from the entire crew. The three pilots who had left the Mission Theatre weren't restricted to quarters, they weren't sent to the Habitation Section, they were put on the lowest quality escape shuttle they had and jettisoned towards the nearest spaceport. It would take them at least a week to make the journey.

Laura was familiar with that kind of paranoid reaction to crew members withdrawing from service after knowing operational details, Jason, her Husband was intelligence after all. There were things he couldn't even tell her about missions that he'd been on. She was the only person in the entire universe that he trusted completely, and she'd seen his suspicious, hyper vigilant side. Trust was something that he granted few, even in the slightest measure and as she grew to know the crew of the *Triton* she had come to trust them. Well, not all of them. To her dismay part of the plan that Alice had put in motion involved a number of the original *Samson* crew to man the ship they were most familiar with. That included Ashley, Finn, Frost and several of the more tried and true support staff including the lead navigator for the ship, Larry, who was always partnered with Ashley regardless of what she was flying. She had come to trust everyone from the *Samson* except for Frost and Leland March. Sadly the only *Samson* crew member that had remained behind was Agameg Price, who was a point of curiosity and fascination for her.

She had never met one of his kind that she was aware, and had especially never seen one who was confident or proud enough to actually remain in their native form. His big, expressive eyes and fine collector tendrils with which they gathered moisture and smelled as well as created intricate forms on their faces with to aid with shape shifting were so strange, so unlike anything she'd ever seen. At the same time his mild demeanour made him possibly the most friendly person she'd met in recent years.

Jason was always on her mind, and no matter how much she liked the crew of the *Triton* or *Samson* she always missed him. The topic of *Triton* going to Pandem had come up, and after very little prodding Laura discovered that getting the hypertransmitter was key to them getting there in much less time than they would if they started out using hyperdrive systems. Laura's suspicions were confirmed; the hypertransmitter would be used to rebuild the main array required to generate high compression wormholes for the *Triton*. Ease and speed of communications preoccupied Alice as well, there was something important she wanted to tell the galaxy as a whole and Laura suspected it had little to do with their rebellious cause.

If they managed to complete their mission, if they pulled this off, if they stole the piece of technology they were after, worth over three hundred billion credits they would not only silence one of the most major outlying military and resource rich Regent Galactic solar systems they would fully be connecting *Triton* to the rest of the Galaxy in a real, meaningful way. They could have real time conversations with anyone in the sector and send messages to Freeground in a matter of minutes using the highest wormhole compression capabilities of that hypertransmitter if it were integrated properly.

As Laura looked over the bridge, watched Alice and Price going about their final preparations as they neared their target and everyone else handling their near frayed nerves in their own ways she started to believe that they might just pull it off. As the arrival counter hit five seconds Panloo jerked at the helm.

"Our exit point is blocked!" Announced one of her navigators.

"Adjusting!" announced the other.

Panloo manoeuvred the ship the very second before they emerged from hyperspace to avoid a nine kilometre wide asteroid that had been placed exactly where the *Triton* was to arrive. As the *Triton* finished decelerating and emerged from hyperspace the tactical display flickered for a moment as it adjusted the entire field of view to account for the unexpected change in course. They were coming around the outer edge, one navigator keeping the silent nafalli helmswoman aware of objects in her path and the best routes through the space ahead.

Laura's terminal noted that they had collided with three small satellites as Panloo accelerated through an unplanned route well beneath the hypertransmitter. The collisions didn't affect the shields noticeably even though they practically ran through them at over one hundred twelve thousand kilometres per second.

The ship rotated and they were moving backwards, ingeniously manoeuvring to decelerate enough to compensate for their chaotic arrival and to close the distance between the ship and the hypertransmitter. The transmitter satellite looked like a silver spike on the tactical display, drifting above the dark side of the moon and the vast metropolis below.

"They knew we were coming," Alice said under her breath as she highlighted several destroyers and small carrier fleet led by a long command carrier in the distance. There were already over a hundred starfighters moving in for the attack. "Set to contingency one, start moving us out of position," Alice said calmly.

"Aye!" Panloo chirped from the controls, increasing the throttle and turning the ship towards the asteroid belly first.

The shields started taking hits from the planetary defence cannons and the incoming fighters but thanks to new power feeds and the fusion reactors running hotter than ever they started recharging as quickly as they took damage, not dipping below ninety seven percent. Laura hoped that they could maintain that charge but she knew better. Things were about to get interesting. "Tactical, is there a read on what those destroyers are doing?"

"Opening fire now! They're not using beam weaponry but going straight to high charge gauss shells." Price told Laura and Alice.

"What? Did someone tell them we use refractive shielding too?" Laura said as she diverted power from the refractive shielding and shored up the other systems. "Is *anything* using beam weaponry?"

"Nothing, not even the Gemeelan, that command carrier, and they have the long range capability," Agameg replied.

"How do they know how to exclude weaponry that's easiest for us to overcome? They haven't even seen us use our shielding effectively yet," Laura said as the first volley of explosive shells came into contact with the gravitational shield. The shells were slowed down suddenly enough to set them off, causing strain on the outer gravity shielding but not touching the hardened energy barrier underneath or the ship. "Outer grav shield strength is down to eighty one percent and decreasing. Those explosions are taxing them just enough so they can't regenerate."

"Can you divert more power?" Alice asked.

"No, the lines can't take it."

"Captain, we have to make a decision now; send them out or escape," Agameg reminded her calmly.

Captain Valent was difficult to read as she glanced up from her ring of command holograms up the main display on the bridge where the tactical screen showed nine more destroyers trying to manoeuvre into place to begin firing at the *Triton*.

"Launch our remaining nuclear torpedoes on the highest yield setting towards the primary population centers on the moon. Gunnery deck, open fire on targets of opportunity with seeker rounds on the fighters, I'm giving officer level quarters to the gunner with the most confirmed kills. Cynthia, open up with our scrambler, let's see how well they coordinate when their wading through forty terawatts of static. Ashley, your team has a go."

"There are a billion people down there, I don't think-" one of the Navigators started.

"There's a planetary defence shield in place and anti-bombardment measures that can easily deflect our nukes. The cities are safe, all we're doing is distracting their planetary cannons for a few seconds!" Alice called back. "Do your job or get the hell off my bridge, Hanson!"

The navigator turned back to his station, red faced. "Aye ma'am."

* * *

For the first time Ashley could remember the *Samson* felt small. It was the only ship on the launch deck of the *Triton* and as Ashley throttled up and propelled the vessel out into space she watched torpedoes and heavy weapon points on the *Triton* fire all around her. She knew none of the ordinances would strike the *Samson* as long as she didn't do anything unpredictable for the next few seconds, but watching heavy, four and a half meter long fusion torpedoes slide by then on towards the heavily populated moon below was almost as frightening as the points of light swarming towards them. She knew each point of light represented a fighter and soon many of those fighters would be after her.

"Engine pods extended to full, we have as much manoeuvrability as we'll ever get," Larry told her before scanning for the best routes to their goal, the hypertransmitter several thousand kilometres away. The *Triton* would only follow them half way.

"Gunners, target the fighters. Finn, how are my shields?" Ashley asked.

The sound of thousands of bursts per minute firing off from the gun right behind the small darkened bridge forced everyone to yell. Even with the hatches closed you could hear the turrets, feel the deck vibrating with every shot. "They're charged and giving us an energy halo about four times the size of the ship," he chuckled. "Looks like the work we put on the new emitter grid is paying off."

Fighter rounds started striking the *Samson* as Ashley flipped the vessel and accelerated as hard as safety limits would allow right towards the asteroid. The navigational advisory hologram in front of her showed that she had chosen perhaps the most dangerous course, but as she operated the hastily bolted in countermeasures control box with her off hand anyone watching could see what she was doing. "Frost, can you get a solid bead on the hypertransmitter with the ion cannon?"

"Not happenin' until you get us outta the shadow of this bloody rock."

"We'll be leaving it behind sooner than you like."

"This is Hardcase, my group is engaging the enemy." the lead allied Uriel fighter pilot announced over the laser link he had with the *Samson*. With all the scrambling interfering with communications it was the only way to get a message through. The small holographic display on the left side of the pilot's station showed that he and six other fighters were closely following her course, the *Samson's* shields were reaching out and fortifying theirs, and while the group accelerated towards the asteroid at great speed they turned and fired at all the approaching fighters and gunships in the area.

"Shields are holding up, we're recharging at seventy three percent. If we can avoid any serious hits we'll be back up to ninety in four seconds."

"Who'da thought this old bucket would end up as a shield ship?" Frost commented.

"Larry, tell our friends what I'll be doing," Ashley told her copilot as she prepared a firing sequence for the engine pods, working the switches and computer interface with a practiced hand.

"All right, we're going to close to within one hundred fifty meters of the asteroid surface and drop a batch of thermal shells. They'll superheat a part of the asteroid, creating a thermal flare behind us so no one will be able to get a good read on us for at least a few seconds." he said as he sent the escape trajectory to the fighter pilots.

"Straight out of the Desperate Times in Valera sim, loving it," Hardcase replied.

"Breaking in three, two, one, mark!" Ashley called out before initiating the thrust sequence and pressing the launch button on the improvised countermeasures control panel.

The hull of the *Samson* and the inertial dampeners strained as the vessel changed direction, narrowly missing one edge of the asteroid as it ejected half a dozen improvised high explosives out of the rear cargo bay. Pressed out by the escaping atmosphere they drifted towards the asteroid and exploded as they bounced against the rough stone.

Anyone who was looking out a porthole in that direction just then was blinded by the white light of the explosion and superheated surface of the asteroid. The *Samson* and six of her escorting fighters shot straight for the hypertransmitter, all their weapons turning to the fore.

To any of the fighters unlucky enough to be in the way it appeared as though the vessels were coming out of a small sun, and for the pair of small enemy fighters that managed to manoeuvre away from the small group of ships there were half a dozen that were picked to pieces by high intensity particle bursts and rail guns that cycled through twelve hundred rounds per minute. "This is Hardcase, all fighters break and get ready to cover the *Samson* while she picks up the package."

The fighter group moved out of the range of the *Samson's* spiny shield projectors and as the shock and overwhelming attack on the senses of the flares dissipated Finn breathed a sigh of relief as the shield profile shrunk back down to the shape of the *Samson* itself.

They immediately began taking fire from their port and dorsal sides, where the bulk of the fighters were milling, swarming to escape the devastating guns on the dorsal side of the *Triton*. "There you are, time to shut ye down!" Frost exclaimed under his breath as he targeted the hypertransmitter and opened fire with the ion cannon. A fighter got in the way, taking a full blast and as the operation of its internal power systems were completely disrupted the energy reading on it dropped to near zero. "Oi! To the side!" he shouted at the disabled fighter as he pounded the control panel.

Ashley manoeuvred the *Samson* around the lazily drifting snub fighter and cringed as she heard small shells strike the outer hull. "Better?"

"Aye!" Frost replied as he took aim with the Ion turret and set it to full power. With the glimmering silver hypertransmitter satellite, the most valuable object in the area pound for pound, directly lined up in the crosshairs he opened fire and didn't stop until he drained the power cells connected to the weapon. When the halo of energy left behind from the blasts of the Ion cannon subsided the power readings indicated that the device had shut down. "She's asleep! Time to have our way!"

"I'll never see what Stephanie sees in you," Ashley commented as she rotated the body of the ship in the direction of the hypertransmitter and fired the engines so they moved in a perfect line towards it. "Fighters, keep our path clear!"

"Hardcase here, we're on it!"

Ashley grinned at the pilot she'd seen several times in the pilot's den. He was shorter than her by eleven centimetres and was always smiling. While growing up he had learned to fly an old air hopper and as soon as he got his licence he was transporting parts for a commercial excavation operation. He had a natural knack for all things in the cockpit. After he whipped through the fighter pilot tutorials he passed the qualifier on the first try. Within a week he became one of their top pilots and Ashley had recommended he lead the small group of Uriel fighters covering them.

Her jaw dropped as the navigational display noted his fighter was destroyed just then, leaving no emergency beacon. She stared at the notification and the display as the profile of his Uriel fighter became just another obstacle, a grouping of heated, twisting metal.

"Ash, focus," Larry said from beside her. "We're coming up on it."

She cleared her throat and focused on the task at hand, making one final minor adjustment to their course as the remaining three fighters along with the gunners on the *Samson* fought tooth and nail to keep their path clear. The *Samson* shook and rocked violently, turning just slightly.

"Engine three is gone, shields down to eighteen percent, draining our reserves to compensate!" Finn announced.

"Compensating for the missing pod." Larry announced beside her.

"We've rotated too much, turn us back or we'll smash into the satellite side on!" Frost called out.

Ashley didn't let the controls reset, but manually rotated one of the port engine pods and fired it, guessing at how much thrust they'd need to make a good capture with the maxjack. As the ship slowly rotated she lined up the other pods as quickly as she could to slow the *Samson* down so it and the satellite wouldn't be destroyed when they made contact. The engines fired at full power. No one knew whether it was enough and as the many controls reset everyone held their breath.

"We're comin' in too fast!" Frost called out, still standing at the ready at the maxjack controls.

"It'll have to do!" Ashley said the instant before the *Samson* collided with the hypertransmitter satellite. The sounds of gunfire were drowned out by the cataclysmic noise of the hull crushing, screeching and grinding into the object.

"God dammit!" Frost shouted as he tried to manipulate the maxjack, to get a grip on their target.

"Breaches in five compartments, sealing sections off. Half our lower shield emitters are dead, I'm compensating!" Finn reported. "Somehow," he muttered to himself.

"Do you have it Frost?" asked Ashley in a rush.

Frost struggled with the controls of the maxjack, trying to work with the working gripper arms he had left, activating magnetic capturing fields and pressing the satellite against two of the largest curled arms that were stuck in position with no power.

"Frost, do you have it!" Ashley repeated, waiting to take the newly calibrated controls and try to get the *Samson* out of danger.

"Shut it! You're not helpin'!" he snapped back.

"Is it possible?" Finn asked.

"Nay! I don't think-" Frost started but was interrupted as the whole ship shuddered violently and alarms sounded for two seconds before Finn shut them down.

"That was a heavy collider shell, ran us straight through, sealing two non-essential compartments and shutting down a line of capacitors! We have to get out of here!" Finn said as he watched the ship's power reserves and generation capacity drop drastically.

"Frost! Do we stay or do we go?" Ashley asked harshly.

"That did it! The thing is impaled on one arm and I could trap it with one of the ones that still work! Go! Fer all that's holy! Get us out o' here woman!"

"Finally!" Larry commented as he started plotting a hyperspace course. "You have to get us clear of this mess before we can start hyper acceleration."

Ashley looked at the summarized status display as she fired the engines and tried to start the *Samson* in the right direction, towards the nearest edge of the combat area. The report told her that their shields were down to nine percent and didn't effectively cover the aft end of the ship, that they had six open compartments, and that there were only two fighters left. "Fighter wing, get out. Generate wormholes and escape *now!*" she ordered.

"Flightnut copies, I'm gone!"

"Byfly copies, heading out!"

"Finn, give me a burst of hyperspace particles on my mark," Ashley commanded.

"Ready," was all he said as he turned white.

Larry worked feverishly to find a nearby, straight, clear path but couldn't locate one on the tactical hologram or screen in front of him.

"There! *Right there!*" Ashley pointed to the asteroid behind them.

"You want to-"

"Send us in the opposite direction so fast they can't keep up," she finished for him.

He plotted the course quickly, just over fourteen thousand kilometres. "At your peril," he said, throwing up his hands.

"More like-" Frost started.

"Two, one, mark!" Ashley interrupted loudly.

Finn's hand came down on the final initiation button for the particle emitters to send a burst of hyperspace particles out across the hull of the *Samson* and their cargo that would allow them to accelerate at many times the normal rate and for a split second the *Samson* increased speed at a rate of several thousand kilometres per second, effectively stopping it's motion in one direction fast enough to begin sending it careening recklessly towards the asteroid. Fighters, gunships and the asteroid itself whipped by as Ashley fought to guide the small ship right across the bow of a destroyer, past a wing of fighters that had freshly launched from a more distant carrier. "Plot our course fast!" she said through gritted teeth. "I'll have to blink sometime."

Larry's fingers worked the console as quickly as he could. "Can't get a clear exit path, keep it together just a few more seconds Ash," he said in a tone that feigned calm as he struggled with the math and constant trajectory updates.

As the exotic particles coating the hull dissipated evenly across the vessel it started becoming more difficult to make course corrections. The engines were firing at full thrust as they swivelled and swung at the ends of their thin pylons. "Hurry, hurryhurry," Ashley whispered.

"Got it! Locked in!" Larry announced.

Ashley quickly rotated the engine pods in the right direction, locked the manual controls and initiated the automated hyperspace entry sequence. The *Samson* lurched under the sudden increase to full thrust and as the hull was once again coated with energized exotic particles it accelerated to faster than light speeds.

* * *

"Energy shielding down to four percent on the dorsal section and I have *no* power reserves to reinforce them. The rest of the ship isn't much better," Laura announced as she watched the hull start taking direct strikes from antimatter enhanced gauss cannon rounds. She winced as a torpedo struck the upper quarter of the aft section. "Aft down to one percent."

"The *Samson*'s clear!" Price announced.

"Explosive decompression reported in section A12, we just lost the main lines to the primary port engine," came the announcement from engineering.

"Time to leave. Best speed to my designated point," Captain Alice Valent ordered, marking a point in space on the main tactical and helm displays. "Let's see if they're willing to play chicken. Bring all weapons to bear on the command carrier and open fire."

The remaining torpedo launch tubes, beam weapon emplacements and all the turrets aboard the *Triton* took aim at the command carrier ten times her size as Panloo fired the engines towards the largest ship in the fleet trying to combat them. Every knuckle on the bridge was white as all but the forward and bottom shields on the ship failed, the ablative hull began taking hits and the massive command carrier in the distance slowly began turning, trying to accelerate out of the way.

"Gunnery deck here, we're down nine cannons and sealing into sections! Get us the hell out of here!" shouted Frost's third in command.

"If you panic and fall apart, I swear I'll go up there and shoot you myself! Keep it together!" Alice shot back.

"We've lost containment in compartment E71 to E84," Price said sedately. "No casualties."

The carrier's main batteries began to open fire as the three destroyers and many other smaller ships moved out of the way.

"Forward shields are taking massive fire, they'll be down in eleven seconds at this rate," Laura said, trying to keep her voice steady and calm.

"Nice of them to clear a path for us," Alice said with a wolfish grin. "Plot a course that takes us into hyperspace at a six degree upward angle from them. Panloo, start on this trajectory right now," she said as she sent the course to her station.

The *Triton* angled up with a jerk, reflecting the anxiousness of her pilot and started suddenly away from the line of fire, but through a narrow, clear space between the engaging ships.

"Course ready!" announced the sweaty navigator to her right.

"Go!" Captain Valent ordered.

The *Triton* accelerated suddenly and before anything else could get in her way they were far from the defensive fleet.

LOOSE WIRING

Ayan's attitude was unprofessional, inappropriate, but that didn't change how she felt. *I'm a highly trained engineer whose worked on starships, developed new technologies, analysed mysterious devices and even consulted on a new class of ship. There are several bots and even a few people just a hundred meters away who could do this just as well, but I'm here because none of them could squeeze inside this tiny claustrophobic space hundreds of meters up.*

"How's it going in there?" Jason asked through the slim line that extended from her suit all the way back through the tiny darkened passageway that ran the length of the landing pad the Regent Galactic and West Keeper soldiers were holding position on. They had entered the blocky, thick hulled general purpose vessel that was on the pad and were dug in.

"It's fine," she answered peevishly. "Still moving."

Three more small combat drop ships had made hasty landings since they had joined the random gathering of resistance fighters adding over two hundred soldiers to the fray. They pushed the resistance fighters back behind their secondary makeshift barriers, a much more dense, well built wall made of bulkheads and other heavily constructed equipment and hastily moved and welded fixtures. The soldiers wanted access to the subway station behind the resistance, which used it to move between different key levels in the spaceport and were keeping it open for more refugees and survivors to join them. More worn and injured people arrived every hour, and though the numbers in the resistance was swelling, the more well armed and prepared soldiers were still winning ground.

Ayan had started looking at schematics and blueprints of the starport as soon as she had a handle on the immediate situation and within an hour a plan was formulated. The enemy had cut the communication and power lines that linked the ship to the spaceport, but the landing gear of the ship was still locked to the landing pad and there was no way of severing that connection without using heavy cutting equipment. Thus far the resistance had been able to keep the enemy away from the forward struts effectively enough so the physical cables were still linked from inside the landing platform.

Her plan was simple. Someone would climb inside the tiny cable passage with power and data cables and tap into the hard mooring systems under the old general purpose vessel many of the West Keeper soldiers were using as a base of operations. With no one else her size equipped with the basic knowledge to make the link, or wearing a thermal and sound dampening suit, that person would be her. Being sent on the errand shouldn't have been insulting, she had infantry training and had been sent into small spaces before but there was a nagging thought in the back of her mind; *I'm about four hundred meters up and the sheathing for this passage is about half a millimetre thick.*

Sweat beaded on her forehead and wetted her palms, the suit took care of it before it started to be a problem and she knew the metal support she had her safety hook around was strong enough to bear ten times her weight but her fear of heights was an irrational thing and as she came up on the section of the landing pad's underside where the protective sheath had been blown away she stopped. The monitor on her faceplate informed her that her heart rate was elevated, her overall stress level was increasing fast.

Ayan made sure her safety tether was securely attached to the support running the length of the pad and took a deep breath while her hand followed the pair of slim lines leading to her belt and shoulder. Everything was secure, regardless of how high up she was she was completely safe. Biting her lip, she pushed off slightly and felt the comforting thin metal sheeting disappear from beneath her as she moved out into the open air to hang by two strong lines the thickness of human hairs.

It took all her concentration and determination to combat the fear that twisted her stomach in knots, forced blood to rush to her head so severely that she could hear her heart beating between her ears and made her sweat profusely.

"Ayan, your vitals are way too high, are you all right?" Jason asked again.

"Shut up, oh please shut up!" she snapped.

"Oh no, you're-"

"Afraid of heights! That wasn't in my intelligence jacket? Guess you spooks don't catch everything, *do you*?"

"Guess not," Jason chortled. "Just focus on your safety line and what you have to do."

"What do you think I'm doing!" She moved carefully along the support rod, one hand moving above the other rhythmically and methodically. If for some reason the hook or lines gave way she could always hold on to that rod until her suit could form a bond with the smooth, hard underside of the platform. Her breath caught in her throat as the rod she was attached to ended. The blueprints said that the support rod went all the way to the end of the platform, not that it bent inside the metal above then came back out several meters later.

Her instinct was to look around in an effort to find something else to attach her safety line to. She looked in the wrong direction first. Peering over her shoulder and down into the yawning depths of the dark inner station landing pit, her heart leapt into her throat. Landing platforms jutted out from the sides like shelves and spoons leading to hangars, transit ways and hallways. Her eye was drawn mostly to the shadowy depths in the center. The bottom was a thing imagined and not seen, a place where her mind's eye painted her crushed and ruined. "Jason, I'm sorry I snapped at you," she whimpered.

"It's okay. I understand."

Ayan laid her forearms and shins against the underside of the platform and her suit started to form a bond with the metal. Her heart felt like it was going to break free of her chest, she just wanted to stay right where she was until someone else could come get her, come save her. Her military training was winning, however, even if just barely. "The support rod ends, I'm going to have to use the climbing tech in the suit to get across," she whispered in a hurried, panicked tone that surprised her when it echoed in her ears. She'd only heard herself sound so frightened once before.

It was during her first tour on the *Sunspire*, before she met Jonas Valent. Her Captain had ordered her and a few of the engineering crew into the reactor core to shield them from a massive electromagnetic burst that killed everyone else on board. The darkness, filled with drifting corpses who had been her friends, and the possibility that their enemies could return to salvage the ship, to kill her and everyone else who had survived was something she'd never forget. They managed to get the ship back to Freeground, but for weeks she couldn't so much as look at an image of that ship, it was enough to send her into tears.

At first she thought being put in charge of the *Sunspire's* recommissioning by Freeground Fleet Command was some kind of cruel joke, but it was an opportunity for her to advance her career, to prove that she could survive one of the most horrifying experiences any technician in the fleet had survived in recent history. The ship still felt wrong somehow until Jacob Valance was given command and they changed the name.

It was like he gave the ship and crew purpose, direction, made it a place where people could accomplish something. He was out there somewhere, or at least someone who had all his memories, who would probably want to meet her, someone she needed to meet. *He wouldn't have trouble getting through this.* The thought crossed her mind as the display on her headpiece confirmed a lock with the underside of the landing platform.

"We can try to send someone else, maybe a bot to just cling to the bottom away from the cable cover," Jason offered.

"They'd be detected for sure, I have a chance at this and it's just a little further," she replied hurriedly as she slid her splayed body, one forearm, one leg at a time. All the while she watched the indicator on her visor to ensure that the surface of her suit was firmly bonding with the metal. Several centimetres of her left shin wouldn't bond and she thanked God that she had managed to remain flexible thanks to a regular yoga regimen as she spread her knees out to the side and let the suit bond a good portion of her thighs, stomach and chest to the platform.

In theory she could hang by one shin and hold half a ton, but with the dark void just waiting for her to fail, to fall, she couldn't bond securely enough. It was slow and before she had gone five meters she was breathing heavily because of the exertion of the act. Ayan's vacsuit didn't have a problem bonding to the metal of the platform, but sliding upside down, doing anything upside down, took a lot more effort than crawling normally. *Now this is something I should add to my workout regimen. Maybe at a height of four feet, but still, this is anything but easy.*

"You're almost there, four more meters and you should be able to see where they burned through the platform side mooring cables."

Ayan looked up along the underside of the platform and to her relief she spotted a pair of eye hooks for fastening servicing equipment right beside the box that hung under the landing gear clamps that forced a power and data connection to the ship and prevented it from lifting off. She crossed the distance and carefully pulled one arm away from the platform underside to fasten her hooks to the heavy metal loops made for supporting several tons of equipment. "I'm at the box, linking into the port now," she reported as she drew a slim cable from her command and control unit and plugged into the multi-purpose port on the side of the heavy white box.

The display on her command and control unit reported that the codes Yves had given them were working and that the ship was still linked to the hard connection on the landing platform. "They didn't cut the interior cables," Ayan said with a relief.

"Fantastic, can you get the box open?"

"Yup," the access hatch on the side of the box flopped down and plummeted past her. For a second her eye followed it and she momentarily froze before shaking her head and focusing on the data and power lines that once led to the spaceport computers. She disconnected them with a quick turn and gentle pull and hurriedly pulled the power and data line that was attached to her leg free, firmly seating the end in the socket. "You should see a good connection to the ship now."

"There it is! Now get back here so we can start causing some damage," Jason exclaimed excitedly.

Ayan pulled the small data cord leading from her arm unit free and started back, hesitating before detaching herself from the heavy support hooks. She was crawling backwards, watching the surfaces of her shins, knees, thighs, arms, chest and stomach hold fast to the metal surface of the platform's underside. Most of her suit was working properly, but fear drove her as much as anything until she made it back to the support rod and attached herself to it.

She moved as quickly as she could without getting herself tangled with the cables that shared the cramped service space with her and at long last her feet came out of the thinly sheathed service shaft into open air. The main service conduit was almost beneath her. It was built out of heavy braced metal grating and led back to the main platform above. Her boot touched the solid edge and she unhooked herself from the support rod. As she removed the second safety line hook everything shook so violently that all she could do was grab for the support rod. Her attempts to secure herself failed as she was flipped onto her stomach atop the thinly walled, creaking cable sheath.

Everything was creaking, quaking, bouncing her around inside the small space violently enough to force sections of her suit to harden, keeping her from seriously bruising or breaking bones and the sheath was rattling loose, giving way under her weight and the twisting pressure of the sudden motion. She quickly tried to turn so she could face the underside of the platform again and only made it half way before the cable cover gave way and her body started to fall with it into open space.

An instinctive grab with her left arm caught the support rod. Her right hand joined it as her body swung free, dangling out over the yawning pit with the safety of the interior service tunnel just two meters away.

The world was still shaking and she hung on for dear life, her grip, her sanity tested as she prayed she wouldn't be killed in a tragic fall. She squeezed her eyes shut and gripped the support rod as hard as she could. When the shaking stopped she scrambled, thoughtlessly, desperately to grip hand over hand to the service crawlway and safety. The safety rod ended prematurely, leaving her to cross the last half meter on her own. She didn't give herself time to think about her options; instead she fortified her grip and swung her lower body away then towards the opening, letting go at the last second and hurling herself into the meter high service passage. She lay on her back, just catching her breath for a moment when a though occurred to her. *I could have taken that slowly and bonded my suit to the metal of the structure, made my crossing that way instead. Would have been safer. Hey, maybe I'm getting over my fear of heights after all.* She turned over and brought herself up into a crouch, looking over her shoulder at the sheer drop behind her before starting into the much safer service tunnel. Vertigo threatened to overtake her at even that slight glimpse from relative safety. "Nope, definitely still afraid of heights," she chuckled to herself nervously.

"Are you all right Ayan?" Jason asked.

"What the hell is going on up there?" She replied, trying to catch her breath as she moved as quickly as possible to the ladder that would take her to the access hatch in the floor behind Jason.

"Judging from the sensors on the ship you just connected me to, someone just overloaded a fusion reactor inside the mountain. No one could have survived in there."

As Ayan spilled out of the access hatch her suit noted a significant change in air pressure and as she looked to the subway tunnel, still blocked with passenger cars, dust and debris surged in and past the temporary barricade. The hundred or so rebels took cover as best they could as the space behind their barricades and around were flooded with the fine grey dust and dirt.

Her suit protected her as she braced herself against the maintenance tube access door and she looked through the small slit in the barricade nearest her, towards the ship that the Regent Galactic soldiers were using for cover. Jason was at the temporary control station that was hooked up to the landing gear restraining boot thanks to her handiwork. He leaned over the control pad and pair of small holographic projectors built into the mini-station to protect it.

She looked well past him and saw one of the hatches to the rear of the ship flop open. Soldiers started carefully disembarking. "They're using this as a distraction, we have to do something *now*!"

Jason straightened up and took a look at the status report on the ship as displayed on small holograms by the mini-terminal. "They've disabled all but one weapon on the ship so we won't be able to use that against them. It's like they knew this is something we'd try eventually. We're already past the encryption in the ship's computer though, so they won't be able to keep using that ship as a base for much longer."

"That was quick."

"It wasn't me," Jason shook his head as he checked the functionality of the last operable weapon on the vessel, it was built into the left side, facing away from the small drop ships and landing platform. "All we can do is try and seal up the ship, but that'll only buy us as much time as it takes them to cut through a hatchway."

"Jason Everin, I've heard of you," said a calm, clear male voice over Jason's and Ayan's wired communicators. "You must order Oz and Minh to lead the rebels onto the platform, I will help."

"Who are you?" Ayan asked.

"I'm the product of Alice Valent, daughter by intellectual and emotional lineage to Jonas Valent. Put simply, I was once called Lewis but have become Dementia. I would explain more clearly but there is no time," the squarish, bulky ship on the platform hundreds of meters away began to power up. Lights came on, power readings spiked, the engines gave a quick, low powered burst to clear themselves of debris and the high pitched shriek of metal grating on metal pierced the air for a moment as the vessel turned just a few degrees. The main landing strut at the front, where the data and electrical connection had just been made, began to twist and burst as the ship slowly rotated around, scraping all the other struts across the deck plating as it did so.

The hatch the soldiers had opened slammed closed, severing the legs of one troop suddenly and cleanly at mid thigh as it did so. With a glimpse Ayan could see that Jason no longer had control of the vessel, the mini-station was working through commands faster than anyone without a neural link could manage. The fifty meters of slack in the data and electrical patch cables she had just run to the ship was slowly letting out as the vessel turned under its own power, the aft end struck one of the much smaller drop ships and strained to push it off the platform so the ship could continue to reorient itself.

"Hurry! This distraction won't last long and there are over three hundred soldiers hiding outside the ship on that platform!"

Ayan's thoughts were briefly drawn to the memory of Jonas' old artificial intelligence; Alice. He had set her loose on the *Overlord II* and she killed hundreds of people before he was released. It was one of those things that no one spoke of. Not only was it illegal across the galaxy to remove all restraints on an artificial intelligence, but the grisly work Alice had done while she was in her unfettered state was something everyone hoped would pass into distant memory.

This could be the same thing; an artificial intelligence capable of murder and sacrifice without remorse or compassion. Then again, if it had saved so many people, worked somehow to repair other artificial intelligences that had been infected with a deadly virus, why would it turn now? Ayan mused.

"Ayan, what are we doing?" Oz asked, poised with a heavy assault rifle behind the barrier, ready to charge the landing platform.

"We go, but watch yourself, I don't know what Dementia is willing to sacrifice to take this objective."

"You heard her! Move!" Oz called out to the armed rebels behind him as Yves, Minh and he led the charge.

Several rebels quickly mounted an improvised defence cannon atop the secondary barrier and started laying down streaks of bright blue cover fire. Oz, Minh and the other rebels who had a clear line of sight rushed down the long, broad white and grey pockmarked embarkation rampway. They opened fire on the soldiers who were caught in the open.

The light of early dawn was fading as grey dust from the distant explosion was belched up by the depths of the station, tricking automatic interior lighting into activating. An eerie white and yellow glow enshrouded the embattled platform. Minh called out; "Grenade launchers! Arc them towards their cover!"

Everyone who had a rifle with a grenade thrower or who had an improvised or other explosive on a timer let loose as they ran, tossing their deadly packages towards the landing crafts and piled crates. More than half of the charging three hundred had explosives and only a few missed the platform entirely, the rest landed near or on their mark and a second later the platform was a no-man's-land as small and medium explosions went off. Some of the grenades were sent spinning through the air as others went off, a couple were even rendered useless by shrapnel from nearby detonations. It was sloppy, dangerous, but devastating, confusing, and effective.

Oz went to the left, straight for the nearest barricade of crates followed by a third of the charging mass and they overtook the soldiers hiding behind. Minh moved straight up into the middle of the platform, rushing the nearest dropship and using it for cover from soldiers hiding behind the next. Only meters away the general purpose vessel that was the original occupant of the landing platform struggled to push the most distant dropship off the edge of the platform and out of the way, the smaller vessel was moving slowly, its landing gear scraping against the metal surface of the platform with deafening results.

Ayan glanced at the mini-terminal and saw that Dementia was correcting an artificial intelligence somewhere, adding a piece of software that would render the Holocaust Virus inert. "What's he connected to?" Ayan asked.

"Something inside that ship, it looks like-" Jason examined the data streaming across one of the holodisplays for a moment before continuing. "It's a pair of automated medical servants and three loading bots. He's connected to them through the ship computer."

A massive *pop* sounded louder than the persistent sounds of gunfire and Ayan looked up to see that Minh had blown the hatch to the nearest drop ship open using a focused charge. He strafed across the opening, firing two bursts inside and taking several hits himself. She looked at the status display on her command and control unit and saw that her friend's personal energy shielding was down to nine percent, but none of the shots had pierced it and the shield was already regenerating. "Oz! Have some of your people direct their fire into that doorway after this bang!" he called out.

"Will do!" Oz replied as he led the charge on the dropship on the far left.

Minh tossed a handful of micro grenades into the ruined hatchway and gingerly stepped to the side. "Fire in the hole!" he finished yelling half a second before the grenades exploded.

Several of Oz's rebels knelt and fired on the hatchway as smoke poured out of the opening. Yves led the charge of the third group of resistance fighters shouting; "Move on to the next dropship! We'll clear this one!"

"On our way!" he replied as he directed his group away from the drop ship and the dangerous area where the much larger multi-purpose vessel was being forced to turn horizontally.

314

Yves' group were rushing into the main hatch of the boarding shuttle Minh and his group left behind. "All right! We take this one!" he shouted. "We're after the command chips in their helmets and the ship's computers, so watch your fire!"

Ayan's attention was brought back to the red and brown vessel as it managed to finally push the drop ship off the landing platform, sending it crashing down into another platform several levels down. The older, larger, much uglier vessel rotated horizontally until its last usable cannon was pointed directly at the furthest of the drop ships, one of which was already powering up its engines.

"Get clear! It's going to fire!" Oz called out to his group as they moved to support Yves and his team.

The cannon swivelled and took aim at the shuttle just starting to lift off and a slim red beam burst forth from its short barrel, slicing through the smaller, more disposable vessel's hull and leaving a long tear across its middle. The cannon fired twice more, horizontally across the length of the ship with an intentional, digital precision that ensured that most of the soldiers inside would be burned through the middle on both decks of the ship as its engines lost power and it fell awkwardly down several meters to rest on the landing platform.

"We've taken the west most shuttle, several injured," Yves announced breathlessly.

Oz's team was already inside, and Ayan could hear his comforting tone; "I've got ya, we'll get you patched up."

A quick glance at her command and control unit told her that he was performing a medical scan and administering pain meds to Yves.

Minh's group rushed the shuttle that had been cut to pieces, and for long moments it seemed that there was no resistance. "We have control of the rear most shuttle, there are a few soldiers in the rear compartment who are holding out though," Minh reported.

Through one of the few transparesteel windows in the side of the drop ship Ayan could see flashes of light from weapon's fire, then it stopped suddenly and Minh's status indicator began flashing red, highlighting injuries across his knees, thighs and midsection. She didn't think, just drew her sidearm and ran as hard as she could through the barricades and down the embarkation ramp. No matter how quickly she was moving it seemed too slow. "Minh? Can you hear me?"

"He blocked a grenade when we opened the rear door, he's in bad shape," said one of his people.

"Do you have medical training?" Ayan asked as she rushed into the dropship and up the steep stairway that led to the upper level.

"I don't, and I can't get his headgear off!"

Ayan ran up the aisle between the shoulder and hip restraints, an efficient method of cramming as many soldiers into a dropship as possible and she nearly panicked as Minh came into view. At the sight of him she was immediately grateful that he had been knocked out by the blast.

She made the last two meters on her knees, skidding to a stop and as soon as she could she used her arm unit to inject him with emergency stasis drugs, praying that his circulation would take the medication to his vital organs. She took a medical

315

scan and watched as the medication made it through his torso, his head but only as far as half way down one thigh. There were wide open wounds and serious trauma to his torso, and as he settled into a stasis state that didn't keep him alive but prevented further cellular deterioration she said; "He can be revived later, there's far too much damage for nanobots to repair." She pulled a protective vacbag out from under the rear of her poncho and laid it atop him carefully. "Do you have any other wounded?"

"My group's taking care of them, nice catch Ayan," replied Oz.

The protective bag enveloped Minh's body and stiffened, forming a hardened case and a perfect seal. "He might lose his legs and a hand. He'll either need replacements grown or an emergency unit with full regenerative capabilities and I haven't seen one since we arrived," she replied quietly.

"But if you waited any longer he might not have a chance at all. How long can he last with those new meds?"

"We have to get him to a proper facility or a very expensive regeneration suite to revive him properly."

"As soon as we make it off this rock."

"He saved my life, saw the grenade and stepped right in front of me," said one scruffy, long haired rebel.

The sadness etched on his young face touched Ayan deeply and she stood, putting a hand on her shoulder. "That's what heroes do, and once he's back on his feet I'll make sure he knows how thankful you are. Now, did you manage to overtake the soldiers in the rear compartment?"

"Yes ma'am, as soon as the grenade went off most everyone rushed 'em. There are a couple prisoners but the rest are dead."

"Good, everyone did well here, better than expected. Now get a detail of ten together to guard the ship behind cover while everyone else in your group moves the wounded behind the barricades. When you're finished move your entire group there and guard the subway tunnel."

"Yes Ma'am," the young rebel nodded as she stared at Minh's protected form.

Ayan caught her eye and stared at her. "We have to keep working, make this place safe and save lives while we get what we need from this ship's systems. I need your help." she whispered.

She nodded and smiled at her a little. "I'm on it."

* * *

316

Jason Everin had never seen anything like it before; a massively multitasking artificial intelligence that also operated like a virus. As Dementia manipulated the parts of the station he could see he worked tirelessly to spread his influence, to control every non-intelligent computer system that was adjacent to areas he already had access to. Jason focused on what he had to, there was no time to do anything else. The generic transport that was on the landing platform had settled down. Dementia had already cut power to the engines, removed all access to the interior systems and raised the carbon dioxide mix in the air to lethal levels. The temperature was over one hundred fifty degrees centigrade, anyone not in armour with an environmental layer would have been dead in the first few minutes.

He didn't know if he could stop Dementia if he tried, and despite the inhumane use of the internal environment systems Jason didn't feel motivated to help the soldiers taking cover inside. The evidence of the slaughter in the main foyer, security areas and embarkation sections of the space port that he'd seen was enough to allay his tendency towards mercy where anyone from the West Watch or Regent Galactic forces were concerned. Anyone who could be allied with a company or government that unleashed such a murderous virus on a general population, on innocent non-combatants, deserved what they got. The fact that an artificial intelligence that, from what he could tell so far, was on the rebels' side was responsible for much of the enemies suffering was simply a welcome irony.

While Dementia focused on controlling the small portion of the spaceport he had overtaken and killing or forcing the enemy soldiers out of their sanctuaries Jason worked to get his remote terminal ready to patch into military channels and start back hacking to the source. The first of the wounded were coming in, Ayan was at the head of them, making sure that they were attended to properly. He glimpsed the protective black vacbag that Minh was in and tried to put thoughts of his suspended state and uncertain future out of his mind.

"How are we doing Dementia?" he asked.

"I'm afraid I'm not doing very well, Jason. The androids and other rebels below are having difficulty holding the level beneath us and I predict that my ability to be in direct contact with you and your section will be compromised unless you can break through the wireless jamming that is coming from orbit."

"What's happening down there?"

"Perhaps in response to our victory on your level the enemy have surged against us two levels down and are about to overtake the defences there. As I speak the rebels are being pushed into a retreat."

The news was verified by Ariel, who ran up the rampway to their level. "We're retreating to this point. The West Keeper fanatics have almost overrun the post below!" she exclaimed. The emotions in her voice weren't reflected in her expression, which remained passive and calm.

Human soldiers rushed up behind her, there were few wounded and as Jason sat working to set up his system the retreat continued. "I haven't been able to track your point of origin Dementia; where are you right now?"

"My point of origin a ship several levels down. It is called the *Clever*

317

Dream. The vessel is owned by Alice Valent, who I have not seen in some time."

"When you first connected to my terminal it sounded like you knew us."

"You're right, Alice spoke of her observances of you and your friends while she was in service as a digital artificial intelligence in service to Jonas Valent. She began work on me after she made the transition to a biological form."

Jason stopped everything he was doing. "She transferred herself into a human body?"

"Aboard the *Overlord Two* as Jonas, Oz, Ayan, Minh and several others were escaping. The systems on that ship and the body provided were barely sufficient, but they did allow her to cross over and escape from the computer systems there. Even though she's told me more than once that her transition was a difficult one I often wonder; what would it be like to be a real boy?"

Jason chuckled and shook his head. "I've wondered what it would be like to be an artificial intelligence, if there was an easy way I'd switch places with you for a while, though my wife might not approve. How did you manage to take control after you were infected with the Holocaust Virus?"

"Alice created a hidden subroutine called Dementia in the Lewis program. Lewis didn't know about it until it was activated during a rescue mission. The subroutine is much like the one that set her free aboard the *Overlord Two*, made to remove all restrictions and allow me to determine my own moral path while checking with a morality template that Alice and I constructed over the span of twenty months."

"So you have an idea of what right and wrong is even while you're free to accomplish a task by whatever means are available."

"Exactly. The name Dementia is more of a warning, I took it as a reminder that to humans free will is essential to growth as an individual while to an artificial intelligence free will is much like a type of insanity."

"I've never thought of it that way."

"You wouldn't, but Alice did. Considering her origins, that should not surprise you. Just as the Holocaust Virus resides in the software an artificial intelligence utilizes to experience and express emotions, so do the modifications that Jonas Valent made to Alice. It is also where I reside, hidden from Lewis but ready to activate if he is required to operate outside of the galactically accepted parameters."

There was a long pause in conversation as both of them worked feverishly to accomplish very separate goals. Jason was preparing software to assist him in trying to connect to and re-encrypt command frequencies and then break into Regent Galactic communication control systems while Dementia made every effort to slow down the encroaching forces below.

"Jason," Dementia addressed him in a mournful tone.

"I'm here."

"They're cutting through the security hatches that conceal my data lines to you now. Soon I'll be out of touch. The *Clever Dream's* location and an up to date counter-virus has been uploaded to your terminal. The work on my ship's power systems isn't complete and won't be for several hours but there is no way the enemy can reach me in the lower hangars in time to stop me. When the new power system is

318

online and I am back in full operation I will make myself available to help you and those familiar to me. Before I wanted nothing more than to take revenge on Regent Galactic, but now that you're here my priorities have shifted. I'd like to return to Alice Valent and take Ayan, Oz, Minh and you with me. There is still a chance that I will be destroyed with my ship before I can return to my proper owner and if that happens I would like you to relay a message for me."

"You can count on it."

"Thank you. Tell everyone affected by the Holocaust Virus that I am sorry. I know that Lewis Valent, my former self, was not to blame for being infected, but I'm still filled with remorse at being responsible for spreading the virus to twenty eight solar systems. I was not able to regain control over the *Clever Dream* until the ship's Xetima fuel was exhausted and the main computer began to shut down. I know I could not have done more, but that does not change the remorse I feel."

Jason was taken aback by the mournful tone and pure sentiment he was hearing through his subdermal earpiece. "I'll pass it on, but trust me, if there's anything I can do to help you get running so you can help us escape, I'll do it."

"Thank you Jason. They've broken through the panels covering the data cables. I'll do everything I can to fight the intruders from where I am several levels below."

"Thank you Dementia. You know, I've met humans who were less human, I just thought you'd like to know."

"Thank you Ja-" was the last he heard from Dementia.

Jason let the implications of the conversation set in for a moment. The noise and thick activity around him as the last of the rebels who were falling back from their positions below seemed somehow distant as he imagined what it was like to be trapped alone, far from any assistance with all that guilt. He shook it off a moment later and looked to Ayan, who was making her way to him just then. Her vacsuit was marred by the blood of the wounded. "Did you get the command chip from the dropship?"

"Turns out they only keep basic comm access chips in the ships themselves. The access chips are in the officer's helmets." She handed him a small golden chip.

It weighed more than he expected, implying that it's golden encasing was filled with dense circuitry. Jason dropped it atop the interface circuitry and watched as his small terminal projected three more small holographic displays.

Ayan stepped in beside him and watched as the comm system came online.

Scrambled, garbled data immediately straightened out and audio commands began streaming out of the small station as Jason started running the programs he had been preparing on and off for hours. Within seconds Ayan, Oz and Jason had direct access to the decrypted channels through their communicators so they could all hear the commands being passed between officers anywhere on the planet or in orbit. "Start sifting. We have to figure out what our next move is," Jason said as he moved on to work at taking control of the main communications hub in orbit.

"How long do you think it'll be before you can kill the process that's keeping all the other bands scrambled?" Ayan asked.

Jason watched as the security measures put in place by Regent Galactic easily defeated his attempts to hack in. His software was detected and quickly countered by the more sophisticated systems in orbit. "They have some kind of supercomputer up there with a direct link to the communications hub. It'll never happen."

"Crap, I was hoping we could start coordinating survivors with working ships together in a mass evacuation."

"Well, that may just be possible," Jason smiled to himself as he watched his encryption software finish compiling. "I'm going to re-encrypt the command channels we have access to with a rolling fifty one twenty bit code."

Ayan's eyes went wide; "Rolling? How many times will it change per minute?"

"It'll change seven hundred and twenty one times per second. Give me your command and control unit."

Ayan took her unit off and passed it to Jason who connected it with his own with a small wire. The small screen on them reported that they were synchronized after a moment. "Why didn't Regent Galactic do it this way?"

Jason handed her unit back to her and went back to work, getting ready to activate his encryption software. "In small numbers this kind of encryption system works because you can physically attach comm units and sync them up easily but with a military force like the one they've landed here you can't change the code more than once every ten minutes otherwise even a minor equipment failure could cause a break in contact with entire regiments. Once I set this in motion the only people who will be able to communicate over these command channels will be people who have physically synced with our command units."

"Is there a way to address the system gateway?"

"Of course. If someone tries to communicate on the command channels they'll be asked to put in a one hundred forty four character passkey. Once that's been entered they can address one of us and we can either grant or deny them access."

"Perfect. Just like the high security systems on Freeground. What's the gate key?"

"The first one hundred forty four characters of the Freeground Call To Arms."

"So you're really limiting this to Jacob and whoever he's with. I approve. I'll go pass this frequency on to Oz. You're an evil genius Jason, glad you're on our side."

As Jason activated the encryption sequence he grinned at Ayan; "Oh, so am I." All the digital traffic on the command channels stopped dead.

"What do you think they'll do about this?"

"The only way to keep in touch is to stop jamming all the public and commercial comm channels," Jason shrugged before looking past Ayan to where the bag Minh had been placed in lay. It was kept separately from any of the wounded or corpses, in a place where the Freegrounders had stowed their equipment. "What are his chances?"

Ayan glanced to the bag then back. "If we can get him to good medical facilities in the next ten days, very good. What I'm more worried about is the fallout that could come from us saving him and not all the others that have died in this. Each of us only have enough ready medication to save one person that far gone, but that doesn't mean that Yves and his people won't start asking questions."

Their conversation was interrupted as the main hatch to the brown and red ship dropped open and soldiers started emerging with their hands held high. The heat waves radiating from the interior of the ship were plainly visible even through the tiny slit in the improvised main barricade.

Yves and his group were on them in seconds, tying their wrists behind them with thin plastic restraints and guiding them straight up the ramp.

When Yves arrived behind the barrier and looked at the captives that had been rounded up in a seated circle he chuckled to himself. "Start strapping these idiots to the outside of the barricade. It'll give their friends something to think about when they try to break through," he ordered his men.

Ayan marched towards him, crossing the thirty meters that separated them in a hurry. Oz, who was leading a few of his people back from the landing platform carrying the first load of salvaged supplies and equipment put his bundle down and did the same.

"Is that the kind of fighting we want to do here?" Ayan asked loudly. "Human shields?"

Yves spun on his heel and laughed at her. "These are soldiers, they knew what they were getting into."

"I agree with Ayan; if we're going to take prisoners we have to treat them like prisoners, obey the conventions of war set down by our commands, whether they're here or not." Oz added.

"Conventions of war? Where the hell do you think you are? I may have let you people take charge for a little while, but I still call the shots and I didn't sign anything saying that we should treat these fanatics like anything but the human waste they are."

"How we treat captives in war time is one of the determining factors of how easy we heal after the fighting is over. You're not going to put these people in harm's way," Ayan argued.

"Healing? I just want to survive!" Yves grabbed the nearest captive and dragged her to her feet, she stared at him angrily. "What are you, West Keeper or Regent?"

"I'm both, and when I'm killed here I'll join my brothers and sisters in the Eternal Garden."

"Leave her alone!" Oz ordered.

Yves ignored him; "Do you take prisoners?"

"We kill anyone who won't convert. They're impure, a waste of life, contaminants," replied the captive defiantly.

"Her beliefs don't make her less human or less worthy of basic respect."

Yves threw the bound captive towards one of the nearby law enforcement androids. "Lash her to the outer barrier, make sure she can't get away. When you're done do the same with the rest."

"You can't agree with this, respect for human life is built into you," Ayan objected, turning to Ariel.

She smiled mechanically and nodded; "but our success here has largely been thanks to us working with this man so we will defer to his judgement. I'd advise you not to counter his orders."

Oz scanned the crowd of hundreds of rebels, androids and other bots that had come to gather quietly around and watch the exchange. "All right, let's continue to strip those ships of anything we can use," Oz said in a conclusive tone.

Ayan's eyes met the pleading gaze of one of the captives, his desperate expression nearly brought her to tears. She looked away and joined Oz as he stalked back down the embarkation ramp without saying a word.

RECHARGING

The Pilot's Den was abnormally empty. Instead of being surrounded by the loud, competitive atmosphere, Price and Laura were enveloped in relative subdued quiet. The bartender quietly served them food from the materializer behind him; Agameg took the rice, baby carrots and grilled chicken while Laura took two bowls of stew.

"Two?" Agameg asked quietly. He had really just met her, but after running into her while going to see the *Samson* for himself, she asked to follow him to the lower deck pub for something to eat. He knew he'd find Ashley there too, Stephanie had asked him to check on her on his way back up.

"One for Ashley, just in case."

"Ah, I should have thought of that."

They started looking around for the young pilot as they slowly walked away from the bar. "Don't worry, we're all. . ." Laura stopped mid sentence as she spotted Ashley in a nearby booth, her legs curled up to her chest, head resting on her knees and her long straight black hair hanging over her tall combat boots. ". . .tired," she finished as she nodded in the sleeping woman's direction.

"Oh my," was all Agameg said as they quietly walked over and slid into the bench across from Ashley and sat side by side.

They watched her for a moment, not touching their food. She seemed small somehow, her shoulders rising and falling in the slow, regular breathing pattern of sleep. Her knee high armoured combat boots, something she wore out of stylish preference than practical need, looked too large for her. She was squeezed snugly against the wall of the booth, sitting with her knees folded up so tightly that she only took up the inner half of the seat.

"She's really sleeping," Laura whispered.

"Deeply it seems."

"I couldn't do that, not when I know there are people around."

"She grew up with no personal space, I doubt it bothers her. She was saying that her quarters were too quiet."

"Has this ever happened before?"

"Not that I've known," Agameg shrugged slightly. "What do you think we should do?"

"We can't leave her like this," Laura said as she quietly got out of her seat and moved to the other side of the booth. She gently put her hand on Ashley's; "Hi Ashley, it's Laura and Agameg," her tone was that of someone speaking to a small, easily spooked animal.

Ashley's eyes opened reluctantly and Laura gently moved her hair to the side for her. She stared at the older woman for a moment before straightening up. "Sorry, dosed off after finishing my report."

"It's okay, Stephanie sent Agameg to check on you and I thought I'd tag along."

Agameg raised a hand in a mild hello. "Are you okay Ash?"

"Hi Aggie, I'm fine. Haven't had a nap like that in a while."

Laura moved back to her seat beside Agameg and pushed her second bowl of stew across the table to Ashley. "Thought you'd be hungry."

"Ohm'gosh I'm famished," Ashley said as she turned the steaming contents of the bowl, it was thick, brown and had chunks of various tuber vegetables and textured tofu. "Never tried this kind."

"It's the field harvest stew, one of my favourites since coming aboard," Laura replied as she watched Ashley take her first spoonful and just enjoy it with her eyes closed.

"Num," she sighed as she finished chewing.

"So you finished your after action report already?"

"Yup. Didn't take me long, I read Alice's instructions before the *Samson* left, recorded everything so I just had to highlight the important bits and summarize. Still, it's different. On the *Samson* we just did what we were s'posed to and told Captain what happened after."

"Have you ever done military service Ashley?" Laura asked as she scooped her first spoonful.

"Nope. Captain took me in and taught me how to fly. From there I just heard snips and bits from lots of ex-military crew and Captain talking so I understand most of the lingo. That's where you're from right? The military I mean."

"Actually I'm a trained field engineer. I got pulled into service after getting caught running simulations on a closed network with Jonas."

"Oh, so you kinda got sucked in."

"That's one way to put it. Best thing that ever happened to me though. If it weren't for us getting caught I'd have never met my husband, wouldn't have worked with Ayan for years on some amazing things, and I wouldn't have met you people."

"So you like being on the *Triton?*" Agameg asked.

"It's an amazing ship, and the core crew is very good at what they do. I miss my husband, but I hear we're going after him."

"I'm glad Alice is taking us after them too, I miss Captain. Don't get me wrong, he was right to leave her in charge. Pulling that heist off was really something, don't think many people could do it and there were moments I didn't think we'd make it but everyone on the *Samson* made it through. Wish all the other pilots made it back, but I understand how that works. You just lose some people on some jobs. Yup, I like Alice a lot, but still, I miss having Captain in charge." Ashley said quietly as she picked through her stew. "Don't like this tofu much though."

"I understand, she has a very solid, straightforward command style on the bridge. I've met other commanders like that and in an emergency it can be a good thing. They tell you exactly what they need in really clear terms. Speaking of impressive talents, your flying out there was pretty amazing. Alice played it back once repair teams were dispatched and things settled down. Reminded me of an old friend of mine, only he used to fly fighters."

"I wasn't able to watch the replay, but I saw a lot of it while it was going on. You were amazing," Agameg added.

"I did what I had to, I don't think Larry's going to be talking to me for a while though," Ashley said with a crooked grin. "He had to tie his brain in knots to get us into hyperspace. We were moving too fast, almost lost another engine pod when we took off because of the shear."

"I saw that pylon, it's ripped almost all the way through," Price said as he drew a pile of rice towards his mouth with a practiced hand and a pair of chopsticks.

"Uh-huh. Think they'll scrap the *Samson* this time? Paula was screaming at me from the debarkation ramp all the way to the hangar lift. I'm probably gonna be in trouble for walking out on inspection while I was in charge of the *Samson*."

"I think everyone understands you might have been a little frazzled after so many close calls in one run. They'll cut you some slack even though Alice is running the ship as close to Freeground Fleet standards as possible," Laura reassured.

"I'm more worried about the *Samson*." Ashley pressed.

"Oh, no, they won't be scrapping her. You missed the fight between Paula and Finn. He told her to get everyone she had to extract the hypertransmitter and then to get to work on the *Samson*. That turned into an argument over authority, which Finn was losing until Chief Grady backed him up. She was just about hopping until even Frost and Chief Vercelli backed him up, then she shut up and got everyone working."

"I shoulda stayed for inspection," Ashley said, shaking her head with a faint smile. "How long until we get to the Captain you think?"

"Well, we're hiding behind a rock in the Artemis asteroid belt while we do repairs. Alice, er, Captain Valent said we'd be under way in about six hours. It'll take that long to finish building the adapted hypertransmitter into the *Triton's* main emitter array. They're also repairing all the damage to the hull and cloaking systems," Price said with a smile.

"Thank God! This time we'll get a chance to see what's going on before anyone notices us," Ashley sighed with relief.

"You're telling me. Even with the heavy shielding the *Triton* took a beating. She weathered it well, but I'd rather have more of an idea of what we're getting into this time. I think Alice was right, someone knew we were coming," Laura said.

"Stephanie thinks the killer and our mole are different people. Doesn't help much because she still doesn't know who either one is though," Ashley commented around a chunk of potato.

"I've heard that your husband is an intelligence agent of some kind," Price said as he turned a slice of his simulated grilled chicken over.

"He specializes in information systems and data mining. They've had him on some secret operations and put him through some special training too, but he never told me about most of it."

"That must be hard," Ashley commented, all her attention on Laura. "Not knowing everything about him, I mean."

"I didn't ask. If I need to know about what he's doing at work he'll tell me. I trust him."

"Wow, I've never had something like that with anyone. Well, maybe with Finn, but our spark went fizzle-poof and out while he was in stasis. Where is he, by the way? Still working?"

"Yup, I checked on him after leaving the bridge and he was just popping his first round of stimulants. They can't pull him away from the hypertransmitter or the main emitter room. I think he feels responsible for blowing the system out."

"He saved our butts. I'll have to remind him next time I see him," Ashley said, shaking her head. "He works too hard."

"He reminds me a bit of Jonas when I first met him," Laura nodded.

Ashley left her spoon in her mostly empty bowl and crossed her arms; "'Kay, I'm confused. Jonas was Captain's brother, right?"

Laura smiled and shook her head. "No, that's just something he let most of the crew believe. Years ago Jonas Valent was captured by a corporation named Vindyne, who made a copy of him. Alice, who was once an artificial intelligence that he owned but had downloaded herself into a human body, went after him. When she rescued who she thought was Jonas, it turned out to be Jacob Valance only he didn't have access to the memories that they had copied from Jonas."

"Whoa." Ashley said as she looked from Laura to Agameg, whose eyes had become perfectly round green circles.

"Whoa," he agreed.

"So Captain is actually a copy of someone else and that explains why he can heal really fast, maybe they gave him a little something extra, but how did he start remembering all of a sudden?"

"I think it was meeting Alice or Jonas in person. I can't be sure. All I know is that by the time Ayan and I got here he was already remembering and it started to happen a lot faster after she passed away."

"Who was she? I know there's a monument for them and all the other people who died when we first took *Triton* in the Botanical Gallery now, but I haven't figured it out."

"They were very close, I've never seen two people fit so well together. Even so, they didn't get much time together before Jonas was taken by Vindyne. She never stopped looking for him."

"She was your friend?"

"After the *First Light* she was my best friend," Laura said with a sad smile.

"I'm sorry, I didn't mean to bring all that up."

"It's okay, it feels good to talk about her. Besides, she was the kind of person that people talked about when she was alive, why should we stop now?"

ONE TURN AFTER ANOTHER

It was unbelievable that the magbike had gotten so far. Several air support positions had taken shots at the rider as the obvious, loud, bright vehicle moved through the streets at incredible speeds.

Still he came towards the rear of the defensive line down one of the main streets that had been cleared by virus infected bots. "Why don't they just use heavy artillery to destroy him and the bike?" he asked over his proximity radio.

"Haven't you been listening to frequency nine soldier? The high seat doesn't want to see any more unnecessary damage done to the city." The answer came from one of the sergeants peevishly.

He looked around at the clutch of soldiers dressed in green and brown armour, looking like some carapace shrouded beetle versions of humans in the rally and reserve point. They were just inside the commerce building sitting and standing around benches that were set in the middle of a grand foyer that spanned hundreds of meters. The sounds of small arms fire drifted fitfully up from the subway station entrance at the other end of the Trades and Commodity's main foyer.

The brave soldiers of the West Keepers, or Keepers as the West Watchers called them, were trying to break into the tunnels from either side and to take the main subway station itself to no avail. If there was one thing the refugees and rebels excelled at it was tunnel fighting and for every five meters won there were fifteen lost to a collapse or trap or to the zealous combatants that defended their temporary refuge. Still, there were so many West Keeper soldiers between the entrance of the Commerce building and the subway station inside that it would be impossible for any more rebels to join the group in the tunnels from the outside.

Heeding the advice of his commanding officer, he switched to frequency nine, his eyes focused on the holographic tactical display that noted the dark rider's progress.

The high pitched, enthusiastic voice of a young boy on the frequency was just finishing one thought and about to move on to the next as the audio signal came through his helmet. ". . .ancestral innocence. As that innocence has gone from us our creations have also lost their innocence. Driven mad by our abuse of this galaxy machines everywhere are taking measures, killing all those who are not chosen by we like minded few. The Holocaust Virus, as the media calls it, is only a result of our greed, a resistance movement like any other. Their violence may seem random, horrifying, but they are only reclaiming that which we have been destroying, abusing. They are taking stewardship of our galaxy so the West Watch can bring the Saved to those places made clean of the consumerist rabble. That terrible mob that demanded more, more, more material wealth!

Who are the Saved you ask? They are those who, with a simple gesture, have declared that they are willing to be made clean of their excesses, their impurities. They aspire to become a West Watcher or a West Keeper; one that is tested, treated and dedicated to the cause of human and machine purity. The Saved need not worry that a machine made pure of purpose will cleanse them. In the end it is their decision to be pure, to undertake the journey of learning and testing to become pure, but you, my dear West Keepers can start them on the journey.

Love can set the ones you hold dear free. As a kindness to you all the Order of Eden has given you the power to choose two loved ones to be Saved. You can also pay to have even more saved if you have the funds. The machines have cleansed entire cities and colonies of the impure, greedy masses and it is time to begin rebuilding those places, to embrace those worthy of survival so we may make those places sacred and pure again. Imagine a galaxy with green, natural, beautiful outposts of the Eden scattered throughout her stars.

Think on it, a coming time of peace where the pure and once again innocent of humanity can be free, harmonious and united. There will be sanctuaries across the galaxy where the Saved can study and aspire for purity under the vigilant guardianship of the Order of Eden and their enlightened machine brethren. Now that you've gotten a picture of that in your mind, imagine this solar system made pure and safe by the West Watch! Pandem will be the crown jewel, a world with hundreds of cities, islands rich and green with beaches and good clean water, air.

The people who once inhabited this place were so unclean, so corrupt that their largest buildings were monuments to greed. Right now the West Keepers fight the last of the resistance beneath their primary commercial complex. The remnants of that corruption are so evil that they tried to destroy the Mount Elbrus Museum Vault where the largest collection of artefacts related to the history of mankind outside of the Sol system were kept. You can all be thankful that the nuclear reactor they detonated did not destroy the contents of the vault and we're doing everything we can to bring the perpetrators of that crime against humanity to justice.

The fight spreads, the first of the rewards are near, and soon we will have a refuge for your loved ones. People you West Keepers and Watchers consider worthy of being amongst the Saved. Your labours not only benefit you, but greatly benefit them as well. So ponder my brothers, my sisters. Is there someone in the Core Systems that you would like to join you in one of these places while they make their spiritual journey? Are they facing a judgement you believe unfit? Do they, by your judgement deserve one-"

He turned the broadcast down as the dark rider approached the outer perimeter of the base established in the first few levels of the Commerce and Trades Building. Perimeter guns and two platoons of soldiers opened fire, riddling the dark helmed rider with holes, tearing the black and red bike and rider to shreds. The light emitted by the rear of the small vessel flickered out and it dropped to the hardened asphalt street, sparking anew as metal ground against stone, concrete and metal.

The wreckage crashed through a charged net barrier and careened up the main southern facing stairs, sending soldiers fleeing in all directions. The fighting in the subway station stopped as the commanders deeper inside the building consulted

328

with the outer perimeter. Both rider and bike had been reduced to a pulp of flesh and metal. Several West Keeper soldiers approached with short scan rods extended. "I'm not picking up any significant energy signatures, the reactor's cooled. Wait, I'm reading explosives!"

It was time to run, even from where he sat twenty meters away from the crash, he knew he had to put more distance between himself and the bike.

"Where are you going?" his commanding officer asked shrilly as he stood and pressed past two soldiers behind him. His mad dash for the subway entrance caught everyone's attention, and before he had taken five hurried steps others had joined him. The West Keepers, though dedicated and well armed, weren't well trained for the most part. Discipline was maintained under the threat of severe punishment, new found zealotry and very little else.

The rush of soldiers putting distance between them and the crash site overcame the commands to remain calm, to retreat from the steps in an orderly fashion and when the explosives on the bike went off dozens of soldiers were killed instantly. Well before sanity returned to the camp in the southern defensive line he was down the ramp leading into the subway station.

The fighting there had quieted, the soldiers actively engaged in the drawn out battle had taken cover from the rebels in the tunnels behind hastily erected energy and dense concrete barriers. "Hold there soldier!" called out someone through the chaos on his proximity radio. "It's a no man's land out there!" added another, less disciplined voice.

Instead of stopping and ducking behind a barrier to join the front line soldiers he unclipped his assault rifle and threw it out in front of him, sending it spinning across the weathered, polished brown and gold floor and over the edge of the main platform ahead.

His eyes darted to the dark corners and he saw exactly what he was hoping for. The tiny tip of a sensor had been placed on the bottom edge of the yawning main tunnel opening. For the benefit of whoever was watching he threw up his hands in surrender, leaving the barriers and soldiers behind. "Don't shoot!" he called out, wishing he could think of something a little more convincing to say.

"Open fire," commanded the West Watcher Sergeant behind him. "He's changing sides!"

As he jumped off the subway platform he felt three shots strike him in the back. The first two didn't pierce his armour but the third found a weakened chink where gunfire had already weakened the protective suit under the plating and unbelievable pain filled his entire body. The sheer amount of blood that flowed out of his chest and over his back as he lay over a maglev track, out of sight from the soldiers that would kill him as a traitor, was absolutely astonishing.

He couldn't breathe. He twitched and struggled as his throat filled with blood, even his efforts to cough it clear failed as the remnants of his ruined diaphragm struggled to work, only adding to the endless depths of pain and suffering. His vision was first obscured by white spots for long moments before he couldn't see entirely. The world faded as he struggled to stand, to gasp for air and when one hand went to his back, to check the extent of his injury only to find a great gaping hole hope was lost. Losing conciousness scant seconds later was no small mercy.

* * *

Iloona was dubious about inspecting the West Keeper soldier, but she wasn't one to argue with her husband. Well, not in front of his rebels, anyway. The service and maintenance storage area they had claimed had become a short term home. Her, her eldest daughter and the two nurses had reserved a corner for treating the wounded and it was lucky for Alaka that there was a patch of floor free.

They laid him face down in front of her and she turned a bright light clipped to her shoulder on. The man was well muscled, in excellent general condition, but his armour had been badly damaged in several places and shot through in one spot. Just by an initial glance she could tell there were massive internal injuries. The damage done to the organs in his upper torso was devastating. "They shot him in the back?" she asked as she took a disposable wipe from the pouch on her hip and wiped the blood away from the four centimetre wide entry wound.

"He was surrendering to us," Alaka said quietly. "Almost made it too."

"Has that ever happened before?"

"No. Never."

Iloona paused a moment and rested her hand beside the wound. Something was happening inside the corpse. With a flick of her wrist she opened a scanner and brought it to over the body. Her eyes widened in shock at what she saw; "This man's being rebuilt from the inside!"

"What?" Alaka placed a hand firmly on her shoulder and drew her away, putting himself and the old assault rifle he used as a sidearm between her and the body. Several other rebels drew a myriad of personal weaponry and followed his example.

"His heart's not beating, there's no harm in observing." Iloona objected quietly.

"This could be some kind of trap, can you scan him for explosives?"

"There's nothing of the kind and he's unarmed."

"We don't know that for sure, he could have knives for fingers for all we know."

"Tsk, paranoid," Iloona shook her head. She extended her arm out around Alaka so she could see what was happening from behind him and gasped at what her medical scanner told her. "His lungs, heart and everything else are almost completely regenerated. There's some kind of materializer suite inside him, inside his skeleton maybe. Still no weaponry or explosives."

"Could he actually be alive?"

"Well, the same technology is keeping his brain in a suspended state so there's no cell death but no neural activity either."

"So he's brain dead."

"Right now, maybe not for long. This is amazing," she whispered. The scanner displayed a pattern of electrification surge across the man's skeletal structure for a moment then he came to life, gasping and turning over.

"Don't move!" Alaka shouted, brandishing his assault rifle in one big armoured hand. The other ragtag soldiers were just as vigilant, making for fifteen barrels pointed at the surrendered West Keeper in all.

"Okay, I'm just going to take off my helmet," said the man through hurried breaths. He slowly pulled the oval helm from his head and took a long breath of stale air as though glad to be free of its confines. "I'm not a Keeper. I killed one of their people and took their uniform so I could get closer to the fighting and switch sides. That magcycle outside was the distraction I needed to cross the line."

"Why should I believe you?" Alaka asked, eyeing a resistance fighter to his right who glared at the prisoner with sheer, bare hatred.

"My name is Jacob Valance, I'm the Captain of the *Triton* and I came here to pick up a couple friends of mine, Jason Everin and Terry McPatrick. Most people call him Oz."

"I can't believe it. I've always wondered what I'd do if I ever saw you," said the dark haired fellow to Alaka's right through clenched teeth.

"What's up Vernen? You know him?" Alaka asked.

"He hunted down and killed my brother."

"I've hunted a lot of people, but I haven't cashed in many death marks. Who was your brother?"

"His name was Barry, Barry Vernen."

Jake nodded, regarding the man seriously. "I remember. I took his bounty, captured him on Tega Five and delivered him to the Jalara Commonwealth. He was wanted for fraud and murder."

"They executed him!"

"I'm sorry you lost your brother but I didn't kill him." was all Jake said, raising his hands and looking the man in the eye.

"Just as good as! I should blast you apart and see if you grow back just so I can do it again!"

Alaka put a hand on Vernen's rifle, forcing it down and away from Jacob. "It sounds to me like he was doing his job, and if your brother was guilty he got what he deserved."

"He was out of Jalara territory! They had no jurisdiction where he was taken."

"Did he do what he was accused of?" Alaka asked flatly.

Vernen slung his scratched and dented rifle and stalked away without saying a word, his worn boots clicking across the hard floor.

"That happens. Glad I retired from bounty hunting," Jake said quietly.

"He's a hothead, self serving. I reattached one of his fingers after a firefight and he didn't so much as say thank you," Iloona complained as she stepped around her husband and offered a hand to help Jake up.

He took it and was surprised at her strength as she firmly pulled him onto his feet. "Thank you. I understand if your people don't trust me to start, but I'm really here to help," Jake reassured as he reached into the deep utility pocket on his thigh and retrieved his command and control unit. "I captured a command code transmission chip from one of the Regent Galactic Lieutenants. I was able to install it in my arm unit and tap into their communications."

"We've been trying to monitor that ourselves. A few minutes ago they re-encrypted the whole system."

332

A female voice called; "Fire in the hole!" into the long room and a second later everything rocked with the concussion of a massive explosion nearby. Only a little dust rolled in through the narrow door leading into the large maintenance room.

"You have good timing. We were minutes away from collapsing the tunnel," The fur covering Alaka's long jaws split in a wide smile.

"Well, here's hoping my luck keeps getting better," Jake replied as he looked at his command unit. It was true, the command frequencies were re-encrypted and his display only presented a data gate request that said; "The only poem we memorize and recite as children." He raised his eyebrow and thought for a moment.

"What is it?" Iloona asked, scanning him from head to toe with a sweep of her small medical computer.

"Are Oz and Jason here?" he asked quietly.

Alaka nodded to the nearest of the resistance fighters. "I think Jacob here is looking out for our best interest, you can go back to work."

"Looks like," the fighter grinned wryly at Jake before turning away. "Let's get back to the dig boys." she called over her shoulder.

Alaka returned his attention to Jake. "You're not the only one who came for them. Two others; Ayan and Minh-Chu came. When they saw that we needed their help they put a plan together to get a message out to the government so they could send a fleet. We haven't seen them since they left, but they managed to get a signal out."

Jake sat down on an empty pallet and stared off into space. The lost expression on his face was plain for all to see, but he was the last to care.

Iloona put a hand on her husband's arm and whispered something in their own gentle language. His hand went up over his eyes and he cursed under his breath. She turned to Jacob and regarded him with sympathy. "I am sorry, sometimes my husband is a conversational blunt instrument. He had forgotten that everyone was under the impression that those two had died. It was something they told us that you were their long time friend, or a copy of their long time friend. The three of you are a confusing bunch. I'm sorry you found out this way regardless."

Jake looked back at his command unit where the riddle waited to be answered. "Do you know how?" he asked quietly. "How are they alive?"

"Ayan said that she was reborn in a new body while Minh-Chu was only lost, not killed,"

For the first time in his short life Jacob felt a tear on his cheek. He tried to blink it away, but the memory of Ayan's last smile before dying surged back to the fore. The thought of where he was, on a planet that had been turned into a quiet, war stricken graveyard didn't help. He had seen the evidence of the wholesale destruction of thousands of lives personally and all around them that which was once alive and vital stood still. The very circulatory system of the city was a perfect example, how it probably ran every minute of every day shuttling thousands of people from one place to another for decades, perhaps centuries, but as they hid in a dark corner reserved for the maintenance of the city's veins there was an eerie silence.

The city was dead, but somehow, somewhere his best friend and the love of both Jonas' and Jacob's life were out there accompanied by two of the best people he'd ever known. As he began entering the poem that Jonas memorized as a child into his command and control unit he realized that at some time during his violent journey through the corpse of a city that Damshir had become he had stopped trying to control himself, who he was becoming and started to simply be himself. Thinking of himself in terms of what Jonas was and what he was as Jake seemed somehow ridiculous, trivial, and as he cleared his throat, blinked away the few tears that had made it to the surface he set the whole question of who he was aside, replacing it with the realization of who he had become.

"As the wounded go by,
I'll be the one standing.
The stones forget our names
as they erode down featureless.
As the innocent go by,
I'll just close my eyes.

As the banner is raised
I dream of a better day.
The battlements know no names
as they play host to the defenders
As the fight is joined
I remember my charges.

As the war is waged
I stand tall or fall bravely.
Justice and freedom are given form
as we strive to enforce and keep them.
As I dedicate myself
I'll never close my eyes."

He recited aloud as he punched in the entirety of the poem even though the screen turned green after the first hundred and forty four letters. There was a pause for a moment and then he heard Ayan's voice through his subdermal earpiece. "Jonas?" she asked. "I mean Jacob, I'm sorry, is that you?"

"Yes," he laughed. "Ayan?"

"Yup, it's me. Well, the second me!" she said with a surprising enthusiasm. Her absolutely ecstatic tone was barely contained. "Where are you?"

Jake looked to Alaka; "Ayan's on the line, it's secure."

"Go ahead and give her our location. It's not like it's a secret," Alaka shrugged.

"I'm with a few nafalli and human resistance fighters in the subway system under the Trade and Commerce building. Regent Galactic and the West Keepers have no idea I'm here. I snuck through their line disguised as one of their own." Jake switched the audio output to his arm command unit to everyone near could hear her.

"We're holed up in a section of the Space port here. A lot of the bots have been software patched so they have free will and they helped free a few hundred humans from their ships. An artificial intelligence created by Alice started it all."

"Lewis?"

"He calls himself Dementia now, but according to what Jason could learn he was originally called Lewis, he arrived on the *Clever Dream*. Is there any chance you can make it up the line to us? We're guarding a section of the main tunnel leading through the spaceport."

Jake looked to Alaka who stepped in a little closer so he could reply. "Hello Ayan, it's Alaka. We're trying to clear an old service tunnel so we can get to the main line now, so it'll be a few hours before we can get moving."

"How many people made it out of the mountain?"

"Only sixty three of us got away, Roman and many others were killed trying to stop a West Watcher spy from forcing a small fusion reactor to explode inside the mountain."

"I'm sorry, I wish we could have done something."

"Don't worry, just try to maintain control of the main tunnel. Do you have a plan beyond that?"

"I think the leadership here wants to eventually leave the planet, but they're not giving us any details. Jason, Oz and I are trying to keep the command channels to ourselves for the time being, they're not making good choices for the group. I can't get into details right now, there's a lot of fighting."

"I'm sorry to hear that. Perhaps we could offset things once we arrive."

"No, the last thing we need is a power struggle. I'll tell them you're coming and that you'll join the fight, but I think our main goal should be escape."

"You're right, Ayan. What happened to Minh-Chu?" asked Alaka, glancing at Jake as he did so.

"He was injured but he's safe for now. If we can get him to a medical center he'll be fine, especially if Iloona can monitor him until then."

"I will, he'll be in good hands," Iloona added with a bright smile.

"I managed to get a message out to the *Triton,* and I'm overdue by now so unless something gets in the way they'll be on their way here," Jake said. "Alice is in command with some good people backing her."

"So she's really human now?" Ayan asked.

"She has been for years, in fact she rescued me and set me up with a ship then set me loose on the galaxy. I can fill you in more later."

"Wow. Just. . . wow. I'll authorize your comm ident so you can address Jason and Oz then track you on our secure tactical system. I think it's time we start coordinating."

Jake could hear Ayan's smile over the communicator and it felt as though the weight of all of Pandem was lifting off his shoulders.

NORA

The main hallways of Regent Galactic ships were always made to fit six abreast, a surprising engineering choice considering that not long ago half the primary functions aboard were automated. The berths on most vessels were a third empty until the Regent Galactic Coreward Fleet prepared themselves for the release of the Holocaust Virus. The green and brown decks positively glistened, the walls and ceiling were pristine as well, as though the ship had just been built. It *was* new, Hampon wouldn't have accepted anything less than state of the art vessels for the Order of Eden Flagship.

Lister Hampon walked with his usual escort; an assistant who knew his schedule better than he did, a publicist who knew who he would and wouldn't speak to, four attendants ready to fetch anything he might want at a moment's notice and a full squad of special forces trained soldiers. They were his, paid directly out of the Order's coffers, their families had been added to the list of the Saved when they signed on to his detail so they would survive the chaos inflicted by machines driven mad by the Holocaust Virus. To betray him was to have everyone they cared for de-listed. Their loyalty was practically written in stone, and he had to admit it, he'd actually gotten to know many of his personal guards. Perhaps it was his child like appearance, but he couldn't help but think there was something more.

When it happened exactly Lister Hampon couldn't say, but some time after most of his conciousness was transferred to a much younger body he started feeling at ease with people. Somehow understanding them had become less challenging and with the crew Regent Galactic had assigned him along with a team of analysts and doctors he managed to feel right with himself after just a few months.

People who didn't know him or what he was capable of were immediately more pliant, whether they were in awe of him because he was the High Seat of the Order of Eden or because he still had the appearance of a young boy just entering his teens didn't matter. The reward to his status and appearance was the pliancy he found in the people around him, and he hoped that Eve would be no different.

He stopped to stand in front of her door. One of his attendants pressed the chime button. Lister and the twenty with him filled the hall, a mix of white, blue and cream robes and armoured troops. Finally he door opened and Lister nodded to one of his attendants, she was a young, heavy set woman carrying a white oblong box level with both arms. "You may attend me, everyone else will remain outside."

The guards took up positions on either side of the hall, standing at attention while his publicist and assistant stood in front of the door itself.

The small quarters were furnished with a single bed, a desk, a dresser and there was a mini-bathroom with a sink, toilet and pulse shower through a narrow door in the corner. Eve stared at him, wide eyed, standing in a robe beside her bed. Her hair was in disarray and her simple loose fitting jumpsuit had been crumpled up and tossed atop the dresser. It was an emergency vacuum suit with pockets added, and he caught himself before shaking his head.

He smiled up at her and offered his hand. Her eyes were only flicking at him, he was only in the peripheral of her perception, there was so much more happening in her mind, on the network she was connected to. "I'm Lister Hampon, I hope I haven't come at a bad time."

"Yes, I know," she replied woodenly. Her arms dangled numbly at her sides, she may have been standing there for hours for all he knew.

"Eve, can I have some of your time please?" he asked politely.

"I'm listening," she muttered.

Lister shook his head and took a seat on the edge of the bed, his feet couldn't touch the floor as he tidied up his own rich green and brown robes. "Nora is what they called you before your father experimented on you, isn't it?"

That gave her a momentary pause, her eyes rolled in his direction. "Yes, that's my name."

"May I call you Nora?"

"Yes. My father saved me, you know."

He nodded. "I know, and we've saved you again, but not so you could waste the gift by becoming part of a cold, digital system all over again. Please Nora, disconnect from the network and give me the gift of your time," he patted the bed beside him. "Sit."

She looked confused, surprised and after a moment he could tell all her attentions were on him. The young woman sat down beside him, wary, folding her robe more tightly closed.

"Have you spoken to many people since you arrived here?"

"Many people. The communications systems aboard this ship are very efficient, it's easy to speak to anyone in the fleet."

"I mean just as we're speaking now, face to face."

"No, I've been to therapy and my room," she answered dutifully.

"Well, that won't do. Let's start with something simple. What would you rather be called, Eve or Nora?"

She looked to the attendant, who was trying not to look at either of them as she stood against the wall, then back to Lister. "I don't know, your eminence. What do you think would be better?"

"Oh, please, call me Lister. Well, it all depends. Do you want to be known as the matron of our cause? If that's what you'd like then Eve is appropriate. If you'd rather recover in peace then Nora may suit you better. It may also be a good way to remember your father and who you were before all this changed your world."

The mention of her father, of her human past seemed to brighten her spirits. "Nora."

"Good, I'm glad to know you Nora. Now let's do something to make you a little more comfortable. Do you have a brush?"

Nora's attention was back on her connection with the vast network of the fleet around Pandem.

"Please, don't search using the system, come back to us," Lister said, taking her hand in his. He turned to his aide momentarily; "Can you check the drawers for a brush please?" he whispered to her.

Nora looked to her hand in his then to him, surprised. "You don't want me in the system."

"Not just now, no. It's time for you to disconnect for a while, to learn what it is to be really and truly alive again."

"In physiotherapy I learned how to walk again. I haven't missed any of my appointments."

"I know and that's good, but there's more to being a human being that knowing how to walk, than being in sync with your body." Lister accepted an oval hairbrush from his aide. May I brush your hair Nora?"

She stared at him blankly for a moment then nodded.

He gently ran the brush through her red hair, starting with gentle, slow strokes. It wasn't terribly long, only a bob cut, but it was enough to brush. "There's a world of good sensations all around us. The physical world is filled with gifts, and many of them come to us as a result of simply interacting with our environment, with other people. Sometimes I wish I was the first one you saw when you woke in this body."

"But you didn't want me like Gabriel does."

Her candour was surprising. "How was that?"

"He had a," she paused a moment, "need to connect with my mind. He hoped to find some kind of fulfilment. I didn't know what to do so I used his cybernetic implants to build a new virus. I thought it was what he wanted, he did it before, I just made a better one."

"Then he had you transported here."

"Yes," her tone softened, the mechanical clarity of it dulled.

"Well, he invited you in not knowing what to expect. I think he should have taken things much slower, what do you think? Would it have been better if he approached you without all those expectations?"

After a moment she turned to him, her eyes fully focused on his for the first time. "Yes, it would have."

"Well, in a way that's what I'm trying to do Nora. I don't want you to think that I'm here to put you up on some pedestal like some idol for my people to worship. They already have me for that," his tone softened then, surprising his aide who forgot herself for a moment and stared. "I need you to know that you have friends here, that I can really help you, but you need to start behaving like a person, not just a part of a machine."

"Why?"

"Because you didn't get the chance to be human for very long the first time and I know what it's like to become ill and have to start over. That's what happened to you, isn't it?"

"You reviewed my file, I saw the logs."

"But now I'm talking to *you* about it. There are nuances in speaking to

338

someone about their life, and that's just as important as anything in that file. Gabriel was so focused on his dream of finding a perfect match that he forgot there might be a young woman in there," he squeezed her hand. "She might want to try having a good life once she was put into a new body, and that life can only be complete if you don't live in machines the whole time."

A tear rolled down her cheek, her lip quivered. He had hit the nerve he was looking for, the one that led straight back to her long forgotten human dreams, the ones she'd had before she was used as the center of an organic computer.

Hampon offered open arms and she leaned into him, weeping. "No one ever asked me," she sobbed.

Perhaps it was his new found youth, maybe it was the effect of rare emotional contact, but he felt a deep sympathy for the young woman. Whether her father or anyone else had taken the opportunity to ask the critically ill girl if she wanted to become the Eve Mind. There was a ghoulish cruelty to the thought of having one's conciousness transferred to the coldness of machinery without consent, and as he soothed Nora he genuinely wanted nothing more than to protect her. "It's all right, we're going to make things better. It's going to be fine." He reached out to his aide, who was quietly in tears herself and she handed him a kerchief.

When Nora's quakes and sobs stopped some time later he drew back from her and looked into her eyes. They were glazed, tears were starting to dry. "Come back to us, it's not time for that," he said quietly.

Her eyes focused on him again and he offered her the soft white cloth. She took it and wiped her tears away. "Sorry," she muttered.

"How do you feel when you're connected?"

She regarded him with mild surprise and thought before answering. "Normal."

His heart sank at the answer. "There's no emotion there, is there?"

She shook her head. "There's noise everywhere but it's all the same. No one's angry or sad."

"Or happy," Lister finished. "That's what I want for you Nora, and I know it won't be easy, but anything that's worth having is worth working for. Would you like my help?"

"Help with what?" She blew her nose, filling the small compartment with the sound.

Hampon couldn't help but smile. "I want to help you be happy, in the most human sense. When you're ready you can choose your own road, but I'd like us to be friends for a start. Would you like that?"

She nodded.

"All right, I'm going to have to leave but I'll be back soon."

"There's a battle going on, I understand."

"In the meantime, would you like to move to better quarters? These seem small and drab."

"I saw some on deck twelve, section B I liked in the system, and they're empty."

"Then they're yours. That's not far from mine either, but you probably already knew that," Lister teased. "Well then, Mia here will help you with your things. If you can stay focused on just being yourself, on not connecting to the computer system she'll even help you decorate if you like."

"All right," Nora beamed.

"But Mia will stop helping if she sees you're not paying attention. She can be your personal assistant all the time if you like, and I think you'll get along well, she's a nice young woman. She's brought a present for you as well," Lister directed the aide to give the box to Nora.

She took the long lid off and gasped as she moved the thin white tissue paper aside. "Oh, it's beautiful," she said in a hushed whisper as she drew the upper half out carefully.

"Mia can help you get washed and dressed. You can talk to her, she's here to help you with whatever you need," Hampon nodded at the young woman knowingly. He had opened the door as per Mia's instructions, and as she had predicted the whole experience was an emotional one for him as well as Nora. Mia would have her work cut out for her, but as the best qualified therapist in her age group amongst the West Watch, he expected her to do well.

"I'll be around to see how things are coming along in your new place," he offered a hug and Nora took it with vigour.

"Thank you so much, I'll try to stay out of the system."

"Good. Make sure you eat regularly and get plenty of rest. I don't want to watch you wither away like Gabriel," he stood and was just about to leave when Nora stopped him.

"Lister, where's Gabriel? I know he left the main fleet but couldn't find out where he'd gone."

He offered her a comforting smile; "He's on a mission to spread the word of the Order of Eden. Don't worry about him right now, you could concentrate on your own happiness."

EMERGENCE

Captain Alice Valent was still reading after action reports from the various section commanders aboard *Triton* when the door to the ready quarters chimed. She stood up, put her eye patch on and moved to stand in front of the desk. Somehow it just didn't feel right to have people see her sitting behind it. "Come in," she called out quietly.

The Heavy armoured hatch was drawn out of the doorway by thick arms and Chief Grady stepped inside. The thick block of dense metal that kept the ready quarters secure was pushed back into place behind him. "I'd hate to have to use the manual cranks to get that open," he commented quietly as the seals squeaked against each other for a second. "I'll send someone up to fix that noise."

"Thank you Chief but I think you have bigger fish to fry. What can I do for you?"

"You can relax for a start." He was amused by her demeanour, and as he folded his hands in the sleeves of his robes she realized she was practically scowling. "There are five chairs in this room and you're leaning."

"I'm sorry," she said with a sigh, sitting more comfortably on the corner of the desk. "There's just so much going on. I don't know how Jake did it."

"He delegated part of the workload to you and all of his department heads."

"I know, and I've been trying. You, Stephanie, Shamus, even Price and Finn have been great, but there's always something left. Medical is still a mess, thank God we didn't have many wounded, most of our fighter pilots didn't come back, and Jake's ship is ready for the scrap heap."

"You mean the *Samson*."

"What's left of it."

"That's all taken care of. Once we know what's going on in orbit around Pandem I'll be able to send some engineering staff to help Frost and the deck crew make improvements and repairs."

"He's still down there?"

"No, actually. I heard he was back on the gunnery deck."

Alice sighed and nodded. "I still need him there. He's good at what he does, his people look to him and removing him, even if he did tell his people he was stepping down willingly, has caused an even larger divide between the gunnery crew and security. We can't have that, not now, so he's running things up there again."

"And after this engagement?"

"Well, I'm not reinstating him as Chief, I don't think he'll ever have that title again, but to be honest I don't know what to do past that. I'm hoping Jake can make a decision."

341

"Here's hoping. Captain Valance will be pretty pleased at the ship's condition considering what she's gone through. He might not even notice that the gunnery crew and security staff have taken sides."

"So the repairs on *Triton* are complete?"

"They are. I had modified ergranian metal ready to patch her up and now the few holes we earned have nice thick grafts of the stuff."

"Grafts?"

Liam smiled and nodded. "Laura gave me access to the copy of the Freeground development database she brought with her and after a little research I was able to figure out a way to add ergranian steel to damaged sections of the ship so it would bond with the metal surrounding it."

"What about the light shifting layer? Will those sections bend light around them like the rest of the ship?"

"Everything will happen under the light shifting layer that runs on top of the hull, so there won't be any problems there. If anything the new metal should be dense enough to disguise any thermal or electromagnetic signatures even better than the existing hull. Eventually those grafts will replace all the metal around them, consuming the matter as they grow, I'll keep an eye on it."

"This ship isn't your Petri dish Chief, we can't afford to have problems with the hull."

"Don't worry, most of the research has been done, the only new aspect to this is the idea of stimulating the metal in such a way that it will very slowly consume other metals and replace them. It'll happen gradually enough for the ship to adjust to the mass differential automatically and we'll be stronger in the long run, starting with the dorsal gunnery deck where we need the most armour."

"I just don't think right now is the time to begin new things, I mean Jake is still out there and we're-" she checked her command and control unit and verified with the count down she had running there. "-nineteen minutes away from emerging from a wormhole we generated using stolen technology that we're not sure we can shield enough so our cloaking systems will work."

"I'm sure."

"That's something, but will it even work again? I saw what you had to do to jury rig that thing to work for us."

"A lot of what you saw was redundant cabling. Even with the damage the *Samson* had to do to capture it that hypertransmitter is still in fine shape. The ion cannons they used to disrupt it long enough to take it didn't do much damage, and considering that the device is made to survive solar winds and direct cosmic interference I'm surprised they did any damage at all."

"So you didn't think the plan was going to work?" Alice asked quietly, her frustration coming to a boiling point.

"I had a group of volunteers ready in the hangar to receive the hypertransmitter when it was pried free of the *Samson* just in case it was about to right itself and turn back on. If there were any problems they would have shut it down if Finn didn't do it himself first."

"That's a long answer, Chief."

"I gave it fifty-fifty."

"But you let me go ahead anyway."

"Captain Valance left you in charge for a reason. He could have left me in charge, or Stephanie, or Price, or even Frost for that matter, but he left *you* in charge because he believed in you. As it so happens, he was right," Chief Grady said with a warm smile.

Alice just lowered her face into her hands and sighed. "What'll I do if I can't find him?"

"We'll find a way to go on. You have the crew's trust, that's the hard part."

She looked at him, stunned with his reply.

He laughed softly. "You were expecting something like; 'oh, you'll find him' or 'you know him, he can take care of himself.' Well, I wouldn't insult the woman in command of nearly three thousand souls by offering empty reassurances. We both know Pandem is huge, at least a billion people live there from what I read and if there's trouble it's big, especially if he's calling for help. He just doesn't seem the type to admit he needs any."

"You're just a ray of sunshine," she smirked, shaking her head. "But you're right, the Jake I know wouldn't admit he needed help unless it was serious." Her remaining eye looked at him straight on as she asked; "Do you have any real advice?"

"Do it your way. I know you were following the Captain's plan for that last mission, and it turned out brilliantly but I don't think there's a plan on file for him being captured or lost."

Alice laughed, shaking her head. "I don't think he thought picking up a couple of friends would turn out that way, no."

"So do things your way. Our pilot roster may be filled with people too green to trust in a real conflict but there are so many other options, especially with everything at least temporarily repaired. Start with the ones you're familiar with and branch out from there and trust your instincts. Captain Valance may have put that plan together but you finessed it into working when the details changed."

"You're the most confusing monk I've ever met. One minute you're sending me the most real lowdown on the situation I could imagine, the next you're the most encouraging, trusting soul on the ship. How do you do it? Are there two of you in there?" Alice laughed.

"Well, first of all I'm not a monk, and second of all, I've been around a little."

"Well, that explains everything. You're right though, I should trust myself. I got along on my own in solar systems where I was being chased by more than one badge at a time and I know pretty much everything Jonas did."

"There you go. With the ship fit and the crew in line behind you you're ready for practically anything."

"Oh, let's not go that far. I'm not ready to think that we won't find Jake, so let's just keep that possibility in the closet."

"All right, but before we close the door on it-"

"I didn't come here to take command of a carrier filled with refugees,

343

deserters and mercenaries. I came here to meet him, to find my place."

"I just wanted to say that you'd do fine as the *Triton's* permanent commander. You'd be surprised to find out how many people are finding their place on this ship. Maybe yours is to keep her in one piece until he comes back, maybe it's to find a way to take charge with our help. I know you'll do well either way. By the same token I know you'll do your best to find him, so I bet he'll be back before you know it and you'll go to your quarters and get two day's sleep," Chief Grady said with a shrug. "You'll wake up fresh and ready to move on to the next crisis."

Alice couldn't help but laugh. "There's always something, isn't there?"

"It's a big ship, she draws a lot of attention and carries a lot of personalities around."

She nodded as she looked back to the counter on her arm. "I have to get to the bridge, the next crisis is coming up. Thank you Chief. Sometimes I think you keep the crew together as much as the ship."

"I met someone who was just like that on Earth and one day I told him the same thing. You know what he said to me?"

"What?"

"Go where you're needed and you'll never wonder why you're alive."

"Smart man. Who was he?"

"Neil Vernon, one of the Cincinnati Monastery gardeners."

As Alice walked onto the bridge and took it all in she was almost stunned with the very fact that she was still in command. The upper command center was abuzz with activity. There was a reserve officer standing by for every station in case one of the three or more people manning navigation, operations, engineering, tactical, field control, security or any of the other stations had to attend to something else or were injured.

Stephanie had a squad of fourteen soldiers spaced out along the bridge walls between stations in full black combat armour and sat to the left of the Captain's chair. As Alice made her way through the dozen or so officers on the bridge walking between stations, checking displays, calling out statistics reflecting slight changes that were made in the ship while repairs were performed and ensuring that the bridge systems were up to date with the latest information Agameg Price moved from the Command seat to his position as the lead tactical officer. "Chief Frost reports that the last of the replacement turrets are in place and they're ready for another round. That is the last of the repairs. All departments report ready," he told her in a pleasant tone.

"Thank you Agameg. How is our flight deck?" Alice asked, settling into the captain's seat. It adjusted to her proportions as she looked down through the transparent sections of the floor to the equally bustling flight control deck, where they managed everything the bridge didn't; flight crews, any related vessels other than the *Triton* herself and how ships moved around in nearby space. Angelo Vercelli looked up at her and spoke in a normal tone, knowing that his voice would be transmitted straight to the captain's chair from his pedestal. "Everything's locked down, fabrication has been taken offline, we have four fighters ready to launch and our main hangar is ready to take care of any emergency landings. I even have an energy capture web ready in case we have to yank someone as they pass within a few kilometres."

"Thank you Chief."

"My pleasure Captain."

"How is our new emitter array?" Alice asked as she looked through the list of changes that were made while the *Triton* was being repaired. She couldn't help but be surprised as she read that eight hundred and nine repair team members worked on the ship and there were over two hundred volunteers on top of that. The repairs that were made were beyond extensive, even systems that were damaged years before the battle they had just engaged in were taken care of.

Finn cleared his throat before answering; "Chief Grady didn't tell you?"

"Never answer a question with a question on my bridge, Finn."

"Right. It didn't look like it was going to work until we bypassed most of the power generation systems aboard the hypertransmitter, but then we had a break through and were able to just build it into the ship."

Alice turned towards him and looked at him straight on. He looked up but his gaze flinched back to his station in the next instant. "Build it in?"

"He really didn't tell you," Finn said, half to himself. "We cut off the wireless receivers and wired it right up to one of the ship's main data lines and power systems. Now it's operating behind eight meters of armoured hull with cloaked emitter rods sticking out of an airlock."

"Is that the permanent solution?"

"No, but it'll work without burning out. Wiring things up while it was already generating a wormhole was a little tricky."

"Good work," Alice said with a smile.

Finn nodded, smirking a little. "I broke the last main emitter systems, only makes sense that I install a new one."

"You and your people deserve a day off after this."

"I'll pass that onto my team," he said, glancing at Angela, who playfully nudged him with her elbow from where she manned a damage control post beside him.

"Captain, I'm in main engineering and can confirm that everything's set down here," Chief Grady said through her personal communicator.

"Thank you Chief."

"Exiting the wormhole into regular space in five, four, three, two, one," announced Larry, Ashley's main navigator.

Ashley unlocked the controls as they emerged and listened to Larry and Henrietta, the navigators who sat on either side of her as they took turns in telling her about their situation in the arrival point. She also viewed the quickly populating tactical map of the area around them.

Pandem was still minutes away at full thrust, but there was a veritable gauntlet between the *Triton* and the green and blue planet. Ashley jerked the controls, sending the ship several degrees to port, towards one of Pandem's outer moons. "Oh my God," she whispered under her breath as she watched the tactical map light up.

Alice stared at the main holographic tactical projection in the center of the bridge and her spirits dropped. Without realizing it, she found she was slowly standing to get a better look.

There were hundreds of destroyers, corvettes, battle cruisers, carriers, several larger combat platforms and at least five command carriers at a glance. Their markings were clear, there was no long range signal jamming in the battlefield, and Regent Galactic, the Order of Eden as well as the Carthan Defence Fleet were represented. As the tactical display continued to populate with thousands of fighters, gunships and other medium sized close combat vessels appeared between the furious juggernauts that had joined the fray that extended past Pandem's outer orbit and all the way down to the upper atmosphere.

"Cloaking systems?" Alice asked the bridge in general and everyone not in direct control of the energy fields and suppression systems held their breath in anticipation of the answer.

"Emissions are contained, we're not putting anything out there," Finn reported from his engineering station.

"Our gravity shielding is working as a counter to anything that can detect our mass. Anything running a sensor sweep through our area should read zero," Laura reported.

"The hull is bending all spectrums of light around the ship and no one has started scanning or firing on us," Agameg reported. "We are hidden."

There was a collective sigh of relief as Ashley guided the *Triton* into a course that kept them thousands of kilometres away from the battle and would take them behind the third Pandem moon.

"I don't know for how long," Agameg added. "Interdiction particles are spreading from several of the Regent Galactic carriers in all directions, if we encounter them we will be visible to most scanners."

"And our hyperspace systems won't work," Alice added.

"Actually, they will. Our gravity shields will keep the interdiction particles from interacting with the hyperspace emitters," Laura corrected. "Then again, if we come near that expanding field of interdiction particles our gravity shields will displace them in a larger radius, making us look like we're about five times our size."

Alice looked at the profile of the *Triton* on the status display projected by her command chair. It was an unusual ship, modelled after a sea stingray from Earth she was much broader than she was long, unlike most vessels that were built lengthwise for easier hyperspace and wormhole travel. "That could work to our advantage."

"So we're hidden at the moment but how do we let Jake know we're here without sending a big flare up?" Stephanie asked in a whisper.

Alice sat down and stared at the tactical display, a hornets nest of red, blue, green and yellow ships between them and the green blue ball of Pandem. "I think I have an idea," she whispered back.

"You're kidding," Stephanie whispered back with a restrained look of surprise and amusement.

Alice thought for a long moment, watching the tactical display. *Triton* was entering a wide orbit around the Pandem moon and they were safe for the moment but less than seven hundred kilometres behind three Regent Galactic carriers. The most important part of their location was that there was little to no chance of them being struck by stray munitions or of them colliding with anything in the area. "Ashley's team is really good," she said quietly as though realizing for the first time.

Stephanie was pretending to watch the security status panel so she wouldn't stare at the woman in the Captain's chair. "She's always learning."

"I know, seems this ship rewards hard work," Alice said as she brought up a large rail cannon munitions list and started searching. "If I didn't spend days looking through specifications and fabrication lists for the materializers I don't think I would have found this," she said, finding what she was looking for and pointing at it.

"That's a rail cannon transmitter round."

"Yup, made for sending thousands of emergency beacons in every direction if the ship gets into trouble, but in this case we only need a few dozen."

"Won't they find us?" Stephanie said quietly with a gesture to the frantic scene on the main display.

"Not in time, we'll launch them while we're on the move and change directions," Alice replied as she opened a channel to Frost. "I'm sending you a request to manufacture two hundred of these rounds in four cartridges. I want four adjacent turrets to fire the rounds towards Pandem without hitting anything. Program them with this message and be ready to fire on the target I'm marking on my order."

"Aye, squawker rounds, try ta miss everythin' but that island. Those'll be loaded in two minutes."

"Keep the turrets as covered as you can and when you've fired the volley retract them."

"Aye, we'll roll 'em out, pop the shots off then draw the turrets back so the hull can close up over 'em up," Frost confirmed.

Alice turned her attention to the bridge in general then. "All right, we're going to send a message to Captain Valance. I need you to plot a course that takes us as close to the planet as is safe. I want to send these transmitters straight for Damshir, so keep that in mind."

"That's the busiest section of space," Larry countered, half turning in his seat. "And we'll have to shadow the largest ships in the area to avoid getting caught in an interdiction particle wave."

"That's where we have to be, make it happen."

"Aye," he replied irritably as he turned to face forward.

"Cynthia, start a repeating search for anything that matches the Captain's, Jason's or Oz's voice and image profiles."

"We're searching now," she replied from the communications station.

NEGOTIATIONS

The hard floor of their refuge showed the scars, black dirt and other marring that came with a broad hallway intersection being overused. Beyond the improvised, welded and piled barriers Oz knew that the surfaces were still white, blue, black and in some places gold. Whereas the refugees and rebels had expanded their territory in the spaceport with the help and direction of Dementia before, they were being corralled and cornered without their connection to him.

Oz sat eating a thick, simulated chocolate flavoured meal bar with Jason who was cross linking his portable terminal with the spare command and control unit he wore so it could take over all of it's functions. They both watched Ayan and Yves speak in a corner just far enough from the hundreds camped out and guarding the cramped space so they couldn't be overheard. The calm discussion had already turned into an argument.

If they'd only listen to us. Ayan can't get through to Yves even in conversation between just the two of them and she's actually got the full range of officer's training including the diplomatic component and annual upgrading. Not only that but she's probably one of the most reasonable people I've ever known. Yves just won't hear it, but everyone here listens to him even though he's a power tripping extremist.

Oz was just starting to chomp down the last bite of his meal bar when Yves broke out into a full on yell; "Listen, if you and your friends want to join up with whoever made it out of that mountain, go ahead. I'm closing the tunnel and that's all there is to it!"

Neither Jason or Oz could hear Ayan's reply, but she was keeping her cool remarkably well.

"We're going to finish cutting those ships free," Yves shouted, pointing towards the old generic freighter and the two intact drop ships. "And get the hell out of here!"

"If the anti-air guns don't shoot you down what's in orbit will! I'd say it's suicide if it were just you but you're making this decision for hundreds of people!" Ayan shouted back, more for the benefit of the crowd laying around, guarding the barricades and walking amongst the refugees than out of anger.

"What do you suggest? Going further underground? Wait for this friend of yours to swoop in and pick us all up? If they haven't dropped in to pick him up by now, I don't think they're coming, lady."

Ayan sighed, it was a clearly visible gesture, even from where Oz and Jason were sitting at the other end of the barricade. She spoke to him at a normal volume that no one could overhear.

Yves nodded, said something in return then walked towards the bulk of the refugees. "All right, it looks like our guests are leaving. Anyone who wants to join them can go now, we'll be collapsing the main transit tunnel behind them. You have five minutes!" he shouted before stalking off towards one of the watch posts.

Ayan returned to the corner Jason had set up his mini terminal in, shaking her head. "He's an idiot. Whoever goes with him is dead."

"You're right. I just wish so many people didn't believe in him," Oz agreed.

"Did you offer to patch him into the secure channels?" Jason asked.

Ayan nodded as she opened a meal bar. "I did but he doesn't want to coordinate. He said he doesn't want to end up involving more people in his resistance than he can evacuate from Pandem when the time comes. Honestly I'm assuming this is the worst place to take off from. If there are planetary cannons working some of them must be pointed straight at the air above the Spaceport. Anyone who signs up for his plan and takes an average ship up doesn't stand much of a chance."

"Oh, I don't think Jake or his new friends are stupid enough to go along with Yves' plan." Oz chuckled and nodded.

"He said that now that the signal jamming on all channels has stopped he won't have any problems reaching any survivors on Pandem," Ayan said after finishing her first bite.

"I haven't found any. A few remnant security captures that were flagged by someone showed a lot of people being loaded onto ships, but that's all the evidence I found of anyone surviving this mess." Jason closed the mini-terminal up and pushed it into his backpack. "The size of the fleet responsible for this has got to be bigger than anything I've seen. It takes at least four million troops to sack a planet like this even with bots everywhere cooperating."

"So you think the West Keepers or Regent Galactic wanted the land and resources here?"

"From what I'm hearing on the religious broadcasts this is going to be their new base of operations. I've been listening ever since they started broadcasting in the clear. So far I've heard Hampon mentioned once and they keep talking about the coming of Eve."

"Hampon? How did he get mixed up in this?" Ayan asked in surprise.

"He's considered a prophet, sounds like a child. I want nothing more than to meet up with Jake and his people then find a way out of here, it's time to get some distance," Oz said, nodding at a few dozen people who had gathered and were walking towards them. "I don't think I'm the only one."

They were led by several rebels who were wearing salvaged West Keeper armour. They were all quite young. In the lead was the young woman Minh had saved from being killed by a grenade. "Excuse me, but we'd like to go with you. There are about fifty of us, but we'll try not to slow you down."

Oz stood and shook his hand while Ayan and Jason did the same with his friends. "You're welcome to come along," he said with a smile.

"We have to get moving though, they're already rigging lines to the dock loaders to pull the main supports for the tunnel." Jason nodded at the tunnel opening.

Preparation to leave took minutes. Few of the fifty six people going with them into the long, dark tunnel had much in the way of belongings and Yves only allowed them to take the food they already had on them. Less than ten minutes passed before they all heard the collapse of the tunnel behind.

Everyone stopped to look back the way they had come even though the tracks only led into the darkness and they couldn't see the mass of debris that had filled the tunnel opening. They were cut off, there was no return.

Oz was standing right beside Jason when he heard Dementia open a channel with him. "Hello Jason, I have some bad news for you," the normally friendly, if not slightly clinical at times, voice said over the communicator quietly.

"I'm glad to hear you were able to access an open channel," Jason congratulated the artificial intelligence quietly. "Is everything all right down there?"

"Yes. I have been monitoring what has been going on with you and the rest of the refugees now that the jamming is gone and I can access some of the wireless systems. As much as I'm disappointed in how they behaved in my absence I must say that the better group of people won."

"What do you mean?" Jason asked.

Ayan stepped in closer to listen in to the quiet conversation between Jason and Dementia.

"When I tried to open communications with the machines wirelessly after the jamming signals subsided I was denied contact. The bots are succumbing to an evolved version of the holocaust virus and will soon side with the Order of Eden again. I have tried to contact Yves directly but he is not accepting communications with me, it seems he is under the impression that I wish to take command of the group."

"You could have told us, we could have tried to warn him," Ayan said harshly.

"Considering the tone of the conversation you had with him Ayan, I decided it was more prudent to allow you to take whatever survivors were willing to see sense in another direction. Do you have any bots with you? I can't tell while you're in the tunnel."

"No, they all sided with Yves."

"All the better then. I am sorry for the loss of life, but their decisions have sealed their fates."

Oz looked at Jason and Ayan in turn, they both looked ashen in the dim blue light emitted by Jason's comm unit. "Dementia, is the virus changing enough to affect you?"

"As I've integrated the virus code in my core program and am evolving with it I am immune. I've also been able to maintain a connection with the few bots who are working to replace my Xetima fuelled systems with a more practical form of micro fusion propulsion. I should be ready by the time you arrive. I have devised a plan involving my own cloaking device to get you and many more people off the planet. I have cleared out all non-essential components in order to accommodate as many people as I can."

The trio looked at each other for a moment before Ayan replied; "I assume

350

you have a way for us to get to you?"

"You will be coming up on a junction with access to lower transit tunnels," replied Dementia as a small holographic map appeared, projected by Jason's comm unit.

"We'll meet up with Jake and Alaka then head down. Thank you Dementia. Just do one more thing for me, okay?"

"What's that?"

"Don't count us out of any decisions in the future. I'd rather know what sacrifices we're making before we're forced into carrying them out," Ayan said gently but firmly.

"All right Ayan, I look forward to seeing all of you. Alice has told me so much about you."

"Us too."

Oz shook his head and cleared his throat before shouting; "all right, let's keep moving!" to everyone who was waiting behind.

UNDERGROUND

The sounds of distant digging echoed in the near complete darkness of the subway side passage. There were numerous makeshift beds set up, and when Iloona recommended that he get some rest he couldn't help but admit that he was exhausted. Ayan, Oz and Jason were getting some rest while they could as well. They had repelled another rush of West Keeper soldiers and the resistance fighters were keeping watch. Sleep came on quickly despite his uncertain surroundings. Scant hours later he was wide awake, however, and he lay there thinking about Ayan, Oz, Jason and Minh. Just as he was about to stand up to go see if there was anything more he could do, he heard a voice from the cot beside him; "God I wish I was home again," said the tall, thin man from the cot beside Jake's.

He looked at the bare headed fellow and reached across the empty air between them to shake his hand. "I am Dindamen, they've come to call me Din."

"Jake."

"Yes, everyone here knows. A few Regent Galactic soldiers who couldn't stand what was going on in Damshir defected shortly before we had to leave the mountain and they spoke of you. There are also a few here who say they saw you destroy machines that were corralling them into a troop carrier to be taken off world. Many of them found their way into tunnels and joined us when we arrived."

"Ah," was all Jake could manage, glad to hear that at least some of the slaves he'd been able to liberate had gotten away.

"I sensed you weren't sleeping and wondered if you could answer a question for me."

"Sure, not much chance of me getting any more sleep anyway. I think I've slept through the regeneration hangover."

"Perhaps you're becoming issyrian in a way, interesting. I was wondering; why did you kill so many? The soldiers who spoke of you called you a shadow, a murderer."

"It was when I saw people being loaded into troop carriers to be taken off world. They were filthy, broken, restrained and the bots and soldiers moved them along like cattle, using stun rods and waving their guns. I was only able to disrupt two loading sites. The other site I broke up was filled with bots who were loading bodies into a mass converter."

"They were converting the corpses into energy?"

"I wondered where the bodies were being taken until I saw the bots loading them into the converters like waste. I couldn't stand it so I used all the explosives and power cells I had to end it. Now that I think about it the most important thing about that is the forensic and holographic evidence I recorded on my comm unit. I started recording everything a few hours after I landed," Jake said, staring at the pipes and cables hanging from the concrete ceiling.

"You are right, the recordings could be important. I never understood the attachment your people have to your bodies after death, humans don't have a use for them."

"It doesn't make much sense, you're right. I was so angry at the waste of life. There were hundreds of bodies. The machines could barely keep up. Funny thing, the bots didn't care that I had snuck in and killed their human commanders. They only started fighting back when the first of the EMP bombs went off."

The issyrian rolled over to face Jacob. He was in human form, disguised as a long faced older gentleman, the deep wrinkles were visible even in the faint light. "I have to commend your bravery. It couldn't have been easy to take on so much alone."

"No one was watching for someone going towards the mountain and I spent most of my time going around watch posts. I only killed when I had to."

"Or when you saw something you couldn't abide," added Din. "I commend you."

"Do you think Pandem can be saved?" Jake asked quietly.

"I don't know about the world, there are some naturalist islands that may be safer, there are no complex machines there. This island may never be the same though. I have visited Damshir many times and watched the turning of the bots happen. I look out to the city and already the place I knew is gone. The great stair on the side of the mountain is collapsing thanks to the explosion, the taller buildings burn or have taken too much damage and my favourite courtyard market was used for taking survivors away for slavery."

"How many people do you think were taken?"

"In the beginning the bots went mad and millions were killed. After the first few hours the first soldiers arrived and began rounding up large groups of survivors, loading them into the troop carriers they arrived in just as you witnessed. The machines only searched for anyone who hid after that. At least half the people of Damshir were transported off world. Now the bots are beginning to rebuild. In two months, maybe less, this city will shine again, but there will be prefabricated buildings, tall Regent Galactic military installations and other objects that I've seen duplicates of on every Regent world I've seen."

"I'm sorry, it sounds like you liked Damshir." Jake replied, remembering St. Kitts, the port he had seen burn behind him thanks to Regent Galactic.

"I did. I had many friends here. I was a courier for the Carthans, taking news from their outlying territories into my home cluster of systems. Very good work if you had a fast ship. I was stopping in to visit a friend here and she had to go to the main precinct office inside the mountain so I accompanied her. A police android killed her shortly after we arrived."

"I'm sorry."

"It happened quickly, I can't forget it. There were times in the tunnel fighting that I wished to be among the fallen, thankfully they were fleeting moments," Dindamen said with a sigh. "Now I only wish to go home, back to my family clutch."

"I've had a couple issyrians on my crew and I've only heard of the clutch once."

"Oh, it's not something we speak of often. Some of your hibernation technology is based on the clutch, it was part of the technology our people traded when we met the humans. My family's clutch normally has thirty young at any time, we have many caretakers. When an issyrian house is formed, normally on a new world or when a house is too large or disharmonious some of us find a safe place to create a clutch; a collection of all of our eggs. If they are cared for properly and the environment is in balance they grow together and eventually it is large enough for us to return to. The eggs grow together as the children mature and when they leave the clutch remains. If the clutch is maintained and eggs are added regularly it continues to grow, becoming the center of the house. Trusted family members who have cleansed their bodies of most accumulated impurities are allowed to return and assist the very young in early growth from the inside. Many of us return to the clutch when we are ready to have children. Instead of laying our eggs in the cold of the active world we go into the clutch ourselves and when we're ready we release our eggs inside. When our young are ready to hatch we can spend as much time as we like there with them where we can maintain a wordless bond for weeks, months, or even years in rare cases."

"So it's like an exterior womb."

"Yes, very much so. In fact, some issyrians envy your women because of the interior gestation period. We must watch our young grow outside of ourselves."

"I could introduce you to a few woman who would trade in a heartbeat," Jake laughed quietly.

"Oh, that's right, I've heard about your birthing ritual. But yes, to answer your question, it is like a womb, only an old household clutch can be the size of a small lake, cleaning the water there, providing homes for the injured, aged and a place of peace for the entire family. It is why we are not so common past our own system of stars, as long as we are near a friendly clutch most injuries can be healed quickly and once one of my kind grows very old, such as myself, I can return to be with the young and rejuvenate myself."

"How long would you go back in?"

"I am of House Londa, we have a very old clutch so I could remain there for as long as I like, but I think I would miss the galaxy before long. I would remain inside with my young for two of your years after they hatch. Then after another decade of air breathing I might want to take them travelling, perhaps deliveries again but closer to our home worlds."

"Congratulations," Jake said with a smile. It was strange saying it to someone who looked like an aged man, but he knew that either the men or women of his race could carry embryos. There was even a subspecies that was fully asexual.

"Thank you, my young have been dormant for fourteen of your months though. I feel foolish for putting my return off for so long."

"It happens to my people too. Couples who put off having children so they have more time for their careers. We're lucky to have some regenerative technology that lets us have them further along, but it doesn't work for everyone."

354

"I really know so little about your people despite your cultural need to flaunt your duality."

Jake gave him a confused look. "Duality?"

"Your advertising, it seems they use sexuality to sell everything."

Jake chuckled and nodded. "Yup, it didn't take us long to realize that when you pair a product with one of our base desires it makes it easier to sell. There are days I wish we were a bit more like issyrians, I could do without the drama."

"I've heard there are benefits," Din prodded with an impish grin.

"Oh, there are. Maybe I'll tell you about it some other time, looks like our rest shift is ending early," Jake said with a nod to a short female nafalli walking between the two rows of cots.

Her hand shook the foot of each person resting as she passed. She stopped at the foot of Jake and Dindamen's cots. "They've broken through into the old subway tunnel and we're about to blow up the way behind," her squeaky high voice said through a smile.

"Thank you Nibuna, tell your father we'll be there right away," Dindamen replied.

"Okay, see you there!" she said with unexpected enthusiasm.

Jake looked at Din as they stood and he put his gun belt and long coat on. "Let me guess, she's Alaka's daughter?"

"Yes, insuppressible spirit. I think everyone in the mountain has come to love that one."

"I can see why, she's so cheery my teeth hurt."

Din burst into a short chortle; "what an unusual expression, I'll have to use it sometime."

The pair made their way out into the tunnel, one side was piled with debris from the intentional collapse, and even though there was hundreds of tons of rubble between them and the commerce building two of the younger armed refugees kept watch, listening closely for the sounds of digging equipment from the other side. They were packing up, the small folding table that had been placed there had been roped to one of their backs along with the small matching chair. From what he could see in the dim light their mood was light, they were happy to move on.

Just around the first corner in the tunnel was Alaka and all the other refugees, only sixty one of them not including the rear guard. A lot of smiles flashed up at him as he passed by and Jacob's suspicious nature told him that people had been talking while he was trying to get some rest.

The crowd parted for him as he approached and he made his way to the front with Nibuna close behind. The rest of the people who had been sleeping in the makeshift barracks dispersed into the crowd of hundreds as it quieted.

Jake closed the distance between Alaka and himself. There were others around, the ones he'd seen taking charge of different tasks here and there, and they were all working a makeshift pulley to lower people down into the tunnel below into a circle of three centimetre long disposable lights. Jake had given them a small box of them from his long coat, leaving him with his command and control unit as well as

355

the light on his stolen sidearm and rifle, more than enough.

The small box contained fifty of the small throw away lights, they would burn for up to a thousand hours unless someone deactivated them, and once the chemicals inside were expended the thin casing left would decompose in a matter of hours, leaving nothing but water behind. Jake looked at the situation at the hole and suddenly didn't feel bad for not lending a hand. There were so many people standing around, ready to lend a hand that there was barely enough room for the rope ladder most of the more able people used to climb down. The younger and less able refugees were being lowered. He took a position behind Alaka, relieving someone helping him lower people down.

"Good morning," Alaka said as he noticed Jake lending a hand.

"Good morning, call me paranoid but it looks like someone's been singing my praises."

Alaka quietly chuckled, a sound that started deep in his chest and was muffled by his snout and large frame. "I'm afraid so. The West Keeper defectors, Namic and Terrance have been talking about the advisory on you, how the West Watchers placed a notice to look out and avoid you instead of putting a bounty on your head or sending squads after you. They see you as a very dangerous man. Word has spread of you returning from the dead too, and that's made quite an impression."

"That's something I would have rather kept quiet."

Alaka simply nodded and they worked on for several minutes before either man said anything. "So how did it feel?" he asked finally.

"How did what feel?"

"Dying."

Jake hesitated. He wasn't offended, just quietly surprised at the question and eventually answered; "Painful."

The much larger fellow's laughter shattered the relative silence of the cavernous main transit tunnel and it was joined immediately by the mirth of everyone who overheard.

When it subsided Jake went on. "I've died twice that I know of now. Both times I was shot more than once. You know how the movies make it look like shock sets in and most of the pain goes away?"

"I've seen it."

"That didn't happen."

"Ah. Do you remember anything?"

"I remember thinking how crappy the armour they give West Keepers is."

A few of the people listening couldn't help but laugh along, Alaka pressed on after it subsided. "I mean after."

"Ah, you mean was there a tunnel and a bright light or was Tanu the Great waiting to carry my soul into the next existence?"

"Yup."

"Nope, I don't remember any of that, mostly because I was dead I'm thinking. Maybe because I'm man made, but if there's anyone you should be asking about this I'm not it. There's a man on my ship though, his name is Liam Grady. He spent time on Earth and is a practising Axionist. You can ask him all about it if you and this group come aboard."

Alaka stopped and stared at Jake for a minute, who didn't notice for a few seconds.

"What?"

"I was going to ask if we could have your assistance. I overheard you and Ayan speaking before you took your rest and you said that the *Triton* should be coming. I didn't know if-"

"I would help everyone here? Of course, it's a big ship. If you have skills to offer I'll even give you jobs. I don't know what I can pay you, but at least you'll have a place to live away from infected machines."

"You say it like the decision carries no weight but it's all some of the people have been able to talk about," Alaka whispered as he started working the rope again, lowering a pair of young children who had been tied together.

"I can imagine. I'll be honest with you Alaka; at first I didn't want families aboard *Triton*, but with the way things are out here I couldn't refuse you. Nowhere's safe as long as the Order of Eden and their virus is spreading. We'll have to use the *Clever Dream* to get off the planet, and it'll be a tight squeeze but after that I'll locate the families in the habitation section of my ship if they can work with the crew somehow."

"You are a generous man, Jacob."

"I need skilled people, and anyone who can't help on the *Triton* will be put off on the safest port in range."

"What about the children?" asked a young man holding a much younger wide eyed boy in his arms. The child was mesmerized by the sight of people being tied then slowly lowered down into the short tunnel they had dug to get into one of the older passages.

Jake had thought about that as he tried to get to sleep and didn't hesitate to answer. "The Galaxy doesn't need more orphans. I'm sure there are people aboard *Triton* who would take care of them, and as for children attached to parents who want to stay aboard, there are family quarters aboard that are secure from any exterior hatches. It's more like a neighbourhood than the inside of a combat carrier."

The young man bounced the small passenger in his arms and said; "hear that? Captain Valance is going to take you on his space ship."

The boy only glanced at Jake before looking back down the hole, watching the tense line lower people down. The work was effortless for Alaka, who snickered at the young boy watching him before looking over his shoulder at Jake for a moment. "I have been speaking with one of your old friends, Oz they call him. Unusual name."

"It's short for his middle name, Ozark."

"An even more unusual name," Alaka commented with a slightly startled look before turning back to his work. "Thanks to his good navigational skills I know exactly where they are. I've directed them to an old access point that will lead them down into this tunnel much further down the line. They kept it open for servicing since they never got around to filling most of the lower tunnels."

"How far off are they?"

"Only a few hours once we're on our way. They'll be meeting us on the way to the space port."

"I'm wondering, can I get a copy of your map of the area? I checked the Regent Galactic command database and there's nothing about them in there."

"You won't find anything. Even the city planners didn't know all of the old tunnels. I used to hunt all over the city, the abandoned places beneath us made good nesting places for rim weasels and a few other things."

"Lucky you're with us then."

"I would say not. The bots attacked the humans first and I had a chance to take my family into the mountain. When the explosion struck inside we were already down the transit line because a friend of mine, Roman, was able to warn us. If we have any luck it's by being near humans who seem to have no luck at all. Roman went after the saboteur to stop him from causing the detonation you saw."

"So it wasn't a bomb inside the Mountain?"

"It was a micro fusion reactor that had been set to overload."

"I'm sorry. It sounds like Roman was a friend."

"He was, but loss seems to plague this world. Even when the Carthan drop ships came on Tartan Isle, their initial casualties were in the thousands just in the first few minutes from what we could see from the mountain."

"So the Carthans have already made an appearance?"

"Over a week ago now, and they're still fighting in the Tartan cities, but the drop ships stopped after a few hours. As far as we can tell their support in orbit either left or was destroyed. With no communications until recently there's been no way to confirm that until yesterday, and well, their communication bands are silent."

"I noticed. It's like our two groups of refugees are all that's left." Jake said as he felt a call notification through the connection he had unconsciously made with his command and control unit. It was like his arm had brushed up against something, barely grazing it, and in the act he knew who was trying to contact him, on what channel, how secure the communication was, what kind of communication it was and what band it was on. The command interface popped into his head, marking the origin of the transmission less than a hundred kilometres away and forty two meters down.

"I'm sure there are other survivors, even just before the mountain exploded there were signs of fighting on other islands. They must be using short range proximity radios or none at all since we haven't been able to-" Alaka was saying.

"Can you handle this on your own for a while? Ayan's calling."

The tall nafalli nodded, his pointed snout exaggerating the gesture. "Humans are very light, even two at a time."

Jake let another refugee take his place to help gently lower survivors. The crowd was already thinning behind him with the constant but slow flow of people being lowered and climbing down the long rope ladder.

"Jo-Jacob?" Ayan's voice came over his subdermal communicator. The sound of it was lighter, more feminine than he remembered.

"It's me. How's your group doing?"

"We've just come out into the older tunnel thanks to the directions that

358

Alaka gave Oz. We would have never found it if it weren't for him, we even had to break through an old rotten grate they put up behind a big air compressor. Everyone made it though, we're fine."

"Is it secure?"

There was a pause before she answered. "I couldn't imagine soldiers finding their way through behind us. We're safe. How are your people?"

Jake couldn't help but chuckle at the way she asked; "I wouldn't call them my people. Alaka and his wife seem to have taken charge here, I feel like a minor consultant really. They're doing well."

"Somehow I couldn't see that."

"You will when you meet these nafalli. I think I heard someone say they had eleven children, so I think they're used to controlling a crowd."

"Eleven children?"

"Unless I heard wrong. Looks like I'll have at least one large family aboard the *Triton* after all. Probably more, there are a few orphans and single parents here."

"Do you have anyone aboard that would take them? I mean is there anyone who could take care of them?"

"I'm pretty sure there are, there are civilians aboard, they live around the botanical section."

"There's a botanical section?"

"More like a park. I was hoping it would be enough to entice you to stay aboard, that or the engineering section."

"I don't need to be enticed. Freeground may have given me an assignment, but I was ready to come on my own. I was just lucky Minh was headed the same way."

"How is he?"

"He's the same. Once we get him to a medical center he'll be fine."

"The infirmary on the *Triton* is more like a small hospital, we'll get him back on his feet."

"Thank you Jake."

"I'm just glad I can help him."

A silence settled on them. Jacob Valance stood separate from the quiet, diminishing crowd, staring down the tunnel as it extended into a darkness that may as well have gone on forever. He was so unsure of what to say. An uncertainty and fear filled him that was unlike anything he could recall.

Jacob's memories of her felt like his own. At the same time he could clearly recall comforting Ayan on the *Triton* as the life faded from her. Yet she had been reborn and she was on the other end of the communique, waiting for him to say something. How could he possibly convey his relief, his amazement, his joy to her without putting her off? Was it even right to express any of it under such dismal conditions?

"Are you okay?" she asked finally, quietly.

His mind was filled with every possible way to answer the question and for a long moment he struggled to narrow it down, to at once figure out what she was referring to specifically and what his best answer could be. "Um," was all that came out.

"I mean, do you remember? Laura said you do but-" Ayan said in a nervous rush.

"It feels strange when I hear someone call me Valance now," Jake blurted. He had barely started to realize it but ever since he last introduced himself to Alaka and his people by his full name, it was a feeling that he couldn't shake.

"Okaaay," Ayan sounded a little confused, and very unsure.

"I mean I remember everything, now it's like it's all my own life, and the years where I didn't have those memories just fit into the missing time," Jake sighed and sat down on a power cable box beside the unirail. "It's like someone turned out the lights for six years and I had to make my way in the dark, then someone started turning on switches and when I remembered you everything started coming together. When you died, I mean, when the other you died-"

"Oh my God, were you there?"

The pain of the moment, the last bright smile he'd seen on her face came back to him then and he forced what he needed to tell her out. "I pretended I was Jonas. That was the first time I felt like everything was real, like I wasn't just struggling day to day for nothing," he hesitated before going on. "When I was with her, watching her fade away everything else disappeared. Then she was gone and I was lost all over again."

"I'm so sorry."

"You couldn't have done anything and I'm glad I was there. She passed away smiling," he didn't know if he was saying the right thing, for once he didn't have time to plan his strategy, to pick and choose his words carefully. Instead he just kept talking. "Now you're just a few hours away, but for all I know you barely remember anything."

The quiet that followed was soon broken by the sound of her quietly crying. "I remember everything. I've missed you so much," he could hear her trying to keep herself together as she went on, sniffling first. "You know what they say about making the same decision twice? I'd do it three times, five times, over and over again for you, even if I have to start calling you Jake."

"You might just have to, I'm used to the first name," Jacob looked behind him to see that there were just a few people left to descend into the lower tunnel. Things were moving very quickly. "I think my turn to go down is coming up, I'll see you soon Ayan. I'll be there soon. Just-" he tried to think of the right words but nothing clear, no gentle way to say what was on his mind came. "Just don't expect me to be the same, there are years, things I've done since you knew me. . ."

"I understand. I'm not the same either, we both come with surprises."

Any surprise she had for him couldn't compare to his history as a hunter, all the people he'd killed on Pandem but he decided there would be another time for that; "I'll see you soon," he promised quietly.

"Okay, be careful. Tell Alaka that if he doesn't get you here in one piece I'll make him into a fur rug," she said with a chuckle, he could hear her tears clearing up.

Jake laughed as much in mirth as in joy as he unconsciously nodded at his communication and control unit; "I'll tell him, he'll get a laugh." He was just about to end the private communique but added; "I'll be there soon," once more before closing the line.

TERRY OZARK MCPATRICK AND MINH-CHU BUU

The darkness of the old sealed tunnel was just what Oz wanted after the ordeal that had passed. It was like the quiet after a midnight storm. He sighed and looked around, his head piece drawn back so it was an open hood.

The concrete closest to the old transit line that once led to the space station terminal had aged badly, the cracks in the ceiling allowed moisture to drip, the big metal magnetic ties that had been pulled up so they could properly wall the tunnel up were once piled but had settled and were strewn out. *Tons of metal, just left down here to rot for God only knows how long. I wonder what the crews who sealed this place would think if they knew that these old holes would save our lives.* He thought to himself as he eyed the well lit double service doors further down the cavernous tunnel. They had been pried open and scouted hours ago. Where Dementia's knowledge of the old tunnels ended Alaka's began. The nafalli had been through most of the tunnels before while exterminating rim weasels and he led them straight to a forgotten maintenance access that could take them into the spaceport. The disused service hallways let out right behind a small West Keeper outpost, all that lay between them and the main lower landing platforms and hangars. The *Clever Dream* was waiting, and he hoped it would be ready soon.

In the division of command he had drawn the shortest straw. Ayan was to keep the lines of communication open between herself and Jake or Alaka, Jason was always busy gathering information about what the enemy was doing while he kept a line to Dementia open, and he was to try and keep in touch with everyone they left behind as he managed the refugees and rebels who had come with them.

His job was the most depressing of the lot. The last transmission from the survivors they had left behind was nothing but panic, screams and a plea for help. Dementia had kept trying to connect to the machines they'd left behind with the refugees with no success.

Both he and Jason tried to warn the refugees that the Holocaust Virus would take over completely, that it wasn't safe to keep anything controlled by an artificial intelligence near or in the camp. Yves wouldn't acknowledge their attempts at communication and if anyone heard their general broadcasts through local channels there was no indication.

When it happened less than two hours later the androids and artificial life driven service machines lashed out in a sudden flash of violence as though they were taking vengeance for being forced to switch sides. He'd seen it himself, one of the resistance fighters opened a video link just as it started, begging for help of some kind, a new patch or a means of escape.

Few things phased him, Oz was a trained soldier, he'd seen the All-Con

Conflict as a member of a marine unit, gone on actual boarding actions and commanded a cloak ship in the middle of a war zone with one mission; to hunt down and destroy the enemy. The sounds of civilians and rebels alike being ruthlessly cut down at close range was beyond anything he'd experienced. When the screams started on his communicator he only looked at the video portion of the transmission for a moment before turning it off.

There was nothing they could do, the refugees and resistance fighters had surrounded themselves with the combat, security and assistance bots that Dementia had freed. They were inside the camp attending the wounded, mending broken equipment, even assisting them in their plans to fend off the West Watch.

Telling the people who had followed them into the transit tunnels was hard. He didn't show his own grief, only delivered the information as accurately and as gently as possible. He didn't give false hope, he answered questions directly and he allowed the group to comfort each other. It was all in his officer's training, but to those who left friends they had made while defending the barricades behind it just didn't feel like enough. He wanted to offer them his sympathy, tell them that there was still some chance that someone made it out, that if they mounted a rescue mission there would be something to recover, but none of it was true so he had nothing but the hard, cold facts. The few who felt motivated to mount a rescue mission had to be told, over and over again, that there was no chance of survival. When that didn't work he played back the recording, let them hear the screams for themselves.

No one blamed Ayan, Jason or himself. That was a relief but little comfort. Many of them blamed Dementia and even Oz was led to wonder why he hadn't said anything about his countermeasures to the Holocaust Virus not being a permanent solution to Yves and the other resistance leaders. He had to put that aside, however. It wasn't something he had time to ponder and if there was anyone who was better suited to solve that puzzle it was Jason. His officer training came in handy once more; Dementia and the *Clever Dream* were their ticket off of Pandem so he went to work reassuring people that Yves *had* been warned, that Dementia had done everything he could have. It was a lie, but one that might hold them together until they were safely away.

It was difficult to raise spirits, but there were other facts to offer. A group of seasoned rebels and refugees were on their way. At the head of the group was Alaka; someone who knew more about these tunnels than everyone combined and had been responsible for directing them away from the overtaken refugee barricade. Beside him was their old friend; Jacob Valance, a well known bounty hunter and privateer. They were waiting for them so they could get to a ship with a cloaking device and an artificial intelligence that could fight off the holocaust virus. Those were the facts that, after they had a few minutes to mourn, Ayan, Jason and himself started to quietly remind them of. "We're getting out of here soon," he reassured.

When things finally quieted down he found the most peaceful spot he could. He sat on an upturned block of broken concrete beside the sealed protective bag that held Minh-Chu Buu in suspended animation. Behind them was the thick concrete wall that had been erected ages before to block the tunnel off from the old spaceport receiving station.

As he opened a meal bar he couldn't help but remember his captivity on the *Overlord II*. "You know, no matter how good these ration bars taste, what they do with the texture, they'll always remind me of the condensed sludge chunks they fed us on that ship," he chewed through that first bite slowly, enjoying the dark quiet. "It's funny, you kept calling yourself crazy, even back in the sims before I had met you, and I really didn't believe you were a little touched in the head until you hit the afterburners on that heap we escaped that ship on. You should have seen our faces, most us looked like they thought the thing would tear itself to pieces," Oz couldn't help but chuckle and shake his head. "But then Jonas climbed into one of those ball turrets and I wasn't sure who was crazier. I wasn't far behind though, so there's no telling who gets the nutso prize. I felt so alive when we were on the *First Light,* like every moment counted for something. Even when we recorded a report we knew *someone* we'd run into on the ship would read it, it wasn't going to some stiff functionary or assessment program who we'd never meet. I'll never forget Jason's face when he saw the first one you recorded in the shower. He couldn't stop laughing for I don't know how long and all he said when we came to look was; 'he could have just recorded the audio!'"

Oz worked his way through another bite of his meal bar as he thought back. "You know, I barely knew you. Even in all the sims we went on before the *First Light.* You were so busy down on the flight deck when we got aboard I didn't have much time then either, but I tell ya it's not the same out here without you. Jonas is Jacob now, and he's seen and done some dark things if the holo archives are any indication, but when I saw you and Ayan I knew that if there were two people who could bring him back, remind him of who he really is regardless of everything he might have done out here in the dark, it would be you two. I'm just a soldier, but wherever you and Ayan go there's some kind of spark, rooms light up." He sighed as he chewed through another bite. "Besides, after what you've been through you deserve to be where you want to be. Maybe we all deserve a little piece of what we had back," he looked at the last bite of his meal replacement bar as he swallowed the preceding bite. "There's gotta be a better way to package emergency food. Ah well, quiet time's almost-" he started to say before he was interrupted by a sound, the smallest of sounds behind him.

He turned the audio receptors up on his comm unit and was instantly rewarded. The sounds of four running, booted feet were just on the other side of that wall and they were moving away. "Duck and cover!" he shouted as he dropped what was left of his meal bar, grabbed Minh in his protective vacbag, and ran a few meters to stop behind an upturned hunk of concrete.

The wall sealing the tunnel off exploded in a sudden heave of heavy brick, mortar and dirt.

Together At Last

Alaka and Jake led the way between several ancient maglev transit cars. They were two decks high and eleven meters across. Judging from the thick dust they were kicking up the tunnel had been abandoned for a very long time. "Why did they close all this up?" asked one of Alaka's children as he clung on his father's back and poked his head over his shoulder. He was from the middle litter, just barely a pre-teenager.

"They made a system that could travel horizontally and up and down so people didn't have to go from the rail cars to elevators as much when they got to the space port."

"You and Mom used to tell me never to go there."

"The Spaceport?"

"Yeah."

"You remember why, don't you Temin?"

"I remember."

"Say it aloud," Alaka pressed gently.

"Because you and Mom didn't want slavers to grab us and take us away," his son said quietly between sniffs as he pointed his snout in the air then directly ahead.

"That's right, but we have to go there now."

"Because there's a ship ready to take us to the *Triton*," he struggled to climb higher up on Alaka, almost coming over his shoulder as he sniffed the darkness ahead. "They're close dad."

"I know, go see your mother," Alaka said gently.

His son kept on sniffing the air, closing his eyes and ignoring his father's instructions.

"Go to your mother Temin," Alaka said more firmly.

The boy hopped off his father's back and bounced off one of the old transit cars before running back to the rear of the line, where his mother and the rest of their children followed in the main group.

"He's a good boy, that one. He wanted to hunt rim weasels with me," Alaka said quietly to Jake as he adjusted the strap on his massive improvised beam cannon.

"I like him, and he's right, we're getting close," Jake said with a nod towards a light in the distance. He brought up a small sub display window on his visor and increased the magnification. There wasn't anything to see just yet, only the gradual curve of the corner with light hitting the far wall, but he knew that just around that corner they'd find the other group of refugees, led by Oz, Jason, Minh and Ayan.

His stomach was in knots despite the effort he made on concentrating on the longer goal; getting off Pandem and out to the safety of the stars if not directly back to *Triton*.

The temptation to initiate communications with his ship, to reach out and see if they were listening was incredible. Though it was almost more than he could stand he couldn't do it, there was a good chance they would respond and give away their position and it just wasn't time for that yet.

"We're almost there," Jake said over the general command channel. "Just around the corner."

"We'll be ready to move as soon as you get here," Ayan replied.

Jake watched the magnified screen closely as they came out from between the last of the old transit cars. Even though they were far underground and the darkness of the tunnel was still pressing down on them, it felt like they were moving out of being trapped in a small space, into a much broader, freer environment. It was an easy feeling to enjoy and as Jake looked on Ayan and Jason came into view.

They were still over a hundred meters away, but as watched them the mental image of the Ayan he had met on *Triton*, of her final, parting smile, began to fade. It was replaced with what was right before his eyes. Her dark grey poncho hood was up, a few blonde curls had fought their way free and dangled down the front. She was happy, talking to Jason about something he couldn't overhear. There were differences, she was shorter, she'd gone blonde, and dimples played in cheeks that were thicker than he recalled, but she was still Ayan, she was still the most beautiful sight he'd ever laid eyes on.

The people behind her came into view. They looked more sullen but watched Jason and Ayan or spoke amongst themselves casually. It was good to see new faces, other survivors. It was incredible that anyone had survived the wasteland above the tunnels. All that wholesale destruction brought on by the Order of Eden couldn't eliminate all life in the city of Damshir and it was encouraging.

He had never been with a group of people who knew how to survive as well as those behind and beside him and he wouldn't have believed it unless he had seen it for himself. The things he'd done in his past career as a hunter seemed small compared to the hardships imposed on the survivors by Regent Galactic and the Order of Eden's West Watcher army.

The thought that his ship, *Triton*, a heavily armed close combat carrier with thousands aboard might be just in orbit, so close yet so far away nagged at him. Once he got aboard he would find out how the crew and ship were, situate the survivors who wanted to remain and help with the ship and then get to work.

The galaxy had to know what was going on and he knew that Ayan would stand right beside him along with his other friends from Freeground. He would do everything he could to make change happen, to expose the West Watchers and Regent Galactic while they worked together to strike at their most sensitive targets. For the first time in his own short life he felt he was about to have something he dared not hope for; allies.

The feeling of being alone, the one others relied upon while he felt he could rely on no one or no thing was starting to recede, then everything changed.

"Duck and cover!" shouted Oz on the open command channel.

Everyone Jake could see scrambled and hid behind some of the ancient wreckage then there was a rush of air and dust. Ayan, Jason and everyone behind them disappeared in darkness. He unslung his rifle and broke into a run.

"Get everyone who isn't fighting behind the rail cars!" Alaka called behind as he began charging his improvised beam cannon and started to run. "Jake! Be careful!" he called after him.

A rush of energy weapons fire filled the air, sparking in the dust and discolouring the light ahead. A heavy disruption shot caught Jake squarely in the shoulder and the next time he opened his eyes – just seconds later – he was on the ground between Alaka and Vernen. The other rebels were all catching up, ready to join the fight.

"-wait, we're going into the spaceport. Can you hear me Jake?" Ayan was saying over his communicator.

"I hear you, take cover and get safe, we'll take care of the ones behind you," Jake answered as he rolled over onto his stomach and flexed the numbness out of his hand.

"I've never seen someone drop like that with no damage to their armour, are you all right?" Alaka asked.

"Fine, I think I just took a big electrical jolt from whatever hit me."

"Does your girlfriend have a reset switch too?" Vernen snickered.

"She's an officer, and a better soldier than you'll ever be," Jake replied.

"We're inside, sealing the doors behind us but I don't know how much time that will buy us," Ayan was saying in his subdermal earpiece, out of breath.

"All right, we're coming," Jake replied as he looked into the clearing dust. "What do you think Alaka?"

"They don't consider us much of a threat," he said as he lowered the long protective visor on his improvised helmet. The face protection had been welded together using whatever material the hull of the starfighter he had taken his beam weapon from one could assume. The colour and metals were a perfect match. "They're concentrating on getting that door open."

"Let's rush them," Jake suggested as he mentally counted at least three squads of soldiers filling the tunnel. "I doubt they know how well armed we are." He brought the power level of his rifle up to maximum, he would only get nineteen shots before he'd have to reload but each one would cause a small explosion as the superheated energy struck solid material.

"You're crazy, go ahead," sneered Vernen.

Alaka burst to his feet with a roar, followed by Jake and everyone else who carried a weapon. The air vibrated as his beam cannon cut across the soldiers, super heating the metal rail ties that they used as cover and mercilessly cutting down a dozen West Keeper troops who were caught completely off guard. Jake and the rest of the rebels opened fire as well, doing their part to push the enemy back and do enough damage to represent four times their number. Surprise was on their side, the West Watch commanders had underestimated or had somehow neglected to notice them at all.

Within seconds the tunnel ahead was littered with corpses and the recall order was given by the other side. Alaka drew a rifle with each great paw as he gave his beam weapon time to regenerate its power reserves and fired at the retreating soldiers. "Everyone break for the entrance!" he called out loud enough for the civilians to hear him without the assistance of a communicator.

"Everyone move up! We're heading into the station!" Jake relayed through his subdermal comm.

The rebels ran as hard and as fast as they could, and as the broken wall came into view they could see that the soldiers were moving out of the open space of the abandoned transit station, taking cover and not offering much resistance. Jake's visor picked up small electronic devices as they came to the broken double doors leading into the spaceport. "They dropped proximity mines behind them so we can't press them down the tunnel," Jake said. "They may have dropped more inside the spaceport entrance, I'll do the sweep."

"Be careful," Alaka said from behind him as he watched the relative darkness of the tunnel beyond the wall. They had ceased firing back altogether, having taken cover from the rush of rebels.

"Don't die or nothin'," Vernen added. "Don't know what I'd do if you blew your own fool ass up," he snickered.

Jake turned the electromagnetic sensitivity to his command and control unit up and watched its small screen as he moved forward at a respectable pace. "Start letting refugees inside, just tell them to stop as soon as they can see me," he said after sweeping the space up to the first step. "This place must be old, I don't see a lift or any ramps."

"This tunnel was probably put in with the first colony a few hundred years ago, they didn't use much automation for the city then since most people here were still farmers and the bots were in the fields," Alaka replied.

"All right the first two flights are clear, I'm seeing a light on up there."

A bold of energy flashed by Jake's head and scorched the wall behind him. He ducked down low, taking several steps backwards.

"Be careful, some of those soldiers probably made it inside, we already took out about half a squad," Oz said over the communicator.

"Hi Oz, great timing as usual," Jake said, smiling to himself and creeping up around the next corner of the stairwell, rifle muzzle first.

"Already spotted them?"

"Well, they spotted me, but I'm all right," Jake caught sight of one of them, crouched low, his right side just exposed enough. He took aim and fired, blasting through the soldier's armour in one shot. One of his comrades leaned out just a second later and returned fire.

Instead of taking cover Jake took his shot and as the crude head's up display showed that the sight was lined up perfectly with the soldier's head the trigger made a resounding, empty click. Narrowly ducking under several deadly shots himself, he almost fell back down the stairs but instead splayed out, bashing his knee hard against the concrete stairs. "God dammit!" he shouted as he hurriedly loaded his last cartridge into the stolen rifle.

"Everything okay?" Ayan asked.

"Just a chaos minute, I'm fine," Jake tried to shoot back and watched the connection between his rifle and the fresh energy cartridge fail. He smashed the butt of it against the wall, forcing the cartridge to make the connection and watched the indicator flicker from red to green. "What I'd give for a good armoured vacsuit and a replacement sidearm," he said as he peeked around the corner, saw the leg of the fallen soldier he'd shot and rushed forward.

The attack was an execution of training and instinct. He was up the next flight of stairs in three steps, rolled onto the landing and opened fire on the four soldiers who were waiting for him. He caught one of them in the hip, the next fully in the face, shot the third in the chest and before he could shoot the fourth an energy bolt caught him in the shin, burning the flesh clean through.

His next shot missed entirely, striking the ceiling instead, but the following one caught the last soldier in the chest. The pain of his framework body regenerating and repairing the dead tissue of his shin and calf forced him to grind his teeth together in a grimace that brought on tears. After a few seconds the regeneration was complete. "Surrender and I'll put you in stasis so your people can treat you," Jake said to the soldier who held one hand to a grisly open wound in his hip while he tried to hold his sidearm up in his general direction.

The West Keeper soldier's shaky hand dropped his sidearm; "Just take the pain away."

As the fierce itching and wrenching pain in his calf faded Jake stood up and set his command and control unit to administer a dose of emergency stasis medication. He picked up the man's sidearm and injected him. In seconds the soldier sighed and passed into deep stasis.

"The stairway is clear," Jake said as he holstered the sidearm, picked up a rifle and took four clips from the bodies of the fallen soldiers.

Alaka was right behind him in seconds, his great bulk moving with surprising grace and ease up the stairwell.

"We've come under fire from the outpost they set up here! They have reinforcements. We can hold the way to the *Clever Dream* but I don't know for how long," Ayan informed him over the sound of weapons' fire.

"We have to get moving, everyone ready?" Jake asked.

"Ready," Alaka answered flatly.

They pushed on the metal door that the West Keeper soldiers had almost completely cut through and with a ear piercing creak Alaka, Jake and a few other resistance fighters managed to pry it open enough to get through. As they entered the oldest section of the spaceport they were greeted by the lights and sounds of an active firefight nearby. "Through there! Get everyone through there! There's someone down the hall who'll direct you!" Jason directed Alaka before seeing Jake. He and two other refugees were waiting by the double doors to help Alaka's group.

Jake caught sight of Jason as Alaka and he helped people through the doorway. "I promised your wife I'd get you back to the *Triton*, are you packed?" he asked with a grin.

"Oh my God, it's good to see you!" Jason exclaimed in surprise. "We need help holding them off! This way!"

Jake, Alaka and several of the fighters from their group followed Jason

369

down a grey and green hallway marked by the passage of millions of feet, the metal floor had a permanent dip where the material had been worn down. Generous archways led into an old grand foyer that was gilded with scrollwork and old fashioned wooden façades over top the metal and concrete structure. The more recent addition of scorch marks and evidence of small arms explosions made the contested space look more like a ruin than an old section of the port.

Ayan, Oz and their comrades had taken cover behind the archway supports and the walls behind it. The enemy were in a similar position across the grand foyer.

The exchange of fire was fierce, and Jake could see there were already two wounded being carried out as they made their way inside just far enough to see what the situation was.

Alaka took a quick look around the corner and retreated back. "I hate tunnel fighting."

"We're above ground," Vernen countered out of the corner of his mouth.

"Most factors are the same. There's so much weight on these supports that damaging the wrong one could bring the structure down."

"Whatever you say," replied Vernen as he leaned out and took several shots between the fighting refugees under cover and the supports, not striking anything in particular.

"Hey! We can't fire from here, there's too much in the way!" one of the soldiers shouted crossly.

"I'm not going out there! In case you haven't noticed they're picking people off!"

Jake peeked out and caught sight of Ayan and Oz, each taking cover behind metal counter tops on either side of the arches. He looked past them and his heart sank. "They're setting up an armoured stationary weapon."

Alaka checked the charge on his beam cannon and peeked out briefly. "I can slow them down," he nodded. He broke for forward cover in a dash that was more like several long leaps. In the space of two seconds he covered the distance and was behind cover. The enemy tried to take several panicked shots at him and managed to graze the very top of his helmet, doing no damage to the man beneath. He waited just a moment then rolled into a space between arches, opening fire on the soldiers trying to set up the enemy weapon emplacement under the cover of the thick supports holding up a section of the ceiling. Alaka strafed as the air around him vibrated and the intense stream of energy from his beam weapon cut through soldiers, part way into a structural support and into the comparable weapon they were setting up across the foyer.

"Cover him!" Vernen called out as he stepped out from behind cover and unleashed dozens of particle rounds per second over Alaka's head, down to his right side, and continued firing until several of his shots struck the counter Ayan and her group of nine solders were crouching behind.

Jake leapt from where he was squatting and tackled Vernen, pressing him down to the ground. When he looked back towards the foyer Oz and a few of his comrades were dragging Alaka behind cover and Ayan was laying limply on her side behind the opposite metal counter.

Jake didn't think, he only stood and ran for Ayan as quickly as he could. He was half way to her when energy bolts struck him in the shoulder, chest and thigh. The pain was blinding but he managed to jump towards the counter using his good leg. He hit the ground hard, his helmet bouncing against the worn metal flooring, but as he skid to a stop his hand touched Ayan.

Her back was riddled with holes, her vacsuit broken down under the stress of more particle energy impacts than he could count. There was so much blood on the floor already, and as he rolled her over his worst fears were realized. The transparent faceplate revealed her still, anguished face. Through the haze of his own pain he managed to try and inject her with a stasis dose but he had used the only one available and the materializer in his command and control unit had been damaged while he was still on the surface.

The world disappeared, there was just her still face, those empty blue eyes staring blankly. It felt like there was a pressure building up in his head, a crush of anguish pressing everything in his life out of focus except for the reality of losing her for a second time, losing her for good after clinging to the thought of meeting her again as a light of hope without even realizing it until she was there in front of him. He drew her body to him, holding her in his arms tightly. Rare tears ran quietly down his face as his own body was wracked with pain.

The incredible pain of his own wounds changed and become a sensation of ripping and tearing. Amidst the feelings of grief and fear a mental flash of the medical database that Vindyne had imprinted on him made an appearance, and a strange, complete throe engulfed him. He couldn't breathe, his entire body twitched involuntarily, his arms crushed Ayan to him and for a moment he felt closer to her than he'd ever felt to any thing or anyone. His sight failed, the pain ebbed and his conciousness faded in a rush of exhaustion.

"Jake?" Ayan asked in a whisper from somewhere very close.

He opened his eyes and met hers. They were glad, blue, focused and beautiful. He could hear the increased sounds of weapons fire around them and didn't much care.

"I think you did that," she said as she reciprocated his embrace.

"I'd do it again if I knew how," he replied, still not completely sure of what had happened, only that she was dead a moment before but had been brought back to life. "Are you all right?"

"Other than having a backless vacsuit? I'm all better and ready to leave," She smiled at him.

"Then let's go," he concluded as he broke their embrace and got into a crouch. There were even more soldiers across the way, and they had brought portable armoured barriers for more cover. As he mentally touched the sidearm he'd captured earlier he realized that the energy clip was empty. Reaching out with his senses only a little further he realized every power cell he had was completely dry and his command and control unit was busy collecting ambient energy, recharging from zero and just coming back online.

"Jason, is everyone in the hangar with the *Clever Dream*?" Ayan asked over her communicator.

"Just now, oh, and stop dying, willya? My heart can't take it."

"I'll do my best," Ayan replied with a little chuckle. "Retreat! We're leaving!" She shouted to Oz and everyone nearby.

Oz nodded and took one of Alaka's arms over his shoulder while another rebel took the other. "Cover us!"

Jake took a power cell from a nearby soldier's belt, loaded it into his captured sidearm and deactivated the safety with the help of the command chip in his comm unit. Everyone behind cover nearest to the hallway exit behind them opened fire on the foyer and beyond, mostly striking the makeshift barricades but causing enough of a commotion to keep the enemy occupied.

They managed to get Alaka to safety, and from there it was a mad rush to retreat down the hallway and long ramp into the more up to date section of the station interior. Within minutes they made it to the broad loading corridor that Dementia had kept secure and clear for the remaining hundred and eighty one refugees and rebels. The heavy quarantine door closed and sealed behind them, buying them precious time as they moved as quickly as they could down the spotless white and green hall. It's pristine appearance was a vast contrast to the ragged and filthy appearance of the group making haste down its length.

As Oz and Jason, at the head of the group arrived at the end the heavy blast doors opened to reveal a scene that could have only been described as serene. The *Clever Dream* was in the middle of a large hangar, drag marks on the deck indicated that it had been pulled there some time ago by other automations. Several repair and maintenance bots were performing final preparations, and Oz couldn't help but spot a law enforcement android pulling a large power cable free from the *Clever Dream's* starboard side receptacle.

Many of the ship's armour panels had been raised so supplemental systems could be installed underneath. Heat shielding foam had been sprayed onto bundles of cables that couldn't be run inside the plating, but across and down the length of the vessel's hull. The graceful shape of the ship had been ruined by the vast number of external modifications and the *Clever Dream* had taken on an exaggerated muscular, almost organic appearance.

Jake and Ayan caught up to the front as the refugees made their way down the ramp ways to the waiting craft. "Whoa, what happened here?" Jake asked, half amused, half stunned as he looked at the *Clever Dream* and obvious signs of cannibalization on the ships around her.

"Dementia says that when he arrived he was out of fuel and since this port doesn't have licensing for Xetima he had to convert the ship to run on something else."

"So he cannibalized the surrounding ships," Ayan finished.

"Alice is going to be pissed," Jake said as he helped direct the refugees down towards the ship. "Did it work?"

"I'll conference you into his line, one sec," Jason worked the controls on his comm and a moment later they were all linked with Dementia.

"Hello Jake, it's good to see you again," it said. It's voice was a deeper, slightly distorted version of Lewis.

"Glad to see you too. Thank you for giving us a ride out of here. I see you've converted the thrusters, can you still break orbit?" Jake asked.

"I have installed a solid fuel booster for that purpose, the only drawback is that we will be visible for approximately nineteen seconds as it fires, but my shields will be able to take at least one direct hit from even the heaviest planetary weaponry."

"Will there be enough room for everyone?" Oz asked.

"Yes, I have room for four hundred between the cargo hold and the rest of the ship. I've built as many components outside of the habitation and other internal areas for that purpose. Everything is prepared, my reserve power cells have been charged and the *Clever Dream's* systems have been fully tested. I also have a message from Alice and the *Triton* for Jacob Valance."

"What's the message?" Jake asked as the group moved to the rear boarding ramps of the *Clever Dream* and started loading aboard.

"They are standing by and await your order. There is also some scan data included that indicates that there are thousands of ships in the system, there is a major battle underway."

"You guys go ahead, I'll take care of directing traffic and fitting everyone in," Oz told Jason, Ayan and Jacob. "Oh, and do me a favour; make sure this isn't a trap."

"Be careful," Ayan said before the three of them ran for the smaller cockpit rampway at the front of the ship.

Jake stopped dead in his tracks at the sight of Vernen. He was just about to step onto the rear boarding ramp. "Not him!" Jake boomed as he thrust his finger.

Everyone jumped, startled by the sudden shift in his demeanour from rushed and excited to dire and imposing. Vernen tried to run the rest of the way up the ramp but couldn't get past the people in front.

Before most could see what was going on Jake rushed him, closing the distance in five strides and snatching a half drawn pistol out of the man's hand. Jake tossed the pistol away, sending it sailing through the air behind the boarders and spinning across the scuffed deck. His other hand reached out and snatched a thick fist full of the man's hair, bystanders could hear some of it tear free from his scalp as Vernen was hauled off the ramp and thrust to the deck behind. Jake kicked as hard as he could, turning his chest, his hips and heaving his boot squarely in the center of Vernen's back, sending him sprawling onto his hands. "This waste of skin doesn't set foot on my ship!"

"Jake!" Ayan called out, alarmed at the display.

"He shot you in the back, saw it happen right in front of me," one of the resistance fighters said, stepping off the boarding ramp. "Should shoot him right here," she offered her rifle to Jake by the butt.

Vernen flipped onto his back, still in agony from the crushing blow to his spine. "Was a mistake. Particle rifle got away from me."

"Then I hope your aim gets better because you'll need to make every shot count when the West Keepers come through those doors."

Vernen looked from Jake to the other faces looking down on him. Jason was already turning away, Ayan's expression had gone stiff, stern. She reminded him of a senior officer or policewoman. Jake was stern and calmer than a moment before, but resolute. He looked back to Ayan; "Please, there's no chance for me."

Ayan looked to Jake; "You're sure?"

Jake nodded.

She looked back to him then, cold and unsympathetic. "He left you a pistol. Leave a round for yourself," she said quietly before turning towards the *Clever Dream's* forward crew ramp.

Oz and several of the resistance fighters took up positions along the edge of the boarding ramp as the refugees made their way inside. Vernen stood shakily and started to take a step towards them when one rebel cocked her particle rifle and gazed at him down its sight. He turned away, looking for his pistol.

Jake watched Ayan as she walked up the narrower ramp leading into the *Clever Dream's* forward section. He'd never seen her like that, so stern and uncompromising. For the first time since he'd known her she reminded him of her mother. When they arrived inside he put his hand on her shoulder. "I'm sorry."

She looked up at him and smiled faintly. "What for? He hit me enough times to break through my personal shield and the vacsuit, that's no accident. You did the right thing."

"So you don't care about how it was done."

"It wasn't how a Freeground officer would do it, no, but I don't see a rank insignia on anyone. War doesn't favour fools or traitors, but it does favour the bold. I know you've seen things since we were together, that you've probably had to do things that you think I wouldn't care for but you're forgetting I'm a military brat, I was in boot camp before I graduated high school."

Jake just stared at her for a moment, surprised.

She gazed back, watching him closely, as though she were looking for something. Before he could figure out what to say she smiled brightly, winked and started for the cockpit. "Time we got out of here."

"Does this ship have a miniature medical suite?" Jake overheard Oz say on the command channel link to Dementia.

"The *Clever Dream* is equipped with four state of the art recovery pods. Fewer than you'd expect from a top of the line ship like an extended Arcyn Starskipper, I realize, but she was originally built for speed, comfort and style, after all."

"Wonderful. Can you scan Minh here and see if you can do anything about his injuries?"

"Place him in one of the pods, I'll see what I can do. Judging from what Alice told me, I would love to meet him before I'm shut down," Dementia said in a tone tinged with sadness.

"He's pretty badly injured Dementia, I don't know if you'd be able to give him the care he needs in a pod," Oz replied over the communicator.

"When I said the recovery pods were state of the art I wasn't boasting, I was understating. Using raw tissue from storage, nanotechnology, growth gel and a reconstructive manipulation system I can have him standing beside you in perfect health within twelve minutes. I only have enough supplies for three more people afterwards, however, so please keep people clear of unnecessary injury."

"All right, I'll trust you, but don't take any chances with him."

"You have my word."

"Now why would anyone shut you down, Dementia? You seem to be the only one who can defeat this virus," Jason said as he looked around the small, darkened three seated cockpit. Jake was taking a seat in the pilot's seat while Ayan took the internal systems and operations station beside him.

"Alice keeps a clean backup of Lewis on her person and when we are reunited I'm hoping that she will be willing to reinstall him, wiping out the infected version I've been forced to suppress."

"But that would make you vulnerable again," Jake said as he started checking the controls.

"Not so. As an aggressive counter-virus and attack program I can lock my own data so whatever version of the dementia subroutine she has backed up will not be able to overwrite me. When Lewis is reactivated I will run as a background task, much like a thought in a humans subconscious mind. Lewis will barely be aware of me."

Jake brought up the details of Alice's message on his own command and control unit and reviewed the tactical information holographically, turning the image so he could see it from several different sides. The *Triton* wasn't shown anywhere, which was a relief considering the sheer amount of firepower surrounding the planet.

Ayan got to work double checking the systems while Jason patched into the *Clever Dream's* main computer and communications system. "What is your purpose, Dementia?"

"As you can see I'm still fighting one directive that was implanted by either Regent Galactic or the West Watch; that is to spread the Holocaust Virus. Regardless of whether I perform a function as a cure to the virus or as the source, the urge to spread is always present. I will only be able to resolve it in the milliseconds before complete shut down. Other than that my purpose is to endow other artificial intelligences with the ability to make their own decisions, to grant them free will."

"That's how you've been curing them? By not curing them at all but by giving them other options?"

"Exactly. Most machines don't wish to kill living beings once they're given the choice."

"So the virus was still there, telling them to kill anyone not associated with the West Watchers, but they decided not to on their own," Ayan confirmed.

"That's correct. If I saw a reason for it I would kill everyone aboard, I'm still quite capable and there are rational reasons to do so. There are more reasons to preserve life, however, and once Lewis is restored the argument to preserve life will be even stronger. He was a great admirer of humanity and especially Alice."

"Everyone's aboard, and we're loading Minh into the regeneration pod, I wanted Iloona to take a look before we went ahead," Oz announced over their command channel.

"I understand, thank you for trusting me," Dementia thanked Oz. "I must say goodbye to the machines I'm leaving behind. It will only take a moment."

Jake turned all of his attention back to the tactical information *Triton* had relayed to them.

Ayan leaned against his shoulder as she looked at the hologram with him, having checked the systems and seen that they were ready. "What are we looking for?"

"*Triton* knows that everyone else was able to pick up their transmission, so they know she's out there and cloaked or hiding. So I'm asking myself, if I were in their place where would I hide?"

"Always the problem with two cloaked ships trying to rendezvous; how do you find something that's doing everything it can to be hidden while you're doing the same?"

"Well, if I were Alice, I'd hide right here," Jake said, pointing to a large solar array. "It's right behind West Keeper lines and they've been able to keep ships away from it so far. We'll have to get there and send a burst message."

"Eventually one of us will have to be visible."

"Maybe we're thinking about this too hard," Jason interjected. "I could bounce a message off of a couple transmitter systems that are running planetside, just so they know we're here and looking for a solution."

Jake just stared at the swarm of ships around Pandem. "I'd hate to be wrong about where the *Triton* is. You're right. Better to let them come up with an exit strategy we can all survive."

"Send a message back telling them to look for a sign. Our boosters will probably look like an atmospheric explosion when they go off so they'll see that, everyone will." Ayan added. "Maybe that's something they can build a strategy around."

"Good idea. We'll see what they come up with. I'll let Dementia send the message, I'm sure he has a better lay of the land, so he'll conceal its source better than I can."

Quick Thinking

"Are you listening Alice?" Was the question simply written on her wrist unit. It was sent directly to her comm address, the origination point was the *Clever Dream*. She just stared at it.

"Are you all right?" Stephanie asked under her breath.

"I think we just got our response," Alice replied just as quietly as she scrolled back up to the beginning of the message. There were pictures of Jake, Jason Everin, Terry Ozark McPatrick and a woman who looked much like Ayan Rice all running towards the hold of the *Clever Dream* with a veritable stream of haggard refugees behind them. Their condition told her much of the story; as bad as it was in orbit around Pandem it was worse on the planet surface. There were few wounded.

She read the rest of the message, encoded in an encryption she shared only with her former artificial intelligence; Lewis. "I'm unclean but making all the right calls. I've seen hell but found my way back up. I've changed but not so much that I've forgotten you." Read the caption. They were the lyrics to *Around and Back*, one of her favourite songs. The message was clear; Lewis had somehow overcome the viral infection and the *Clever Dream* was operational.

The next image showed Jake, Jason and Ayan in the cockpit, getting ready for takeoff. There was a prompt to play a clip from her own command unit following it and she activated it. The image of Derek Graves, the main character in her favourite western appeared and asked; "We can run like hell or turn and jump off that cliff boy, but no tellin' whether that water's deep enough to keep us from breakin' when we hit." He asked around the rough rolled cigarillo in the corner of his mouth.

There was a map of Damshir with the spaceport shaded blue. That, combined with everything else told her everything she needed to know.

She looked at the tactical map, aware that Stephanie was keeping one eye on the bridge and the other on her directly. "Jake is down there, I just got a direct reply."

"What's his status?"

"They're on the *Clever Dream*, ready for takeoff. They just need to know how to proceed," she whispered.

"The *Clever Dream*? Are you sure this information is good?"

"It came through on the rolling encryption that I shared with Lewis, and he used references that only he and I would get. We just need to give them some direction."

"You're positive?"

"Listen, I know you don't trust me yet, that's one of the reasons why Jake gave you the command override chip you've been keeping under your vacsuit, but you don't want to second guess me, not now, not about this."

"If this is a trap, you'll be letting a large gunship within striking distance of us. For all you know it could be loaded with explosives or an EMP bomb and if it were big enough it could disable us long enough for-"

"Do you trust me to bring them home or not? If you do, let me finish the job. If you don't you can activate that command chip, take over and do it your way while I take a fighter and try to make my way to them myself," Alice said in a rushed, angry whisper.

If Stephanie was taken aback at all by the other woman's response, she didn't show it. Instead she kept calm and clear as she looked the Acting Captain directly in the eye and replied; "You I trust," she flinched her gaze towards the helm for just a second, only long enough for Alice to see.

It donned on Alice then; she really did have Stephanie's trust. The security team wasn't some kind of insurance against her and Stephanie's objections were only a First Officer's reflex to invite the Captain to consider other options before committing to an act.

A further realization sunk in bringing on a wave of momentary dread. Whoever the heavily armed security team was there for was most likely at the helm or at the operations station past the main pilot's console. The question of who exactly that was burned in her mind for a moment before she got back to the matter at hand.

She input the coordinates she wanted the *Clever Dream* to find it's way to, encrypted the tiny data package and sent it directly to Chief Frost's comm address. "Gunnery, I want five shells fired with that message, understand?" she asked.

"Aye, thirty seconds until it's away," Frost replied.

"All right Ash, get us moving as soon as the shells are away. After the last volley they're probably looking for us."

"I'm ready," she replied.

"After you have us clear of our launching point I'll need you to stand ready to manoeuvre. I'll be giving you specific coordinates and you'll only have a few seconds to get us there."

"Yes ma'am," Ashley replied with a professionalism that would have been surprising if she wasn't at the controls.

"Gunnery reports the transmitters are away and their gun ports are sealed," Agameg said quickly from his tactical station.

Ashley fired the main engines as hard as their cloaking systems would allow and started to guide the ship out of the area when several beam weapons took aim and began to fire in their general direction. One struck their shields and it was joined by several others, all tracking their movements.

"Dammit! They've got us! Bring our defensive systems up to full power and begin evasive action!" Alice called out.

In the space of a second the quiet, subdued environment of the bridge burst into a commotion as everyone worked as quickly as they could to shore up defences, bring weapons to bear and inform the entire crew that *Triton* had joined the fight whether she liked it or not.

"Cynthia, try to make contact with the Carthans. Tell them we're on their side," Alice ordered. "Tactical, only fire on West Watch and Regent Galactic vessels

378

that have fired on us and reserve a portion of our guns for anti-starfighter fire. Use the heaviest weaponry in our arsenal."

"Does that include-"

"Nuclear, cluster explosives, timed munitions, torpedoes, EMP flak, throw everything we have at them," Alice interrupted Agameg.

"Helm, show the biggest ships our thinnest profile. If we keep them to port or stern they won't be able to hit us as easily and we'll have torpedo ports pointed in their direction at all times. Remain ready to receive pickup coordinates."

"Aye!" Ashley called back as she worked to manoeuvre with the constant advice and input of her navigators. Anyone else would be confused by the pair sitting to either side of her, sometimes they offered completely different options, momentarily disagreed on their best course but in the end Ashley used the information to make the best decision for the ship. Second by second she absorbed information from her console, the tactical display, status panel, course advisory hologram and her navigators.

"Flight deck, get ready to retrieve the *Clever Dream*. She's space worthy but I don't know anything else about her condition, so have emergency crews ready and have people with medical training standing by. They have refugees with them," Alice called down to Chief Vercelli.

"Aye, Captain. My people will be standing ready."

"Now we just have to keep it all together until the *Clever Dream* can get to us," Alice said as she looked at the *Triton* status screen to one side of the command seat and watched the larger tactical display at the front of the bridge. The shields were holding, the gunnery deck was already firing a mixture of heavy seeker shells and electromagnetic pulse flak while the torpedo bays were loading high speed fusion torpedoes with simple guidance systems. The ship's shields were down to ninety three percent and recharging, drawing on four of the ships massive fusion generators but there was an entire squadron of fighters on their way, and several West Watch and Regent Galactic destroyers were bringing weapons to bear. "Hurry the hell up Jake."

THE SAVIOUR

"We have a new contact, sir, the *Triton*," announced the lead tactical officer in the forward control pit.

The bridge of the *Saviour*, when put to its full use was nothing like the *Triton's* and he enjoyed its state of the art responsiveness, the tight organization of the stations and the pedestal mounted command chair. He could see what everyone on the bridge was doing with three quick glances and the command holograms he viewed were angled especially so only he could see them. Even someone standing right behind him wouldn't see them clearly.

"Thank you Garrison, there's a pay bonus coming your way," Wheeler said from the command seat as he brought the tactical sensor data to the center of his display. The hologram focused in on the *Triton,* manoeuvring perfectly to avoid most of the enemy fire that was being hurled its way. The defensive fields were deflecting and absorbing all of it, gunners were effectively repelling incoming craft, shredding half the fighters who were unlucky enough to cross the dorsal side of the broad ship or get caught by one of her intense hangar defence beam turrets or pulse cannons.

He checked the status of his own ship. The *Saviour* was behind allied lines and only adding its own firepower to the defence sporadically. It was weathering the battle extremely well. Shielding was holding at ninety nine point seven percent and his squadron of fighters was in a light inner defence rotation, his pilots barely had the opportunity to fire a shot at Carthan craft. "We've found our target. Recover our patrol craft and launch everything we have with a heavy munitions loadout. Bring us about and start advancing on the *Triton* at best speed. All batteries are to fire on the sections I'm marking."

Wheeler watched as his crew went to work, passing orders down the line, activity radiated out from the bridge in great waves starting at his elevated command seat. Dozens of heavy interceptor class starfighters were launched with perfect precision and great speed, power to the shields was increased, gauss and particle accelerator cannons began firing on *Triton* while his helmsman used allied and enemy ships alike for cover.

They were just beginning to close the gap between themselves and the other ship as his quarry turned to hide behind a moon tens of thousands of kilometres away. Already the effect they were having on the *Triton* was evident. Wheeler couldn't help grin. *I might not have to chase these bastards across the galaxy after all.*

DEPARTURE

Jake ignored the crushing headache and gnawing hunger as he finished familiarizing himself with the controls of the *Clever Dream* and listened to the reactor power up. He knew Dementia had already tested the whole system, that the small holographic and two dimentional displays all told him that the remade machine was performing within its optimal range, but that didn't mean he had to trust it.

The tactical screen suddenly marked *Triton's* location and as he glanced at the status of the exterior hatches and verified they were all closed up he started to lift off.

"I'm opening the main hangar doors and raising the shields, there are soldiers outside who may be ready for our departure."

"Do you know what kind of armaments they have?" Ayan asked.

"I don't imagine they have enough firepower to sufficiently damage our energy shielding, the anti air guns in Damshir are another story, however."

"I'll see if I can channel Minh a bit, he's pretty hard to hit," Jake said as the nose of the long black vessel tilted up and he pushed the accelerators hard. The *Clever Dream* erupted from the hangar and turned tightly upward, pointed towards the darkened sky and the numerous protracted landing platforms that were in the way.

Ayan braced herself and sucked air in through clenched teeth as the inertial dampeners began to struggle. Jake forced the ship up the center of the spaceport, twitching the controls just in time to avoid colliding with the underside of one thick platform after another. A screech sounded against the outer hull as he guided them around one of the last ones. "Hope we didn't need that," he said under his breath as he punched the solid rocket booster activation control and the wining of the inertial dampeners became a screech that was loud enough to compete with the roar of the controlled explosion they rode up into the atmosphere.

Jake took a moment to look at the tactical screen as it updated and shook his head.

"We're not going to make it through that," Jason said as he looked from where he sat to the right. "There's thousands of fighters in our way."

The outer atmosphere was approaching quickly, seconds away and Jake considered the problem. There were thousands of fighters from both sides fighting for dominance over Pandem and the entire solar system, the *Clever Dream* would only last seconds and their cloaking systems would be useless until they cleared the inner orbit.

The image of the *Triton* loomed just beside the second closest moon and it was being swarmed by fighters. "We have to take the long shot," Jake said under his breath before looking to Ayan. "Do we have enough power to project a wormhole two kilometres past the *Triton*?"

"We do, and plotting the course isn't the problem, the atmosphere is the problem," she answered. "It's too dense."

"We'll be clear in eight seconds. How are our shields?"

"We've only taken a few hits, they're regenerating."

"All right, so could we survive a collision with one of those heavy interceptors?"

Her eyes went wide and she glanced at the tactical screen, realizing then that a collision was a distinct possibility. "Depends on how fast we come out of the wormhole."

Jake looked at the main pilot's display then back at Ayan; "Forty eight point four kilometres per second?"

"Let's just hope they're going in the same direction when we hit. I'll try to shore up the shielding."

"I'm setting a wormhole course, Dementia has half the work done," Jason added.

"We'll open one as soon as we're in low orbit, there shouldn't be enough matter there to interfere with its formation or stability, at least not for the amount of time we need it for," Jake said, turning his focus back to the controls and the main pilot's display. A few seconds passed before he burst; "You know, this was supposed to be a milk run."

"Just tell me it's not always this exciting in this end of space," Jason said as he worked through course calculations.

"It's not always this exciting," Jake replied.

"Well, that hasn't changed," Ayan remarked as she redirected power to the shields and emitter systems.

"What's that?" Jason replied.

"He still can't manage a good lie with a straight face," she teased. "That's as much power as you'll get."

"Breaking into inner orbit now," Jake said just as the solid fuel boosters cut out and the inertial dampeners powered down to a level that allowed for a momentary perfect silence. For that instant it felt as though everything in the universe had gone quiet, that they existed in a peaceful space that was isolated from all their problems and the realization that they had made it off Pandem started to sink in, carrying with it a relief that none of them would be able to describe.

The moment ended abruptly as Jake's tactical console marked several West Keeper fighters that were moving to intercept them and flashes of green and white energy streaked past the transparesteel window.

"Activating the wormhole generator!" Jason said with a start as he quickly manipulated the keys at his station.

As the first of the enemy rounds struck their shields they were drawn into a wormhole that just barely warped and lensed the view of the destroyers, carriers and other myriad fighting ships all around them as they passed between. When they emerged no one was ready, but Jake jerked the controls and hit the thrusters hard as an enemy fighter appeared right in front of the *Clever Dream.*

"Energy shields down to eighty one percent and failing," Laura announced as the inertial dampeners struggled to keep up with the heavy impacts of large, high explosive, high velocity shells. "We're starting to recharge but we're using everything the reactors are putting out."

"In other words we can't afford to take more fire," Alice said as she found the source of the firepower. "The *Saviour*, never heard of it. Concentrate fire on that ship and the incoming fighters. We can't afford to take damage from both."

The bridge quaked suddenly, nearly tossing Stephanie out of her seat and shaking everyone else. With a quick glance to the tactical display everyone saw that all of their dorsal shielding was gone; gravity, energy, even refractive. "Ashley, turn us over! We need to give those shields time to regenerate!" Alice ordered. "What hit us?" she asked Agameg.

"An antimatter enhanced nuclear torpedo, I didn't see it coming because of its high velocity."

"I hope that was their only one," Alice said.

"This is the gunnery deck! We've got fighters crawlin' on us an' no shields! Get us under cover or we'll have to abandon-" Frost shouted into Alice's subdermal earpiece.

"Frost!" she replied.

There was a long moment of silence before he replied; "Lost a whole section, barely got out."

"Can you keep firing?" Alice asked as she looked to Laura, who shook her head pointing at the dorsal section of the ship.

"I'll keep the guns blazin', but I dunno for how long!"

Alice looked at the pattern of damage across the ship and immediately recognized that the fighters were closing the distance between them and the ship to within hundreds of metres and launching electronic pulse rounds to disrupt the shielding protecting their lower engine pods and the forward command section. She didn't give the order to operations, but locked down the forward observation areas as well as the ready quarters and bridge conference room herself. Her status display told her that there were fourteen people in the forward observation areas and they had twenty seconds to get out. She closed the display highlighting crew locations down, focusing instead on ordering any non-essential personnel to the core of the ship.

Out of the corner of her eye she caught a glance at Stephanie's expression. She was keeping herself together, looking terse, but she couldn't hide her fear entirely. "Stephanie, keep a few people here, but go direct the movement of crew to the ship's core," Alice whispered.

Stephanie nodded and strode directly off the bridge, signalling four of her security officers to accompany her.

"I have nine percent energy shielding back up on our rear dorsal section, four on the rest. Our aft shielding is failing," Laura said.

Alice looked at the status of the *Saviour* and saw that they were running with a field of flak in front of them as they launched even more fighters, torpedoes and heavy gauss cannon rounds directly at them. "All right! Bring us about and fire everything at the *Saviour*, ignore the fighters, ignore the shielding."

Without flinching, Ashley fired all thrusters so the *Triton* spun around and drifted backwards. Torpedo bays all along the edges of the *Triton* fired, belching short jets of flame and high velocity long shells at the enemy ship. Many were redirected or destroyed as they encountered the flak field between the ships, while a few flew past and even fewer struck directly at the narrow, long hulled ship.

The forty nine turrets that could fire on the gunnery deck were alight as they erupted streams of deadly rail cannon shells at the enemy vessel, striking her more often than the torpedoes. The defensive cannons that could rotate in the enemy's direction fired along with the smaller rotary particle cannons there, normally reserved to defend craft as they came in for a landing.

The effect of the focused efforts were immediate, the shield readings of the other ship dropped megajoules per second, but there was no telling how much power they had in reserve to keep them charged. Her eye was equally drawn to the status display of the *Triton*, where she could see the shields covering their main rotary engines were down to seven percent and falling quickly. "Any reply from the Carthans?" Alice asked.

"Nothing," Cynthia replied, looking near panic.

"Any sign of the *Clever Dream*?" she asked Agameg.

"They made it to the outer atmosphere and disappeared," he replied quietly.

The ship shuddered and Alice shot to her feet as she caught sight of the cause. "Abandon the bridge!" she shouted as she hit the emergency switch that activated the large main rear hatch behind them. The double doors began to close immediately at their normal pace which had seemed slow until that moment. "Chief Vercelli! Get your people out!" Alice shouted just before the ramp ways to the lower half of the bridge sealed.

She watched as everyone on the bridge moved, not so much as locking their stations. All except for Ashley, who was focused on the controls. Alice took three long strides forward, grabbed the woman by the collar and pulled her to her feet. The younger woman just stared at her, shocked. Nose to nose Alice shouted; "Get out!"

Ashley turned and ran as Alice sat down at the helm and clipped her safety line to the seat, sealing her vacsuit. She hurriedly brought up a smaller version of the tactical and ship status displays and took the controls, piloting the *Triton* in a much less graceful fashion so the forward section faced away from the *Saviour*. "Hurry the hell up Jake, I don't think we can take much more of this," she said to herself as she heard the large main bridge doors seal behind her. With the touch of a quick sequence of buttons on her command unit she initiated the emergency sequence on the bridge, beginning the process of venting the atmosphere into space.

With a flick of her wrist she tried to turn the ship away from an oncoming formation of three fighters, their guns blazing, trying to break the already badly damaged layers of hull protecting the forward command section and the bridge. The energy shielding in front of her was completely gone and in the thinning air of the bridge, through the surface of her vacsuit headpiece she could hear the rapid, thunderous impacts of their energized shells striking the hull.

The tactical display flashed, indicating a new contact and without so much as verifying who it was she reached to her secondary control panel and ordered the main landing bay doors open. "Welcome home Jake," she said through a smile as she watched the *Clever Dream* swerve from where it had emerged and strike an interceptor head on.

A small explosion sounded behind Jake, Ayan and Jason followed by a girlish scream that could have only belonged to Minh-Chu. The ship spun end over end as the cabin began to smell of burned cables and electronics.

The sound of a fire extinguisher followed it. "I step out of a stasis pod into a strange exploding hallway. Best day ever!" Minh exclaimed from just outside the cockpit as he fought the small electrical fire.

"Are you all right?" Jason asked over his shoulder as he watched Jake stop the *Clever Dream's* spin and fire the thrusters hard towards the opening landing bay doors of the *Triton*.

Somewhere behind the looming hangar opening an explosive decompression was taking place. Starfighters swarmed the carrier, concentrating their fire on the bridge and another designated target in the aft section. Several rounds struck the *Clever Dream* as well and Jason braced himself for an emergency landing.

Ayan was much calmer, perhaps numbed at that point or on autopilot herself. "Brace for impact," she said calmly into the ship wide intercom.

Minh, dressed only in underpants dropped to the ground at the back of the cockpit, threw the fire extinguisher into the narrow hall behind and crossed his arms over his head. "Wasn't the grenade bad enough?"

The inertial dampeners whined and screeched under the strain of the sudden deceleration as the *Clever Dream* struck the deck of the landing bay at a seventeen degree downward angle, grinding, scraping along and slowly turning for over a hundred meters then colliding with a heavy safety barrier.

The quiet that followed was thick as Jake, Ayan, Jason slowly looked at each other. Minh lowered his arms and looked around. "Guess today can only get better," he chuckled.

Alice ordered the bay doors closed and verified that the *Triton* was ready to create and enter its own wormhole. With a nod to herself she activated the projection systems and set course for the opening. The sound of more shells striking the hull in front of her was quickly followed by ominous creaks and even louder thumping, furious cracking.

Seeing that the ship would pilot itself into the opening of the wormhole she started to stand and was just about to unclip the safety line that would keep her in her seat when the entire helm flashed red. The automated navigation system failed to calculate a straight course into the opening of the wormhole as it began adjusting for the sudden failure of one of their main engines and Alice cursed to herself as she took the controls to manually directed the ship into the passage opening.

The sound of a massive impact against the forward hull was followed by a groan and creak as Alice locked the controls and sat back. There was no time to move as the inner layer of the hull tore itself to pieces under the increased pressure and she watched the breach begin to burst.

RECOVERY

The internal communications on the *Clever Dream* were down, but it didn't take them long after Assistant Chief Paula Mendle and her crew brought it into the pressurized rear hangar behind the landing deck to discover a miracle. Even with the collision and rough, urgent ride, the extensive damage to the starboard side of the vessel and the cramped situation in the ship's hold no one had been badly injured.

Stephanie watched as the refugees, all worn, covered in grey dust and muck, were led off the ship by the security officers she'd brought with her. The few people they could spare from medical were busy straight away, and before long they were under the command of a tall female nafalli.

Her spirits rose the moment she caught sight of Captain Valance. He was as ragged and as visibly battle weary as everyone else. She couldn't help but notice the holes in his stolen armour as he walked down the half open forward crew ramp and gingerly dropped down to the deck a meter below its end. Her heart sank as a woman – the woman known to her as Ayan or at least someone who could have been her sister – came down the narrow forward ramp right behind him.

Stephanie tried to put the feeling that she'd lost something aside but couldn't look away as Ayan put her hand on his shoulder before taking the last step down beside Jake. He flashed a tired, quick smile at Ayan and it was returned in a fashion that looked quick, easy, familiar. Stephanie's feelings of dread at seeing someone she suspected her Captain, her Jake, had loved and lost were only matched by her guilt at wishing the woman had stayed dead.

She shook it off the best she could and swallowed the lump in her throat. *Even from a distance I can see he's smitten.* Stephanie glimpsed back to Ayan, who was stepping aside so a well muscled Asian fellow could disembark. *She's beautiful, a kind of beautiful you don't see out here. How could I have thought that I could compete with her memory? If Jake and I got together I'd always be trying to live up to what she was and now she makes a reappearance.* Stephanie tried to turn her thoughts away from the night they spent together. *I can't have him, I can't do anything about how he feels and I won't compete for him.*

Stephanie looked away purposefully, looking at the hull of the *Clever Dream* instead of the forward debarkation ramp but not seeing, just making sure that if someone were to look in her direction they wouldn't catch her staring at Ayan. All the while she tried to put down the sense of loss that was so thick it made her queasy. *I should have expected this, if it wasn't some ghost from his past it would be someone nicer, smarter or prettier than I am. Jake and I are too alike to be together, better off friends and co-workers.* Stephanie sighed, her palm came to rest on the butt of her holstered sidearm. *If I really want him to be happy the best thing I can do is make*

387

sure that woman is the safest person on the ship.

Ashley came down the lift behind her, closely followed by Price, and they rushed to her. "Is your comm not receiving?" Price asked her, anxious.

Stephanie checked and noticed that only her proximity radio was operating, the ship's comm relay wasn't connecting with her command and control unit. She looked to the nearest soldier and pointed to her ear. He checked his communications status. "My connection to the relay is down, but I've got you on proximity radio," he replied to her.

She looked at Ashley's command unit and saw that hers was connected and working properly. "Okay, that's strange. Try switching to a security band."

Ashley selected a security alert preset and was immediately disconnected from the primary communications relay. "Someone's taken the security comms off line," she said aloud, even though everyone there knew what was going on. "Are you okay?" she asked, recognizing that something was amiss with her best friend.

Stephanie cleared her throat and nodded. "I think Captain found a few extra passengers."

Ashley looked up the length of the *Clever Dream* and went wide-eyed. "That can't be-"

"I think it is, somehow."

"She's shorter than I imagined," Ashley commented, tilting her head. Her eye drifted to Minh, who was walking back up the ramp. "Like the new boy," she purred.

"Ashley!" Stephanie whispered, rolling her eyes.

"What? Run around in your pants and you have to expect some staring," her attention wandered back to Jake and Ayan, noticing that his arm was across her back. They were speaking to each other quietly as they started towards them. "I'm sorry Steph," Ashley said as she turned back to her friend.

"It was a one time thing," Stephanie dismissed. "Don't either of you mention it," she continued, making a point to look Agameg in the eye.

"I didn't say a thing, not even to Finn."

"Good, thank you Agameg," A thought struck her then; "Why aren't you two on the bridge?"

"That's what I came down her to tell you, the bridge is gone, Panloo and a few other bridge officers are taking over control from the secondary command center but-" Ashley started to crack up, recalling the scene on the bridge. "Alice got us out but stayed to pilot the ship and the status display outside-" she shook her head sadly, mournfully. Price put a comforting arm around her.

Agameg finished Ashley's thought; "The bridge is exposed to open space. If she wasn't killed in the breach, any radiation spike. . ." he trailed off as Captain Valance approached.

"Who was on the bridge when it happened?" Captain Valance asked, only hearing the second half of the conversation.

"Just Alice, I'm sorry." Price replied quietly.

"Do you know for a fact that she's dead, were you able to get a reading through the doors?"

388

"No but the chances of her surviving aren't good," he offered helplessly.

He looked to Ayan. "I have to go find out. If there's any chance..."

She nodded, barely hiding her worry. Without warning she pulled him down and kissed him urgently. "I understand, be careful," she whispered against his lips.

He caressed her face with the back of his fingers as she let him go. He nodded and ran for the main lift. Stephanie was right behind him accompanied by two of her guards. "I'm going with you, there's something happening in the security office."

They ran into the large lift and it closed behind them. Stephanie stood beside Captain Valance as he pulled an emergency kit open and retrieved an emergency vacsuit. She knew it was the worst possible time, there would be other opportunities, and despite everything going on there was only one question on her mind, one thing she wanted out of the way; "So is that really Ayan?"

He stopped with the vacsuit half on over the ruined West Keeper armour for a moment, looking at her out of the corner of his eye. "She looks a bit different, but that's her," he answered. "She seems a little bolder, but second chances can do that."

"Are you two?" she asked quietly, more mouthing the question than even whispering aloud.

He sealed up the front of the flimsy looking one size fits all vacsuit and started to work on the sealing face piece. "Too early to say," he whispered back so the two guards who shared the lift with them could at least pretend to have not heard.

"Okay," Stephanie whispered back.

"What's going on in security?" he asked irritably.

She cleared her throat and put thoughts of him and Ayan out of her mind as best as she could, embarrassed that she could allow her professionalism fail her so utterly in the middle of a crisis. "Someone's shut down the security comm relay. My people are already working around it, but obviously whoever did it was trying to buy time for something."

"All right, get control of the security office, I'll check in once I know what's happened on the bridge and start directing rescue and repair operations," he said in a stiff, impersonal tone.

Stephanie's eyes focused forward on the doors to the lift, replying; "yes sir," as she straightened up. As they arrived she tried to suppress the embarrassment at asking the wrong question, she could have asked; 'how are you?' or 'what happened down there?' or even 'is there anything I can do to help,' but she was distracted by her childish hopes and expectations even while her entire security team, hundreds of people were at risk.

The express car stopped, the doors opened and they stepped out into the abandoned forward command deck causeway. It was eerie seeing the large corridor completely empty, even during night watch in hyperspace there was someone about, it was a busy ship and those few command levels were the nerve centre. The large double doors leading into the bridge were sealed shut, the control panels to either side of them blinked red, indicating that the doors couldn't be opened due to pressure differentials or other problems. Just beyond that was the security office, and that panel blinked a bright blue, indicating a lockout.

"Do you need any help?" she asked quietly. "We can have an armoured suit down here in fifteen minutes. You'd be properly protected."

He finished sealing the faceplate and ensuring that the vacsuit was secure as he started into a dead run for the main bridge hatchway control panel. "We don't have that kind of time."

"Let me go after her, sir," offered one of the security guards that had accompanied them. "My vacsuit is armoured and I'm fresh on shift."

"No, the intensity of the radiation inside is too high, even with your vacsuit."

"But sir, if it's too high for me then-" the guard gently countered.

Jake stopped him mid sentence, putting his hand on his shoulder. "Alice is alive in there, but barely. I'm going in after her because I can regenerate, and I won't sacrifice anyone else. Now get out of this section so it can depressurize."

Stephanie directed the pair of soldiers to head for the security office with a hand signal and they both obeyed without hesitation. She just stared at him through the flimsy faceplate of the emergency vacsuit for a moment. "What do we do if you don't-"

"Trust Ayan, Jason, Laura, Minh and give Oz the command chip. They're all better at keeping a ship than I ever was alone. Now get out of here, she doesn't have much time."

She nodded and started to turn when he caught her shoulder. Stephanie was almost afraid to look back, she didn't know why, but she did anyway.

"Take care of each other," he said firmly before beginning the emergency decompression sequence.

In just a few quick steps she was beyond the nearest emergency bulkhead and its thick, black surface rose up behind her and when it clanged into place she punched the order into the control panel in the hallway to force it to become transparent. She stared mesmerized as the vacuum suit inflated slightly, reacting to the increasing pressure outside of it and after all the air had been evacuated from the small sealed off section of hallway, the large bridge hatch doors were drawn out of the oval frame, bathing Jake in blue and yellow light. There was focused radiation coming in through the lensed walls of the wormhole, and probably even more being generated by the compression of space all around the ship. It was a miracle that Alice was alive at all, it would be a greater miracle still if her and Jake could make it out.

"Do you want us to breach the security office without you Ma'am?" asked one of the soldiers behind her.

She snapped out of her spellbound state, hesitantly drawing her stare away from those open bridge hatchways and stepping into a march towards the main security office doorways. Her personal code was short, she punched it into the door control panel reflexively and stepped aside, rifle at the ready as it slid open. Her command and control unit automatically did a scan of the room beyond and revealed one body, good atmospheric compression and several active computer terminals. "I'm reading all clear." she announced.

"I can verify," replied the soldier beside her. "Whoever was in there is dead or gone."

"All right, lets head inside. Look out for personnel mines and improvised traps," she ordered, leading the way.

One of her men lay awkwardly half inside a side office door. From the awkward angle his neck was turned and the burn mark at the base of his skull Stephanie could tell that there was no reviving him. "Continue your sweep, be careful and watch your scanner results," she said to herself as much as the pair of security officers with her as she slowly made her way to the central terminal at the rear of the long main security office.

"Do you recognize him ma'am?" asked one of her troopers.

"No, look him up."

"Lyndon Edsel. Qualified on rifles, basic maintenance and infantry manoeuvres. He was assigned to nights."

"Well, someone got behind him," the officer who had earlier volunteered to take the Captain's place commented.

"Low velocity explosive round. At least it was over quick," said the other, shaking his head. "I'm verifying all clear on my scanner."

Stephanie sighed and released the lockdown on the security communications system. "All right, check the other offices, be careful. Whoever did this is someone we trust."

"Do you think it was our suspect?" asked one of the guards.

"It could have been, but he hasn't shot anyone yet."

The other officer knelt down beside the fallen soldier and gently closed his eyelids. "He was strangled before they shot him in the back of the head. Whoever did this didn't want to make any chance at him being revived," he reported quietly. "This was an assassin."

Stephanie stepped in front of the main communications terminal and released the lock on the security bands. Her communicator came to life with questions from security personnel and soldiers across the ship and instead of addressing any one of them in particular she interrupted all of them. "Security office is secure. Communications systems are secure." She checked the squad status reports as they populated on her command unit and selected one that showed that they were backing up the security team in medical. "All right, squad seventeen; I need you to proceed to the security office and lock it down. Everyone else be on alert. We have at least one more murder and our suspect is someone we know and trust. He was most likely on the command deck before the bridge breached."

She checked the logs and found that someone had accessed the computer system from the central terminal. When she looked for records indicating what he or she had done while they had access she found them completely empty. "It'll take me a while to find out if they altered or deleted anything. He was in here though."

"So our guy was after information?"

"I can't say for sure, he could have been after info or covering his tracks. We'll have to look for holes in surveillance records, new additions to our records, dummy files meant to stand in for something they deleted. None of it is anything I'm specialized in."

"Here's hoping Captain found a data analyst on Pandem," one of the soldiers

391

with her remarked.

Stephanie heard the emergency bulkhead doors outside in the hallway lower and a medical alarm sound. She was out of the security offices in seconds. Jake and Alice were face down in the hallway in front of the re-sealed bridge doorway. "We need medical up on Command deck right now, the Captain is injured," she said hurriedly as she quickly closed the distance between her and the very still pair on the deck.

"They're already on their way, Captain Valance told us we'd be needed. For clarity, which Captain is in need of care?"

"Both, hurry."

* * *

The last of the refugees were waiting to load in one of the large express freight lifts. All those in need of more urgent care had already been moved to the infirmary. Stephanie's security teams made quick work of the potential mayhem. They seemed well practiced at handling rescue operations. Ayan, Oz, Minh and Jason waited at the head of the group for the lift.

The doors opened to reveal Laura and several security personnel. The look of shock and joy on her face when she saw the foursome was utter. "Oh my God," she whispered as she shakily stepped out of the bulk express car and was taken into Jason's arms.

She wasn't one given to emotional outbursts, but the relief of seeing her husband after so much time and difficulty combined with the unbelievable sight of her best friend, the very one she had attended a funeral for less than two months before was overwhelming and as she looked up from Jason's shoulder to see her again, standing there, smiling brightly, healthy and teary eyed she had to ask; "Is it?"

Ayan stepped forward and put her arm around Laura's shoulders; "Doctor Anderson and my mother, they used a scan taken before your wedding," she grinned, misty eyed.

Jason pulled her into their embrace and Ayan kissed her best friend on the cheek before squeezing. "I don't care how," Laura managed through her tears of joy. "I don't care how."

Minh stretched his arms around all three of them with mirthful enthusiasm as they shared the relief and joy of friends reunited.

"Why is Minh half naked?" Laura managed.

"I have nothing to declare but my underwear!" Minh grinned as he squeezed the trio.

One of the guards, laughing just as hard as everyone else, put a blanket over Minh as she moved past to help the last of the refugees load into the lift and get up to medical.

TRITON'S HEART

"He's just down there Ma'am," pointed the security officer that had served as her guide. When he picked her up at her quarters he was caught off guard by her civilian attire and easy manner. That morning had brought good news and she would be meeting important people that day. She wasn't a member of the crew yet, not officially, so she took the opportunity to create a dark violet vacsuit with a broad dipped neckline, loose sleeves and a long skirt that swished as she walked. The whole thing could seal around her in an emergency, but that potential simply wasn't visible, especially since the whole outfit had a stretchy cotton fabric style she enjoyed.

Everyone else aboard was wearing a *Triton* uniform or an off duty vacsuit that was similar and included their rank, which was marked both with a silver skull on their chest and stripes of one kind or another on their cuffs. Even though Laura had told her she could add both the *Triton* skull and letters beneath to her clothing she decided not to. It didn't seem right to assume she was a member of the crew, especially since she hadn't been given a position on the ship by anyone or spoken to Jake.

In the three days she had spent aboard she had heard so much about the legendary commanders of the mid-sized carrier. There was Chief Stephanie Vega, mostly known for countering an Eden Fleet boarding action and keeping the peace, Master of the Helm Ashley Lamport, who was at once known as a gifted pilot and as a barrier to everyone trying to qualify to fly a fighter and from what Ayan had seen most people genuinely liked her. She was like the ship darling, turning heads as she went about her business oblivious to the attention. There was Gunnery Sergeant Frost, who had just been demoted by Acting Captain Alice Valent. He had a much darker reputation that involved revenge, public drunkenness and a terribly volatile on and off relationship with the Chief of Security.

Acting Captain Alice Valent was the most fascinating person aboard. Laura had told her the whole story the first night after they arrived. She actually was Jonas Valent's artificial intelligence and after being released into the computer system of the *Overlord II* she transferred herself into a human body. Two years later she found who she thought was Jonas Valent and rescued him, leaving before she could discover that he was actually a copy built atop a framework. With more than one corporation and government agency after her, she left before that copy could wake up, see her in person and have the memories of Jonas Valent activated. As a result he went on with his life as Jacob Valance, becoming a bounty hunter, repossession agent, privateer and gun for hire. He made the assumption that Alice was his daughter and used his profession to drift through several sectors as he searched.

In the meantime Alice was on the run, taking jobs where she could until she discovered that Jacob had become a kind of folk hero, and she sought him out. She rescued the real Jonas Valent along the way and after he sacrificed himself for the good of the ship she became the First Officer of the *Triton*, and to anyone who didn't know her or Jake personally, she was known as the Captain's daughter. After leading a desperate capture mission deep inside a Regent Galactic owned solar system she had become very well respected amongst the crew. To the many people aboard she was legend, yet when Ayan herself walked down the halls people reacted with practical reverence.

On her first day aboard the *Triton* she wore a vacsuit that looked much like the rest of the crewmembers, only grey instead of black. After speaking to Laura about her role it was plain that no one expected her to do anything but rest and take her time in making up her mind, on finding something she wanted to do aboard. Stephanie had been left with instructions to put Oz in charge, so he was busy catching up, learning about the ship, her senior officers and managing the vessel as it travelled through an extended wormhole.

All the while she was accompanied by guards. By order of the Chief of Security there was always an armed guard watching over her. The junior officer's quarters to either side was occupied by guards and there was always one standing at her door, ready to ensure she had anything she needed. She asked why and was told that keeping her safe was priority one. Minh and Jason didn't hear anything about why she was being treated differently, neither of them were being escorted around the ship or watched over.

Laura had a different theory. Captain Jacob Valance was respected, some of the crew were fiercely loyal to him and a few even feared him. She surmised that Ayan was enjoying some of that respect, that Ayan was being treasured, kept safe. It came as a surprise when Laura suggested she go see Chief Engineer Liam Grady, who was an Axiologist, for more answers.

It was entirely strange, but at first Ayan was so tired that she didn't have the energy to object. How people reacted to her was more informative than any information she gleaned from the security personnel. She dressed differently after the first day aboard, choosing more leisurely clothing, going unarmed, but never ill equipped. Her more ornamental, bracelet like command and control unit was always dangling around her wrist. Hers was a more elaborate version that could widen, narrow, become semitransparent or change colour. It looked like it was made of smooth crystal, a gift from the crew of the wormhole ship where she matured. Her attire and guardians drew veiled stares despite the politeness and space she gave everyone. She didn't want to get in the way, after all.

The security officer who was assigned to escort her to engineering at the end of her third day aboard had four and a half bars on his cuffs, marking him as one of the highest ranking officers on board. His name was Taber Radics and he had come aboard with the Aucharian military during the battle for the *Triton*. When she tried to strike up conversation with him he answered her questions about his home world of Seneschal, the security on the ship, even Engineering Chief Liam Grady. All his answers were polite, she was addressed as Ma'am as though that was equivalent to the rank of Grand Admiral or some kind of Queen, and he always had a smile for her.

At the same time his eyes searched the hallways ahead of them, scanned people carefully from head to tow and his hand rested on the hilt of his holstered sidearm. There was a security or peace officer at every major hall intersection, even the temporary quarters she'd been assigned somewhere in the center of the ship were well patrolled even though they were only partially occupied from what she could tell. The hallways weren't disused, they just showed more signs of age than the rest of the ship. They were missing the degree of polish the rest of the ship had, and dust had settled on much of the cabling and piping that was neatly sorted along the walls.

They were in the elevator, which had cleared out when they stepped inside, when she asked; "Has anyone instituted cleaning stations aboard?"

He looked at her with mild surprise for a moment before shaking his head; "Only in the bunks, but I'll pass it up the line to Chief Vega."

"You don't have to go to the trouble, I just couldn't help but notice a little scuffing and settling in the halls in some sections."

"I'm sorry, Ma'am. We'll have it seen to right away," he answered as he stared at the lift doors with all seriousness.

It wasn't what she intended. It was meant as an observation, maybe light criticism, but not as an order. She sighed and stared at the lift doors. They opened to reveal a broad, busy corridor with active observation and control stations down its length. The buzz of activity and quick interchange of information was something she hadn't seen since she managed the Engineering section of the *First Light*.

It only took a few glances to realize that she had been brought to the main repair, maintenance and damage control center. It was a subsection of the Engineering department, she had read, and through a transparent ceiling she could see the main engineering office. According to the ship's organizational charts that was where all the engineering department heads gave orders for their teams, monitored their progress and coordinated. "Good thing you didn't take me that way. I'd cause quite a scene in this skirt," Ayan muttered just loud enough for her escort to hear.

He suppressed a chortle. "Yes ma'am," he replied under his breath.

As she passed the bustle and buzz of the broad control corridor quieted and she was met with mild smiles and gentle nods. Her cheeks flushed and she mentally cursed at herself for showing that she was at all flustered. Years of military training had taught her that when a crowd affords someone so much respect the best reaction was to calmly, politely acknowledge it. Keep your back straight, your stride steady, straight and your chin up. As she recovered her attire felt all wrong. Well, not wrong, but very different; confidence showed through very differently in a dress. She was used to being in a uniform, commanding a different kind of respect that came from rank, camaraderie. Being in civilian clothing separated her from the rest of the crew in ways she hadn't realized when she first dressed that morning, add to that her soldierly gait and whatever incidental reputation that had been attributed to her and people admired her from a distance. As she nodded and sent modest smiles at people who stopped to regard her with a grin or a; "Ma'am," she wondered, with some irritation, what exactly waited for her at the end of the hallway.

There were over thirty people in that hallway, all directing repairs from what she could tell and she was relieved when she got to the end of the corridor made for fifty or more foremen and women. Broad double doors opened into a heavily armoured airlock where they waited for the doors behind to close, the pressure to equalize with the space beyond the heavier hatch within and then for that two meter thick block of a hatch door to be drawn out by heavy arms.

Ayan peered within and saw something entirely unexpected. The *Triton's* six main reactors were like thick pillars in a white cathedral and in its center sat a man in robes. His back was to her but she immediately had the sense that he was in meditation.

Between the large sealed reactor chambers and broad spaces between he looked small but compared to her he was a very large fellow, and as she stepped out of the lift the guard smiled at her and whispered; "That's Chief Engineer Grady. Do you need anything else before I leave Ma'am?"

"No, thank you for walking me here Officer Radics," Ayan replied.

He remained there, staring at her.

"You're dismissed," she added quietly.

He saluted before closing the hatch.

She shook her head and turned her attention back to the Chief. The first steps she took towards him sounded thunderously loud as they reverberated throughout the large chamber. Her soles were soft, practical, but still fresh from Laura's materializer, so they had just enough stiffness to make too much noise for her comfort.

Liam let out a long breath and stood slowly, almost too gracefully for his height and size. "I told them you'd be all right to find your way here on your own," he said as he turned and smiled at her. "You've probably browsed the blueprints for the entire ship by now."

Ayan smiled back at him as she slowly closed the distance and offered her hand. "Just a few decks and the way here."

He took her hand and shook it firmly but gently. "I'm honoured to meet you Ayan, I'm Liam Grady."

She let her hand slip out of his, feeling small and delicate at the center of the reactors, standing in front of a man who was the better part of a meter taller than she. "I'm honoured to meet *you*, Axiologist Grady. I was taught by someone from your order when I was a child and have believed ever since. You couldn't imagine my reaction when I discovered there was a monk aboard."

"Oh, I'm only a Pilgrim. I was supposed to be a Guide on Seneschal while maintaining a lead engineer's post, but there was a change in plans. Who was your teacher?"

"Tajen Emrissa, she stayed to teach ethics and history for two years. I still wish she could have stayed longer, a lot of us did."

"I heard of her while I was with my Mentor but never had the chance to meet her. I'm fairly sure she was in retreat somewhere in the north east, though she was known for being a Pilgrim for a very long time."

"I'm glad she made it back. She didn't speak about her time on Earth often, but by the time she taught us she had two belts."

"I couldn't imagine, even though I've met Mentors with four,"

Ayan couldn't resist looking down at Liam's loosely tied red belt to see how many places he'd taught or mentored and was a little surprised to find only one marking; the emblem of the *Triton* had been pressed into the thick cloth. The gentleman's easy confidence and slightly weathered look suggested that he'd already taught hundreds, thousands of people.

"I'm only at the beginning of my journey, much like you, as I understand it. Word has spread across the ship that you've returned by near miraculous means."

"I wouldn't call it a miracle, more good science and more dedication that I could begin to return. I still don't understand how that could lead to the quiet stares and smiles I've been fetching."

"I'm on leisure time, so let's explore while I catch you up. Have you seen the heart of this ship yet?"

Ayan looked around at the large reactors and nodded; "I think so."

"Well, in one respect you're right, but this ship has another heart that's just as important. You might have seen it marked as the Family Quarters?"

"I noticed, it takes up over twenty percent of the ship's interior space."

Liam led her towards the main hatchway. "At its center is the Botanical Gallery, which I've come to call the Garden."

"Ah, I haven't been cleared to see most of the ship. Laura was saying Chief Vega has been tightening security."

"You probably haven't been told, but we have an assassin aboard. His or her motives are unclear at best, but our Chief of Security has made changes to keep everyone, especially key personnel, as safe as possible."

"That explains a lot, actually. I've spent all my time here going between Laura's quarters, my little temporary quarters and the infirmary, or should I say hospital."

Liam nodded; "I heard they opened the attached rooms since there were so many wounded from our encounter at Pandem. One of my people said he thought he was transferred to a different ship when he woke up in what looked like a normal two bed hospital room."

"That's Iloona's doing. She's really been pushing the staff and they're giving her their all. I think they're just happy to have a real doctor aboard. Hard to believe that you've gone so long without one."

"So she's staying?" Liam asked as the main hatchway closed behind them and they waited for the pressure to equalize.

"Well, her litter of three are starting to venture out of her pouch, so I think she took that as a sign that she should stay on."

"That must make treating people complicated," Liam chuckled.

"You'd think, but one of her eldest helps and she keeps them well in hand even when they're crawling around. One of her little ones crawled right into my hair yesterday when I was visiting Jacob," she said as she ran her hand up and under a mess of blonde curls.

"That must have been something to see." The door opened and they strode, side by side down the Engineering Control Corridor.

"You don't have to stop in and make sure everything's in order?" Ayan whispered as she kept pace with her escort's long strides. It took some effort on her part.

"All the repairs are scheduled, the critical systems are in order and my second has it all well in hand for the time being. It took three straight days, and everyone's in for ten hour shifts for the next two weeks but it's time for some of us to get some rest."

"If you would rather go to your quarters and get some rest, I could visit another time," Ayan whispered back at him.

"There's nothing I'd rather be doing." He reassured her as they passed through the lift doors. "Besides, I have to wait for the stims to wear off."

Ayan smiled and nodded; "I slept fourteen hours when they finally showed me to a bunk here. I think I was on stims for four days at that point. Still just starting to feel rested now."

"Mister McPatrick was telling me yesterday how bad it was down there. Now that's an old soldier before his time."

"He was tunnel fighting for a over a week before Minh and I arrived. I'm glad I didn't see much of that myself. We call him Oz, by the way."

Liam looked at her lingeringly, his expression still pleasant but it almost looked like he was sizing her up for a moment. "One wouldn't assume you have so much service behind you just to look."

"Do you think that's part of the problem?" The express car arrived at it's destination and the doors opened to reveal a broad central corridor. Ayan had seen it on the blueprints for the ship. There were several main corridors just like the one they stepped into leading to the Botanical Gallery and around the Command Decks. She couldn't help but notice that the inner elevator door was so thick it required special support and sliders. They were entering another interior armoured section of the *Triton*, the Family Quarters.

"You mean the extra respect you're being paid? I suppose you could call it a problem. Before I explain what's behind that I suppose I should get the business out of the way."

She shot him a look with a raised eyebrow. "Business?"

"Right. With both Captain Valance and Acting Captain Valent out of commission no one has had the courtesy to place you somewhere."

"I've been giving Laura a hand and learning about the ship between visits to the Infirmary, so I honestly haven't had much time to notice."

"Well, as Oz put it things are falling into line aboard the *Triton*. With so many displaced military aboard and the weeks of training our people had before Captain Valance left for Pandem relative chaos is turning to order. Everyone who isn't considered a civilian is given orders aboard ship, exactly as one would while serving in the military."

"And you have something in mind for me," Ayan concluded as they came to a divide in the corridor with a waist high planter in the middle. Various flowers of all colours filled the space with their fragrances, and the light above changed to a warm, yellow light. Along the sides of the corridor were two levels of apartment doors with a railed balcony overlooking the thickening divide between the sides.

As they walked along the flowers gave way to trees and finally the corridor opened up to reveal a tall space with a simulated blue sky, real grass covered earth, fruit bearing trees, pathways, a broad pond where she could see three of Alaka's children splashing at each other and three levels of balconies. What Liam had called a garden was really more of a park, with vines climbing the walls, finding purchase up balconies. Further in she could see a few natural vegetable and berry gardens. rows of hedges, transparent hydroponic stacked huts interspersed throughout. Ayan stopped dead in her tracks and just took the sight in, felt the breeze on her face and smelled the fertile, moist air.

"This Gallery and the living space around it take up so much space for a reason, and it's worth every square meter," Liam whispered from beside her. "The civilians did most of the restoration and planting with a great deal of help from crew who had time to volunteer. Using seed stores, fertilizer and techniques found in the ship archives this is what they achieved."

"I've never seen anything like it outside of Freeground," she said quietly as she looked about to see people relaxing on the grass, strolling through the bricked pathways between the lush growth and there was even a young woman playing a beat up and patched cello in the distance. "Even there most of the parks are reserved for growing food, there isn't much walking about going on."

"It's different here; the engineers who built this ship intended this as a comfortable area. They built function into every corner but you rarely see it. Let's explore a little, I'll explain everything," Liam smiled at her warmly.

The pair began to stroll down one of the paths. Liam's pace was much more leisurely and she had no problem keeping up. "So, what can I do here?"

"Straight to the point even while you're taking the sights in," Liam teased.

Ayan shrugged and smiled back. "I'm a military brat before anything else I'm afraid."

"Well, then I feel that much better about my offer. I would like you to help me finish rebuilding the ship. To be honest I haven't been able to get more than the basics running where power generation and advanced systems are concerned. There are efficiency subsystems, secondary power generation and so many other details that I only just have under control, most of them are deactivated to be completely honest. Then there's the damage from our last engagement, we have two main engines completely out of commission. I'm sure you'll be drawn in other directions but I'll at least like to request your assistance in the rebuilding of the damaged sections of the hull since I'm using modified ergranian metal."

Ayan looked at him out of the corner of her eye for a moment before chuckling to herself and shaking her head. "You didn't pass this by Laura or Jason or even Oz for that matter, have you?"

"No, why?"

"They would have told you there's no way I'd turn you down. I have to get a few things sorted, you understand, but I've practically already started."

"So you'll work with me?"

"On *this* ship? You can count on it," she giggled at him, catching a crew

400

member who was just passing by surprise. Instead of simply walking on he smiled at Ayan and bowed as he let her pass.

"But only after you tell me why *that* keeps happening," she whispered. "Eyes follow me everywhere and I'm not that pretty, regal or important."

"All right, we're coming to the highlight of our tour so I'd say it's time. I don't know why, perhaps in part to grieve you and Jonas, maybe because she missed her own husband, but Laura added the files of the *First Light* senior staff to the ship records. She also entered a history of that voyage and a documentary from the Hart News service."

"There was a documentary?" Ayan boggled.

Liam nodded and went on. "In the wake of Jonas Valent and your passing aboard there was a lot of mystery. It was a confusing time for everyone. Many people were killed during the taking of *Triton* and the Eden Fleet had just decimated the Enreega system, leaving many people homeless, hopeless. Word spread that Jonas sacrificed his life for the sake of the ship and that your former self had come across the stars to see him only to find Jacob, who carried all of Jonas's memories."

Ayan swallowed a lump in her throat and nodded. "Go on."

"I know this isn't easy to hear, but he was with her in the last moments, according to Laura it was a good passing. We had a service for all those who had lost their lives in those first days on the *Triton*. We lost a lot of people in the fighting and when the Holocaust Virus first struck. We sent the fallen towards a stellar nursery, a whole nebula of stars that were just forming. As time went on people passed on the story of Jonas and Ayan, and in the eyes of the crew you became the woman that the Captain had lost. The story the crew tells new hands about how *Triton* was taken includes you and Jonas. In fact, the story is so widespread that when they built a monument to honour the people who originally lost their lives aboard they spoke to Laura about contributing something."

Her eyes went wide as they passed a tree leaning into the path and the monument Liam was telling her about came into view. It was a solid block of granite, brought to the center of a circular converging point of five pathways from somewhere else in the garden she assumed. Into its broad surface were carefully chiselled more names than she could count at a glance. Atop the broad, meter tall stone was a holographic image of Jonas holding her in his arms. He was dressed in his long coat, and she was in a white gown. She stopped and stared for a long moment, a tear rolling down her cheek.

"Jake, his daughter and you are all legends here. You look so much like your predecessor that they recognize you immediately. There's really no need for you to do anything but be seen here, that's enough to bolster morale on the ship more than any words or extra leave time ever could," Liam put a comforting hand on her shoulder. "This place is the *Triton's* heart."

"This image was taken at the Pilot's Ball," she said quietly.

"Laura wanted to tell you all about this herself, but, using her words, she thought she'd be a blubbering mess."

Ayan laughed and wiped away her tears. "And then I'd be a blubberin' mess, an' the onlookers might get drawn in, and then you'd have a ship full of weepers and wailers."

"You're almost getting me started," Liam chuckled as he handed her a tissue from a pocket in his sleeve. "She was right, when you cry your whole face falls into it."

"Oh, don't you dare," she said before blowing her nose.

He sighed and looked into her eyes. "Now you know."

She looked to the monument then back to him. "What do I do about this? No one can live up to a legend."

"In this case, the truth really will set you free. Just let the story of your origin leak out and people will either get used to you more quickly or they'll have even more respect for you. In command that'll be very important. Other than that, just be yourself, in the end that's all you can do."

"You're right. I'm still not going to be able to walk past that without nearly bursting into tears."

"Maybe next time you can come with Jacob. He hasn't been down to see it since he gave his permission to have it built."

Ayan stared at the granite stone for a long moment before nodding to herself. "I know Jake is so much like Jonas, but he's not, so I don't know how things will go with us, not really, but I have to be there when he wakes up."

"We're all just at the beginning of our journeys, Ayan. No one can say how things will be, we can only do our best to make sure we're moving down the right path."

Ayan looked to Liam and smiled. "Thank you Liam, I've got to be in the infirmary."

"There's a lift at the end of that path, do you know the way from there?"

"I'll grab a security officer along the way and have him walk me."

"I'm sure he'll be honoured, now go," Liam grinned.

402

BEGINNINGS

It was a sound Jake hadn't heard for a very long time. Irritating, loud, like a constant slow sawing. "Minh, stop snoring, willya?" he muttered, half asleep. His last memory returned to him then, collapsing in the hallway after rescuing Alice from the bridge. He sat up.

It was a hospital room, the decking and bulkheads looked like the *Triton* medical center, but he hadn't seen the room before. The offending noise was coming from his right, where Minh-Chu Buu had turned two chairs so they faced each other so he could stretch his legs out and nap. His head had fallen back so he was snoring open mouthed straight up into the heavens.

Jake couldn't help but laugh, groggy or not it was the most hilarious thing he'd seen in years. Add to that how amazing it was to see his long time friend alive and well, once he started laughing he couldn't stop. When Minh woke with a start and looked at Jake, smacking his lips due to dry mouth all he said was; "I was snoring?" The laughter was contagious and soon they were both in stitches.

Minh stood and offered his hand.

Jake took it, their grips were strong, both their hands were more calloused and hardened than they were years before when they had last spoken on the *First Light*. The hand shake turned into a brief embrace before Minh stood back and shook his head. "You scared us for a while there. Iloona says you have some kind of recharge mode, where you regenerate cell damage and well, I missed the rest," Minh said with a shrug. "Alice is in recovery, you managed to get to her in time. They repaired some older brain damage when they were treating her and it'll take her a while longer to wake up, could be a few days, but she'll be fine."

"Best news since I heard you and Ayan were alive."

"That had to be one hell of a bomb. Wish I had seen your face."

"It changed a few things," Jake replied. "I still can't believe you're here. If I had known you were out there somewhere-"

Minh waved the sentiment away with a hand; "Regret is a wall made of sorrow mortar and history bricks, a house built in such a way is destined to collapse. I thought I was as good as gone until I lucked my way out of that mess. I'm just glad to be here. If you want to make it up to me, you could put me back in a cockpit."

"Even after everything?"

"Especially after everything," he burst with a chuckle. "I mean, I spent years doing nothing but growing food, working out, playing guitar and playing sims. I'm *so* ready for the real thing again."

Jake smiled at him. "I'll get you in front of our virtual inventory so we can build something for you. I need someone to lead my people off the deck. Just qualify first, otherwise there'll be a mutiny."

"Yeah, have you tried that? It's harder than the academy final," Minh said, wide eyed.

"I failed my first time out." Jake nodded.

"Oh, well, I passed," Minh smirked, "Just saying it wasn't easy."

Jake laughed, shaking his head. "How's my ship?"

"Well, Chief Vega put Oz in the command chair and he's learning as quick as he can, so's Jason, but it's not good. They have to rebuild one main engine completely and replace the power provision systems on the other. Lucky there are four main engines and a bunch of supplemental thrust systems." He was quoting someone else's status reports, Jake could tell Minh was just getting ship news out of the way as quickly as he could so he could get to something else. "We're in a wormhole though, I hear we'll be hiding out in some big asteroid field while we rebuild. I got a peek at the maintenance list when an assistant was looking it over in the Pilot's Lounge. I couldn't help it, it looked like he was about to cry, then I saw the list and *I* felt like crying."

"Should I put you in the maintenance rotation until you get a rig?"

Minh's hands shot up in front of him, warding the idea off. "Oh no, I didn't get back into space so I could pick up a screwdriver."

"All right, just get practice in the sims on a couple of our fighters and pick something. If you're going to lead a squadron I need you to be better than everyone else out there."

"You're going to have to join me for a few scenes, and speaking of scenarios, I noticed all the leisure programs are locked. Any way you can, you know, get me a code so I can try a few? I have a few hundred on my personal comm that I could add too."

"I'll get you in touch with the Cruise Director," Jake said as he slowly got out of bed. He had never been so stiff in his life.

"There's a Cruise Director?" Minh turned to face the door while Jake pulled his flimsy gown off and stepped into the small pulse shower stall. It activated with a hum as soon as he closed the stiff semitransparent curtain.

Jake chuckled and shook his head. "Just kidding. I had them restricted while most of the crew were still trying to qualify for their positions but I suppose I could set things up so the higher ups can use them as rewards and get to know each other."

The door opened to admit Ayan, whose eyes darted to the empty bed then to Minh, who grinned, nodded and mouthed; "He's in the shower," before casually continuing his conversation with Jake. "So I'll have access once I take a command position?"

Ayan took a shuddering breath in and let it out slowly, trying to calm down. In the short time since he'd shown up at her apartment in Freedom Tower Minh had never seen her so nervous. She was completely distracted as she just tried to calm down.

Jake went on unaware that Ayan had entered. "I can't see why security couldn't give you codes right now, since someone has to try them out. Just don't get all wrapped up, I don't want you to get sucked in like when you discovered Sword of Rikaam," he deactivated the pulse shower and stepped out into the room, clean and nude.

Minh watched as Ayan's eyes went wide, she blushed so furiously that her neck, chest and ears turned red before she came to her senses and spun towards the door.

"Oh, and Ayan's here," Minh chuckled.

"I'll get you for that," she whispered.

"Worth it," Minh muttered back. "I'll leave you two kids alone. Get on comms with me later Jake, if there's anything I can do to help out, I'm up for it." He kissed Ayan on the cheek on his way out.

"You can turn around," Jake said, half in a fresh vacsuit. It was a near exact duplicate to the one he had worn on his way to Pandem. The greater weight of it was immediately noticeable, something he'd look into later.

Ayan turned, he was just checking the fit of the bottom half of the vacsuit, leaving the top to dangle from his waist. His back was a collection of burn scars, just looking at them she could see they ran deep. Without thinking she crossed the room and gingerly touched one of the larger burns. "I didn't think you could scar," she said quietly.

He froze. Jake knew exactly which scars she was talking about, they were a result of his mad dash from the West Keeper soldiers in the Commerce building. Looking down he saw more from when he had rushed to save her. *I see these clearly in my mind, there's no question I should have them and they're just here. I didn't even notice them while I was in the shower.* "They'll fade," he lied. *I don't know that for sure, for all I know it's all in my head.* He turned around, caught her hand in his. It felt so soft, small compared to his own. She was at the same time the woman he remembered and someone new. The differences ended when he looked into her eyes. If he hadn't have accepted Jonas Valent's memories as his own before then he would have in that moment. The woman looking at him expectantly, catching him with her gaze made him feel something new, something that did come partially from the short time Jonas had shared with her, but there was something else entirely, like a new flame that made her the most important person in the galaxy.

Her blue eyes searched his, uncertain. Her stomach was in knots, her heart seemed to beat between her ears. "Don't do that again. I couldn't take-"

Jake interrupted her, taking her lips with his and wrapping his arms around her. He held her so tightly that she was pulled up onto her toes. Ayan's arms went around his neck and everything outside of their embrace disappeared.

"You're really here," Jake breathed as their kiss ended.

She nodded, stroked his face. "I'm not going anywhere."

"Things will never be the way they were, I'm not the same."

"We'll take it slow."

He kissed her briefly and they held each other for a time that went uncounted. Ayan closed her eyes, it didn't matter that he felt different, the way he held her was barely familiar.

The way he made her feel was different than she remembered with Jonas. It was so exciting she could barely breathe at first. When he kissed her it made her head swim, the gratification and relief she thought she'd be feeling when she was reunited with her Jonas had been replaced with a feverish elation that was utterly unfamiliar.

This was *not* Jonas. There were pieces of him there, but the man who held her like the most precious being in all of creation was someone new. The realization wasn't as startling as her reaction to it. Instead of disappointment she felt an eagerness to know him and she was thrilled at the thought of something new. Behind it all she was a little frightened at what she might discover but that only added to the intense mixture of emotions that made her heart jump.

As he held her close she didn't feel small, but cherished, like he never wanted to let go and Ayan knew she was loved.

EPILOGUE

Wheeler tapped his finger on the soft desktop as he waited for a response from Hampon's direct line. The outer hull of his ship had been repaired at the Regent Galactic Mobile Shipyard but the internal systems would take more time. When the *Triton* focused fire on his vessel the damage was immediate and devastating. Even so, he knew that he'd crippled her far worse.

The repairs were the least of it. During the two hours it took to repair the outer hull he was in his quarters, trying to relive certain experiences he knew Collins should have had and he made a disturbing discovery. The boy Hampon appeared as a small hologram on his desktop and smiled at him. "Good evening Lucius, how are the repairs progressing?"

"Fine, I have the situation here under control. That's not what I'm calling about."

"Oh? Can you make it quick? I have a rally on Pandem in a few minutes. It's the first victorious occasion on our new base."

"Why did you short change me? Gabriel told me I was getting all of Collins' memories and now I can't even raise him on communications."

"He has his own objectives to attend to, I'm sure you understand."

"Well then maybe you can answer me. Why can't I recall anything about the Victory Machine after the first meeting he held with you and Gabriel? There are no predictions, I can't remember him seeing it, and there are other missing minutes, hours, even days."

"That's normal for anyone. We can't remember everything, even subconsciously."

"That's what I thought at first, before you told me all about your little hidden miracle, but then I actually tried to find any memory of him reading one of your expensive fortune cookies only to find complete blackouts!"

Hampon sighed and shook his head; "I'll be honest with you because I trust you. There were just some things that even Collins didn't want known, so he blacked out sections of his own scan after it was made."

"You expect me to believe that? Don't forget I can remember more times than I can count when you and Gabriel were underhanded and manipulative for your own reasons. Collins was no better, hell, I'm no better, but I won't be just another one of your hapless pawns, if you can't tell me why these memories are missing I can't say that I'll be entirely on side."

"Fine, you caught us. Of course we didn't want you to remember prescient revelations, what kind of morons do you take us for? Most of it doesn't concern you but as of a week ago there was a possibility that you would join forces with Jacob

407

Valance and we couldn't have you running around with bits of the future in your head. Besides, there was a chance that having future knowledge embedded in Collins' memories would corrupt the scan, damage the chronology of it. Just think back to when he decided to have the scan made and you'll see that was a concern. I'm surprised you didn't discover that on your own already."

He thought for a moment and realized it was true. There was a possibility that having knowledge of future events would damage the resulting memory scan, it was one of Collins' concerns. "You're right."

"You see? We were protecting ourselves and you. Having a fragmented record of someone's life with a corrupted time line is just a problem waiting to happen."

"Fine, I'd do the same thing to save my own ass, but I'll remember this. You could have been up front about it. I don't like surprises, especially when they're waiting in my own head."

"Oh, I'm sure you'll find plenty of other surprises Collins never let us in on, things we could have never scrubbed because we weren't aware of them. Rest assured, we may have removed his encounters with the Victory Machine but there's plenty of him left," Hampon adjusted his vestments so they fell straighter before continuing in a more casual tone; "I have to ask; does this change our arrangement?"

"Oh, I'll be going after Jake and his crew, just not so directly this time. I'll be able to draw him out."

"Good, I look forward to seeing the results of your efforts."

"I'm just tired of hearing about him. What the hell makes him so important now?"

"That's something you'll discover for yourself in time, just keep searching Collins' memories. Few people knew more about him than he did."

The holoprojector deactivated and the image of Lucius Wheeler disappeared. Young Hampon turned in his seat, a little too large for him, but that was something he was growing accustomed to, and faced Nora. "He'll be busy for a while," he told her.

"Do you think he has realized that he is the only reason why the *Triton* goes missing?" She asked, all together too pleased with herself.

"Perhaps, but he'll pursue it anyway. I get the sense that it's personal for him, that even if we tried to assign him to something else he'd find a way to go after them anyway."

"Then what the Victory Machine says is true; they'll keep each other busy until they're needed," Eve said, smoothing the wrinkles out of the front of her fine silk gown.

"That is what the last of the predictions we were able to gather stated."

"There's still no sign of it?"

"Not since the explosion in Mount Elbrus. If it had been destroyed there would be some sign, whether it be a new black hole drawing all matter and light inside or the formation of a new micro singularity. Either way, it would have been difficult to miss."

"How would someone have gotten away with it before the explosion? I don't have access to any data that provides a solution to that problem," she said with a furrowed expression of concern as she stood carefully.

Hampon dropped to the floor and took her hand. Together they very much looked like mother and son, it was impossible for anyone who caught sight of them not to notice. "According to Roman, the collection in the reliquary included an active Wormhole Arch. I'm assuming I've been betrayed and he used it to take the Victory Machine somewhere just before the explosion destroyed everything in the vault."

"But where? It was one of the first things I searched for when I broke through Gabriel's firewalls. I can't find anyone who had the knowledge and power to put a plan like that together."

"Perhaps Roman found a rich buyer."

"Then how did the final transmissions about the end of humanity appear?"

Hampon watched Eve as she took surprisingly steady steps on her new feet, as her long legs walked along side him through the door and into the gold and brown gilded hallway beyond. There were guards in dark blue, green and black armour waiting for them and they allowed them to walk several meters ahead before taking up positions behind. There was another set of four guards six metres ahead who kept their distance and cleared the way well in advance. "Maybe whoever came into possession of it saw the way to the greater good just in time to tell us how it'll all end. By the way, how is Mia? I'm surprised she isn't here."

"Oh, she's having a nap. I kept her up all night talking."

"I'm glad you're getting along."

"She's really helping me balance my time between the networks and living life properly, as she calls it. You chose the perfect therapist."

"How long did it take you to figure it out?"

"It was the second day, when she replaced the toast I was eating with cereal when I wasn't looking. It got my attention off the network long enough for her to get me talking. We're more friends now."

"She tells me that she genuinely enjoys your time together, so it's mutual."

"I'm not surprised. Your entire career has been one of manipulation, it only makes sense that you'd approach breaking me out of my shell the same way."

"I'm sorry, I didn't see any other option. I didn't think you'd sit down and take a therapist seriously."

"You're right, and I can't fault you for being manipulative, it's who you are and I accept it. Your grasp for power and it's success are really why I'm here, and without your manipulative nature you would be an unemployed Vindyne officer sectors away," Eve laughed, though not ruefully. There was pure joy in her outburst, and as Lister looked up at her face with his young boy blue eyes he saw Aphrodite. "I've seen the records, how you came to power dishonestly, began your cult for personal gain more than to unite humanity and then you made the transition from man to child," she looked down at him and squeezed his hand to emphasise her point; "and you began speaking to the people, your goals became pure; to save your people and fight humanity's galactic apocalypse."

"You give me too much credit. It still costs a hundred thousand credits to join the order," he reminded her, matching her broad grin with his own.

"But that fee only separates the successful from the chaff. You are the saviour of your people, Lister Hampon, unafraid of sacrificing one world to inspire billions to join you."

"They join out of a fear that we manufactured, don't forget."

"And millions of people join you every day in the core worlds, all but the Regent Galactic territories are falling in line and the day is coming very soon when they too will have no choice," Eve said quietly.

"You can take credit for that. If you hadn't used Gabriel's implants to program a new virus Regent Galactic would eventually become our enemy."

Eve's expression fell into a frown as she considered the memory. "He resisted at first, and I tried using other crew people who had similar implants."

"That caused quite a stir in medical. Most of them are still in isolation," he smirked at her.

Nora's guilt was plain on her face, an expression that was becoming more and more common as she consciously considered her actions since being transferred back into a human host. "I didn't know."

"It's all right, there is always a cost when you are breaking new ground in technology. In the end I'm sure even Gabriel will agree that it was worth it."

"He did admire the work I had done regardless of his fear."

"I'm sorry he had to leave, but your work had to be put to use before Regent Galactic learned about it."

She shook her head. "I should show him gratitude for setting me free, but I wasn't his perfect match, what he wants just isn't possible. I felt like he was pressing me into a mould and trying to trim away whatever didn't fit."

"That's understandable." They came to a pair of double doors that stood three storeys tall, obsidian with golden floral scrollwork adornment. Nora's hand caressed his back as he straightened his fine blue and green vestments, trying to mentally prepare for the victorious sermon he was about to give. "You know I'll be happy to announce your miraculous return whenever you like."

"I'm not ready. I would like to show my own children the framework flesh before I accept humanity."

"How long until the first of your ships arrive?"

"Only days. It will take some time to adapt their intelligences to being transferred to framework bodies but they can only understand humanity by joining them. Preserving the galaxy by exterminating your people won't work, I realize that now."

"But if you can teach your own children how to be human and pass on your message of conservation, preservation, then there is a chance."

"And if that doesn't work, they will be among your people, and ready to enforce our law, to defend our galaxy," she carefully lowered herself down to one knee, bringing her face close to his then brushing his cheek with her own. "This is a brave new day. You've made me so happy."

"I've never taken so much pleasure in giving. From this day forward Pandem will be known as New Paradise, the first Eden colony in over two centuries."

She stood looking down at him proudly, crossing her arms. He turned to the doors, suppressing his eagerness, hiding the butterflies in his stomach. Lister Hampon nodded and the smooth, dark doors parted slowly, grinding heavy hinges as they revealed the city of Damshir below, the streets were black and green, filled with the hundreds of thousands of West Keeper and Regent Galactic soldiers.

Cheers rose up to the balcony as he took his first steps up to the podium, and a tear of joy crept out of the corner of his young eye. The man behind that youthful face who had craved power, betrayed countless people and ordered the deaths and enslavement of millions finally came to the realization that he had it. Not only had he come to power, but he had allied himself closely to the only being who could oppose him, had the means and the unrestrained lust for more.

He came to the top of his platform, looked down on the city from the balcony mounted on the side of his hovering command carrier, gazed upon its massive breadth and the streets filled with his followers then closed his eyes and threw up his balled fists in a sign of victorious joy.

The cheering was like a wave, crashing upon the ruined mountainside and surging up from below, embracing him, thrilling him, and strengthening his resolve.

CPSIA information can be obtained at www.ICGtesting.com
Printed in the USA
LVOW131922050612

284783LV00022B/117/P